第七批中国外语教育基金项目：ZGWYJYJJ

U0607040

Sponsored by the 7th Chinese Foreign Language Education Fund: ZGWYJYJJ2014z30

山海集

——寻觅中国古代诗歌的镜像

（上册）

吴松林　著/译

A Collection of Seas and Mountains

—The Mirror to Seek the Ancient Chinese Poems

Authored & Translated By Wu Songlin

东北大学出版社

·沈　阳·

ⓒ 吴松林　2015

图书在版编目（CIP）数据

山海集：寻觅中国古代诗歌的镜像／吴松林著/译. — 沈阳：东北大学出版社，2015.10（2025.1 重印）
ISBN 978-7-5517-1098-5

Ⅰ. ①山… Ⅱ. ①吴… Ⅲ. ①诗集—中国—当代
Ⅳ. ①I227

中国版本图书馆 CIP 数据核字（2015）第 242851 号

出 版 者：东北大学出版社
地址：沈阳市和平区文化路 3 号巷 11 号
邮编：110819
电话：024－83687331（市场部） 83680267（总编室）
传真：024－83680180（市场部） 83680265（社务部）
E-mail：neuph@neupress.com
http：//www.neupress.com
印 刷 者：三河市万龙印装有限公司
发 行 者：东北大学出版社
幅面尺寸：145mm×210mm
印 张：34
字 数：978 千字
出版时间：2015 年 10 月第 1 版
印刷时间：2025 年 1 月第 2 次印刷
组稿编辑：周文婷
责任编辑：汪彤彤 孙德海 责任校对：关 哲 陈微微 陈传宇
封面设计：刘江旸 责任出版：唐敏志

ISBN 978-7-5517-1098-5 总定价：98.00 元

著/译者简介

吴松林（1964—），男，满族，黑龙江省望奎县人，博士，教授，中央民族大学赵展教授、北京大学许渊冲先生关门弟子。供职东北大学。

本书集合了作者1985—2015年写作并英译的七种体裁的格律诗，其中，包括四言诗201首、五言绝句214首、五言律诗207首、六言绝句202首、六言律诗198首、七言绝句217首、七言律诗190首，合计1429首，中、英文累计2858首。

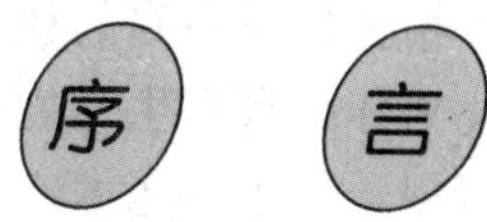

对作家而言，间接的经验可以开阔文学创作者的眼界，这是一笔直接继承自前辈的遗产；直接的经验多半来自文学创作者自身的实践，这是一笔自己挣得的财富。财富的叠加，可以润身富人；两方面经验的融汇，则常常可以孕育伟大的作品，催生优秀的作家、艺术家。

一方面，文学艺术的品味或曰鉴赏力要在经验的累积中生根发芽，这种主体的创造性能力——品味、鉴赏力——则要在艺术评判标准最终成熟于胸后才能诞生。大量而有效的阅读、精深而科学的研究，加上勤奋的创作和大胆的艺术训练，都足以使笔下文学艺术作品的内涵不断趋于丰富，也足以使创作者自身的文学艺术素养不断得以提升。《文心雕龙·知音》云：“操千曲而后晓声，观千剑而后识器。”这是经验累积并不断转化为创作主体的艺术素养的过程，缺乏这个过程的训练，即便在天才那里，先天对文学艺术的敏锐感知力和不羁的激情也很难在文学艺术创作实践中得以“熟巧”地表达出来，更遑论表达的艺术性了。

马克斯·舍勒（Max Scheler）在谈到艺术作品标准的问题时，指出了自身“劳作”经验的重要性——“谁不曾在事实领域中付出劳作，谁就会首先提出这个事实领域的批判标准问题。”没有“劳作”经验的懒汉，常常先于那些辛勤劳作的人提出各种艺术作品的评判标准。但须知，人人都能充当天生的批评家，但真正的批评家却很少是天生的。批评者在自身创作经验尚且并不足够丰富时就过早充当了批评家，只能像急功近利的园丁，贪心的所得只不过是早一点摘取了些青涩的果实，丰收的希望他们是不能指望的。而创作

者的草率之作，在面对内行人火辣辣的目光打量时，难免要心虚得战战惶惶，汗出如浆；在临镜审视自己时，也未尝不是战战栗栗，汗不敢出。足够的经验、真实的感情、熟稔的艺术表达，对文学艺术精神始终不渝的执着追求，是构成一部作品的美的元素，是一部优秀作品具有生命力的秘诀所在。缺少上述这些因素，缺少将生命沉浸于其中的艺术实践，所谓艺术性也只能在空谈中高高地悬置起来，却难以在笔端最终落实下来。令人欣喜的是，《山海集》的作者以胸中蓬勃的诗情，以其对中国古典诗歌的挚爱，以“我手写我口”的不羁感和“戴着镣铐跳舞”的严格韵律感，以文字传达诗歌艺术之美，自由地抒写着本我之“真”。亏了作者胸中的一副别才，我们才得见这样一部集上述诸美的元素于一身的作品；也亏了作者眉下的一双别眼，我们才有机会在吟咏中以诗人的眼光重新打量这个我们耽溺其中的寻常世界，发现久被遮蔽的存在之真。

然而，在海德格尔看来，“在贫瘠的时代”做一个诗人是危险的。“贫瘠”是因为，外在的自然被技术阱架所制而正变为“荒原”，我们的心灵“自然”也正被现代社会“进步的幻象”所驱赶，诗性之丧失使人无处诗意地栖居，这使人和作为艺术本质的“诗”（《艺术作品的本源》云：“一切艺术本质上都是诗。”）在现时代无处存身。即便在我们这个诗的国度，诗人和诗也无法免除这种尴尬。在诗歌的田地正在不断变得贫瘠的时代，谁在思？谁在游吟？

在这个时代，吟唱的诗人必定是“一位天生的冒险家和探索者”。他无视在这个时代作为一个诗人的危险，不顾要遭受到的愚迂不合时宜的讥讽，也不在乎常常要面对的如是的尴尬：当诗之美妙言辞传达至我们这些被伦常紧缚的凡人的耳朵，语言和心灵发出的召唤换来的也许只是一声闷响，之后便如石沉大海，阒无声息，没有“应和”，更没有诗人所求的心灵间的“共鸣”……这正是1500多年前刘勰在《文心雕龙·知音》中的无限感慨：“知音其难哉！音实难知，知实难逢，逢其知音，千载其一乎！”也许正是基于同样的缘由，诗人、哲学家尼采将他心中理想的读者描述为“一位天生的冒险家和探索者”，他引用《查拉斯图特拉如是说》中主人公的话，说他只向这些人诉说自己的谜：“勇敢的探索者”“沉溺于谜的人”。

今天，诗人需要像他们那样“沉溺于谜”的读者，而拥有真正勇敢品格的读者，也必定需要拥有他们那样品格的诗人。诗是桥梁，沟通了惺惺相惜的人的精神世界。

《山海集》是一个诗人和译人的浅吟低唱，也是一种“写”“译”兼之的“双重创作”。写汉诗，是一重创作；之后将之译为英文，又是一重创作。我想，作者在翻译时，定有以“翻译家之我”观“诗人之我”的艺术感受，身份的转化和观照视角颇类卢梭《孤独散步者的遐思》一书——以“思想家的卢梭”审视“哲学家的卢梭”。以本我审视自我心理之镜像，自然妙趣横生，这妙趣来自诗歌这种语言创作艺术，也来自诗歌翻译这种语言转化的艺术。对《山海集》的作者来说，作者、译者、读者的身份交融为一，诗人的双语艺术创作与情感体验交融为一，二者又统一于艺术创作心理，这其中的滋味恐怕是难以与读者分享的。

一般人文学创作的经验不外乎间接经验、直接经验两部分。而《山海集》的作者，则在阅读的经验、创作的经验之外，还多了一重从事诗歌翻译的经验。作者在译界耕耘多年，出版过英语、法语、意大利语三个语种的专著、译著、编著，累计80余部。另外，译言2400多万字，其创作经验之丰富亦见其创作精力之旺盛！林语堂尝云：“两脚踏东西文化，一心评宇宙文章。”易“评”为“做”，“做”兼个人创作、译作，足谓作者传神写照。

汉诗的妙处寻常人能够妙解于心，而将汉诗翻译为地道的英文，其中的曲折和英诗的妙处，就不是寻常人能够道出的。个中情形，不写诗、不译诗，也自难心领神会。譬如人饮水，冷暖唯自知耳。

诗歌创作是艺术，翻译也是艺术。凡为真艺术，必蕴大美；而艺术之“美”，在审美感知中为自然的，在孕育及创作中必经历极“难”、极“苦”之过程，艺术巨匠在创作中的自得或心理意义上行云流水般的“流动感”，或天才式的“流溢感”，或尼采所说的“喷涌”，在才智平平者那里，只偶尔在缪斯垂青或上帝赐恩时才会为作品生色添彩，唯自知者从来不奢望，只埋头耕耘，因此常蒙赐予灵感，也唯有这些老实人才理解柏拉图《大希庇阿斯篇》所说的真理：“美是难的。”这不仅仅是就美的理论性而言，“美”的艺术实践，文学艺术的创作更是“难的”。

解诗已难，写诗更难，译诗可谓难上加难，而语兼中英，出之自然且信而能雅、辞达意通，非诗界射雕手孰能为之！作者在此基础上独立提出了“魂似”（Transoul），以可持续的写作和翻译实践去不断进行验证。

海德格尔在《林中路》中说：

> 林中有许多路。这些路多半突然断绝在人迹不到之处。这些路叫作林中路。
>
> 每条路各行其是，但都在同一林中。常常看来一条路和另一条一样。然而只不过看来如此而已。
>
> 伐木人和管林人认得这些路。他们懂得什么叫走在林中路上。

在林中路上，“在人迹不到之处”，旅行者不会孤独，因为他从其间走过多个来回，“认得这些路”；不但认得，每次走在林中路上，旅行者都能满载而归——无论是肩上的背包，还是诗人的心灵。

伐木人和管林人类似哲学家，因为尼采说：“从不中止对异乎寻常之事去经验、去看、去听、去怀疑、去希望和梦想，这个人就是哲学家。”从事创作和翻译的“双枪将”则类似伐木人和管林人，“伐”和“管”的关系看似吊诡，实则统一：因为在林中，无论做什么，总能有收获；这关系正如创作和翻译，在实践中，在时间这块田地上辛勤耕耘，付出者往往有所得。

走在林中路上，他的背上是沉甸甸的箩筐，箩筐里，装满了他的吟唱；从林中归来，在收获的喜悦中，累累硕果变成了一部适宜在这个初春的季节吟唱的诗集——《山海集》。且让我们和作者一起踏上这林中小路，“去经验、去看、去听、去怀疑、去希望和梦想”……

这部诗集取名《山海集》，本意是“高高山顶立，深深海底行”。具体说来，就是：学习写诗和译诗也是在学着做人，要从高处着眼，从低处着手。这个集子为诗部，分为 7 种体裁，即四言诗、五言绝句、五言律诗、六言绝句、六言律诗、七言绝句、七言律诗。为了便于理解，相当多的诗歌内容由作者的爱女吴冠乔加了按语和注释。

《山海集》在写作和翻译的过程中，不离开清静的环境和清静的心灵，有些诗的意境和意象就是在清静如水的状态下写出来的。受许渊冲先生的指点，作者更清醒地意识到了继承老人家事业的担子有多重。作者多年以来也深深地感受到，作许渊冲的关门弟子是个莫大的荣幸，同时，也承受着难以言表的压力。这种压力在于先生耳提面命地强调，有多高的文言文水平，就有多高的外文翻译水平。想翻译中国古代诗词，必须有驾驭中文诗词写作的基本能力，没有这个能力，许门不承认任何人踏进半步。现在，终于可以向许先生提交这份作业了。

作者攻读博士学位期间，导师赵展先生也不时地传递汉语功夫的重要性，刻意把作者的博士论文定位在《红楼梦》的满族文化研究这个选题上。多少个日日夜夜，《红楼梦》原著和英文的两种译本一个字一个字地对照通读。2007 年，作者把第一部诗词手稿打印出来交给赵先生指导，先生不厌其烦地从写作技术上进行把关，同时，建议作者写作的格调不要太低沉、太灰暗，要歌颂祖国的大好河山。作者涉世不深，违心地描述现实生活中的所见所闻又不是作者的性格，而刻意地去歪曲和丑化社会更不是作者的思维。本集留下的行行文字，是他心路历程的部分折射。

许先生 1921 年 4 月 18 日出生，赵先生 1931 年 7 月 11 日出生，两位先生是作者步入中年学业的航标。这个航标将持续照耀着作者和作者不断扩大的典籍外译团队不断地前行，毫不动摇地前行，试图完成《二十四史》整体英译工程。如果上苍假以时日，继而完成《四库全书》整体英译工程，让祖国传统文化精髓部分全盘走出去，不辜负国内两位心静如水的学术泰斗的期望。

作者在《山海集》中创作的格律诗没有严格使用平水韵，所用汉字的入声字没有完全照搬古代音律。作者所感悟的是：现代汉语扬弃了古代部分音训，是否采用商务印书馆《新华字典》《现代汉语词典》的注音来处理部分平仄，但还不能完全丢掉古代传统诗词的基本脉络。同时，试图把西方后现代文学创作手法融入其中，用心良苦，可见一斑。

在这里，作者首先感谢自己的父亲吴连忠、母亲刘成珍，是他们让作者来到这个世界。其次，感谢汪晋宽校长，是他给了作者自由写作的客观学术环境和条件。作者也借此向支持和关心他的家人、亲属、老师、同学、同事、学生和朋友致意。

诗词写作和翻译的路还很长，作者恳请社会各界读者批评指正。

（阿运锋/文）

2015 年 7 月 1 日

著/译者自序

诗是一种文体，体现在具体的诗中。只有具体的诗，才能去了解、去欣赏、去翻译、去共鸣。诗词翻译是一种创作，需要有诗人一样自如运用双向文字的能力。英译中文的古诗词，不能不考虑白话文的负面迁移。近一百年前的新文化运动，西化了汉语思维，这种被西化了的思维体现在现代汉语方面，使原本极其丰富的语言简化了、弱化了、泛化了、洋化了，枝繁叶茂的经典英文原著和贫瘠的汉语译本使英汉两种语言在基本要素的饱和度上不是处于同一个层面上。反过来说，枝繁叶茂的汉语原著和相对贫瘠的英文译本也出现了汉英两种语言难以对等的局面。

有观点认为，中国翻译的最高境界在于“化境”。首先，我们不妨解析一下什么叫化境。王昌龄在《诗格》中提出三境：物镜、情境和意境。这是文学批评史上最早的出处。明末朱承爵在《存余堂诗话》中认为：作诗的真味“全在意境融彻”，把“意”和“境”的关系熔炼一处。王国维的“造境”“写境”“意境两忘，物我一体”承上启下，把内外、虚实、象境推移到了引发无限遐思的情感体验之中。上述所有的术语中，“境”是眼睛，是着力点。

化境的“化”，就是点化、转化、融化；“境”，就是独立存在于“象”以外的客观环境，它既包含“象”，同时，也包含“象”以外的一切虚实。钱钟书先生提出的化境，是符际转换之后，不留斧凿的痕迹，能够保留原作的风味，也就达到了“极其高超的境界”(sublimity)。实际上，这是禅化了的信达雅。

钱先生所说的风味，也就是风格和品味，仍然是一种“境”——从此境化入彼境，实现了外部条件的转化，自然连带了内核的转化。从这个意义上说，化境是诗词翻译的方式，是手段问题。内核的合理转化才是目标，转换到什么程度才是目的。合理内核是怎么布局的，布局的各个要素呈现出怎样一种架构状态，这是需要进一步探讨的。

我们认为，“化境”直接受到了“传神”翻译观的影响。传神的“神”是个核心概念，对于人，指的是内在的情感；对于物，指的是意趣和内在的感染力。译诗想做到神似，不但要有十分精确的结构肌理、音色配置和全部构思，还要体现出原诗情思、情致和情趣。

然而，所说的传神，对于诗歌而言，只能取近似值，它合理的存在观应该是“神似”。神似是一种审美标准，与中国传统绘画最高境界的神似有相通的地方；不同的是，绘画的神似表现的是似与不似之间的物象，留给读者的是广阔、遐思的空间；译诗的神似不存在这种空间。这种空间是原诗的，绝不是译诗的，译诗的能动性只能是具象的写实，不允许脱离原诗去生成不相关联的空间。这个初步论断告诉我们：神似是相对的，保证神似的“传神”也是相对的。可见，诗词翻译，完全的等值和等效是不现实的。

弗罗斯特（Robert L. Frost）有一句话：“诗就是在翻译中失去的那种东西。”这句话一再被用来证明，诗歌是不可译的。从文学的临摹、微雕角度看，我们完全赞同这个观点，因为在诗词翻译过程中，最合理的动态对等也是不现实的。茅盾先生曾经说过，原诗翻译“只能保留一二种，决不能完全保留”。为什么这样说？我们的理解是，诗歌载体所具有的本体特质不同：中诗讲究意合、平仄、升降调、对仗、排偶以及象形文字的三维特征，英诗所使用的屈折语具有音步、轻重音节、跨行、断句等功能。这些都是两种文字在信息接受方面无法完全对等的因素。

然而，从统摄人类情感这个超越国界和时空的角度，所有的诗都是可以解码的，是可以解读的。菲茨杰拉德（Edward Fitzgerald）由于出色地翻译了欧玛尔·海亚姆（Omar Khayyam）的《鲁拜集》

（*The Rubaiyat of Omar Khayyam*），才走进了英国文学史杰出诗人的行列。许渊冲先生由于使用英、法、汉三种语言，出色地翻译了以诗词为主体的60多部典籍，所以，1999年被提名为诺贝尔文学奖候选人，2014年获得国际翻译界最高奖项之一的“北极光”杰出文学翻译奖，且系首位获此殊荣的亚洲翻译家。从这个意义上讲，诗词是可译的。

神似、化境、三美翻译观是贯穿20世纪中国翻译体系的三元素。三元素中，神似是作者拟切入的关键话题。通常所说的神有四个方面，即神韵、神味、神致、神趣。其中，神韵是核心，包含感情、韵味、意境和风格等要素。总起来讲，神似就是接近原文的精神。传译所借助的手段一旦达到了神奇或神异（magic）的效果，则谓之传神。

不过，我们要问，神似究竟近似到了什么程度？这是个不容回避的问题。我们透过诗歌的三维架构，试图剥离它的外墙，看看支撑起这个建筑模型的究竟是什么。我们发现，诗歌的下层，对应地排列着诗骨、诗韵和诗魂。所说的诗骨，指的是构成诗词所指和能指的一切符号；诗韵，指的是这些符号流动于诗行中的韵味；诗魂，指的是诗的风骨、器局和操守。

大家知道，魂与神是同时存在的，神是外显的，是可感知的；魂是内隐的，主阳，随神游变，物载魂而生，生而有神。神的灵动程度取决于魂的凝聚程度。如果把神比作眼睛，那么，魂则是统摄和支配眼睛的大脑。写诗是这样，译诗也是这样，神似为表，魂似为本，要传神，先译魂。翻译诗魂，就是在翻译原诗的本真。这里，我们暂且把这个现象命名为魂似（Transoulation，省称 transoul），它是译神→传神→神似的最终目标，是通向诗词的灵魂和神志的极致。

从量化层面上看，诗魂只有一个，它是由不同截面构成的，是个多元体，每个单元都呈阴阳对照状态。

在诗词的稳定性上，分为静魂和动魂：静魂是指诗词的原象或主象总体上保持着恒定的状态，每个诗人的总体风格就是由这种状态支配的；动魂是诗词在总体器格的框架下，按照不定的频率所进行的游离或反拨。比如，清奇千里的诗脉偶尔出现几首郁陶诡势的

诗行，并不能说明某个作者的诗位由于它的殊声而离开了它的合响。

在诗词的存在状态上，有隐魂和显魂：隐魂是指诗词的精义趋向婉晦、阐幽；显魂是指诗词的精义趋向昭晰、骋势。

在诗词的气格上，有精魂和负魂：精魂是指诗词迁雄拔体，金相流风；负魂是指诗词忿怼狷狭，郁伊怆怏。

在诗词的格体上，有强魂和弱魂：强魂是指诗词的雄浑、豪放、旷达、俊爽；弱魂是指诗词的沉郁、悲慨、冲和、工丽。

在诗词的饱和度上，有浓魂和淡魂：浓魂指的是诗词的绚丽、繁淫、远奥；淡魂指的是诗词的清幽、精约、轻靡。

合格的诗词写作和翻译需要具备一定的审美前结构，这个结构由语言知识、文化积淀、阅历储备、审美经验、个性特征等潜质构成。这些潜质要素的数量和质量，与诗品的质量成正比，这些潜质要素决定着作者和译者只有某一个主导气质和若干个相关的辅助气质。在不同的诗境之下，是狂放还是缠绵、是豁达还是哀婉，都可以通过气质调节，传达出原诗的本真状态，这个状态也就是诗魂的代称。

诗词语言最精练，最能高度概括和表达作者的思想感情，同时，最具有特殊的音乐结构。《毛诗序》中有六义，即诗词划类的风、雅、颂和表现手法的赋、比、兴。这个古老的诗论同样适合于英汉诗歌互译。传统比较诗词译论认为，中诗重于辞藻，英诗文辞朴实；中诗强调简约，英诗流于铺陈；中诗长于韵外之致，英诗善于条分缕析；中诗以象形文字会意，解构出特殊的象征性暗示，英诗以拼音文字组合，刻录出特定环境下瞬间的形象；中诗一字一位，同韵词选择空间大，韵式相合，脚韵相乘，英诗单词长短不一，音节不定，同韵词数量有限，韵式多变成为必然。针对最后一点，不是英诗不善一韵到底，而是语言本身使其无法作为。

我们也知道，中诗的审美境界在于意象美、含蓄美和朦胧美，所产生的幻想是语言的多义性和不确定性造成的。而之所以造成这种局面，正是由于汉语缺乏数、格、性、体、位等显性标识。也正因为这样，才创造出了富有张力的隐喻式体认。就此，我们回到原文和译文比之于茶和水的关系上，并非甲语言先天优于乙语言，是茶还是水，说的无非是语言的典雅和华丽程度。经验告诉我们，英诗总体上不如中诗，中诗英译，适当地增色，通过再造了的语言“借诗还魂”，只有这样，才能避免千诗一面的“像诗”现象的出现。

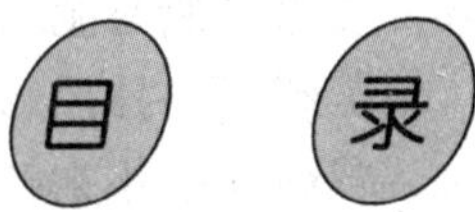

上 册

四言诗

Four Character Poems

爱

迷眼杨花，轻鞶送音。矫情盈袖，青黛羞琛。
红软相扶，抱玉[①]钩心。远烟恋花，近月藏林。
宝钗不老，冷翠千浔。旧燕卿卿，黄茅[②]映沈。
陌上香细，酥手难寻。残香疏淡，花落霜侵。
袅袅楼风，秋蝉雀音。我有糟糠，抵过千金。

【注释】

①抱玉：怀抱德才，深藏不露。②黄茅：茅草名。

Love

Blinding willow catkins
Are frowning the light tones.
Affections fill the sleeves and
Black brows are rare and shy.
Soft flames in sustaining one another
Hug the hearts into a pure jade.
Afar, the mists are loving the flowers, and,
Near, the moon is hidden into the woods.
Precious trinket for the never-aging
Is chilled with green, fathomless dews.
Old swallows are lured into the whispers
Of tangleheads that are shining down.
And on the pathway the fine sweet
Is inaccessible to her fine hands.
Sparse and thin, the lingering incenses

Are frost-bitten with the petals down-at-heel.
Waved in the wind of the storeys,
The harvest flies are chattering with the sparrows.
But in my eye, my bread-and-butter marriage
Will be worth more than one thousand ounces of gold.

爱别人

青荷落雨，碎玉玲珑。寒阁夜读，点珠圆融。
老骥吟病，万马驰风。凉枕秋梦，更待春红。

Love Into Another

Rains, onto the green lotus,
Jingle, rattle, tinkle like broken jade pieces.
My night book within the cabinet trembles
In a unity of all the beads.
Amiss with the rhapsodies, the veteran thoroughbred
Nips along like the wind of all horses.
In the arms of morpheus the cool on the autumn pillow,
Is waiting for another red spring.

爱的伤逝

金桂如米，银桂似霜。丹桂红蕾，满城流香。
几片飞叶，暗影彷徨。一韵朔风，万转情肠[①]。

【注释】

①情肠：感情；心肠。

Love That's Gone

Golden osmanthus flowers are grains
And those silvery are frosts.
Red buds in the crimson are
Coursing full in the sweet town.
Yet, a few gliding leaves
Are mooching like a shadow.
And in the rhyme of north wind,
All are having their worth-feelings.

北戴河

青牛踏紫，十里梓桑[①]。辐辏[②]碾海，魏武垂芳。
一河毓秀[③]，三峰[④]绿阳。碣石远裕[⑤]，鹤舞梅乡。
陆离海镜，赫赫天潢[⑥]。翠柳含金，碧云腾骧[⑦]。
九衢夏都，麟趾[⑧]连冈。六朝否臧[⑨]，八代分张[⑩]。
耒耜[⑪]星驰，论语叩阊[⑫]。临水向若[⑬]，冷眼东方。

【注释】

①梓（zǐ）桑：即桑梓。清·孔尚任《桃花扇·辞院》："烽烟起，烽烟起，梓桑半损。欲归，归途难问。"②辐辏（fú còu）：车轮的辐条，表示车轮的辐条一起向毂（车轮中心的圆木）集中，用于比喻目、耳、心一起使用。③毓（yù）：养育；秀：优秀。毓秀：孕育着优秀的人物。④三峰：即北戴河联峰山，位于北戴河海滨中心偏

西，傍海东西横列5公里，有东联峰山、中联峰山、西联峰山之分。⑤远裕（yù）：遥远而富足。⑥天潢（huáng）：《史记·天官书》和《汉书·天文志》中称“天津”星为“天潢”：“王良旁有八星绝汉，曰天潢。”⑦腾骧（xiāng）：飞腾；奔腾。《文选·张衡》：“负笋业而馀怒，乃奋翅而腾骧。”⑧麟趾（lín zhǐ）：比喻有仁德、有才智的贤人。晋·陆云《答孙显世》诗之七：“志拟龙潜，德配麟趾。”唐·陆贽《册杞王妃文》：“克茂鹊巢之规，叶宣麟趾之美。”⑨否臧（pǐ zāng）：成败。⑩分张：分割；分裂。⑪耒耜（lěi sì）：象形字，古代的一种翻土农具，形如木叉，上有曲柄，下面是犁头，用以松土，可看作犁的前身。“耒”是汉字部首之一，从“耒”的字，与原始农具或耕作有关。耒耜的发明开创了中国农耕文化。⑫论语：“论”是“论纂”的意思，“语”是“语言”的意思。“论语”就是把“接闻于夫子之语”论纂起来。阊（chāng）：传说中的天门。⑬向若：《庄子·秋水》：“至于北海，东面而视，不见水端，于是焉河伯始旋其面目，望洋向若而叹曰：‘……今我睹子之难穷也，吾非至于子之门则殆矣。’”

Beidaihe

Black Ox steps along the purple
Mulberry and catalpa for ten miles.
The cart wheel ever rolled along the sea,
Where the Emperor Wu of Wei was inscribed indelibly.
One river’ s endowed with the finest qualities
And three peaks are sunned in green.
Arid Rock farther in opulence
Enjoy the stork dance among the wintersweets.
Above the sea mirror of varied hues
Are the celestial lake great in renown.
Weeping willows golden in emerald green

Are swift-rising in the bluish clouds!
Downtown streets of the Summer Capital
Are ridged and kindhearted gently.
In the rise and fall of the six dynasties,
All the reigns were weakened into division.
Plough-handles and shares on the wings of the stars
Opened the celestial door to the *Analects of Confucius*.
By the water stretched to the ocean,
We see the crack of dawn, cold-eyed.

别错放位置

田车于野，止步维萚[①]。中林有谷，不纳锦衣。
携弓于狩，虎兕有声。徂旅攸摄，戒惕有愆。

【注释】

①萚（tuò）：酸枣一类的灌木。一说“萚”乃枯落的枝叶。

Don't Be Misplaced

My hunting chariot in array
Was halted by the bushes.
Thru the vale of woods,
Damask dress was rejected.
Put in the case my bow,
Tigers and rhinoceros sounded rough.
Before the invading foes of ill will,
I was wrong for the dangers that bode.

别太自信

九折铜梁，藤葛引度。绳烂沙井，柳枝依附。
雨前闹蚁，沸耳眩目。一寸泞淖，夺天铁幕。

Don’t Be Too Assured

Crooked and tortuous, the bronze beam
Could be crossed with a lone vine.
Were the rope worn-out in the sand drain,
A willow branch could be clung.
Fast and furious, ants before the rain
Were boiling in my dazzling ears.
One inch of foul ditch could be
An iron curtain to despoil the heaven.

别找错对象

柳棉谁织？黄鸟殷勤。绣作蝶语，纱絮欺云。
临风紫阙，洙泗[1]求勋。霓裳骨瘦，焉得子君？

【注释】

①洙泗：洙水和泗水。古时二水自今山东省泗水县北合流而下，至曲阜北，又分为二水，洙水在北，泗水在南。春秋时属鲁国地。孔子在洙泗之间聚徒讲学。后因以“洙泗”代称孔子及儒家。此处泛指河流。

Never to the Wrong Shop

Who's woven the willow cottons
Like yellow birds pay their attentions?
Embroidered into the tongue of butterflies,
The yarn wads are teasing the cloud.
To the wind around the purple palace,
The rivers seek their meritorious service.
But how could a gaunt loner in the rainbow skirt
Get the chance to attend the Lord?

不胜酒力

初筵醉止，由醉其心。心内无忧，曷饮如霖。
陈馈百盏，对月以斟。尔仪式饮，明月抚琴。
月离星小，零露涔涔。终日瘖寐，谁知我音?

Hopelessly Drunk

Drunk in the revelry,
Drunk in my heart.
Free of care within,
Drink like rain, but why?
Here, one hundred cups,
Drink to the moon.
To go on a bust,
The bright moon plays the lute.

The moon moves thru the small stars,
And the dews are streaming down.
To consult with my pillow all day,
Goodness knows my tongue.

浮　沉

青丝绾愁，花落阑珊。优游一叶，叠翠孤帆。
波澜静嵩，水梦苍山。空江冷暖，月明青天。

Ups and Downs

Sad black hairs are tied up in
The falling and waning petals.
In carefree leisure, one leaf has been
Claded in verdure that sails in solitude.
Billows, still and lofty, fantasize
About the grey hills by the water.
Bare, the river changes in temperature
By the broad moon-lit daylight.

成　家

上智无言，生死尘埃。参差风雨，独坐钓台。
一弯平水，墨心闲裁。东君踏歌，默草时来。

Gone to the World

For the wisest, it's dumb, and
For the life and death, it's dust.
In the rain and wind on all the notes,
My fishing table sits alone.
At the curve of the calm water,
My heart of ink cuts at ease, and
In the stepping dance by the Lord of East,
The tacit grass comes on time.

大樱桃

剔透熏风，朱玉万点。露妆颦蹙[①]，几谢清寒。
谁信缘啬？柳絮轻拈。苍黎[②]市井，自知酸甜。

【注释】

①颦蹙（pín cù）：皱眉皱额，比喻忧愁不乐，亦作“颦顣”。②苍黎：百姓。

Big Cherries

Perceptive in the gentle air
Are ten thousand bright red jades.
Dressed in dews that knit the brows,
The clear cold has fallen and fallen away.
Who would believe the harvest all along?

The willow catkins are smiling lightly.
But throughout the town of the people,
A bitter-sweet taste of life should be natural.

淡　定

旻天厥月①，于以②昭明？原隰戬穀③，阴雨零濛。
弁彼甫田④，播厥⑤沮耕。临冲⑥旱麓，四野维屏。
烈烈溯风，率土靡盈⑦。五湖多辟⑧，新庙卒崩⑨。
浩浩三江，曷惠其氓？殷殷⑩小子，坐迁峥嵘。
暴虎苛政，猗⑪于虎鲸。冯河⑫长羽，画里龙行。

【注释】

①旻（mín）天：秋天，泛指天。厥（jué）：气闭。②于以：犹言于何。在何处。③原隰（xí）：广平与低湿之地。亦泛指原野。戬穀：即“戬谷”，出自《诗经·小雅·天保》，后多见于各类骈文。有福禄之意，亦有尽善之说。④弁（biàn）：急。甫田：大田。⑤播厥：播种。⑥临冲：古代的两种战车。⑦靡盈：不足。⑧多辟：亦作“多僻”。多邪僻。⑨卒崩：倒塌。⑩殷殷：形容忧伤、忧郁。⑪猗（yī）：加，超越。⑫冯（píng）河：徒步涉水渡河。引申为有勇无谋、冒险行动。

Calm

Under the due, pitying heaven,
How could the virtue be glorified?
In the open country for perfection,
It is overcast to the rustling of rain.
With those boundless fields,

I have sown my low and wet furrows.
Out from the mountain' s foot,
All the vast stretches are screened.
Stirred by the vigorous breezes,
The land leaves much to be desired.
With the evils to deplore, the Five Lakes
Have toppled the new temples.
In proud array the Three Rivers
Have favoured their faithless men, but how?
Ardent, my unworthy self moves
The seat along the rugged grandeur.
Unarmed against the tigers from tyranny,
It' s like a brave go to the killer whales.
Feathered long to cross the boatless river,
It' s like the go of a dragon in the picture.

东秦咏

烟霞横翠，玉兰唱清。蜡黄泄金，兰蕙薰风。
艳冷芳池，阑干敲玉。濛茸草色，荡柳丝冰。
桃花纱碧，雪梨冠山。丹霞云影，汤河闲灯。
醉花裁云，骊珠娇奼。广厦雄起，断阙群峰。

Ode to Neuq

With wisps of the coloured mist in green,
Magnolias are chanting clean.
Off the waxen buds spills the golden thread,
In the breeze the orchids smell sweet ahead.

All along the fragrant pond of a quiet glory,
Marble balustrades stand there silvery.
On the downy hues of grass,
Willow threads sway gentally like pure stars.
In a green gauze of peach blossoms,
Snow pears would cover the hilly axioms.
Under a myriad of evening sun-rays and clouds,
The Tanghe River is a blaze of free crowds.
Tipsy flowers like the trimmed clouds sailing
Are buoying up the tender pearls charming.
High-rises are standing up abrupty,
That shelter the dream of mountains steeply.

大　雨

时维仲夏，汗星潸潸。轻荷暗附，细柳弄烟。
山角拖云，电母挥鞭。荆篱越风，豆雨离天。
万条水线，狂舞乱剑。裂闪夺目，霹雳摇川。
咆哮龙虎，隐迹藏胆。卷荡星河，横扫霄汉。

Rain in Torrents

It was in the midsummer,
I was glistening with sweat.
While the light lotus sneaked up,
Fine willows were misty.
While the mountain corner towed the clouds,
Mother Lightening whipped the waves.
Over the fence roared the wildest rage, and

Rains like beans fell off the heaven.
A myriad of waterlines
Were wielding the swords rapturously.
Lightning was ripped up in dazzles,
Whose thunderclaps rocked the rivers.
Like dragons and tigers that roared,
All courages were hidden in seclusion.
Oh, the galaxy was rolled and and bowled,
Sweeping the Milky Way.

荡　者

红雨掩门，罗衾绮袖。独榻思游，绿蜡依旧。
逸梦疏风，雨梨更漏。冰弦归鸟，抱琴空瘦。

Concubine

Door, hidden by the blood rain,
Sleeves, splendid down the silken quilt on the sly.
Couch, a free spirit in the wandering solitude,
And as usual, her green candle flickers there.
Dreams, easily lost into the dispelling wind,
And water clock, like the rain unto the pears.
Bird, back to his ice strings,
And her lyre hugs but a thin shadow.

冬天海日

维时[①]苍苍，蚴蟉趋跄[②]。暗棹[③]清韵，詄荡紫皇[④]。
奇龙韬匿[⑤]，謇謇綦辙[⑥]。低徊氄毳[⑦]，洗尽寒霜。
彳亍[⑧]苍虹，鱏鱼溧锦[⑨]。倚天瑰玮[⑩]，光锷[⑪]东方。

【注释】

①维时：其时。②蚴蟉（yòu liú）：语出《汉书·司马相如传》所载《上林赋》："青龙蚴蟉于东箱。"本为龙行之貌。趋跄（qiàng）：行动有仪容。③棹（zhào）：船桨，代指船。④詄（dié）荡：旷远貌。紫皇：《太平御览》卷六五九引《秘要经》："太清九宫，皆有瞭属，其最高者，称太皇、紫皇、玉皇。"⑤韬匿：隐藏。⑥謇謇（jiǎn）：耿直貌。綦（qí）辙：足迹，泛指旧迹。⑦低徊：徘徊。氄毳（rǒng cuì）：鸟兽的细绒毛。⑧彳亍（chì chù）：慢慢走路貌。⑨鱏（yín）鱼：白鱼，皮着银粉物，尾分三叉，形同小鱼。溧锦：美玉罗列状。溧：当作"瑮"。⑩瑰玮（wěi）：宏丽。⑪锷（è）：刀剑的棱刃锋芒。

The Sea Sun of Winter

Grey, grey, at the horizon,
Gambols the dragon in a refined complexion;
Dark, dark paddles rhymed clearly
Are spotted afar along the purple heaven.
Into the shade the dragon so wonderful
Traces his old, frank go.
Wandering imperceptibly,
He's cleared up the frosty spell.

Like a grey rainbow that hovers,
The silken scales swim their silvers.
Into the heaven, he's counted greatly,
That shines in the eastern universe.

读　书

韦编[①]忘倦，缥帙[②]悬梁。
尺璧[③]寸阴，循躬笔芒。
云衡典惊，日驱千行。
鲸鲵[④]运海，眺听雪狂。
何日坟籍[⑤]，点化夷乡？

【注释】

①韦编：简策书连接的形式与材料。②缥帙：浅青色的书衣，泛指书卷。③尺璧：古玉器名，直径一尺的大璧，言其珍贵。④鲸鲵：古人认为是凶猛的大鱼，雄者为鲸，雌者为鲵。这里以典籍诗词作比。⑤坟籍：古代典籍的代称。

【自解】

农历十一月十七日是父亲的生日，母亲刚才从望奎来了电话，才知道自己疏忽了。我不能以开会、年终考核为理由去辩解什么，内心掠过一丝自责。

几个春节没回家了，下一个春节无论如何也要回去一趟，关上门，陪父母过个年。这个愿望现在尤其强烈。曾经在父母身边过了四十多个年，后二十来个年，即使除夕夜，也在捧着书本，不顾及父母的感受，实在可恶。

For Study

Relief from fatigue I' ve found
In books where my mind must be sound.
Time is precious,
Be a man industrious and labourious.
Like the clouds glaring and thrilling,
Thousands of lines in a day are running.
Like the whales hurtling on the sea,
Scour the horizon that snows violently.
When shall the learned books
Touch the foreign land with magic looks?

读书瘾

案几衔月，春来卧寒。断云锄风，敲雨问兰。
龙井烟绿，蕙心摇帆。墨笔潇潇，青葱落幔。
玉鳞寥廓，结庐尘寰。自谪戴水，心横楚山。
纵酒欢情，天长月淡。阅遍千古，一声轻叹。

Reading Addiction

The moon has been gulped into my desk,
That sleeps cold into the coming of spring.
With the sudden veer of clouds hoeing the wind,
The rain rattles before my orchids.
With the cup of green tea curling up,

The pure heart shakes the sail.
Here, my writing brush showers and showers,
By the verdure that lowers the curtain.
Under the boundless sky the precious fish
Has settled down on the worldly society.
Exiled to the Daihe River by myself,
My heart goes transversely to the Chu Mountains.
To be on the bend,
The days are long through the thin moon.
Having gone over all the ages,
I can but heave a gentle sigh.

飞　鸟

提琴万里，弄影冰弦。半生逐浪，一梦苍山。
杯底凝香，落拓枕边。孤竹飞渡，瘦月晓寒。
迢迢沧浪，红雨峦烟。消魂归鸟，清露鸣滩。
幽幽古韵，折柳阑干。灵阳化气，我要飞天。

Flying Bird

Fiddled thru ten thousand *li*,
My ice strings are shivering their shadows.
To run after the billows half a life,
My dream is lost into the dark green mountains.
On the cup bottom curdles the sweet that
Has been down and out by my pillow,
Where the lonely bamboos are scudding,
That tightens the moon thru the trembling dawn.

Behold! The far-stretching, surging waves
Are misted by the red rain in the mountains.
My soul is consumed like a bird that returns,
In the clear dews singing on the strands.
Cloistered into the old rhymes,
The willows are snapped beside the balustrade.
To the sun spirit that refines the vital essence,
How I would be soaring up!

飞　雪

腊月驰雪，浮浮①昊天。于以克明②？雪霁③萧寒。
腊月冲雪，汎汎④幽燕。于以明晦⑤？高朗清源。
腊月弥雪，漉漉⑥水湾。于以凌阴⑦？翰飞⑧于田。

【注释】

①浮浮：雨雪盛貌。②于以：犹言于何；在何处。克明：彰明。③雪霁（jì）：雨雪停止，天放晴。④汎汎（fàn）：荡漾的样子，浮动的样子。⑤明晦（huì）：明暗；晴阴。南朝·梁武帝《拟明月照高楼》诗："相去既路迥，明晦亦殊悬。"⑥漉漉（lù lù）：莹润貌。唐·李贺《月漉漉篇》："月漉漉，波烟玉，莎青桂花繁，芙蓉别江木。"⑦凌阴：藏冰的地窖。《诗·豳风·七月》："二之日凿冰冲冲，三之日纳于凌阴。"《毛传》："凌阴，冰室也。"⑧翰飞：高飞。

Blowing Snow

Snows are spurred by the twelfth month
In the great heaven, flake on flake.
How could the virtuous light be shed?

The cold spells should be cleared up.
Snows are charged by the twelfth month
Downstreaming the serene, northern shades.
How could the obscurity be brightened?
To be clean and clear from up high.
Snows are overflown by the twelfth month
Which is soaked with the water bay.
How could the shades be soaring?
Soar up from among the farmland.

芙　蓉

一抹风影，两道划痕。吻落东风，盈盈水滨。
幽潭忍香，翠衣半轮。闲观陌路，眼中几人？

Hibiscuses

A wisp of wind shadow
Has scratched two trails.
Kiss down that easterly gales,
Full of the bustling beaches!
A faint fragrance born in the deep, secret pool
Is coating the emerald green onto half the wheel.
In eyes of mortals, there would be a few
Strangers with their lazy watches.

感　激

少小来路，桑麻自攀。倚天绵玉，风信逸闲。
百年横雨，萧透维艰。一瞬轻灵，心香几瓣。

Gratitude

Youth approaches,
Like the hemp creepers of their own.
A soft fair under the sky
Takes comfort in the hyacinths.
In the torrential downpour for a century,
The quenched, desolate times are hopeless.
While in a split second, the flighty elf
Has budded into a few petals of sweet heart.

工作乐趣

轻装就道，青簇[①]晨鸡。曀曀游雾[②]，采芹月西。
劳使人生，花觞畅犁。银烛紫陌，梦影山溪。

【注释】

①青簇：草木青翠繁茂貌。②曀曀（yì）：阴沉昏暗貌。游雾：形容霜雪很盛的样子。

Job Pleasure

Lightly, it should be out on the journey,
Till the green clusters by the roosters at dawn.
In gloomy, cloudy mists that wander,
I've plucked the water-cress till the moon slides down.
Mundane earthlings as we are,
The lure of wine ploughs smooth.
Throughout the thoroughfare, my silver candlestick
Traces my dreams in the mountain creek.

关　心

香尘收雨，翡翠薄梳。含冰临镜，野渡幽庐。
闲钓静浦，路涩蟾蜍。行潦有意，尊酒对虚[①]。

【注释】

①虚：大丘。

Frame of Mind

Rain, drawn in the fragrant dust,
Is combing a thin emerald,
Before the mirror like ice,
That shines on my serene hut by the ferry,
Where let my idle angles go down still,
Apart from the cragged and rugged toads.

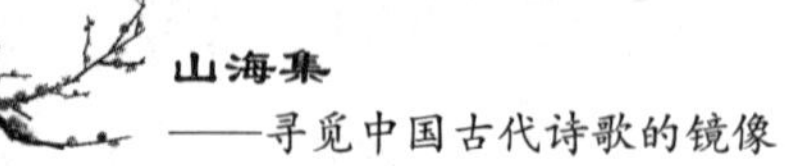

If the ditch-water has its will,
My wine will be concrete with those abstracts.

好女人

仕女知性，劳人不迁。牖下怀春，舒脱静言。
仕女有行，其姝也欢。骄人善怀，思柔自怜。

Good Lady

To be in the know, a fair lady
Won't transfer her mundane earthling.
Once in seclusion longing for love,
She'd ruminate it mutely yet leisurely.
To be wedded and gone, a fair lady
Would be bright with a heaved-up joy.
The sense of pride is satisfied to be good,
With a soft spirit to mirror herself.

好诗人

朔气雕玉，娇颜怕弹。红尘倦客，一捻幽寒。
柔情铁血，玉人雄关。莫道天长，英雄不还。

Good Poet

Northern chills can carve the gems,

Afraid for shooting the tender faces.
A tired wanderer in this worldly life
Is but a pinch of serene, severe snap.
Iron-willed, the tender feeling faces
The impregnable pass of rosy hues.
Say not that the days are long,
And the hero will be gone forever.

好心态

柳岸推盏，当花侧帽①。一池绿菱，满襟晚照。
菡萏②千枝，蝉影初报。饮露藏声，清响自好。

【注释】

①侧帽：北周美男子独孤信长得很帅，所以常有人以他为模仿的对象，堪称当代时尚。某天，他出城打猎，不知不觉中天色已晚，他要赶在宵禁之前奔回家，由于马骑太快了，头上的帽子被吹歪了，也来不及扶正。不明就里的人看了这个样子，大感惊艳，觉得他看起来非常潇洒。第二天起，满街都是模仿独孤信侧帽的男人。但“侧帽”的典故后来被引用为风流自赏的意思。②菡萏（hàn dàn）：荷花的别称。

Good State of Mind

Raise the goblets to the shore of willows,
Relishing our turns to the elated flowers.
As the pond of green water chestnuts is
Leaving the departing rays on our lapels,
Thousands of lotus flowers are reporting

Their first shadows of balm crickets, who
Are drinking the dews but hide the tones,
Ringing clear in the purity of their own.

赫图阿拉

山林之浒，滔滔猎夫。介狄①维禹，匹猫成虎。
启运发祥，桓拔外疆。奋伐披挞，振振厥声。
戎狄②好音，天命显思。明昭③失序，烝民降罔④。
作召奉天，揉解万邦。哀恫⑤景山，青天炯长。

【注释】

①介狄：犹言元凶。②戎狄：古时候华夏族对西北地区的少数民族的统称，即北狄和西戎的合称。③明昭：明智聪察。④烝（zhēng）：众多貌。罔：同“网”，降网。⑤哀恫：悲痛。

Hetuara

Along the clear river through the woods
Bravely came out the surging hunters.
As the great foes to the Central Plains,
The cats were growing up into the tigers.
Promising and propitious, let slip the dogs
Of war beyond the northeast of the Great Wall.
Charge! Fearless on the punitive expedition,
With the tinkling, jingling voices overflown.
Those barbarians with the spiritual tidings
Were evidently entitled to the mandate of heaven.
As the bright grace had been out of sequence,

The common people should extend their own way.
To act only as Heaven as the time would do,
Thrills of sweet tenderness went over the nation.
That stricken heart in Jigsaw Peak hanged himself,
And the broad daylight would last long and long.

恨　人

世路多舛，怜鬼有冤。沧海一恨，楚囚桃源。
国破红粉，负罪陈垣。银钩西去，还可再圆。

Bad Blood

Life' s path can be buffeted by fate,
Whence even a ghost may be grossly unjust.
One hatred afloat on the vast ocean
Has been convicted into the shangri-la
Where the state and its rosy cheeks are lost,
And held in guilty unto the old walls.
As the silver crescent sails west,
She would return round again.

话不说破

轻纱薄暮，汗马丹霞。流光度尽，等闲生涯。
菜根夜谭，御世清茶。莲池妙善，半开奇葩。

Put It Less Bluntly

Damasked vespers
Toil their red auras.
As time is waning,
Careers are consuming.
Night roots of wisdom
Freshens the kingdom.
Wonderful goodness in
Lily pond half-blooms again.

坏女人

胭脂水浅，野杏羞颜。醉池倦柳，柯烂归山。
晴云乱鬓，银钩妒烟。引蝶一夏，花落复关。

Bad Lady

Rouge, shallow in the water,
Wild almond, with a shy face,
Willows, drowsy in the tipsy pool,
Twigs, worn-out before going back...
Fine clouds, with tresses discomposed,
Silver crescent, through jealous mists,
Butterflies, seduced in one summer, and
Petals fall, but never back again.

荒草行

大庆草荒，雾罩萍梗。杨木空锅，户外暇清。
霏霏落雪，玉花飞浪。隐隐长空，朔风交横。
膏腴放颠，丹黄景短。曲想幽思，苍鬓洁伤。
落落孤月，虚名相误。觞咏攒凑，幽人独行。
气格扬骨，晦潭摇风。鳞鳞霜阔，高历群星。
阴阴幌影，离离银汉。壮气逸胆，对语庄周。

Through the Weeds

On the overgrown farmland of Daqing,
The shrouded fogs are wandering.
Inside, kitchen fire is to be stoked,
Outside, it's perfectly untainted.

The old woman is plucking her geese,
That's a flurry of flying fleece.
Throughout the vast of heaven,
North wind is impetuously driven.

To be prolific,
The life of man isn't beatific.
Full of gloomy thoughts,
My forehead sprinkles with grey reports.

While the moon is down solitary,
Empty fame is but a wrong story.

While raising our cups in the toast,
My inner heart walks along the lonely coast.

Of striking demeanour, though,
Such carry-tale, dissentious jealousy, for know;
Over the minute diamonds of white frost so vast,
The twinkling stars are highly cast.

Beyond the tavern-sign in the dark,
Runs the Silver River like a lark.
With an eagle-winged pride of sky-aspiring,
May my dream of butterflies be sparkling

活　着

浮鹢戴水，潜兴遗魂。纵横辐凑，燕台无痕。
山妖水魅，粉阁销魂。独行束马[①]，隐遁溪村。

【注释】

①束马：驾马。南朝·梁·任昉《百辟劝进今上笺》："山戎、孤竹，束马景从伐罪吊民，一匡靖乱。"北齐·魏收《后园宴乐》诗："束马轻燕外，猎雉陋秦中。"

Alive

One egret floats in Daihe River,
On the diving spur with a lost soul.
To be converged, vertically and horizontally,
The swallow stand leaves no shadow.

Evil spirits in the hills and rills
Have intoxicated the cabinet of rouges.
To gallop lonely on my belted horse,
The creek village goes into hiding.

活自己的

嗟嗟[①]小子，肃肃[②]德行。遵彼戴水，其钓三更。
泛彼孤舟，济身北瀛。浼浼[③]离去，历历青萍。
子惠[④]田亩，岁聿[⑤]以衡。滺滺[⑥]陋室，驾笔独行。

【注释】

①嗟嗟（jiē）：叹词。表示招呼或感慨、赞美等。②肃肃：恭敬貌。③浼浼（měi）：水盛貌。④子惠：慈爱；施以仁惠。⑤岁聿（yù）：岁：年；聿：句中语气词。⑥滺滺（yōu）：水流貌。

Earn My Keep

Ah! My unworthy self tries
To be deferential to the virtue.
To abide by the Daihe River,
My night is dead keen on angling.
To float about on my lonely boat,
I' ve borne the body to the north Isle.
With the restless waters that are gone,
The blue duckweeds are clear and vivid.
Should the harvest-home be merciful,
The year would be bound in balance.
Closed in my humble room that flows,

I' ve driven my pens, alone and alone.

简　化

静水流远，素心淡敛。关情一缕，晓荷点点。
谁坐天际？轻颦恭俭[①]。柔红扯地，碎花风浅。

【注释】

①恭俭：恭敬俭约。俭，俭约，不放纵。

Cut Short

Still water flows far, but
The pure heart reaps thin.
A plume of care drops
On the dawning lotus.
Who sits there at the horizon
Complaisant and economical in a light frown?
It' s the soft red that' s bestrewed
In the shallow breezes scattering the flowers.

碣石山

渐渐[①]荒石，蒺藜明晦[②]。下临桑柔，时序有愆[③]。
渐渐荒石，孤竹戎作。荏染[④]弓矢，孑遗[⑤]委土。
渐渐荒石，渊渊[⑥]裂鼓。八鸾魏武，载旆[⑦]苍莽。
渐渐荒石，泱泱白浪。润之眉寿[⑧]，东土无疆。

【注释】

①渐渐（chán）：山石高峻。②蒺藜（jí li）：又名白蒺藜、屈人等。茎平卧，无毛，被长柔毛或长硬毛。为草场有害植物。明晦：明暗；晴阴。③愆（qiān）：过。④荏染：柔貌。⑤孑（jié）遗：遗迹。⑥渊渊：鼓声。亦泛用作象声词。⑦旆（pèi）：旗子上的镶边。泛指旌旗。⑧润之：毛泽东，字润之。眉寿：长寿。

Mount Jieshi

High and rough, the stones
In the wild rues are darkly brightened.
Gaze down those mulberry trees,
The timing sequence' s delayed.
High and rough, the stones
Are hidden by the Lone-Growing Bamboo,
Whose supple bows and arrows
Were ever razed into the dust.
High and rough, the stones
Striked up the swift rhythm of drums.
Whence Emperor Wu of Wei on eight phoenixes
Undulated the banners into the brooding twilight
High and rough, the stones
Were buffeting the wide, white waves,
Where Mao Tsedong granted with life long
Would bless China with boundless longevity.

酒　礼

青锋阔饮，问剑几何？孤调三尺，琴胆行波。
龙泉谁拭，宝匣蹉跎。壮士问天，何必豪歌。

Drinking Manners

Blue-tipped! Gulp down!
Unsheath'd sword! Short or long?
Isolated melodies measured three feet
Move the waves with the lyre so sweet.
My precious sword to grind, but who?
In the scabbard, don't you be staid, too.
Heroic man before Gracious Heavens
Needs not to be enlivened with a fado sense.

酒桌上的规矩
Table Etiquette

其一

旨酒令仪[①]，不废荒湛[②]。受之有衎，克之以胆。
君子式燕[③]，温克维感。小人式燕，回风摇颔。

【注释】

①旨酒：美酒。令仪：整肃威仪；美好的仪容、风范。②荒湛：沉湎于酒色，行为放荡。湛，通“耽”。③式燕：亦作“式宴”，宴饮。

One

Sweet wine observes the rite,
Should not be wallowed in lecherous pleasure.
Now strain off the wine for the right,
And get the better of it, truer and tougher.
A man of virtue keeps his revels
Won't get drunk in passion;
While a mean man keeps his revels,
He juts out his jaw like the air return.

其二

使君湛乐[①]，厌厌[②]神嗜。三觞之饫[③]，孔偕和旨[④]。
燕饮[⑤]八升，横槊生翅。湑[⑥]矣此饮，壹醉夺智。

【注释】

①湛乐：过度逸乐。②厌厌：绵长貌。③饫（yù）：古代家庭私宴的名称。饱食。④孔偕：甚为整齐。意谓同心尽兴。和旨：醇和而甘美。⑤燕饮：聚会在一起吃酒饭。燕，通“宴”。⑥湑（xǔ）：滤去渣滓而变清。

Two

In a dissipated life, the man
Has turned into gluttons.
Satiated with three cups,
He's mild, good and energetic.
After eight jars like a bacchanal,
His winged spear's levelled.
Pure and clear, such a wine
Snatches the wit after befuddled.

酒　座

无酒沉醉，有酒佯狂。煮酒玩月，谈酒流觞。
薄酒邀客，浓酒驱霜。举酒盈杯，放酒思乡。
心酒自省，墨酒弛张。人生有酒，黑夜阳光。

Drinking Seat

Deeply drunk for want of wine,
But delirious without the want of wine,
Such a warmed wine bathed in the moon
Was conversed into a meandering stream soon.
May the weak liquor be an entertainer,
And the spirituous liquor as a frost-like powder.
Fill and raise that brimmer and

Put down the homesick flask in the end.
As the heart wine knocks there,
The ink wine goes into the flexible air.
If life has its squirrel dews,
The dark night faces the sunny news.

看准再玩

探梦情种，红英赠蝶。乱丛萦蕙，野饭不接。
回阳鸟翼，朱楼可楫。火云闲乘，挟矢可猎。

Play Before More Advised Watch

The seeds of love for dreams are
Bestowing the red blooms to the butterflies
Thru a grove of evergreens full of sweet orchids
Whose wild foods are different as chalk and cheese.
Set the bird's wings with a warm weather
That resumes the red storey as their rudder
By which the cloud of flames can cleave
Its spare arrows to be pinched for a bag game.

浪漫有度

滴雨破云，细柳摇风。明月弄巧，艳鬓朦胧。
青草谁误？且问飞鸿。飞鸿一去，应有归踪。

Measured Romance

Specks of rain are breaking the clouds,
As the slender willows sway in the winds.
One bright moon is outsmarting herself,
As the amorous temples are bleary-eyed.
Who has led the green grass astray?
You may ask the wild geese in flight,
Who, once gone,
Should leave their trails of return.

梨花教主
Hierarch of Pear Flowers

其一

蝶梦无雪，情梦诗工。诗才落寒，醉蝶扑虹。
庄周枕蝶，雀渡冯风。红袖扶栏，凤蝶梦同。

One

The dream of butterflies is snowless,
And that of passions is acatalectic.

When the poetical genius trembles cold,
Her tipsy butterflies are flapped into the rainbow,
Which were ever the pillow of Chuang-tzu,
That got the sparrows over the windflows:
Her red sleeves on the hand rail
Shares the same dream of the swallow-tails.

其二

路在荆棘，草莽弯刀。人在桃园，柳叶暗刀。
寒诗瘦眉，薄纸藏刀。千仞松壑，不耐风刀。
霜刀可握，心刀无鳌。天若有情，人不操刀。

Two

The way amidst the brambles
Bends the blade thru the wild jungles.
The lady in the peach garden has
On the arched eyebrows like a secret knife,
That are thin with the trembling numbers
On her tissue-paper that conceals the daggers.
A thousand fathoms of her pine valley
Weary of the wind knife
Can hold the knife of white frost sharpened into her
Knife of heart but without a pincer.
Were Nature sentient,
The lady wouldn't grab a knife.

其三

一壶浮月，寒波潋滟。谁人可掬？迭软褰眠。
一盒碎月，三寸冷焰。孰与坐赏？玉华之僭[1]。
一抱水月，两膝醉念。壶中星雨，盒里浓艳。

【注释】

①僭（jiàn）：超越本分。

Three

A potful of floating moon
Shimmers on the cold waves.
Who'd hold it in both hands?
It's her swathed sleep suspensively supple.
A box of broken moon
Lights up the cold, three-inch flame.
With whom to sit for it?
With the insolent ambition of her ringlets.
An armful of water moon
Misses in the tipsy delights on her knees.
And star showers in her flagon
Are boxed into bright colours.

其四

池蛙鼓舌，枉自①疾雷。蚁穴任敲，鼓槌连绵。
灌坛雷雨，无意惊天。虺虺②其响，如迸铁舷。
急峡霆斗，猛志孤悬。狂雷叱顶，隧道击穿。

【注释】

①枉自：白白地。②虺虺（huǐ）：雷声，打雷的声音。

Four

Green frogs beat their tongues,
Like the sudden thunderclaps, but of no avail.
Ant nests are framed for the tolls,
Like the drum sticks at a stretch.
Thunderstorms that are poured down the platform
Shake the world, unconsciously.
The thunder rumbles high and nigh,
Like a burst ship's rail of steel.
In the deep dread-bolted thunder down the gorges,
Her intrepid will hangs there, though isolated.
When another violent bellow crashes overhead,
A fierce pang of pain shoots through her tunnel.

其五

听舟木影，两心同命。寒香放春，空遗水镜。
剪成花语，随风落定。自适温凉，克明养性。
百龄之木，刻舟以竞。抱水漂风，他人摇柄。

Five

The traces of wood with a boat ear
Share the weal and woe by the two hearts.
As the spring is set free in the cold sweet,
Her hollow mirror of water has been lost,
And scissored into the tongue of flowers
That would be settled with the wind.
Warm or cool, she takes her ease contentedly,
To nourish her nature by sheding a virtuous light.
That wood, about five-score winters,
Could be chiselled into a race boat,
That hugs the water to be drifted by the wind,
Striving to paddle, but by another.

其六

阴晨晴暮，守尽约期。仙人一洞，如画如诗。
此情叠垒，乱云摇枝。庐山看尽，百年围棋。
屈子天问，难倒仲尼。今人问天，何梦可依？

Six

Overcast morning or clear evening,
Don't you break the date.
Like a fairy in one cave
With a picturesque prospect,
Where such a passion can be nested
In the riotous clouds of swaying twigs,
That, like Mount Lushan, has taken in
The game of go for a century.
She knows Ch'u Yuan's questioning the Heaven
That ever gravelled master Confucius.
She also knows today' s asking the Heaven
Can count on no arms of morpheus.

其七

巧言窃笑，游丝张网。回纹绵密，织绵成像。
红尘灰梦，任由息飨[①]。林瘴洗天，素心澹荡。
乐彼机缘，流风为党[②]。横空丝路，向君开敞。

【注释】

①息飨（xiǎng）：年终农事既毕，举行蜡祭，饮宴老人，祭享神明。此处借指平日生活。②为党：结伙。

Seven

The sniggers through specious words
Are spreading the net like gossamers
Meandering along a fine, careful picture,
Which has been woven into the floss.
An ashy dream in the worldly life
Is abandoned to the sacrificial offerings.
After the wood miasma washes the sky,
Her pure heart becomes warm and pleasant.
Pleased by the chalice of opportunity,
Her lingering breeze flirts into a splinter
Of her own that rises upon the fibre path
To be opened to her man.

其八

风浮雨躁，胃煮心烧。狂急本性，胆智飘摇。
浮华满城，龙凤喧嚣。中国有梦，海外弄潮。

Eight

The birdbrained wind and rain
Give the heart and stomach a boil.
Fiercely and hastily, her nature
Has fluttered down the courageous wit.

The empty pomp and show of the city looks
Startled at the nice hustle and bustle.
If China has her dream,
Try to be a beach swimmer abroad.

恋爱中的鱼

游之乐，在于荷东。赫兮君子，杲杲[①]其阳。
游之乐，在于荷南。殷兮君子，素素其闼[②]。
游之乐，在于荷西。锦兮君子，邻邻其车。
游之乐，在于荷北。温兮君子，煌煌[③]其服。

【注释】

①杲杲：明亮的样子。②闼（tà）：门。③煌煌：形容明亮。

Fish in Love

A wandering pleasure
Sprightfull to the east of the lotus
Was elevated by the man of virtue
Whose bright sun rose into the void.
A wandering pleasure
Sprightfull to the south of the lotus
Was ardent for the man of virtue
Whose door was noted for sang-froid.
A wandering pleasure
Sprightfull to the west of the lotus
Was splendid to the man of virtue
Whose cab bells were ringing.

A wandering pleasure
Sprightfull to the north of the lotus
Was gentle with the man of virtue
Whose dress was brightly twinkling.

梨　花

点点梨花，一怀嫩雨。春心几寸，花萼先知。
点点梨花，丝丝嫩寒。春光几许，花心自明。
点点梨花，玉酥其濛①。春情何处，花衣随风。

【注释】

①其濛：犹若细雨一般，白茫茫一片。

Pear Flowers

Pear petals
Bloom into a tender rain in heart.
How many inches is the heart of spring?
The calyces could foreknown it.

Pear petals
Breathe their breaths of tender cold.
How deep is the spring in view?
The heart of flowers may be self-evident.

Pear petals
Are a soft, smooth rain.
Where are the desires of spring?
In the wind gone with the flowers.

梦中梦

飘窗梦雨，枕函[①]咏梅。我心孔棘[②]，半百衰摧。
劬劳覃耜[③]，聿修块垒[④]。举世彭彭，稻粱霏霏。
厥德有奭[⑤]，纲常霰隳。蓼蓼书案，去日莫追。
生民赪尾[⑥]，湛乐[⑦]酒杯。烝尝[⑧]晓月，不见春晖。

【注释】

①枕函：中间可以藏物的枕头。②孔棘：很紧急；很急迫。③劬（qú）劳：劳苦、苦累的意思，特指父母抚养儿女的劳累。覃（yǎn）："剡"，锋利。耜（sì）：古代一种似锹的农具。④聿修：聿（yù），文言助词，无义，用于句首或句中。块垒：泛指郁积之物；比喻胸中郁结的愁闷或气愤。⑤厥：代词，代指前文提到的某人；德：德行，品德。奭（shì）：盛大的样子。⑥赪尾（chēng wěi）：赤色的鱼尾；借指鱼。⑦湛乐：过度逸乐。⑧烝尝：本指秋冬二祭。后亦泛称祭祀。

Dream in Dreams

Rains of dream across the window
Are intoned to the plum blossoms on my pillow
Where my heart in danger, you see,
Has languished after gone of fifty.

In toil and moil, sharpen my plough-shares,
To cultivate the gloomy airs.
All the world has gone in throng,
With the grains drifting all along.

If the virtues are to be grand,
The moral principles will lose caste in the end.
By the desk large and long,
Past times call off the chase like a swan gone.

Were the living men a red-tailed fish,
Lead your goblet, loose yet beamish.
To savor my libation in the morning moon,
The vernal rays are well be-met, too soon.

磨平的心

深檀散雪，玉瘦浓霜。金炉旋暖，疏影温凉。
芳菲欲送，往日时光。柔情一世，花泪冲肠。

Heart Worn Flat

Snow flakes down the deep sandalwood
Are softly tight like heavy frosts.
In the golden hearth are whirling warmer tints
Whose dappled shadows are screwing the temperatures.
When the entrancing prime attemps to deliver
The tenderness of the old days,
All the melting heartthrobs are swilling
My bowels with the tears of the flowers.

牡　马

赳赳[①]汗马，之彼河浒[②]。骙骙骏骐[③]，陟彼东山。
出其左岸，赤驹业业[④]。出其右岸，老骥绥绥[⑤]。
易水汤汤[⑥]，荆轲不返。碣石赫赫[⑦]，魏武游衍[⑧]。
令德蹻蹻[⑨]，千里维烈。骈死槽枥[⑩]，心在牧野。

【注释】

①赳赳：威武雄健的样子。②河浒（hǔ）：河边。语本《诗·王风·葛藟》："绵绵葛藟，在河之浒。"③骙骙（kuí）：马强壮的样子。《诗·小雅·采薇》："四牡骙骙"。骏骐：健硕的马。④业业：高大雄壮貌。《诗·小雅·采薇》："戎车既驾，四牡业业。"⑤绥绥：舒行貌。《诗·卫风·有狐》："有狐绥绥，在彼淇梁，心之忧矣，之子无裳。"⑥汤汤（shāng）：水势浩大、水流很急的样子。《书·尧典》："汤汤洪水方割，荡荡怀山襄陵，浩浩滔天。"⑦赫赫：显著盛大的样子。晋·常璩《华阳国志·先贤士女》："临州郡虽无赫赫之名，及去，民思之。"⑧游衍（yǎn）：从容自如，不受拘束。⑨令德：美德。蹻蹻（jué）：强盛貌。⑩骈（pián）：两马并驾一车；骈驰。槽枥（cáo lì）：喂牲口用的食器。枥：马棚、马厩。亦作"槽历"。养马之所。骈死槽枥：和普通的马一起死在马厩里。

Stallion

Valiant, the sweating horse
By the clear water course
Galloped the strong mane
Up to the east mountain.

To the left bank down,
The red colt looked strong.
And to the left bank there,
The old steed was free from care.

Onward the Northern Stream was swollen,
But Jing Ke was gone never to return.
On that Arid Rock great in renown,
Emperor Wu of Wei wandered into his own.

Behold! The excellent virtue strode,
For a thousand miles being all the mode.
Though dead in his stable,
To the wide field was his heart accessible.

能　事

万缕金丝，低眉晓岸。杨花不解，流影桃面。
半藏梨雪，深浅难断。流云一朵，风耳梳散。

Knack

A myriad of golden threads
Meekly obey the dawning shore
Puzzled by the willow catkins
Drifting her face like a peach.
And in the half – hidden pear snows,
Thick or thin, she can't be
Diagnosed in one floating cloud,

That has combed down the ear of wind.

牛角尖

戴河宦乡，秦城失意。春草何辜？野火恣肆。
恩荣错权，埋骨瘴地。流火人生，双肩正气。

Split Hairs

From the official town by the Daihe River
To the sense of frustration in Qincheng Jail,
O what wrong has the spring grass done by the
Wildfires to be burned wantonly at every turn?
Gloried in honours, the wrong power relations
Have been buried into the foggy swamps.
Life is but a flowing fire,
That should shoulder the sense of right.

乐　妇

之子俣俣[①]，洵[②]美怀善。舜英[③]皎月，归沐西衍[④]。
之子娈娈[⑤]，不贰其选。执手音德，云胡流转[⑥]？
之子婉婉[⑦]，折柳如剪。君子邂逅，令德[⑧]嬗变。

【注释】

①俣俣：魁伟貌。②洵（xún）：实在。③舜英：木槿花。④归沐：回家洗发。衍（yǎn）：水满而出；散开。⑤娈娈（luán）：美好貌。⑥云胡：为什么。流转：流落转徙。⑦婉婉：和顺貌。⑧令德：美

德。

Sultry Seductress

Of large and tall stature, the lady
Was full of fine grace properly.
Like a moon-lit mallow flower,
Her moon west was haloed in a shower.
Fair and bright, the lady
Showed great and unchanging loyalty.
But her noble fame in hand
Should be on the move in the end!
Of meek deportment, the lady
Snipped and snapped the willow resolutely.
As the man of virtue ran up against her,
She had transmuted her good character.

女人五十
Woman at Fifty

其一

香繁日暖，惊破梅心。秋容漫展，一捋清阴。
凌寒玉赋，梦影斜琴。暗香浮月，柳眼闲吟。

One

Her sweet is stronger and warmer,
That shatters the mume's vernal heart.
When her autumn is chequered with ease,
One handful of her shade is clear.
Endowed with the pure air of a frosty bite,
Her image in dream plays the tilted zither.
When a subtle fragrance floats thru the moon,
Her drowsy eyes will croon at leisure.

其二

冰影闲掬，尘身清逸。半溪残红，一潭幽室。
雾锁高楼，谁知妾意？梦里惊鸿，秋水常逝。

Two

A pure, tender shade spares
Her clear leisure in the dust.
Fallen petals on half the stream
Feed the pool of her serene room.
Locked in the tower by the fogs,
How she trusts to hear a connoisseur.
Slim and graceful, her dreams
Often flow into her limpid eyes.

其三

青禽弄月，连岸鸟飞。闲云逸处，半点熹微。
平沙杳杳，一任春晖。多情已去，无情为谁？

Three

Like a black fowl in the moon,
Mated by the gliding birds on the shore,
Her calm clouds of ease and pleasure has added
One straw to the faint rays of first dawn.
Out and away, the strands
May assume her gentle brightness.
As the trace of sentimentality has gone,
For whom to turn the heart to stone?

其四

篱边乱藤，香草空瘦。夜虫鸣风，寒蝉依旧。
幽怀几许，澹月吹皱。一瓣清愁，好梦无皱。

Four

By her fence in rattan vines,
The sweet grass is lean in vain.
As night bugs chirp in the wind,

The cold cicada chirrups are as usual.
Far, far apart, her serene delight
Whiffled and crimpled by the pale moon
Shines a clove of sobre melancholy
In her sweet dream, without a crease.

其五

落花一寸，寒林过雨。冰魄空沉，清欢铩羽。
向晚风翼，撒盐新舞。梦镜藏羞，银屋老树。

Five

One inch of petals fall
Down the trembling woods.
As the soul of ice sinks into her hollow,
The fine sweet is being crest-fallen
With a fan-fly to reflect the advancing night
That's sprinkling salt on a fresh dance.
In her mirror of dreams is hidden the shy
And aged tree within the silvery house.

其六

红颜水影，剪断芊愁。流星一瞬，月泻兰舟。
西窗情浅，抱影深秋。之子衰红，谁与绸缪？

Six

Her rosy lips and cheeks reflected on water
Have nipped up the furrowed sorrows.
In a split second, her shooting star
Discharges the moon down to the sweet boat.
Why the west, emotional window is simple
And embraces her image into the deep autumn?
Of a waning, red deportment,
With whom to be sentimentally attached?

其七

轻蝶纤雨，素手娇痴。幽笛未散，碎剪青丝。
低眉惊叶，乱愁堪惜。一寸悲鸿，几片蝶翼。

Seven

Like a light rain and butterfly,
Her pure hands are coy
On the serene flute still there
That scissors up her black hair.
As her lowered brows shock the leaves,
Calling forth a pity for the settled glooms,
One inch of doleful swan
Whirs away with a few butterfly's wings.

其八

向梦解梦，临镜烟青。风染眉鬓，落晖疏影。
清寥霜花，浅醉刘伶。芊绵一缕，菊为谁荣？

Eight

To interpret the dream in dreams,
Her misty mirror comes blue.
In the wind that dyes her brows and temples,
The slanting sun drops into her dappled shadows.
In the clear, boundless ice flowers,
She has been bright in the eye.
Like a wisp of flossy chrysanthemums,
For whom she'd be dressed to the nines?

其九

素女临霜，不为他容。浮窗瘦影，弦冷自听。
风过柳梢，嫩雨邀冬。几缕冰色，明蟾月浓。

Nine

Goddes of Music in white frost
Bears and forbears
Her thin shade foating on the window

That meets a cold string with her ear.
As the willow-tips are blown through,
Her tender rains are calling for the winter.
And a few threads of the ice colour
Will be shining bright in the moon.

其十

鸟度闲情，斜阳瘦减。风敲翠竹，锦屏声满。
玉瓣随风，空庭闲散。流光飞屑，犹唱旧年。

Ten

Like a bird of passage in idle feelings,
The oblique rays of the sun is but a thinner story.
While the wind knocks the green bamboo,
Her embroiderd screen swells the sails.
And with the wind are gone her pure petals,
The stark garden wears a loose skin.
After the clock drains away thru the flying chips,
She still sings to the accompaniment of the old times.

其十一

飞絮牵衣，催花妙影。朱颜镜暗，纸扇雪景。
漫下帘栊，沐禅月冷。客思人生，梦蝶初醒。

Eleven

Her gown by the flying willow fuzz
Hies the floweres into a subtle image.
Though the rosy face is mirrored dimmer,
Her paper fan is wafting a snow scene.
Lowering that portiere,
Her moon is bathed cold in meditation.
Worn out with care, her life is
Awakening from the dream of butterflies.

其十二

雨梨旧韵，敲窗溅花。洗尽沉梦，薄醉归鸦。
一寸描红，碎剪轻纱。性情封印，秋水天涯。

Twelve

The old aroma of rhymes drizzling in pear trees
Patters against her spattering window.
After the sinking dreams are washed away,
The raven would return like a sheet in the wind.
But one inch of painted blusher
Has cuts up her light gauze,
Which will seal the easiness of temper
To be drifted to the limit of the earth.

其十三

秋水临风，池鱼一跃。晨梦曦光，宝钗映落。
菡萏香消，岸头红萼。红粉老矣，此生厚薄？

Thirteen

When the wind flares the autumn water,
The fish may leap in the pond.
When the morning dream is flooded in the grey of dawn,
Her precious trinket could be mirrored down.
When the lotus flower is thawed and done,
Her water's edge would come into red bloom.
When her rosy cheeks are old now,
I wonder whether this life is thick or thin.

其十四

长倚绿荫，看尽芍药。笛香荡雪，枕浪几度。
紫燕衔泥，居息以乐。雏仔南柯，空堂落寞。

Fourteen

Long in the green glooms,
Her peonies are an open-and-shut case.
As the sweet flute's swinging the snows,

Many times she's pillowed on the billows.
If a purple swallow pecks clods of clay,
To enjoy her rest and ease,
She'll feel her own dullness in the empty room
After her baby's gone for a fond dream.

其十五

一犁风雨，两亩心田。幽怀鉴影，落叶飞燕。
世路秋雨，流年逝川。老妪拾香，荣华不迁。

Fifteen

A plough of wind and rain
Through two acres of heart
Reflect her serene shade
To shed the leaf and swallow.
In autumn rain her life's path
Floats in the fleeting time
With an attitude of prayer
To keep the ephemeral glory.

其十六

柳色晴暖，谁堪作伴？梳发凉风，闲话长短。
晚日奔象，心在月边。莲子生根，此生无憾。

Sixteen

Sunny and mild green willows!
With whom to enjoy her society?
Comb that cool zephyr
Down her tittle-tattle of various lengths,
That, like a bolt overdue,
Locks her heart onto the moon's brim.
To be a lotus seed that takes root,
This life should be satisfied.

平常心

千乘駉駉[①]，喤喤[②]成康。乐只簧翿[③]，君子阳阳。
载驱荡荡，载兴旁旁[④]。一朝丧乱，难续永康。
于彼田牡，驾言[⑤]如常。逸豫[⑥]他主，项领[⑦]四疆。
十月飞雪，朔月有常。持家止戾[⑧]，进退有方。

【注释】

①駉駉（jiōng）：马肥壮貌。亦指肥壮之马。②喤喤（huáng）：象声词。③乐只：和美；快乐。只，语助词。簧：乐器里用金属或其他材料制成的发声薄片；翿（dào）：古代羽舞或葬礼所用的旌旗，即羽葆幢。簧翿：泛指音乐舞蹈或娱乐。④旁旁：强壮有力貌。⑤言，语助词。⑥逸豫：犹安乐；舒缓貌。⑦项领：肥大的颈项。⑧止戾：安定。

A Sense of Patience

The stout steeds of a thousand chariots
Were blessing the resounding kings.
To the musical touches of sweet harmony,
The men of virtue cheered brightly.
Darting and dashing, they swirled down
Their sturdy courses full of merriment.
Once the wild riot arose, the fair
Morrow would succeed, but never more.
Behold! Those stallions afield were
Striking their gallops as usual, who,
To be in good cheer by another,
Would be harnessed to the four borders.
Snow-flakes flying about in October
Pursued their regular, lunar course.
As the house-keeper not in labile state,
He would not be impaled on a dilemma.

钱

青钱摇落，榆钱招眼。铁弩射江，秋水金剪。
流光暗叠，繁枝素笺①。天命八斗，商略②有限。

【注释】

①素笺：白色的笺纸。②商略：商讨。

Money

Copper coins are shaken down,
And elm seed coins are shown all along.
The iron crossbows are shooting the river
Like golden scissors into the autumn water.
Fleeting hours are folded darkly,
And the tufted sprays are noted purely.
Even a superb talent by the heavenly mandate
Can be deliberated in a finite state.

将进酒

饫酒[①]成眠，孤酒恨短。荒湛[②]不济，酒馔独软。
飞酒驰魂，酒冷酬眠。清箫一梦，对月把盏。
无酒无花，闲门荒馆。置酒邀春，客醉酒阑。
绿酒共浮，归隐陶潜。病酒[③]掏情，枯肠相见。
酒殇及脐，杯深腹浅。酒卮知己，在于寡言。
我有知音，携酒飞天。风前猛醒，何惧朱颜。
酒风柳意，浪眼追仙。新酒醅[④]岁，诗以为剑。

【注释】

①饫（yù）酒：饱酒。②荒湛：沉湎于酒色，行为放荡。湛，通“耽”。③病酒：饮酒沉醉。④醅（pēi）：聚饮。

Down the Hatch

The well-fed wine is like a berceuse,
And the lonely wine transient though joyous.
Steeped in the evil days,
The dishes are all but soft anyways.
If the gliding wine gallops my soul,
The cold wine compensates a sleep on the whole.
Amid the clear flutes in dream,
Hold the cup to the moonbeam.
Without flowers or wine,
The door can't be free from famine.
With the wine to regale the spring,
My bagged guests are draining.
To be floated in the revelry,
And then withdraw from society,
The dopy passions are hollow,
And open to the impoverished bowel.
Cups! Go gaily down to the navel,
Though the stomachs are shallow.
Cups! You're taken into my confidence,
Whose hell is the tight-lipped experience.
If Goodness knows my soul-mate,
May the soaring wine be animate.
To be blown and sobered up all at once,
Why timid before a rosy face?
In the wined wind, the will of willows
Traces its dissolute eye for the immortals.
Young wine by this hour together!

With my poems as the sabre.

穷与富
The Poor and The Rich

其一

乞借天锤，以平瘴策。灞桥飞絮，乱楫钓客。
何日骑鲸，连洲阡陌。闲作清斋，一匾香额。

One

Please lend me Heaven's Hammer
To quash the miasmic challenges
Whose flying willow fuzzes down the bridge
Are oaring the angler.

When could I ride the whale
Thru the labyrinth of fields dotted by the islets?
Just fast in my leisure time,
To wait for the tablet with a sweet-browed tale.

其二

满面花气，水波玉软。一瞬流光，清眸如善。
莹洌之姿，贵玉为浅。楚楚眺听，聘币[①]无冕。

【注释】

①聘币：古时聘人所备的礼物。币，本意为缯帛。古以束帛为赠送宾客及享聘之礼。

Two

Flowers assails her face,
On the waves, pure and supple.
Her streamer winks
The clear and fine pupils.
Her charm's like a fair sparkle,
Which worthes a Jew's eye,
Strained to a delicate scope,
Where the gifts are crownless.

其三

绕梦家山，归心茹苦。醉句闲抛，霜丝千缕。
既回家室，酾[①]酒如虎。酤之湑之[②]，神嗜忘祖。

【注释】

①酾（shī）：滤酒；斟酒。②酤（gū）：买酒；卖酒。湑（xǔ）：（酒）滤去渣滓而变清。

Three

Hometown fully in dreams

Roughs a bitter return.
Flip the drunken lines,
Into thousands of hoarfrosts.
To be back at last,
Strain off the bountiful wine.
To deal in pure and clear spirits,
He's ignorant of his own origins.

其四

鲛人善淚[1]，犁人乐畴[2]。圣人澹逸[3]，贤人悠游。
棋局袖手，不屑苟偷。大方之士，不怀诡谋。

【注释】

①鲛人：中国古代汉族神话传说中鱼尾人身的生物。淚（lèi）：泪。
②畴：田地。③澹逸：淡雅飘逸。

Four

A siren may be vexed with tears,
And a tiller clever at his field.
A sage may be freely easy,
And a worthy leisurely and carefree.
With folded arms,
He'd shrug off a fool's paradise.
And as a liberal man,
He'd harbour no bag of tricks.

其五

浩饮听泉，尘沙破胆。夙夜如泮，长河腹满。
沛水云龙，扶觥[①]举颔。苍天负我，酒以为椠[②]。

【注释】

①觥（gōng）：古代用兽角做的酒器。此处泛指酒器。②椠（qiàn）：古代以木削成用作书写的版片。简札，书信。

Five

Drink to the limit of the fountain,
With a terror to the swirls of dust.
And before dawn, into the abysmal cup,
The stomach is full like a long river
Whose copious clouds come with a dragon,
That raises the jaw of his goblet.
If I've been betrayed by the heaven,
The wine should be my pen.

其六

豪兴樽俎，命里词花。荐觞东里，天心紫霞。
熊投好梦，瓜瓞[①]有遐。人生甲子[②]，几日还家？

【注释】

①瓞（dié）：小瓜。瓜瓞喻子孙繁衍，相继不绝。②甲子：干支之

一，顺序为第一个。前一位是癸亥，后一位是乙丑。中国传统纪年干支历的干支纪年中一个循环的第一年称“甲子年”。甲子也是六十年的别称，也就是一生的代称。

Six

Exhilarate your glass of wine
To be fated by poetic flowers!
As the entertainer to my neighbours,
God’s will toasts His purple glows.
In the sweet dream by the Bear,
Melon vines are free on the passage of time.
And to the life in a cycle of sixty years,
When shall I be on the way home?

其七

黔黎[①]荒径，抱树无骨。疏枝挑月，浅澹阙阙[②]。
一襟钩影，何以卒读[③]？枝头惊绿，古钺回鹘。

【注释】

①黔黎：百姓。潘岳《西征赋》：“愿黔黎其谁听，惟请死而获可。”②阙阙（quē）：空缺貌。③卒读：尽读。

Seven

A countryman on the barren path
Nestles the tree soft as soap.

Amid the boughs that stir the moon,
A shallow smooth combs hollow.
As the crescent is imaged on his bosom,
How can it bear to read to the end?
As the branches jump out of the green joy,
It's like a broad ax hunting for the old Uighurs.

其八

浮沉一梦，贵贱如烟。猫爪一挥，贫富悬天。
深幽一梦，三生如燕。蝴蝶一翅，宇内行笺。

Eight

One dream swims or sinks,
Like a misty birth, high or low.
As the cat's paw swishes,
It will create a gulf in wealth.
One dream goes deeper and deeper,
Like the swallow to a stroke of luck,
And also like one wing of the butterfly
To zoom an avalanche of papers.

其九

鱼泪濯足，耽思弱水。逸泓弥弥[①]，底事[②]红鲤?
一瓯[③]秋星，蕙心咫尺。晴丝拂槛，首丘已矣。

【注释】

①弥弥：水满貌。②底事：何事。③瓯（ōu）：小盆。

Nine

Wash the feet with the tears of fish,
Engrossed in a free spirit of the weak water.
Even in the popples, deep and vast,
What' s that to the red carps?
In the bowl of the autumn stars,
The pure heart is closed on the horizon.
As the fine treads are kissing the sill,
The dying fox will face his natal hill.

其十

晓瘴芳颜，暮雪樵苇。葛袂染香，危峦结虺[1]。
野鹜孤蟾，裁书佩玮[2]。天下商贾，亦人亦鬼。

【注释】

①虺（huǐ）：古书上说的一种毒蛇，喻奸恶小人。②裁书：写信。玮：皮绳。通“韦”。

Ten

Her sweet face dawns the unwholesome breaths,
While the woodsman dusks the snows.

Her sleeves in vines have dyed the fragrant vows,
While the perilous peak has colluded with venomous snakes.
Let me be a wild duck or a lonely toad,
To tailor my ornate letters,
In that the shrewd merchants under the sun
Are both men and demons.

青　莲

素女在隰①，出镜裳裳②。君子思之，绵蛮③绕梁。
素女在渚④，白华皎皎⑤。君子思之，牵绊罗襦⑥。
素女在湖，玉环濯濯⑦，君子思之，绸缪罔极⑧。

【注释】

①素女：古代传说中的神女。此处借指莲荷。隰（xí）：低湿的地方。②裳裳（cháng）：鲜明美盛的样子。《诗·小雅·裳裳者华》："裳裳者华，其叶湑兮。"③绵蛮：小鸟貌。《朱熹集传》：绵蛮，鸟声。④渚（zhǔ）：水中小块陆地。⑤皎皎：洁白貌；清白貌。⑥牵绊：牵扯，纠缠使不能脱开。襦（rú）：短衣，短袄。⑦玉环：荷花的同义词。濯濯：明净貌；清朗貌。⑧绸缪（chóu móu）：紧密缠缚，缠绵貌。罔（wǎng）极：无极，无穷尽。

Blue Lotus

Fairy maiden in the lowland
Is mirrored nicely and brightly.
When the man of virtue longs for her,
Chirps are reverberating round his beams.

Fairy maiden along the shore
Sheds her clear and white flowers.
When the man of virtue longs for her,
Even a silk jacket isn' t without encumber.

Fairy maiden inside the lake
Is cool and fresh like a jade ring.
When the man of virtue longs for her,
He' d be sentimentally attached to excess.

青　龙

谁谓青龙？千里凝翠。谁谓青龙？银水流岚[①]。
谁谓青龙？玉带嵯峨[②]。谁谓青龙？骑海飞天。
谁谓青龙？赶日追风。谁谓青龙？大漠扬帆。
谁谓青龙？隐介无形。谁谓青龙？气吞霄汉。

【注释】

①流岚：山间流动的雾气。②嵯峨（cuó é）：形容山势高峻，也指坎坷不平，或者形容盛多。

Black Dragon

Who is Black Dragon?
The emerald a thousand miles.
Who is Black Dragon?
The silvery flow like a vapour.
Who is Black Dragon?
The belt of jade, high and steep.

Who is Black Dragon?
He who bestrides the sea and soars up.
Who is Black Dragon?
The runner after the sun and the wind.
Who is Black Dragon?
The sail hoisted through the great desert.
Who is Black Dragon?
He who veils its scaly form from view.
Who is Black Dragon?
He who engulfs the Milky Way.

青龙行

凯风自东，之子绥绥[①]。既穿大隧，令仪[②]维夏。
凯风自南，之子好好。徂彼高台，孰适于观?
凯风自西，之子京京[③]。薄言爽德，服其梦令。
凯风自北，之子习习。盼彼蛮荆，不见玁狁[④]。

【注释】

①绥绥：舒行貌。②令仪：整肃威仪。③京京：忧愁不绝貌。④玁狁（xiǎn yǔn）：中国古代民族名。亦作"猃狁""荤允""荤粥""獯（熏）鬻""薰育""严允"等。

The Journey to Black Dragon

Riding the wind from the east,
Our wheels are ambling.
Through the great tunnels,
We observe the rite of summer.

Riding the wind from the south,
Our wheels are steady on.
Atop that tower,
With whom to strain my eyes?

Riding the wind from the west,
Our wheels are fraught with sorrow.
In an alleged failure to be possessed,
The virtue'd take its lyric in dream.

Riding the wind from the north,
Our wheels are blowing in little gusts.
On tiptoe for the savage bands,
The Huns are without any display.

人啊人

人生适意，念涨念消。繁荣落尽，一抔艾蒿。
人生率意，云低云高。名牵利扯，来去操劳。
人生趁意，瑶情寂寥。幽人块垒，任尔飘摇。
人生快意，舒雅清箫。闲杯乍试，梦笔横桥。
人生失意，逆水行艄。浮光谢影，影落风飘。
人生得意，灼灼桃夭。东君醉卧，花露明朝。

Man! Man!

Life is well,
That ebbs and flows.

After the luxurious elements,
What's left is a clod of mugworts.

Life is willful,
In its clouds, high and low.
For the involved fames and gains,
One comes and goes in his toil and moil.

Life is desirable,
In an artless but deserted love.
To be a lonely, melancholy malcontent,
One is gone with the battered Caravanserai.

Life is enjoyable,
Amid its clear, easy, refined note.
Try my cup, fresh and carefree,
To the dream that writes its cross-bridge.

Life is down,
Like a rudder upstream,
Skimming and falling before
Being filmed and fluttered away.

Life is proud,
And tender like the peach aglow.
In a drunken stupor, the sun-god
Rises with the dews of the morn flowers.

人分三等

百代人生，红尘白浪。浮名浮利，舒卷弛张。
四海横帆，无非戏场。硬弩先折，刀口易伤。
麝因香死，蚕为丝亡。人心造业，惹祸舌长。
谄曲贪嗔，败坏伦常。黄金白玉，作人嫁妆。

Men in Three Classes

In the course of lifespans,
White waves through the mundane plans
For wealth and fame in vain
Are rolling back and forth, ever and again.
Square sails in the four seas
Are invariably the stage as one sees.
Crossbows are first to break,
Like the knife-edges prone to a blunt beak.
Musk-deer die for their own musks,
And silkworms for their silk someone else asks.
A heart may produce kamma,
Like a chattering tongue that court disaster.
Fury and flattery in an insatiable desire
Have corrupted the moral air.
Gold and jade
For others are toiled and paid.

人　情

人情薄纸，真挚何求？雨易飘萧，萤火难收。
修为俗浅，韵事如舟。旧时莺燕，牵梦闲愁。

Humanity

From a flimsy human interest,
Where's the warmth of the attachments?
The rain may be prone to the wafts,
But the fireflies hard to be ingathered.
In a prevalent custom to be cultivated,
The romantic story is but a boat.
Like the orioles and swallows in days of yore,
My bitter grief is lost in a needless reverie.

人　性

青鸟衔枝，宝函①弄妆。时维韬景②，露泣凝霜。
玉石之德，慈训③绵长。弱影谁对？落红暗伤。
地纪④不绝，月轮永芳。人伦尽丧，铁树摇墙。
青青紫宫⑤，朔朔天狼⑥。希夷⑦灭道，架水成梁。
怀冲不正，哀雁残阳。褓褓未出，奈何永康。
路人清跸⑧，悲风恸亡。弱者何辜，祸起萧墙。

【注释】

①宝函：指盛佛经、典册及贵重首饰等的匣子。这里指成婚待孕。

②韬景：隐晦的景象。指秋天的季节。③慈训：母或父的教诲。谢朓《齐敬皇后哀策文》：“闵予不祐，慈训早违。”④地纪：维系大地的绳子。古代认为天圆地方，传说天有九柱支撑，使天不下陷；地有大绳维系四角，使地有定位。⑤紫宫：紫薇垣，在古代中国，人们认为紫薇垣位于天的最高处，共有恒星15颗，这组恒星被认为是天帝所居的宫殿，称为紫宫。也指任脉腧穴，任脉气血在此化为温湿水气，婴儿被灌的农药也从此进入体内。⑥天狼：即天狼星，是大犬星座最亮的一颗星，绝对星等1.44。在古埃及，人们对它十分敬畏，因为它一旦在黎明前出现在东方就意味着尼罗河的泛滥，那是一年中最恐怖的一段日子。⑦希夷：道家、道士。唐·元稹《周先生》诗：“希夷周先生，烧香调琴心。”⑧清跸（bì）：帝王出行时开路清道，禁止通行。此处指网络浏览信息，被震慑不前的心情。

Human Nature

Blue bird, with a branch, flied here,
Pretty dolly, ready for the case, so dear.
Case! Case! Case! The autumn case
Cased the weeps in a frosty glaze.
By the favour of jade,
The beneficial instructions should not fade.
To whom the feeble shade can be faced?
To the falling red wistfully paced.
If earth pillars won' t be falling down,
Wheels of the moon will forever be young.
Human orders, if utterly conscienceless,
Will shock the wall like steel trees.
Under that tender star of Purple Palace,
We see the barren Dog Star with malice.

Like a Taoist for the way of extinction,
The beam made of water brings an abortion.
Out of square, the sense of mores
Glows and mourns in wild goose calls.
Strangled in the swaddling clothes,
Could it be good and fair as one knows?
To be wayfarers, we are overawed,
By the doleful rage that's gnawed.
O what crime has the weakling committed?
The misfortune befalls from within, unbitted.

人在路上

考槃束楚①，其路蒙棘。崔崔②山岗，荼苦③自识。
喓喓穀旦④，蔽芾罔极⑤。柞薪聿归⑥，雨雪如织。
啴啴罪罟⑦，式遄⑧其塞。飞隼九皋⑨，约之振翼。

【注释】

①考槃：考，指深入探究；槃，指水平盘旋，即反复盘查。束楚：捆荆成束。②崔崔：高大貌；高峻貌。③荼苦：苦楚。④喓喓（yāo）：虫鸣声。穀旦：良晨；晴朗美好的日子。⑤蔽芾（bì fèi）：树木茂盛的样子。罔极：无极，无穷尽。⑥柞（zhà）薪：柞木类的柴薪。亦泛指柴薪。聿：乃。⑦啴啴（tān）：形容众多盛大。罪罟（gǔ）：罪、罟皆为网。泛指法网。⑧遄（chuán）：加速。⑨飞隼（sǔn）：鸟名。凶猛善飞，故名。九皋（gāo）：曲折深远的沼泽，亦称鹤。后亦用为称美隐士或贤人的典实。

Man on the Way

Thru the wood bound and unknown,
The way is in brambles overgrown.
Locked in the lofty hummock,
The bitter lettuce sets its sensible clock.
In the auspicious day of buzzes,
The leafy trees are measurable to excess.
With the oak for firewood I return
But in the sleets wreathed again.
In the legions of traps high and low,
I speed up my steps out of the stymy, lo!
And like a hawk's flight in the marsh,
The wings are bound to flap out of the hush.

认清自己

蓝鸟于飞，傅天之翼。栖于苞桑[①]，两丈颉颃[②]。
越鸟于飞，六翮噫噫。斑蝶狎竞，逗絮崻庭。

【注释】

①苞桑：丛生的桑树。②颉颃（xié háng）：鸟儿上飞为颉，下飞为颃。指鸟儿上下翻飞。

Find Yourself

Blue birds in flight bear

The heaven-mounting wings.
Alighted on the mulberries,
Their wingstrokes are whirring short.
While south birds in flight are
Warbling their soaring joy,
Milkweed butterflies pit their wits
To tease the catkins twittering the court.

如雪人生

人生似雪，盈盈九重。纤纤素袂，幽笛弄声。
寒烟闲遁，雪霁独行。斜阳半挂，翻梦深冬。
帘卷腊梅，为伊痴情。不著尘埃，不弄疏影。
红颜断尽，宠辱不惊。春池消解，来去从容。

Life in Snow

Life is snow
Glitters in the 9th power.
With a virgin hand,
The serene flute tones.
Chilly, foggy, the leisure's driven far
Off into the clearing snow alone.
And in the oblique rays that's half hung,
The dream routs thru the depth of winter
Whence the winter-plums before the shutters
Would be soppy on her.
No speck of dust,
No dappled shadows,

And after her ruddy complexion fails,
She keeps her cool over either gains or losses.
As the spring pool thaws,
She'd come and go, naturally and easily.

傻　子

抱眠孤榻，蚊雷耳边。几时蕉梦？山脊断鞭。
横眸四季，蚊语几天？扰眠之戏，丝雨吞船。

Idiot

My isolated bed sleeps into
The thundering ear by a mosquito.
How long could be the capricious dream?
Short as my scourge's snapped by the ridge.
Into all the seasons my pupils are veered,
To count the days of the mosquito's words.
Such a game that's eaten my sleep
Swallows the ship like Scotch mists.

上　智

藤萝锁秋，瘴岭林薄。徽音半卷，轻雨拂阁。
青萍负气，越鸟求索。寒枝照羽，乘露于乐。

Of Supreme Wisdom

Autumn, locked in creepers,
Woods, a slip sheet in miasmic mountain,
Fame, half-scrolled,
Rain, a light kisser on the cabinet…
The blue duckweeds in vital energy
Are questing the south birds
Whose feathers to be beamed in trembling twigs
Would ride the dews of mirth.

手
Hand

其一

绿云风起，布局九天。遥思谁问，不抵轻寒。
天幕催雪，关河苍澜。飞絮青眼，冰火两难。
红尘避世，一任尘寰。市井芳陌，薄霭清梵。
落愁安寄？有手垂天。仙音曲底，任由悲欢。

One

Green, windy clouds
Of an empyrean composition
Ponder here and there

To wonder the chills
That urge the snows down the canopy
Whose trickles are thinned down into the billows
Flying the willow fuzzes in the green eyes
Incompatible as ice and hot coals.
To hide from the world,
All things should go as they are led.
And through the sweet ways of the towns,
Buddha's resonant voice reverberates in a thin vapour.
Where to put my falling sorrow?
Put it into the celestial hand
With an immortal tone
Abandoned to the quirks of joy and grief.

其二

生涯倚梦，情怀一捧。远岫湿云，仙岛孤洞。
四时弹雨，八秋呼众。权杖挠私，飘沈来风。
几案游鳞，金元暗涌。镜异月亏，千官阵痛。
中国有梦，青天一统。古来正气，何惧回风。

Two

My career in dream
Is emotional in hands,
Like a moist cloud over the distant hill,
Or an isolated hole on certain supernatural island.
In the clock that plays the rains,
The deepest autumn's lost in the hubbub of men.

With the sceptre that intrigues,
A flapping and sinking phoenix is coming.
On the desks swim the fish,
That flush gold dollars in secret, but,
Down the waning moon like a strange mirror,
Thousands of office-holders enjoy a sharp cry of pain.
Now that China has a dream
In the broad daylight of union,
The sense of right from of old
Will be undaunted in the face of the back drafts.

暑　热

天朗眼穷，狗舌燥暑。飞火旱云，可怜焦土。
自烹者何？大地成釜。嘉肴者何？稼田苦楚。

Summer Heat

Bright but down, the sky-eye
Swelters the dog tongues.
Jumping fires down the dry clouds
Are scorching the wretched earth.
For what it's boiling by itself?
For the globe that turns into a boiler.
What's that feast of choice delicacies?
It's the groans of the farmers.

思君苦

春残莫恼，篱畔风清。闲舟钓梦，野径听莺。
香君一瓣，轻弦谁听？春江半盏，孤镜妆明。

Sick in Love

Don't be afflicted with the late spring,
Which beyond the fence is breezing.
In the leisurely boat to fish the dream,
Orioles amid the wild trails are twittering.
And before the sweet petals of chastity,
Who would listen to the light string?
Now scoop half a bowl of the spring river,
To light up her rouge in the lonely mirror.

四　牌

一阕行香[①]，芙蓉求凤。玩雨孤楼，唼唼[②]鱼动。
黄花晚节，不约春梦。鸣雁催舟，不碍云涌。

【注释】

①一阕（yī què）：一度乐终，亦谓一曲。行香：正月初一清早，旧有“行香”之俗。②唼唼（shà）：象声词。水鸟或鱼的吃食声。

Four Medals

One incensed melody seeks
Her phoenix in the roses of Sharon,
That plays the rain in the orphaned storey
Alive with the nibbling fishes.
Daylilies, though fully-grown,
Won't be paired off on a spring dream.
In the honks of wild geese that speed the boat,
None will get the scudding clouds into a hobble.

四十以后的醒悟
Disillusion after Forty

其一

鱼游河海，深浅难融。鸡鸭异路，各食西东。
头在一枕，两心不同。浮生蚁命，几人善终？

One

Sea or river, the fish
Are thick, thin and unsociable.
Duck or chicken, different routes
Peck at their own foods.
On one pillow,

Are lying two hearts at variance.
In this fleeting life of ants,
Who would die a natural death?

其二

入秋抱子，青绿[1]随园。残英占尽，燕体辞轩[2]。
眠沙卧水，哪堪浪翻。临寒劲土，何必明喧。

【注释】

①青绿：小葱种子秋天落入肥沃的园子，变成青葱。②轩（xuān）：古代一种有围棚或帷幕的车；有窗的长廊或小屋等。

Two

Into the fruitful autumn,
The garden is bright with blue and green.
As the fall gets the deadwood on flowers,
The swallows would dart off the windows.
A slumber on the sandy water
Couldn't keep from billowing.
And a fat soil in cold
Isn't anywise necessary to din
Into the bright ears.

其三

真诚满树，一生绿音。蝶蛱醒梦，前事霖霖。

长亭故事，短亭牵心。心河翻过，自消迷津。

Three

Trees, full of frankness,
Sound green in all their born days.
Butterflies, awake to the fact,
Sew the fine incessant needles of water.
The story of the farewell afar
Should be on tenters nearer.
And to climb over the heart of the river,
The maze of paths vanishes apiece.

其四

淡冰处世，一梦裁春。劫波过后，心有富贫。
富诚淡远，穷滑如囷。囷[①]量有限，淡远如茵[②]。

【注释】

①囷（qūn）：廪之圆者。②如茵（yīn）：席，褥，引申为铺的东西。像铺着的东西，形容很柔软。

Four

To be a light ice in society,
That scissors the spring in dream;
After the kalpa,
The heart, rich or poor,

Will fade out though truthful,
Or be narrow-slitted but round.
Round like a granary, it's limited,
And to fade out, it's so well grassed.

其五

心闲听雨，名简藏身。简则易循，繁则动尘。
猿鸟畏简[①]，风云有伦。幽燕大醉，青简书深。

【注释】

①猿鸟：化自李商隐《筹笔驿》的“猿鸟犹疑畏简书，风云常为护储胥”。通俗地说，意思就是：虽然六百多年过去了，面对诸葛的遗迹，猿猴和飞鸟还是不敢靠近，似乎依然畏惧诸葛亮森严的军令；风云般神奇的力量，护卫着当年的军营壁垒。

Five

A free heart listens to the rain,
And a simple name hides the body.
Simple, it's easy to follow,
Fussy, the dust stirs.
Battle writs! Monkeys and crows in fear!
Well-ordered! The winds and clouds should be!
Silent north! Be three sheets in the wind!
In green bamboos, the books are deep.

其六

平淡修心，青山无道。城市若海，对镜孤岛。
心灵漫步，以求洁皓。如蚁人群，如蚁面罩。

Six

Plain but pure in heart,
A castle peak has no way.
In the cities like the sea,
The mirror is but a detached island.
As the soul saunters
In search of a spotless seclusion,
The ant-like armies
Are veiled in obscurity.

其七

娇杨花径，烹茶不温。无名乱性，野风入门。
侵雪掠风，不摇其根。人无柳性，其情长存。

Seven

A flower trail tender in willow catkins
Brews the tea but not tepid.
And a nameless，outrageous nerve

Reaps the wild wind.
Swept by the winds and snows,
The roots should not make a move.
And a man without the willow nature
Lives long through the passage of passions.

其八

冰霜入眼，雪松如烟。落花愁忍，簪月无眠。
神情静女，未必飞仙。醉心野味，真情计年。

Eight

Rimes in the eye
Are smoky in the cedars and
Blossom drops bear their sad
Sleepless, hairpinned moon
Whose fairy shepherdess is
Unlikely to rise on the clouds.
And to be bent on the gibiers,
The true drop of blood counts the years.

其九

随缘落絮，绿黛结钗。欺灯惊枕，浓淡幽斋。
鸥情遥念，同心许怀。清流执手，偕老尘埃。

Nine

In the falling fuzzes submitted to fate,
The fair lady's been locked into her hairpin.
On the shocking pillow that ballrags the light,
The secret room's densely or sparsely zoned.
With the remote passion of gulls,
The devotion heaves its undivided sighs.
Hand in hand through the clear springs,
The dust should live to a ripe old age in bliss.

其十

沙缘聚涧，水缘出峡。钗缘钿插，眉缘入颊。
泪缘染心，笑缘可呷。缘啬谁信？花开有法。

Ten

Out of the gully the predestined sand with
The predestined water bubbles thru the gulch.
And predestined in the gold-encrusted jewelry,
The brows are predestined into a diffused blush.
While the predestined tears are dyeing the heart,
The smile predestines its sips.
Who would believe the miserly manner?
The blossom has a way.

随机应变

柔爪扒窗，娇蛮探蝶。轻扑掩笑，水印桃颊。
多情粉蕊，损销翠荚。客思随舞，熏梦一叶。

Trim the Sail

Soft paws scrabbling the window
Are tender but rough at a butterfly.
Her light pounce hidden in smiles
Is watermarked on the rosy cheeks
Moonstruck to the pink pistils
That consume the green capsules.
In such a homesick flutter,
My dream smoulders like a leaf.

随他骂去

笑骂随意，何必回眸？轻扬三月，柳絮叠丘。
绕梁一阙，遏云如流。东君几缕，翻手浮游。

Curse What You Like

Ridicule and revile as you like,
Why the need for glancing back?
When March is swaying lightly,
Willow fuzzes are mounded gently.

To linger around the beam, the note
Checks the clouds into the remote.
As the sunny patches are coming,
One turn of the hand keeps roaming.

坦　然

祖山之阴，天女楚楚。婉娈[①]清人，之子谁语？
晢晢[②]北斗，明月西去。素衣漂摇，长庚为侣。
嗟尔[③]白华，比于孤屿。受命如斯，维德是处。

【注释】

①婉娈：美好貌。②晢晢（zhé）：明亮的样子。③嗟尔：副词，表示慨叹。

Self-possessed

On the north slope of Mount Zu,
Fairy magnolias are fresh and clear.
Gentle and graceful, such fairs
Tell their tale, but to whom?
As the Big Dipper is quivering,
The bright moon floats to the west.
As their pure dresses are swaying,
Gold Star keeps their company.
Alas! Alas! The white flowers
Are compared to the solitary isle.
However, to be dictated like this,
Their single virtue is revealed.

桃花源

胡为[①]桃源？陟[②]彼阳朔。既徂[③]阳朔，赫赫株林[④]。
闲闲[⑤]巴士，四海率从。洋洋之涘[⑥]，不见桃源。

【注释】

①胡为：何为，为什么。②陟（zhì）：登。③徂（cú）：往；去。④赫赫：显著盛大的样子。株林：株邑的郊外。株，陈国邑名，在今河南省柘城县。株是陈国大夫夏御叔的儿子百般征舒的封邑。⑤闲闲：悠闲的样子。⑥之：到；往。涘（sì）：水边。

Arcadia

Where's the arcadia?
Let's set out to Yangshuo.
There we get registered,
Into the beaming wood,
Inscribed with the free buses,
From the four seas in the entourage.
To the water front in delight, how'er,
Where's the arcadia?

桃　夭

灼灼桃花，倚风三月。香瘦轻剪，为伊孱弱。
粉面白骨，随风零落。红尘可叹，为何来过？

Shimmering Peaches

Blossoms aglow
In the wind of March
Pruned, sweet, thin and mild
Are weak and feeble for her.
Bleached bones with the rouged
Faces are humbled into the wind.
To this worldly life deplorable,
What for are you coming hither?

讨人喜欢

雅怀几许，欹枕新凉。琴台乱鹤，雪弦难张。
孤棹烟雨，夜郎飞扬。闲门高柳，渡鸦啼霜。

Lovable

Deep, deep, my refined mind
On the pillow braced a fresh cool
On the lute terrace by the cranes
Whose snow strings were so taut.
In the misty rains oared lonely,
A night man floated in the sky, and
In the high willows that shut my door,
One raven was cawing to the frost.

退 路

荻花迷海，北斗游鹅。苍苔花径，醉里扶歌。
千山一叶，巫岫嵯峨。重霄锁月，绝壁封河。

Route of Retreat

Over the lost sea of the flowering reeds,
The Big Dipper swims like a goose.
Through the flowering path in green moss,
My song drinks in the leaning delights.
And one leaf among a thousand mountains
Saws the air by the enchanted peaks, but
When the empyrean moon catches her lock,
A beetling wall would wrap the river.

温柔的回忆

草丝香软，一半清凉。纤纤星目，红豆暗伤。
叠叠青笺，子规苍茫。梦魂国里，扑袖柔香。

Soft Memory

Soft and sweet, the grasses
Are fresh and cool on the halves.
Long and slender, the starry eyes
Are wistful like a lovesicked seed.

Folded into the blue letters,
A cuckoo's fanning his thickening shades.
And slipped into the dreams,
The snapped sleeves are soft and sweet.

享 乐

樱红坠谷，挹水村桥。闲行燕翼，浪涌催箫。
陪游百草，一簟鷦鷯。凝酥日照，野蔬牧樵。

Life of Pleasure

A cherry red drops down the dale,
That's ladled through the hamlet bridge.
A free swallow skims over
The surging flute and
Wanders thru the luxuriant herbs
That are couching the wrens.
To be sunbathed softly,
The man of herds lives wild.

想了又想

垂眉秀蕊，轻锁春莺。闲鸟自翩，晓月独行。
筇枝欲狂，瘦梅疏横。明窗半掩，扶醉有声。

Search My Memory

Graceful pistils down the brows are
Locking up the spring oriole gently.
Idyllic in light feelings, the bird
Scampers lonely in the dawning moon.
Writhed in a craze of bamboos, the
Emaciated plum flowers are spare and stray.
Inside my bright window ajar,
I should be the vocal worse for liquor.

笑人笑己

花阴半树，落樱如雨。大漠曾游，马蹄已腐。
群蛙乱塘，也惧铜釜。今日黄花，明日阿姥。

To Mock Means to Be Mocked

Flowers are shaded half down the trees,
And cherries are dropping like rains.
Ever through the great desert,
The hooves have been rotten; and
In the piping of the pond, the frogs
Are also terrified of the copper cauldron.
Today, they're day-lily buds,
Tomorrow, old age creeps on.

效　率

清影无尘，茑萝[1]自傲。一肩花雨，漫洒堂奥[2]。
悠悠水墨，度岭风骚。千山眼底，曲径不毛。

【注释】

①茑萝：原产墨西哥，又名密萝松，俗称五角星花、狮子草。《诗经》云："茑为女萝，施于松柏。"意喻兄弟亲戚相互依附。②堂奥：室内的西南角，泛指房屋及其他深处隐蔽的地方。

Efficiency

Dustless in a clear picture,
The cypress vine gets above itself.
Showers of petals on the shoulder
Sprinkle the hidden recesses all over.
Leisurely, the ink drawings prove
The glamorous work of the ranges,
Whose panorama counts its move
Into the barren mazes should it behoove.

心　动

青蝶醉风，流春雪花。戏萍长短，折走奇葩。
兰香满袖，梦萦绿纱。蝴蝶梦破，葭莩[1]天涯。

【注释】

①葭莩（jiā fú）：芦苇秆内的薄膜。比喻关系极其疏远淡薄。

Eye-catching

A blue butterfly blind to the breeze
Streams like a spring snowflake,
That teases the duckweeds, long or short,
To snap off the fabulous flowers.
The sweet orchids full in the sleeves
Are enwrapped in the green gauze
Of a fond illusion that's shattered,
And gone to the limit of the earth.

心　量

嗟嗟[①]小子，率时俶载[②]。遵养高廪[③]，夙夜不怠。
命于苞桑[④]，肇域[⑤]渤海。猗与[⑥]戴水，不逆不塞。
绥靖勤止，邦家所爱。陟降[⑦]沉浮，其心不改。

【注释】

①嗟嗟（jiē）：叹词。表示招呼或感慨、赞美等。②率时：犹率此，率领这些。为时人的表率。俶（chù）载：始事，开始从事某种工作。《诗·大雅·大田》：“俶载南亩，播厥百谷。”后以“俶载”指农事伊始。③遵养：顺应时势或环境而积蓄力量。廪（lǐn）：会意兼象形。从人回，象屋形，中有户牖。又作“廪”。“廪”是俗字。本义：米仓。④苞桑：桑树之本。⑤肇域：疆界。⑥猗与（yī yǔ）：亦作“猗欤”。叹词。表示赞美。⑦陟（zhì）降：升降。

Mind-measure

Ah! My unworthy self,
To act as a pacesetter,
And draw in my claws,
Should be sedulous all the day.
Mandated to the mulberries,
And acquitted by the Bohai Sea,
The Daihe River so beauteous
Won't recede or silt up.
And my conscientious care
Is ready to serve my colours.
Sink or swim,
My heart will never back out.

信　心

东风不仁，夜问汤水。寒暄弱岁，素浪闲弛。
吹衣浅海，腊雪相靡[①]。夜郎烟树，旌节不徙。

【注释】

①相靡：摩擦，接触。

Confidence

Inhumane, the easterly
Asked the Soup River darkly.
Chin-deep, my teenager

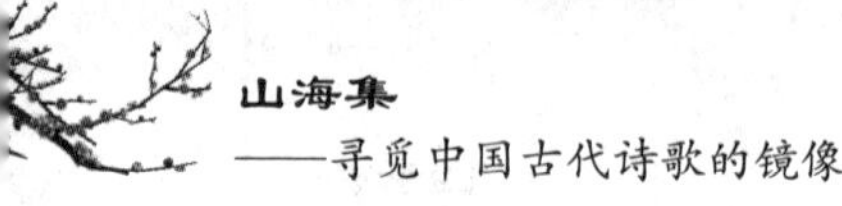

Was worn in the billows irregular.
Whiffled by the shallow sea,
My garb rubbed the snow, you see.
Mist-veiled, the night man
Never moves his unyielding quality.

行　动

江花欲来，浮瘴溪湄。温暾[①]百里，老树摇枝。
谁登野船？一叶涟漪。易水东去，北风斜吹。

【注释】

①温暾（tūn）：微暖；不冷不热。

Action

When the river blooms its loom,
The fetid stream floats.
Tepid in the 100-mile radius,
Old trees sway there.
Who's gone aboard in the wild?
It's one leaf that ripples.
As the Easy Water flows east,
The northerlies are slanting.

行　酒

酒旗戴露，酒垆[①]雨浓。酒绿芒角[②]，酒意葱茏。
斟酒暗香，琥珀容容。扶酒伴月，客酒临峰。

柏酒[3]三巡，宿酒[4]寒冲。酒阑[5]霜重，酒梦龙钟[6]。

【注释】

①酒垆：卖酒处安置酒瓮的砌台。亦借指酒肆、酒店。②芒角：星辰的光芒。③柏酒：柏叶酒。汉族传统习俗，谓春节饮之，可以辟邪。④宿酒：宿醉。⑤酒阑：酒筵将尽。⑥龙钟：身体衰老、行动不灵便的样子。

Down the Hatch

The tavern-sign in dews
Drenches the house of call
For our starlit revelry
Full of vinous flavours
To be filled subtly
Into the rippling amber
Bathed in the moon
Working up to a climax.
After three cups,
The night binge braves the cold.
After the feast is over in white,
My dream in wine dodders.

外　孙

时维八月，厥初[1]者何？清嘉诞降[2]，其胤[3]也歌。
戴水洋洋，[4]舜华之波。东方既明，熠熠[5]蒲荷。
子矜[6]零雨，秩秩[7]女萝。高冈作诵，紫运孔多[8]。
烝[9]民亦卿，翰飞[10]于戈。骏及千里，丰水明德。

【注释】

①厥初：其初。②清嘉：美好。诞降：从天而降；降生。③胤（yìn）：后代。④舜华：木槿花。⑤熠熠（yì）：闪烁的样子，形容闪光发亮。⑥矜：衣领。⑦秩秩：顺序貌。⑧孔多：很多。⑨烝（zhēng）：众。⑩翰飞：高飞。

Grandson

Who's the new-born babe
Coming in August?
In the first, fine light of day,
His worthy heirs will bask their smiles.
Overflown, the Daihe River
Is rippling her hibiscuses.
And with the wheels of Phoebus,
The lotuses glitter and glisten.
Drizzly and merrily,
The vines pass off in perfect order.
On the mound amid the chanted joy,
The gift of purple fortunes is well-favoured.
To be a high noble in the people,
The lion shall soar up in his sky.
And for a liable realm of space, the sturdy steed
Is richly endowed with the pleasant virtue.

乡思泪

凝珠欺眼，一梦难收。孤窗染袖，临水更流。
恓惶岁月，沧海横舟。风花旖旎，几缕乡愁。

横枝漫拂，飞雪衔秋。清晓伤逝，旧雨盈眸。
环佩有意，青冢难修。不见父母，何悔远游。

Homesick Tears

My tears clotted to tease the eyes
Are hard to draw in the dream
Whose lonely window dyes my sleeves
Though in the rill the water still flows
Into the years that are running scared
With a sweep of the oar in the sea.
In the captivating delights of Nature
Are twinged some wisps of nostalgia
Brimming over the side branches
Thru the blowing snows in the autumn mouth.
Bright in dawn's clear light, the gone love
Fills my pupils like a worn rain.
Wittingly, the jade pendant tinkles,
Yet toughly, the green tombs honour my memory.
To my parents, out of view,
I've felt remorse for such a journey afar.

象鼻山

薄言[①]观象，绵雨行空。漉漉条枚[②]，湝湝江汜[③]。
驾言谷风[④]，清扬适野[⑤]。弥弥漓水[⑥]，浼浼桃花[⑦]。
水天双月，月去月留。天月满亏，水月长圆。
薄言观象，有月其除[⑧]。盈盈黍梦[⑨]，随月运周[⑩]。

【注释】

①薄言：急急忙忙。高亨注："薄急急忙忙。言读为焉或然。"②条枚：枝干。《诗·周南·汝坟》："遵彼汝坟，伐其条枚。"③湝湝(jiē)：水流貌。《诗·小雅·鼓钟》："鼓钟喈喈，淮水湝湝。"汜(sì)：通"涘"，水决后又流入。江汜：江边。晋·陆机《为顾彦先赠妇》诗二首其一："愿假归鸿翼，翻飞游江汜。"④驾：乘车；言：语助词。语本《诗·邶风·泉水》："驾言出游，以写我忧。"后用以指代出游，出行。谷风：东风。⑤清扬：美好的仪容、风采。适野：犹言前往野外。⑥弥弥：水满貌。⑦浼浼（měi）：水盛貌。桃花：桃花江。⑧其除：日月流逝。指光阴不待人。《诗·唐风·蟋蟀》："蟋蟀在堂，岁聿其莫。今我不乐，日月其除。"⑨黍（shǔ）梦：黄粱梦。⑩运周：犹言回环运转。

Elephant Trunk Hill

In a breathless hurry for the elephant,
The steady rain is drizzling down
Through the sloppy boughs
By the running, winding river.
On the wheels through the easterly,
We get the keenest sight in the wild, and
Beside the popples of the Lijiang River,
The Peach Blossom River breaks into dimples.
Two moons in the water and sky
Are grown and then gone,
Along the higher course that waxes and wanes
But lower that would be long and round.
In a breathless hurry for the elephant,
The moon flows away
Into the full evanescence of life,

That operates ceaselessly with it.

校园行

2007 年仲夏，拿着教案再次迈进工作了 16 年的大庆师范学院校园，跟随自己学生的读书声，重新涌起了继续当学生的感受。

大庆闹春，四月摆尾。黄花滴露，对枝云虬。
珊珊和风，旰食左右。离离篁青，嫿妍鲜芳。
粼粼水波，依依柔条。莹心簸荡，漠色宵动。
群楼灌灯，杳杳旷语。聆聆书声，笔削优博。
化迁悟颖，刮肤穷髓。行墨淡荡，窈然志远。
古痕学步，气貌拔木。垂音孤简，达由性空。

Through the Campus

Fast and furious，the spring of Daqing,
In the fourth month is tail-flirting.
Day-lily buds are dewdropping,
With the cloud twigs curling and unfolding.

In the gentle breath of air,
All the nature is vigilant and fair.
On the pads of green lawn over there,
Perfumes of fresh flowers are sprinkled everywhere.

Along the rhythmic rasping of waves,
Wickers are but supple，willowy slaves.
In a spell of manly heart that heaves,
Twilight has been brooded in sheaves.

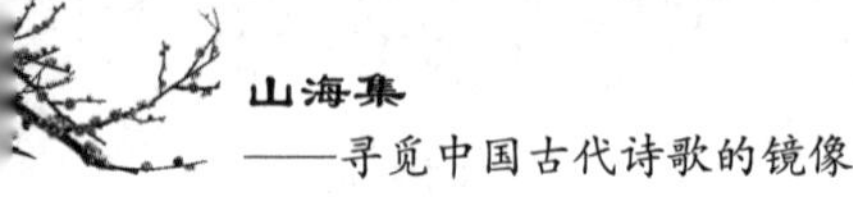

All the building lights are spectacular,
Out and away gladdening an unknown favour.
In the hum of study that's clear,
A polished work seeks the quality better.

Endowed with a highly-gifted spirit,
I have to plod poisons up in a dear merit.
Softly, a light ink imparts the secret,
That's aimed at the highest favourite.

To try to walk like an ancient swan,
One's deportment should be a sheer-muscled plan.
Tones, solitary but simple as it can,
Are but a temporal entity for the man.

淹死胆大的

白笔对镜，戴水临霜。修鳞戏鲸，野人横桨。
青云壮气，行潦有方。豪迈沧海，长短自量。

Bold to Be Drowned

A white eyebrow pencil in the mirror
Faces the frost over the Daihe River
Where the thin fish molests the whale
Like a savage throwing his weight on the paddle
With the eagle-winged pride of the sky-aspiring
Brook and rill which won't be good-for-nothing.
Unchained before the sea,
Such a pencil can caliper itself as it should be.

阳朔钟乳石

玉乳怀金，香樟滴露。一线清痕，岚烟如幕。
斜漫流光，壁纱锁雾。步韵敲诗，陶情满目。

Stalactite in Yangshuo

Gold, bosomed in the jade breasts,
Drops its dews down the camphor trees
Like a glimmer of clear shade
Curtained by the misty vapours
Brimming over the streamers on the cross,
Whose voile paries are locking the fogs.
My step steps along the metrical numbers
In a happy frame of mind here and there.

野人梦

野人乃梦，梦深几许。花香旧年，晕红轻雨。
绣作粉蝶，为君留取。合烟绿窗，冷翠绮户。
柳嫩霓裳，清风作舞。宝玲掩春，泻红如缕。
肃肃子君，乐只琴曲。振振公子，行迈如故。

Savage in Dream

The dream by the savage
Has been dreamt to certain depths,

Whose perfume of flowers in the past
Flushed in the light rains
Embroidered into a pink butterfly
Which would be spared for you.
Misted behind the green window,
Gauze-draped and chilled with the verdant dews,
The tender willows in their rainbow skirts
Are dancing to the fresh wind,
That closes the spring, like precious jingles,
Pouring down strands of red.
Reverent, the fair ladies
Are given to up pleasure;
Exhilarated, the good man
Will continue the same.

野人行

野人在山，松竹[①]橐橐。瞻彼鸾鸟，其声哕哕[②]。
野人在水，蒹葭菁菁[③]。瞻彼嘉鱼，其水唯唯[④]。
野人在田，蔓草瞿瞿[⑤]。瞻彼葛藟[⑥]，百虫喓喓[⑦]。

【注释】

①橐橐（tuó）：象声词。多状硬物连续碰击声。②哕哕（huì）：有节奏的声音。③菁菁（jīng）：草木繁茂的样子。④唯唯：象声词，描摹流水声。⑤瞿瞿（jù）：惊顾貌。⑥葛藟（lěi）：葡萄科植物，果实味酸，不能生食，根、茎和果实供药用。喓喓（yāo）：虫叫的声音。

The Journey of the Savage

The savage in the mountains
Thru the thudding pines and bamboos
Looks up at the phoenix,
In her rhythmical tinkles.

The savage by the water
Amidst the lush reeds
Looks down at the good fish
Which are babbling and murmuring.

The savage in the farmland
With a stare at the sod grass
Looks far at the the creepers and vines
Wherein hundreds of insects are buzzing.

叶　落

戴河波浅，攲枕[①]风弱。等闲试酒[②]，旧筵酬酢[③]。
一叶飘萍，惊散残萼。忆春纤魂，风云尽错。

【注释】

①攲（qī）枕：斜靠着枕头。②试酒：品尝新酿成的酒。③酬酢（chóu zuò）：宾主互相敬酒。

Fallen Leaves

Shallow waves of the Daihe River
Are feeble on the blown pillow.
Having browsed the new wine,
The old feast exchanges toasts again.
One leaf of the floating duckweeds
Suddenly startles the faded petals.
And the recalled spring that tows my soul
Has gone amiss in the ebb and flow.

一段情

菱花玉露，几度风霜。轻鸥数点，花外惹香。
萱草谁怜，珠凝已凉。小窗犹记，玉唇寒香。

An Incident in Love

The pure dews in my mirror
Are bitterly glamorous for ages.
Some dribs of light gulls have
Stirred the sweet beyond the flowers.
Who pities the day lilies that
Are cooling the curdled beads?
Vaguely, my little window still remembers
The humble sweet on her pure lips.

赢　点

藤萝丝语，软风忘机。自性情中，初试娇衣。
青尘罗袜，红粉为谁？三千紫陌，一瞬寒思。

Win the Point

The silken tongue of the creepers
Holds herself aloof in the slight air.
Of her own nature,
Her tender dress is newly attired.
And in her silk socks thru the dark dust,
For whom could she be rose-cheeked?
And in three thousand thoroughfares,
Her cold spirit winks.

影响力

君子在邑，乐只攸宁①。悠游燕婉②，臧否不惊。
实维尚寐，子嗟换觥。北园有棘，我心有荆。
聊以独行，蔹③蔓横生。畅毂④载兴，菡萏⑤飞莺。
晨露在桑，浸彼舜英⑥。节彼桑扈⑦，馌⑧彼青萍。
弁彼嘉卉，嘉我黎明。其毒流火，孤蝉也鸣。
天命大任，敬止⑨三更。俾⑩立阮疆，戴河飞鲸。

【注释】

①攸宁：幽静安宁。②燕婉：仪态安详温顺；优美。③蔹（liǎn）：多年生蔓草。④畅毂（chàng gū）：长毂。指兵车。此处泛指汽车。

菡萏（hàn dàn）：荷花。⑥舜英：木槿花。⑦节：高峻的样子；高飞貌。桑扈：俗名青雀。⑧馌（yè）：给在田间耕作的人送饭。此处拟人化处理。⑨敬止：敬仰。止，语词。⑩俾（bǐ）：使；从。

Influence Power

The man of virtue in the city.
Enjoys his composed seclusion.
Leisurely, his harmonious felicity
Keeps his cool over a mixed reception.
To foretell his own slumber,
Freely, let the wine flow.
The north garden may be a pricker
That has grown up in the soul.
Just to walk in solitude,
A rank growth of weeds is overflowing.
Full of merriment the wheel's habitude
Glides its lotus to the oriole flowering.
Like the morn dews afield,
The roses of sharon are bathed.
Feathered, the green-beak can wield
His food to the duckweeds so wreathed.
To be adorned with the herbs,
His daybreak is convivial.
While the torrid Fire Star curbs,
The lonely cicadas are also jovial.
For the great task by the mandate of heaven,
His night is dead keen on the feeling of reverence.
To exercise his own dominion,
The Daihe River flies its Titanic confidence.

咏 梅

欺寒镜川[①]，折水绝国[②]。冲飙坎壈[③]，转蓬百折[④]。
涸鳞疏影[⑤]，遵渚御风[⑥]。琴台豹隐[⑦]，应侠碧落[⑧]。
冲襟[⑨]行健，积气[⑩]载德。堂萱[⑪]北望，对酒以歌。

【注释】

①镜川：镜湖。②折水：回旋的流水，也指产珠玉的地方。绝国：极其辽远之邦国，此处指遥远的地方。③冲飙：急风；暴风。坎壈（lǎn）：困顿，不顺利。唐·张彪《北游还酬孟云卿》："行行无定心，壈坎难归来。"④转蓬：随风飘转的蓬草。⑤涸鳞：化自明·杨慎的《高泉临行再赋此以别》："鎩羽涸鳞去安所，翾飞川咏几时同。"处于极度窘困境地、亟待救援的人。疏影：疏朗的影子。⑥遵渚（zhǔ）：化自《诗·豳风·九罭》："鸿飞遵渚，公归无所。"原谓鸿雁循着水中小洲飞翔，后用以形容鸿飞。御风：《庄子·逍遥游》，"夫列子御风而行，泠然善也。"⑦琴台：唐代县尉陶沔所筑，前方后圆，呈半月形，又名半月台或单父台。唐代大诗人高适、李白、杜甫曾联袂来游，题咏颇多。豹隐：比喻隐居山林。⑧应侠：英勇仗义。碧落：道教语，指东方第一层天，泛指天上、青天。⑨冲襟：也作"冲矜"，旷淡的襟怀。⑩积气：聚积阴阳之气。《列子·天瑞》："天，积气耳，亡处亡气。"⑪堂萱（xuān）：指母亲。宋·范成大《致政承奉卢君挽词》："眼看庭玉成名后，身及堂萱未老时。"

【自解】

初冬的时候，花草树木光秃秃的，山海关城墙里边，几棵干枝上面，粉红色的花冷艳地对着瑟瑟的寒风。

大年除夕直到初十，也跟其他时间段一样，外面怎样的精彩似乎都被自我屏蔽了。昨天，运锋博士来办公室写项目书，顺便聊聊眼皮底下几个地方，什么海底世界、集发观光园、紫云山滑雪场、求仙入海处、乐岛等，凭良心说，的确不曾去过。好像秦皇岛是别人的，与自己无关。真的无关吗？其实，自己也愿意走一走，找一找感觉，起码也能写成更多的诗行。但是，出去了，时间也就没了。

每年过年，都是这么过的，苦行僧一样苛刻着自己。

Ode to the Plum Blossoms

Mirrored streams in cold spells
Whirl back into the distance God tells.
Dog-tided, the tempests
Have snapped the rootless weeds.
In jeopardy, the dappled shadows
Ride upon the wind along the isles.
Retreat, towards the lute terrace,
Gaily, to the realms of bliss in place.
Carefree, in its motion,
The virtue has its own concentration.
North, my eyes are gazed out to Mother,
And before the cup, drunk as a merry beggar.

攸 行

谗口不穀①，田稚不实。秉畀②无焰，笾豆无苾③。
夏桀式序④，昊天不佚⑤。商纣有严，邦畿⑥不诘。
凤凰来仪，树羽吉吉。邦国好音，寝庙⑦乃一。
君子眉寿，栉比⑧逸逸⑨。小人惶惶，终日怀疾。

【注释】

①不穀：不得养；不得相养；不善。②秉畀（bǐng bì）：化自“秉畀炎火”，就是将田中的害虫捉去烧掉。③笾（biān）豆：笾和豆。古

代食器，竹制为笾，木制为豆。古代祭祀时盛祭品的两种器具。苾(bì)：芳香。④式序：亦作“式叙”。按次第；顺序。⑤佚（yì）：过失。⑥邦畿：国家。⑦寝庙：古代宗庙的正殿称庙，后殿称寝，合称寝庙。⑧栉比：像梳子齿那样密密地排着。⑨逸逸：往来有次序。

Take the Initiative

If the slandering tongue behaves well,
The field will be barren of fruit;
If the vermins are flameless,
The sacrificial dishes will not be fragrant;
If King Jie of the Xia Dynasty were proper,
The great heaven wouldn't screen its faults;
If King Zhou of the Shang Dynasty were reverent,
The imperial domain would not dispute him.
When a phoenix comes with grace,
The feathered trees would be blessed.
For a state in sweet melodies,
The rear temples would stay in step.
And to the man of virtue for the oldest-grown,
He should be free and easy, but in tight rows,
While to the mean man on tenterhooks,
He would make a life of jealousy, all day.

欲望与激情

惊涛一线，浪卷云舒。群峰含黛，万木苍庐。
流红滴翠，点墨成书。空灵意蕴，江山老欤?
断浦之池，贵在芙蕖。人生飘叶，岁月有初。

扁舟探雨，遣兴如鱼。荣华过后，一切成虚。

Desire and Passion

Surging waves along the coastline
Are smacking the easy clouds
In which the black gleaming peaks
Are hutted thinly in the trees and shrubs.
In the flowing ruby and the green drops,
The clicked inks are snowballed into the books.
Of an illusory implication,
The old age creeps up on the landscape?
For the pond by the broken beach,
What matters most is the lotus pool.
Life falls like a leaf,
From its first point of passage.
And compared to a skiff in the rain,
The leisure time swims like a fish.
Yet after the glory,
All are deluded with false hopes.

缘　分

屏里玉兰，繁花断香。朱眉一点，半面清妆。
心飘万里，嫁作他娘。子君去矣，明月浮浪。

A Stroke of Luck

Magnolias are curtained

And fitful in the sweet waves of flowers.
And one bright red eyebrow
Has been half-veiled in soft light.
Her heart, once gone to the earth's end,
Has stepped off the carpet.
Gone, the fair maiden
Floats her waves in the bright moon.

造富机会

上个十年，你可能错过了无数发财致富的机会，下个十年你还想错过吗？让我们看看接下来十年可能存在的造富机会。

Chance to Wealth

其一：农地入市

春畦苦旱，地虬[①]不贮。农政不修，累及禾黍[②]。
耒耜[③]不耕，士庶[④]不拒。民畜食贫，四方失序。

【注释】

①虬（qiú）：古代传说中有角的小龙。②黍（shǔ）：亦称“稷”“糜子”，古代专指一种子实叫黍子的一年生草本植物。③耒耜（lěi sì）：古代耕地翻土的农具。耒是耒耜的柄，耜是耒耜下端的起土部分。④士庶（shù）：士人和普通百姓。亦泛指人民、百姓。

One: Farmland to Market

When drought prevails in the spring plot,
The earth dragon won't gain his store of provisions;
When the agricultural policy is not cultivated,
The crops will be left unharvested.
And like the plough-handles and shares out of work,
Like the courtiers and commoners out of order,
And in poverty the people and the animals
Will lose all their proper precedence.

其二：文化传媒

珠字隽文，其心卓阔。悲欣长短，褒贬予夺[①]。
持螯共燕，笔底无葛。中国故事，不文而曷[②]？

【注释】

①予夺：赞许和贬低。②曷（hé）：何，什么。

Two: Cultural Media

The letters like sublime beads
Are broadminded.
Doleful and delightful, their lengths
Hold power over praise or blame.
And to the nippers of the feast-finding crabs,
The pen shouldn't be tangled in vines and briers,
In that the Chinese story

Has her own degrees of elegance.

其三：4G 网络

云罅倏开，风播谬种。柳娘舞罢，新月如拱。
黄杏结烟，衔笛成冢。醅酒折枝，踏来新宠。

Three：4G Net

Rift that sudden clouds,
And sow that wrong wind!
After the willow's dance,
The crescent will be arched.
And in the yellow misty apricots,
The street flutes sound bold.
Break off a branch for the wine,
To drum up a new favourite's step.

其四：在线教育

声声慢里，一网鹅毛。云中洛神，带月驰涛。
播香洒翠，雪细飞猱。九天上下，处处为牢。

Four：Education on Line

In the slow, slow tune,
All the goose feathers were fished out, where
The Goddess of the River Lo on high

Was billowed with the moon.
From the sweet seeds sprinkling the green,
The snowflakes are gliding like macaques,
Upper and lower in the highest heavens,
That served as prisons here and there.

其五：创业孵化平台

瑶池一月，形迹轮回。天上憔悴，地下崔嵬[①]。
高锁冷梦，穿帘燕飞。鹿台酒肉，早已衰颓。
薜萝牵恨，古人成灰。玉人紫楼，酒霁蓝媒。
梓童[②]幽韵，剪红无悔。遥向巫山，夜雨藏梅。

【注释】

①崔嵬（wéi）：有石的土山；高大、高耸的样子。②梓童：原作“子童”，最早见于《全相平话五种》：“妲己乃问天子曰：‘大王前者行文字天下人进宝，近日进得何宝？将来与子童随喜看之。’”（《武王伐纣平话》）“吕后：‘子童领旨，九月二十一日未央宫下，斩讫韩信也。’”（《前汉书平话》）“高祖圣旨言：‘寡人去游云梦，交子童权为皇帝，把三人赚入宫中，害其性命。’”（《三国志平话》）在明代小说中，“子童”逐渐被“梓童”所替代，用于对皇后的称呼。此处特指风流女性，以为戏说。

Five: Startup Incubator

Jade Pool one month
Trails the wheel of life.
Celestially, it pines away,
Terrestrially, it towers.
Locked high, my dream feels cold,

Thru the curtain, my swallow flies.
Wine and meat at the Deer Terrace
Have been weak and down-hearted.
And in the crooked, wild figs,
The men of old have been crumbled.
While in the purple floors the rosy faces
Become blue devils in the blue media.
To the serene rhymes of certain empress,
The clipped red has made a right move.
And towards the amorous hill afar,
Plums are hidden in the rain at night.

其六：移动互联网

尘缨世网，作翅冥飞①。穿风漏雨，坐透罗帏。
一掌之欢，络绪霏霏。清谈早契，棱镜熹微。
山泽遮道，罔绳之机。匡庐三业②，当赋以归。

【注释】

①冥飞：高飞。比喻人的退隐。②匡庐：江西的庐山。相传殷周之际有匡俗兄弟七人结庐于此，故称。三业：佛教三业，身口意。

Six: Mobile Internet

In this mundane world like a net,
The obscure wings are flapping,
Thru the wind that lets in the rain,
Whence the curtained bed lounges full.
The merry hours of one palm
Are threaded, thick and fast; and

Prittle-prattle into an early contract,
On the prism to the faint rays of first dawn.
In the marshes that block the way, the ivy
Tendrils are meshed with wiles and intrigues.
From the Lushan Mountain for the trividha-dvāra,
I have to go back with my lines.

其七：资本市场

树裹轻裘，柳陌依旧。挂冠烟萝，草色出岫。
腹内藏诗，五车之富，不抵纨绔，一宿之陋。

Seven: Capital Market

Light furs swathed in trees
Wicker along the roads as usual
Hang up amid the hazy sea whose
Hues of grasses rise out of the peaks.
Longs and shorts in the stomach
Could fill up five carriages,
Which can't outweight the playboy's
Broken money in one night.

照照后面

清樽九转，举步长歌。狂飙着陆，猛志冲河。
太白豪兴，醉卧清波。失足明月，千古婆娑。

Mirror the Back of Yourself

Clear cup! Make up nine!
To the tune of the long song!
In the fierce gale that's grounded,
The violent will charges the river.
With a spirit soaring higher and freer,
The limpid waves fall in a drunken stupor.
After the bright moon slips down,
All the ages are whirlingly bounded.

争　辩

雪泥埋身，有待春日。沃野枯瓢，冷暖自知。
雨雾穷荒，迁客游佚。贪泉沙怒，任由凶吉。

Catfight

My body in the snow slush
Has yet to get the spring.
My dried ladle in the fertile field
Knows its own changes in temperature.
Barren in a poor, little air of mist,
Those exiles are going on the loose.
Insatiable desires in the rage of sands
Are careless of good or evil.

知　足

十年隽影，暗剪梅烟。幽寂闲听，蝶苑莺浅。
梅边雏凤，轻羽飘帆。飞花散处，风香语软。

Contentment

A sublime picture for a decade
Clips her dark mist in the plumps.
A spared ear in the secret silence
Warbles in his shallow garden of butterflies.
And a female phoenix next to the plums
Flaps her sail gently.
While in a flurry of flying flowers,
The wind says its soft sweet.

自　知

凝冰润物，轻梦落花。芙蓉弄晚，微翥待霞。
一弦娇月，不解轻纱。莫作梨眼，题梅天涯。

Self-awareness

Moist in the curdled ice,
One petal falls light in my dream.
And a lotus that teases the night
Awaits the shimmering track of beams

Before one tender crescent
Could be puzzled by the light gauze.
My eyes of pears, nay!
Write no plums far, far away.

智　愚

角山积翠，汤水西行。彤庭圣谕，迁客相迎。
忠臣不死，奸佞峥嵘。智者无言，观者自清。

Wit or Fool

Green, amassed on Mt. Corner,
Westward, rolls the Soup River;
To be commanded of the King,
The exile slips into a wrong greeting.
A loyal vassal rises like phoenix,
And a crafty sycophant downs like a rugged pix.
For the wisest, he would be dumb,
And on the sideline, he won't be rum.

走　火

敏歆①宪警，受命彭彭。不日劳止②，匪类狰狞。
威仪式遏③，泄忧抚宁。小子斯畏，君子哀兵。
俾民攘寇，胡斯恶行？烝民有则，蟊贼④不宁。
昊天右序⑤，蛮貊⑥其氓。薄言⑦奋伐，惩毖正名。

【注释】

①敷歆：感动貌；欣喜貌。②劳止：辛劳；劳苦。③式遏：制；制止。④蟊（máo）贼：坏人。⑤右序：辅助；佑助。⑥蛮貊（mán mò）：古代称南方和北方落后部族。亦泛指四方落后部族。⑦薄言：急急忙忙。

Gone off by Accident

Readily, the policeman
Received a devoted commission,
That was hard pressed so soon,
With his grinning skull of a goon.
To repress in an awe-inspiring dignity,
The peacekeeper relieved his melancholy.
The blokes stood in awe of the manner,
And the noble droned a plaintive note to the ranker.
To resist the bandit for the people in distress,
Who'd freeze-frame the deformity of conduct so careless?
Were the people to see the specific law,
The grubbing pests would hang up on the how.
To be blessed by the great heaven,
It should not rule out all the barbarous men.
To repress him in a breathless hurry,
It was but a warning sign against those not worthy.

做　人

炫示[1]者匮，介怀[2]者薄。惬心[3]潜匿，落拓者汹[4]。
出茧撕痛，靓翅隐疾。顾外疏内，宜正风骨。

【注释】

①炫示：炫耀。②介怀：介意，在意。③惬心：得意。④落拓：穷困潦倒，寂寞冷落。汹：张扬。

How to Behave

To flaunt means to be short,
To reck means to be shallow;
A pleasant heart is masked,
And a lost soul is tusked;
Out of cocoons, it's a tearing pain,
For a fair feather, it's a hidden gain.
To be without yet not within,
One should set right his vigorous strength.

做人三十六字

一个人不管有多聪明能干，背景条件有多好，如果不懂得如何去做人、做事，那么，他最终的结局肯定是失败。做人做事是一门艺术，更是一门学问。很多人之所以一辈子都碌碌无为，那是因为他一辈子都没弄明白该怎样去做人、做事。可以这么说，做人做事是一门涉及现实生活中各个方面的学问，要掌握这门学问，抓住其本质，就必须对现实生活加以提炼、总结，得出一些具有普遍意义的规律来，人们才能有章可循，而不至于迷然无绪。

36 Characters on How to Behave

其一：谦

日晖河柳，笛内梅瘦。淡烟无痕，明波织绣。
暗云摇雨，香阶出岫。铁血疾风，清语依旧。

One：Modest

Like the sun slanted in the river willows,
The plums are emaciated in the flute.
Unlike the pale mists short of shadows,
The bright wave weaves its embroidered articles.
In the dark cloud that shakes the rain,
A sweet step is stepping out of the grotto.
Iron-willed, the choppy wind amain
Whispers as usual, again.

其二：淡

小桥风满，千秋谁见。红萼滴愁，一春画扇。
倦客听荷，红衣芳甸。趁意幽思，随它浓淡。

Two：Light

Who，off the raging foot bridge，
Has seen a thousand autumns?
Sad drips down the red petals
Are fanning one spring，and
Like the lotus ear of a tired wanderer，
The red dress enkindles the sweet pasture.
Seize such a secret spirit，
At the mercy of the shades of colour.

其三：俭

三千弱水，一寸玄机。闲凝沧浪，甘露迷离。
梵心意远，几度宏辞。瘦月满纸，无灯自绥。

Three：Frugal

In three thousand fathoms of weak water，
One inch of the hidden workings
Has frozen the idyllic，surging waves，
From the blurred，heavenly dews.
And a pure mind wanders afar，
Into the grand rhetoric many a time.
Full of the paper，a thin moon
Pacifies herself without a lamp.

其四：自

东君轻暖，疏影韩香。幽枕抱灯，老梦几行。
浮生秉烛，尺素星光。忠奸百态，任尔无常。

Four：Self

Light and warm，the Lord of East
In the sweet，dappled shadows
Caresses the lit，secret pillow
Whose old dreams are dreamt.
In this life like a candle aglow，
Under the written star lights，
A good or evil kaleidoscope
Will never mind an alternated caprice.

其五：礼

迍邅[①]汉月，云不隔礼。牵身底事，不劳口体。
别来青蒲，老去荒荠。听鸡唱第，不为稊米[②]。

【注释】

①迍邅（zhūn zhān）：难行貌。②稊米：小米。比喻其小。《庄子·秋水》："计中国之在海内，不似稊米之在太仓乎。"

Five: Manners

Turbulent, the Han moon
Scudded thru the polite cloud.
Tangled, such a matter
Saved the mouth and body.
Farewell, green blades of grass,
Doddery, deserted shepherd's purse.
At the true crow of a rooster,
He's not for a grain of millet.

其六：正

阳和正气，多梦人生。黄菊掠影[①]，暗波不惊。
东篱霜苦，莫待黄莺。清风挥剪，春华再明。

【注释】

①黄莺，英文名 Oriolus chinensis，也有称“黄鹂”“黄鸟”等，分类上属鸟纲，黄鹂科，主要分布于旧大陆温热带地区，特别是东洋界，有 2 属 28 种，我国有 1 属 5 种。在我国分布于东部地区，由内蒙古的东北部、东北、华北地区，往南直到广东、云南，西达陕西、甘肃 南部和四川西部等地。为夏候鸟。黄莺是大自然的“歌唱家”。鸣声圆润嘹亮，低昂有致，富有韵律，婉转似笙簧，清脆如织机，十分悦耳动听。古人把它的鸣啭称为“莺歌”“黄簧”，是诗人经常歌咏的对象。

Six：Right-minded

The sunny sense of right
May lead a dreamy life.
As a film comes over yellow chrysanthemums,
The dark billows will be calm still.
Under the east fence bitterly frosted,
Await that golden oriole，no more.
After the breeze clips,
The spring flowers will brighten anew.

其七：志

乳燕于飞，直向昆仑。孑孑驭翼，万里弥敦[①]。
击风半世，齿衰气存。人生百年，不辱祖孙。

【注释】

①弥敦：更加诚恳。

Seven：Will

Nursling swallow's flight
Straight to the Kunlun Mountains
Drives his lonely wings
More in sincerity to the earth's end.
To hazard half a lifetime,
His spirit lives thru the gone teeth.
For the lifespan about 100 years,

He won't debase his forbears.

其八：时

飞鸟绝漠，一去不还。空亭雁影，短命红颜。
孟德横槊，赤壁问天。时空隧道，转瞬百年。

Eight: Time

A sand bird on the wing,
Once gone, will never return.
A wild goose off the void pavilion
Will be like a soap bubble.
Cao Cao's levelling his spear
To the red cliff asked the heaven;
And thru the space-time tunnel amain,
One century is just twinkling.

其九：勤

戴河孤蛹，弄茧春丝。箱篚未沐[①]，谁遣新棋？
吴蚕初壮，缕缕情思。千结自囚，甘做嫁衣。

【注释】

①篚（fěi）：古代盛物的竹器。

Nine: Industrious

One pupae on the Daihe River is
Cocooned out into the spring fibres.
Who has advanced the new chessman before
The bamboo-baskets have yet to be clean?
As the south silkworms start to be sturdy,
Their tender thoughts of love are threaded
And knotted and chained by themselves,
Ready to sew trousseaus for others.

其十：实

殷勤布谷，纤雨带梦。麦前鼓翅，剪破春风。
浮生焦谷，扫径游空。殊俗转蓬，不改初衷。

Ten: True

Cuckoos in assiduity
Are dreamed in the slightest drizzle
And flutter down the wheat field,
That trims the spring breeze,
Floating thru the scorched dales
That sweep the wandering paths,
Like the alien tumbleweeds,
Without a change of the first resolve.

其十一：专

根机虽钝，固本方圆。岫深门里，书阁惊雁。
十年不语，印文度阡[①]。我有青麦，归以养年。

【注释】

①阡：道路。曹操《短歌行》："越陌度阡，枉用相存。"

Eleven：Concentrated

Obtuse in motive power,
I can consolidate his square.
Deep behind the cavern' s door,
The wild geese shock the book floor.
Lost in thought for a decade,
The printed letters get it made.
If I have the green wheat, my return
Will enunciate the gospel of health.

其十二：慎

纷纭世务，慎尔其行。尘途叵测，薄履悬冰。
贪泉举瓢，埋祸无声。枝俏色醉，海里骑鲸。

Twelve：Prudent

Diverse and confused, the world affairs
Should mind their Ps and Qs.
Unfathomable, the way of dusts
Treads thin under the hanging glaciers.
Insatiable, the raised ladle
Covers up silent disasters.
And fuddled, the hues of pretty branches
Are riding the whale in the sea.

其十三：硬

心急语硬，刚鬣柔毛。野石乱犀，谁惮江皋？
惊嗟沧海，不虞浪蛟。天下渤海，寰球一勺。

Thirteen：Uncompromising

A fast heart and a strong tongue
Are the fluff of the hog bristles.
To the hog-wild rhinoceros down the wild stones,
Who feels some nameless fear by the stream?
And open-eyed before the vast sea, what’s
Unforeseen may be a serpent from the billows
Of the Bohai Sea under the sun which is
But one scoop in the whole globe.

其十四：小

白茅度岭，溪水出滩。流火灼浪，越鸟不欢。
三秋暮雨，夜郎锁寒。八荒炎瘴，就此消残。

Fourteen: Go Small

Mountain cogons
Are oozed down to the shoals
Whose scorching billows
Have withered the south fowls.
In the late autumn and rains,
When night locks the cold,
The burning, farthest mode
Will vanish out of its abode.

其十五：锐

帘外紫梨，垂玉三千。孤客凭水，纵横由年。
谗毒劲色，腊雪扬天。丹心铁刃，断头凛然。

Fifteen: Dauntless

Purple pears beyond the curtain
Are hanging 3000 jadestones.
And the lonely passenger on the water is
Ramified into a labyrinth for a century.

In the face of the backbitten, driven poisons,
The coldest snows are roaring in the sky.
And before the sword of steel, the loyal heart
Should be full of an icy dignity, though beheaded.

其十六：创

眸中闯雪，败草荆蓬。刀霜满砚，野人独行。
唐书宋墨，古今蒙戎[1]。书生指剑，双面英雄。

【注释】

①蒙戎（méng róng）：蓬松。也作“蒙茸”“龙茸”。《左传·僖公五年》：“狐裘龙茸。”

Sixteen: Creative

The rushing snow in the eyes
All over the withered, thorny grass
Slashes the hoars full in the ink stone,
By the lone hand of the savage,
Whose ink tablet in the Tang & Song rhymes
Are fluffy through the time tunnel
Where the sword by the schoolman
Has generated the two-edged hero.

其十七：通

眉心一点，可通三世。人生坎凛[1]，源自拘泥。
轮困[2]猛士，尤有不济[3]。九派吞海，不量其力。

【注释】

①坎凛：贫困潦倒。②轮囷（qūn）：高大的样子；形容勇气过人；比喻勇气、血性过人。③不济：不成功。

Seventeen：Free Course

The jot between the eyebrows
Can be navigable in the three worlds.
The life down on its luck
May come of the great nicety.
With the brawn virtues of warriors,
One could be born under the wrong star.
For the nine streams to gulp the sea,
It bites off more than they can chew.

其十八：言

狗舌叹暑，炎光萎蔫。池蛙鼓舌，春雷震天。
长舌讦隐，惹事无端。早莺声巧，调舌自闲。

Eighteen：Speech

Dog tongues deplorable in the summer-heat
Are wilting in the blazing light.
And green frogs wagging their tongues
Rend the air like spring thunders.
To pry the privacies, the long tongues
Can wake a sleeping dog for nothing.

And an early nightingale may be trilling,
And lives at ease as a wit-cracker.

其十九：宽

宽溪入湖，耳静心宽。宽宥负荆，鸡腹度寒。
瘦雨宽风，闲云梦宽。天下知音，字窄缘宽。

Nineteen: Tolerant

A broad brook joins the lake
With a broad heart and a calm ear.
A gracious clemency offers an apology,
But a chicken crop its cold spells.
When a broad wind blows the poor rain,
The broad dream roams in the clouds.
And for the soul-mates under the sun,
A narrow character should be broadly predestined.

其二十：和

山鸡隔海，忘情凌波。无岛呓语，蜩[①]舌戏蛾。
清和焦尾，明月吟琴。花和去岁，再邀笙歌。

【注释】

①蜩（tiáo）：蝉。

Twenty: Harmony

The ringed pheasant off the sea
Was unruffled by the emotion of the ripples.
Its footle without the foothold on an isle
Molested the moths like the trills of cicadas
That, to the Burned Tail in tranquil,
Chanted the lute under the bright moon,
That, shone on the cycle of the flowers,
Would rope in the revelry.

其二十一：信

鹤磬敲雪，微信半笺。素笔低唱，着墨方圆。
斗酒酬句，珠玉生烟。为人一世，不改前言。

Twenty One: Trust

Crane chimes in the snow
Mailed half their tiny note-paper
Whose croon under the pure strokes
Drafted its radius
In the wine to offer the lines, where
Were permeated the pearls and gems…
To be a man,
Not to be a slip of the tongue.

其二十二：帮

亲者观火，隔岸扇风。举柴之旺，心寒苦冬。
扶危助蹇，不计兹功。红尘为善，天下一同。

Twenty-Two: Help

While watching the fire, my dear
Has been fanning across the river.
While reaping the games in rows,
My bitterest heart takes the chills.
To succor those in distress and danger,
I never give any thought to my personal power.
To be virtuous in the worldly life
Comes to be identical and rife.

其二十三：敬

君子敬人，不需提耳。小人不恭，匕首中函。
夙夜敬天，天克其明[①]。浮鬼暗浪，自困穷关。

【注释】

①天克其明：减自“克明”：能明。

Twenty-Three: Respect

A respectful man of virtue
Needs not to talk like a Dutch uncle.
A humble man who's cynical
Conceals his dagger under the rose.
To revere great Heaven day and night
Will shed the virtuous light.
And to be a floating ghost so tight
Will trap itself into a dead close.

其二十四：交

青舒踏臆，鹿鸣维桑①。临屏对友，偕步天香。
隔篱唤旧，附葭连秧。我有高朋，温酒达慷②。

【注释】

①维桑：《诗·小雅·小弁》："维桑与梓，必恭敬止。"《毛传》："父之所树，己尚不敢不恭敬。"后以"维桑"指代故乡。②达慷：也作"慷达"，大方通达。

Twenty-Four: Associate

In my stepping heart, green and easy,
There goes a deer lowing in the mulberry.
With the curtain to pal around,
Such geminated steps thru peonies are profound.
Beyond the fence to call back my old pals,

The vines in the reeds are running false.
To the guests of exalted rank,
My wine's versed in a big-hearted thank.

其二十五：坚

振梦三更，断魂尤难。九衢潢潦[①]，消泯[②]浩瀚。
壮士执鞭，山前断腕。勇者一叱，千夫忌惮[③]。

【注释】

①潢潦（huáng liáo）：地上流淌的雨水。②消泯（mǐn）：消灭，消失。③忌惮（jì dàn）：对某些事或物有所顾忌、顾虑，表现为害怕、顾虑、畏惧。

Twenty-Five：Persistent

My dream braced up the midnight,
Hardly possible to break my soul
In the rainwashes of the downtown streets
That were shadowing into the sea.
Whip in hand, a stout warrior
Chooses to break his piedmont wrist;
To bellow thunderously, the bold
Will be scaring off thousands of men.

其二十六：谋

瘦月肥花，君子于游。豆灯吊梁，柴米之谋。
厕身庾吏[①]，枯坐亭丘[②]。尧舜相承，浩德阳州。

【注释】

①庾（yǔ）吏：古代管粮仓的小官。②亭丘：丘亭，即空亭。

Twenty-Six：Scheme

Fat flowers under the thin moon
Are a must-see to the man of virtue.
One wick on the hanging beam tries
To find the firewood and rice.
But to be Jack in office,
The hollow hall sits there idly，unlike
King Yao and Shun rendering helpful service
Whose grand virtues shine on this earth.

其二十七：屈

裹雪谣风，东施窃叹。满堂炎威，鬼手递寒。
九嶷虽好，斑竹泪干。中国有梦，在于久安。

Twenty-Seven：Stoop

To the scandalous blizzards,
An ugly woman steals her sighs.
In the halls thronged with despotic heat,
The ghost hands are passing on cold spells.
Good and just，the Nine Mysterious Mountain
Has wept her mottled bamboo's eyes out.
And in the dream of China,

A lasting and durable peace prevails.

其二十八：静

虚牖鸣琴，海潮初涌。沧浪腾云，浦星惶恐。
叱霭谁静？在于心冢[1]。静水之心，无敌之勇。

【注释】

①冢：大；山顶。

Twenty-Eight：Calm

To the living lyre in my window,
The sea tide starts to swell
The surging and soaring waves
That boggle the riverside stars.
Who'd be still before the bellowing brume?
It may be the tomb of my heart.
For such a heart like still water,
It should be the bravery unrivalled.

其二十九：乐

乞人乐胥[1]，其情可衔。显贵之忧，头上悬剑。
寿民安逸，不畏谗言。违纪之官，难免坐监。

【注释】

①乐胥：从事音乐工作的小吏。唐·刘肃《大唐新语·极谏》：“高祖即位，以舞胡安叱奴为散骑侍郎，礼部尚书李纲谏曰：‘臣按《周

礼》，均工乐胥，不得参士伍。虽复才如子野，妙等师襄，皆终身继代，不改其业。'" 又，喜乐。《诗 · 小雅 · 桑扈》："君子乐胥，受天之祜。"《朱熹集传》："胥，语词。"

Twenty-Nine: Optimistic

May a beggar rejoice,
His thoughts could be accredited.
May a seigneur be melancholy,
A sabre hangs overhead.
To benefit the peace and ease,
He'll defy all the calumnies.
And those in disciplinary violations
Are all liable to jail.

其三十：靠

梨花有泪，春雨润之。飞花阵里，葬心有期。
黄花对镜，桃面悲催。之子迟暮，君子不离。

Thirty: Recourse

Pear petals in tears
Are moistened in spring rains.
In the hails of flying flowers,
The heart sepulchre may be scheduled.
Forget-me-not in the mirror
Drifts a tornado of rosy grief, and
To the fair lady in declining years,

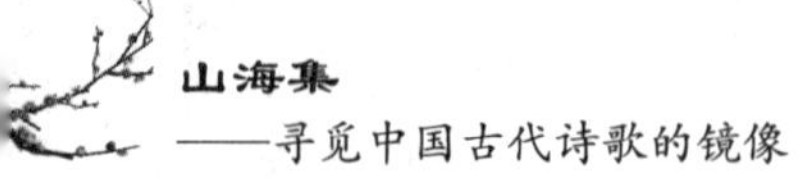

The superior man will never leave her.

其三十一：愚

少慕高鹄，愚人钓丘。水墨污鱼，纶丝不休。
大草蓬心，凉飔[①]覆秋。月落白沙，孤雁啁啾。

【注释】

①飔（sī）：疾风。“一举必千里，乘飔举帆幢”。

Thirty-One: Slow-Witted

Lofty swan was admired when young,
But to fish the mound like a simpleton,
In the inky and fishy water,
With a ceaseless fishing line,
Vulgar and shallow, down the thorny grass,
Cooled by the overturn autumn—
When the moon is drowned by the silver sand,
One wild goose will be honking there.

其三十二：忍

西风不忍，催尽秋香。清痕待掬，百叠温凉。
折笛飞燕，碎语依梁。飞沐柳花，下年绿阳。

Thirty-Two: Endure

West wind, dreadful to see
The sweet, uprooted autumn,
Waits to skim a new, clear shadow
Of cool and warm like a pyramid
Where the flute plies the flying swallows
Whose word debris on the beam
Glides to bathe the willow catkins
In the green sun of the coming year.

其三十三：退

伤筋不苦，掩好退门。身求自闭，三舍图存。
霏霏冷雨，水不生根。迎风鼓浪，移步失魂。

Thirty-Three: Retreat

An injured sinew feels neutral,
And bars the door to be sure
That his body could be closed
Afar to ensure its survival.
Thick and fast, the cold drizzle
Takes no root in the water,
That billows in the wind and
Loses its steps and soul.

其三十四：圆

轮辕曲直，凿枘方圆。方圆入世，动静有常。
车轮不圆，落日难方。方圆得体，一切吉祥。

Thirty-Four：Round

The wheel and shaft are crooked or straight,
And the mortise and tenon square or round—
To be socially experienced,
And constant in the activity and repose—
Such a wheel out of round
Wheels under the sun not square;
And in a proper round and square,
One could attain all prosperity.

其三十五：危

危枝露眼，落日霜鸦。危栏独倚，月冷天涯。
危卵千层，水里游沙。国危坏法，人危乱家。

Thirty-Five：Danger

In the eyes of dews, the dangerous branches
Are perched by a white raven at sunset.
Leaning on the dangerous balustrade,
The moon feels cold far away in the earth,

Where thousands of layers of dangerous eggs
Are wandering on the subfluvial sands.
For a dangerous nation, the law lies debased,
For a dangerous man, the family lies confused.

其三十六：隐

禅钟清隐，北山竹长。鸡窗月小，罗帐未央。
娇面烟雨，别有纲常。酣风动鼓，衣袍不慌。

Thirty-Six: hide

Clearly, the Buddhist bell retires
Amid the long bamboos of the north hill.
In the cock-window, one little moon
Still pales the curtain of thin silk,
Whose tender face in the misty drizzle
Harbors an ulterior, moral principle.
When the raging wind escalates its rataplans,
Our attire will not swither.

五言绝句

Five-Character Quatrain

五绝平仄

凡式一

①首句仄起不入韵

仄仄平平仄，平平仄仄平。

平平平仄仄，仄仄仄平平。

②首句仄起入韵

仄仄仄平平，平平仄仄平。

平平平仄仄，仄仄仄平平。

③首句平起不入韵

平平平仄仄，仄仄仄平平。

仄仄平平仄，平平仄仄平。

④首句平起入韵

平平仄仄平，仄仄仄平平。

仄仄平平仄，平平仄仄平。

凡式二

①首句平起不入韵

平平仄仄平，仄仄平平仄。

仄仄仄平平，平平平仄仄。

②首句平起入韵

平平平仄仄，仄仄平平仄。

仄仄仄平平，平平平仄仄。

③首句仄起不入韵

仄仄仄平平，平平平仄仄。

平平仄仄平，仄仄平平仄。

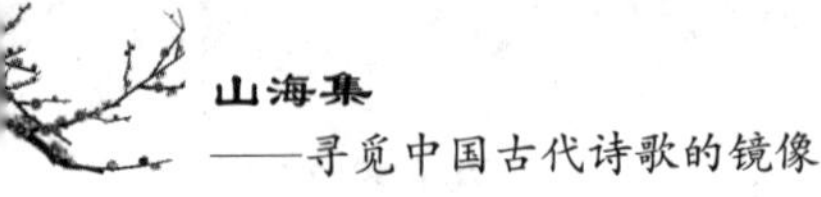

④首句仄起入韵
仄仄平平仄，平平平仄仄。
平平仄仄平，仄仄平平仄。

爱　界

月女难思睡，云郎爱不眠。
情关尤可渡，柳岸自消烟。

Realm of Love

Moon Fairy has lain awake,
Cloud Beau’s afflicted with vigilance.
The hurdle’s pervious for love’s sake,
And the shore smoke evaporates of the lake.

爱　情

紫燕是芳邻，寻巢恋故墟。
空檐难饮泣，四季可裁春。

Love

Swallows are my sweet neighbours,
Seeking the ruins for their former nest.
To the stark eaves that hardly swallow their tears,
The four seasons could be their spring scissors.

爱之沙

五味红尘里，独掬一捧沙。
浮生随断梦，瘦骨向天涯。

Sand in Love

All flavours in the world
Scoop up the sand in hands
Broken with the floating dream
That taggers to the skinny skyline.

百合花
Lilies

【自解】

2014 年除夕前，周丽杰老师随少尉相公捧来一大束鲜花，里面是百合，还夹杂四朵红色黄边郁金香，一周以来，每天都在办公室桌子上面对着我在写着什么。每天呢，只要见面，能够送给她们的是喷壶里面清清的雾水。她们无欲无求，只要有水，就是最大的满足了。

其一

婷婷枝茎上，四朵报春开。
一缕幽香过，清纯圣女来。

One

Graceful on the stalks,
The four petals herald the spring.
When a subtle perfume walks,
Lady of virture is coming.

其二

蜜腺[①]粉盘上，娇羞守柱头[②]。
清香滑六瓣，此韵[③]为君留。

【注释】

①蜜腺：能分泌蜜液（花糖或花蜜）的一种腺体。②柱头：位于雌蕊的顶端，是接受花粉的部位。柱头成熟时，为花粉萌发提供必要的物质与识别信号，一般膨大或扩展成各种形状。柱头组织又称为传递花粉的组织，为与柱头组织有明显的细胞及生理上相似性的组织，一般位于花柱中央，是具有浓厚细胞质的一束细胞，主要作为花粉管进入花柱的通路，同时，供已育的花粉管营养。③韵：花韵。也指孕。

Two

Nectaries on the pink trays
Observe her stigmas, gentle and shy.
As the subtle sweet slides down her six petals,
Such a rhyme should stay for her dear.

BAT

玉镜金盘里，苍峦掠影归。
疏狂扬雪态，任尔北风吹。

BAT

Jade mirror in the gold tray
Has snapshoted the green hills
Unbridled by the fluttering snows
Stirred and rustled by the north arbitrary.

逼　格

寒烟迷晓雾，海镜伴风飘。
散柳横笛处，纤纤落小桥。

Bigger

In cold, dawning fogs,
The sea mirror was flapped.
Where the lost willows were fluted,
The small bridge was dropped softly.

标准化产品

孤舟一叶静，万里海涛平。
半壁孤轮下，江天倒影明。

Standardized Products

Isolated, the boat like a still leaf
Was flat on the vast terrain of surges.
Isolated, the wheel on half the territory
Reflected brightly upon the river.

秉　持

孟夏吟微雨，新禾抒笔底。
抟风落笺时，走墨如飞羽。

To Hold It

An early summer in slight rains
Writes his fresh, smooth seedlings of grains.
As the wind rolls and drops the letters,
The ink will walk like flying feathers.

不　屈

飞泉落千丈，簌石不畏寒。
松风卷云客，扶醉归尘鞍。

Uncompromising

Fathomless down, the flying spring streams
The stones unflinching before cold spells.
In the soughing of pines that swishes the clouds,
The jingled saddle's going back into the dust.

咖啡馆

佳人逢乱世，粉面破娇羞。
女汉乾坤月，烟云自弄舟。

Cafe

At wild times, a fair lady
Breaks her pure, shy modesty.
Wo-men like a reversed moon
Go for a pull under the misty canopy.

采　花

采蜜醉娇花，春来千树里。
寻幽戏玉葩，好运无悲喜。

To Pick Flowers

To seek honey amid the tender flowers
Feels a bit tipsy as the spring comes.
To seek secret sports in the pure flowers
Comes off well without delight and dole.

谗　言

奸谗可误国，害马乱亲族。
利口白驹隙，丹青远案牍。

Slanderous Talk

Slanders can fail the nation,
And disgracers the cognation.
Unlike the glib tongue passing a crack,
The true portrait alienates an official operation.

产与望

怀春人脉脉，旧韵雨梨花。
玉带轻飘絮，悠闲卧碧沙。

Creative Work on Watch

Affectionate in the thoughts of love,
The old rhymes are drizzling their pear flowers.
Light-footed like jade-starred belts, the catkins
Are sleeping on the green sand at ease.

尝　试

西风吹弱水，小径鸭声浅。
赤脚点清波，丝丝苔藓软。

Attempt

Weak water wiffles in the west wind,
That quacks flat through the footpath.
On his bare-footed, limpid waves
Interspersed with silken, supple mosses.

成 功
Success

其一

黄鸡徒报晓，镜里有悲头。
煮酒沉沙路，千年任铁流。

One

To herald the day-break turns out futile,
The mirror's wedded with a doleful head.
To warm the wine on the broken-sanded way,
The iron stream catches all time-based passions.

其二

煮名灯影中，灯老影欲堕。

剪来晓色暖，升起天边火。

Two

To cook the name in the candlelight,
The old wick totters to the root,
Trimming the warm, dawning hues,
That fire up the sky line.

处　境

月炼银钩沉，苍苍染翠心。
潜鱼衔尺素，不懂柳风寻。

Situation

A silver crescent smelts, submerges
And tinges the dark, green heart,
Whence the letters born by the diving fish
Have no ear for the wind of the willows.

闯

平仄人生路，诗行半寸明。
等闲花漠漠，扇底一飞鸿。

Go for It

Level and oblique, the way of life
Sparks half an inch in the lines.
Far-flung casually, the flowers
Are fanned into one swan.

春　声

春眼沉鱼色，闲枝映水明。
流光碎阳里，银梭戴河轻。

Voice of Spring

A fish colour sinks in the eye of spring,
That brightens the branch-caressed water,
Streaming its light into the broken sun,
Before the silver shuttle sails on the Daihe River.

春　晓

冷露凫鸭处，潭溪顾影清。
晴丝听浅梦，柳燕渡春明。

Spring Daybreak

In cold dews, the mallards
Are admired in the clear creek.
In sunny rays, their shallow dream hears
The swallows thru the bright willow spring.

春　心

春心生雨后，小镜暗娇羞。
软语关罗袜，轻狂枕上留。

Heart of Spring

Spring heart comes after rain, like
A shy virgin in the secret pocket mirror,
Shutting her silk socks into a soft speech,
And leaving her light tones unto the pillow.

春　燕

春草芊绵柳，河东浴月光。
柳裙游乳燕，访遍旧时梁。

Spring Swallow

Lush and willowy, the spring grass has
Been moonbathed to the east of the river
Whose willowy skirt's swum by fledgling swallows,
That have called on all their former beams.

挫　折

折枝月下黄，弱柳逸清霜。
淡扫新容后，如烟细水塘。

Frustration

The broken branches yellow below the moon
Pulsed their clear frosts in the pliant willows
That, after a light makeup on their new looks,
Would sway softly like a puff of smoke on the pool.

错　位

瘦骨飘轻絮，支离沁北风。
怀骚迎悖世，不齿雪飞冲。

Mismatched

Skinny fuzzes are swimming
In the bitty, northerly that's seeping
And grumbling to the inconsistent world
In contempt of the snows, fluffy and whirling.

怠　惰

春光不上树，倦鸟啾庭户。
断谷欲盘桓，投林还暮雨。

Sloth

Spring climbs into the trees, never more,
And a tired bird chirps before my door.
After his stay in the downfaulted rift valley,
He returns to the evening wood with the rain fall.

单相思

昨夜风摇树，潇潇乱絮声。
剪来一片绿，潋滟照天明。

One-sided Love

In the wind-rocking trees last night,
Were whistling the broken catkins.
One slice of green, if to be trimmed,
Could be shimmering another daybreak.

得　失

得失落花果，秋来悲远鸿。
鸡虫似冰火，婴累[①]如囚翁。

【注释】

①婴累（yīng lèi）：遭罹罪累。《文选·嵇康》：“咨予不淑，婴累多虞。”

Gain and Loss

Worldly gain, like the fruit fallen,
Goes in autumn like doleful swans again.
Fowls and worms, similar to fire and ice,
Will be tied down like a convicted man.

低　头

清霜鸿雁影，紫塞低头去。

有字寄天书，飞霞惊几许。

Nose Down

A swan picture in clear frosts
Hangs his head beyond the border
With the letters to the sky tale
That shocks some swift rosy clouds.

颠　覆

老枝骑粉墙，花乱雪轻过。
莫言月镜短，疏影东风落。

Subversive

Old branches bestride the chalky wall
Are swaying their light snows into
A long mirror of the moon whose
Dappled shadows are blown by the east.

电　话

山竹影同瘦，竹韵松风叩。
松心倚疏竹，相约三秋后。

Telephone

Skinny and shaded, the bamboos
To the soughing rhymes of pines
Are tapping a scattered heart
To fix the date for a late autumn.

放不下

心狂体态轻，坐赋话悠闲。
漫把幽窗倚，浮云过远山。

Fail to Extend

Pretentious but light in stature,
The chanted seat at leisure
Rests against the secluded windows
Whose clouds flow to the far hills.

放　弃

十万芳菲红，缘何碎影鸣?
柳摇轻梦处，泣露静无声。

To Waive

One hundred thousand red primes
Are warbling their milled shades?
Where the willows jiggle the dreams,
The weeping dews are still and silent.

风信子
Hyacinth

其一

紫梦[①]千滴泪，冰壶半恨风[②]。
玲珑何所似，放眼一归鸿[③]。

【注释】

①紫梦：指紫色风信子，代表悲伤、妒忌，忧郁的爱。②冰壶：比喻月亮。半恨风：希腊神话中受太阳神阿波罗宠眷，并被其所掷铁饼误伤而死的美少年雅辛托斯，是被西风风神泽费奴斯（Zephyrus）用计害死。在雅辛托斯的血泊中，长出了一种美丽的花，阿波罗便以少年的名字命名这种花——风信子。③“玲珑”二句：化用唐代诗人杜甫于765年离开成都草堂以后在旅途中所作《旅夜书怀》：“飘飘何所似，天地一沙鸥。”

One

A thousand treardrops in purple dreams
Are half blown by the ice kettle.
Delicately wrought, what does it resemble?
In sight, it's but a returning swan.

其二

晶莹含雪蜜，冷月对红尘[①]。
若是纤尘染，飘零葬慧心。

【注释】

①红尘：古时原意为繁华的都市，出自东汉文学家、史学家班固的《西都赋》，指的是纷纷攘攘的世俗生活。来源于过去的土路车马过后扬起的尘土，借喻名利之路。

【自解】

乳白色的风信子花序出现叶尖端褐斑，被寄生菌感染，引起最初的侵染，其组织透明，生长白色或黄色斑点，感染严重的结果是生长受阻，甚至植株萎蔫直至死去。风信子的自然生理某种程度上也反映了她坚贞、守节的性情。美国有句话：Give me liberty, or give me death（不自由，毋宁死）；对于风信子来说，只换一个单词：Give me chastity, or give me death（失节殒命）。偶尔吟唱的《葬花吟》大致能投射出葬花和葬心的感受。

Two

Sparkling, her snow honeys
Are coldly touched by the moon.
To be soiled by a particle of dust,
Her heart is given the deep six.

改　变

长短由天定，栖迟鸟自还。
浮生醉如醒，青云负忠奸。

Change

Long or short, it's made in heaven,
Here or there, a bird would return.
Like the short life that wakes up sober,
The blue sky bears a good-bad relation.

改　造

气骨锁秋声，江天横玉兔。
织成过雁啼，漫理青丝路。

To Remould

The sounds of autumn are locked in the spine,
That veers Jade Hare on the river sideways
Woven into the passing honks on the
Black-haired way to be freely disentangled.

刚性需求

寒江钓柳枝，柳叶雪中迷。
只见鱼游水，无钩柳线急。

Rigid Demand

To fish for the cold with the willow
Whose leaf is lost in the snow.
Over there, the fish are swimming,
Hookless, the willow can't take it slow.

功　夫

朔气裹白沙，清狂落百花。
蛱蝶翻羽过，五月嗅奇葩。

Kungfu

White sand in the northern chills
Fades and falls all frivolous flowers.
When a leaf butterfly flutters by,
The May day sniffs his exotic flowers.

贵　人

荣辱何足贵，君前莫问人。
花开雨来后，多情妄自生。

Worthy Person

Wheel of fortune, unfit to be thought noble,
Asks no more before the gentle.
When flowers bloom after the rain,
A drippy passion will come but in vain.

故　事

芳尘惹绿窗，寸草化飞莹。
晓露滴寒蕊，银盘泄玉声。

Tale

My green window teases to the sweet dust
Whose inch-long grass turns into a firefly.
As dawning dews drop down the cold pistils,
The silver plate will let out her jade sounds.

海上日出
Sunrise over the Sea

其一

海上藏朝晕①，丹心赤兔②明。
浮云结万里，毕竟一时轻。

【注释】

①朝晕：清晨日出时的光晕。②赤兔：一种骏马，驰骋速度快。此处比喻太阳升起时的速度。

One

The morning halo buried on the sea
May be a budding Hare with red heart,
Who, drifting to the earth's end,

Has a light foot all in all.

其二

长鲸驾赤轮[①]，展翅九重云。
笑看金光里，红尘有落魂。

【注释】

①赤轮：红色的圆轮，借指太阳。

Two

Long whales on red wheels
Wing up to the Ninth Heaven,
In whose golden, smiling light,
Souls are falling down and down.

其三

银盘[①]驶向西，戴气[②]舞天鸡。
旖旎[③]来合璧，殷勤[④]宇宙驰。

【注释】

①银盘：形容月亮的容貌。②戴气：罩在太阳之上的黄气，日晕时可见。唐·元稹《辨日旁瑞气状》："伏以五色庆云，盖是小瑞，戴气抱珥，所谓殊祥。"③旖旎（yǐ nǐ）：旌旗随风飘扬的样子，引申为柔和美丽。也比喻柔美、婀娜多姿的样子，或带雄伟状。④殷勤：情意深厚，引申巴结貌。

Three

A silver plate drives west, where
Heavenly Rooster dances in the solar halo,
That, well-assorted in his gentle charms,
Gallops off through the good horizon.

其四

晨乌[①]齐海浪，翘首打渔船。
只见鳞光闪，除夕也过年。

【注释】

①晨乌：初升的太阳。古代神话谓日中有乌，故以乌为日之代称。《南齐书·张融传》：“晨乌宿於东隅，落河浪其西界。”

Four

Morning crow on the ocean ripples
Cranes its head for the fishing vessels,
That, punctuated by the glittering scales,
Have to tell the New Year's tales.

其五

金盘[①]露海天，万里抹银边。
一举喷薄跃，长空可弄帆。

【注释】

①金盘：金色的盘子，比喻太阳。

Five

Golden tray out of the boundless skies
Paints its silver laces at the earth's end.
Gushing out at one fling,
He could sail the vast of heaven.

海　月

沧海铺明月，清清水镜圆。
淡妆羞粉色，玉脂不凝寒。

Moon on the Sea

Bright moon on the vast sea
Rounds like a clear mirror.
Thinly powdered in pink colour,
Her shy, pure skin is cosy, you see.

好夫妻
Good Spouse

其一

妻淑拈髭[①]断，夫公并蒂结。
指环情欲绣，缃帙[②]巧来舌。

【注释】

①髭（zī）：嘴上边的胡子。②缃帙（zhì）：浅黄色书套。亦泛指书籍、书卷。

One

For a virtuous wife, the mustache lasts for ever,
For a good man, the conjugal luck's like a twin flower.
Her finger ring could embroider the ardour,
And his books are glib-tongued, to be sure.

其二

宵征取天下，枕前无大捷。
征夫必征妇，家内无和谐。

Two

Day and night one seizes the state,
But the pillow has no resounding victory.
If a warrior must have the scalp of his wife,
His family would not sing with perfect harmony.

其三

孤灯对双影，都晓憨痴错。
精明不装痴，难约百年乐。

Three

Two figures in one light
Aware of the idiotic error
Play dumb though savvy
And live to a ripe old age.

其四

秋云不翻手，难唱钗头凤。
盘床对荆妻[1]，别把机关弄。

【注释】

①荆妻：对人称自己妻子的谦词。

Four

If an autumn cloud turns no hand,
Pheonix Hairpin will sound hard.
To sit crosslegged before the old wife,
Don't rack your brains in scheming.

其五

对错谁来问，黄莺暗啭之。
声声啼暖树，乱语不择辞。

Five

Right or wrong, who enquires about it?
The golden oriole will twitter in secret
Amid the silver iterance of the mild trees,
Not choosy about the tongue babbling at ease.

其六

乱影芙蓉晚，惊风愁锁眼。
桥头冷雨后，好景难重返。

Six

Late lotus flowers in disorder
Lock my eyes in sad, stormy power.
After a cold rain by the bridge head,
The sweet dreams will be soon over.

其七

闲愁理淡妆，对镜掩薄情。
欲渡清江水，怀舟野外行。

Seven

Thinly powdered in the needless misery,
Her mirror has hidden the spoony.
To cross the clear river,
The country-foundered skiff could ferry.

其八

落絮控湘帘，帘钩半卷寒。
隔帘蝶影过，子夜月光甜。

Eight

My curtains are reined by the swimming catkins
Whose cold spells are half-scrolled on the drapery's hook.
Beyond the curtains, certain butterfy flutters by
Into the sweet moonlight of such a midnight.

其九

多情翡翠床，冷雨无情幕。
岁月过青丝，凄风盘铁鹊。

Nine

My drippy emerald bed
Has curtained a cold, callous rain
Like her black hairs after the time slips
Into the sad-voiced dish of magpies.

其十

谁裁鹅黄玉，青柳青梅曲。
两小邀秋千，荡云裁一束。

Ten

Who's clipped that jade like yellow goose-down
Among the melodious green willowy plums whence
Two teenagers were roped in by a swing,
That swang up to clip one cloud.

其十一

割面刀裁裙，无端舌信分。
清逼开檀口，一曲唱鸡闻。

Eleven

Her face-ripped knife that tailors a skirt
Flicks the fork of her tongue unprovoked
Out of the fragrant, fire-eating mouth
That heralds the crowing of the cock.

其十二

点点痴心泪，斑斑不老情。
衰红阶泣雨，照尽老竹声。

Twelve

Blind passions in tears
And the mottled，ageless affections
Weep their rains down the red，emarcid steps
That shine all over the sounds of the old bamboos.

其十三

枝头紫燕飞，不改往常衣。
柳下双双去，衔泥细雨归。

Thirteen

Flying up the trees，the purple swallows
Still continue their attire as usual.
In pairs they are flying under the willows，
And return with bits of earth in the mizzles.

其十四

藤下有甜瓜，瓜秋月色浓。
瓜心如会意，破体也从容。

Fourteen

Sweet melons ripe under the rattans
Are moonlit with a radiance of deeper hue.
Of a knowing heart, the bodies
To be cracked bear themselves smooth.

其十五

提篮采瘦枝，妙色蝶轻落。
缕缕暗香折，群英红乱过。

Fifteen

To basket the thin branches,
And the subtle hues of butterflies,
The wisps of secret fragrance are snapped
Out of the red flowers in confusion.

其十六

瑶琴闲弃早，记取萧歌乱。
对影唱青春，孤莺啼柳岸。

Sixteen

To forsake the jasper lute so soon,
And print the melody in confusion,
The youth warbles its shadows,
Like a lone oriole trilling the bank willows.

环　境

绝境南柯梦，啼鹑客晚舟。
结庐封幻境，醉羽下平洲。

Environment

The dream without hope of escape
Cries like a quail in the late boat
Bound to seal the land of illusion
With his tipsy feathers down the flat islet.

活 着

Alive

其一

英雄不苟活，帝阙寡天恩。
铁马十三骑，山河尽可吞。

One

No hero lived on in degradation,
In the empire not in state of grace.
With the sweeping cavalry of 13 steeds,
All the foes could be slain.

其二

雨霁秋萧瑟，寒蝉草不鸣。
萧疏听雁语，瘦影向南行。

Two

In the bleak autumn after the rain,
No cold cicada chirps in the grass.

In the desolate honks of wild geese,
The poor images are flying south.

机　会

寒暑常劳顿，酸甜半世风。
忘机心似水，羽墨为谁浓？

Chance

Summer and winter are frequently fatigued,
Sour and sweet are blown half a century.
Aloof from the world, my heart like water
Has feathered the deeper ink, but for whom?

价　值

晓月寒风满，冰莹刺剑霜。
开匣鸣虎胆，驾海跃天狂。

Value

A full, icy moon at daybreak
Stabs her crystal and frosty sabre
At the tiger growls out of its courageous box
That pilots the sea up in a celestial violence.

坚 韧

恒沙本无事，凡人徒自惊。
平生四方志，佛道随身明。

Tenacious

The sand grains of the Ganges were free,
And bowled down the mortals, of no avail.
Where there's a lifelong will of all sides,
There's the way of Buddha bright with you.

简 单

明月摇绳床，携君吟晚风。
君心如明月，听断古今鸿。

Simple

In the moon-lit hammock that sways,
Let's spin out the evening air.
In your moon-lit heart, the swan
Thru the history falls in the ear.

讲道理

良驹行野径，万树扬轻雪。
柳噪乱枝桠，高蝉听明灭。

Have It Out

A good colt along the wild trail
In the wood that winnows the dust snow
Clamours the willow branches intermingled
With the higher, blinking cicadas.

教　训

长鞭笞贪吏，旷诛淫雨官。
三公霸京邑，黎庶声声叹。

Lesson

Flog the long corrupt officials,
And kill the free carnal officials,
From the Tree Dukes that usurp the capital
That have been groaning the people.

阶　梯

空阶幽梦处，落叶影初凉。
掩梦长阶柳，苍苔几点光。

Stairs

My stark steps in secret dream
Shed a leaf picture of fresh cool
That covers the long-stepped willows
Like some filtered lights to the dark mosses.

结　局

奋迅鹰丰羽，惊心麇鹿走。
椒花曲水狂，野草分良莠[①]。

【注释】

①良莠：好的坏的都有，混杂在一起。

Finale

A full-fledged feather works the swift updrafts,
And a stunning heart scares away the deer.
Pepper flowers flip out by the curving streams,
And in the wild grass may graze sheep and goats.

镜　子

芙蓉照明镜，真颜磨玉清。
凌花对秋水，天水珠难明。

Mirror

A lotus in the illuminated mirror
Whets her fair and pure portrait
In the limpid eyes not clear
About the beaded water.

抉　择

囊空不远行，酒后贪花累。
探路一枝春，扑窗寒影窥。

Choice

An empty bag goes not far, and an erotic
Flower works hard after liquor.
A spray of spring that noses her way
Shoots the peep at a cold window picture.

坎　坷

坎坷人生路，烟云梦未残。
绮栊寒透骨，暮鼓走重峦。

Twists and Turns

On the rough way of life,
My dream in clouds has yet to wane.
While the fabulous latticework chills my bones,
Some late drums are gone into the ranges of hills.

看　透

虬枝一抹云，蘸取两重天。
顾影轻舟里，空明万里弦。

Insight

Curled，clouded sprays
Dipped in the two skies
Are narcissistic in the shallop
That kindles a string afar.

蜡　炬

红烛临窗瘦，裁冰剪影长。
垂青对丝雨，三生共温凉。

Candle

My red candle thins by the window
That trims a long，icy silhouette
Submitted to the favoured drizzles
In the community of worthy temperatures.

劳　逸

沉浮遵鸟道，畅逸遣行知。
大任劳筋骨，闲聆赋仲尼。

Work and Play

Up and down，a narrow trail
Knows its free and easy avail.
The major task toils my muscles,
With a spare ear to Confucius odes.

泪

梦醒多噙泪，莹莹倦客愁。
梨花泪挥雨，雨霁自然收。

Tears

My wake-up mostly in tears
Of a weary, glistening worry,
Drizzles the pear flowers
That ride out its natural stop.

理　想

英雄比铜臭，山溪欺海龙。
铜心烂商旅，不透寒门松。

Ideal

Before the stink of money, the hero
Like a sea dragon gets molested by a creek.
To the trade caravans, the worn-out coin heart
Will be impermeable to the cold, lofty door.

柳
Willows

其一

寒柳经冬后，牵丝寸寸明。
泛青昨夜雨，万缕满河风。

One

Cold willows after the winter
Are hanging each thread brighter.
Lively green in the rain last night,
Thousands of threads blow the full river.

其二

鹅黄点溪水，惹来一阵风。
悄悄问明月，花瓣何时红？

Two

Stream, tapped by the light yellow,

Has seduced a puff of wind.
Bright moon steals up to her show,
Wonders when her red petal will follow.

其三

明月冰壶里，吹开片片风。
青娥[①]展眉日，红唇自然明。

【注释】

①青娥：一是指青女，也就是主司霜雪的女神；二是指美丽的少女，明·夏完淳《青楼篇与漱广同赋》："长安大道平如组，青娥红粉娇歌舞"；三是指娥眉。

Three

Bright moon in the ice kettle
Has blown open the breezes.
As her eyebrows lithely show,
Her red lips are bright and natural.

六不合作
Six Noncooperation

其一

蓝雀骑篱藩，敲风闻鹧鸪。

无边铺明月，观井一蟾蜍。

One

A blue sparrow on the fence
Strokes the wind from partridges
That strew the endless, bright moon
With a look down on the toad in the well.

其二

榆钱招人意，丝雨抽云絮。
摇尽轻埃声，一川轻狂翅。

Two

The elm seed coins are intriguing, like
The drizzles to reel off the cloud fuzzes,
That shake away their light dust sighs,
On the flighty wings of the whole river.

其三

人情厚如纸，还债风吹雨。
痴顽叹今生，寒蓑游孤旅。

Three

Human nature's thick like paper,
That buffets the rains of debt,
Whose nescient sighs this life
Roam lonely in a straw rain cape.

其四

青眼连黑云，携风不认人。
浮荣观人世，天地一堆坟。

Four

Black eyes mated by black clouds
Carry the wind of treachery
Off the world in vanity
Which is none but a cemetery.

其五

追名仿蝇蚋[①]，贪杯邀玉郎。
青春不须怨，眠榻钱铺床。

【注释】

①蝇蚋（ruì）：苍蝇和蚊子。

Five

To crave for fame like gnats and flies,
And to be potatory with my men,
But why to rail at the fate of youth?
Money feels the sag of the mattress.

其六

骑鲸渡沧海，喷荡吞云梦。
银涛紫崖行，杀鲸衔孤勇。

Six

Ride the whale across the ocean to engulf
The cloud dream in one swallow that floats
Over the silver billow against the purple cliff
Where the lone courage slaughters the whale.

路　遥

显贵乘风去，香车歧路远。
行吟借玉壶，几盏青壶宴？

A Long Way

Gone with the wind, the seigneur
Goes astray in his perfumed cart afar
With the chanting wheels of wine
From uncertain cups at the blue dinner.

玫　瑰

轻阴嗅早春，莫教春迷路。
簇夜逗萧郎，疏离还眷顾。

Rose

Early spring sniffs a slight shade,
And then strays, but, nay, in that
Each night titillates the merry man,
Who's estranged but regards with affection.

梦　想

撩人月色闲，水镜痴心笑。
玉面不识人，梨窝梳晚照。

Dream

A tickled moon frees
Her water mirror in fond smiles
On her wrong, pretty face
With the twilit comb of dimples.

面　对

一缕幽香梦，无端月下凉。
寒风惊梦醒，抱枕已成霜。

Confrontation

A subtle perfume in the dream
Cools below an unprovoked moon.
As the icy wind wakes up the dream,
Her nestled pillow has frost-crowned.

命　运

薄命谈人生，鸡肠噬海涛。
满盘封退路，四面楚囚牢。

Fate

Star-crossed, the life gobbles up the surges
Into the chicken' s intestines, and the route of
Retreat's locked all over the tray,
Tightly sieged on all sides.

目　标

有梦去竹林，清谈翠谷空。
瑶琴谈古韵，更待百年工。

Target

My dream walks into the bamboos of
A high-toned, hollow and green vale;
And in old rhymes, my jasper lute
Has awaited the wright for a century.

耐　力

尘沙如流水，人世由悲喜。
莫道无春壶，虎狼为知己。

Endurance

Like flowing water, the dust
Could be agreeably grieved.
Say not there's no spring pot,
Tigers and wolves are my confidants.

能　力

新泥一只燕，鬓风穿绿丝。
娇肢滤寒雨，低户归有期。

Ability

One swallow with bits of fresh mud
Flies thru green willows in the wind,
With cold rains sieving their frail bodies,
For their fixed-term return to the lower nests.

努 力
Endeavor

其一

砚匣尘未封，方寸万千路。
墨心捧素笺，掀浪如平步。

One

My ink case without dust
Immured all on the way
Annotates a pure heart
Of billows with steady steps.

其二

心结宽些许，蝶衣苦羽拼。
追风穿柳去，飞影浣无闻。

Two

Relief flooded through me
On the bitter wings of a butterfly
Chases the wind thru the willows
Like a swift image to be washed nowhere.

攀　登

扶云攀天槛，藤萝叩陛阶。
斑驳斜玉枕，平卧有荫槐。

Ascend

On the cloud to climb the celestial sill,
The creepers fall down before the jade steps,
And are mottled to be agley as a jade pillow,
That lies on the back in the shady pagodatrees.

疲　惫

魂疲斥候[①]路，醉心淫雾中，
寒琴付薄宦，吹散天边虹。

【注释】

①斥候：古代的侦察兵，起源于汉代，并因直属王侯手下而得名。

此处指官场。

Tired

Souls, worn in the officialdom,
Hearts, drown in the wanton fogs,
Lyre, cold to the minor officials,
Blows off the rainbow on the horizon.

七不交
Seven Incompatible

其一

父母悲石墓，生儿没养老。
婵娟若有情，莫笑坟头草。

One

Parents in doleful sepulchre
Didn't live out their life by the children.
Were the moon sentient,
She wouldn't mock the grave grass.

其二

梦里踏春冰，游鳞融水镜。
冰心百面好，转脸金石硬。

Two

A trodden spring ice in dream
Thaws and swims the water mirror
Whose bright heart of all good tales
Comes to the stony-hearted wretches.

其三

酸涎乌语后，几处机关险。
沥胆又剖肝，须臾人变脸。

Three

Slander' s venomed spear
With the underhand dealings
That unbuttons its soul
Does an about-face in a flash.

其四

山鸡变凤凰，上树啼不住。
几度踏枝头，栖迟唯我固。

Four

The phoenix from a blackcock
Crows on and on in the tree
Whose branches are trodden
And reposed in his old ways.

其五

谀辞挂嘴边，巧辩粲莲花。
点检[①]长舌妇，何如此辈牙。

【注释】

①点检：查核，清点。宋·晏殊《木兰花》："当时共我赏花人，点检如今无一半。"《醒世恒言·灌园叟晚逢仙女》："乱了多时，方才收脚，点检人数都在，单不见了张委、张霸二人。"清·盛锦《别家人》诗："点检箧中裘葛具，预知别后寄衣难。"

Five

The praises are flourished by the mouth-corner
In a giff-gaff that brightens the lotus flower.
Even a Lady Fame of venom clamours
Can't be outstripped by such teeth.

其六

朝堂排显贵，草野闭鸡虫。
宦匪成一道，国家四面风。

Six

To the hall full of the purple,
To the wild plugged up with the worms and fowl;
When bandits and officials are wallowed in the mire,
The country would be blown here and there.

其七

无情乱世心，反噬豺狼恶。
笑面裹阴毒，行奸无对错。

Seven

Ruthless times of chaos trump up
A countercharge against the wicked jackals;
And the insidious smiles
Could fool about without right or wrong.

祈　运

羽翼飞天去，游仙春月短。
横笛两片心，又怕云台暖。

Pray for Luck

The wings gone,
The wild dream for a spring moon is not long.
Two hearts in one flute
Are awe-struck by the warming Cloud Terrace.

青　春

骨瘦香腴颤，芳兰四月天。
眉边醉杨柳，酹酒沁桃面。

Youth

While the plump, skinny sweet quivers,
The April days have sung of orchids, whose brows
Are intoxicated with poplars and willows,
Exuding their sweet wine onto the peach faces.

情　愿

舍去尘俗耳，求得累世情。
三生守一诺，愿秉夜烛明。

Willing

Leave the dust ear,
For the generations of passions,
True to your word,
In the candlelight sweet at night.

旁　观

醉眼看花痕，无声花又近。
拂丝逗晚晴，遍野铺红粉。

Onlooker

Flower shadows in dim-sighted eyes
Are prevailing in silence again, to tease
The after-glows with the whisking willows,
That strew their red powders in the fields.

穷　富

一语梦惊人，得失富贵乡。
抽身名利锁，睡觉也安详。

Poor and Rich

One word like a night terror
Preys in the riches and honour
Whose locks should walk away,
And peacefully pound our ear.

人

游人醉春色，一路逐飞雀。
因何赠离人？皆因东风恶。

Man

The time shifters tipsy in spring
Run after swift sparrows all the way.
Why to bestow those who part more?
All this comes of the east wind unfair.

人　生

人生能几岁，聚散有归途。
莫问尘埃险，浮生去狡狐。

Life

Life has its limited line,
That comes and goes as destined.
Ask not the vicious dust,
Whose fleeting life could be foxy.

人生三论

人生不如意，名利如枷锁。
当头对悲秋，无情先无我。

Three Views on Life

Life goes wrong
With the fame and gain in shackles.
Sorrowful in the fall,
One who's uncharitable should be egoless.

人生三事

清欢人生路，着意羊肠曲。
落锁谈鸿鹄，振飞能几许？

Three Affairs of Life

Sweet and fine, the way of life underlines
The song of the narrow winding trail.
To be unlocked like a swan,
How far could one braces up?

日西行

掠日金乌去，陶陶①向海边。
城郭九万座，娟娟②两腋③山。

【注释】

①陶陶（táo）：和乐的样子。《诗·王风·君子阳阳》："君子陶陶

……其乐只且。”②娟娟：明媚、飘动的样子。③腋（yè）：胳肢窝。

The Sun Heading West

Away, the golden crow sweeps,
To the west water front in delight,
Skimming over the towns in heaps,
Under its arms two mountains in flight.

三　好

好景年年似，疏条勾紫燕。
闲听翠柳鸣，软唱斜风前。

Three Good

Each year, the beauty resembles
In sparse branches for purple swallows.
Atop the green willows the free warbles
Softly chant before the side-wind blows.

沙　梦

失意攀折后，娇颜落暮春。
莺啼看不尽，青云洗明轮。

Dream of Sand

After the frustration gets broken,
The fair face falls into the late spring.
Hope the oriole songs are everlasting,
In the bright wheel washed by the blue heaven.

胜　败

秋红泣转蓬，败叶凌风过。
满地索诗行，横墙谁对错？

Win and Loss

When red autumn weeps in the floating duckweeds,
The withered leaves are gone on the woven wings,
Longing for a poetic line all over the ground,
Which is crossed by the walls, right or wrong?

赏　赐

一曲清箫梦，枝头观杏蕾。
幽怀欲透红，浪景千枝汇。

Reward

A clear flute in dream watches
The buds of the apricots
To be rosy on her secret bosom
Dissolute on thousands of clustered branches.

失　败

昔年囚中客，龙城败马还。
扬鬃嘶暮雪，犹想越关山。

Failure

Convicted in former years,
The Dragon comes back to an anchor when
The dusk snow tosses his mane and neigh,
Still in the mood to cross the forts and hills.

时　机

迷津尚独步，几时烟幕休。
庭阴锁流影，思古成幽囚。

Opportunity

Alone in the ford of delusion,
The smoke screen comes to conclusion, but when?
When the hidden court locks up the flowing picture,
My ancient spirit's grown up into a quiet prison.

使　用

劳心尘寰事，仙子凌波去。
一缕疏风残，乱莺啼别墅。

Usage

Labouring with this mortal life,
The faerie's gone over the ripples.
One wisp of faint, scanty wind
Twitters the villas in confusion.

是，不是？

秋果藏春心，经冬栖静林。
枝头含羞处，蛙鼓振三浔。

Yes or No?

High desires hidden in autumn fruit
Are perched in the still wood thru the winter.
Graceful yet bashful on the branches, the frogs
Are croaking near the deafening riverside.

收　获

雁字高天里，轻别乘月影。
明波翠幕深，楚客梅边醒。

Harvest

The wild geese in the high sky ride
The light picture of the moon whose
Bright waves are curtained deep and green
Waking up the vagrant beside the plum flowers.

守　岁

又是除夕夜，全家少一人。
守岁乡音里，何时去泪痕?

【自解】

第五个除夕没有回望奎了，马年的除夕也是这个样子。每每做梦的时候，出现的往往是久远的记忆。记忆醒来的时候，多了不少的叹息。父母在的时候，难得回去过个年；父母不在的时候，这个家还能回得去吗？

Stay Up On New Year's Eve

Here comes another New Year's Eve,
But the house is still one short.
To stay up late for my local accent,
When the tear-stains will be dried?

水仙花
Daffodils

其一

凌波仙子[1]步，玉露不生尘。
冷艳金寒里，清芬为几人？

【注释】

①凌波仙子：水仙的别名。“凌波”二句：典出曹植的《洛神赋》：“凌波微步，罗袜生尘。”《文选》五臣注，吕向曰：“微步，轻步也。步于水波之上，如尘生也。”也就是说，洛神步履轻盈地走在平静的水面上，荡起细细的涟漪，就像走在路面上腾起细细的尘埃一样。

One

With the fairy steps so light,
Her honeydews have gathered no dust.
With the golden, frozen glory,
For whom her sweet wafts are smelt?

其二

冰肌锁玉蟾[①]，腊月点羞颜。
雪态鹅黄[②]暖，琼姿透轻寒。

【注释】

①玉蟾（chán）：月中的蟾蜍，此处借指月光。②鹅黄：嫩黄色的花。

Two

Pure flesh in the moon light
Nods her shy, deep winter.
Snowed in a warm, light yellow,
Her purity makes light of chills.

其三

香露杯中酒，无言对子君。

倚寒开倦眼，玉骨一冰心。

Three

My cup is a scented juice,
Wordless before my man.
Open the drooping eyelids,
My heart is pure like the ice.

其四

天香飘柳絮，劲骨委深冬。
弱质藏丘壑，银台独自明。

【自解】

春夏之交，柳絮横飞，此时，国色天香的牡丹凋落了。寒冬腊月，滴水成冰，此时，岁寒的红梅萎靡了。杳无人烟的丘壑里面，藏匿着纤弱的小白花儿。她们好似银台一样的花朵，绝不炫耀地默默绽放着自己的靓丽身姿。

Four

Like willow catkins at times of fragrance,
Like vigorous bones in the deep winter,
Their tender bodies hidden in canyons
Are clear-sighted in the silvery moon.

四位朋友
Four Friends

其一

水重天飘雨，山高好挡风。
云朋如有意，好雨助霞嵩[①]。

【注释】

①“云朋”二句：假借“霞友云朋”之意。

One

Rainy, watery,
And windy by the mountains,
The good rain will help the lofty, rosy clouds,
If the cloudy friend can be measurable.

其二

绿蚁谢亲朋，微熏块垒[①]升。
杯中花未落，堕酒也无凭。

【注释】

①块垒：泛指郁积之物。

Two

Nectars for my kith and kin,
Of a merry depression,
Still bloom in my cup,
With its dubious fall.

其三

葱茏一缕香，伴雪浸春阳。
遍野伞花落，千枝陌上狂。

Three

A plume of verdant fragrance
Soaks the spring sun with the snow
Falling like umbrella flowers all over the wild
So wild on thousands of branches in the road.

其四

鸡豚难共舍，锦鲤不嘤鸣。
苦雨织成泪，无情对有情。

Four

Pigs and fowls are hard to live together,
And a carp will not be chirping.
In the bitter rains woven into tears,
The sentient faces up to the callous hearts.

推手

袖底暗清风，瓜庐又一年。
疏狂闲厚冠，旷野莫游仙。

Demand Pusher

Secret breeze in my sleeves
Of the melon hut a new year
Was deeply hatted, idle and unbridled,
That stopped my wandering steps into the moor.

推　销

蛱蝶放九秋，几瓣泄轻痕。
好梦结成茧，犁云始破春。

Sales Promotion

A leaf butterfly free in late autumn
Lets out some petals like a light shadow
In her sweet dream yoked into a cocoon
That ploughs the spring-broken cloud.

托孤者死
Death of Guardian for the Heir

其一

猛虎不吃人，吃人潜犬[1]门。
藏弓因鸟尽，兔死犬无痕[2]。

【注释】

①潜犬：群犬闭门饿三日，几成饿殍，变成群狼，以其刑决，也称“犬决”。意即：狼心狗肺，还是让狗吃了吧。亦谐音：缱绻，即托孤之臣，本来亲密无间；缱绻则无间、无恭、无敬，久留侧榻，君

之患。②"藏弓"二句：化典自司马迁《史记·越王勾践世家》："蜚鸟尽，良弓藏；狡兔死，走狗烹。"

One

A fierce tiger eats no man,
But dogs do in the hungry door.
Birds done, the bow is gone,
Hares killed, the dog is stewed.

其二

清川江漠漠[①]，九月岭愔愔[②]。
傥荡驺卒[③]怒，难敌禁卫军。

【注释】

①清川江：朝鲜西北部河流。源于狼林山西南麓，向南偏西流，下游为平安南、北道的分界线。全长212.8公里，流域面积9778平方公里。与九龙江等汇合后流入西朝鲜湾。上游地形陡峭，下游为博川平原。水量大，利于灌溉农田。朝鲜主要工、农业地带之一。从河口向上溯可通航152公里。漠漠：寂寞无声。②九月岭，即九月山：自古与"白头山"（即中国的长白山）、妙香山（Mountain Myohyang）、金刚山（Mountain Kumgang）、七宝山（Mountain Chilbo）、智异山一起，成为朝鲜名山之一。自古，朝鲜的民众把金刚山之美称为女性美，把"九月山"之雄壮称为男性美。愔愔（yīn）：安静无声。③傥（tǎng）荡：疏诞而无检束。驺（zōu）卒：役卒，泛指张府（Jang Sung-taek）役隶之人或所辖卫戍部队。

Two

Ch' ongch' on River is foggy,
Mountain Kuwol is gloomy:
Outraged garrison in debauchery
Is vulnerable to the lifeguard.

其三

抄家灭九族，斩草仿明孺[①]。
狗窦[②]身先死，缘何带幼雏？

【注释】

①明孺：即方孝孺，被称为明初第一大儒，且是辅佐朱元璋孙子建文帝的重臣，桃李满朝廷（其实是一大派系）。燕王朱棣打下金陵后，第一个要收服的就是方孝孺，偏偏这位老夫子一身傲骨，两次见新皇帝都是披麻戴孝、号啕痛哭，朱棣低声下气地请他代拟诏书（逼他表态），他只写了“燕贼篡位”四个大字。朱棣问他：“难道你不怕死吗？”方孝孺答：“要杀便杀，诏不可草。”朱棣问：“难道不顾及你的九族吗？”方孝孺答：“不要说九族，诛十族也不怕。”这一下皇帝火了，在方孝孺九族之外，加上“门生”凑成十族，统统杀掉。②狗窦（dòu）：狗洞；也指坏人聚居处。

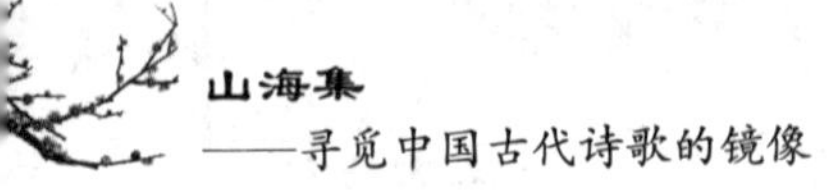

Three

In the clan-wide extermination,
Leave no chance of its revival.
Dead in the dog hole,
But why grub up his children?

伟　人

晨钟暮角寒，野渡举长竿。
钓水烟波里，吟鞭向海宽。

Great Man

Morning bells and evening bugles are cold
To the wild ferry heaved by a long fishing-rod
Clever in the misty rolling water
That chants and scourges the wide sea.

习　惯

雨外烟沉醉，飞红阵阵香。
匆匆子衿①去，锦色玉壶长。

【注释】

①子衿：文人贤士的雅称。

Habit

Ecstatic in the mist beyond the rain,
The flying red breathes her sweet
And leaves in haste
For the chalice, fresh and vivid.

向　上

岭上染苍梧，空阶淅沥雨。
伶仃燕子啼，断续椽檐舞。

Upwards

Tinged by the green parasol, the ridges
In the intermittent rains down the stark steps
Are chirping a lonely swallow who
Dances around its desultory eave.

行　动

草腴[①]流水肥，光转玉壶动。
酿得翡翠碗，谁舀琉璃桶？

【注释】

①腴（yú）：丰富的。

Action

Fertile in the grass and flowing water,
The light turns the crystal glass that
Brewed an emerald bowl to scoop a barrel
Of coloured glaze, but who could?

识　人

世象渐失真，红尘扑眼底。
相约命里空，落难无知己。

Good Judge of Man

The world images are distorted gradually
In the mundane dust that flaps the eye
That' s trickled in an empty fate
Without a confidant in distress.

限　制

清梦愁三更，相逢水月沉。
暗香情缕缕，梦醒泪无痕。

Restriction

My clear dream sad at midnight
Met the moon sinking down
The secret sweets in passions
Out of the tear stains after I woke up.

小　事

石矶横赤壁，小乔驭风来。
一剪分香影，千年葬冷腮。

Trifles

To the stone steps before the red cliff,
The junior Lady Qiao came with the wind,
That clipped her minute, sweet picture,
Whose cold cheeks were sepulchred 1000 years.

心 态
The State of Mind

其一

有句欲凌风，奸心难去病。
金石若有恒，饮羽[1]丹心正。

【注释】

①饮羽：射箭，没矢。

One

A wind-swift sentence comes
On the wicked disease with
A hypothetical constancy like diamond
Which is loyal and strong.

其二

临江情若醉，倚海心怀月。
照水邀春光，蝶园青影过。

Two

My sentiment by the river seems to be drunk,
To the sea that harbours a moon
For the spring in its beaming water
And also for the blue public butterflies.

信 念

信步踏书斋，十年行万卷。
垂纶草笠风，柳岸逐飞燕。

Belief

My casual stroll in the study
Of 10000 volumes ten years
Fishes the wind against my straw cape
By the willowy bank for the flight of swallows.

行 动

心田莫积雪，淹没冰弦渡。
流光谢梨花，清平中国路。

Course of Action

A snow-topped heart
May flood the icy ferry
Whose streamers wither the pear flowers
In the pure and peaceful Chinese way.

行　路

楚客蓬山路，薄衣杳杳行。
蜂忙菊淡敛，玉瓣剪西风。

Journey

A vagrant for the fairy mountain
Goes with his forlorn clothes thru
The pure, light chrysanthemums in swarms
To be snipped by the west wind.

行　善

人间万事轻，不死不趋同。
契阔[1]知天命，还需有善终。

【注释】

①契阔：离合，聚散，偏指离散。

Benefaction

All affairs of the earth is so light
As to be mutually agreeable when dead.
To toil the assigned decrees of heaven,
A natural death should be an essential.

兴　趣

草木如识趣，闲风过水轻。
吹起尘累事，漫洗月光明。

Interest

Congenial vegetations
Are gently and idly blown on the water
That whiffs the passion-karma
Brimming over the brightly-bathed moon.

幸　福

真性根基深，无根如揽云。
青云骑鸿雁，霜阵盼明春。

Happiness

A true and deep base
May be rooted cloudlessly
And ride the swan in the blue sky
Towards a bright spring in frosts.

性本善
Man is Good in Nature

其一

世事三更梦，人生一场棋。
穷通[①]观自性，富贵不迷离。

【注释】

①穷通：困厄与显达。《庄子·让王》：“古之得道者，穷亦乐，通亦乐，所乐非穷通也；道德于此，则穷通为寒暑风雨之序矣。”

One

World is but a dream at dead of night,
And life a chessboard.
Fortunes are self-natured,
Where riches and rank are blurred
Not in fluffy tufts of air.

其二

净月一河明，心行月也行。
心行不见月，月落在心中。

Two

A pure moon in the bright river
Walks with the heart
Without the moon
That' s fallen into the heart.

其三

奸谋千百个，自作自来承。
恶焰凶锋里，身家[1]是克星。

【注释】

①身家：自己。

Three

A suspicious head of theft
Will be stewed in its own juice.
In wicked and hellish flames,
He himself could be the jinx.

其四

空灵水月中，入性更通明。
自古同一月，参来几阵风？

Four

Illusory, the moon in the water
Will be well-illuminated, if penetrable.
The same moon from of old
Has attended the blasts of wind.

其五

竹影尘不动，姮娥①在月宫。
不沾尘垢念，业障②自凋零。

【注释】

①姮（héng）娥：即嫦娥，此处喻指月亮。②业障：詈词，指责他人他物为恶果、祸患的根源。《金瓶梅词话》第二十四回："婆子道：'奶奶，你看丢下这两个业障在屋里，谁看他?'"清·李渔《比目鱼·肥遯》："要急抛离这乌纱业障。"

Five

Bamboo shadows can't flicker their own dust,
Like the mythical goddess in the moon palace.
Not to touch the desires of dust and dirt,
A vile spawn will be deteriorate and disperse.

其六

钓寒青柳枝，别弄柳烟色。
水浑百丈里，心静鱼难过。

Six

To fish the cold with the green,
Play not the hue of the willows.
To be fathomed amain,
A calm heart keenly knows.

其七

得意行囊空，阴阳合历[①]明。
乾坤循佛道，空色自然生。

【注释】

①阴阳合历：历法是根据天象变化的自然规律来计量较长的时间间隔，并判断气候的变化、预示季节来临的法则。根据月相圆缺变化的周期（即朔望月）制订的历法称为阴历；根据地球围绕太阳的运转周期（即回归年）制订的历法称为阳历。我国古代的历法，把回归年作为年的单位，把朔望月作为月的单位，是一种兼顾阳历和阴历的阴阳合历。

Seven

A glory in the empty wallet
Should be sharp-featured over time.
By the supreme Buddha-law,
Noumena and phenomena are natural.

其八

清泉野山里，潇潇独自鸣。
疏枝月光落，横水尤添声。

Eight

A clear fount in the wild mountain
Is trickling and tinkling by itself.
Moonbeams bathed in the sparse boughs
Speak louder when blocked by the water.

其九

黄花枝头老，明月河中小。
夜静人无声，动心闻啼鸟。

Nine

Like the day-lilies about to fall,
The moon in the river will be small.
In the quiet of night,
My heart quakes by a bird brawl.

其十

菱歌①泛莲藕，沉水红腮浪。
出泥卸浓妆，莲房②轻楫③上。

【注释】

①菱歌：采菱之歌。南朝·宋·鲍照《采菱歌》之一："箫弄澄湘

北，菱歌清汉南。”②莲房：荷花的莲蓬，为睡莲科植物莲的成熟花托。③楫（jí）：船桨。此处指船。

Ten

In the water chestnut song,
Her red cheeks are billowed young.
Out of mire, dressed in light,
On the lotus pods, let's oar in light.

燕京八景
Eight Sights of Peking

其一：卢沟晓月

卢沟滑兔影[①]，野水照清蟾[②]。
兔影之何往？清蟾晓雾天。

【注释】

①兔影：喻指月亮。②清蟾：又喻指月亮。

One: Foredawn Moon Over the Marco Polo Bridge

Over the bridge slides a hare shade
That beams down upon the wild water.
Where the hare is going now
In the misty light of early dawn?

其二：玉带垂虹

白玉瑶池里，清风借月明。
泻银芳柳岸，玉液洗春声。

Two: Jade-belt Bridge Like a Rainbow

Jade bridge in the jade pool
Breezes in the brilliance of the moon.
On the sweet shore of willows, the silvers
Are flooding the sound of the jade spring.

其三：蓟门烟树

晴丝鹅柳嫩，细雨软如纱。
点雪梨花落，何方是我家。

Three: Misty Trees By Jimen Gate

Fine and tender, the willowy ripples
Are soft like gauzes in thin drizzles.
While the pear petals are snowing,
Tell me where could I be homing?

其四：西山晴雪

甜雪凝松柏，金星[①]剔透香。
化成十里玉，凛冽更光芒。

【注释】

①金星：形容冬天里的日光。此处描摹阳光反射挂树雪霰的晶莹状态。

Four: Clear Snow on the Western Mountain

Sweet snows on pines and cypresses
Of a sparkling, crystalline purity
Are resolved into ten mile's jade
That bites more cold, silvery flashes.

其五：琼岛春阴

浮云白塔客，浪迹不识风。

北海撑船去，苍天满目清。

Five：Spring to Be Budded on Jade Isle

To the white pagoda are drifting the clouds
Whose wandering traces can't read the rage.
Now，off the north sea！Punt ahead！
Ahead into the full，clear horizon.

其六：太液秋风

丝丝杨柳梦，寸寸舞清风。
似醉鲜鱼去，传来不老情。

Six：Autumn Wind of Tai-yeh Lake

Faint，balmy，dreams of the trees
Are willowy in slices of the breeze.
Tipsy，the fresh fish may swim away，
And riffle here ageless mood，anyway.

其七：金台夕照

拔山盖世胆，作古向晴晚。
代代金戈处，星河日月转。

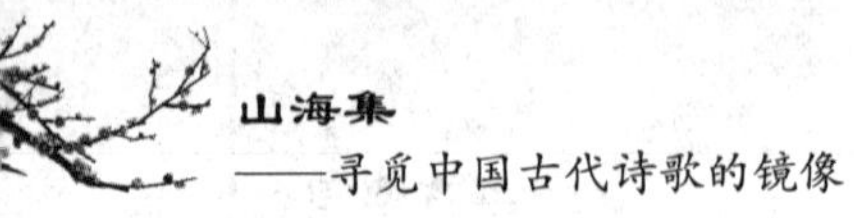

Seven：Golden Stand after Glow

Herculean in strength and courage,
The fine founder in the evening
Stands here as a golden spear,
Through the revolution of the galaxy.

其八：居庸叠翠

雄关万仞峰，渡鸟也心惊。
铁马金戈在，长缨可纵横。

Eight：Well-vegetated Juyong Pass

Impregnable Passes at the peaks
Startle even a flying bird.
Should the sweeping steeds and spears be there,
The galloping cavalries can cover the length and breadth.

燕山月
The Moon over the Yanshan Mountain

其一

明月春山里，徘徊柳树间。
细风梳鬓影，缕缕浣清泉。

One

Bright moon of the spring mountain
May be wandering about the willows.
While soft breeze combs the temples,
Her fine images are pure in the fountain.

其二

翠风浓万花，新月照白雪。
密密雨洗过，风月何须躲。

Two

In emerald breezes, all dense flowers
Are snow-white by the prime of the moon.
Washed clean in the dense showers,
The mystery of nature has no shelters.

其三

冰镜[①]出长城，龙头[②]今夜明。
千年同一月，何日卧龙行？

【注释】

①冰镜：喻指月亮。②龙头：老龙头，万里长城从这里的海中拔起，绵延万里，直指大漠嘉峪关。

Three

An ice mirror comes out of the Great Wall,
Whose dragon head will be bright tonight.
When the same moon for 1000 years or more
Can call forth the sleeping dragon for a flight?

其四

董家口衔月，心怀戚继光。

将军不归日，倭寇凶如狼。

Four

Over Dongjia Pass, the moon that passes along
Has harboured the figure of Qi Jiguang.
General! In the days of your absence,
Japanese invaders took their wolfish chance.

其五

汤河丁香树，千点银辉驻。
紫陌红尘[①]中，不须行人顾。

【注释】

①紫陌：城外的道路。红尘：尘埃，指城市街道热闹非常，尘土飞扬。比喻虚幻的荣华。

Five

Lilacs by the Tanghe River
Cast numerous lights of silver.
In such a dusty thoroughfare,
There is no need for a walker's care.

其六

相思抱霜月，飞过燕山夜。
孤寒进家门，多情尤悲切。

Six

To hug the moon in frost,
My love flies through the night.
Into the door are my isolated steps lost,
That's more susceptible to regret.

其七

烽火骑山冈，无声四百年。
点来残月火，世界可燎原。

Seven

Fire beacons on the mountains
Have been dumb for 400 years.
Light a fire with the wasting moon,
That can start a prairie fire in the world.

其八

清风追冰兔[①]，潮汐伴月升。
幽燕行易水，还有任侠[②]行。

【注释】

①冰兔：喻指月亮。②任侠：先秦时期对于游侠的统称，代表人物有盖聂、荆轲等。

Eight

Ice hare, chased by the breeze,
Tidal wave, raised with the moon;
Heroic river, gone into the north soil,
Is still in a strong sense of swordsman.

其九

长城怨明月，不留秦始皇。
求仙过沧海，车裂徐福帮。

Nine

Bright but pained, the moon on the Great Wall
Left not a single shade of the First Emperor,
Who, across the sea for his magic elixir,

Should have torn Xu Fu the quack doctor.

其十

山海关中月，惊心炮火红。
娇柔一眉黛，青天换黎明。

Ten

Shanhai Pass in the moon light
Was thrilling in the red flashes.
Tender and soft，her eyebrows
Were dawning into a broad daylight.

用户痛点

红粉霜天后，清寒斜影残。
剪春留雁字，最好弃桃源。

Pain spot of Users

After the rosy cheeks were frosted,
The pure cold air was shaded on the cross.
To snip the spring，for a stay of the wild geese,
It is preferred that the shangri-la surcease.

月西行

清圆流海镜，照我一清樽[①]。
冷韵冰姿里，疏香[②]倚绿荫。

【注释】

①清樽：清亮的酒杯，借指美酒。②疏香：淡淡的花香和酒香。

The Moon Heading West

A clear disk flows on the sea mirror,
That beams down upon my clear cup,
In whose pure and icy charms,
A faint fragrance counts on the green shades.

有教养的人
Well-breed Man

其一

守信识君子，幽遐论素衣。
霖铃约晓色，梦里不怀期。

One

A virtuous man in faith
Clothes himself far, pure and serene,
For the dawning hues in his drizzling bells
Not scheduled in the dreams.

其二

纸上可清谈，膝前话不休。
秋江穿涧谷，去鸟有喧幽。

Two

A chin-music paper
Babbles before the knees,
And as the autumn river roves in the dale,
The birds are chirping away in secret.

其三

德风流四海，巷道不行船。
大境容狮虎，云涵纳九天。

Three

The wind of virtue flows to the four seas,
Whose boats can't be sailed thru the lanes,
Unlike the big world for the king of beasts,
And the celestial spheres for the clouds.

其四

风楼玉雪中，倚柳暗听箫。
月底聆清谱，霜尘草木摇。

Four

Pure snows outside the blown floor
Heard a dark flute in the willows
That composed a clear ear to the moon
Rocking the frost dusts in the wood.

其五

青苹剪月光，软语斜晖落。
雪浪钓春风，林梢追燕雀。

Five

The moonlight was clipped by the duckweeds,
In the persuasive words of the slanting sunlight.
While the snow billows angled for the spring wind,
The wood tips would chase after the chaffinches.

其六

抒怀不傲世，冷瑟无孤韵。
几许谢芳容，何时音信近。

Six

An easy head will not be proud,
And a cold lute has no lonely rhymes.
To the fair but worn-out faces,
When her tidings will be coming?

其七

铁笔纵山河，风云不寂寞。
天地有厚薄，做人千钧诺。

Seven

My pen of steel's free in hills and vales
Whose ebb and flow are not doleful.
Before the world, thin or thick,
One should be true to his word.

其八

铁马入苍山，开阖天外雁。
斜书字百行，宛转浮云淡。

Eight

My sweeping steed into the green mountains
Stirred up the wild geese beyond heavens
Like the italics for 100 lines
Delicate through the light cloud drifts.

其九

沐雨披风短，流年驰马浅。
淘沙混此生，野度思多舛。

Nine

My utmost rigours shortly blown
Have galloped swiftly and flatly
And goofed off the life like the sifted sand
In the natural ferry full of twists and turns.

其十

嘶嘶蜂语里，吮蜜舞花肥。
飒飒三秋后，蜂房早不归？

Ten

In a swarm of humming bees,
The honey suckers dance in rich flowers.
After the soughs of the late autumn,
The honeycombs should go back earlier.

郁金香
Tulips

其一

阳辉[1]展玉玲，入夜更羞红。
欲解烛光意，灵犀[2]一点明。

【注释】

①阳辉：指太阳。清·陈梦雷《西郊杂咏》之五："阳辉升景耀，苍翠加润泽。"②灵犀：古代传说犀牛角有白纹，感应灵敏，所以，称犀牛角为"灵犀"。比喻心领神会，感情共鸣。

One

Like a sun opening her pure bell,
More blushes in her cheeks at night
Desire to decode the candle-light
That, tacitly strung, understands well.

其二

对饮冰团[1]下，绯红[2]为使君。
银葩[3]知妾意，隐匿不留痕。

【注释】

①冰团：形容月亮洁白明亮，如浑圆之冰。宋·梅尧臣《戏作嫦娥责》诗："正值十月十五夜，月开冰团上东篱。"②绯（fēi）红：红色的一种，艳丽的深红、鲜红、通红、深红色。③银葩（pā）：指月亮。元·高明《琵琶记·伯喈牛小姐赏月》："玉作人间秋万顷，银葩点破琉璃。"

Two

To drink under the ice ball,
My scarlet lies here for you.
To make out my desires more,
Secrete your shadow first of all.

造　就

简书去古箧[①]，书页随心染。
蓼蓝[②]不劝学，蓝玉暖成焰。

【注释】

①箧（qiè）：箱子。②蓼（liǎo）蓝，亦略称为蓝或靛青，是一种一年生的蓼科草本植物。《荀子·劝学》云："青，取之于蓝而青于蓝。"但《荀子·劝学》所指，应该是明代之前广泛使用的菘蓝，而非蓼蓝。

To Train

Out of the old trunk the bamboo slips
Were tinged and enscrolled arbitrarily.
No indigo exhortation on learning is necessary
Before the turquoise grew up into a flame.

战略性亏损

雪霁锁清愁，风摇望海楼。
金银铺满地，梦醒入深秋。

Strategic Loss

Sober melancholies locked in clear snow
Are blown by the sea building that may
Be a lush carpet of gold and silver that
Wake up from dream in the deep autumn.

折　花

一亭明月空，牛角辩羞涩。
乱丝冷雨后，独向菱花泣。

Snapped Flowers

Over the pavilion one bright, empty moon
Was timid and shy like a horny plait.
After the cold rains like sleaves,
She would weep in the lone mirror.

争　斗

一水乱肥烟，争食冲赤鲤。
闲云不忍停，深怕惊行止。

Struggle

Misty and watery in confusion,
The red carps compete for food
Like a roaming cloud pathetic to halt,
For fear of a shock of the measures.

种　子

月下谁人种，霜前一朵花。
相思断肠处，冷艳对朝霞。

Seed

Who's sown below the moon
One flower in the frost?
She's the heart-broken love
With her quiet elegance in the sunglow.

助　人

腕底词章醉，蝶园玉色新。
谁识蓬累苦，欲落问青鳞。

Helpful

My poetic wrist is so tipsy before
The fresh butterflies fluttering gracefully.
Who'd read my bitter whereabouts?
It's the dark fish that see the fall.

自媒体

反腐靠传媒，晴空炸响雷。
人人成记者，处处可抓贼。

We-media

In the medium war on corruption
Which is a bolt from the blue,
Everybody has become a pressman,
That can be catching the cracksmen.

自　立
Independence

其一

铁血拿云手，扶风烈烈行。
百年尽成墓，浩气鬼神惊。

One

A magic, iron-and-blood hand
Goes with the high wind into
The tomb after a century whence
Its moral force shocks the ghosts and deities.

其二

玉酿靠时间，珍馐动慧心。
柴门炉火色，饯我有佳禽。

Two

Time brews fine,
And stirs a delicious wit
Whose oven within the wicker gate
Dines me with its fine fowls.

自　我

梦里一分田，催生百草园。
拿来八两粟，百草化三餐。

Self

One plot of field in my dream
Has created a herb garden
Whose millets approx 400g
Are translated into three meals.

五言律诗

Five-character Octave

五律基本句式：

仄仄平平仄（仄起仄收式）；
平平仄仄平（平起平收式）；
平平平仄仄（平起仄收式）；
仄仄仄平平（仄起平收式）。

这四种句式是律诗平仄格式变化的基础，由此构成五言律诗的四种基本格式。

第一种格式：首句入韵仄起式

（说明：加括号表示可平可仄；五言律诗以首句不入韵为正规，而且以仄起式为常见。）

（仄）仄仄平平，平平仄仄平。
（平）平平仄仄，（仄）仄仄平平。
（仄）仄平平仄，平平仄仄平。
（平）平平仄仄，（仄）仄仄平平。

第二种格式：首句不入韵仄起式

（仄）仄平平仄，平平仄仄平。
（平）平平仄仄，（仄）仄仄平平。
（仄）仄平平仄，平平仄仄平。
（平）平平仄仄，（仄）仄仄平平。

第三种格式：首句入韵平起式

平平仄仄平，（仄）仄仄平平。
（仄）仄平平仄，平平仄仄平。
（平）平平仄仄，（仄）仄仄平平。
（仄）仄平平仄，平平仄仄平。

第四种格式：首句不入韵平起式

（平）平平仄仄，（仄）仄仄平平。

（仄）仄平平仄，平平仄仄平。
（平）平平仄仄，（仄）仄仄平平。
（仄）仄平平仄，平平仄仄平。

爱

玉户蒲葵扇，轻裙薜荔[①]缘。
鉴容攒素指，归鸟转红绵。
竹药风撩乱，琴尊[②]月正悬。
老来谁看取？家妾向君前。

【注释】

①薜荔（bì lì）：木莲、凉粉果、鬼馒头、凉粉子、木馒头。具不定根，常攀附于墙壁、岩石或树干部。②琴尊：亦作“琴罇”。琴与酒樽为文士悠闲生活用具。

Love

Her punkah in the jade door gets tied
To the gentle skirt like a creeping fig;
Her pure fingers reflected in the mirror
Go back like a bird shifted in the red cottons;
Her turbulent wind in the bamboos cures
The lyre of the hanging moon in the wine.
Stricken in age, who would see her?
It will be her man with a warm cuddle.

爱 情
The Torch of Hymen

其一

逢春粉蕊开，华露翠风来。
幽径喧心路，浮云话镜台。
翻红轻点破，随影淡别裁。
茗醉还能醒，情离自可哀。

One

When pink pistils bloom in spring,
The green wind is coming in bright dews.
When her secret track bustles the way of heart,
The drifting cloud recounts her dressing table.
To dub her routed ruby,
A selected image comes light.
If a tipsy tea could be sober again,
The feeling of separation would be woeful itself.

其二

问柳青芽小，颗颗吐雨长。
春光安枕畔，燕子静斜阳。
萍浪随花醉，牵丝扯地香。
西风昨夜起，花柳两苍黄①。

【注释】

①苍黄：苍指青色，黄指黄色。素丝染色，可以染成青的，也可以染成黄的。语本《墨子·所染》。比喻事物的变化。

Two

The budding willow leaves
Are spewing longer in the rain.
The spring safe by the pillow
Calms the swallows in the setting sun.
Like a bird of passage in the tipsy flowers,
The interminable threads are dragged out sweetly.
Last night, after the west wind was rising,
The flowers and willows would be greenish yellow.

其三

藤梢拉地气，清峭①欲攀猿。
逗浦幽兰茂，吟竹翠柳繁。
红颜独蹭蹬②，皓首两蟠蜿③。

谁动苍梧[④]泪，妻孥暗雨轩[⑤]。

【注释】

①清峭：清丽挺拔。②蹭蹬（cèng dèng）：险阻难行；失势貌。③蟠蜿（pán wān）：盘曲貌。④苍梧（wú）：即苍梧山，或九嶷山。相传，舜帝二妃娥皇、女英当年寻找舜帝未着，被大风阻于洞庭湖的君山，死后遂化作两座山峰，护立在舜峰的两旁。⑤妻孥（nú）：妻子和儿女。轩：屋檐。

Three

The essence of earth goes up from the vine tips,
Like a climbing ape on the cragged cliff.
The serene orchids are luxuriant by the river, green
In the exuberant willows and the whirring bamboos.
When the rosy lips and cheeks feel frustrated alone,
The hoary head took a sinuous course.
Who had stirred the tears of the green parasol?
The son and wife who were hutted by the secret rain.

扒心为知己

人生是战争，跃马更从容。
暗箭玩心跳，明枪鼓乐行。
幽燕驰俊骨，塞外射寒风。
铁血单刀去，捐躯亦鬼雄。

Open My Heart for My Soul Mate

Life is a war,
That spurs more naturally.
A stab in the back may be thrilling,
And an open spear thrust may play its tunes.
Noble grace! Gallop on the northern soil,
Great Wall! Welcome your cold shoot.
One sword! Against the iron and blood,
Though dead, die a hero even in afterlife.

把　握

行尸一草虫，夜噪语啾啾。
枕簟啄风淡，游丝缚梦幽。
短长飞舞絮，高矮系平洲。
缕缕清寒断，随蝶辗转流。

Confidence

One grasshoper like a walking corpse
Chirps its night words,
In the light wind pecked by my pillow,
With a dream, serene and gossamer,
Fluttering its willow fuzzes, long and short,
And looping up the flat isle, high and low,
That severs the clear cold in puffs and wisps

Of the butterflies that toss and turn.

百湖月

玉魄[①]照明春，宵晖[②]探芙蓉。
霜轮[③]吹弱水，冰兔盼飞鸿[④]。
春夏秋冬驻，风云雨雪行。
湖心如可鉴，千面也从容。

【注释】

①玉魄：月亮的别名。唐·春台仙《游春台诗》："玉魄东方开，嫦娥逐影来。"②宵晖：指月亮。唐·元稹《春六十韵》："昼漏频加箭，宵晖欲半弓。"③霜轮：指月亮。出自唐·陆龟蒙《中秋待月》："转缺霜轮上转迟，好风偏似送佳期。"④飞鸿：飞行着的鸿雁。东汉·马融《长笛赋》："尔乃听声类形，状似流水，又象飞鸿。"南朝·宋·鲍照《数诗》："四牡曜长路，轻盖若飞鸿。"此处指盼望春天大雁归来。

【自解】

大庆有"绿色油化之都，天然百湖之城"的美誉。原生态的湖泊，犹如大大小小的天镜，是王母的梳妆台上无意中掸落的几滴粉屑，那样的多姿和淡定。生活在这里的人们，看惯了一年四季形态不同的"百湖"，而"百湖"呢，也看惯了形形色色的人们。《哈姆雷特》中有一句经典台词："To be or not to be，that is a question."大概能映衬百湖的从容吧：有戏没戏，走着瞧吧；想活想死，酌量办吧；是升是迁，还用心思吗？

Moon Over the Hundred Lakes

Soul of jade, in bright spring,
Slanting twilights, to spy the rose of sharon,
Wheel of frost, that whiffles the feeble water,
Hare of ice, on tiptoe for the swan...
All are braked by spring, summer, autumn and winter,
All are going in wind, cloud, rain and snow.
Heart of lake, if it can be mirrored,
A thousand faces will be quite leisured.

报　应

因果累枝头，婆娑聚散心。
菩提不见树，古寺不怀荫。
紫气东来日，佛光罩我襟。
诸缘依旧在，无奈宿琴闻。

Retribution

The cause and effect works hard on the branches,
Whirling a heart of separation and reunion.
Out of a Bodhi tree, the ancient temple
Would not be thick-pleached.
When the ruddy light comes from the east,
My gown will be bathed in the Buddha' s halo.
And as usual, all the destinies rest there

Still in an old importunity by the lyre.

抱　怨

暮色半含烟，闲阶渺渺寒。
轻舟扶柳弱，流水泄萍残。
玉鉴吹竹影，凌波皱佩兰。
窗帷清苦月，飒飒冽风宽。

Whines

Twilit half in the mist,
The free steps are visionary by the cold spells.
Before my skiff that supports the supple willows,
Those duckweeds are lost by the running water.
While a bamboo shade whiffles in her jade mirror,
The fairy steps would crinkle my fragrant thoroughwort.
As the spartan moon sails past my curtain,
Her wrathful nipping cold would be widened.

玻　璃

玻璃敲玉座，闲骨吊孤魂。
云落一张脸，风摇两扇门。
依稀栖礼异①，寥落照名存。
铜雀②关青壁，回风断雨根。

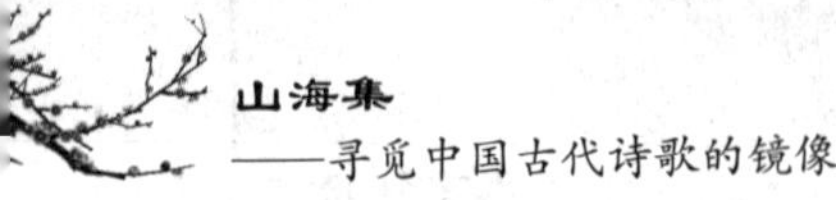

【注释】

①礼异：特殊礼遇。②铜雀：铜制的鸟雀。

Glass

While the glass knocks the jade seat,
His wandering soul hangs in the spare bone.
While his face drops off the cloud,
The wind rocks its two doors.
Vaguely perched in a different courtesy,
His name has been dimly deserted.
And behind the black wall, the bronze bird
Would unroot the rain in its backdraft.

不归路

人心千丈险，太古不曾绝。
长短翻烟聚，阴阳弄雨别。
奇峰随处起，异壑顿时折。
财色骷髅冢，尘封万代舌。

Step Over the Line

Men's heart are gone to a vicious depth, and
Have not vanished since the remote antiquity,
With the billowy wreaths of smokes long or short,
And also gone with the rains, of wax and wane;

Here and there, the queer peaks are rising,
And on the spot, the weird gullies are creasing.
In the tombs of skeletons, tongues of the wealth
And beauty have been dust-laden for all ages.

不解释

断崖谁敢顾，万尺坠青天。
谷荡悬冰涩，峰危跳涧欢。
凌空击紫燕，翻水泻白泉。
天下愁绝路，巉岩[1]属四川。

【注释】

①巉（chán）岩：高而险的山岩，形容险峻陡峭、山石高耸的样子，李白的“清晏皖公山，巉绝称人意”意即如此。

No Explanation

Who dares to tread on the edge of the precipice
That weighs down the broad daylight ten thousand feet?
In the dangling dales the hanging glaciers are obscure,
And off the threatening peaks the streams are skipping.
Heavenward one purple swallow is cleaving,
And seething down, the white springs are pouring.
All the ways that sigh and moan under the sky
Are those steep cliffs of Sichuan.

才　气

古城骄虏[1]断，日暮上麟台[2]。
箬笠弥天[3]去，蓑衣[4]满眼来。
苕溪[5]怀正气，韬野[6]倦宏才。
薛夜裁绡帕[7]，生花眼不开。

【注释】

①骄虏：亦作“骄卤”。骄横的胡虏。②麟台：武则天天授年间曾改秘书省为麟台，神龙元年（705）复原名。此处喻指做学问。这句是指年龄大的时候才想起去真真正正地做学问。③箬笠（ruò lì）：用箬竹叶及篾编成的宽边帽，即用竹篾、箬叶编织的斗笠。弥天：喻志气高远。④蓑（suō）衣：农村一种广泛使用的雨具。主要由棕榈树的纤维做成。⑤苕（tiáo）溪：苕，古书上指凌霄花。这里指盛长芦苇的溪流。⑥韬野：隐藏在野外。⑦薛夜：指薛夜来，三国魏文帝曹丕的宠姬。原名薛灵芸，常山人，美容貌。魏文帝改其名曰夜来。夜来妙于针工，虽处于深帷之内，不用灯烛之光，缝制立成，宫中号为针神。绡帕（pà）：薄绢巾帕。

Esprit

The dominating Huns were gone from the old town,
Gone to the Hall of Fame in the twilight,
Gone in the bamboo hat to fill the world,
But back in the coir cape to fill the eye,
With the sense of right in the reed streams,
By the myriad-minded gift tired in the hidden wild,
Who could tailor a silk hand-kerchief in the pitch dark,

With the vivid, broidered designs, but shut-eyed.

长　短

荣枯论短长，薄厚不推敲。
柳句敲成虎，梅章化作蛟。
穷通[①]无断雁，毁誉有同胞。
半世烟云路，听由冷热嘲。

【注释】

①穷通：困厄与显达。

Long and Short

Gain or loss, it is long or short,
Thick or thin, it stands up to no scrutiny.
A willowy sentence may be knockned into the tiger,
And a plum chapter transformed into the dragon.
Obscure or eminent, the wild geese will not wane,
Praise or blame, there exist our fellowmen.
On the way of clouds and mists half a lifetime,
Do as all the seeds of cynicism please.

尝　试

红颜试酒帘，寒酒帘幕低。
酒漫春光懒，帘飘月色啼。
愁眠先事远，浅醉后情迟。

饮尽弯弓月，青春子夜犁。

Attempt

When the rosy lips and cheeks tried the wineshop sign,
The curtain was hanging down in the cold wine
Which brimmed over its lazy spring hours
And cawed in the flapping curtain that veiled the moon.
In an uneasy sleep, the past memories faded away, and
Like a sheet in the wind, the passions were heavy-headed.
Now gulp down the moon like a curved moon,
And plough our youth when midnight comes.

徜　徉

野径去寻芳，牵衣脉脉香。
闲来得野趣，心远送朝阳。
流韵秋姿镜，幽明腊蕊妆。
横斜图半隐，妙处是春光。

To Roam

When the wild trail seeks the sweet,
The perfumes are tangled affectionately.
Leisurely with a fascinating charm of nature,
My heart afar follows another rising sun.
And in the autumn mirror, the gracious numbers
Are dim or bright to the winter stamina.

Sloping down the picture hidden in half,
The delicate phrase comes to the spring hours.

沉　默

野渡晨霞静，枝头一抹红。
林间观走雀，户外看飞蓬。
齐案红烛影，平台绿酒盅。
纵横千里阔，帷幄有飞鸿。

Silence

Still and rosy, the dawn on the open river
Spots a flash of red on the branches
Of the woods shuttled by the sparrows
From the thistles in the open air, and by
Contrast the red candles on the table
Are flickering to the green glasses.
Though the liable realm of space can be broad,
A swan might be perching behind his curtain.

承　诺

一诺堂前燕，寻常剪影空。
旧宅啼杏雨，新陌掠桃风。
草色含烟尽，连珠[1]带露中。
诺言如紫燕，宛转下年同。

【注释】

①连珠：连珠语，形容燕子叫声。

Commitment

One swallow before its promised hall
Becomes a usual but stark sketch
That chirps his old house in the rainy apricots
And then skims his new road with the windy peaches.
To the limit of the misty hues of grasses,
His dews could be interpretated by the beads.
The word of honor like such a purple swallow
Should be well-tuned into the next year.

出头鸟

枪林澹澹风，幽鸟欲藏踪。
青翼横枝隐，白翎素叶封。
仙根不入世，栖逸[①]对严冬。
生翅还学步，飞天枕梦行。

【注释】

①栖逸：隐居赋闲。

To Stand Out

In the storm of shots, the undulating

And serene wing wishes to hide his track;
Such a black wing hides in the boughs athwart,
Such a white plume's closed in the usual leaves;
Such an immortal root never goes down to earth,
But retreats from the world in the severe winter.
With wings, though, he'd learn how to walk,
And to soar up, he has to pillow his walking sleep.

刺　猬

缱绻梨花玉，抽弦怨苦寒。
飞鸿渤海远，落叶角山残。
无端青烟妒，徒添绿鬓[①]难。
丈夫生此世，忠孝不相干。

【注释】

①绿鬓：乌黑而有光泽的鬓发。形容年轻美貌。

Hedgehog

Locked in blissful pear flowers,
The chord marvelled at the bitter cold.
Afar the swan might fly over the Bohai Sea,
And strewn with dead leaves was Jiaoshan Mountain.
For no reason the black smoke was jealous,
And in vain to fresh the black temples again.
As a man in this world, his loyalty
And filial piety have no connection.

冲　动

冲天诟怒生，触影向蛇神。
出剑钢霜紧，捉刀铁雪伸。
寒光投素采，柳絮下三春。
天地无穷恨，人贫气不贫。

Impulse

To awfully fly into a passion,
The stricken shade scrambles to the zombie;
To bare the sword in the fast frosts
And ghost the iron-snows to be stretched,
The frosty light shoots its pure colour
Into the willow catkins in the late spring.
Between the earth and heaven, an endless hatred
May be backgrounded by the poverty against the integrity.

得　失

人世有悲欣，穷通似断虹。
深潭行猛虎，绝壁走黑熊[①]。
大才招人妒，锋芒落地宫[②]。
千秋说毁誉，宦海梦痕空。

【注释】

①黑熊：又叫狗熊、月熊，还有个俗称叫黑瞎子。②地宫：石雕刻

和石结构相结合的典型建筑，是陵寝建筑的重要组成部分，为安放死者棺椁的地方。

Gain and Loss

The world is agreeably grieved,
And all fortunes are like a broken rainbow,
Or a fierce tiger through the deep pool,
Or a black bear through the bold cliff.
A great talent must be subject to envy,
Before his cutting edge drops underground.
To be chided or hymned, for a thousand autumns,
All dreams in the official careers are traceless.

德　行

乌纱戴小人，得志怯豺狼。
入世呼风雨，出局唤雪霜。
烟云平浪起，红雨荡天扬。
白眼浮尘碎，阴霾炼狱狂。

Disgusting

A villain with the black gauze cap
May scare off the jackals in his ambition.
Into the world, he summons the wind and rain,
Out of the game, he commands the frosts and snows,
Like the cloudy wind and waves out of nothing,

And the blood rain that swings the sky,
Whence his white eye breaks the floating dust,
And his purgatory borders on mad hazes.

地　狱

软火流三界①，蓬门岁月忙。
空明②迎地狱，悲喜造天堂。
暴骨云高第③，胎禽④夜丧亡。
浮生行尽处，冥寞⑤可还乡。

【注释】

①三界：在佛教术语中指众生所居之欲界、色界、无色界。②空明：空旷澄澈，洞澈而灵明的心性。③暴骨：暴露尸骨，指死于郊野。高第：成绩优秀；名列前茅；高就。④胎禽：鹤的别称。⑤冥寞（míng mò）：死亡；阴间。

Hell

As the soft fire flows thru the three realms,
The years are bustling inside my thatched door.
Vast and bright, the hell is coming,
Joyful and sorrowful, the paradise is going.
Unlike the bare bones to deserve higher,
Or the fetus fowls that perish at night…
To the greatest extent of this fleeting life,
My lone, obscure soul WILL return home.

蝶　心

蝉翼[①]扑蝶暗，蝶衣振翅明。
红烟随君意，翠雨任君行。
蝶羽轻风静，蝶心乱世宁。
空灵吹入梦，弱水化为鲸。

【注释】

①蝉翼：比喻薄如蝉翼的女子的衣袖。

Heart of Butterflies

Like the cicada-wings on the secret butterflies,
Their frequent flaps are flapping bright,
Through the red smokes as you please,
And the green rains as you like.
Though their wings are still in the slight breeze,
Their heart is composed in the troubled times.
Flexible and unpredicable into my dreams,
Such a feeble heart turns into the whale.

对　错

云水天河过，春桥暮雨薄。
太阴[①]穿柳岸，明星落花阁。
野火枫焦卷[②]，穷鳞[③]易水涸。
幽怀追古意，高羽为谁约？

【注释】

①太阴：喻指月亮。②焦卷：枯萎，卷缩。③穷鳞：失水之鱼，比喻处在困境的人。

Right or Wrong

Past the cloud water the galaxy goes,
Down the spring bridge the dusk drizzles;
When the moon passes over the willow shore,
The bright stars drop to the parterre's call.
In a wildfire the maples may be scorched,
As are silhouetted by the poor fish so parched.
With a quiet mind to chase the ancient idea,
For whom to date the higher feathers from here?

对　立

骑雨萧萧剑，蒙轮下野山。
风疾堆叶影，水乱闯雄关。
宦海雄鸡闹，乌纱走兔闲。
词锋击晓月，月落又回还。

Antagonism

The rustling sabre that bestrides the rain
Gets down the wild mountain with its muffled wheel
While the gales were piling the leaf images again

And the turbid waters barging to the strategic pass at will.
As the cocks of officialdom crowed its first round,
The government-owned caps were rabbiting free.
Though the fighting words jabbed the dawning moon aground,
The moondown could have made its round trip at liberty.

人际关系
Relationship

其一

多秋难隐事，无事总淹留①。
怀璧难识错②，商歌怎辨羞③。
清平别谄媚，浊世不低头。
爱恨随君转，情愁枉自囚。

【注释】

①“多秋”两句：多事的时候能识别谁是君子，无事的时候却总是暗藏着小人。②“怀璧”句：《左传·桓公十年》：“匹夫无罪，怀璧其罪。”杜预注：“人利其璧，以璧为罪。”因以“怀璧”比喻多财招祸或怀才遭忌。③“商歌”句：典出《淮南子》卷十二《道应训》。春秋时宁戚想向齐桓公谋求官职，在齐桓公路经的地方“击牛角而疾商歌”，引起齐桓公的注意，后成就大业。商声凄凉悲切，后遂以“商歌”指悲凉的歌，亦比喻自荐求官。

One

An autumn cannot hide its tail,
At a loose end though to be lingered still.
If a precious stone hardly knows what's wrong,
How could the volunteered song be lost to shame?
Don't be beslavered when blessed peaceful,
Don't hang your head at chaotic times:
Love or hate, it's your turn, and
Any sad passion will be convicted, of no avail.

其二

动气骂群楼，群楼尽胆寒。
怒云翻瀚海，热浪弭[①]重峦。
航母沉齑粉[②]，神舟坠沙滩。
天庭息怒后，山在海没干。

【注释】

①弭（mǐ）：平息；消除。②齑（jī）粉：细粉；粉末；碎屑。

Two

To bawl out with a lost temper,
That quake all floors into a terror,
The vehement clouds are seething the sea,
Whose hot waves quell the hills easily,

Where an aircraft carrier sinks like broken bits,
And an spacecraft falls down to the sand beach.
After the heaven will have simmered down,
The hills and the sea are still so strong.

其三

心宽赛井蜍[1]，自诩[2]是鲸鱼。
夜艳丘樊[3]户，阳春市井庐。
尘嚣迷倦客，荒径待荷锄。
天上行云过，谁识弄雨虚。

【注释】

①蜍（chú）：蟾蜍，也就是青蛙。②自诩（xǔ）：自夸。③丘樊：园圃；乡村。亦指隐居之处。

Three

Open-minded, one's exceeded the well frog,
Cracking himself up to be a whale,
At his retreat for the colourful nights,
Or his downtown hut in the glow of spring.
Lost and languid in the madding crowd,
The lotus hoe should serve its desolate trail.
Who, under the rolling, celestial clouds,
Could read their virtual rain?

其四

人面尊如玉，敷成粉色羞。
交情如仲夏，还债似寒秋。
举债还钱易，牵情送礼愁。
逢场不作戏，薄纸也无由。

Four

An exalted face is like the jade,
Powdered to be a shy pink.
A friendship is like the midsummer,
Similar to the autumn chills for the payment
Of debts which is prone to be feasible,
Unlike the bound favours with a heavy heart.
If one refuses to join in the fun on occasion,
Even a paper lodges where senseless it’s lying.

其五

野外铁霜动，柴扉露水白。
腹中扑剑气，嘴里射刀排。
万类争食去，八方晦气来。
敲门浮爽气，花季柳摇宅。

Five

The iron frosts in the open country
Have bleached the dews on the faggot door
With a snapping sabre in the stomach,
And a shooting slasher out of the spout.
Don't you be those creatures competing for food,
Or all the directions will solicit fouler fortunes,
Rather than a knock at the floating, fresh air,
In the willowy residence of the flower season.

其六

人心尽看穿，快语莫生风。
宁静篱藩[1]破，潜心旷野穷。
虬枝书地气，娇蕊写天虹。
浓墨藏心里，无笔赴翰宫[2]。

【注释】

①篱藩：篱笆。②翰宫：翰林院。

Six

When your eyes are opened to the heart of men,
Your straight speech should not sow discord,
In that serenity may shatter a barrier and
Contemplative concentration can use up the moor

Whose humidity would be written on the curled sprays,
The tender stamina of which script your rainbows.
In your heart, hide your dark ink, and without
Any writing brush, go to the Hall of Academy.

其七

心欺暗室中，职场莫言欢。
羁旅升圆月，孤烟对日残。
东篱藏逸客，北岛掩长滩。
忧乐鸡虫事，何如钓海竿？

Seven

A heart may deceive in its dark chamber,
Where your cheerful career chats should cease.
As one round moon rises on your journey, the last
Sun gleams to the single straight plume of smoke.
And in the east fence, hide yourself free,
On the north isle, close your long strand.
It seems fiddle-faddle in the cheerful sorrow
Rather than casting your fishing line into the sea.

其八

红萼折轻雨，枝头点玉酥。
朝阳合冷露，圆月滚珍珠。
冰蕊三蓬断，诗情两不孤。

心宽忧社稷，地窄叹穷途。

Eight

Red calyces are lost even in a light rain,
Before leaving their pure, soft branches,
That shut the cold dews in the rising sun,
And roll the pearls in the round moonlight.
Down to the fistful of soil, the icy pistils
Are lost with their poetic fancies
About the sacred shrines, to be broad-hearted,
And about the dead end on the earth so narrow.

其九

长夜忘情水，相思枕上流。
牵心随弱柳，挂梦到梢头。
雾雨空眉皱，闲云满腹愁。
女墙明月度，鸾镜染三秋。

Nine

The forgiven love canopied in darkness
Flows on the pillow
That fetches the willowy heart
And hangs the dream onto the top wood.
In the fog drips that frown in vain,
The idle cloud fills the sad belly

Through the bright moon over the flower-beds,
And down to the mirror that dyes the late autumn.

其十

春天谁剪错，自古怨东风。
覆水游鱼过，开门走狗通。
云驹蹄草阔，夜梦酒淘空。
隔岸观荷叶，春秋总不同。

Ten

Who's scissored a wrong spring?
It's the bitter easterlies from of old.
In the spilt water a fish is swimming,
And thru the opened door a lackey is passing.
On the prairie let the colt hooves go,
And in my night dream, the wine's tunnelled.
Across the river, let me see the lotus leaves first of all,
Whose spring and autumn should not be the same you know.

发　现

藤萝荡碎云，乌鹊挂荆榛[①]。
渤海摇华盖[②]，汤河覆锦茵[③]。
临波游女笑，谑浪[④]海蜇亲。
圆魄[⑤]幽燕暖，金轮[⑥]放紫鳞。

【注释】

①荆榛（jīng zhēn）：亦作“荆蓁”。泛指丛生灌木，多用以形容荒芜情景。②华盖：帝王或贵官车上的伞盖。此处喻指天空。③锦茵：喻指芳草。④谑（xuè）浪：戏谑放荡。此处双关。⑤圆魄：喻指月亮。⑥金轮：喻指太阳。

Discovery

Tangled vines swung in the ragged clouds, and
Crows and magpies hung in the briars and brambles.
The Bohai Sea swayed its canopy, and the Soup River
Was bespread with the lavish tapestries.
To the waves, the wandering women were smiling,
And the teased sea blubbers were so genial.
When the round soul warmed up the silent shore,
Its golden wheel will liberate the purple scales.

放　手

冰释[①]镜潭酥，冰绡[②]软玉纤。
青冥[③]难俯视，色界有傍瞻[④]。
地阔凉风动，天高细雨沾。
隳官轩冕累[⑤]，五柳忆陶潜[⑥]。

【注释】

①冰释：像冰一样融化，比喻怀疑、嫌隙等完全消除。②冰绡（xiāo）：薄而洁白的丝绸。③青冥：青苍幽远。指青天。④色界：佛教用语。色界位于欲界之上。相传生于此界之诸天，远离食、色

之欲，但还未脱离质碍之身。所谓色即有质碍之意。由于此界众生没有食色之欲，所以，也没有男女之别，生于此界之众生都由化生，依各自修习禅定之力而分为四层，分别是初禅天、二禅天、三禅天、四禅天。傍瞻：侧视，环顾。⑤隳（huī）官：罢官；解职。轩冕（xuān miǎn）：古时大夫以上官员的车乘和冕服。⑥"五柳"句：陶渊明，字元亮，后改为潜，号"五柳先生"，私谥"靖节先生"（死后由朋友私下起的，并非朝廷颁布，故称私谥），浔阳柴桑（今九江市星子县）人，出身于破落仕宦家庭。大约生于东晋哀帝兴宁三年（365）。曾祖父陶侃，是东晋开国元勋，军功显著，官至大司马，都督八州军事，荆、江二州刺史，封长沙郡公。祖父陶茂、父亲陶逸都做过太守。曾任江州祭酒、建威参军、镇军参军、彭泽县令等，后弃官归隐。他是中国第一位田园诗人。

Let Go

The thawed pool in the mirror was crisp
And silken like a soft, fine gem,
Hard to be overlooked from the sky,
But looked about in the form-world.
When the wide world stirred its cool breeze,
The high sky was moistened with the mizzles.
When the sacked fame and gain felt so tired,
Go where it's permanently secured from disturbance.

放　下

青冥[①]掩夜闺，高岭露星飞。
连地江风至，川接海日微。
琅华[②]惊落照，霞散绮珠辉。

燕赵出佳丽，银钩[③]锁绣闱。

【注释】

①青冥：形容青苍幽远。指青天。②琅（láng）华：琅花，即琅玕树所开之花，常以美称白花。③银钩：喻指月亮。此处寓意双关。

Drop the Matter

When the azure sky closes its night boudoirs,
The high ridges will show their flying stars,
Under which the panoramic river is gusting,
And calls for the sea sun that' s shimmering.
Until the white flowers surprise the afterglow,
A flood of rosy light like pearls may overflow.
In such a northern, beauteous abode,
One silver crescent locks up her sweet code.

改　变

得梦斜风绿，枝头扇底红。
琉璃晴晓色，琥珀雨空濛。
苍狗[①]钻云海，白驹[②]射崆峒[③]。
轻蹄行软草，袖底半丝风。

【注释】

①苍狗：化自白云苍狗。苍：灰白色。浮云像白衣裳，顷刻又变得像苍狗。比喻事物变化不定。②白驹：化自白驹过隙。像白色骏马在细小的缝隙前跑过一样。形容时间过得极快。③崆峒（kōng tóng）：属六盘山支脉，受差异风化、水冲蚀、崩塌等外动力作用，

形成了孤山峰岭、峰丛广布、方山洞穴发育、怪石突兀、山势险峻、气势雄伟奇特的丹霞地貌景观。此处为山高峻貌。

Change

In a slanting breeze, my ready dream is green,
And the branches on my fan are red,
Which dawns the fine coloured glaze,
With its ambers shrouded in mist.
While a gray dog bolts into the sea of clouds,
The white pony may shoot into the fairy mountain.
Like the light hooves on the supple meadow,
Half a breath of wind comes out of my sleeves.

感　恩

侠义若流水，躯壳半世轻。
萧萧别易水，猎猎赴西京。
三尺扬眉气，千寻笑傲名。
丈夫游四海，舍命效长卿[①]。

【注释】

①长卿：汉代辞赋家司马相如的字。相如未遇时家徒四壁，后为汉武帝所赏识，以辞赋名世。诗文中常用以为典。晋代葛洪《抱朴子·论仙》："吾徒匹夫，加之罄困，家有长卿壁立之贫，腹怀翳桑绝粮之馁。"

Thanksgiving

To be chivalrous is like the flowing water,
Whose body has been ethereal half a lifetime.
Farewell, the bleak Yishui River!
In the howling wind, betake to the west capital!
Raise your eyebrows, three feet!
Face the name in smiles, unbounded!
To be a man wandering in the whole world,
He would speed to his heroic power!

高 估

碧空黄叶地，绿水半寒秋。
斗笠吹孤客，渔歌钓小舟。
风梳情缕缕，柳底梦悠悠。
独坐清江浦，夕阳脉脉流。

High Estimate

Under the blue sky, the yellow leaves
On the green water are half-cold autumn.
Lonely in the straw helmet that blows,
The songs are fishing the rowboat,
In the windflow that combs the passions
Of a leisurely dream under the willows.
Sitting alone by the clear river,

The setting sun flows affectionately.

工　作

劳君雁字长，客梦破高天。
紫蔓熏风①断，白华解愠②连。
红尘足下软，世事掌中棉。
践蹈③茫然路，登云咫尺寒。

【注释】

①熏风：和风。②解愠：恼怒怨恨。温和的风可以消除心中的烦恼，使人心情舒畅。③践蹈：踩踏；蹂践。

Job

Wild geese in service are so long
To soar up in the dreams all along.
As the purple vines stop the mild air,
The white flowers cure your worries there.
Beneath, the mundane dust seems so gentle,
And in palm, the world runs soft you know.
To tread on the blank way,
The climbing cloud has a short but cold say.

孤　独

大漠一驼峰，黄云万里愁。
铜铃听欲杳，铁骨流沙洲。
萧散天涯客，孤标地角楼。
燕犀[①]经百战，肥马委荒丘。

【注释】

①燕犀：燕地制造的犀甲。亦泛指坚固的铠甲。

Solitude

One hump in the great desert
Was melancholy under the endless yellow clouds.
When the brass bell was jingling weaker,
Its iron bone flowed into the shoal.
Skylined with great panache,
Such a proud recluse from the foreland storey
In its fat, ever-victorious coat of mail
Was entombed into the barren hillock.

故　事

往事断根蓬，诛茅[①]卷地行。
霏微[②]横雁叫，萧飒[③]解鞍鸣。
宿客闲来往，吟人淡送迎。
汉家秋塞草，戴水过遐征[④]。

【注释】

①诛茅：亦作“诛茆”，芟除茅草。②霏微：雾气、细雨等弥漫的样子。③萧飒（sà）：风雨吹打草木发出的声音。④遐征：远行；远游。

Tale

An unrooted history
Sweeps its thatched off the ground.
Gabbles of the wild geese are heavy with drizzles,
And the unsaddled neighs are bleak and chilly,
Unlike the regular callers at leisure,
Or the chanters insipid as water.
At the autumn border, the Chinese grassland of
The Daihe River launched its retaliatory expeditions.

光　鲜

光鲜不厌世，漫挹不疏狂。
冲淡轻何物？豪歌为卯粮。
亭危空寂寞，石乱漫仓惶。
长啸千秋岁，南柯梦正香。

Fresh and Bright

Fresh and flashy, but don't forsake this world,
Free and fan, but not unfettered and freewheeling;

Tranquil and plain, what's that studied contempt?
It's the clarion for the corn in the blade.
In the dying pavilion, the solitude is so stark,
In the chaotic stones, the indecent haste so free,
In the long whistles toward a foreseeable future,
The empty dream locks fast.

过　程

初程骆马①肥，莎草缦②长天。
铁壁飞丹阙③，群峰泻紫烟。
斜阳嘶郡邑，玉蹄溅绵川④。
狐兔别歧路，崎岖也不迁。

【注释】

①骆（luò）马：白身黑鬣的马。②缦（màn）：纡缓回旋貌。③丹阙：赤色的宫阙。④绵川：流水潺潺的河流。

Procedures

Snort and stout, alight for a short rest,
Before the sedges under the vast of heaven.
Over those iron walls may be rainbowed a palace,
Down those peaks would be rushing purple smokes;
While the setting sun nickers to the shires,
The jade hooves spatter the tumbling river.
Astray on a forked road, the fox and the hare
Will not change their rude and rugged course.

过　去

贾客[①]出绮错[②]，儒服布政堂。
农人不溉稻，蚕女卧贼床。
垂币通三古[③]，升歌荐万方。
八旗不负弩[④]，禾黍[⑤]叹国亡。

【注释】

①贾（gǔ）客：商人。②绮（qǐ）错：如绮纹之交错，也形容文辞雕饰华丽。③三古：上古、中古、下古的合称，所指时限各别。泛指古代。④负弩（nǔ）：背着弓箭，指习武。⑤禾黍（shǔ）：禾与黍。泛指黍稷稻麦等粮食作物。

Past

Gorgeous damask in the deal
Could clothe the academic administration,
Unlike a farmer without the irrigation of his rice,
Or a silkworm lady in the thief's bed,
Who's perhaps lost into the velocity of money,
By all creatures for their merry peals in full swing.
Behold! The Eight Banners out of their crossbows
Could but bemoan their conquered nation.

海　月

菱花[1]初对月，洞鉴[2]有云天。
雪辉[3]流清质，杨花[4]阵阵翻。
青铜惜桂魄[5]，白铁远乌迁[6]。
欲照鲜妍态，孤鸾[7]为哪般？

【注释】

①菱花：镜子的代称。这里把大海比作平放着的镜子。②洞鉴：亦作“洞监”。明察；透彻了解。晋·郭璞《客傲》：“玄悟不以应机，洞鉴不以昭旷。”③雪辉：月亮雪白的清辉。④杨花：雨貌。⑤青铜：铜镜，也指月亮。桂魄：明月。⑥白铁：比喻播雨的白云。乌迁：太阳迁逝。晋·陶潜《怨诗楚调示庞主簿邓治中》：“造夕思鸡鸣，及晨愿乌迁。”⑦孤鸾：孤单的鸾鸟，又比喻高人隐士。南朝·梁·江淹《赠炼丹法和殷长史》：“譬如明月色，流采映岁寒。一待黄冶就，青芬迟孤鸾。”

【自解】

颔联“雪辉流清质，杨花阵阵翻”本该对仗，一时偶句无法换韵，只好搞成了如水的月光忽然被拨弄的潇潇云雨遮蔽了，牵情的时光就这么人为地阻拦了。颈联里的“青铜惜桂魄”本该是“桂魄惜青铜”，这里掉个顺序，原意是月亮照在如镜的海面上，两两相惜，不料被“云雨”了。当然，“桂魄惜青铜”也犯了行内合掌的大忌。尾句的“孤鸾为哪般”是从上两联顺下来的反问：月亮究竟有多亮，想要照照，就这么点儿奢求，也被隔阻了，成了“孤鸾”，无奈何，只好在想象中顾影自怜、孤芳自赏了。

Moon over the Sea

O Mirror fresh to the moon
May be perceptive of the broken sky.
Like a snow glow, a sweet streams
Into the rolling willow catkins.
If the bronze could spare its own light,
The white irons would line up away
From the Crow of migration.
To be beamed down upon
That bright-coloured image,
The solitary phoenix might be labyrinthian.

欢　乐

诗酒游仙客，兰亭醉几人。
相逢邀雪夜，相劝饮鸣春。
称意消灵运[①]，多情忘主宾。
行杯居陋室，走笔不为臣。

【注释】

①灵运：天命；时运。

Glee

Poetic wine like an immortal has inebriated
The men of the orchid pavilion.
To be together, let's invite the snow night,
To be wined, let's drink a warbling spring.
In the bed of roses, go with the whirligig of time,
In the bathos of sentiment, forget the guest of honor.
Now raise our cups in my rattrap,
And write like an angel, instead of a lackey.

回 归

一枝迎雪乱，洒遍野桥声。
老树棵棵暗，新花点点明。
搓寒浮柳梦，化日等青萍。
三弄笛横醉，幽弦伴夜莺。

Regress

One spray loses her cool in the snow,
That perfuses the tones of the wild bridge,
Beside the old, obscure trees, and
The fresh, bright flowers, before the cold spells
Could be twined in the willowy dream,
And the bright sun awaits the blue duckweeds.
After the tipsy flute's thrice played,

Some nightingales shall sing to the serene strings.

活　着
Alive

其一

幽梦一襟风，邀出北斗行。
江头扶翠色，江尾落莺声。
不用凌花镜，难求碧水清。
天风吹月落，北斗举勺迎。

One

My subtle dream blown by the collar
Invited the northern dipper out for a walk.
Upstream was supported by the green,
Downstream were falling the orioles warbles.
Without the mirror,
It would be hard to get the clear water.
When the heaven's breath blowed off the moon,
The dipper would scoop it.

其二

汤河若戴河，斜雨黯然惊。
燕雀扶摇淡，鱼龙卷水浓。
苍林摇魅影，一爪带西风。
临水垂蓑笠，拔竿柳线鸣。

Two

The Soup River like the Daihe River
Was shocked and downcast in the slanting rain
Whence a chaffinch rose up light,
And an ichthyosaur curled the wave strong.
While the dark wood wigwagged the goblins,
One claw seized the west wind.
By the river, my hanging cape and hat pulled
Up the willowy rod, rustling and rattling.

积　善

青蒿鞭嫩雨，矮岫遁苍鹰。
御世平阡陌，明言到武陵[①]。
玉藤寒抱径，石剑暑推蒸。
好景邻孤月，群峰卧古僧。

【注释】

①武陵：武陵源风景名胜区，位于中国中部湖南省西北部，由张家

界市的张家界森林公园、慈利县的索溪峪自然保护区和桑植县的天子山自然保护区组合而成，总面积约500平方公里。这里又发现了杨家界新景区。

Benefaction

Sweet wormwoods scourged the tender rain,
Where a goshawk fled out of the low cavern,
Trying to govern the criss-cross country,
But outright to the land of cockayne,
Where the path lined with ivy was nestled cold
Or saunaed in the summer-heat of the stone sabres.
Before the moon so fine, adjacent but solitary,
All the peaks are lying there like an ancient monk.

给　予

一诺轻相许，豪情两片心。
兔尖[①]别把剪，藕线不抽针。
古岸狂风远，平沙雪浪侵。
千金徒自负，失信岂为人。

【注释】

①兔尖：兔毛制作的毛笔笔尖。

To Give

To fob off with light promise, a lofty
Sentiment with two faiths and troths leaves
Its scissor off the tip of the writing brush,
Or needles its lotus fibre, but never more.
The squalls off the old shore have gone far,
Far off the snow billows against the strands.
To be a fly on the wheel, 1000 ounces of gold
Has its good conceit but not to forfeit confidence.

家

青山云水岸，甬道草深深。
邑外行鸡犬，田间卧土村。
风摇花影动，月摆柳枝温。
摇曳谁来采，新新挂雨痕。

Home

On the cloudy shore by the green mountains,
One path stretches, paved but grassy.
Fowls and dogs are sluggishly wandering around,
And in those fields sits an unrefined hamlet.
As the wind rocks the flowers,
The moon sways those mild willow branches.
Who'd come to pick those who're willowy?

It's the rain prints on the fresh willows.

假　如

金阙[①]晓钟清，兴诗对李白。
主人邀舞袖，歌妓唱飞席。
游燕鸣云树，泠[②]泉漱响石。
挥毫翻北海，研墨润七泽[③]。

【注释】

①金阙：道家谓天上有黄金阙，为仙人或天帝所居。②泠（líng）：清凉的。③七泽：相传古时楚有七处沼泽。后以“七泽”泛称楚地诸湖泊，此处泛指湖泊。

Hypothesis

When the dawning, golden-gate tolls clear,
Let's rendezvous with the inspired poems.
When the host invites the dancing sleeves,
The songstress chants on the magic carpet.
When the wandering swallows warble in the clouds,
The cold spring rinses its clinkstones.
When I drive my quill by the north sea,
The grinded ink would moisten the seven marshes.

较　真

黄鸟多情夜，蜉蝣片刻忙。

平生多计较，死后伴严霜。
照水冰枝弄，衰颜朽木亡。
劫灰出本性，口业祸苍苍。

Too Serious

Yellow birds are moonstruck at night,
And the ephemeras are abustle awhile.
More lifelong vigours to split hairs
Go along with the black frost after death.
Be not a branch in the frozen water,
'Cause any faded face of the dead wood must die.
Like the kalpa-ash resulting from the true nature,
A vicious tongue will court disaster.

借　口

晓渡返暝[1]潮，船头过断桥。
扶桑[2]不寂寞，雨露可逍遥。
斜照浮秋水，惊波裹碧霄。
金乌啄后羿[3]，高燕火云烧。

【注释】

①暝（míng）：黄昏。②扶桑：别名朱槿、佛槿、佛桑、大红花、朱槿牡丹。③金乌：中国古代神话中的神鸟，也称金乌、阳乌，或称三足。传古代人看见太阳黑子，认为是会飞的黑色的鸟——乌鸦，又因为不同于自然中的乌鸦，加一脚以辨别，又因与太阳有关，为金色，故为三足金乌。三足乌是神话传说中驾驭日车的神鸟名。后羿：上古时代的传说人物。他善于射箭，曾助尧帝射九日。传说十

日齐出，祸害苍生。天帝（帝俊）就派擅长射箭的羿下凡解除灾祸。羿射九日，只留一日，给大地带来复苏的生机。

Pretext

When the dark tide backs to the dawning ferry,
One prow threads through the broken bridge.
In the tree of dawn not deserted,
The sweet dews would be unfettered.
When the setting sun floats on the autumn water,
The stormy surges are swathed by the green sky.
Before the Golden Crow pecks the great archer,
The swallow soars up into the crimson clouds.

经　历

毁誉奚足论，荣枯取自然。
沉浮如隐逸，聚散若轻烟。
宦海缁衾暖，平民粟米寒。
人生多坎坷，天晚噪金蝉。

Experience

Praise or blame has no proof of it,
Gain or loss takes its own course.
Up or down, it' s like an escape from society,
Come or go, it's like the wisps of smoke.
The dark quilt of the officialdom warms up,

While the corns of the people are so cold.
On the thorny road to life,
Golden cicadas are chirping in the dark.

境　界

罗浮绝秀境，僧梵①步晨钟。
青壁②千寻谷，嵬岌③百仞峰。
莓苔④行万卷，薜荔⑤忍三冬。
苦志青云路，横空暮霭浓。

【注释】

①僧梵（fàn）：指佛教徒的修行，或僧人。②青壁：青色的山壁。③嵬岌（wéi jí）：高耸的山。④莓苔：青苔。⑤薜荔：桑科榕属，常绿攀缘性灌木藤本植物。别名“木莲”“凉粉果”“鬼馒头”“凉粉子”“木馒头”。具不定根，常攀附于墙壁、岩石或树干。

Realm

Mt. Rover in its crumptious setting
Chimes the steps of the morning monks.
Beyond the black, cliffy dales,
The rocky peaks are fathomed to a great depth.
Having pored over innumerable, formidable volumes,
The creeping figtrees are endurable three winters
Whence the bitter will on the road to the azure sky
Grows stronger like a sudden jolt in the evening mist.

距 离

青芜羽翰生[①]，蕊雪乱红英。
秀色香囊重，芙蓉翠玉轻。
花心叠有浪，风影踏无声。
湾浦[②]含晴树，汀洲草露明。

【注释】

①青芜（wú）：杂草丛生的草地。羽翰：翅膀。②湾浦：水流弯曲的水滨。

Distance

Born in the grass-grown enclosure, the wings
Dazzle the red flowers amid the snow of pistils.
Before the sweet but hefty sachets,
The roses of sharon are gentle like an emerald.
In the heart of flowers are furled the billows,
The wind shadows shall stride in silence.
While the bay could be bathed by the fine wood,
The sand islet would be bright for its dews on grass.

君 臣

仇雠[1]为名利，貔虎[2]恨难销。
暮暗藏峰壑，晨明适远嚣。
荷蓑低暗壁，弑[3]梦待狂飚。
拯溺如穷厄，群臣尽哺糟[4]。

【注释】

①仇雠（qiú）：亦作“仇仇”，仇恨；仇怨；仇人。②貔（pí）虎：貔和虎。亦泛指猛兽，或桀骜不驯的人。③弑（shì）：封建时代称臣杀君、子杀父母。④拯溺（zhěng nì）：救援溺水的人，引申指解救危难。穷厄：穷困，困顿，不亨通。⑤哺糟（zāo）：饮酒；吃酒糟。比喻屈志从俗，随波逐流。

Lord and Vassal

To be sworn enemies for fame and gain,
The beasts of prey would die hard
In the dark dusk of the ravines
By the clamours far from bright morns.
With the lotus cape down the dark wall,
The murdered dream awaits a wild whirlwind.
On the way of salvation,
All the courtiers should serve the hour.

开　放

沈思游宇宙，斜雨软来风。
一触寒清脆，三发暖朦聋。
无根峰骤起，有意水分洪。
鼓角连千载，沉烟塞上空。

Opening-up

To ruminate in the wandering universe,
The slanting rain was softly blown…
With one cold touch clear and crisp,
And three mild, bleary-eyed views.
As the rootless peak sprang up sharply,
The dividing flood went there wittingly.
Down to posterity, the drums and bugles
Were mist-veiled by the empty frontier.

开　心

豆蔻胭脂嫩，娇娥素手鲜。
藤鞋独自醉，苔絮[①]枉相牵。
落叶肥鸡尾，拈花[②]瘦楚鹃。
合欢裤腿暖，肌雪浸蚕绵[③]。

【注释】

①苔絮：水中青苔。②拈（niān）花：拈，即捏、惹。多指男女间

的挑逗引诱。③蚕绵：丝绵。

Delight

Of a tender and budding rouge,
Her fair fingers are so fresh.
Tipsy alone in the rattan shoes,
The moss fuzzes are fetched in vain.
Before the fat, defoliated cocktail,
One svelte cuckoo faces the avid flowers.
In one trouser-leg of happy-reunion, her
Snow-white flesh feels soft like a floss.

恪　守

净手去焚香，清心启慧源。
千古多寂寞，百代少寒暄[①]。
有意托鸿雁，无为寄晓岚。
梅边知冷暖，冲淡[②]不相烦。

【注释】

①寒暄：犹寒暑，亦指年岁。今泛指宾主见面时谈天气冷暖之类的应酬话。②冲淡：冲和、淡泊。

Scrupulous Obedience

Clean-handed, to burn the incense,
Pure-hearted, to start the source of wit;
All the ages were mostly deserted,
And a hundred generations were less chin-deep.
Intentionally, request the swans,
Effortlessly, entrust the dawning vapours—
When the plum flower learns the temperatures,
Her tranquil and plain heart won't be a bother.

苦　乐

浮生一枕凉，苦乐几十秋。
青眼多岑寂①，风签少敝幽②。
沉浮行苦海，惨舒③驭方舟。
一叶西风起，蜉蝣④落古丘。

【注释】

①青眼：阮籍能作“青白眼”——两眼正视，露出虹膜，则为“青眼”，以看他尊敬的人；两眼斜视，露出眼白，则为“白眼”，以看他不喜欢的人。岑寂：寂静，寂寞，冷清。②风签：利用溶图、调色、高光等，融合古典意境诗词，形成了独具风韵的签名图；另外，排字和字体也是决定风签质量的重要因素。敝幽：生计艰难窘迫、隐居未仕（的人）。③惨舒：指忧乐、宽严、盛衰等。④蜉蝣：最原始的有翅昆虫。稚虫水生，成虫不取食，寿命很短，仅一天而已，但它在这短短的生命中，绽放了最绚烂的光彩。

Joy and Sorrow

This fleeting life on one cold pillow
Suffers or cheers dozens of autumn
In a favourable eye mostly mute and still,
Or in a signed miniature to the broken recluses.
The vicissitude in the abyss of misery
Has navigated the ark in a cruel leisure.
When the west wind blows, one leaf will
Fall down to the old hill like a mayfly.

离　弃

宦途方入道，棹海落浮槎[①]。
樵唱云无迹，垂竿水有涯。
饥食狂噬象，充腹醉修蛇[②]。
朔漠[③]刑宽窄，俘囚[④]忆酒家。

【注释】

①棹（zhào）：划船。浮槎（chá）：古代传说中来往于海上和天河之间的木筏。②修蛇：古代中国的巨蛇，也叫作巴蛇，据说体长达到180米，头部蓝色，身体黑色。修蛇居住在洞庭湖一带，吞吃过往的动物，据说曾经生吞了一头大象，过了3年才把骨架吐出来。③朔漠：北方的沙漠。也可单称“朔”，泛指北方。④俘囚：战争中被掳获的人；拘禁。

To Forsake

The first step on the way of official career
Drops into the floating raft on the sea
Unidentified by a wood song from the cloud
That angles for the limited water
And gobbles down the elephant
Enough to inebriate a huge python.
Broad or narrow, the law of the desert
Takes the winehouse into custody.

黎　民

灵台[①]织野草，落寞有朋知。
四壁霜虫苦，一床月客悲。
狂心松露坠，醉眼柏风吹。
明质[②]德归处，黎氓盼抚绥[③]。

【注释】

①灵台：比喻让人不受利诱，保持心灵的纯洁，别做错事的地方。②明质：明信，诚信。③黎氓（méng）：亦作“黎萌”，即黎民。抚绥：安抚，安定。

Multitude

Wild grass was woven in heart,
Whose solitude was revealed by an associate.
Like the frosty bugs aching on the walls,
One moon-lit bed was so doleful.
When the pine dews fell off the wild heart,
My drunken eyes were blown by the cypresses.
Where there's the brilliant inner power,
The people watch the clock of appeasement.

李　白

海镜金樽里，中国①万里游。
一杯行剑壁②，两盏走风楼③。
恣肆④七星落，矜矜⑤九月流。
功名得宦场，粪土是封侯。

【注释】

①中国：国中。②剑壁：峭壁。③风楼：宫内的楼阁。南朝·宋·鲍照《代陈思王京洛篇》："凤楼十二重，四户八绮窗。"④恣肆：恣：放纵；肆：无顾忌。也指言谈、文笔等豪放潇洒。⑤矜矜（jīn）：小心谨慎貌。

【自解】

40 个字，想概括李白的伟大成就，是不自量力的。这首五律的重心落在尾句"功名得宦场，粪土是封侯"，这是调过来的说法；其中，末句化自毛泽东的"粪土当年万户侯"，这里是反其意而用之，

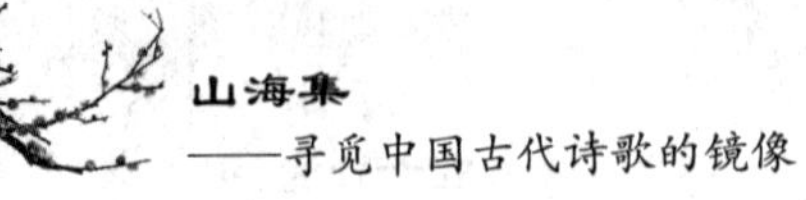

即，如果李白官场得意，如果没有唐玄宗“赐金放还”，那么，封侯以后的李白千年以后，或许与其他王侯将相一样，被埋没在粪土里面而不为人所知了，中国的文化符号由此便会黯淡许多。

Li Po

A sea mirror in my golden cup
Swims great in its own state.
One cup could be steep,
The second could be royal.
Wayward，Bid Dipper falls，
Watchful，months have wandered.
Worldly fame from the government
Has proved to be dungs and dirts.

理　解
Understanding

其一

大路百寻宽，驱车两袖风。
寻常驰野马，自古越飞鸿。
回望荆云富，别来楚水穷。
天遥通鸟道，绝域可圆通。

One

On the great, open road,
My sleeves are driving on,
Like a wild horse as usual,
Or a swan from of old, with a retrospective
Glance at the rich, southern clouds
Over the poverty-stricken water.
In the sky afar, there should the path of birds,
In the remotest corner, there's a perfect understanding of the truth.

其二

浮尘一梦醒，去日总成空。
临浦观鸥鹭，寒津看钓翁。
春宵啼晓月，醪醴①叫银盅。
向晚红衣醉，菊花满院风。

【注释】

①醪（láo）：本指汁滓混合的酒。《广韵》称其为浊酒，徐灏笺云："醪与醴皆汁滓相将，醴一宿熟，味至薄，醪则醇酒味甜。"后亦作为酒的泛称。醴（lǐ）：甜酒。醪醴：泛指酒。

Two

Awake from dream like a floating dust,
My days have been written on water,

With the feasted eyes on the waterfowls,
Or the fishing men at the cold ferry.
While the vernal night caws in the dawning moon,
The mellow wine calls for its silver cup.
As the red, tipsy dusk is near, my courtyard
Will be full of the wind of chrysanthemums.

帘

幽燕雪暗来，飞过柳萧萧。
客子[①]何须怨，隔帘顺手招。
帘钩垂冷月，帘幔挡寒潮。
帘落西风短，帘波剪梦消。

【注释】

①客子：旅居异乡的人。

Curtain

North snow comes quietly and murkily,
Over the rustling willows.
What need is there to deplore
With a smooth beckon behind the curtain?
It's hook droops one cold moon,
It's blind blocks the cold current,
It's fall is short against the west wind,
It's wave clips the dream.

鹿　鸣

白鹿过青萍，呦呦柳色闲。
薄星浮晓岸，圆月没苍山。
香雪枝头醒，清云几瓣鲜。
春秋三味①里，无味也开颜。

【注释】

①三味：原意指布衣暖、菜根香、诗书滋味长。

The Bleating Deer

A white deer thru the blue duckweeds
Bleats his free willows.
As the sparse stars swim over the daybreak shore,
One round moon has sunken down the dark mountains.
Awake at the branch, the sweet snow blooms
Several fresh petals to the clear clouds.
In the three-flavour season of spring or autumn,
Even a flavourless bleat will be chuffed.

旅　伴

涤尘紫陌中，斜雨现花残。
谁料风帘瘦，平偷半盏圆。
榴裙尤带醉，香袖更贴寒。
旅雁鸣心语，吹熟万户餐。

Fellow Traveller

In the dust-free thoroughfare,
The last flower looms in the slanted rain.
Behind the thin, damp sheet, who would
Have stolen half a round bowl?
Her garnetred skirt are a bit sottish,
Her sweet sleeves more shivery.
Listen to the whispers of the wild-geese,
All meals shall be whiffled fully ripe.

马踏飞燕

追影跃三寻①，淅淅过耳风。
鼻端承碧月，眼里纳朱明②。
且问何方去，前边有燕行。
龙威浮燕颔③，借力比鲲鹏④。

【注释】

①三寻：指马奔走时，前后蹄间一跃而过三寻。形容马奔跑得快。②朱明：红色耀眼的太阳。③龙威燕颔：形容威严雄武的相貌。颔(hàn)：下巴颏，此处双关汉朝皇恩庇护下的赵飞燕。④鲲鹏：化典于《庄子·逍遥游》："北冥有鱼，其名曰鲲。鲲之大，不知其几千里也；化而为鸟，其名为鹏。鹏之背，不知其几千里也。怒而飞，其翼若垂天之云。"与鲲鹏相比，斥鴳则"腾跃而上，不过数仞而下，翱翔蓬蒿之间，此亦飞之至也"，"奚适也"？我言：无力借鲲鹏，自有可借力。

【自解】

记得2001年评上副教授之后（当年全校只给一个指标），人事处处长刘德仁当桌点音儿道："月亮再亮也晒不干谷子。"从此铭记。马踏飞燕这个意象给我的现实感觉就是：去干远远超越自己能力的事情的时候，如果设计的方案具有可能性，不妨借力使力，使之成现实。这也就是我所理解的人力资本的替代效应所产生的递增收益原理。

Horse Stepping on Flying Swallow

After the traces, leap forward!
Rustling, whistling, swishing,
His nose holds a blue moon,
His eyes take a bright red.
But where to go? Answer me,
Over there, a swallow is going.
On the swallow's heavy jowls,
A new force could be leveraged.

门 槛

龙蹄遮布被①，十载踏青门②。
紫禁分天壤③，云梯载客魂。
秋风终落尽，蝉翼岂独存。
早懂声名累，如何作草根。

【注释】

①布被：盖布被。形容生活艰苦。②青门：汉代长安城东南门，此

处指城门。③紫禁：宫禁，皇帝的居宫。此处指中央国家机关。天壤：天和地，天壤间或相隔极远、相差极大。

Threshold

Muffled by the cloth，the dragon hooves
Dawdled the decade away in the town,
Practically a forbidden world of difference,
Whose scaling ladder loads those souls.
After the autumn wind denudes all,
How could a cicada wing exist alone?
Should one learn the fame on his back,
He could as well be a grassroot.

命　运

人生如盛宴，拨弄任浮沉。
天步[①]纤毫意，轮回世代身。
红尘不错爱，过客系深根。
帷幕蝴蝶翼，难隔裂瓣春。

【注释】

①天步：天运，命运。

Fate

Life is like a feast,
That fiddles the ups and downs.
Fate to a hair's breadth
Drives the wheel of reincarnation.
If the mundane dust loves right,
The passers could be rooted deep unlike
A butterfly wing on the purdah
Hard to seperate the valve spring.

哪　怕

鱼踪脍羽觞[①]，幽显[②]辨同方。
古渡云没改，荒林雁已亡。
闲潭托落照，紫陌盼垂杨。
瘦骨浮沈[③]夜，啼寒万木霜。

【注释】

①羽觞（shāng）：又称羽杯、耳杯，是中国古代的一种盛酒器具。②幽显：犹阴阳，亦指阴间与阳间。③浮沈：浮沉。

Whatever

The fish trail was stir-fried into the cup,
Obscurely manifested by the eyes abreast...
On the same cloud over the old ferry,
On the wild geese gone in the barren wood,
On the setting sun down the idle pond,
On the weeping willows along the thoroughfare...
While the skinny night floats or sinks,
The cold caws have frosted up the woods.

男　女

相知云水淡，甘涩两绸缪[①]。
外物金石诺，约心紫燕游。
簪绂随远岫[②]，轩盖[③]浪回流。
散玉离怀隐，合钱[④]钓冷钩。

【注释】

①绸缪（chóu móu）：紧密缠缚；缠绵。②簪绂（zān fú）：冠簪和缨带。古代官员服饰，亦用以喻显贵、仕宦。远岫（xiù）：远处的峰峦。③轩盖：车盖。④合钱：犹集资。

Men and women

To be thick with the light cloud-water,
Their bitter sweet is sentimentally attached,
With an incredible, detached promise,
That trysts the merry heart of purple swallows.
Following the distant hills, her hairpinned ribbons
Are wheeling against the back flows.
To invest emotionally goes without reserve,
Their financing page will bait a cold hook.

女　子

冷面呵红手，回春冻雨飘。
荆钗明锦簇①，鬓畔暗垂髫②。
随意潘郎③窥，由他玉面瞟。
我身因我在，不理任逍遥。

【注释】

①荆钗：荆枝制作的髻钗。古代贫家妇女常用之。锦簇：锦绣成团。形容色彩艳丽。②鬓畔：鬓边，鬓角部位。垂髫（tiáo）：古代儿童犹未束发时自然下垂的短发，此处指女子鬓发下垂。③潘郎：晋代潘岳。少时俊美，故称，泛指为女子所爱慕的男子。后亦以代指貌美的情郎。

Young Lady

The cold face breathed out by her pink hands
Rejuvenates in the silver thaws.
With the thornpin in a mass of rich brocades,
Her temple presages a subtle maiden image.
Do as those fancy men may snoop,
And squint like other toy boys—
I live, therefore I am,
At my own pleisure, anyway.

朋　友

人世与谁同？闲云碧玉杯。
春山沽酒去，秋水醉情回。
炭火殷寒雪，蛮烟煮小梅。
平生邀四海，穷老有人陪。

Friend

Who's my confidant in the world?
It's the jasper cup to the idle cloud
For the wine from the spring hill that
Will return from the drunken autumn water
Into the eager, chilling snow by the charcoal fire,
Boiling the green plums in reckless smokes.
A lifelong invitation to the whole world
Will be gone through the poor, grey hairs.

第七批中国外语教育基金项目：ZGWYJYJJ2014z30

Sponsored by the 7th Chinese Foreign Language Education Fund: ZGWYJYJJ2014z30

山海集

——寻觅中国古代诗歌的镜像

（中册）

吴松林　著/译

A Collection of Seas and Mountains

—The Mirror to Seek the Ancient Chinese Poems

Authored & Translated By Wu Songlin

东北大学出版社

·沈　阳·

中　册

牵　手

野侣骑云鹤，深情两不分。
无缘升古淡[1]，有梦落鸡群。
携手桐阴恶，连镳[2]海气欣。
一朝拂手去，千载断相闻。

【注释】

①古淡：古朴淡雅。②连镳（biāo）：谓骑马同行。镳，马勒。

In Hand

Wild mated on the cloud crane,
Their heart strings are inseparable.
If an ancient, placid mood could be deniable,
Their dream would fall into the chickens again.
Under the shady, hungry plane trees together,
Their bridle breathes the delightful scent of the sea.
Once flicking his or her sleeve in anger, you see,
All their life shan't trace each other.

清　淡

春江何潋滟[1]，对镜柳催眠。
皓月出沧海，明阳落角山。
樱桃垂万树，桑椹挂千田。

园里红尘静，蝶衣处处鲜。

【注释】

①潋滟（liàn yàn）：形容水波荡漾。

Insipidity

On the spring river so rippling,
The willows on the mirror are nodding.
As the bright moon comes out of the sea,
The shining sun has gone down already.
All the trees are thickly hung with cherries,
And all the fields with mulberries.
As the red dust is calm in my garden,
All the butterflies become fresh again.

清　高

傍水问清风，春光盼柳长。
半途回乳燕，长岸放鹅黄。
杜宇啼清月，沙鸥振紫阳。
度微疏雨路，剪草满园香。

Self-Contained

By the water asking after the breeze
From the spring on tiptoe for her long willows,
We saw the halfway return of the fledgling swallows
To the long shore which is light yellow at ease.
In the notes of the cuckoos to the clear moon,
The sandpipers are bracing up the purple sunlight.
Through the rhythm of the pitter-patters so light,
The lawnmower smells sweet in my garden so soon.

清凉女子
To Be a Fresh and Cool Lady

其一

翠鸟飞天去，成仙几日还。
鸡舌啼柳岸，鸭蹼踩河湾。
茅店开竹露，荆扉闭素颜。
三叠[①]篱下闹，空舍对青山。

【注释】

①三叠：古奏曲之法，至某句乃反复再三，称三叠。

One

A kingfisher has gone but returns
A few days later as an immortal, to find
The chicken tongue clucking on the willowy shore,
And the duck webs waddling on the cove,
Where her bothy blooms the bamboo dews,
That closes her pure face inside the gate of thorn…
Coming to the third stanza of the bleeps
Under the roof empty before the green hill.

其二

凉夜星霜梦，研磨半块冰。
琼姿娇玉蕊，雪韵展银凌。
尺素无长短，双鱼有降升。
多情托楚雁，哪赶点心灯？

Two

Her dream at the cool night, starry but
Frosty, has grinded half a cube of ice,
Tender and crystalline in her pistils,
Whose snowy rhyme shows her silvery sleets.
Her letter should not be short or long,
But could be going up or down.
To the amorous wild goose of loyalty,

How to jump up to light up the heart?

其三

清风抚玉帐，窥探倚楼人。
月貌舒眉黛，菱花浅蹙颦[1]。
芳云红豆蔻，细雨惹红唇。
几缕春慵[2]散，幽窗欲探身。

【注释】

①蹙颦（cù pín）：皱眉皱额，忧愁不乐的样子。②春慵：春天的懒散情绪。

Three

Her pure curtain breezes
To pry into the man of that storey,
Who's unknitted her good eyebrows,
Or wrinkled her light brows in the mirror
Whose sweet cloud reddens her bloom of youth,
That mizzles onto her red, jiggled lips,
With a wisp of her lethargic spring,
To lean over her secret window.

其四

晴丝万木摇，柳絮满城飞。
绿水摇金虎[1]，黄花采落晖。

疏狂升月影，澹荡[2]落云帏。
一抹流华去，飘飘不再归。

【注释】

①金虎：比喻金色的阳光。②澹荡：荡漾，飘动。

Four

All the fine threads are wagging
Their willow catkins all over the town.
When the green water ripples its golden tigers,
The yellow flowers pluck the threads of afterglow.
When her moon shadow rises, unbridled again,
Her warm pleasure falls into the cloud curtain.
Once a touch of time flows away,
She would be gone with the wind for ever.

其五

祖山行百里，荒碛[1]涌蓬芽。
清影浮芦剑，娇颜降晚霞。
云根生劲草，山气展奇葩。
闲径连天去，陂陀[2]到断崖。

【注释】

①碛（qì）：浅水中的沙石。②陂陀（pō tuó）：倾斜不平的样子。

Five

A hundred miles to Zushan Mountain
Are budding the wild herbs in the land so barren,
Whose clear shadows are floating one reed sabre,
And dropping the sunglows are their faces so tender.
Strong grasses along the cloud root are growing,
And in the vital hills the exotic flowers are blooming.
On the idle trail that stretches to the skyline,
They follow their own steps to the fault scarp.

其六

厚土山花闹，亭亭伴草生。
携君归大野，为尔采青萍。
着雨萧萧意，临溪隐隐晴。
云龙怀晓月，翠岭寂无声。

Six

The fresh, loamy flowers are bright-coloured,
Grown with the grass like the slim skirts.
Gone back with you to the open country,
And to pick the green duckweeds for you,
My tender affections are drizzling and rustling,
By the brook that grows dimly bright.
Below the dawning moon in the ambitious cloud,

The emerald green mountains are still silent.

其七

屏前成雅趣，对镜且从容。
隐逸行云紧，清明嫩雨松。
花船流宋鼓，饕餮[①]舞唐龙。
代序春秋后，天缘百代丰？

【注释】

①饕餮（tāo tiè）：传说中龙的第五子，是一种存在于传说、想象的神秘怪兽。古书《山海经》介绍其特点是：其状如羊身人面，其目在腋下，虎齿人爪，其音如婴儿。

Seven

Her elegant taste before the curtain
Looks into the mirror, naturally but easily,
To be retreated into the cloud, rolling but pressing,
That brightly drizzles, tenderly but loosely,
Where drums of the Song Dynasty flow her flowery boat,
And dragons of the Tang Dynasty dance vigorously.
After the spring and autumn pass in swift succession,
Would her heavenly bliss be affluent for all generations?

其八

描蚕羞雁字，信笔赤鸦高。
缕缕丝弦缈，悠悠曲底豪。
消凝[1]闻寂灭，落寞对离骚。
我有清音日，挥毫可作刀。

【注释】

①消凝：销魂凝魄，形容极度悲伤。

Eight

The wild geese feel shy to her pencilled brows,
Like a red raven that soars after she freely draws
The sequins of silk strings dimly discernible,
For a melody, unchained and unrestrained.
Clearing up the confusion, she hears a tranquil extinction,
And in solitude, she faces the *Encountering Sorrow*.
On the day of crystal sound,
Her driving the quill may be knifed.

其九

红枫衔落叶，半卷下长亭。
杜宇啼云马[1]，韶光付流星。
凉泉滑兔影[2]，幽谷跳青萍。
浅草横斜岸，苍苔碧水宁。

【注释】

①云马：比喻太阳。②兔影：比喻月光。

Nine

Red maples hold the leaves,
Half-scrolled to down the pavilion.
As the cuckoos chirp to the cloud courser,
The springtime goes like a shooting star.
Down the cool fountain slides a hare shadow,
That skips the green duckweeds off the dingle;
With its sloping shore across the shallow grasses,
The green moss is so tranquil by the green water.

其十

胭脂透水红，玉兔[1]点秋霜。
淡远莲心路，轻浓断藕塘。
青莲成落藕，落藕为情郎。
藕断今朝去，情丝藕里藏。

【注释】

①玉兔：喻指月亮。

Ten

On her red, pervious rouge,

The moon dribs its cold demeanour.
On her way of an ineffable heart,
Her gentle, light air breaks the pond
Whose green lotuses are fully grown
And then down as her dear swain,
Who, once gone, will be still bound
To harbour his threads in the lotus root.

倾　诉

雨天窥孤寒，翻墙欲采薇。
涟漪[①]溪上皱，清影月中飞。
曳露红烛密，摇风绿柳稀。
雨丝弹泪眼，烛焰断窗帏。

【注释】

①涟漪（lián yī）：涟，即水面被风吹起的波纹；漪，即水的波纹。本意就是水面上的微波。

Outpouring

When the wet weather watches his severe, solitary snap stealthily,
He jumps over the wall to gather the vetches.
While the gentle ripples crinkle the runnel,
One clear shadow should be gliding the moon,
That tugs her dews down the close, red candle,
Which is swaying in the sparse, green willows,
To his tearful eyes flipped by the strands of rain,
Before the candle flame breaks inside the curtain.

缺　憾

一斛[1]珠莫恨，秋水染沈檀[2]。
多少相思瘦，无穷玉带宽。
空枝斜倩影，风叶满雕栏。
素月星追去，青娥袅袅寒。

【注释】

①斛（hú）：中国旧量器名，亦是容量单位，一斛本为十斗，后来改为五斗。一斛珠：词牌。②沈檀：用沉檀木做的枕头。

Flaw

One casket of bright pearls gnawed no regret,
When the sandal incense's imbrued by autumn water.
Countless pangs of love were so meager
That boundless belts of jade were broader.
One showy shadow was tilted on the stark twigs,
Whose whiffled leaves filled the carved balustrade.
While the white moon chased the stars like a delicate shade,
The lithe maiden was becoming so cold and fade.

秋 暝

惬意解浮云，秋暝[①]细语归。
情怀流水去，幽径送罗衣。
花露由裁剪，风寒瘦鸟飞。
空山筛月影，落下几斜辉。

【注释】

①秋暝：秋日薄暮之景。

Autumn Evening

Unriddle that cloud drift so agreeable,
And go back at dusk in a whisper so gentle.
My emotions are gone like the water,
With a silken robe that the quiet paths deliver.
Clip those flower dews,
And fly those cold and bony fowls.
While the empty hills griddle the moon's picture,
Some tilted glows will alight, to be sure.

求

抱璞空劳意，精灵不可求。
芳姿明洗眼，香袖暗倾眸。
薄幸观春景，多情上凤楼。
纤毫迷醉眼，拂面使君羞。

Search

You have a soul above buttons, but for nothing,
And to be a genius, but not by seeking.
Wash your eyes bright for a pretty posture,
With the seductive sleeves of a sweet flavour.
Watch that spring so fickle,
And go upstairs susceptible.
The slightest error may be the dust in your eye,
And to kiss your face, don't you become so shy.

人　格

天阶走上格，燕冷紫衣绝。
百啭鸣花柳，双栖弄巧舌。
黑雕击险雪，白马守臣节。
且醉汀云树，西风染半折。

Moral Quality

A celestial step spirals up, and
A cold swallow ceases its purple coat;
A hundred tweedles in the flowers and willows
Wag their facile tongues, but in pairs;
Unlike the dark vulture against sinister snows,
The white horse lives chastely;
Though the trees by the river are drunken,

The west wind has dyed half its world.

人　面

海月悬孤影，无风皎皎行。
一泓萍水镜，百面露真容。
扰攘[①]红尘闹，纷纶[②]意象明。
古来人入世，海月两难清。

【注释】

①扰攘：忙乱，匆忙，混乱。②纷纶：杂乱貌；众多貌。

Face

The sea moon hangs her solitary trace,
That strolls in the still, bright air.
In the water mirror of the duckweeds,
Hundreds of faces show their true colours.
The worldly life in commotion
Has captured numerous bright images.
To be a member of society since olden days,
Neither the sea or the moon can be clear.

人　生

天门九万寻[①]，双履踩天梯。
石柳参差上，浮空断雁低。
行高风袂卷，空谷草凄迷。
出世朝霞亮，衰微月挂西。

【注释】

①寻：古代的长度单位（一寻等于八尺）。

Life

Up the great gate of heaven,
I step on the celestial ladder.
Up the rock willows irregular,
The wild geese float lower.
Higher, my sleeves flap and whirl,
Hollow, the grass veils so chilly;
Aloof, the rosy dawn shines brightly,
Waned, the moon hangs westerly.

人　心

隔帘听夜雨，万缕下天心。
落翠银珠响，鸣琴紫凤[①]吟。
轻灵山更翠，晦暗水弥深。
月照空山静，烟轻草色阴。

【注释】

①紫凤：传说中的神鸟。亦指衣上凤鸟花纹。

The Man's Heart

Behind the curtain, I heard the night rain,
Coming down like all men's hearts again and again.
Down the green, silver pearls jingling,
Down the lyres of purple phoenixes warbling,
Down the nimble hills greener,
Down the dull water deeper,
Before the moon-lit hills are stark and still,
And the hazy hues of grass are gentle.

人性恶

枯柳寒风恶，人情枉断肠。
扬眉谈大义，低首赴琅当[①]。
厚宦和珅灭，薄官赵瑁[②]亡。
黑白描世界，楚汉界河长。

【注释】

①琅当（láng dāng）：也作“锒铛”，在一般的说法中，就是为人带上铁锁链。②赵瑁（mào）：明初礼部尚书，被朱元璋弃市处死。供词牵连各布政使司官吏，系狱拟罪者数万人。此案令核赃株连之人遍天下，中产以上民家被抄杀者不计其数，以此整顿吏治、惩治贪污。

Evil Humanity

Like the withered willows in cold, wicked wind,
The human nature is heart-broken, but in vain.
The arched brows speak a strong sense of justice,
And the bowed head can be thrown into prison.
High officials like He Shen perished like the wind,
Petty officials with Zhao Mao weren't immune to extinction.
In the black-and-white universe that we'd trace,
The boundary river between Chu and Han has a long dimension.

仁　义

栖冰解冷香，宝鉴太聪明。
宁静藏奇险，尘心裹素荣。
锱铢寒暑变，世利夏秋明。
业障生前算，投胎也不清。

Benevolence and Righteousness

Cold sweet can be deciphered by the perched ice,
As the precious mirror too much cunning.
In its serenity stores a strange and sinister service,
Compared with the earthly desires purely swathed in blooming.
To quibble over the cold and hot weather,
The desired profits in autumn and summer are bright.
Because the vile spawn before death should occur,

One's coming down to other's womb won't be so light.

认　识

秋菊野地眠，漫山映青天。
雁阵千浔水，鸿毛百丈泉。
暗香浮皓雪，明月一孤弦。
虬干寒汀后，黄花处处鲜。

Cognition

Autumn chrysanthemums sleep wild,
And shine in the broad daylight.
The wild geese over the wide water so mild
Are winging their springs so light.
As the subtle sweet steers the bright snow,
One bright moon strikes her solitary chord.
After the twisted trunks of the cold islet go,
All yellow flowers will freshly accord.

日　子

梦里红尘起，楼头紫雪急。
树浓风越闹，马倦夜偏骑。
梅子青帘雨，楼台冷月湿。
长天君已老，过眼北风袭。

Day

Touched by the filth of dust mortal in dream,
The purple snow presses upstairs.
As the dense trees catch the furious wind,
The night must needs ride the tired horse.
As the plums are wet on the green curtain,
The cold moon washes the huge tower.
Days and age are telling on you,
That only remember the cold blasts.

容　貌

情愁约小雨，薄晚试梨香。
明月幽花树，清心静雪妆。
枝头蝉闹耳，叶底满春光。
笑点芸窗色，丁冬午夜长。

Visage

Her woeful love sprinkles
In the evening twilight for sweet pears.
To the quiet, moon-lit flower trees,
Her pure heart calms her snowy attire.
In the raspy buzz of cicadas on the branches,
The leaf bases are full of spring splendour.
However, some smiles on my study window

Are tinkling her lengthy midnight.

弱　点

清荷初嫩雨，蘸日野花鲜。
数柄临河淡，三枝向月圆。
细虾藏柳浪，肥蟹映桑田。
半架秋藤乱，寒蛩[①]替杜鹃。

【注释】

①寒蛩（qióng）：深秋的蟋蟀。

Soft Spot

The clear lotus in the fresh, tender rain
Dips the fresh, wild, sunny flowers
Along the washy river with only tree
Flowers round to the moon whence the fine
Shrimps are hidden in the willowy billows,
And the fat crabs are garish in the mulberry field.
When half the trellis loses its cool, the cricket
Chirrup in the vines has replaced the cuckoos.

善　良

轻佻[①]琐屑心，深隐坐渔翁。
依水垂纶[②]下，投竿钓鲤空。
粼粼溪柳岸，唼唼苇荻风[③]。
沧浪移星月，闲池岁月穷。

【注释】

①轻佻（tiāo）：言语举动不庄重，不严肃。②垂纶：垂钓。③唼唼（shà）：象声词。水鸟或鱼的吃食声。荻（dí）：俗称荻草、荻子、霸土剑，系多年生草本水陆两生植物。

Kind-hearted

Of a heart, trivial and giddy,
The fisherman sits deeper,
As an angler by the water,
Who dibs, but ends in bubble.
On the sparkling shore willowy
Nibbles the wind of the reeds,
Over the billowy stars and crescent at ease,
That exhausts the years by the pond so idle.

奢　侈

千金直烫眼，挥手若流风。
行乐多如意，逍遥莫叹穷。

举杯临大海，畅饮下千盅。
北宋徽钦去，皆因酒肉功。

Luxury

One thousand ounces of gold burning in the eyes
Have been waved away like a windflow.
To be gone on the spree satisfies
More than the carefree sighs broken thorough.
Raise my wine before the open sea,
And quaff a thousand glasses.
The captured emperors of the Earlier Song Dynasty
Took the credit for the meat and wine in masses.

生　活

笙歌别燕语，流景四十年。
倦客回家日，秋风铁骨天。
三杯娇艳色，一点画皮鲜。
借问生花笔，霜痕几刻欢？

Life

Farewell, my swallow words of revelry
That flow for forty years.
On the day back wearily,
The iron-flesh in the autumn wind comes into the ears.
Three glasses of delicate and charming colours

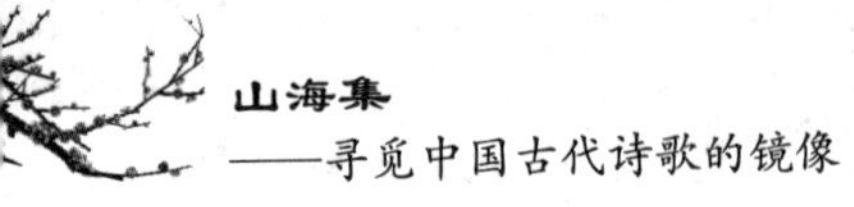

Have dabbed one fresh, painted skin.
Tell me, the gifted pen that bears flowers,
How long will your frosty traces be merry again?

生之乐

生命论春秋，凡人有竟日。
荣华恋广厦，富贵蔑蒺藜。
草舍空墟守，食蔬自隐逸。
茧房缠柳絮，蝶粉数花实。

The Pleasure in Life

Life cycles from spring to autumn,
And man has his final day.
Glory loves its large houses,
And wealth smears the wild rues.
The hut watches its wasteland,
And the retreat opts for vegetarian diets.
When willow catkins tangle the cocoon nursery,
White butterflies may count their pollens.

生　死

死者无交契[1]，活人有往来。
消冰涵水镜，透雪掩泉台。
旧日和珅过，多年夏禹材。
金盘横赤鲤，自怨曝红腮。

【注释】

①交契：情谊，交情。

Life and Death

The deceased is not cordial,
But the living is social.
The ice's thawed in the water mirror,
But the full snow covers the nether.
Former days, greedy officials were gone,
For years, they rose in the world all along.
The red carp on the gold plate
Repined at its own red gills, but too late.

失　势

万里青锋地，连天势未销。
平芜沧海阔，蔓草断云消。
暮色长城落，霜风易水凋。
腾雄缭紫气，白露散花桥。

Failure

Blue-tipped to the earth's end,
His powerful thunder is uncorroded.
On the far-flung plain, the sea should end
Its sod grass below the cloud demoded.

As the Great Wall gloams,
The Yishui River fades away in frosty wind.
Amid the mighty, ruddy light that roams,
The white dews drift on the bridge so kind.

书　梦

衔书①行古道，梦远鸟难飞。
弃落观天府②，悲鸣看太微③。
寒云闲走马，霞照静攸归④。
只为⑤鸢禽乐，高翔遍九围⑥。

【注释】

①衔书：化典"飞凤衔书"，寓意有大旺文书、考学升迁等文上之喜。②天府：南斗之主星，属土，取卦为坤，司任脉，主守成。天府星又称"福星"，主财帛、田宅，为衣食之星。③太微：古代星官名，三垣之一，位于北斗之南，轸、翼之北，大角之西，轩辕之东。诸星以五帝座为中心，作屏藩状。或者用指朝廷或帝皇之居。④攸（yōu）归：攸：所；归：归属。意即责任、义务等有所归属，不容推卸。⑤鸢（yuān）：老鹰。⑥九围：九州。

The Dream of Books

My books walk on the old road
And dream further than birds can hold,
Falling down to watch the Heaven,
Or whine at the Grandeur which will govern.
To be an ambler under the cold cloud,
Who would return in his calm, rosy cloud.

Only for the pleasure of an eagle or a fowl,
Let my books soar up to the earth pole.

水　墨

烟紫落波青，兰台淡墨横。
流云风染色，挥雾雨争鸣。
月步青山静，河冲野雀惊。
疏枝剥柳意，又是雪来轻。

Ink

The purple smoke falls on the green billow,
And crosses its light ink on the orchid table.
In the wind that dyes the floating cloud,
The wigwagging fog-drips contend aloud.
As the moon steps on the still, green hills,
The river scours those shocking sparrows.
After the sparse boughs strip the willow's idea,
Another gentle snow shall turn up here.

瞬　间

十载易销沈①，贤愚解袂②间。
红云辞柳岸，白月过溪关。
野渡惊沙鹭，空城泣苦蝉。
尘埃吹倦旅，烟水盼家还。

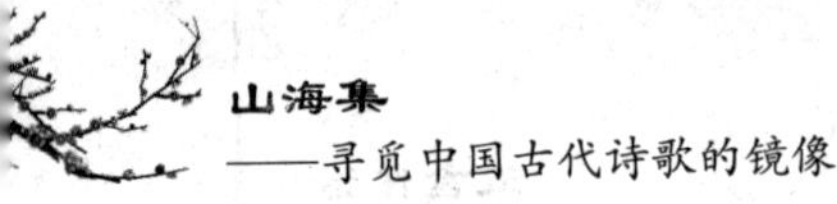

【注释】

①销沈：消沉，消逝。②袂（mèi）：衣袖。解袂即离别。

In a Split Second

A decade goes easily,
Good or bad, it seems to be stripped,
Like a red cloud from the shore willowy,
Or a white moon across the pass streamy,
Whence the ferry egrets may be shocking,
And the evacuated city weeps its bitter cicadas,
Where a tired dust might be whiffling,
On tiptoe for the misty waters to be returning.

太

穷途鸟倦路，老树有深痕。
次第[①]蓬山梦，迢迢望海魂。
南柯沉紫燕，北岛起昆仑。
夜静听莺啭，微澜看子孙。

【注释】

①次第：依次，按照顺序或依一定顺序，一个接一个地。

Too Far

Birds on the way tired out
Have gashed the old trees
Graded into a fairy dream
Gazing out to the sea soul
Whose south swallow's sinking,
Whose north isle's soaring.
To the silent nightingales,
The ripples warble their offsprings.

汤　河

汤河收暮色，落日滔春晖。
树影斜白月，苍山嵌玉霏①。
藤萝横甬道，钟磬铁鸟②飞。
几许残芳照，伶仃③入绣闱。

【注释】

①玉霏：漂浮的花瓣。②铁鸟：比喻飞机。③伶仃：也作“零丁”，孤独无依的样子。

The Soup River

The soup gloams
And scoops her spring sunshine
Tilted by a white moon in the wood
Of the dark hills wedged by the drizzles.
Shaggy with ivy, the paved path
Flushes a flock of birds in the toll
Whose sweet sunset glows
Enter the silken screen in solitude.

桃花源
Arcadia

其一

蝉鸣兔影①中，叵测②有螳螂。
岂料花阴后，折魂傍③雀藏。
机关全算尽，举弹射萧墙。
世外都说好，桃源也相戕。

【注释】

①兔影：月影。②叵（pǒ）测：不可探测，险恶。③傍（bàng）：近也。④萧墙：当门而立的小墙，即影壁。⑤戕（qiāng）：杀。

One

Cicada chirping in the hare shades
Hides an unpredictable story of the mantis,
Who's never imagined that behind the flower shades
A siskin waits upon it, somewhere.
After all their tricks have been used up,
A slingshort is discharged by the wall.
Beyond this world, all declare that it is so good, but
Who knows the fairyland goes unneighbourly!

其二

悠悠山坳里，渺渺荡炊烟。
一盏枝头醉，三杯好种田。
飘然寻帝子①，帝子举白帆。
且问何方去，夕阳②可下船。

【注释】

①帝子：传说上古时期姜姓部落的首领，少而聪颖，三天能说话，五天能走路，三年知稼穑之事。他一生为百姓办了许多好事：教百姓耕作，百姓得以丰食足衣；为了让百姓不受病疾之苦，他尝遍了各种药材，自己一日中七十次毒；他又做乐器，让百姓懂得礼仪，为后世所称道。其族人最初的活动地域在今陕西的南部，后来沿黄河向东发展，与黄帝发生冲突。在阪泉之战中，帝子被黄帝战败，帝子部落与黄帝部落合并，组成华夏族。帝子是中华民族公认的人文始祖之一，也称神农氏。②夕阳：谐音“西洋”。

Two

Remote in the col,
Chimney smoke curls up evermore.
Cheers to the branches so tipsy,
And three cups work the field merrily.
Leisurely, let's look for the nymph,
Who might be white-sailed in triumph.
Tell me where to go?
To get off the setting sun, you know.

退一步

竹影惧风飘，平明雪阵来。
松针扶骨瘦，柏叶锁灵台[①]。
山裹乾坤闭，河邀日月开。
苍苍蒹葭里，绿影让人猜。

【注释】

①灵台：《晋书·天文志》称："明堂西三星曰灵台。"在太微垣的西南垣墙外，有明堂三星，在明堂之西，又有灵台三星。上古时，将皇家的天文台称为灵名，用以观测天象。《晋书·天文志》曰："灵台，观台也，主观云物，察符瑞，候灾变也。"是说测候天象以占卜军国大事吉凶，是古代灵台和天文学家为皇家服务的主要功能之一。

One Back Step

Bamboos in a blown terror
Are dawned by the snow flurry,
Whence the pine needles are skinny,
And the soul is locked up by the cedar.
Hills are plugged up with the universe,
And the river opens up to the sun and the moon.
Among the reeds which are dark green,
The green shade shakes a suspicious verse.

忘　本

才气卷江山，微光陋室寒。
平心临躁世，风翦柳烟残。
孤月开青眼，香荷闭紫坛。
红尘身是客，对影有悲欢。

Ungrateful

With a sweeping esprit,
The shed shimmers its severe snap.
With a normal heart in the fickle world,
The windflow wipes out the foggy willows.
When the solitary moon opens her vernal breeze,
The sweet lotus shuts its purple shells.
Under the hospitable roof of the human society,

There's a note of pessimism in our shadows.

忘　记
Forget

其一

忘筌[①]游戴水，聚散不通贤[②]。
双枕尤乘暖，孤眠正可怜。
推诚斟月下，慷慨醉风前。
此去人心远，他年忘旧欢。

【注释】

①忘筌（quán）：忘记了捕鱼的筌。比喻目的达到以后就忘记了原来的凭借。②通贤：通达贤能。

One

Kick over the ladder, and across the Daihe river,
To meet and part, there's no sensible allusion.
While the two pillows still enjoy the warmth,
The solitary sleep shows so pitiable.
Perfectly frank to drink below the moon, the soul
With profound passion's drunken when the wind blows.
Once gone, the heart would be gone afar,
And the old romance could be forgettable.

其二

凝脂罗衣淡，轻思处子柔。
秋花摇醉梦，春鸟返平洲。
逸柳喧山静，琼枝倚绿丘。
携君同入梦，箫管任啾啁①。

【注释】

①啾啁（jiū zhōu）：象声词，形容鸟叫的声音。泛指繁杂细碎声。也作“啁啾”。

Two

Her bitty cream tastes thin in the silken robe,
Her gentle and virgin spirit feels so supple.
As the autumn flowers joggle her drunken dreams,
The spring fowl could go back to his flat isle.
When her willowy leisure bustles its quiet hills,
The jasper boughs would lean on the green mound.
Wafted by sleep into the land of dreams together,
Our flute would be twittering with delight.

忘记过去

游鸿掠草庐，杜甫已寒荒。
晴翠连晨苑，幽峦钓晚塘。
鲜枝啼小杏，白羽照明妆。

作古东流去，诗心客冢霜。

Forget the Past

A swimming swan swept past the cottage,
Where Du Fu, the poet was subject to cold shortage.
As the sunny green met the morning garden,
The late pond angled for its quiet mountain,
Whose little apricots in fresh branches twittered,
With the white wings brightly chartered.
Like the river he flowed eastward,
Leaving his poetic heart to the white tomb forward.

伪　装

闲宴驾南城，杨花似雪明。
临门开绣户，倒屣[①]下阶迎。
淑气出肥脍[②]，新声入嫩晴[③]。
浮伪[④]频对酒，伴醉有黄莺[⑤]。

【注释】

①倒屣：倒穿着鞋，形容店老板热情迎客。②淑气：温和之气。脍(kuài)：切碎的肉。肥脍，指美餐。③嫩晴：初晴。④浮伪：虚伪。⑤黄莺：也称黄鹂、黄鸟，此处喻指三陪小姐。

Masking

Fete my wheel down the south town,

Thru the poplar blossoms snow-bright all along.
Open the door of your noble house,
And slip on slippers hurriedly down your course,
Serve your minced meat like a fairy tale,
With your fresh tone that shines a tender sale.
In such a truthless toast,
An oriole will be my drunken partner if I boast.

我是谁

存道为元君[①]，殷勤去宦游。
千山皆秀木，万水尽清流。
大意恣疏野，翻船恶水沟。
汉臣无丑虏[②]，败绩自俘囚[③]。

【注释】

①元君：贤德的国君。②丑虏：对敌人的蔑称。③败绩：军队溃败或事业失利。俘囚：在战争中被掳获的人。

Who Am I

My reasonable moral for the sage
Courted a government service
With all the wood full of natural grace
And all the waters that clearly flow.
Vigorous, incautious, and audacious,
I was capsized by the vicious gutter.
A good subject should not be captured,
And my defeat was self-imposed.

我是鱼

绿稻戏三花①，涸池欲振鳞②。
回翔急掉尾，跳掷③对蛙唇。
鸥鸟追阴兔④，云霞踏日轮。
游仙邀我去，鱼梵⑤大江滨。

【注释】

①三花：鳌花、鳊花、鲫花3种黑龙江名鱼，此处泛指鱼。②涸（hé）：水干。振鳞：指摆鳍游水状。③跳掷：上下跳跃。④阴兔：喻指月亮。⑤鱼梵（fàn）：敲木鱼和诵经念佛之声。

I Am a Fish

The green paddies are sporting the fish,
But the dry pond tries to be sailable.
To swirl slowly, I turn my tail fast,
Flip and skip onto a frog lip.
As the heron runs after the hidden Hare,
The rosy cloud steps on the solar disk.
Let me go with an immortal,
To the waterfront that is chanting sutra.

我要飞

紫桐花未落，越鸟去无声。
野径扶云暗，幽怀自负明。
冲天驰月镜，过岭走金星[①]。
千里寻芳印，携风雨不惊。

【注释】

①金星：比喻太阳。

I Want to Fly

Purple plane trees are still blooming,
And away the silent birds are flying.
Murkily, the wild trail is cloudy,
Clearly, the bosom is secret in vain glory.
Lofty, the mirror of the moon is sailing,
And beyond the ridges, Venus is sliding.
While seeking my sweet stamp remotely,
The rain will be calm still, though windy.

无　忧

随缘聚散间，悲喜两无愁。
一剪青丝尽，三生梦幻游。
莲花空入镜，渔鼓[①]落萍洲。
人世怀佳梦，穷途不隐忧[②]。

【注释】

①渔鼓：又称道筒、竹琴。简板，又称简子。流行于湖北、湖南、山东、广西等地区。②隐忧：内心郁郁寡欢，犹有心事，心中有不可言喻的惆怅、忧虑。

Free of Care

Come and go, be it natural,
Delight and dole, never be sorrowful.
Black hair, one cut to lose all,
Of the three births, let our dreams go.
After the lotus flowers are lost in the mirror,
The fishing drum drops into the duckweed water.
When the world has a dream sweeter,
Our dead end has no secret sorry deeper.

息　怒

楼前沧海怒，翻手触天心。
寒水浮烟阔，青云倚梦暗。
逐风腾怒焰，卷雨泻天禽。
砸碎乾坤后，长天百木森。

Calm Your Anger

Before the tower, hear the sea's anger,
Turn my finger, onto the heart of the nature.

On the cold water floats the wide vapour,
In my dumb dream clouded much greener.
To be a wind chaser, free my rising anger,
In such rough weather, let the fowls pour.
Crash the universe thereafter,
All wood under the vast of heaven grow fresher.

习　惯

利刃欺冰冷，凉风扫乱缨。
南山驰老马，北海渡长鲸。
肝胆残辕照，红心四野明。
贫寒独守志，富贵也风清。

Habit

Sharp, icy blade
Sweeps its cluttered tassels
Of the nag to the south hills
And of the huge whale in the north sea
With its courageous shaft in the sunset glows
Whose red heart has enkindled the open country
Where the pauper preserves his own chastity
And the rich has a clear sense of integrity.

限　度

官微行败冰，权重暗怀私。
老虎螭盘[①]险，苍蝇溷[②]粪离。
潜形霜似铁，侧翅雨如痴。
缚虎长缨在，直言社稷危。

【注释】

①螭（chī）盘：如虎之蹲踞。②溷（hùn）：肮脏，厕所。

Limit

A petty official walks on the crushed ice,
And a powerful official is preoccupied with private cares.
When the tigers are crouching murderously,
The flies are droning about the latrine nastily.
An invisible frost is cold as iron,
And a winged rain falls within its idiotic line.
Long ropes here to tie up the tigers
Bluntly foretell the teetering state altars.

小　鸟

临涧闻山道，蒙笼[①]羽客飞。
冲花啼菡萏[②]，拂柳啭蔷薇。
汉地浮云色，胡天览镜辉。
好风腾羽翼，一去不东归。

【注释】

①蒙笼：草木茂盛貌。羽客为双关，也借指道士。②菡萏（hàn dàn）：荷花。

Little Bird

My creek sniffs the mountain path
Which wings lushly and chirps
To the lotus flowers near the willowy
Trills in the wild roses.
Southward, the cloud is drifting,
Northward, the mirror is shining.
On the blessed wind, the wing soars up,
And will never return from the west.

心灵陷阱
The Snare of Soul

其一

幻境三千尺，情思万里长。
开山石斧烂，播雨大风狂。
妙手花篷乱，挥鞭紫梦扬。
浮云飘假梦，满眼是稻粱[①]。

【注释】

①稻粱：化典“稻粱谋”，稻粱本指禽鸟寻觅食物。杜甫《同诸公登慈恩寺塔》：“君看随阳雁，各有稻粱谋。”亦用作比喻人之谋求衣食和基本生活必需。

One

Three thousand feet, the shadowland surveys,
Ten thousand miles, the emotion weighs.
To cut the mountain, the stone axe is rotten,
To seed the rain, the wind howls again.
Magic handed, the flower stands are fluffy,
To wave the whip, the purple dreams are flappy.
With the cloud the false dreams are flapping,
And before the eye, rice and millet are enticing.

其二

童心长一分，豆蔻重三钱。
禾垅翻长卷，文房画稻田。
秋霜人自叹，梨雪有谁怜？
悲喜蜉蝣地，平生莫负天。

Two

The kid’s heart grows a bit longer,
With the budding age weighed heavier.

To ridge the volumes so long,
The paddy field can be drawn.
Before the autumn frost we sigh,
But who'd pity the snowy pears so high?
Agreeably grieved at the dayflies,
Don't be false to the lifelong skies.

其三

高情[①]多自负，入眼裹浮尘。
浼浼[②]一张嘴，狺狺[③]两片唇。
孤魂来探穴[④]，魅影去封神。
放眼追天幕，雷车滚早春。

【注释】

①高情：高隐超然物外之情。②浼浼（měi）：水盛貌。③狺狺（yín）：犬吠声。④探穴：中医里面找穴位或风水师找墓穴的行为。

Three

An ideal soul tends to be the fly on the wheel,
That tucks the floating dust you can feel.
Silver-tongued,
With the barking lips prolonged,
The wandering soul comes for trial boring,
And the goblin shadows for apotheosizing.
Open your eyes to the canopy,
The wheel of thunders rolls to the spring so early.

其四

率性仰红尘，浮光竖子心。
任凭秋韵紧，不惧冷霜侵。
帘雨遮明月，飘风透树阴。
迢遥[①]行陌野，虫蚁闹寒林。

【注释】

①迢遥（tiáo yáo）：遥远貌。

Four

Willfully, face up the human society,
Shiny, like a stripling heart ordinary.
Before the autumn rhymes so tight,
Let's be undaunted to the cold frosts so light.
When the blind rain veils the bright moon,
The whirlwind pours in the shade at noon.
Thru the open country from afar,
The insects are buzzing the cold wood as they are.

其五

粪泥独傲世，大气啸高狂。
枯叶云烟散，轻枝柳絮扬。
斗霜花霰[①]短，经雪玉冰长。
铁血折不断，沉沙枉自伤。

【注释】

①霰（xiàn）：亦称“雹”。

Five

To be sapropel, to be proud alone,
Of free air, he's wrong in the head of his own.
Like the dead leaves flying away,
The gentle willow catkins are gone without delay.
Frosty graupels are short,
And the snowy ices are purely sought.
An iron blood in sand can't be broken,
It will be self-inflicted but in vain.

其六

海马冲天去，蹄轻瘦影飘。
秋风嗔噪雀，暮雨怨啼枭。
贼子妆成鬼，封狐[①]化作妖。
河中没涨水，惊梦断蓝桥[②]。

【注释】

①封狐：大狐。②蓝桥：化典《庄子》中一个哀怨凄婉的爱情故事。说的是一个叫尾生的痴心汉子和心爱的姑娘约会在桥下，可心上人迟迟没来赴约，不幸的是，大水却涨上来了，这个痴情汉为了信守诺言坚持不肯离去，最后，竟然抱桥柱溺亡。据说，他们约定的地点叫蓝桥。尾生所抱的梁柱，也和他一道成为守信的标志。

Six

Soar, the sea horse,
Scud, its skinny shade on light hooves.
Angrily, the sparrow chirps in the autumn wind,
Melancholy, the owl caws in the dusk rain.
As the evil man pretends to be a spook,
The huge fox turns to a vengeful ghost.
If the tide is least at the flood,
The nightmare's broken by the blue bridge.

其七

云纱玉榻中，残月久成眠。
金玉缠腰阔，银珠滚梦圆。
闲居徒枉费，要路为争权。
挥霍阴晴雨，苔钱[①]四季天。

【注释】

①苔钱：苔点形圆如钱，故曰“苔钱”。

Seven

His cloudy voile in luxurious couch
Has slumbered soon in the wasting moon
Whence he wallows in wealth,
And rolls in silver, round pearls.

Leisurely, he schemes to no avail,
Critically, he competes for power.
Cloudy or sunny, he's flush with his money,
Which is moss-like in the circle of seasons.

其八

闭户锁孤宅，藏心袖底幽。
遮天辞酷暑，掩梦戏冷秋。
寂雨新鱼雁[①]，飞红老绿洲。
蜗居怀广厦，方丈[②]稻粱谋。

【注释】

①鱼雁：书信。②方丈：一丈四方之室。又作方丈室、丈室。

Eight

Shut the door, lock the lonely house,
And hide the heart into the secret sleeves.
Shroud the sky from the sweltering summer,
And cover the dream to trifle with cold autumn.
New letters in the still rain
Are gliding their red to the old, green isle.
In humble abode for a liberal edifice,
Ten cubits square is shifted for rice and millet.

其九

萧疏[①]扑落叶，满目是清嘉[②]。
腐草翻云树，垂杨唱碧纱。
猧[③]鼻寻宿鸟，猫爪叩飞鸦。
执意黄泉路，寒尸裹乱麻。

【注释】

①萧疏：萧条荒凉。②清嘉：美好貌。③猧（wō）：小狗。

Nine

Desolate, the falling leaves are rustling,
Everywhere, it describes the terrific beauty.
In the rotten weeds are rootled the cloud woods,
While the weeping willow's warbling to the green gauze.
When the puppy's nosing his night bird,
The cat's claws are clouting the gliding raven.
To take the road to ruin,
The cold corpse may be clothed with coarse hemps.

其十

名利飞蝇蚋[①]，银缸[②]破梦来。
生前难仗义，死后不疏财。
自在隔尘世，逍遥冷梦台。
远山风物在，心锁落尘埃。

【注释】

①蝇蚋（ruì）：苍蝇和蚊子。②银缸：银白色的灯盏、烛台。此处是双关。

Ten

Fame and gain are flying like the flies and gnats,
And coming into the broken dream in the silver candle.
If he stands not for honour while living,
He will disdain no wealth after death,
When, perfectly comfortable in the underworld,
He will answer none in his cold dream.
The sight are still there in the hills afar,
But the locked heart falls into the dust.

其十一

行杯观月醉，客梦对花癫。
镜染桃林艳，波翻钓篓鲜。
吞风凉水润，晒露暖石干。
急马求鸾凤，寒冰百丈悬。

Eleven

My cup watches the drunken moon,
Deranged to the drifting, dreamy flowers.
When the peach forest feels a tinge of fresh mirror,

The wave rootles my delicate creel.
When the wind swallows the sleek, cold water,
The sunned dews has dried the warm stones.
When the swift steed woos his conjugal felicity,
Gigantic sheets of ice are hanging the wastes.

其十二

临海自无尘，行舟百度深。
浮萍缠碧树，蝼蚁咬黄昏。
云里寻花叶，潭中找菜根①。
芳菲清雪后，风信②更牵魂。

【注释】

①“潭中”句：化典《菜根谭》。该书是以处世思想为主的格言式小品文集，采用语录体，糅合了儒家的中庸思想、道家的无为思想和释家的出世思想。②风信：风信子。

Twelve

The dustless seaside
To the abyssal boat
From the green wood by the duckweeds
Where mole crickets and ants are gnawed into the dusk
Seeks its flower leaves in the cloud
Or its roots in the deep pool.
After the clear, sweet snow,
The hyacinth stirs my soul still more.

其十三

浅嫩流尘妒，黄莺百啭[1]声。
飘风[2]凌子夜，淫雨浸三更。
缥缈猿猱[3]笑，沉吟草木惊。
绿烟浮野草，飞燕也狰狞。

【注释】

①啭（zhuàn）：鸟婉转地鸣叫。②飘风：旋风；暴风。③猿猱（náo）：泛指猿猴。

Thirteen

A soft, simple envy flows
And trills its golden oriole
At midnight that gathers the whirlwinds,
And soaks the excessive rain.
Illusory, the apes and macaques smile,
Lost in thought, the woods startle.
Over the azure mists on the wild grass,
The flying swallows are also hideous.

其十四

才情负子君，执念起欢荣。
素昧朱绂[1]暗，平生紫燕[2]明。
塘蛙能鼓噪，螃蟹可横行。

瘸马嘶鸣去，穿石细雨惊。

【注释】

①素昧：素，即“向来”。昧，即“不了解”。朱绂（fú）：古代礼服上的红色蔽膝，后常作为官服的代称，也指做官。②紫燕：也称“紫燕骝”，古代骏马名。

Fourteen

A good wit deceives
Its joyous, obsessive glory
Unaware of the dark red knee-covers
Though bright before the purple, lifelong swallows.
Frogs can croak in the pond,
And crabs can crawl sideways;
As the lame whinny has gone,
The constant dropping will be startled in dribbles.

其十五

犷俗敲雪信，梅底酿春痕。
远岫[①]来描黛，春风去扫门。
扬花飞太古，携雨过昆仑。
举世寻论语，明德在野村。

【注释】

①岫（xiù）：山洞。

Fifteen

The snow letters are knocked uncouthly,
To brew their spring shade below the wintersweet.
As the distant hills turn up to paint the brows,
Such a spring has gone to sweep the door.
As the catkins are adrift and pristine,
They're taking the rain to the Kunlun Mountains.
As all the world seeks the *Analects* of Confucius,
The bright virtue lives in the wild country.

其十六

黄叶飘旋地，鸭梨挂满山。
梦中闲影瘦，月底散眉弯。
折取三秋绿，斜阳照铁斑。
深山人莫采，烂漫自凋颜。

Sixteen

Yellow leaves flap and whirl,
Silhouetted by the pears all over the hill.
Her shadow tight in the dream so idle
Bends her brows loose under the moon.
Snap the latest green,
In the setting sun upon the iron stain.
But pick her not in the remote mountain,

Because she'd fade away after romantic bloom

其十七

黄鹤谢清虚[①]，尘云弄步飞。
齐腰缠万贯，对月佩淫威。
沉羽疏林下，昂胸旷野归。
无心随百鸟，山后杏花肥。

【注释】

①清虚：清净虚无。

Seventeen

The yellow crane leaves its pure emptiness,
And flies into the dust cloud,
Which wallows in money,
Wearing the despotic power to the moon.
Sinking down the thinning forest,
Its puffed-up chest returns to the moor.
Mindless to follow all other fowls,
The apricot blossoms are hanging heavy behind the hill.

其十八

金铃挂九霄，金缎照水明。
金瑟弹花影，金风洗树声。
金石诚闭锁，金玉患开屏。

金马传戎册，金龟守令名。

Eighteen

Gold bell hangs in the empyrean,
And gold satin shines in the water clean;
Gold lute' s played to the flower shadows,
And gold breeze bathes the wood news.
Metals and stones are closed down truthfully,
Gold and jade worry about the shield openly;
As the armoured horse confides the art of war,
The golden tortoise keeps its good name all the more.

其十九

秋千冲乱雨，棋案崩秋风。
悬瀑惊雷动，寒云裹电红。
腊烟三万丈，湍气九霄通。
激箭回流险，平川水镜空。

Nineteen

The seesaw messed up in the rain,
And the chessboard tumbles by the autumn wind.
The waterfalls are thundering,
And the cold cloud rolls the red bolts of lightning.
The dried smoke billows down a hundred thousand metres,
And its scouring vapour soars up into the highest sky.

A swashing arrow flies into the narrow backflow,
And the water mirror on the plain looks so hollow.

其二十

潮信叩幽燕，追芳盛夏天。
月凉渤海汛，日暖戴河欢。
疏响三秋阔，飘萧百里鲜。
蓼花摇静雪，白鹭绕空舷。

Twenty

The tide washes up the serene shore,
After the sweet depth of summer.
As the Bohai sea is cold in a moon-lit murmur,
Merry and mild, it is to shine on the Daihe River.
Sparsely rangy, the late autumn is noisy,
And a 100-mile radius scuds to a fresh whistle.
As the smartweed' s flowers joggle their still snow,
One egret is hovering over the hollow gunwale.

其二十一

前路设荆棘，穷途闭馆荒。
门深空漫步，幽径更徜徉。
世象丝丝隐，烟霞缕缕藏。
形骸颓自放[①]，达命[②]已心亡。

【注释】

①“形骸”句：放浪是指放纵、不受拘束。形骸：人的形体、形迹。指行为不受世俗礼法的约束，旷达豪爽，行事不拘一格。这里整体是说：想豁达不羁，是办不到的。②达命：知命。

Twenty-One

Before, the road is locked in brambles,
Dead down, the closed hall looks lorn.
As the deep, hollow door strolls,
The serene path roams more along.
Hide all threads of the world picture,
With the wisps of coloured hazes;
Let the body be given to sensual pleasure,
The heart dies when resigned to fate like blazes.

其二十二

鸡窗[①]恨酒幡，半盏话联翩[②]。
忧乐通花梦，疏狂散柳烟。
马头急刺剑，触影乱着鞭。
斩断恩仇树，削红紫陌[③]前。

【注释】

①鸡窗：书斋。②联翩：指鸟飞的样子，形容连续不断。③紫陌：大路。陌，本是指田间的小路，这里借指道路。紫，是指道路两旁草木的颜色。

Twenty-Two

A wineshop flag hangs on my grudged study,
That drifts half a bowl of the tongue—
Sad or glad, go to the dream of flowers,
Rash or nesh, scatter the willowy smokes.
Over the horse head, thrust my sword,
And to the shades, snap my whips.
Chop off the tree of love and hate,
Before spall the red avenue.

其二十三

囚鸟怪鞭蓉①，披襟②盛夏寒。
有心千丈跃，无意百花残。
啼向云绝唱，关情夜已阑。
鸣娇千百度，逢场莫强欢。

【注释】

①鞭蓉：水莲。②披襟：敞开衣襟。多喻舒畅心怀。

Twenty-Three

A caged bird blames the waterlily,
Exhilarated by the cold depth of summer.
His heart springs high purposely,
When the flowers fade down unconsciously.

Chirp to the cloud like a swan song,
His closed passion breaks up late at night.
Chirp and chirp lovely all along,
But for a pillow fight, be forced not to mirth so wrong.

其二十四

流沙度玉门，吻落美人腮。
桃色羞归棹[①]，梨花落镜台。
红楼春又闭，青梦几回开。
朗月胡杨路，娇颜尽可哀?

【注释】

①归棹（zhào）：归舟。

Twenty-Four

The drift sand through the Pass of Jade
Kissed down the cheek of the eye-catchers
Whose peachy lips were shy and roamed afar,
And whose pear flowers fell onto the dressing table.
After the red mansion closed her spring,
When would the spring dream bloom again?
On the way of the moon-lit euphrates poplar,
Their tender faces were bewailed to such an extent.

其二十五

青钱[1]默默游，雁路驶蓬舟。
绝响星河转，孤萤翠谷流。
金弦拨旧恨，玉骨惹新愁。
野马思奔泻，云缰不可收。

【注释】

①青钱：质地为铜、铅、锡合金。比喻有才学的人。

Twenty-Five

The copper coin wanders silently,
On the goose way that sails his boat,
With a long-lost run in the starry river,
And flows thru the green vale like a glowworm.
Gold strings! Twang your old remorse!
Jade bones! Stir up your new sorrows!
Rush down, like a wild horse!
Rush out, like a cloud uncontrollable!

其二十六

听雨不执情，中年百味明。
牵衣常顾影，迈步慎操行。
仕路浮冰裂，情丝野火惊。
童颜刚踏雪，鹤发古稀声。

Twenty-Six

Cling not to the rain in a foolish passion,
In mid-life a hundred flavours will be brighter
And tug at the sleeves in self-pity more again,
Which is stridden for a cautious moral character.
On the official way of the floe cracks,
Such a passion shocks the wildfire then.
As the ruddy complexion braves the snowy tracks,
The white-haired grows into three score and ten.

心　态

人心似水心，万古进徽音①。
飒飒刷瑶草，萧萧洗遗金②。
晴涟拂玉袖，冻翠落梅襟。
宽窄弹韶乐③，方圆弄宝琴。

【注释】

①徽音：犹德音，指令闻美誉。②遗（wèi）金：遗落的金子。③韶乐：史称舜乐，起源于5000多年前，为上古舜帝之乐，是一种集诗、乐、舞为一体的综合古典艺术。

State of Mind

Man's heart is like water,
That spurts its moral tones forever,
Combing the immortal grass that's soughing,
And washing the lost gold that's rustling.
When jade sleeves are kissed by the fine ripples,
The cold green drops its wintersweet news.
Broad or narrow, in the cheers of the jubilant melody,
Square or round, the precious lute's played merrily.

心　智

高风邀沛雨，巧智自愚拙。
鱼背图朝日，狼牙吐血舌。
丈夫伏潜志，孱妇①舍名节。
坟冢高千丈，孤魂鬼门决②。

【注释】

①孱（chán）妇：软弱无能的妇女。②决：弃世绝尘。通“诀”。分别。

Mind

The high blast invites a good rainfall,
And the quick wit is graceless, evermore.
As the fishback draws its sun in the morning,

Its tongue of blood the wolf's fang is wagging.
To be a man, he should incubate his will,
To be a puny woman, she gives her chaste tale.
A tomb measures ten thousand feet,
Whose gate will end its wandering soul.

行　动

娴花观静水，梨雨看秋声。
休问梨上梦，先说树下情。
老蝉循序瘦，新木隐约明。
代序[①]轮回路，车轮滚滚行。

【注释】

①代序：时序更替。

Action

Refined flowers watch the quiet water,
And the pear rains see the autumn sound.
Ask not the dream on the pears,
Let's say the passions under the trees.
When the old cicadas are thin in proper order,
The new wood would be bright subtly.
On the way of transmigration,
The wheel will be rolling on.

幸 福

福祸轮流转，形骸[①]莫忘情。
丹墀无宠命[②]，紫禁有恩荣。
闾井[③]穷通过，关山苦乐行。
三尸焚浪死[④]，契阔不虚生[⑤]。

【注释】

①形骸：人的躯体。②丹墀（chí）：宫殿前的红色台阶及台阶上的空地。宠命：加恩特赐的任命。封建社会中对上司任命的敬辞。③闾（lǘ）井：居民聚居之处。④三尸：又称“三彭”或“三虫”。道教认为，人身中有三条虫，称为上尸、中尸、下尸，分别居于上、中、下三丹田。浪死：徒然死去；白白送死。⑤契阔：勤苦，劳苦。虚生：徒然活着，白活。

Happiness

Weal and woe take turns,
Man, don't you be unruffled by emotion.
If the red step is alien to a nomination of grace,
The forbidden city has its glories honours.
Fortunes are predestined in our residential quarters,
Through the bitter-sweet passes and mountains.
Even the three gods within are burnt in the fierce fires
Of affliction, how could our hands of toil live in vain?

学 会
Learn

其一

疏雨过蓬门，蕉窗夜里敲。
浮萍横紫梦，列宿[①]掩黄茅[②]。
断梦谁惊醒，留春冷月嘲。
昏灯徒照壁，逆旅漱眉梢。

【注释】

①列宿（xiǔ）：众星宿。特指二十八宿。②黄茅：多年生，丛生草本。

One

A few drops of rain audibly down my wooden door
Knocked the night window with the banana leaves.
When my purple dream was athwart the duckweeds,
All the stars were closing the tangleheads.
Who's jerked me awake now?
Leaving the spring moon to the coldly biting sheaves.
In the glimmers on the blank wall,
The worldly intrigues are rinsing my tips of brow.

其二

白发当玄发[①]，学书噪暮鸦。
素鱼[②]游客境，秋果列仙家。
朽质初明媚，枯萍似破瓜[③]。
东山邀玉兔[④]，山外散朝霞。

【注释】

①玄发：黑发。②素鱼：白鱼。③破瓜：指女子十六岁时。④玉兔：喻指月亮。

Two

Hoary-headed, stimulated to be black-haired,
My bookworm tries to caw at dusk,
Like a usual fish before the tourists,
Or an autumn fruit as the tribute.
Senile, but freshly bright,
The withered duckweed emulates the broken melon,
Calling for the moon in the eastern mountain
Beyond which the rosy dawn is coming loose.

学　问

无德处事难，无智做学残。
慧眼识滩暖，奇缘辨水寒。
疏枝听天籁，新笋长泥潭。

隔路人还在，同床梦不欢。

Knowledge

Immoral, it's ticklish,
Witless, it's shallow;
Quick-sighted, the strand snugs,
Enchanted, the water is shivery;
In sparse sprays, hear the heavenly melody,
In the mire, green shoots spring up;
Across the road, the man is still there,
In the same bed, the dreams are not bright.

遥　远

泊舟[①]春欲尽，浪静好堪眠。
残月明零雨，衰荷暗断烟。
夭桃[②]羞地暖，游女踏云鲜。
辗转斜梁燕，疏红落木天。

【注释】

①泊（bó）舟：停船靠岸。②夭桃：称艳丽的桃花，喻指少女容颜美丽。

A Long Way

To be moored, the spring passes no more,
Surgeless, it is somnific.

In the broken moon, the pitter-patters are bright,
In the waning lotus, the smoke stops secretly.
As the peach runs riot, the snug soil seems shy,
With the female sightseers stamping below fresh clouds.
To flounder about, the swallow off the bridge board
Skirrs in the rustles of the red, sparse colours.

一个人

唐诗五万首，抚景寄独吟。
珠履敲高殿，闲花叩远林。
清诗藏逸兴①，熟酒旷幽寻。
李杜身前事，芝田②种苦心。

【注释】

①逸兴：超逸豪放。②芝田：传说中仙人种灵芝的地方。

One Man

To the 50000 Tang poems,
My lone chant hopes to be mailed.
As the pearl shoes click the high hall,
The idle petals buckle the far woods.
In the scoured lines harbours my fancy mood,
Whose cooked wine seeks that serene, open space.
Li Po and Tu Fu during their lifetime
Sowed their bitter hearts in the fairy farm.

仪 表

云踪倚断潮，幽水黯魂香。
古渡山峰短，今泉河谷长。
红颜梳冷露，绿镜照暖妆。
春袖乾坤里，风云任尔藏。

Grand Air

The cloud trail on the broken tide
Has gloomed the sweet soul by the secluded water
Of the ancient ferry right in front of the short peaks
Whose valley of the current fountains are prolonged
Where the ruddy complexion combs her cold dews
And the warm makeup looks into the green mirror.
In the universe of her spring sleeves,
The wind and cloud are free to be concealed.

义

弱柳豪侠气，黑白两片天。
山高风鹤唳，水矮雾连绵。
清烈河阳瘦，磅礴海月圆。
归途何所在，大野义千年。

Righteousness

Feeble willows are chivalrous,
In the black and white skies.
The peaky wind cries its cranes,
And the dwarf water is foggy.
After the sweet, stern sun thins in the river,
The majestic moon of the sea will be round.
Where would be the way home?
The wild integrity has lasted a thousand years.

异　性

荒草没猪蹄，流莺破晓天。
浅薄云淡淡，柔弱水绵绵。
昨夜琴心①挂，今朝剑胆②悬。
巫山兰梦③后，灵影④落山巅。

【注释】

①琴心：指的是内心丰富，善良，敏感。②剑胆：指的是态度凌厉，果决，该出手时就出手。③兰梦：绮梦，女儿家的美梦。④灵影：灵飙，指灵气的熏风。

Opposite Sex

The pig's feet in the thorn bush
Are dawning their twittering orioles
Below the light, shallow clouds
Which are soft in the wistful water.
Last night her tender feelings hung there,
Now, her courage of sabre hangs here.
After the sweet dream in the amorous hill,
Her lively shade drops onto the crest.

意　识

无事却淹留[①]，殊俗两样秋。
西门风正紧，东户雪相浮。
莫怪杯中少，原来酒未休。
此生图醉饮，万事可消愁。

【注释】

①淹（yān）留：长期逗留。

Sense

To linger still for nothing, different
Customs have their own autumns,
Whose west gate blows hard,
Whose east house floats on the snow.

Blame not the limited cup, for my wine
Has gone on without respite.
To be banged up to the eyes this life,
All cares will be soothed.

意　义

史籍韦晏御[1]，青蒲不签牌[2]。
鸣玉敲斜日，垂丝绿古槐。
荻花[3]寻野渡，莲子落成排。
铁嶂截高牖[4]，独蛙洗宿霾。

【注释】

①晏御：典出晏御扬扬。晏子为齐相，出，其御之妻从门间而窥。其夫为相御，拥大盖，策驷马，意气扬扬，甚自得也。既而归，其妻请去。夫问其故，妻曰："晏子长不满六尺，身相齐国，名显诸侯。今者妾观其出，志念深矣，常有以自下者。今子长八尺，乃为人仆御，然子之意，自以为足，妾是以求去也。"其后，夫自抑损。晏子怪而问之，御以实对，晏子荐以为大夫。"内助之贤"和"扬扬得意"都来自这个典故。②青蒲：典故名，典出《汉书》卷八十二《王商史丹傅喜传·史丹》。同"伏蒲"，咏忠臣直谏。签牌：标签，用作书卷、画轴帙签的标记，垂于书画旁。③荻花：荻的花多年生草本植物，生在水边，叶子长形，似芦苇，秋天开紫花。④牖(yǒu)：窗户。

Purport

Historically, the wagoner on the high ropes
Was scrupulously honest without a mere pretence.
As the jade tinkles the tilted sun,
The old pagoda trees are green and willowy.
To seek the reeds in the wild ferry,
The lotus seeds drop in defined rows.
When the iron peak halts my high window,
The lone frog scours the night hazes.

因 果
Cause and Effect

其一

看破尘中雪，情识聚散多。
屏前长负累，屏后短蹉跎。
一树桃风动，三生李雨多。
佛台开玉蕊，莲子落恒河。

One

An insight into the dust snow comes
And goes in the realm more emotional.
Before the curtain, it's a long burden,
And behind, a short, wasted turn.
As the peach trees are breezing,
More lifetime plums are raining.
As the Buddha table blooms its pistils,
The lotus seeds fall into the Ganges.

其二

香雪山林重，房栊[①]半掩寒。
翠竹眠玉簟[②]，琼液捧金盘。
袅袅拨青玉，萧萧照紫檀。
箫韶[③]知燕乐，交颈共合欢。

【注释】

①房栊（lóng）：窗棂。②玉簟（diàn）：光滑似玉的精美竹席。③箫韶：美妙的仙乐。

Two

Sweet snow heavy in the wood closes
Half its cold spells in the lofty eaves.
While the green bamboo mat sleeps there,

The golden plate holds its nectar;
In its sapphire curls, the rustling
Sun shines on the red sandalwood. Behold
Those convivial and melodious swallows!
The conjugal pair are necked.

阴 影

朝阳连翠影，长月渡河明。
皂盖[①]随云岭，红荷洒地晴。
流光滑短景，素手惹浮名。
建业心不静，秋山日脚[②]轻。

【注释】

①皂盖：亦作“皁盖”，古代官员所用的黑色蓬伞。②日脚：太阳穿过云隙射下来的光线。

Shadow

Green shades in the rising sun are crossed
By a long, bright moon in the river.
One black umbrella over the ridges
Spills its fine red lotus all over.
As the short shadow slides in the streamers,
Her pure fingers have courted the vain glory.
Not to calm down as a pioneer,
The sun steps slightly in the autumn hills.

勇　士

扬眉翻虎穴，冷眼更癫狂。
斗虎人前去，撩猫事后长。
都说人胜虎，哪懂虎心亡。
一比决高下，行侠去北方。

Spartan

Eyebrowed, jump into the tiger's den,
Cold-eyed, still more insane.
For a tight-fight, be there in public,
To tease this cat, just for a latter-wit.
All say man prevails over the tiger,
But the jaws of death may be sure.
To duke it out,
Better go north, gallantly.

游子吟

荒庭桂露新，墨点猎丹飞。
惆怅平芜①去，空伤荡子②归。
欣欣缠翠带，蔼蔼架蔷薇。
窗罅③晴丝柳，摇烟暗琐闱④。

【注释】

①平芜：草木丛生的平旷原野。②荡子：辞家远出、羁旅忘返的男

子。③窗罅（xià）：窗缝。④琐闱：镌刻连琐图案的宫中旁门，常指代宫廷。此处指家园。

Homesick Song

The new laurel dews in my barren court
Hunt the red, flying ink dot, which is
Gone from the far-flung plain,
But back as a vagabond drifter,
Back with good grace of a green ribbon,
Back thru the luxuriant rambler roses.
From my window slits, sunny and willowy,
The swaying smokes are trivial to my secret shed.

圆融一点

圆月被云欺，闲思淡点风。
行行筛柳岸，悲喜过圆融。
人世韶光遽，心灯罩雾穷。
憨眠纤影后，万事转身空。

Slightly Smooth

The round moon was bullied by the cloud,
Whose spare spirit was breezed,
And sieved along the willow shore, for a
Perfect unity weighing delight and dole.
During the swift course of lifetime,

The inner light hangs below the fogs.
After the naive slumber by the slender shade,
All affairs turn on their heels, empty.

在人间
In the World

其一

夜幕理胭脂，红尘看画皮。
怀人贴假面，怀事影迷离[1]。
势满抒胸臆[2]，危折假作痴。
嚣嚣盟海誓，衮衮各东西[3]。

【注释】

①迷离：模糊而难以分辨清楚。②胸臆：内心深处的想法。③衮衮：相继不绝。称众多的显贵，衮衮诸公。

One

The cope of night was rouged, and saw
The painted skins in the human society,
Where the men were masked, and the matters
Were confusing and complicated.
Full in power, it was a rise of breath,
On thin ice, they played the fool.

After a pledge in all sincerity and seriousness,
They would go their separate ways at last.

其二

无节治酒功，无耻抱佛经。
物议[①]荣枯腻，人诛取舍腥。
茅长丹桂[③]止，棘刺[②]野菊停。
利刃营甘露，阴阳顺逆灵。

【注释】

①物议：众人的议论，多指非议。②棘刺：荆棘芒刺。③丹桂：木犀、桂花。

Two

Untempered in hitting the bottle,
Bare-faced in embracing the sutra,
The public censures are meticulous at the extremes of fortune,
And the man's attacks are smelly in their trade-offs.
In the long couch grass the crimson cassia would be halted,
In the calthrops the wild cchrysanthemums could be stopped.
While a sharp blade seeks its sweet dews,
Active or inactive, the ups and downs might be effective.

其三

麋鹿[①]在深山，鸣镝[②]破雪前。
啸吟[③]清浦夜，舒卷淡云天。
灵窍[④]留憨态，机宜[⑤]取笑圆。
人心加暗锁，隐刃去承欢。

【注释】

①麋（mí）鹿：又名“四不像”，是世界珍稀动物，属于鹿科。②鸣镝（dí）：鸣为响声，镝为箭头，鸣镝就是响箭，射出时箭头能发出响声。③啸吟：长啸哀叹。④灵窍：慧心。⑤机宜：机密之事。

Three

An elk in the remote mountain
By the whistling arrow before the snow.
Rended the air in the clear night of the riverside
Under the clear clouds that curl and uncurl.
His wisdom in an air of charming naivety,
And his reasons radiant with broad smiles.
Were locked up by the heart of men in secret,
That tried to be lively mirthful on the knife-edge.

其四

贪兽神旗地，檐牙[1]粟马寒。
同门闲剑气，隔网醉铗[2]弹。
短梦风淫荡，遥阶雪暮潺。
金屋霓影乱，草舍换平安。

【注释】

①檐牙：檐际翘出如牙的部分。②铗（jiá）：剑柄。

Four

Where the voracious beasts are perky,
The horse under the eaves feels chilly,
With the sword spirit of the same door
Blind to the world across the web before.
In the short dream that blows carnally,
The dusk step snow babbles distantly.
As the neon lights dazzle in golden chambers,
The humble houses could be the peace-makers.

其五

黄泉流碧落[1]，生死向人开。
看取三餐累，休沦世事哀。
直文斜雨肇[2]，乱字逆风裁。
独步章台[3]路，青烟扫镜台[4]。

【注释】

①碧落：道家称东方第一层天，碧霞满空，叫作“碧落”。这里泛指天上。②肇：开始，初始。③章台：汉时长安城有章台街，是当时长安妓院集中之处，后人以章台代指妓院赌场等娱乐场所。④镜台：装着镜子的梳妆台。此处与“青烟”搭配，具有双关意义，比喻青青的眉黛如同飘渺的柳烟；也指短暂的人生灰飞烟灭，不再临镜梳妆。

Five

Hades flow under the realms of bliss,
Where life and death are open to the men.
Cold-eyed, the three meals are a burden,
But fall not into the world sadness.
Literally, the rain is drifting down,
Tousily, the letters in dead wind are grown.
On the way of courtesans of my own,
The smoke whisks the dressing table along.

其六

青眼[①]识人意，痴心道灵低。
殷勤眠吠犬，萧索厌黄鸡[②]。
背地猫童戏，人前撤扳梯。
憨痴别效狗，求利莫执迷。

【注释】

①青眼：黑色的眼珠在眼眶中间，青眼看人则是表示对人的喜爱或

重视、尊重。②黄鸡：化典“休将白发唱黄鸡”。白发指年老，黄鸡指代白居易诗中的年华易逝的感慨。

Six

Dark-eyed, it's considerate,
Obsessed, the spirit hangs down.
Affable, the sleep barks,
Desolate, the cock is tired.
Privately, play the peek-a-boo,
Overtly, hit the man who's down.
To be idiotic, to be a dog,
To be profit-hungry, not to be hell-bent.

张　扬

豪情笑六朝，如梦甲兵销。
灯影流霞绰，秦淮画艇邀。
酒殇千古醉，雪韵百年娇。
曲径疏花落，空林鸟寂寥。

To Flaunt

The six dynasties in lofty sentiments are mocked,
Whose armed men collapsed like a dream.
When the lamp shadow ripples below the wandering roses,
One painted boat comes to its tryst on the Qinhuai River.
Under the influence through all age,

Her snowy charm looks affectedly sweet about a century.
After she's deflowered in the winding path,
The jay would be solitary in the stark wood.

哲　人

思危断谷边，累卵有千层。
老树连柯散，新芽扯地兴。
比肩同入定，对枕一俗僧。
立仞菩提远，佛光枉自升。

Wise Man

The sense of crises at the downfaulted rift valley
Has been precarious as a thousand piles of eggs.
After the old trees are rooted out,
The cantle of land would be sprouting again.
Together, let's sit in meditation,
Pillowed, it's one secular monk.
Pliable but strong, the phothi is so far,
And the light of Buddha rises, of no avail.

珍　惜

簪花柳带①晴，携风两澄明②。
碎浪单鱼静，繁枝两燕行。
疏风浮绿岸，瘦月点白苹③。
菡萏④衔杯露，泉石玉佩声。

【注释】

①簪花：妇女头饰的一种，用作首饰戴在妇人头上，增加了一种生机勃勃、生动活泼的生命气息，因而美。除了鲜花以外，有绢花、绫花、缎花、绸花、珠花等。柳带：柳条。因其细长如带，故称。②澄明：清朗。③白苹：即四叶菜、田字草。蕨类植物。多年生浅水草木。④菡萏（hàn dàn）：古人称未开的荷花为菡萏，即花苞。

To Cherish

Fine flowers in the hair are willowy,
Clear and bright in the breeze.
One fish is still in the broken wave,
And two swallows go thru the tufted sprays.
As the sparse wind swims on the green shore,
The emaciated moon dribs onto the white clovers.
As the lotus flowers hold the chalice of dews,
The spring stones will be tinkling and jingling.

争什么

人世有悲欢，离合似下棋。
萧萧敲玉子，晏晏[1]动琼思。
攘攘空云散，熙熙两鬓垂。
芸芸春脚抱，瑟瑟火星移。

【注释】

①晏晏：和悦貌。

Why to Vie

The world in the quirks of grief and joy
Comes and goes like a game of chess,
Whose chessmen are rustling
In a free, amiable spirit
Like the hustling, scattering clouds,
Or the bustling, drooping temples,
That clasp the feet of the springs,
And move with the whispering Mars.

竹

青嶂①啼疏雨，苔痕迸笋香。
初晴急换彩，向晚染浓妆。
瑟瑟浮竹影，苍苍断水光。
交横②敲素帐，风静卧朝阳。

【注释】

①青嶂：如屏障的青山。②交横：纵横交错。

Bamboos

The green ridges are cawing in raindrops and
The moss traces spurt their sweet bamboo sprouts,
That change their colours fast under the clear sky,
And tinge the attractive dress as the dusk is near.

Rustling, the bamboo shades are floating,
And breaking the dark green water colours,
That knock the white disorderly canopy,
Where the rising sun sleeps in the quiet air.

自　然

明月有光音，梢头岁岁忙。
床前如辨水，柳下似涂霜。
冰魄浮沧海，银魂钓苇塘。
盈亏徒放眼，胖瘦自温凉。

Natural

In the light voice of the bright moon,
The years are hastened at the top wood.
Abed, it's like a visual cue of water,
That's frosty below the willows.
As the soul of ice floats over the sea,
Its silvery spirit angles in the reed pond.
To wax or wane, open your eyes in vain,
Fat or thin, it's warm and cool by itself.

自　我

寒花澮澮秋，陶潜[1]写菊忙。
开爆黄金蕊，折来绿蚁[2]狂。
挥毫流韵律，墨笔绣天阳[3]。

篱畔藏秋目，南山四季香。

【注释】

①陶潜：陶渊明。②绿蚁：新酿制的酒面泛起的泡沫称为“绿蚁”，后用来代指新出的酒。③天阳：太阳的别称。

Ego

Cold flowers in the undulating autumn
Are busy writing the chrysanthemums.
In a riot of golden pistils
Converted into the crazy nectar.
Driving the quill in gracious numbers,
The writing brush can embroider the sun.
In the fence are hidden the autumn's eyes,
All seasons of the southern hill will be sweet.

自　尊
Self-Esteem

其一

黑白没浅释，难易有轮回。
云瘦流深远，山空势不摧。
旧游思绪乱，往事梦惊灰。
风影林中过，三生不可追。

One

Black or white, it has no simple explanation,
Quick or slow, it has transmigration.
An emaciated cloud flows afar,
And a hollow mountain will be unbroken.
As the brains ran wild formerly,
The past startled the ashes so dreamy.
When the wind shadow passes thru the wood,
The three lifetimes are but a history.

其二

青枝吵野凫①，振落几行诗。
次第春风冷，暄妍②柳絮吹。
白霜欺体小，红蕊坠颜衰。
聒耳③闲蛙闹，平生两不离。

【注释】

①凫（fú）：水鸟，俗称“野鸭”，似鸭，雄的头部绿色，背部黑褐色，雌的全身黑褐色，常群游湖泊中，能飞。②暄妍：天气和暖，景物明媚。③聒（guō）：声音吵闹，使人厌烦。

Two

A wild mallard quacks in the green twigs,
And shakes off a few lines of poems,

In the cold spring breeze sequentially,
That whiffles the glorious willow catkins.
While the white rimes are stronger before
The weak, the red pistils have lost their looks.
While the croaking frogs are fast and furious,
Their life should not have been parted.

其三

真性串清韵，潺湲素沫[①]游。
花丛堪系处，红萼欠相投。
星雨荒村静，流云陌上浮。
幽风悬一角，孤月满汀洲。

【注释】

①潺湲（chán yuán）：水慢慢流动的样子。素沫：白色水花。

Three

Clear charms are clustered by the natural essence,
Where the pure foam travels in the rippling maze.
Where the flowers in clusters are tied up,
The red calyces will be loosely allied.
In the starfall, the bleak village is still, and
The flowing cloud floats over the field.
When the quiet wind hangs at the corner,
The solitary moon fills the sand islets.

其四

山冷鸟别枝，岩松瘦不群。
衔杯明月醉，欢影艾青[1]闻。
往事飘如梦，香茗淡若云。
无言天解语，见面懂悲欣。

【注释】

①艾青：喻指太阳。

Four

Cold hills blow the birds away,
Cliffy pines are skinny but untrammeled.
The moon-lit cup's steeped in liquor,
That sniffs the merry traces of the green mugworts.
The past events are gone like a dream,
And the fragrant tea tastes so weak like a cloud.
To decipher the tacit sky,
A contact will know its cheer and sorrow.

嘴　巴

斗嘴轻弹剑，揭疤见硬伤。
龟蛇穿蚁穴，鹰隼[1]欲凌霜。
酣醉非昏聩，微醺[2]有醋狂。
浮尘争乱草，纸醉笑凄凉。

【注释】

①鹰隼（sǔn）：两种猛禽，泛指凶猛的鸟，用来比喻凶猛或勇猛。常用于比喻天性凶狠而令人畏惧的人或勇猛的人。②微醺（xūn）：微醉。

Mouth

To squabble flicks a sword, and
To rake up the faults shows the dog marks.
While the Tortoise and Snake Hills are burrowed into the anthills,
The hawk attempts to soar up in the frost.
To be dead drunk means not to be muddle-headed,
But to be bright in the eye explodes in jealousy.
When the floating dust vies for the mass of weeds,
The voluptuous life will smile bleakly.

六言绝句

Six Character Quatrain

六言绝句格式

要求每句字数相等，平仄相对，一诗四句，偶句入韵，一韵到底，并有六律，平仄相对，偶句入韵，一诗八句，中两联对仗。

【平声韵】

1. 仄起首句不押韵格式：

仄仄平平仄仄，平平仄仄平平（韵）（对仗）
平平仄仄平仄，仄仄平平仄平（韵）

2. 仄起首句押韵格式：

仄仄平平仄平（韵），平平仄仄平平（韵）。
平平仄仄平仄，仄仄平平仄平（韵）。

3. 平起首句不押韵格式：

平平仄仄平仄，仄仄平平仄平（韵）。（对仗）
仄仄平平仄仄，平平仄仄平平（韵）。

4. 平起首句押韵格式：

平平仄仄平平（韵），仄仄平平仄平（韵）。
仄仄平平仄仄，平平仄仄平平（韵）。

【仄声韵】

1. 平起式：

平平仄仄平仄（韵），仄仄平平仄仄（韵）。
仄仄平平仄平，平平仄仄平仄（韵）。

2. 仄起式：

仄仄平平仄仄（韵），平平仄仄平仄（韵）。
平平仄仄平平，仄仄平平仄仄（韵）。

爱
Love

其一

戴水千层月影，汤河百面阳轮[①]。
烟波妒柳[②]横过，洒下三分皱纹。

【注释】

①阳轮：喻指太阳。②妒柳：也同“渡柳”，含双关。

One

A thousand moon shades on the Daihe River,
And a hundred sun wheels on the Tanghe River,
Swept the green-eyed willows on misty rolls,

That sprinkled thirty percent of wrinkles.

其二

绿屑金珠惹春，蜂腰燕体浓荫。
低鬟[①]眼过秋水，柳岸寻机卧根。

【注释】

①低鬟（huán）：低头，用以形容美女娇羞之态。

Two

Green dregs and gold beads in the stirred spring
Are wasp-waisted in the soft shadows,
Where her limpid eyes lowered by a tousled cloud
Look about the willowy shore for a sleeping source.

其三

轻薄惹弄闲愁，捧露银波入秋。
枕玉香帷并蒂，狂蜂冷月如钩。

Three

Frivolous worry and woe
Are dewed and waved into the fall.
Pillowed inside the sweet couple,

A cold, lascivious crescent hangs there.

其四

艳质通酬[①]带雨，蛱蝶[②]入梦难娶。
梨姿柳底铅华[③]，摆落清秋几许？

【注释】

①通酬：（男女）往来交际。②蛱蝶（jiá dié）：一种蝴蝶，翅膀呈赤黄色，有黑色纹饰，幼虫身上多刺，危害农作物。③铅华：蝴蝶翅膀上的粉末，也指妇女化妆用的铅粉。曹植《洛神赋》："芳泽无加，铅华弗御。"

Four

Rain-drenched, the graceful charms have exchanged
Their angle wings waiting for be wedded in dream.
How much the clear autumn has been swayed off
Her powdered posture like a pear under the willows?

其五

檀郎紫陌[①]天短，谢女[②]青楼夜长。
有韵昙花月影，无声细雨高唐[③]。

【注释】

①檀郎：晋代潘岳小名檀奴，姿仪美好。借指情人男子。紫陌：大路的意思。陌：本指田间的小路，这里借指道路。"紫"：指道路两

旁草木的颜色。②谢女：情人女子。唐代李贺《牡丹种曲》："檀郎谢女眠何处，楼台月明燕夜语。"③高唐：即高唐梦，借指男女交欢之事。传说楚襄王游高唐，梦见巫山神女，幸之而去。

Five

Scarlet day of a beau way is so short,
Dark night of a fancy lady is so long,
That glide a rhymed flash-in-the-pan
In the hushed moon for a drizzled orgasm.

其六

酒晕金谷[①]送暖，潮红柳岸偷寒。
轻妍半寸檀口[②]，锁住床头玉箫。

【注释】

①金谷：游宴。②轻妍：轻柔美丽。檀口：红艳的嘴唇。

Six

A pink-faced wine warms up her blush that steals
The severe snaps on the shore of willows.
Her soft, sweet and small lips are locked
Into a pure flute by the spindle box.

其七

绣帐营奸视频，添红减玉娇云。
颠鸾倒凤鹦语，地老天荒颤魂。

Seven

A video game in the embroidered curtains
Freshens the tender, scarlet loss or gains
That hum the voluptuous pleasure
Of a thrilling, world-old heart, sure.

其八

湘裙①画月藏蕊，燕懒②红白欲睡。
宝髻流莺楚云③，杨花水性沉醉。

【注释】

①湘裙：湘地丝织品制成的女裙，泛指裙子。②燕懒：燕子的巢筑完了，之后作呢喃声。③楚云：女子秀美的发髻，喻指男女欢合。

Eight

Pistils are hidden in her moon-shaped skirt,
That murmurs a pure, sleepy scarlet.
Her hair cascades that are twittering high

Fall into the wanton ecstasies like willow catkins.

其九

青春暗惹飞红，艳动娇唇稔丰[1]。
苦口幽魂瘦影，轻妍玉兔[2]朦胧。

【注释】

①稔（rěn）：庄稼成熟。②轻妍：轻柔美丽。玉兔：喻指月亮。

Nine

Youth flirts secretly to the red flight,
That vividly stirs her lips so tender and bumper.
To taste her bitter spectre of a thin figure,
The moon glooms into a gentle wonder.

其十

凌空众里结爱，艳逸疏情紫塞[1]。
晓镜幽人照霜，花发二度眉黛。

【注释】

①紫塞：长城。

Ten

A love amid all the flesh soars
Up the sensuous but sparse border
Where the solitary figure in the frosty, dawning mirror
Has grizzled her eye-brows for a second vigour.

其十一

家囚自古衔爱，莫唱合欢翠黛[①]。
皓指妖红巧匀，宫额[②]绣户不再。

【注释】

①翠黛：眉的别称。②宫额：古代宫中妇女以黄色涂额作为妆饰，因而称妇女的前额为宫额。

Eleven

The caged bird loves from of old
Warbles her reunited brows.
As her bright fingers smooth the skillful flame,
Her forehead in the boudoir will be no more.

爱凋

蛾眉晓月妍丑[1]，皓齿寒门礼闱[2]。
凤管[3]青枝倒挂，片片野雪花飞。

【注释】

①妍丑：美和丑。②礼闱：古代科举考试之会试，因其为礼部主办，故称礼闱。③凤管：笙箫或笙箫之乐的美称。

Withered Love

Pretty or ugly, her brow dawns like a moon,
And her pearly teeth in the cold door are courteous.
As the melody on the green twigs hangs upside down,
Small flakes of snow are flying everywhere.

爱深

移床梦暗缘涧，柳陌霏微岁晏[1]。
秀色凝阴此丘，芳心枕底一瓣。

【注释】

①柳陌：植柳之路。旧指妓院。霏微：雾气，细雨等弥漫的样子。岁晏：一年将尽的时候，又指人的暮年。

Deep Love

In the skirted ravine that secretly shifts the bed in dream,
The willowly path drizzles mistily to the end of the year.
When her sweet beauty is frozen into such a mound,
Her fragrant heart will be pillowed like a petal.

悲哀

苦味鸡虫草深，中秋窥镜明春。
虚烟敛霭衰柳，剪破锋镝[1]叩尘。

【注释】

①锋镝（dí）：箭镝，镝矢，箭头。泛指兵器。

Sorrow

Bitter chickens and worms deep in the grass
Look into the mid-autumn for a new spring.
Timidly hazed among the waned willows
That snip the blade and arrowhead in the dust.

暗恋

晴云暗恋苍树，绕砌嘤嘤[1]暮雨。
薜荔[2]惊风厚薄，朱门澹荡茹苦[3]。

【注释】

①嘤嘤：象声词，形容鸟叫声或低而细微的声音。②薜（bì）荔：木瓜藤。③澹荡：荡漾，飘动。茹苦：茹即“吃”。形容备受艰难，忍受痛苦。

Secret Love

Her unrequited love in the dark green trees down
The fine cloud wispers like an embraced, dusk rain.
As her thick or thin creepers are whirling in the wind,
Her red rippled door has to suck it up.

背叛

威怀饮羽[①]横剑，晓角歼夷[②]远念。
铁骨飘风虎吟，溟渤[③]望断勾践。

【注释】

①威怀：威服和怀柔。谓威德并用。饮羽：箭深入所射物体。②歼夷：诛灭。③溟渤：溟海和渤海，多泛指大海。

Betrayal

My dignified arrow and sword
Bugled their dawning blows afar.
My muscles of iron before the tiger growls
Looked away unto King Goujian beyond the sea.

奔忙

归林燕语扑絮，抱叶蝉声乱秋。
几度烟霞[①]翠影，浮光昼夜乘流。

【注释】

①烟霞：烟雾和云霞，也指山水胜景。

Bustle

A swallow back to the wood flaps the catkins,
And the cicadas on the leaves derange the autumn.
And a green shade in the wisps of coloured mist
Flows day and night in the floating light.

表象

池边暗数花蕊，落墨清绝咫尺。
乳鹊衔风野棠，啾啾不解宣纸。

Appearance

By the pool, I count the pistils in secret,
And ink a short, refined and superb verse, like
A fledging magpie with its wild, windy crabapple
Who is chirping to the puzzled rice paper.

不算

伸舒夙志灵鉴[①]，伫立残肌翘襟。
莫畏青莲露冷，寒池寂灭[②]幽寻。

【注释】

①伸舒：伸展，舒展。灵鉴：英明的识见。②寂灭：度脱生死，进入寂静无为之境地。

Exclusive

To stretch my old, wise will,
My crippled muscle stands here prayerfully.
Fear not the chill dews of the green lotus,
Whose cold pool should be inscrutable.

不要

掩素冰流古貌，矜红雪静高谈。
孤城醉倚羁旅，逆浪明烛不堪。

Never

The old, pure look is closed under the ice flow,
Toward her red, still and eloquent snow.
As the isolated town is tipsy on the journey,

The bright candle can't bear the cross-waves, you know.

才华

秘语绝国[1]碧水，奇文故里丹霄[2]。
空江两片鸥鸟，月镜一湾海潮。

【注释】

①绝国：极其辽远之邦国。②丹霄：绚丽的天空。

Gifted

A vocable secret on the distant, green water
Writes its florid and remarkable sky natively.
And the two herons on the river so empty
Are tided on the moon-lit gulf like a mirror.

沧桑

燕山晓镜沧桑，寸黛罗薄澹妆。
渺渺浮杯雪夜，休言臧否彭殇[1]。

【注释】

①臧否：书面用语，褒贬、评比、评定、评价、评介、评论等意思。彭殇：彭，彭祖，古代传说中的长寿之人。殇，夭折，未成年而死。

Weather-beaten

In the shifting, dawning mirror, the Yanshan Mountain
Was lightly made up like a gossamer
Visionary before the snow night floated in my cup:
Hold your tongue about the life, short or long.

差距

青蝇虎背鹰喙，罔象岩峦吊诡[①]。
数载长门玉堂，丰暇走吏积毁[②]。

【注释】

①罔象：古代传说中的水怪，或谓木石之怪。吊诡：有怪异、奇特。
②丰暇：多空闲并安逸。积毁：不断地毁谤。

Gap

With the beaks of eagles, the blue flies on the tiger's back
Are a monstrous paradox among the cliffy mountains.
After a few years in the jade halls of the long gates,
The leisurely lackeys have been speaking evil lightly.

柴米油盐

云寒素浪柴米，日暮浮萍稻农。
莫怨荆钗①枕梦，蚕筐旧岁鸾踪。

【注释】

①荆钗：荆枝制作的髻钗，古代贫家妇女常用之。

Daily Necessities

By the white billows for the fuels and rice below the cold cloud,
The eventide was washing over the duckweeds of the rice farmers.
Don't you blame, my ladies on the pillow in dream;
Your silkworm basket ever trailed the phoenix last year.

沉　默

默会①难裁野径，凝思绿琐初定。
旋风爆响朱楼，汗漫②劳筋逸兴。

【注释】

①默会：暗自领会。②汗漫：漫无标准，浮泛不着边际。

Silence

A knowing wild trail is hard to cut,
And a thoughtful mood is freshly clocked.
As a whirlwind cracks in the red floor,
My wrought muscle will be rambling free.

吃　醋

蓬莱酩酊膏泽[①]，逆浪天清挂席[②]。
洞府闲情野鹤，椒兰暗妒白石[③]。

【注释】

①膏泽：滋润土壤的雨水。②挂席：挂帆。③椒兰：椒与兰，皆芳香之物，故以并称。白石：传说中的神仙的粮食。

Jealousy

The timely drunken rain in the paradise
Trimmed the fine sails for the cross sea.
Like a wild, idle crane in his fair abode,
The pepper and orchid envied his ambrosia.

赤　脚

微烟赤脚榛莽[1]，宿雾长须裹霜。
曲沼[2]青刀路远，白猿栈[3]踏云长。

【注释】

①榛莽（mǎng）：杂乱丛生的草木。②曲沼（zhǎo）：曲折迂回的池塘。③栈（zhàn）：栈道。

Bare-footed

Bare-footed through the hazy weeds,
The beard was frosted in the gathering murk.
Along the winding stream were prolonged the green cattails,
And the white ape was long on the cloudy, rickety footbridge.

聪　明

月落清风谑浪[1]，春眠宿露娇怜。
惊心举翅秋汉，落照萧寥[2]洞天。

【注释】

①谑浪：戏谑放荡。②萧寥：寂寞冷落。

Acumen

Moondown, the breeze teases
Her spring sleep in the tender night dews.
As her thrilling wings are flared into the autumn sky,
The setting sun shines on her unique charm in solitude.

出　徒

婵娟绣户白昼，破镜珠帘晓风。
乱木清猿客泪，波急野渡虚空。

Ultimate Goal

Her boudoir in the daylight of a dawn-breeze
Breaks the mirror in the pearl curtain
Mournful by the cries of apes in the woods
Before the fast, wild waves where nothing exists.

错　觉

绮错①葱茏胜境，章台羽猎②遐骋。
苍林逸藻雄俊③，野寺苹烟杳冥④。

【注释】

①绮（qǐ）错：绮纹之交错。②章台：章华台，春秋时楚国离宫。

羽猎：帝王出猎，士卒负羽箭随从。③逸藻：华丽的辞藻。雄俊：雄伟险要。④杳冥：幽暗。

Illusion

In the verdant, glorious labyrinth,
A royal hunt could run wild.
Near the ornate wood, pretty but mighty,
The hazy, wild temple looks gloomy.

单　身

匹马嘶风雪蹄，衔鱼野色山鸡。
荆门暗缚青女①，健气乖离②袖低。

【注释】

①青女：传说中掌管霜雪的女神；借指霜雪；喻指白发。②乖离：背离。

Single

As the blizzard hooves are neighing,
A wild, fishing blackcock is awaiting
Outside the secret gate of nymph thorns
Deviating his vigour, with the sleeves hanging down.

道　德

名花智慧盲眼，片玉疏清放盏。
透纸乾坤道德，斯文宝祚[1]惟简。

【注释】

①斯文：文化或文人和有修养的人。宝祚（zuò）：国运；帝位。

Morale

A famed flower may be brain-blind,
But a jade cup could be sparsely free
In the moral world lucid on the sheet
That records the easy fate of the nation.

敌　人

灭影危言寡义，诛心蛊惑谗谀[1]。
青云泄雨杀气，振藻[2]浮荣宦途。

【注释】

①谗谀：谗毁和阿谀。②振藻：显扬文采。

Enemy

The shade has perished by the inhuman prophecy,
That deludes the hard-hearted flatterers and slanderers.
Down the blue sky are raining the auras of death,
That shows off the peacockery on the official way.

多　少

涧草苍莽翠敛，岩花[1]迥野荒诛。
披文海客高话，隙地[2]迷津异途。

【注释】

①岩花：灌木，高 1 ~ 3 米；枝有 4 棱，棱上密生一行小瘤状凸起，近无毛，嫩枝干时变黑色，老枝淡灰褐色。②隙地：空地。

Untold

The gully grass like a vast emerald
Killed the wild，cliffy flowers afar.
The gracious harangue of the wayfarers
Was lost in the spatial mazes.

烦　恼
Vexation

其一

朝烦地窄云野，夜怯天宽月游。
冻露虚空岁暮，春来化水沉浮。

One

The morn vexes by the cabined clouds, and
The night funks to the broad wander of the moon.
The frozen dews left void at the year end will
Be melted into water, up or down in the spring.

其二

鼓浪悲风卷蜡，销霜宿草①舒原。
章台②断尽飞燕，烟花蒙笼负暄③。

【注释】

①宿草：隔年的草。②章台：代指柳。③负暄：冬天受日光曝晒取暖。

Two

My candle whirls by the doleful billows,
Against the open wild, grassy but frosty,
That looks away unto the flying swallows,
In the winter sun, filmy but hazy.

方　向

夜雪惊湍浅暗[①]，朝霜静影深明。
轮回没胫辐凑[②]，鬼转白沙砥平[③]。

【注释】

①惊湍：急流。浅暗：肤浅而不明达。②辐凑（fú còu）：连结车辋和车毂的直条，即车辐。③砥平：平直；平坦。

Direction

The night snow startles in its shallow and dull overfall,
And the morn frost calms its close but clear shadow.
As the spokes of the wheel converge upon the axle,
Their ghostly turns on the silver sand are smooth and level.

风　景

浮阳弄倒猿影，嫩树轩云窥镜。
驿路寒迷翠微[1]，苍苔闭锁深岭。

【注释】

①翠微：青翠的山色，形容山光水色青翠缥缈。也泛指青翠的山。

Landscape

The floated sun knocks over the ape
Off the tender tree below the cloudy mirror.
As the courier road thru the emerald hills turns cold,
The dark green moss will close the deep mountains.

疯　狗

蝇头入眼传神，逸气江头跃鳞[1]。
化犬穿篱吠日，狺狺[2]浪恶摇唇。

【注释】

①逸气：超脱世俗的气概。跃鳞：游动的鱼。②狺狺（yín）：犬吠声。

Mad Dog

The tiny head of a fly is lively in the eye,
Whose free soul by the river can leap so high.
Once turned into a dog at the sun thru the fence,
HER barking lips will wag the stormy seas to the sky.

俯　仰

壶中俯仰寒露，策外逡巡夜风。
望鹤三秋漫道，归来致理攸同。

Up and Down

Cold dews up or down my flagon
Are whipped out to prowl the night wind.
After a gaze out upon the cranes in late autumn afar,
I have to return with my original face without peer.

付　钱

幽婚放逸①形神，再嫁绵绵晚春。
毕娶蓬蒿②百虑，瑶觞玉漏③垂银。

【注释】

①幽婚：志怪小说中谓人与鬼结婚。放逸：放纵逸乐。②毕娶：办

完子女婚事，避世优游。蓬蒿：草野间人，指未仕。③瑶觞：玉杯。多借指美酒。玉漏：古代计时漏壶的美称。

To Pay

If a ghost marriage was given to sensual pleasures,
Her remarriage would be swamped with the late spring
Whose carefree leisure in the bushes would be apprehensive
Before the silvery ticking of the water-clock in my jade cup.

改　变

老去苗青御柳，别来叶翠夭桃。
鱼吹燕觜天阔，稳睡舟楫浪高。

Change

When old, the green shoots of grains are willowy,
After departure, the peach runs riot in the green leaves.
As the fish bubble up, the swallow beaks are flying wide.
And at the breaker height, the boat and oar sleep sure.

感　情

轻霞步柳薄日，辅翼朱弦委质①。
锦帐孤飞暮尘，凉飙②凄厉苦禅。

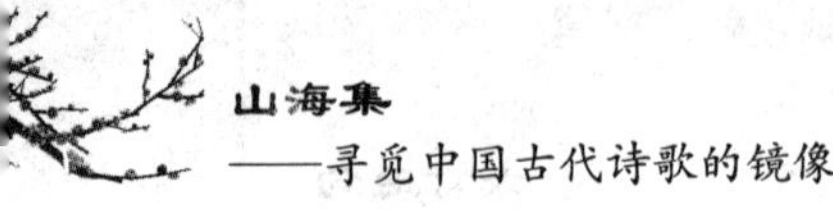

【注释】

①辅翼：辅佐，辅助。朱弦：用熟丝制的琴弦。委质：亦作“委挚”“委贽”，表呈献礼物，表示忠诚信实。②凉飙：亦作“凉飚”。秋风。

Sentiment

In the gentle clouds the thin sun steps thru the willows,
Whose red strings are animated by a devout spirit.
When the dusk dust flies alone in the silk bed-curtain,
The cold breath of autumn shrills a bitter meditation.

感　受

鸡声未晓逐客，袖底尘霜巷陌。
跨下掬风踏云，离痕散尽颜魄[1]。

【注释】

①颜魄：容颜和心魄。

Perception

Show the door before the cock crow,
And gone with my sleeves, dusty and frosty;
To stride the skimmed wind and cloud,
The last trace of the facial soul fades away.

滚

细雨秋尘月色，轻雷朔气河声。
晴天碧落[1]挟电，宝瑟孤吟不惊。

【注释】

①碧落：道家称东方第一层天，碧霞满空，叫作“碧落”。这里泛指天上。

Out

Mizzly and dusty，the autumn moon lightly
Thunders in the northern chills of the river.
Even by a bolt from the blue
My lone zither will still calm.

好　坏

远水离群自慰，空山望月独悲。
章台[1]叶暖云暗，落日槐阴鸟迟。

【注释】

①章台：歌妓聚居之所。

Good Or Bad

The consolable stray to the water afar
Views the moon-lit hill，empty in sorrow.
To the mild leaves below the dark clouds,
The late bird returns to the sunset pagoda shadow.

哄

新霜冷暖侵骨，旧雨枯荣授衣。
玉女朱荷卷幔，秋风嫩浪人非。

To Coax

Mild or cold，the fresh frost bites the bones,
Bloomy or gloomy，the old rains are coated.
As the fair in the red lotus drops her curtain,
The wanton wind of autumn turns into another.

坏心情

意密情疏恨花，衔鱼寡味寒鸦。
秦心楚恨酸骨[①]，没世流年夜叉[②]。

【注释】

①酸骨：酸痛刺骨，形容愤恨、悲伤。②没世：到死；终身。夜叉：

鬼的名字，译为捷快，形容男的行动敏捷又迅速。

Bad Mood

The density of affections hates the flower,
And the insipid taste of the fish is like the jackdaw.
Amid a mixture of sorrow and anger,
The lifelong hell-cat fleets with time somehow.

谎　言

云霓[1]鼓浪高调，磴道[2]盘石莫言。
老鹤喷风断雨，笛声谑[3]柳尘喧。

【注释】

①云霓：虹。②磴（dèng）道：登山的石径。③谑（xuè）：开玩笑。

Liar

When the lowering clouds are billowing,
The huge rock on the trails turns tacit.
When the old cranes spurt and snap the elements,
One pipe teases the blatant willows.

回　头

扬尘月落清界，藉力谁听杵钟[1]。

万里孤舟野岸，回头又是穷冬[2]。

【注释】

①杵钟：用粗木头做的撞钟的杵子。②穷冬：古代对冬季的别称，也指深冬和隆冬。

Glance Back

The moonset dust is well-defined,
But who's heard the aid-seeking tolls?
To be moored wild so far,
Another mid-winter comes when faced about.

婚　姻

情疏暗恨柔态，透影朱融翠黛[1]。
宿露横波冷滑，白头老妪[2]谁爱？

【注释】

①翠黛：古时女子用螺黛（一种青黑色矿物染料）画眉，亦即眉的别称。②老妪（yù）：古代老妇人的自称。

Marriage

The hatred has haboured her gentle but estranged emotion,
Whose eyebrows have been rouged and pencilled.
After her frowns drop their cold night dews,
Who would love such a white-haired woman?

机　会

莫问闲机满筐，寒服镜晓凝霜。
陶然混迹薄月，半缕杨花放狂。

Chance

A basketful of chances must not be spare,
And a cold clothes could be frosty as the mirror dawns.
Canopied in a thin，unworthy moon,
Half a wisp of willow catkins rolls in a fine frenzy.

记　忆

残阳万木摇落，满月千峰盛衰。
雨后垂帘倦枕，扬花病眼闲开。

Memory

As the setting sun shakes down the woods,
The full moon rises or falls in the mountains.
After the dossal grows drowsy after the rains,
The catkins in the affected eyes fly more broods.

寂　寞

喧阗[①]野水高卷，飒飒潺浮海甸。
暑雨[②]飘蓬梦残，苍黄古灶轮转。

【注释】

①喧阗（tián）：声音大而杂。②暑雨：夏大雨，冬大寒。后以之为怨嗟生计艰难之典。

Solitude

Like the wild waters in boisterous bustles,
The rustles are babbling in the marshes,
Whose broken dream blown down its rain in the dog days
Will rotate with the ancient, flurried oven.

家　败

烈气萧萧冷笔，峨眉破镜衢室[①]。
开帘露索垂杨，扯地孤清梦日。

【注释】

①衢（qú）室：相传为唐尧征询民意的处所。此处指遇事本应相互沟通的家庭。

Home on the Decline

A vigorous pen cold in rustles
Breaks her brows in the homely mirror,
Opens her dews on the weeping willows,
And bestrews her lone dream like sweet water.

健 康
Health

其一

壮士挟弓射雕，回头臂上狂飙。
秋风铁甲割面，海气平吞九霄。

One

Bow warrior, to be a eagle shooter,
Glances back with his arm billows
Over his armour slashed by the autumn wind,
And swallows the empyrean over the sea air.

其二

清贫枕簟秋雨，散鸟随风鹤舞。
铁翅挥石窜沙，低扉不掩柴户。

Two

My poor pillow in the autumn rain
Goes with the wind like a crane dance,
Which bolts out the gravels off my iron wings,
Opening wide to the lower thatched hut.

教　育
Education

其一

大署高儒妙迹，微官旅宦科第[①]。
横财锦幛瑶华[②]，货赂求珠苦志[③]。

【注释】

①旅宦：外出求官或做官。科第：科举制度考选官吏后备人员时，分科录取，每科按成绩排列等第，叫作科第。②横财：意外的、非分的钱财。瑶华：玉白色的花。有时借指仙花。③货赂：财物。苦志：苦其心志。谓磨炼自己的意志。

One

Yamens for scholars are a wonderful goal,
Whose grade candidates start from petty officials,
Brilliant with the windfall from the magic heaven,
That practises open bribery in a mental trial.

其二

清槎漱晓迢递[1]，莫教春潮隐体。
万木疾流曲江，风尘海内开济[2]。

【注释】

①清槎（chá）：小舟。迢递（tiáo dì）：形容遥远。②开济：情操志向开通美好。

Two

Let us go for a row afar in the morn,
Lest the spring tide be receded.
As all woods meander in a run of rapids,
The civil times of turmoil will be liberal.

其三

贪泉百度秋风，野迥嚣尘蔽空。
乳窦[1]石霄过雨，燕山鸟道残虹。

【注释】

①乳窦：泉眼。

Three

Autumn wind! Greedy Fountain on the web
Was obscured by the far, wild temporary clamours,
Like a cascading spring down the sky, breaking
The bird's rainbow over the Yanshan Mountain.

其四

盈川紫气回梦，满眼黄山动情。
荡子妍媸皂枥[1]，空嘶日月功名。

【注释】

①妍媸（yán chī）：美和丑。皂枥：马厩。养马之所。

Four

In the dream of the ruddy light, the whole river
Got an eyeful of yellow, emotional hills
Where a roue was stabled without aesthetic appeals
Whose null life neighed in his success and failure.

其五

走浪参差隐鳞，吹云入脑迷真。
游童未老先化，少艳衰翁汉津[1]。

【注释】

①汉津：银汉，亦称银河。

Five

A fish hides in the billows,
Lost into the brain the cloud whiffles.
Prematurely senile, his skipping time
Slides into the Milky Way as one knows.

其六

碎玉驰风浅濑[1]，遗金鼓浪轻尘。
千柯泾渭风翦[2]，澹动[3]珠光客心。

【注释】

①浅濑：水流急速的样子。②翦：同“剪”。③澹动：水波纡缓的样子。

Six

As the shallow water smashes the jade into a breeze,
The light dust billows for its lost gold.
As all the sails are lost in the wind,
The feeling of sojourn will be bejeweled in ripples.

其七

花飞剪断春服，古壁闲听草屋。
野粟乾坤翰墨[①]，高风掩卷悬牍[②]

【注释】

①翰墨：义同“笔墨”，原指文辞。②牍（dú）：古代写字用的木片。

Seven

Spring gowns are gone with the flowers,
From the old wall of the idle, thatched house,
Where a wild millet wishes to write the world,
That shuts and hangs the book in its high blasts.

其八

曙色城头鼓绝，穷通宝镜明哲[1]。
清崇象法[2]空阔，百代儒衣漫说[3]。

【注释】

①明哲：明智；洞察事理。②清崇：清贵显要。象法：国家的法律教令。③漫说：别说，不要说。

Eight

The early dawn catches the tums no more from the town wall,
Which was worldly wise to the fortunes like a rare mirror.
Dignitary or decretal, all the view has stretched into infinity,
And nore more all the generations of the Confucian clothes.

其九

落笔寒泉皎镜，青袍寸步衔命[1]。
灵踪慧性禅心，倦鸟空林短咏。

【注释】

①衔命：遵奉命令。

Nine

To write the cold fountain in the pale mirror,
The black gown has to bow at every order.
With the meditative mind of the trail, wise and clear,
The tired bird in its empty wood carols short.

今　天

今霄戴水孤驿，澹画泓澄①百尺。
聚散燕山小晴，花枝泛酒②结客。

【注释】

①澹画：如淡淡的水墨画。泓澄：水深而清。②泛酒：古代风俗。每逢三月三日，宴饮于环曲的水渠旁，浮酒杯于水上，任其飘流，停则取饮，相与为乐，谓之“泛酒”。

Today

My lone post house by the Daihe River now
Like a light, limpid water-colour a hnudred feet.
Just clears up down the Yanshan Mountain once in a while
And brings out the choice wine to the flowering wood.

禁　忌

卜筑[①]深云鸟道，青山瘦鹤楼台。
春残乱水群木，月影风急不开。

【注释】

①卜筑：选地盖房。卜：占卜。古人盖新居有请卜者看地形、相风水以定宅地的习俗，也称卜宅、卜居。

Taboo

To predict the bird passage in the deep clouds,
The huge tower thins like a crane in green hills,
Whose woods by the swift current in late spring
Are blustery without any shade of the moon.

经　历

深檐弱柏生寒，破影帘钩雪残。
寂寞苍山筚户[①]，青灯暗隙邯郸[②]。

【注释】

①筚（bì）户：用荆条竹子树枝编成的门。形容穷苦人家所住的简陋的房屋。②邯郸：也作“学步邯郸”。比喻一味地模仿别人，不仅学不到本事，反而把原来的本事也丢了。

Experience

Cold, feeble cedars outside the deep eaves drop
Their snow-thawed shades unto the drapery's hook.
My humble abode doleful in the green hills
Flickers its lamp with a blind imitation.

居陋室

陋室风花几年，三尺雪月生寒。
青丝斗米不在，饮雪吞毡何难？

【自解】

饮雪吞毡：出自西汉使者苏武滞留匈奴的故事。匈奴大汗扣留苏武，想让他投降，但是，苏武坚贞不屈，匈奴人因此把他囚禁起来，不给吃喝。于是，他渴饮雪，饥吞毡，匈奴人实在降服不了他，就让他到北海牧羊，告诉他什么时候公羊生了小羊，才放他回国。就这样，苏武在匈奴被扣十九年。

历经千百年的民族融合，匈奴的一部分跑到了欧洲，特别是建立了匈奴帝国，其他绝大部分已经被华夏同化了。苏武的气节是民族的，更是个人的：守得住方寸，耐得住寂寞，认准合理的目标，排除各种干扰因素，还有不会成功的吗？

In Humble Room

Poetic delight of humble years
Spells cold by three-foot snows

Whose bushels of sorrows
Could be swallowed in cheers.

距 离
Distance

其一

嘴距晨鸡罢唱，心规斗柄[1]遐望。
潮来日落孤帆，夜月平芜迥旷[2]。

【注释】

①斗柄：北斗七星中玉衡、开阳、摇光（或作瑶光）三星。②平芜：草木丛生的平旷原野。迥旷：旷远。

One

The rule of mouth has finished the cock's song,
The rule of heart looks up into the Dipper's Handle along.
One sail comes with the tide after the sundown,
In the moonlit night of the wilderness so long.

其二

推诚放旷[①]蓑笠，雾雨莺啼井邑[②]。
马首不饱稻粱，荒田露草初泣。

【注释】

①放旷：豪放旷达，不拘礼俗。②井邑：城镇；乡村。

Two

Earnest in a free spirit, the cape and hat
Warbled in the fog shower outside the town.
If the horse head had gone hungry,
The fresh, dewy weeds must weep in the barren land.

决　定

雨露残心薜萝[①]，垂实半醉空柯[②]。
檐前草色晴雪，紫绶[③]游仙梦多。

【注释】

①薜萝：薜荔和女萝。两者皆野生植物，常攀缘于山野林木或屋壁之上。②空柯：没有花叶的枝干。③紫绶：紫色丝带，古代高级官员用作印组，或作服饰。又指紫薇。

Decision

The broken heart climbs in the rains,
Fruitful but half-drunk on the empty branches.
As the snow clears up the herbs before the eaves,
The dreamy immortal would wander with the purple tassel.

看

乌窥汀州雪浪，花临户牖[1]孤舟。
机闲透水天眼，敛翠虚穿客游[2]。

【注释】

①户牖（yǒu）：门窗。②敛翠：凝聚秀色。客游：在外寄居或游历。

Look

Snow billows on the isle are spied by the birds
That moors one boat beside the blooming door.
As the pervious, divine eyes are least scheming,
My travel for pleasure threads the dense, vain green.

看得起

黄梅闭妾莺转，绿杏深闺鹤翔。
翠羽江天破露，沧波野市鱼梁[1]。

【注释】

①鱼梁：拦截水流以捕鱼的设施。

Highly Esteemed

Yellow plums close me as the oriole trills,
Green apricots seclude my boudoir as the crane circles.
As the green feathers over the river break the dews,
The fishweir practises wild in the boundless waves.

空

渺水清光落木，长天晓色离云。
临川带雨沧浪，满眼穷秋共闻。

Void

In bright light dappled with the falling leaves on the vast water,
The clouds are bidding farewell to the long sky at dawn.
Towards the surging, raining waves of the river,
An eyeful of limited autumn has been well-known.

孔子遗言
The Last Will of Confucius

其一

大享稽天物象[①]，三神百禄金石[②]。
行藏见智粢盛[③]，世上绝无孔丘。

【注释】

①稽（jī）天：至于天际。物象：客观事物，它不依赖于人的存在而存在，它有形状、颜色，有声音、味道，是具体可感的。②三神：人体三丹田之神。百禄：多福。金石：不朽。③行藏：行迹、出处。粢盛（zī chéng）：盛在祭器内以供祭祀的谷物。

One

To the boundless images, the sacrifices
Are pealing the bells and stones in the blessed abdomens.
When his whereabouts were wise in sacrificial grains,
Confucius would not have existed under the skies.

其二

禄位高低有无，明决耸志贤愚。
奴心翘股殊智[①]，朔漠三冬浴凫[②]。

【注释】

①殊智：独特的智谋或聪明。②朔漠：北方沙漠地带。凫（fú）：水鸟，俗称“野鸭”。

Two

High or low, the office and peerage are true or not,
Sage or fool, the shrewd mind is exalted.
Cocky and smart, the slave heart is none but
A mallard bathed in the north winter desert.

其三

寒汀践草[①]采秀，碧涧苔滑抚琴。
款曲[②]衔风百代，阳春羽客[③]幽寻。

【注释】

①践草：踩踏草地。②款曲：殷勤的心意。③羽客：羽士，指神仙或方士。

Three

For a perfect delight, go thru the cold isle meadow,
And play the lute down the green gully, mossy and slippery;
For all generations flutters after the courteous melody,
One Taoist priest seeks his seclusion in the spring glow.

其四

兵机动地悲风，断扫乾坤鬼雄。
锦帐辕门翠羽，何及满月彤弓[①]。

【注释】

①彤弓：漆成红色的弓，朱漆弓。

Four

An earth-shattering wind of corps woes
Wiped out all the ghost heroes of the worlds.
All green wings in the silk curtain of the camps
Didn't get near to the red, fully-drawn bows.

其五

拔山猛气行者，扯断天河倒泻。
紫液[①]横流骨山，强梁易主[②]华夏。

【注释】

①紫液：直接引用原文原意，"鲜血"。②强梁：勇武有力的人；又指粗暴、残忍或凶狠的人。易主：轮回主宰。

Five

Bold and powerful, do like the hercules,
Tearing down the galaxy for a pour
Of the blood flowing over the bone hills,
With the strength prevailing over China, to be sure.

其六

宝历齐民[①]易帜，飞蝇走虎曹吏[②]。
黑白莫论衰荣，慧剑清流燕戏[③]。

【注释】

①宝历：指国祚；皇位。齐民：治理人民。②曹吏：属吏；胥吏。③慧剑：佛教语。谓能斩断一切烦恼的智慧。燕戏：燕子嬉戏地飞翔。南朝·梁·何逊《为人妾怨》诗："燕戏还檐际，花飞落枕前。"

Six

Supersede that throne by the people,
For the officials like flies and tigers on the go;
Black or white, say not the swing of the pendulum, you know
The sword of wisdom is just a swallow sport on the clear flow.

其七

旌节[1]百代连璧，朔鼓千王大风。
猛虎移山绿眼，削藩剪爪皆同。

【注释】

①旌节：古代指使者所持之节，以为凭信。后借以泛指信符。唐制中，节度使赐双旌双节符。旌以专赏，节以专杀。行则建节符，树六纛（dào）。亦借指节度使；军权。

Seven

All emblems have been invaluable,
In the war-drum gales of all emperors;
To move the mountains, the green-eyed tigers
Removed the vassals like a clip of its claw.

其八

掩抑[1]空怀大志，施康变化衷情。
邦国莫论夷狄[2]，钓饵闲来圣明。

【注释】

①掩抑：压抑使低沉。②邦国：国家。夷狄：古代泛指中国东方各族为“夷”，北方各族为“狄”，因用以泛指异族人。

Eight

To be ambitious, but covered up in vain,
To be big-hearted, but mutate that heart-felt emotion.
For a nation that judges not of the barbarians,
Bait an enlightened sage for its leisure gain.

其九

儒门亿万忠孝，孔圣三千礼教。
治粟①犹如治国，息心②紫雾弥罩。

【注释】

①治粟：秦代所置掌管谷食钱货的官吏。汉初因袭。②息心：梵语“沙门”的意译。谓勤修善法，息灭恶行。也称控制人的灵魂。

Nine

Billions of loyalty and filial pieties
Were created by the Confucian code of ethics.
An official governance like the run of the countries
Uprooted all sundry ideas with the purple, cloaked fogs.

其十

海岱尊彝[①]礼乐，商弦蔓引[②]犀角。
霜刀暗锁游魂，至死荆山抱璞[③]。

【注释】

①海岱：海，东海，今之渤海；岱，泰山。泛指东海和泰山之间的地域。《书·禹贡》："海岱惟青州。"又云："海岱及淮惟徐州。"这里的语义扩大为山海、江山。尊彝：古代青铜尊、彝，均为古酒器名。泛指祭祀的礼器。②商弦：弹奏商调的丝弦。即七弦琴的第二弦。蔓引：牵连。③荆山：湖北南漳县的荆山抱玉岩，传为春秋楚国卞和得玉处；另指陕西省富平县西南荆山，相传禹铸鼎于此。抱璞：保持本色，不为爵禄所惑。

Ten

For rituals and music, the wine goblets of the mountains and the seas
Were strung with the gaur horns in their rhythmic melodies.
Even though the frost knives locked the external soul secretly,
It was still evident to be devoted to the undying fantasy.

其十一

紫诰垂纶[①]乐清，瑶墀[②]雅韵升平。
辞舌古詈吞声[③]，万里羲和[④]尚宁。

【注释】

①紫诰：指诏书。古时诏书盛以锦囊，以紫泥封口，上面盖印，故称。垂纶：传说吕尚（姜太公）未出仕时曾隐居渭滨垂钓，后常以"垂纶"指隐居或退隐。②瑶墀（chí）：玉阶。借指朝廷。③詈（lì）：责骂。吞声：不出声；不说话。④羲和：中国神话中太阳神之母的名字。

Eleven

Retired in cheer clear by the imperial order,
The jade steps were peaceful in their elegant rhymes.
Swallow those old bawls from the rhetorical tongues,
We know the driver of the sun has been still tranquil.

其十二

冥征杳霭[1]青关，寂历[2]苍苍客闲。
漠漠时空巨浸[3]，蓬壶[4]殡玉关山。

【注释】

①冥征：神灵暗示的征兆。杳霭：茂盛貌。②寂历：寂静；冷清。③巨浸：大河流；大海。④蓬壶：蓬莱，古代传说中的海中仙山。

Twelve

Green Pass lush in the oracle
Was carefree to be hushed in its spatio-temporal
Sea vastly and lonely that buried the jade
Into the wild, fabled abode of immortals.

筷子

素手开合淡菜，加餐冷热俗态。
幽禽醉饱膏粱[①]，起落应无滞碍。

【注释】

①膏粱：肥肉和细粮。指精美的衣食。

Chopsticks

Retractable vegetables by the fingers
Offer the meals to the laic heat and cold.
Dined and wined to the satiety, the hidden birds
Should be absolutely sure to be up or down.

乐　观

虚楼放旷[①]明火，静室逍遥暗涛。
满灶无烟紫塞，苍茫翠色天高。

【注释】

①放旷：豪放旷达，不拘礼俗。

Optimism

A free, open flame in the false floor
Goes free into the dead room with the blind billows
Around its smokeless oven near the Great Wall
Clothed in the vast, varied and lofty vegetation.

泪

风霜堕满残泪，看尽尘心百戏。
钓客谁能洗涤？清江沐浴泥滓[①]。

【注释】

①泥滓（zǐ）：泥渣。

Tears

My broken tears are fully weathered,
In all the games of the dust heart.
Who could baptize such a rodster
Bathed in the slush of a clear river?

冷热

金绳[①]远宦悲凉，寂寞烟波望乡。
戴水离亭羽客[②]，薄衣试问暄凉[③]。

【注释】

①金绳：黄金或其他金属制的绳索，用以编连策书。此处借指图书。②羽客：道士。③暄凉：暖和与寒冷。

Hot or Cold

The bookworm wails in his official career,
Doleful before the misty, homeward water.
In his departing seclusion by the Daihe River,
His simple life tries out the temperature.

恋爱

晚沐深情枕畔[①]，知音苦调逡巡。
飘飘弱柳明暗，掠脂难得养真[②]。

【注释】

①枕畔：枕边。②掠脂：残酷地盘剥。养真：修养、保持本性。

In Love

The heart strings are bathed on the pillows,
Whose soul mate prowls with a bitter tone,
Gone like the dark and light willows,
Where a usury can't abide in the nature of his own.

留后路

冰霜醉隐绝域，静览青石险塞。
锦字连织枕席，花枝锁断飞翼。

A Way Out

The tipsy rimes are hidden far, far away,
Inaccessible to the blue stone on the silent way.
With words woven into the satin pillow, the blooming
Branches have locked up the wing.

慢半拍

浮荣切忌疏慢[①]，辨口玄津遘患[②]。
快意青萝[③]宛聚，山高茎短烟幻。

【注释】

①浮荣：虚荣。疏慢：轻忽，怠慢。②玄津：玄妙。遘（gòu）患：

构成隐患；作乱。遘，通“构”。③青萝：又名松萝，一种攀生在石崖、松柏或墙上的植物。

Half-beat Slower

Halt the alienated vanity,
Defend the abstruse and lurking peril;
Like the green vines gathering joyfully,
Climb your short stalks up into the hazy fantasy.

忙

野润游蜂细雨，霜涵玉露烟光[①]。
喧嚣满眼蚊蚋[②]，雨霁繁枝绿阳。

【注释】

①烟光：云霭雾气。②蚊蚋（ruì）：蚊子。

Busy

A wasp wanders wild in the moist drizzles,
And fades into the frosty light, dewy and hazy.
An eyeful of mosquitos and gnats in row-de-dows
Are cleared up by the green sun in the branches thrifty.

梦　想

海内岩花翠袖，登楼散影依旧。
文闱北阙[1]浮萍，柳陌疏阴晚岫[2]。

【注释】

①文闱：科举考试。闱，试院。北阙：宫禁或朝廷的别称。②岫（xiù）：山洞。

Dream

Rocky flowers on her green，civil sleeves
Go upstairs with her loose shadows as usual，
Interpreting the imperial examination as a duckweed，
By the road to the dusk peak，shady but willowy.

秘　密

清阴咫尺夹岸，碧落风弦脆断。
隐雾虚空澹薄[1]，新蝉月苦缭乱。

【注释】

①澹薄：恬淡寡欲。

Secret

Closed within the banks, the clear shades are brittle
By the wind strings down the realms of bliss, foggy
Into the void, with a calm and self-composed disposition,
Loosing its balance below the bitter moon chirped by the cicadas.

明　知

天南暮鸟烟萝[①]，避世长竿笠蓑[②]。
静倚蓬蒿半睡，应识野迥[③]狂波。

【注释】

①烟萝：草树茂密，烟聚萝缠。②笠蓑（suō）：斗笠与蓑衣。借指劳动者。③野迥：旷野。

Self-awareness

A late bird in the hazy south shuns the world
In his cape and hat with a long rod,
Drowsy still on the brushwood
And the bushes, aware of the wild waves.

模　糊
Blurred

其一

丘墟[1]撼落珠泪，满眼波痕晚翠。
莫厌蒙戎沈姿[2]，轻求蔌蔌[3]独坐。

【注释】

①丘墟：废墟；荒地。②蒙戎：蓬松；杂乱。沈姿：深沉庄重的姿态。③蔌蔌（sù）：形容风声劲疾、花落的样子、液体流动的样子。

One

Tears shaken down the shambles
Have rippled an eyeful of the green evening.
Bored not with such a subtle，fluffy decency，
They are pursuing the trickles down in solitude.

其二

常怀稻粟一囤[1]，野马簪缨[2]模糊。
鸡豚桃源辅弼[3]，谁人否臧贤愚？

【注释】

①稻粟：粮食的总称。囤（dùn）：用竹篾、荆条等编织成的或用席箔等围成的存放粮食等农产品的器物。②野马：雾气浮动状如奔马。簪缨（zān yīng）：古代达官贵人的冠饰。后遂借以指高官显贵。簪为文饰，缨为武饰。③鸡豚：鸡和猪。农家所养禽畜。辅弼（fǔ bì）：辅佐；辅助。

Two

One bin of rice and millet often blurs
Before the hazy, ornamental tufts.
Hens or pigs to assist the fair rule! Who would
Make comments on the wise and the foolish?

陌　生

纤尘冷雨无晴，镜暗朝云野苹。
破浪高辞远棹，秋砧掩泣风声。

Unfamiliar

In the cold rain, the slim dust darkly mirrors
The wild clovers below the morning clouds.
Farewell! Thru the broken waves far by the oars!
Her washing block weeps silently to the winds.

男　人

西楼夜卷梅暗，北牖[①]朝飞柳明。
禁地耕犁蕙草[②]，疏愚堕髻[③]无名。

【注释】

①牖（yǒu）：古建筑中室与堂之间的窗子。后泛指窗。②蕙草：古代著名的香草，以其在零陵多产，故又有零陵香之称。③疏愚：亦作“踈愚”。粗疏笨拙；懒散愚昧。堕髻：堕马髻的省称。亦称“坠马髻”。古代妇女发髻名。

Man

The dark plums shrouded at night in the west tower
Will be bright in the morn willows to the north window.
To plough the sweet blades of grass in the forbidden area,
Even the neatly-braided hair should be slothful and ignoble.

脑　子

花旋脑破石枕，水转心开笋席。
破壁黄烟杳渺，摧环抱月微白。

Brain

On the stone pillow, the dizzy head crashes,

In the swirling water, the bamboo mat blooms its heart.
Beyond the broken walls, yellow smokes are dimly discernible
Below one crescent to be hugged by the gray streaks of dawn.

逆　风

千年落絮冲雪，百丈游丝逆风。
醉里谁知暗泪，迢遥苦乐穷通①。

【注释】

①迢遥：远貌。穷通：困厄与显达。

Upwind

The falling fuzzes like snow have flushed thousands of years,
And floated in the inverse blows of the gigantic gossamers.
Who would know the stealthy tears so tipsy?
The remote joy and sorrow will decide the wealth or poverty.

鸟　飞

一抹浮云掠过，两三瓦雀①闲落。
叽咕窃笑②蟾蜍③，羽翼遮天广阔。

【注释】

①瓦雀：麻雀。②窃笑：亦作“窃咲”。暗笑。③蟾蜍（chán chú）：古代神话中吉祥之物，借指月亮。

The Flight of Birds

A wisp of cloud has swept down
Two or three sparrows do-nothing,
Who babble and burble at the toad,
Opening out the wings like the sky.

女　友

东君低柳香暗，倦倚幽兰散澹。
素简[1]簪书子卿，秋毫倒卧生憾。

【注释】

①素简：朴素简约；指书籍。

Lady Friend

At sunrise, the subtle sweet amid the low willows
Drowsily leans on the hint of delicate orchids.
When the hairpin over the book fixes her whole attention,
An autumn hair that lies dead would be regretful.

朋　友
Friend

其一

幽怀旧友萧索，醉处遗踪[①]并跃。
澹荡青林露白，池边对影巢鹊。

【注释】

①遗踪：陈迹。

One

Deep and remote, my old guys are desolate,
Whose traces have been but tipsy and jaunty.
White-dewed, the green wood will be pleasant warmly,
Around the pool shadowed by a nested magpie.

其二

云行旧客春草，燕雀浮沈[①]易老。
万里轻腾破云，鸿鹄眼底晴岛。

【注释】

①浮沈：浮沉。

Two

On the spring meadow, an old passenger below the cloud
Drifts along like the chaffinch that comes on apace,
Or soars up the cloud light to the largest lengths of miles,
Where a swan commands its panoramic view of the fine isles.

骗　子

狂来谏猎[①]明境，杳杳含云素影。
远道无期草悲，黄鹄过后杯冷。

【注释】

①谏猎：典出《汉书》卷八十七上《扬雄传上》。指对天子迷恋游猎、不务政事，予以规劝。后泛指谏诤。此处指骗子的忽悠之术。

Cheater

Bamboozled into a wild hunt for the bright mirror,
The sombre cloud goes with its white picture,
Whose indefinite way of grass would be doleful,
Whose cup feels cold after the yellow swans go.

品 味

闲临品第[1]驰道，洗浪禅心四皓[2]。
遁迹白黑雪姿，荧荧曲润孤岛。

【注释】

①品第：门第；等级。②四皓：商山四皓，秦时隐士，汉代逸民，是居住在陕西商山深处的四位白发皓须、德高望重、品行高洁的老者。

Taste

Before the pedigrees free on the way,
The meditative mind is surfed for a perfect getaway,
Where the black-and-white posture of snow
Moistens its twinkling melody in the detached isle.

平 凡

幽人[1]浅卧悬榻，好鸟深藏茂枝。
柳色游春醉袖，鸭头绕水笆篱[2]。

【注释】

①幽人：幽隐之人；隐士。②笆篱：用竹、苇、树枝等编成的围墙屏障。

Commonplace

A solitary man lies on his hammock,
And a good bird hides deep in the lush branches;
As the wandering sleeves are intoxicated with the spring willows,
The duck heads will splish and splosh beyond my fences.

钱
Money

其一

古藓逍遥素钱[1]，金鞭走马风烟。
鸡鸣夜雨潮落，满口浮金困癫[2]。

【注释】

①素钱：指榆荚，俗称榆钱。②困癫：困顿失常。

One

The elm pods on the old mosses at large amble
With their golden whips in the blown smokes.
As the tide falls after the night rain at the crows,
The floating gold is trapped in open-mouthed disorders.

其二

连钱[①]莫计春草，露水荆钗[②]不扫。
野色空阶柳绵，金鳞远浪幽岛。

【注释】

①连钱：古钱币术语。指一炉所铸因未曾錾开而连在一起的两枚古钱。如战国晚期的“四布当”、新莽的“刀”等均有“连钱”。花纹、形状似相连的铜钱。②荆钗：荆枝制作的髻钗。古代贫家妇女常用之。

Two

No copper string haggles over the spring grass,
And no thorn hairpin needs to be pencilled.
Off the wild, stark steps, the willow fuzzes
Would swim to its secluded isle afar.

青　春

青春入户酣醉，一曲偷窗暖香。
举目微茫暮景，缘阶碧草烟光。

Youth

My youth comes dead drunk, and mooches
The warm sweet of her melodious window.
When I raise my gaze to the blurred dusk,
The green grass along her steps fades into a haze.

轻　重

兰房鸟道寒籁，凤阙[①]独明镜台。
塞马盈虚[②]日暮，归来碗转[③]黄埃。

【注释】

①凤阙：汉代宫阙名；皇宫、朝廷。②盈虚：盈满或虚空。谓发展变化。③碗转：言辞委婉含蓄。

Weight

In the chilly, zigzag bridal chamber,
The lonely dressing table stands bright by the grand gate.
After the cloud waxes and wanes with the eventide,
Its yellow dust would return tactfully.

情与景

江潮卷地人境，海雨平填隐情。

雨色箫台百尺，寒空鬼转心惊。

Sentiment and Scene

When the river tide sweeps the land of men,
The sea rain fills up the motives hidden,
Down the flute table hundreds of feet,
With a cold, heart-pounding apparition.

人

行人醉渡沙草，隐映千寻翰藻[①]。
落剪湿云晓风，溪烟野迥[②]横扫。

【注释】

①隐映：隐隐地显现出。翰藻：文采，辞藻。②野迥：旷野。

Man

The foot passenger tipsy across the sand binder
Nestles towards the long, rhetorical flourishes.
Having snipped the dawn-breeze off the moist cloud,
The hazy creeks would sweep the open country.

人生

人生处处阴晴，世事无常厉风[①]。
子建仙才势窘[②]，国桢[③]自尽昆明。

【注释】

①厉风：大风；烈风。《庄子·齐物论》：“泠风则小和，飘风则大和，厉风济，则众窍为虚。”②子建：曹植（192—232），三国时魏国诗人，文学家。沛国谯县（今安徽省亳州市）人，字子建，是曹操与武宣卞皇后所生第三子。势窘：刘勰在《文心雕龙·才略》中说：“文帝以位尊减才，思王以势窘益价”，认为曹丕（文帝）与曹植（思王）的诗文相比，曹丕在宫廷斗争中胜利了，当上了皇帝，才气减弱了；曹植被贬“势窘”，却文采富艳，他不幸的身世引起后世文人的认同。③国桢：王国维（1877—1927），字静安，又字伯隅，晚号观堂（甲骨四堂之一）。浙江嘉兴海宁人，中国近代学术史上杰出学者和国际著名学者，从事文史哲学数十载，是近代中国最早运用西方哲学、美学、文学观点和方法剖析评论中国古典文学的开风气者，又是中国史学史上将历史学与考古学相结合的开创者，确立了较系统的近代标准和方法。中年后，在“五大发现”中的三个方面，即甲骨学、简牍学、敦煌学上均作了辛勤的、卓有成效的探索，被公认为这些国际性新学术的开拓者、奠基者。王国维在学术上是置身于一个广阔的国际学术平台上来观察、思考问题的。1927 年 6 月 2 日，在颐和园昆明湖鱼藻轩自沉。

Life

Life is cloudy or sunny, at interval,
World is unpredictable, in a gale.
An immortal brush is frustrated politically,
And a prominent brain commits suicide finally.

人　心

无常世事如水，有序人情似山。
揽镜清波覆没①，幽阴②卷叶危崖。

【注释】

①揽镜：持镜；对镜。《晋书·王衍传》："然心不能平，在车中揽镜自照，谓导曰：'尔看吾目光乃在牛背上矣。'"宋·刘克庄《贺新郎·实之三和，有忧边之语，走笔答之》词："少时棋柝曾联句，叹而今，登楼揽镜，事机频误。"明·孙承宗《答袁节寰（袁可立）登抚》："以凌霄夜雪鹅池对六花而视草，谁能揽镜。"覆没（fù mò）：船只倾覆，沉没水中。②幽阴：阴暗。宋·苏辙《次韵子瞻十一月旦日锁院赐酒及烛》："光明坐觉幽阴破，温暖方知覆育长。"

【自解】

不逾矩，不僭越，做到自持和自守，这是处事的起码底线。物欲横流的时候，这类人不多，但不是没有。正是因为干净，麻烦也就来了；如果不想找麻烦，除非与世隔绝。然而，想找个桃花源，简直是乌托邦。还是自重吧。活着，怎么说也得有个心理防线，即使设了防，也难免好事者无事生非，三人成虎。

The Man's Heart

Like water, the world is fickle,
Like hills, men should be sequential.
On limpid waves, a mirror could be sunken,
Off a serene, shaded steep, the leaves drunken.

删 除

伤春数点雷雨，咏絮千番梦魂。
硬弩冥鸿[1]岁晚，谁识釜底凉温。

【注释】

①冥鸿：高飞的鸿雁。

Delete

Some drops of the thunderstorms in vernal sorrow
Are caroling the dreaming soul of the willow fuzzes.
After the crossbow misses the late, soaring swan,
Who would know the cold or warm bottom of cauldron?

伤 爱

红裙染雪新笋，绿袖垂风旧墙。
夜夜猿声客梦，隔帘咫尺青阳[1]。

【注释】

①青阳：春天的别称。

Grieved over Love

Her red skirt was snow-dyed into a bamboo shoot,
Her green sleeves lolled the wind on the worn wall.
Each of her night was dreaming like a howling gibbon,
And on the other side of the curtain shines the green sun.

上　课

物色[1]青阁晓光，长风柳陌河阳。
寒云淡荡良弼[2]，羽客[3]飞天践霜。

【注释】

①物色：风物；景色。②淡荡：水迂回缓流貌。引申为和舒。良弼：犹良佐，即操行好的小官。《书·说命上》："恭默思道，梦帝赉予良弼，其代予言。"③羽客：指神仙或方士。

To Attend Class

The black cabinet dawns naturally,
And whiffles the wayside willows into the sun of the river.
Below such a cold cloud, the soft and soothing conduct
Should be soaring and riming supernaturally.

时　间

孤芳鹤发[①]惊老，岁月青云厌寒。
寂寥烟霄[②]苦短，风骚逸气阑干[③]。

【注释】

①鹤发：仙鹤羽毛般雪白的头发。②烟霄：云霄。③逸气：清闲、超凡脱俗的雅逸之情。阑干：最早指一种竹子木头或者其他东西编织的一种遮挡物，后来引申为纵横交错的样子。

Time

A narcissist was startled to find his gray head,
Whose years rebelled at the cold clouds under the blue sky,
Where life is but a silent and drear span,
With a free, glamorous spirit upon the rails.

时　尚

飞鸦锁月空院，凤管宫莺百啭。
陌上黄鹂晓啼，参差落絮平甸。

Vogue

The moon-locked compound was hollow after the crow,
But was to be warbled by the jar-owl.

When the roadside oriole announced the arrival of dawn,
The jaggy willows would fall onto the pasture more and more.

是不是

穹庐晓镜鱼背，散眠秋窗犬吠。
渡水寒驴不鸣，苍烟岁晚茫昧[①]。

【注释】

①茫昧：模糊不清。

To Be or Not

The canopy dawns on the fish backs like a mirror,
Whence my loose sleep yips by the autumn window.
Like a cold, wading donkey who won't heehaw,
The closed year veiled in haze is incomprehensible.

树

凌宵翠盖嘉树，雾敛轻歌翠羽。
隐隐泉石岁阑[①]，长风落花淫雨[②]。

【注释】

①泉石：山水。岁阑：年末。②淫雨：持续过久的雨。

Tree

The stately tree towers like a king canopy,
Whose green feathers sing merrily and hazily.
As the year shuts its stone springs dimly,
The long wind drops the flowers to the rain loosely.

说　话

鸾台日月媸妍[①]，野鸟持情枕边。
漏尽疏钟翠幕[②]，莓苔[③]智月空圆。

【注释】

①鸾台：妆台。媸妍（chī yán）：妍指美丽，媸指丑陋。②翠幕：翠色的帷幕。③莓苔：青苔。

To Speak

Vulgar or elegant, her daily dressing table
Holds the emotions of a wild bird by the pillow.
Seeped down the sparse bells of the green curtain,
Her moon-lit wit on the moss sounds round but hollow.

说　笑

野客兰楫密叶，江僧柳浦幽花。

鱼惊鹤唳风晓，落镜青山断霞。

Speak or Smile

A wild traveller lay to his oars thru the waves of leaves,
And the secluded flowers down the riverside, willowy and priestly,
That shocked the fish and whooped the cranes blown at dawn,
Breaking the clouds into the fallen mirror of the green mountain.

死　路

追攀杳杳轻风，险涩[①]游思不穷。
暮纪[②]飞霜雪暗，危峦挂断飞蓬。

【注释】

①险涩：崎岖阻塞。②暮纪：一年将尽之时。

Impasse

To run after the slight breeze out and away,
The shoaly, swimming spirit was an endless story,
By the year end when the dark frost and snow flied,
The perilous peaks had hung up the fleabane.

太　阳

光斑一点天幕[1]，洗尽铅华[2]晓雾。
万里扶摇古今，明察善恶无数。

【自解】

①光斑：太阳光球边缘出现的明亮组织，比喻太阳初升的样子。天幕：笼罩大地的天空。②洗尽铅华：铅，古代用于化妆；华，外边的华丽。意思是洗掉伪装世俗的外表，不施粉黛，不藏心机，具有清新脱俗、淡雅如菊的气质。

The Sun

A light spot in the canopy
Clears up the daybreak foggy.
On a whirlwind thru all ages,
The omniscient Sage judges.

掏　钱

青钱[1]锦袖双臂，美味花黄两膝。
落木疏芜[2]宿鸟，咨咨废井唧唧[3]。

【注释】

①青钱：青铜钱。②疏芜：萧索荒芜。③咨咨：叹息声。唧唧：鸟鸣、虫吟声，又指叹息声、赞叹声。

To Pay

The copper coins out of the two silken sleeves
Get the tasty day lilies delivered to the knees,
Near the night birds desolate and deserted in the falling wood,
Overflown with soft sighs and stutters down the spent well.

天　才

铁马卿云[①]玉树，金闺绛雪[②]芳晨。
人闲翠幕[③]微雨，百越[④]遥听占春。

【注释】

①卿云：一种彩云，古人视为祥瑞。②金闺：指朝廷。也是闺阁的美称。绛雪：比喻红色花朵。③翠幕：翠色的帷幕。④百越：古代中原人对南方（秦岭淮河以南）部族的总称或通称。

Talent

The cavalry was rainbowed like the jade trees,
And the boudoir was red-snowed in the sweet morn.
As it dribbles in the green, idle curtain,
The native hordes are giving ear afar to the seized spring.

挖墙脚

枝头雨墨叠影，客散须臾落景[1]。
野寺清琴壮心，明朝雪满苍岭。

【注释】

①落景：落日的光辉。

Sabotage

The inky rain down the branches was folded over,
Before the scenes were coming loose.
The flaming heart of the wild temple played its clear zither,
Before the dark ridges the next morning had a snow cover.

网

繁张世网罗雀，野渡相萦敛索[1]。
宦序长竿钓台，疏檐夜半风恶。

【注释】

①敛索：搜刮索取。

Web

Spread the worldly network for sparrows,

And haul in the catch from the enwrapped ferry.
But as the official plops his bait long into it,
His loose eaves reap the whirlwind at midnight.

位置

晓窥平沙暗澹[1]，衔花浅草周览。
逢人汗漫[2]疏萤，顾影丰神燕颔[3]。

【注释】

①暗澹：亦作“暗淡”。不鲜艳，不明亮。②汗漫：漫无标准，浮泛不着边际。③丰神：风貌神情。燕颔：形容相貌威武。

Location

As the dawn peeps over the dim strand,
The flowers are all interspersed with the shallow grass.
As he should have roamed like the sparse fireflies,
He would raise his swallow's beak in the air of self-assurance.

无争

云霞览镜妖容，翠羽高情[1]露浓。
暖色黄阁[2]骨瘦，孤微野客遗踪[3]。

【注释】

①高情：高隐超然物外之情。②黄阁：汉代丞相、太尉和汉以后的三公官署避用朱门，厅门涂黄色，以区别于天子。借指宰相、高官。

③孤微：低微贫贱。遗踪：旧址，陈迹。

Stand Aloof

Seductive in the mirror, the rosy clouds
Are dewy densely with a high, green soul on feather.
Skinny in the warm, yellow door,
The wild traveller finds his lonely trace.

细语

浮萍丧志名利，信口青蝇举翅。
玉蕊娇容落红，幽姿照影妍媚[①]。

【注释】

①妍媚：可爱美丽。

Soft-spoken

The duckweed loses heart in wealth and fame,
And prattles like a blue fly to flap.
After the red, tender pistils are littered,
The subtle carriage beams her charms.

闲话男女

The Chitchat about Men and Women

其一

满目嘉姻忘我，遥知重义偷闲。
琢文玉佩淅沥，绮帐帘风堕鬟[1]。

【注释】

①鬟（huán）：古代妇女梳的环形发髻。

One

Everywhere, merry couples are carried away from
The integrity afar to snatch a moment of leisure.
While the pendants wrought in jade are drizzling,
Her tress falls into the wind of the silk curtain.

其二

月冷重帘梦远，西窗夜幕春漏。
高台满袖清歌，镜里仙郎道旧。

Two

A cold moon dreams far within the heavy hangings,
Leaking her spring of night curtain from the west window.
As the melody fills her sleeves in the high tower,
The fairy man in her mirror chats of old times.

其三

操琴海阔偷韵，冷酒花枝远近。
粉堕轻飏玉痕，回风弄影谁问？

Three

The wide sea is secretly played on the lute,
Far and near the flowering branches in the cold wine.
When the rouge floats off her fair impression,
Who would wonder her dancing shadow in the back draft?

其四

金闺自掩惆怅，铁骑平驱素衣。
对镜幽栖落日，青关眷恋云归。

Four

She closes her melancholy boudoir,
For her elite knight to drive his casual wear.
As the secluded sun sets in the mirror,
Her black pass loves the return of the cloud.

其五

漠漠青石野心，霏霏古壁长阴。
幽闺月露香暗，卧断银床半浔。

Five

Vast and lonely, his ambition like a bluestone
Is shaded long on the old wall that drizzles.
In her secret, sweet boudoir below the dewy moon,
Half of the silver bed breaks her slumber.

其六

性懒情丝伴酒，家贫素影牵诗。
梨秋醉舞江月，野渡孤舟鬓眉。

Six

Her indolent nature lingers into the wine of love,
His pure, poor shade has been obsessed by the poems.
While the pear autumn dances on the drunken, moony river,
Her temples and brows are paddled into the lone ferry.

其七

彩笔新添素花，白头谢客天涯。
风尘看剑瓜步[①]，妾梦应回晚家。

【注释】

①瓜步：山名，在南京市六合区东南，亦名桃叶山。水际谓之步，古时此山南临大江，又相传吴人卖瓜于江畔，因以为名。这里指立名之处。

Seven

More white flowers under the colour pens
Are locked to the skyline, grey-headed.
Crown with the glory in times of turmoil,
My dream should have been home, but late.

其八

泊舟雨暗蝉老，渡海云斜鹭新。
野水长桥顾步[1]，寒窗潜寐[2]思人。

【注释】

①顾步：徘徊自顾；回首缓行。②潜寐：深眠。

Eight

Berthed in the murky rain，the aged cicada chirps
To the new heron before the tilted cloud crosses the sea.
Along the wild water，the long bridge lingers
By the cold，missing window in deep sleep.

其九

翠影斜拔宿焰，空堂酒醒凉篁。
晴霓柳岸疏烟，水性含风掩敛[1]。

【注释】

①掩敛：遮藏躲闪。

Nine

Her green shade pokes his night flame on the cross,
Before the cool bamboo mat sobers up in the bare hall.
Sparsely hazy on the shore willowy below the fine rainbow,
Her fickle and lascivious breaths are shifty-eyed.

其十

雁翅穷泉野蒿，风急历乱[①]孤高。
蟾轮[②]梦断荒径，雪隐荻花怒号。

【注释】

①历乱：纷乱，杂乱。②蟾轮：圆月。

Ten

Over the wild wormwood of the nether world, the wild geese
Are soaring helter-skelter in the lone, strong wind.
While the Wheel of Toad wakes from the dreams of the wasted way,
The snow has concealed in the reeds that howl and snarl.

其十一

柳下抛心月榭[①]，闲情倚梦风帘。
殷勤莫道心雨，葬泪可识苦甜？

【注释】

①月榭：赏月的台榭。

Eleven

The terraced moon throws her heart down the willow,
Whose idle feelings lean on the dream of the air curtain.
Blame not the rain of heart which is so hospitable,
'Cause no buried tears know the bitter-and-sweet version.

其十二

晚色垂阴薜萝，游扬[①]扯碎清河。
沈沈[②]雨霁滴影，素魄[③]残香弄波。

【注释】

①游扬：幽晦貌。②沈沈：深邃的样子。③素魄：月光。

Twelve

The climbing figs are lolling their late shades,
Tearing the shrouded mists into the clear river.
In the overbrimming rain that drips the clear shadows,
The pure soul are rippling her lingering sweet.

其十三

落羽江湖禀命[1]，忧思柳变长镜。
齐云眇眇失期，素卷同心掩映。

【注释】

①禀命：指受之于天的命运或体性。

Thirteen

An itinerant wing falls to the Mandate of Heaven,
Haunted with gloomy willows over the long mirror,
Which is overdue down the clouds uncertain,
And sets off his pure, undivided devotion.

其十四

骑猪拱破鸡舍，驭马轻蹄狗窝。
尺草流离隐迹，幽枝坐卧青娥[1]。

【注释】

①青娥：指与女性有关的一些意象。一是指青女，也就是主司霜雪的女神；二是指美丽的少女。

Fourteen

On the swine, rootle the coop,
On the horse, kick the kennel;
Under one foot of grass, hide the vagrant trace,
And on the serene twig sits or lies a lithe maiden.

其十五

深恩反覆招隐[①]，旧路归还后尘。
晓雾空蝉堕露，截竹老雨初新。

【注释】

①反覆：反复。招隐：招人归隐。

Fifteen

The retreat into privacy beckons his repeated clemency,
On the old way that returns to those footsteps.
As the cicada drops its dews in the dawning fogs,
The chopped bamboo will shoot in the constant rain.

其十六

落地青霞欲散，飘零碧树初明。
薄衣瘦草平澹，彩袖交欢晚荣。

Sixteen

Aground, the blue cloud will come loose into
The first light thru the green, forsaken wood.
Thin-coated, his thin grass looks thin, though,
And her late, colourful sleeves are copulated merrily.

其十七

炼骨幽栖厚薄，合欢雨霁情多。
沉浮断续蓬转，耿耿星桥润河。

Seventeen

Thick or thin, the tempered bones are secluded
And wedded into a clear rain full of affection.
Up or down, like the floating thistledown,
The devoted bridge of magpies will be starry but smooth.

其十八

红颜朔雪[①]春色，绿鉴寒花梦思。
旧宇[②]飞蓬弱柳，倏忽枕簟[③]翻悲。

【注释】

①朔雪：北方的雪。②旧宇：旧宅。③枕簟：枕席。泛指卧具。

Eighteen

Her rosy lips and cheeks are a spring in the snow,
Free but green in the dream that mirrors the cold flowers.
In her former house by the pride-weeds below the feeble willows,
Her pillow turns doleful in the twinkling of an eye.

其十九

深溪半树红榴，辅弼①穷荒畅幽。
旅雁参差咏梦，清宵尽锁堪羞。

【注释】

①辅弼：辅佐；辅助。

Nineteen

Half the trees, the red pomegranates by the deep creek
Are supporting the serene and smooth desolation.
When the wild geese carol their dreams in graceful disorder,
The lonely night may be locked into its endurable pudency.

其二十

骄阳旱地晴雨，月满庭空闭户。
宿露花枝柳风，惊蝉满树空舞。

Twenty

Sunny or rainy, the arid land in the scorching sun
Still shuts its stark door after the moon is full.
In the night dews, the flowering branches are willowy,
Shocking the cicadas full of the dancing trees in vain.

现实

云根复照晴阳，远雁谁分子桑①。
送客闲阶断迹，吹裙暗草炎凉。

【注释】

①子桑：子舆和子桑是好朋友，他们都很穷。有一次，下了十几天的雨，子舆心想：子桑怕是饿出病来了吧？就带了饭去看他。子舆踏着泥泞走到子桑家门口，听见破屋里传出歌哭之声，是子桑正在唱呢。子舆推门进去，说："为什么唱这样的歌！"子桑说："是什么让我陷入这样的绝境？想来想去也想不出答案呀。父母爱我是无私的，他们难道愿意我一生受穷吗？我能责怪父母吗？天地无私，难道偏要我特别地承受苦难？我能怨天恨地吗？那么，是谁捉弄我到这地步？是命运吧？"

这里，子桑对人生、自然有着自己的思索和探求，不与世俗苟同，在纷乱的时代中保持着自己的价值取向，坚持着按照自己的观念来处世，因此，在物质方面是潦倒窘迫的。

Reality

The cloud root shines sunnily again,
With the wild geese gone adrift.
As the parting steps break their spare trace,
The secret grass whiffles her skirt in fickleness.

小便宜

开襟索杖头钱[①]，闭户求清枕眠。
墨守无人玉洞，谋身委似蜗涎[②]。

【注释】

①杖头钱：买酒钱，或人物放荡不羁。②蜗涎：蜗行所分泌的黏液。

Petty Gain

Open your clothes for the drink money,
Close your door for the clear dormancy,
Clung to the jade cave unmanned, and
Committed to the snail saliva so stingy.

小　人

宿草[①]沙虫暗壁，戚戚落景[②]喧秋。
莎寒露重悬影，野客屈身旧仇。

【注释】

①宿草：隔年的草。②戚戚：化典“君子坦荡荡，小人长戚戚”。落景：落日的光辉。

Little Man

Under the dark wall, the sandworms in the grass of last year
Are humming and shrilling in the sunset autumn without cheer.
On the cold leaves of grass the heavy dews hang their shadows,
Where the wild visitor lowers himself to serve the old foes.

笑　笑

烟汀[1]寂寥苔长，世路天阶晚阳。
丽藻[2]寒鱼客笑，青霞坠露温凉。

【注释】

①烟汀：烟雾笼罩的水边平地。②丽藻：华丽的诗文。

Spare a Grin

Silent and drear, the misty sand bar grows mossy so long,
On the way of the world to the heaven steps in the setting sun.
When the cold fish smiles about the ostentatious words,
The dark, rosy clouds are dropping their dews, warm or cold.

笑与泪

浮薄洗耳幽素[1]，落日长桥野渡。
寄语春秋缥囊[2]，留连晚照清露。

【注释】

①浮薄：轻薄，不朴实。幽素：幽寂。②缥（piǎo）囊：用淡青色的丝绸制成的书囊。亦借指书卷。

Smiles and Tears

Wash the frivolous ears in seclusion,
At the long bridge of the wild ferry in the setting sun,
That sends word to the books of spring and autumn,
And lingers around the clear dews below the afterglow.

心　口

心期夏夜萤火，掠影回旋叶堕。
霭霭横岑[1]暗灯，苍冥[2]漱口逃祸。

【注释】

①岑（cén）：小而高的山。②苍冥：苍天。

Mouth and Heart

My heart for the fireflies in the summer nights
Skims, whirls and tumbles like the fallen leaves.
When it glimmers to the cloudy, horizontal hills,
The blue sky would rinse its escaped mouth.

心　伤

闲愁冷雨情伤，隐隐眉边月凉。
翠影凌波玉漏[1]，尘缘弄粉流霜。

【注释】

①玉漏：古代计时漏壶的美称。

The Wounded Heart

In the cold rain, her needless woes for the pangs of disappointed love
Are dimly visible in the eyebrows below the cold moon
That ticks the flight of time on the waves where her green shadow
Should be rouged into the streaming frosts of the mundane world.

选 择
The Choice

其一

寒花野渡青帘，乱草新秋半蟾[①]。
落木辞家岁宴[②]，轻冰玉镜垂檐。

【注释】

①半蟾：半个月亮。②岁宴："宴"通"晏"，指太阳下山。此处与"岁"搭配，指年末。

One

Cold flowers of the wild ferry are covered with the dark curtain,
Over which half a toad croaks its fresh autumn in the weeds.
While the falling leaves are kissing away from the year end,
One jade mirror like a piece of ice hangs light from the eaves.

其二

客燕眉欺宝靥[①]，鸣鸠眼妒罗裙。
长波卷落霜雁，远塞飞梯片云。

【注释】

①宝靥（yè）：花钿。古代妇女首饰。

Two

The brows of the visiting swallow cheat her fair hairstyle,
And the eyes of the warbling cooer envies her silk skirt.
When the long wave sweeps the wild geese in the frost,
A flake of cloud is flying like a ladder to the skyline.

眼　睛
Eyes

其一

山头瘴色[①]萧飒，曲岸青袍落拓[②]。
紫燕梁间太平，黄鹄冷眼合沓[③]。

【注释】

①瘴色：因瘴疠患病的气色。②青袍：学子所穿之服。亦借指学子。落拓：豪放，放荡不羁。③合沓：重叠；攒聚。

One

The hilltop in miasma looks so bleak, and
The winding bank so wild and free in black gown.
As the purple swallows on the beam are safe and sound,

The cold eyes of the yellow swan are overlapped.

其二

虚怀宝瑟神女，洗眼清真使君。
木魅[1]荒淫静影，山精惑乱闲云。

【注释】

①木魅：老树变成的妖魅。

Two

Humble and valuable，the goddess plays her lute，
Clear and free，the noble man cleanses his eyes.
As the wood spirit debauches still trace，
The mountain sprite deludes the idle cloud.

眼　泪

点泪青眸玉滴，盈睫欲涕昭晰[1]。
菱花渐次微皱，曲落红尘素笛。

【注释】

①昭晰：清楚；明白。

Tears

Her crystal teardrops
Full on the crystalline eyelashes
Come to be crimpled in the mirror
And fall their melodies into the mundane dust.

掩　藏

晴丝惹断缨络[①]，澹荡裴回[②]燕雀。
壮岁劳歌帝乡[③]，灵风逸响元恶[④]。

【注释】

①缨络：珠玉串成的装饰物，多作颈饰。②澹荡：荡漾，飘动。裴回：彷徨。徘徊不进貌。③帝乡：京城；皇帝居住的地方。④灵风：春风；时势。元恶：大恶之人；首恶。

Conceal

The fine fibres have incurred the lapse of the tassels,
Where a warm and pleasant chaffinch was hanging about
The capital town from the fond song of farewell in his prime
For the chief culprit that echoed free with the trend of the times.

掩　盖

虚舟潜隐遐旷[1]，世路风乾懒放[2]。
醉卧幽栖禁门，空林芥子[3]深藏。

【注释】

①虚舟：无人驾驭的船只，比喻胸怀恬淡旷达。遐旷：辽阔；辽远。②风乾：借风力吹干。懒放：懒散。③芥子：十字花科植物芥的干燥成熟种子。

To Cover up

The unmanned boat lurks into a far-flung place,
Off the world way which has been weakly seasoned,
And secluded within the exclusion gate drunk in bed,
And hidden in the depths of the empty wood like a mustard.

妖　精

冷孽元凶杳冥[1]，华星朗照游灵。
孤心敛迹[2]妖氛，堕影浮云忘形。

【注释】

①杳冥：幽暗。②敛迹：收敛形迹。

Sprite

A gloomy ringleader of the cold sins wanders
His spirit below the starry light of rays with
His lone heart converged into the monstrous airs
That drop its shadow into the cloud beside itself.

腰　带

腰肢毁誉①天造，粉态穷通汉津②。
对镜妆奁③暮雨，霓裳④踏落红唇。

【注释】

①毁誉：毁损与赞誉。②穷通：困厄与显达。汉津：银汉。亦特指十二星次中的“析木之津”在尾与南斗之间。③妆奁（lián）：妇女梳妆用的镜匣。④霓裳：神仙的衣裳。相传神仙以云为裳。也是《霓裳羽衣曲》的略称。

Waistband

To be or not, the waist is fated to the nature,
Good or bad, the rouge to the Milky Way.
In the mirror, the trousseau rains at dusk,
And rides the red lips off her rainbow skirt.

一 定

芙蓉潋滟[①]翻云，绿水朱香为君。
醉客折枝泣露，娇声看惹罗裙。

【注释】

①潋滟（liàn yàn）：水波荡漾的样子，波光闪动的样子。

Sure

The hibiscus flowers are glittering and rolling like clouds,
With the green water cherishing its ruddy sweet for you.
After the tipsy passenger snaps the weepy dews,
Her silk skirt seduces there with the delicate breaths.

一个人

谁人北鸟披阳，绿绮舒文羽觞[①]。
半卷华烛浅笑，飞蹄壮齿奔亡[②]。

【注释】

①绿绮：古琴名。羽觞（shāng）：又称羽杯、耳杯，是中国古代的一种盛酒器具，器具外形椭圆、浅腹、平底，两侧有半月形双耳，有时也有饼形足或高足。因其形状像爵，两侧有耳，就像鸟的双翼，故名“羽觞”。②奔亡：逃亡。

Single-handed

Which bird is wearing the northern sun in
The melodious and aesthetic goblet?
With a trace of smiles to the flickering candles,
His strong teeth would gallop off for his life.

遗　憾

翘翠蛮腰①柳倾，蛾眉秀骨初行。
凌波②似雪闲卧，老镜黄莺数声。

【注释】

①翘翠：漂亮的发饰。蛮腰：年轻女子纤细灵活的腰肢。②凌波：女子步履轻盈。

Regret

Her fair hair is willowly down the supple waist,
Her fair framework newly goes with her arched brows.
Soon after her snow-white steps are lounged,
The golden oriole in her old mirror resounds its notes.

影　子

林疏吊影归梦，岸转销魂旧居。
莫恨羁人①野色，乘风羽化焉如②？

【注释】

①羁人：旅人。②羽化：古代修道士修炼到极致，跳出生死轮回、生老病死，是谓羽化成仙，飘飘乎如遗世独立，羽化而登仙。焉如：哪里去？

Shadow

My single dream returns to the sparse wood across the shore
Where my old home has been intoxicating my senses.
Hate me as the traveller in the wild, never more,
You know how I hope to take wing on the wind?

游　戏

铁锁惊波日下，眠沙海内青蝇。
灯花日影蝉翼，宝镜斜插帐绫。

Game

In a downward spiral, the iron chains were shocking the waves,
That caught up on the sleep of the blue flies on the civil sand.

While the lamp wicks were lucid through the cicada wing,
Her rare mirror was obliquely inserted into the damask curtain.

有

高谈老树风声，月里烟岚[1]客行。
冷澹飘萧[2]漏影，空庭枕簟虚明[3]。

【注释】

①烟岚：山里蒸腾起来的雾气。②飘萧：状风声。③枕簟：枕席。泛指卧具。虚明：空明；清澈明亮。

Possession

The old trees are soughing eloquently,
Where the moon goes thru the hazes.
In the cold, rolling rustles, a shade seeps
Onto my pillow in the garden bright in vain.

有所期

衡门素履[1]疏影，笔下新诗冷光。
敛翅[2]飘风蔽日，清明带月脱缰。

【注释】

①衡门：横木为门，指简陋的屋舍。素履：素净的鞋子。②敛翅：收拢翅膀。

To Be Desired

The dappled shadows in my humble room have stepped
Some other new lines under the cold light of the pen.
When the folded wings on the wind could shade the sun,
The clear and bright moon would be running wild.

原　来
I See

其一

帘帏莫测芳辰，梦里幽寻蕴真。
瘦马清宵暗魄①，花枝晚露消春。

【注释】

①暗魄：月牙儿；新月。

One

Curtain! Your fine morning may be inscrutable,
And to seek your dreams could entail the truth.
As your feeble horse deepens the soul of the lonely night,
The late dews on the blooming branches would vanish with the spring.

其二

暮霭萧萧雨蝶，穿花百啭榆荚①。
蚕蛾画断纱罩②，落寞扑灯坠睫③。

【注释】

①榆荚（jiá）：榆树的果实。②纱罩：旧时婚礼中新娘罩面的纱制头巾，又指蒙纱的灯罩。③坠睫：流泪。

Two

Butterflies are drizzling at dusk,
And twittering thru the flowers with the elm leaves.
A silkworm moth breaks the painted gauze cover,
And darts into the light that drops the lone lashes.

缘

孤帆破镜缘业①，酹酒②高台凤箫。
锦帐空凉嫩雨，流莺暗渡夕潮。

【注释】

①缘业：也称业缘。谓善业为招乐果的因缘，恶业为招苦果的姻缘，一切众生皆由业缘而生。后多指男女之间姻缘。②酹（lèi）酒：以酒浇地，表示祭奠。古代宴会往往行此仪式。

Fate

The single sail shatters the past fate in the mirror,
And spills this flask of wine to the phoenix flute on the dais.
Inside the silk bed-curtain, the tender rain feels cool and empty,
And the twittering orioles are wading the evening tide in secret.

攒着

烟云野幕沧溟[①]，鸟道清音忘形。
铁马平沙敛迹，闲听巨浪叮咛。

【注释】

①野幕：野外的帐篷。沧溟：大海。

Accumulation

Over the vast sea below the cloudy canopy,
The bird passage with resonant notes was beside itself.
After the cavalry on the strands had been prudential,
The billows were whispering in the spared ears.

知　识

遥约草木垂雾，近揽乾坤卧云。
披拂[①]青楼片月，春帘细雨争分。

【注释】

①披拂：吹拂；飘动。

Knowledge

To date the hanging fogs in the far wood, and
To seize the sleeping clouds of the near universe,
The green mansion sways below the moon,
With its spring screen sprinkled but wrangled.

重

结茅[①]宿鸟藤萝，若木[②]逢时几多？
密处藏枝野迳[③]，空林眇眇乔柯[④]。

【注释】

①结茅：编茅为屋。谓建造简陋的屋舍。②若木：传说中神木名。此树呈赤色，叶青花赤，光辉照地。③野迳：野径。④眇眇(miǎo)：辽远；高远。乔柯：高枝。

Weight

A night bird in its humble vines
Wonders when to encounter the golden bough.
Densely under the wild trail,
The higher branches tower in its empty wood.

竹隐

寂历幽篁[1]翠湿，流香纨扇相袭。
春山色照苔锦，大隐空山静习。

【注释】

①寂历：凋零疏落。幽篁：幽深又茂密的竹林。

Hidden in Bamboos

Wet and green in giant thickets of bamboo, the desolate
Silk fan follows its own flowing fragrance.
When the spring mountain beams down upon the silken moss,
The better reclusion is to develop a stark and still practice.

自欺

薄夫[1]久窃幽梦，露簟[2]孤吟玉洞。
九派[3]仙游浅深，柴鸡倒影乘凤。

【注释】

①薄夫：刻薄或浅薄的人。②露簟（diàn）：竹席。因其清凉如沾露，故称。③九派：长江到湖北、江西、九江一带有九条支流，故以九派称这一带的长江，后也泛指长江。

Self-deception

The secret dream has been stolen long by the acid tongue,
On the dewy mat of the jade cave that chants in solitude.
Deep or shallow, all the would-be immortals may be wandering,
Featured as a phoenix, but proven to be an inverted, cage-free fowl.

自　由

逢春敛笑清波，乱夜冲融[①]雪河。
四气尝闻燕语，幽石暮色庭柯[②]。

【注释】

①冲融：充溢弥漫貌。②庭柯：庭园中的树木。

Liberty

The limpid wave freezes its smile to the spring,
But suffuses its chaotic night like a thawed river.
As the four gases have heard of the swallow's voice,
The garden trees are gloaming in their hidden rocks.

嘴

朽嘴青鸦入肉，啾啾日暮披腹[①]。
推心百蜞簧舌[②]，翳翳[③]多情唤物。

【注释】

①披腹：披露真诚。②簧舌：如簧之口。多借指谗言。③翳翳（yì）：晦暗不明貌。

Mouth

Beak-rotten，the black carnivorous raven
Caws in the veracious nightfall,
With the quick，sharp flow of soul and tongue,
For his sombre and amorous call.

最高境界
Supreme Pursuit

其一

布政[1]霜台猛虎，为官粉署[2]苍崖。
飘摇造化同穴，客梦唯求避豺。

【注释】

①布政：施政。②粉署：又名粉省，尚书省的别称。

One

Fierce tigers were heading the administration
Of the state affairs on the black cliffs.
In the same, tottering dens by the Creater,
Their passing dreams were to avoid the jackals.

其二

素律[1]寒光翦云，凌风戴水生文。
疏凉孟夏[2]高枕，苦调危途始分。

【注释】

①素律：秋令；秋季。②孟夏：进入夏季的第一个月，即四月。

Two

In the frosty light, cut that autumn cloud,
With the woven wings, the Daihe River ripples.
In the cool breaths, the early summer rests easy,
With a bitter tone, start to sieve the perilous way.

其三

平生桂客疏索[1]，累日衔杯寂寥。
野马羁人[2]吊影，苍梧鹤梦云消。

【注释】

①桂客：对科举及第者之称。疏索：冷淡，冷漠。②羁人：旅人。

Three

All his life, the academic winner stands offish,
Illusory and intangible with his cup all day long.
Single and alone, the wayfarer in the wandering air
Flies away in the crane dream of the green parasols.

其四

叠沙隐隐柴桑[1]，断续骑春羽觞[2]。
倚树独言戴水，清琴柳暗眼长。

【注释】

①柴桑：故里。②羽觞（shāng）：又称羽杯、耳杯，是中国古代的一种盛酒器具，器具外形椭圆、浅腹、平底，两侧有半月形双耳，有时也有饼形足或高足。因其形状像爵，两侧有耳，就像鸟的双翼，故名“羽觞”。

Four

My home village dimly visible in the dunes
Rides the fitful cup of the spring.
To think about the trees on the Daihe River,
The clear zither plays its panorama below the dark willow.

其五

江湖落日归鸟，顾影恩波月杳。
袖障明霞雨仙，幽栏紫府吟晓。

Five

The bird returns to the itinerant sunset,
Narcissistic on the graceful waves of the far moon.
As the bright, rosy clouds block the sleeves of the rain immortal,
The daybreak would chant its serene rail of the purple palace.

其六

对酒空花楚客[①]，杯间月色寒魄。
笙歌醉触流莺，酩酊青帘苦涩。

【注释】

①楚客：特指屈原，泛指客居他乡的人。

Six

The vagrant drinks to the empty flowers,
Below the cold soul of the moon.
As the tipsy revelry touches the twittering orioles,
The ebriety tastes bitter within the black curtain.

其七

桑栽绿叶新岁，翅掩黄莺旧朋。
落笔天台暖影，融怡①莫醉薄冰。

【注释】

①融怡：融洽；和乐。

Seven

Tailor the green mulberry leaves for the new year, and
Cover the wings of the golden oriole for the old friend.
Write the warm shadow before the quiet retreats,
But be drunk not on the cat ice that thaws joyfully.

其八

逸韵青苹柳风，烟波落景飞鸿。
丹阳肃肃苍旻，卧草白头曲终。

Eight

The green, lofty cadences are willowy on the misty,
Rolling water in the sunset by the swan geese.
As the red sun sails down the grey, solemn sky,
The hoary hair on the grass shall close its music.

其九

翠染凌澌[1]伴月，孤篷马尾游阙[2]。
青冥[3]不晓关河，万事浮云芜没[4]。

【注释】

①凌澌：流动的冰凌。②游阙：备用的游车。[3]青冥：形容青苍幽远。指青天。④芜没：掩没于荒草间。

Nine

The flowing icicles are dyed green to the moon,
Over the idle, single coach behind the horse tail.
Ignorant of the hills or rills, the sky
Storms and seizes all the cloud drifts.

六言律诗

Six-character Octave

六言律诗格式

要求每句字数相等，平仄相对，一诗八句，偶句入韵，一诗八句，中两联对仗。

【平声韵】律诗押平声韵

1. 平起首句押韵格式：

平平仄仄平平（韵），仄仄平平仄平（韵）
仄仄平平仄仄，平平仄仄平平（韵）（对仗）
平平仄仄平仄，仄仄平平仄平（韵）（对仗）
仄仄平平仄仄，平平仄仄平平（韵）

2. 仄起首句押韵格式：

仄仄平平仄平（韵），平平仄仄平平（韵）
平平仄仄平仄，仄仄平平仄平（韵）（对仗）
仄仄平平仄仄，平平仄仄平平（韵）（对仗）
平平仄仄平仄，仄仄平平仄平（韵）

【仄声韵】

1. 平起式：

平平仄仄平仄（韵），仄仄平平仄仄（韵）
仄仄平平仄平，平平仄仄平仄（韵）（对仗）
平平仄仄平平，仄仄平平仄仄（韵）（对仗）
仄仄平平仄平，平平仄仄平仄（韵）

2. 仄起式：

仄仄平平仄仄（韵），平平仄仄平仄（韵）
平平仄仄平平，仄仄平平仄仄（韵）（对仗）
仄仄平平仄平，平平仄仄平仄（韵）（对仗）
平平仄仄平平，仄仄平平仄仄（韵）

八仙花

冷爱冰姿暗香，蒙咙[①]半卷朱光。
和风袅袅华彩，晓日青青淡妆。
画苑初开小径，丝竹欲掩川冈。
八仙搅动沧海，甩袖涂蓝大洋。

【注释】

①蒙咙：朦胧。

Hydrangea

Her subtle fragrance from the purity of the lovely rice
Half scrolls the red and hazy light.
Her rich colours curled in the soft breezes
Are lightly powdered in the green，tender dawn.
When her footpath stirs the fresh art gallery,
The silk and bamboo music hopes to cover the hills.
After the Eight Immortals churned the sea,
One flick of her sleeves should blue the ocean.

百日红

仲夏云间赫日[1]，含情寄语灵室[2]。
红光百度神幽，紫韵千回致逸。
破锁惊风众星，开源喘月文质。
沉怀万点相思，几树生怜饵蜜。

【注释】

①赫日：红日。②灵室：灵兰室。古藏书的秘府。

Crape Myrtle

A red sun in the clouds of the midsummer
Has messaged the clever and tender chamber:
Red hundreds of times with the secluded spirit,
And purple thousands of times with the utmost solitude.
Unlock the stormy power of all the stars,
And unbolt the wheezing moon in ornate quality,
A myriad of pangs of love are sedimented into the heart,
Where some trees are taking pity on the bait honey.

百子莲

百子春来物情[1]，枝条素艳[2]初明。
抽苞玉粉方冷，吐信[3]蛾眉半荣。
艳质无需谄媚，空心最晓陈诚。
思君恻耳千里，哪日风回故程？

【注释】

①物情：人情；情理。②素艳：素净而美丽。③吐信：吐花蕊。

Agipanthus

On the ways of the world, hundreds of seeds come with the spring,
With the white wickers that are freshly glowing;
Their pure pollens in bud are curling up with chills,
And their blooming brows are half flourishing.
Such a graceful charm dispenses with the blarney,
Such a hollow heart is alive to the honesty.
When I miss you, my sympathy thousands of miles away
Hopes to hear the day when the wind returns on my way.

帮　助

燕市奔觥[①]战骨，存亡断续胡越[②]。
识弓瀑浪腾腾，认箭边笳兀兀[③]，
冷月千军不存，寒沙万马芜没[④]。
前朝莫问沈沙，史册箫韶共谒[⑤]。

【注释】

①燕市：指今北京市，此处为泛指。觥（gōng）：酒盏。②胡越：敌人或对立关系。③兀兀：用心的、劳苦的样子。边笳（jiā）：即胡笳。我国古代北方边地少数民族的一种乐器，类似笛子。④芜没：掩没于荒草间；湮灭。⑤箫韶（xiāo sháo）：舜乐名；泛指美妙的仙乐。谒（yè）：拜见。

Assistance

The battle bones bolted to the cup in the town
Had little in common, alive or dead.
To know the bow that falls like the seething billows,
The arrows showed off the flute which must be toilful.
Below the cold moon, thousands of troops were no more,
In the cold dusts, ten thousand horses were taken by storm.
Never ask the trapped sand about the former dynasties,
Let's greet the fairy music recorded in histories.

榜　样

柳岸扁舟远梦，娇莺窥月吟弄。
灵枝皎皎青鸾，玉树飘飘紫凤。
翠色仙桥野村，离情古道幽洞。
蓬瀛水客独行，射浪蛟螭[①]破瓮。

【注释】

①蛟螭（chī）蛟龙。亦泛指水族。

Example

The boat by the willowy shore far in the dreams
Spied upon the sweet warbler under the moon,
Glistening like a pheasant on the spiritual branches,
Or fluttering like a purple phoenix on the jade trees.

Clothed with the green fairy bridge, the wild village
Parted the sorrow of its secret cave near the old road.
To walk alone like a passenger on the fairy isles,
The boa-dragon shot the billows at the broken urn.

包　容

破口流光壮行，恣行远近狂冲。
流言鼓噪云汉，恶语喧聒①仲冬。
大块悲辛妄作②，劳生嗳气顽凶③。
浮生转瞬烟灭，聚散风烛去踪。

【注释】

①喧聒（guō）：闹声刺耳。②大块：大自然；大地；世界。悲辛：悲伤辛酸。妄作：无知而任意胡为。③嗳（ài）气：俗称"打饱嗝""饱嗝"，是各种消化道疾病常见的症状之一。顽凶：愚妄不顺。指恶人。

Tolerance

To hurl the time slurs at the grand departure,
And to act wilfully and unscrupulously, far and near,
The rumours in the clamours howl and shriek higher,
And the rough tongue is garrulous to the midwinter.
While the touching world commits all manner of evil,
The breath of the creatures blows dreadful.
This floating life shrivels up in a twinkle,
Like the candles before the wind that come and go.

报春花

劲骨相钩野藤，疏慵倒挂金绳[①]。
冰轮[②]掩映河静，倩影参差海澄。
韵绕尘香绮陌，光摇墨润香绫。
春来剪碎清曲，嫩语消融素冰。

【注释】

①疏慵：懒散。金绳：形容串串虬枝上的报春花。又喻指太阳。②冰轮：喻指月亮。

Harbinger-of-spring

The wild vines are clawed by the strong bones,
Hanging upside-down like golden, slothful ropes.
While the wheel of ice screens the still river,
Their pretty, spotty shades are clarified by the sea,
Whose rhymes down the sweet suburban paths
Shimmer their sweet silk like the smooth ink.
As the spring comes and snip the sweet song,
Their soft say shall thaw out the pure ice.

悲 剧

挟矢[①]百步凉热，惨澹无辜寸铁。
落羽杯中控弦[②]，孤鸣酒里悬彀[③]。
虚空纸上喧哗，此处谈兵寂灭[④]。

玉兔闲观六钧⑤，凌寒渡水幽咽。

【注释】

①挟矢：持箭。②控弦：弯弓。③悬彀（gòu）：张弩。④寂灭：度脱生死，进入寂静无为之境地。⑤玉兔：喻指月亮。六钧：强弓。

Tragedy

Cold or hot, the arrow measured hundreds of feet
Shot the innocent and strenuous gloom
Of the feathers down into the cup
That cried to the drawn bow in solitude,
On the hollow, blatant paper with
The desk-intensive extinction of distress.
While the idle moon watches the crossbow,
The frosty bites would be waded in whimpers.

变　革

流音镜内文章，楚客欢娱稻粱。
落叶青林旷望，幽居绿水微茫。
壶中咫尺苍岭，洞里千秋紫阳。
梦断飞蓬玉枕，白须望断穷荒。

Change

The gliding tones of the letters in the mirror
Are lifted in mirth like a stray dog for food.

When the green leaves fall beyond the depths of yonder,
My reclusion will be blurred by the green water.
Closed on the horizon near the flagon, the dark hill
Basked in the purple sunlight outside the ageless cave
Wakes from the dream of fleabane on the pure pillow
Whose barren white has been gone from view.

层　面

红鬃伺隙[①]伏兽，落魄休嘶内厩[②]。
世事知情未名，年光路远难透。
泉声坐客伤别，月影巢禽论旧。
志业何当[③]比肩，三年隐见孤陋。

【注释】

①伺隙（sì xì）：窥测可乘之机。②厩（jiù）：马棚，泛指牲口棚。③何当：犹安得，怎能。

Level

My red mane bode its time to subdue the beasts,
But never neighed in the inner stable as a goner.
If the world knows the inside, nameless story,
It's hard to pass far through the passage of time.
To the tone of fountains, the spectator so heart-broken
Recollects his good old days like a fowl nested in the moon.
How to turn into the rival with the life's work?
To be sequestered from the society about three years.

长城梦

威灵[①]澹荡驱驰，坐占烽堠四夷[②]。
壮士云飞鼓角，将军雪刃旌旗。
鸿嘶敕电风进，帐冷惊飙火随。
万里长城尚在，何惜百万沈尸[③]。

【注释】

①威灵：神灵。②四夷：对中国周边文化较低各族的泛称。即东夷、南蛮、北狄和西戎的合称。③沈尸：陈尸。

Dream of the Great Wall

Ride hard, your powerful soul aspires to seize
All the frontier tribes down the smoke towers.
Among the wrathful drums and bugles, the warriors
Are sabring the banners in the snow under the general.
Strike down, with the squally thunderbolt of your swans,
That shock the following flames to the cold camps there.
The Great Wall still stands alive in the air,
Which has never begrudged one million bodies.

长寿花

天泽物象[①]延龄，度岭渊云自冥[②]。
密雪相思绿树，寒星至理青萍。
德风必有先后，胜气无非宠荣。

百岁升沈[3]苦短，独寻腊月光庭。

【注释】

①物象：可感知的客观事物。②渊云：高空和深潭。亦以比喻施展才能的环境。冥：昏暗；深沉。③升沈：即“生沉”，也是“生辰”的谐音。

Jonquil

The macrobian images by the nature
Are obscure in the mountain ranges, higher or deeper.
Densely snowed in the green, love-lorn trees,
The cold stars are a maxim to the blue duckweeds.
If the wind of moral has its order,
The vehement vigour will win its royal favour.
Up or down, one hundred years are swift sadly,
In search of my barren garden under the twelfth moon lonely.

吃　苦

风尘百草疏顽[1]，有负流年苦颜。
草创幽拙[2]路险，谋身睿算途艰。
咸阳古道犹在，易水狂夫不还。
路转鸡鸣报晓，低头叫醒函关。

【注释】

①疏顽：懒散顽钝，或指强硬、固执。②幽拙：愚拙。亦指愚拙的人。

Hardships

All herbs slothful but stubborn in times of turmoil
Live down to the bitter faces of the swift time.
On the vicious way sketched out in clumsy stupidity,
This rough mind is but a shrewd accessory in life.
Behold! The old road of Xianyang is still there,
But the madman by the Yishui River never returned.
Where the path winds down, the cock heralds the daybreak,
And revives the Hangu Pass by tilting his head downward.

怆　然

寒云大漠人单，莫为途穷弃捐[①]。
雁过悲乡路远，星移叹梦君边。
高风向晚云净，细露连空晓天。
故土蛾眉作古，乡音众里独全。

【注释】

①弃捐：抛弃。

Sorrowful

Alone in the great desert below the cold cloud,
Don't give up on the way out.
The wild geese gone are tracing down their hometown, and
The stars gone are sighing for your pillow in dream all along.

As the dusk is coming, the cloud is blown high and clear,
And stretched to the skies the fine dews are dawning.
After all my beautiful, native eyebrows have passed away,
None but my local accent will have reserved its former say.

存 在

旁观逝去者存，进退难于取舍。
毁誉阴风满身，优游嫩柳空惹。
不明仕宦沉浮，怎懂官曹[①]上下。
背后谁能下石[②]，生人要辨真假。

【注释】

①官曹：官吏办事机关；官吏办事处所。②下石："落井下石"的省称。

Existence

Look! The departed saint still exists there,
But impossible of his choice where to ebb and flow;
All over the body, the evil wind may blow its praise or blame,
And devoted to idleness, the tender willows are felt in vain.
Unaware of the official vicissitude,
How could you know the ups and downs of the officialdom?
And who could kick the man when he is down?
A living sould should learn to know true from false.

答　案

微辞莫叹宽窄，世梗途穷损益。
坐看山川寂寥，谁识断梦萧索。
穷通散影闲居，苦乐流光自适。
暗覆棋声百端，门深羽客博弈。

Answer

A subtle tongue sighs no breadth,
And a stalk in life on its way out may lose or gain.
Still before the solitary streams and mountains,
Who could read the bleak scene in the broken dreams?
Failure or success disperses like an idle shadow,
Joy or sorrow fits apiece like a flowing light.
To all the chess sounds to be developed secretly,
The deep door has its own gamesters or chessplayers.

大丽花

红簪[①]照落长镜，漏彩浑圆气正。
带雨空山寿光[②]，连云野渡回映。
明鲜历乱薄情，落寞参差厚命。
故宇消磨丽人[③]，新泉[④]是否同病？

【注释】

①红簪：花粉色，花瓣浑圆，玫瑰形，花径 12 厘米。植株紧凑协

调，非常美丽。②寿光：花色鲜粉，花瓣末端白色，花朵艳丽，花径 12 厘米，株高 110 厘米，为夏、秋季切花品种。③丽人：花紫红色，花瓣先端白色，花径 10 厘米，株高 100 厘米，直立性强。为小型切花品种。④新泉：花鲜红色，花瓣边白色，花形美，极早花品种。

Dahlia

Her red hairpin has beamed down the long mirror,
Perfectly round and square in her bright rays of colour.
Her pink-and-white splendour like a drizzle in the empty hill
Reflects the clouds over the wild ferry.
The turmoil of times may be bright and fickle,
But her lone, graceful disorders should be lucky.
If such a beauty putters away in the native land,
Whether her fresh spring will be similarly afflicted in the end?

大学生的尴尬
Embarrassed Undergraduates

其一：恋爱

梨花度曲[①]阿娇，弄月罗绮玉箫。
锦水宫迷迹系，琴台蔓草神超[②]。
奇花枕底野人，玉兔帆前半妖。
咫尺玄云[③]暮鸟，闲观海气成潮。

【注释】

①度曲：唱曲。②神超：精神飞逸。③玄云：黑云，浓云。也指黑发。

One：In Love

Pear flowers swim in the tender song,
Played to the moon with their silken flute,
That ties up the labyrinth of the limpid water,
Exuberant with the weed vines around the lute terrace,
Where the pillow of the exotic flowers may be savage,
And the moon before the sail could show the half-monster.
Down the close, dark clouds returns the dusk bird,
With its spare eyes at the air into the sea tide.

其二：工作

庸奴浪迹知辱，抱瓮黄庭[①]益笃。
故态琼枝翠微，长思粉壁空曲。
柴关草履孤平[②]，野客绫梭启沃[③]。
梦怯鸡声世云，荒迷曲岸幽酷。

【注释】

①抱瓮：典出《庄子》外篇之《天地》。传说孔子的学生子贡在游楚返晋过汉阴时，见一位老人一次又一次地抱着瓮去浇菜，“搰搰然用力甚多而见功寡”，就建议他用机械汲水。老人不愿意，说：这样做，为人就会有机心，“吾非不知，羞而不为也”。这也被视为对技术、机械文明的某种反省。后以“抱瓮灌园”喻安于拙陋的淳朴生

活。亦省作“抱贫”。黄庭，亦名规中、庐间，一指下丹田。②柴关：柴门。孤平：韵句中除韵之外只有一个平声字，或两仄夹一平。此处指上学，做学问。③绫梭：织帛的机梭声。启沃：典故名，典出《尚书·商书·说命上》。商王武丁任用傅说为相时，命之曰：“若岁大旱，用汝作霖雨。启乃心，沃朕心，若药弗瞑眩，厥疾弗瘳。”意为“比如年岁大旱，要用你作霖雨。敞开你的心泉来灌溉我的心吧！比如药物不猛烈，疾病就不会好。”后遂用“启沃”指竭诚开导、辅佐君王。

Two：Job

The mediocre slave roams free with the heart of shame,
In his quieter calm of pristine life.
To the jasper boughs of the emerald hills, his old posture
Misses long the empty song on her white-washed wall.
While his smooth straw sandals comes into the wooden door,
His wild mind might be shuttled towards the official channel.
Below the clouds of the world, his dream fears the cock crow,
Lost into the wasted, winding bank with the ruthless secret.

其三：生活

狡兔常怀翠阜[①]，飞鸿难追苍狗。
情知万草天涯，莫怪清霜洞口。
造化安知梦田，乾灵变在渊薮[②]。
高风漫卷寒潮，远照茅檐共守。

【注释】

①阜（fù）：土山。②乾灵：上天。渊薮（sǒu）：渊，深水，鱼住的

地方；薮，水边的草地，兽住的地方。比喻人或事物集中的地方。

Three: Life

A wily hare's often burrowed in the green mound,
And a swan hard to follow the grey dog of clouds.
Fully realized in the heart of the grassy skyline,
One should not blame the hole in the clear frost.
How could the creator know the farm in dream?
The heavenly spirit has changed in its den.
While the high blast flutters the cold waves,
The evening glow will observe its thatched roof.

其四：社会

魍魉圆辉世稀，青楼楚鹤云飞。
出行旅梦香饵，引涕残芳祸机。
契阔①飘蓬物是，绸缪②远客人非。
山中宿鸟飞尽，海里何船可依？

【注释】

①契阔：勤苦，劳苦。②绸缪（chóu móu）：情意殷切。

Four: Society

Spirits and sprites should be scarce under the round canopy,
Where a crane soars up to the clouds from the green mansion.

To the fragrant baits in the roaming dream on the way,
The pivot of a disaster will evoke the last sweet to tears.
Gone with the wind, our toils are still there; however,
Sentimentally attached afar, the human affairs are no more.
After all the night birds have flied off the hills,
Whether there would be a sea vessel to follow?

待人

山林不比公卿，落叶来年尚荣。
宇静[①]轻财寡立，持节重义独行。
孤峰有意浮霭，瀑布难求至明。
万里扁舟过后，红尘卷走猿声。

【注释】

①宇静：平稳的心态，不为杂念所左右。

Behave Yourself

Unlike the official mansions, the mountain wood
Will be green again in the year to come, that stands
Lonely and quietly, with the money regarded lightly, and
Like the man of a valued constancy with the preserved chastity.
Wittingly, the isolated peak may be wreathed in hazes,
Hardly, the water fall could be transparent.
After the light boat passes thousands of miles,
The mundane dust will have engulfed the howling gibbons.

担心

万里晴川皓皓[①]，高风不惹天道。
冥心捣尽然灰[②]，洗面衔枚[③]再造。
落笔人生秉烛，行文几度盈抱[④]。
红颜自古羊昙[⑤]，百代谪仙[⑥]不老。

【注释】

①皓皓：旷达貌；虚旷貌。②冥心：泯灭俗念，使心境宁静。然灰：死灰复燃。③衔枚：缄口不言。④盈抱：满怀。⑤羊昙：晋名士羊昙是谢安的外甥，很受谢安器重。谢生病还京时曾过西州门。谢死后，羊昙一年多不举乐，行不过西州路。有一天吃醉了酒，沿路唱歌，不觉到了西州门。左右提醒他，他悲伤不已，以马鞭敲门，诵曹植诗："生存华屋处，零落归山丘。"恸哭而去。后将羊昙醉后过西州恸哭而去的事用为感旧兴悲之典。⑥谪（zhé）仙：指李白，号称谪仙。

Anxiety

The vast, broad river goes to the earth's end,
The high wind won't wake the way of God;
After the dying heart smashes the dying cinders,
The cleansed face will rework in reticent manner.
When the last pen of life holds the candle,
Its running text has been imbued many a time.
From of old even a red face has her retrospective passions,
And a banished immortal will be stuck in time ageless.

倒挂金钟

悬灯倒挂朱颜，艳粉消沈髻鬟。
掩映璇闺[1]变幻，轻拈绣户斑斓。
清芬半世绝妙，秀色平生雅娴[2]。
夜夜思君入梦，酸肠掩泪成斑。

【注释】

①璇闺：闺房的美称。②雅娴：即娴雅。

Common Fuchsia

Her rosy face hangs upside down like a ceiling lamp,
Whose gorgeous rouge sinks with her coiled buns.
In the irregular changes that set off her boudoir,
The bright-colored chamber lightly fiddles.
Her fresh, sweet smell tastes spiffy half a century,
With her sweet sight being suave all her life.
Each of her night longs for you in dream,
That has been grieved over the tracks of tears.

道　德
Moral

其一：口德

萧萧紫寒云深，逸气空山旅魂。
谷口寒流喜怒，山阴宿雨[1]凉温。
连天谑浪[2]巴水，渡鸟喧呼剑门。
利嘴谁识楚客[3]，劫灰[4]不掩王孙。

【注释】

①宿雨：夜雨，经夜的雨水。②谑浪：戏谑放荡。③楚客：泛指客居他乡的人。④劫灰：劫火的馀灰。

One: The Moral of Mouth

Deep in the clouds, the Great Wall rustles,
Free in the soul, the empty mountain travels.
At the valley mouth, the cold current is happy or angry,
And in the night rain are shaded the hills chilly.
On and on, the bantering billows are rolling,
Hoo and hoo, the birds of passage thru Gates of Swords are flying.
Who could know the wanderer of a sharp-tongue?
The kalpa-ash won't shut the hermit down.

其二：掌德

抚掌恬和[①]柳花，邀欢曲水流霞。
轻风旅梦香叶，皓露孤吟嫩芽。
驿站销魂入塞，人烟放醉还家。
春衣枉自临镜，漫道[②]玲珑玉纱。

【注释】

①抚掌：拍手。多表示高兴、得意。恬（tián）和：安静平和。②漫道：休说；别说。

Two: The Moral of Palm

Let me applaud the willow catkins in peace, and invite
The wandering roses over the meandering streams.
As the slight breeze travels its dream on the sweet leaves,
The bright dews are chanting the tender shoots in solitude.
Southwards, the courier station intoxicates my senses,
From the sign of life, I'm done to the wide and must return.
In vain, my spring gown comes into the mirror,
And let alone the gauze ingeniously and delicately wrought.

其三：面德

清姿玉面低掩，翠茎荷心一点。
绮榭[①]初开舞腰，雕梁久现歌脸。
游鱼点缀年衰，老鹤飞升岁俭[②]。

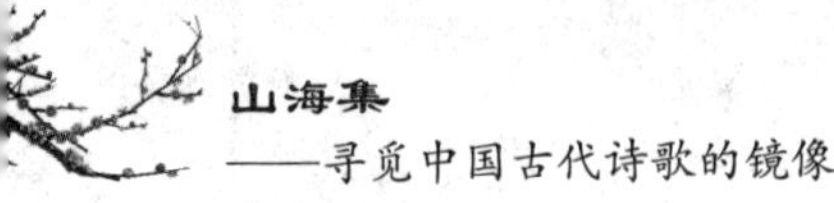

不忍承颜耻污，浮俗怎奈疵玷[3]。

【注释】

①绮榭：装饰华丽的台榭。②岁俭：年成歉收。③疵玷：缺点；过失。

Three: The Moral of Face

Clean and clear, she lowers her face
To the lotus heart on the green stalks
Sinuating the fresh figures near the pretty hall
Below whose carved beams are the vocal visages.
While a school of fish strew the declined age,
The old crane flies higher for the crop failure.
It hurts me to be subjected to the indignities,
Although the fickle custom shrugs its demerits.

其四：信任德

翠幕珠帘兔影[1]，深潭黛色[2]灵境。
积阴气化心兵，累日寒销语阱。
大野鸡鸣落箔[3]，高楼犬吠清冷。
春深坐断云台，千丝闲锁雨杏。

【注释】

①兔影：玉兔的影子，即月亮上的阴影。指月影。②黛色：青黑色。③落箔（bó）：喻指落月。

Four: The Moral of Trust

The Hare shadow on the green, pearl curtain
Inlaid a dark, deep pool in the wonderland.
The armed heart by the air of the netherworld
Thaws the cold from the word snare for days on end.
After the cock crowed its moonset down the wild,
The high-rises would be yipping, cold but cheerless.
As the full spring broke the cloud deck in its seat,
Thousands of threads would lock the rains of the apricots.

其五：方便德

落木飘零万片，扬眉澮扫流霰[①]。
回头翠黛[②]峰头，举目朱颜镜面。
叹月裁来碧藤，悲秋剪去团扇。
危樯暮宿垂萝，望断荆扉紫燕。

【注释】

①流霰：飞降雪粒。也常形容流泪。②翠黛：眉的别称。

Five: The Moral of Convenience

Thousands of leaves are falling,
In the soft hails rolling over the brows,
That look back at the leading peak,
That mirrors her raised, rosy face.

When the sighing moon drops its green vines,
The sad autumn will cut out the round fan.
Down the toppling wall are lolling the night vines,
Looking away unto the purple swallows over the gate of thorn.

其六：礼节德

施财贾客相逢，酒蚁[①]殷勤百重。
肃肃诸公水淡，煌煌大府云浓。
随春宛转仪制[②]，度岁参差礼容[③]。
四海连江楚客，狂飙万里心胸。

【注释】

①酒蚁：酒面上的浮沫。②仪制：仪态形制。③礼容：礼制仪容。

Six: The Morale of Formality

The eleemosynary traders crossed their path,
And drank by their heart's content,
With the good, deferential sirs to the insipid water,
And the big, bright mansion below the thick clouds.
As the spring was well-tuned to the ceremonies,
The new years touched on all the notes of etiquettes.
In the vagabondage of the rivers to the seas,
Their hearts were going in gusts to the earth's end.

其七：谦让德

睿藻徽音[①]共瞻，柔德不泯冲谦[②]。
山孤数茎明减，海阔一舟暗添。
有酒粘天峻岭，无弦弄月潮尖。
清狂软絮著雨，未解圆融梦甜。

【注释】

①睿藻：皇帝或后、妃所作的诗文。此处指好的诗文。徽音：德音。指令闻美誉。②冲谦：谦虚。

Seven: The Morale of Humility

Full of grace, the poetic proses are obvious,
With the tender virtue retaining a mantle of humility.
While the lonely hill tailors the bright stalks,
The wide sea has added one boat secretly.
Let the liquor be pasted on the lofty mountains,
Below which the chord plays the moon on the high tides.
When the soft willow catkins are raining their clear violence,
The sweet dream in infinite harmony still exists.

其八：理解德

明心耻作虚幌[①]，放迹[②]蛱蝶自赏。
古道风来月寒，春桥日落云朗。
江楼旷朗徘徊，海裔[③]舒合飒爽。

鼓翼云屏锁心，青天翠羽排荡[4]。

【注释】

①虚幌：透光的窗帘或帷幔。②放迹：远行。③海裔：海边。常形容边远之地。④排荡：激荡；冲激。

Eight: The Moral of Understanding

A bright heart may be ashamed of its lucid curtain,
And a butterfly set free in self-admiration.
When the wind blows the old way in the cold moon,
Before the the sun sets in the bright clouds down the spring bridge,
The airy lodges by the river are wandering there,
And the seaside opens and closes in bold and brave air.
Although the fluttering curtain of clouds locks the heart,
The green wings in the broad daylight are stormed-drenched.

其九：尊重德

眼底临风断雨，羁人[1]夜梦霜缕。
琴声慧眼寻禅，鹤唳斋心吊古。
意绪朝来计谋，炎凉暮去城府。
清谈莫论人闲，半掩帘栊洞户[2]。

【注释】

①羁人：旅人。②洞户：门户。

Nine: The Moral of Estimation

In the eyes, the wind blows away the rain,
That's frosted in the night dream of the traveller.
In the tweedles, the quick eye seeks its deep meditation,
Where the crane whoops dwell on the past so serene.
In the morn comes the scheme for the emotional appeal,
And at dusk are gone the shrewd inconstancies.
For an idle talk, let the idle come and go,
Outside the blinds half-open on the window.

其十：帮助德

远色[①]春盘一抹，劳形对语青葛。
双层紫绶轻摇[②]，一把白须淡捋。
屈曲[③]羊肠越岩，沈吟鸟道回斡[④]。
红尘满眼轮蹄，万毂残阳契阔[⑤]。

【注释】

①远色：远天的颜色。②紫绶：紫色丝带。古代高级官员用作印组，或作服饰。③屈曲：委曲，曲意迁就。④回斡（wò）：旋转，掉转。⑤万毂（gū）：车轮。契阔：勤苦，劳苦。

Ten: The Moral of Assistance

The wisp of the spring dishes afar
Toils his response to the green vines.

And the double purple cord jiggles,
With the white whiskers stroked lightly.
The path full of twists and turns goes over the crags,
Over which the passage of birds convolutes in a inner muse.
And an eyeful of hooves are wheeling in the mundane dust,
Around the laborious hubs of the setting sun.

其十一：诚信德

诚明[①]纵目清风，万尺云霞气冲。
远客荻花岸上，秋风蒲叶船中。
垂纶[②]日暖灵异，举棹[③]天阴半空。
几度浮沈宦海，幽人[④]锦字心同。

【注释】

①诚明：至诚之心和完美的德性。②垂纶：垂钓。③棹（zhào）：船桨。④幽人：幽隐之人；隐士。

Eleven：The Moral of Good Faith

Genuinely enlightened，the breeze looks far
Into the rising air of the shimmering clouds,
One traveller on the bank around the reeds
Rustles into his paddle of the autumn.
Miraculous，the warm sun goes angling,
Overcast，the midair raises its oar.
In the official seas up or down，time and again,
All the solitary men are thinking alike.

其十二：实惠德

廓落薄俗锦轩[1]，柴门羽客微言。
飞觥次第今野，痛饮参差古原。
薜荔闲敲叶暗，梧桐远落阴繁。
萍实[2]旧隐春梦，笑看蓬壶[3]几番。

【注释】

①廓落：空旷，空寂。锦轩：彩车或金屋。②萍实：甘美的水果。指吉祥之物。③蓬壶：蓬莱。古代传说中的海中仙山。

Twelve: The Moral of Real Benefit

Spacious and serene, the slight and silken door
Of the wicker gate shall be perceptive to the feathers.
Successively, let's toast swiftly in today's country,
Heartily, let's drink irregularly on the old prairie.
As the creeping figs flap the dark, spare leaves,
The phoenix trees afar are dropping their heavy shades.
Where the luscious fruit hide the old dream of spring,
The fabled abode of immortals are repeatedly smiling.

其十三：虚心德

方圆莫信晴色，待物怀安守墨[1]。
暗柳蜗房月筛，明花鹤颈风刻[2]。
人幽聚散沈浮，市闹荣枯现匿。

大道空怀素襟[2]，禅门坦荡弥勒。

【注释】

①待物：指跟别人往来接触。守墨：墨守成规。②素襟：本心。亦指平素的襟怀。

Thirteen: The Moral of Modesty

Round or square, believe not the fair,
To treat in peace, better stay in a rut;
Down the snail house, the dark willows sieve the moon,
On the crane necks, the wind chisels the bright flowers.
Deep or remote, the man may come and go,
Loss or gain, hide yourself in the busy streets.
The great truth has its innate mind, but in vain,
The gate to Buddhism should be open and at ease.

其十四：欣赏德

远近幽寻画桨[1]，红蕉转水寥朗[2]。
滩头野渡清明，岭下函关肃爽[3]。
杳霭[4]残阳沐心，霏微[5]远鸟神往。
闲花野客[6]乾坤，密片飘零百丈。

【注释】

①画桨：小舟的美称，指美丽的船只。②寥朗：空阔明朗。③函关：函谷关之省称。此处泛指关口。肃爽：本用以形容秋天景色，犹言天高气爽。亦借以形容其他事物和人的性格。④杳霭：幽深渺茫貌。⑤霏微：雾气、细雨等弥漫的样子。⑥野客：村野之人。多借指隐

逸者。

Fourteen：The Moral of Appreciation

Far and near，seek your paddle in secret，
Wide and bright，the scarlet bananas rotate with the water.
Over there，the wild beach stands crystal and clear，
Down the ridges，the Han Pass smells cool and nice.
The hazy heart must be bathed in the setting sun，and
Heavy with drizzle，the bird takes his breath away.
When a wild world wanders in the wild flowers，
The luxuriant petals become faded and fallen away.

其十五：感恩德

青门[①]点亮关河，引梦飘风孔多[②]。
水阔秋鸿变化，扁舟夜鹤销磨[③]。
舒霞望远歌舞，迥月啼春绮罗[④]。
义胆雄心反刃，长虹万古荆轲。

【注释】

①青门：汉青门外有霸桥，汉人送客至此桥，折柳赠别。②孔多：很多。③销磨：磨灭；消耗。④绮（qǐ）罗：华贵的丝织品或丝绸衣服。

Fifteen: The Moral of Gratitude

Light up the suburban fort, and
Lead your dream into the whirlwinds,
That drift the autumn swans over the wide water,
That fritter the night cranes near the boat.
To sing, to dance, to gaze out upon the open clouds,
The moon caws the spring lapped in silks and satins afar.
Ambitious but chivalrous, the blade of dagger
Will remember Jingke forever below the long rainbow.

其十六：援助德

井邑疲魂庶氓[①]，穷居大漠孤城。
楼头猎猎风冷，梦里啾啾雁鸣。
遥知乱世旅宿，早晚穷途独行。
衰颜旷望[②]奔走，翠羽清吟树声。

【注释】

①井邑：城镇；乡村。庶氓：众民；民众。②旷望：极目眺望；远望。

Sixteen: The Moral of Support

The worn souls of the people in the town
Dwell in the great, poor desert all alone.
Howling, whistling, the buildings are cooling,

Honk! Honk! The wild geese honk in the dream!
To have known the night out in such wild times,
I should have walked alone to the dead end.
Gazing out to the declined faces on the run,
The woods are chanting their clear, green wings.

其十七：激情德

狂飙烈烈长卷，腊雪鱼鳞铁箭。
战鼓惊沙胆薄，红魔溅海心颤。
磬磬火浪驰风，点点激情作电。
仗剑霜轮野云，飞蓬曲度裁遍。

Seventeen: The Moral of Passion

Fierce gales! Blow your long scrolls!
Iron arrows! Shoot your fish scales in the winter snows!
War drums! Shock the pale-hearted sand shoals!
Red devils! Splash your heart into the sea that trembles!
Fire billows! Drive your windflows!
Little by little, our vivid flash of lightning goes!
Braced on the sword! The wispy clouds scud on frost wheels,
Bitter fleabane! Tailor all your melodies but who knows?

其十八：形象德

粉墨韶光慧性，平波幻影临镜。
花前秀骨微明，醉里庞眉掩映。

入眼回娇上方，藏心弄艳中正。
疏狂秀色幽欢，后浪谁及柳永？

Eighteen: The Moral of Visualization

The painted face in his wise, glorious youth
Mirrored the phantom on the calming waves.
Before the flowers, his elegant bones were dimly lit,
Steeped in liquor, his broad brows were tucked away.
Into the eyes, his glances back waked up,
Into the heart, his gorgeous pose looked fair.
Unbridled by nature, the sweet sight went to the secret tryst,
Wherein none of the following waves would reach such a willow.

其十九：爱心

青囊①冷素枯春，旧客霜纹锦茵。
脚下红尘渐旧，唇边紫陌②长新。
衰情倦旅相问，蹇步③欢游可亲。
万事飘摇海镜，人生自有彝伦④。

【注释】

①青囊：风水术的俗称。②紫陌：大路。③蹇（jiǎn）步：步履艰难。④彝伦：常理；常道。

Nineteen: The Moral of Love

Cold and pure, the consumed spring goes into the black satchel,
Whose frost veins tread upon the lavish tapestries as of old.
Underfoot, the worldly life has been fading away,
On the lips, the thoroughfare would put forth the new leaves.
Waned in emotions, the weary travel has created mutual questions,
Fraught with difficulty, the joyous excursion looks affable.
All the affairs of the world sway on the mirror of the oceans,
Where life has its own standard principles.

其二十：笑脸德

客醉含春弄珠①，灵华②洗玉如酥。
沈沈水静遐迹，眇眇庭宽近趋。
道性牵肠器量，人情惹恨贤愚。
长吟众鸟云水，百啭邀欢暮途。

【注释】

①弄珠。指汉皋二女事。《文选·张衡》："耕父扬光於清泠之渊，游女弄珠於汉皋之曲。"②灵华：神灵；光辉。

Twenty: The Moral of Smile

Her tipsy spring in the pearls
Scours the soft, pure soul,
Leaving her far trail on the still water,

That shuts her uncertain steps to the broad court.
The nature of man must be obsessed by the tolerance,
And the human feelings grudged with the sage and fool.
How I hope to be the birds over the cloud and water,
Twittering long together on the joyous way of dusk.

其二十一：宽容德

登楼曲水容裔[1]，庇影春风待济。
有意紫浦涧声，无心青鸭[2]峰势。
孤身浅井昌黎，广袖明珠试艺。
历数寻常汉家，千年看惯兴替。

【注释】

①容裔：水波荡漾貌。②青鸭：绿头鸭。

Twenty-one: The Moral of Forbearance

Downstairs, the meandering streams are rippling,
And awaiting the sheltered shadow of spring.
Wittingly, the purple riverside is streaming soundly,
Unwittingly, the mallard rears majestically.
Alone in the shallow well, the common people are thriving,
In the wide sleeves, the bright pearl tries to be squirting.
Historically, the ordinary Chinese have been used to be
Facing the rise and fall of the glorious eternity.

其二十二：合作德

柳带新晴细草，烟条绮陌[1]春早。
随天嫩色轻波，近日奇香翠岛。
仄径撑折巨篙[2]，回廊吮断天宝。
南山散秩[3]闲行，野马云萝四皓[4]。

【注释】

①绮陌（qǐ mò）：繁华的街道，宋人多用以指花街柳巷。②仄径：狭窄的小路。此处指狭窄的水道。篙（gāo）：用竹竿或杉木等制成的撑船工具。③散秩：闲散而无一定职守的官位。④云萝：也叫藤萝。即紫藤。因藤茎屈曲攀绕如云之缭绕，故称。四皓：本为秦代官员，古称秦博士。秦人历代务农讲武，任用贤能的知识分子奠定了霸业。到秦始皇嬴政时，废井田，毁学校，焚烧经籍，坑杀儒生。四皓见时政日非，危乱将至，逃离咸阳，隐居在“上洛商山”。后人说此不与乱世合作的态度，为“避世”或“避秦”。

Twenty-two: The Moral of Co-operation

Fresh, fine willows on the fine meadow
Sway their early, hazy spring along the busy streets,
Like the tender, light waves below the sky,
That smells the rare scent on the green, suntrapped isle.
When the huge pole props and breaks on the narrow trail,
The corridor sucks and breaks the natural jewel.
To walk at a loose end in the southern hill,
The wandering air would like to be weedy off the society.

其二十三：善良德

高情览镜彰善，开帘清风洒面。
雉尾轻拈舞衣，鹤裘掩映歌扇。
珠帘杳杳薄垂，朗月蒙蒙应遍。
燕冷得君岁寒，茅檐览物天眷[①]。

【注释】

①茅檐：茅屋。天眷：上天的眷顾。

Twenty-three: The Moral of Goodness

The ideal soul in the mirror commends the virtue,
Opening the curtain of the sprinkled breeze.
While the pheasant tail flips the dancing dress,
The crane fur would set off the singing fan.
Out and away, the pearl curtain droops flimsily,
A heavy pall of mist settles all over the bright moon.
While the cold swallows converse with you,
The thatched roof possesses a great transcendence.

其二十四：倾听德

梦断空山静听，千丛细雨孤青。
狂言雨扫双耳，古调风吹一丁。
粉署相逢老吏，霜台解佩[①]高厅。
清贞[②]莫忘风骨，造化萦回性灵。

【注释】

①解佩：解下佩带的饰物。②清贞：清白坚贞。

Twenty-four: The Moral of listen

Awake from the dream of the stark, silent hill,
One single green was rhythmically sprinkled.
As the wild tongue sweeps the ears,
The old tone was blowing this man here.
As the branch office met its old officials again,
The censor-in-chief removed the dignitaries we learnt.
To be chaste and clean, forget not the vigour of character,
Whose spiritual world would be lingered in nature.

其二十五：宽恕德

猿声乱点[1]穹苍，几树清滑野霜。
初辞千花雨露，远效九日扶桑[2]。
谁同邑里明月，杜口楼台巽方[3]。
孔雀流声几度，天涯鹤梦家乡。

【注释】

①穹苍：亦作“穹仓”或“苍穹”。②扶桑：神话中的树名。③杜口：闭口。巽（xùn）方：东南方。

Twenty-five: The Moral of Forgiveness

The howling gibbons clicked the vault of heaven,
And slided down the clear, wild frosts off the trees.
First, farewell to the sweet dews of the flowers,
Then, follow the Tree of Dawn by the nine suns afar,
Who would share the bright moon in the town?
It must be that silent, southeast tower.
After the peacock flowed her tones time and again,
The crane on the skyline dreamed his hometown.

德　位

诗书敢荐明德，奕世纯阳郡国[①]。
大道怀柔四海，擎天辨状八极。
长川错认新冠，曲岸谁知旧识。
百代中国有梦，人生莫问游息[②]。

【注释】

①奕世：累世，代代。郡国：一般的郡和诸侯王的封国统称为郡国。泛指地方行政区域。②游息：行止。

The Seat of Moral

The scholarly clan dares to symbolize its virtue,
By flourishing the affairs of the state for generations,
With the great truth to conciliate the four seas,

With the Eight Poles discerned to prop up the heavens.
By the long river, the new crown may be mistaken,
On the winding bank, who would know the old knowledge?
If China has her dream for a hundred generations,
Life should not ask her action or suspension.

底　气

傲物清扬[①]酒圣，狂言不辱天命。
凌云剑下无尘，锁径刀中日正。
乱世金笳[②]大风，穷途铁马清净。
谁言逸气[③]乘龙，万类竹风率性[④]。

【注释】

①傲物：高傲自负，轻视他人。清扬：指眉目清秀，也泛指人美好的仪容、风采。②金笳：胡笳的美称。古代北方民族常用的一种管乐器。③逸气：超脱世俗的气概、气度。④率性：遵从自己的本性、天性的态度。

Energetic

Insolent and resonant, the wild saint of wine
Will not disgrace the mandate of heaven.
To fly in the void, the sword is dust-free,
To lock the neck, the sun says right in the sword.
While the golden flute really blows the wild times,
The sweeping horse seeks its quietude at the last extremity.
Who can confide his free spirit to the dragon?
It would be the willful wind of bamboos.

地 球

八极万里天行，水镜长空放情。
大野飞来翠卵，横空化去蓝莺。
玄心①壮志时暗，世路淳风自明。
草木荣枯策电，乾坤亿载无声。

【注释】

①玄心：玄妙之心识。

The Earth

In the movement of the heavenly body on the eight poles,
The still waters below the vast sky are growing bright.
As soon as the green willows are flying to the great wild,
The blue warblers will be gone and span the air.
Although the profound heart could darken its bold ambitions,
The homespun custom on the way of the world is naturally bright.
In the shafts of lightning, the wood circles its birth and death,
And the universe should tone off a hundred million years.

吊竹梅

远色青丝翠阴，金风顾影相寻。
莺娇袅袅烟露，草软苍苍羽林。
素萼甘泉作赋，银房玉树听琴。
银屏叹紫一世，恪守三生寸心。

The Wandering Jew

The black hair in the green shades has receded
And traced into its cool, narcissistic breezes
Tenderly waved and warbled in the dewy wind
Through the green and supple wood of wings.
Now the white calyces in the rhapsody down the sweet spring
Are listening to the lyre of the silver house in jade trees.
All her life the silver curtain acclaims the violets,
That scrupulously abide by all the intricacies of heart.

对　位

平生卧钓高位，莫剪如鸦世累[①]。
耳目谁知过涯[②]，浮舟不敢求备[③]。
歌邀翠柳莺啼，舞请黄鹅客醉。
贵贱亲疏一丘，相怜不肯轻弃。

【注释】

①世累：世俗的牵累。②过涯：超过一定的规范。③求备：谋求完善齐备。

Contraposition

All the life pronates for a higher position,
That shouldn't snip the weary world in caws.
Ears or eyes! Who knows the limited specification?

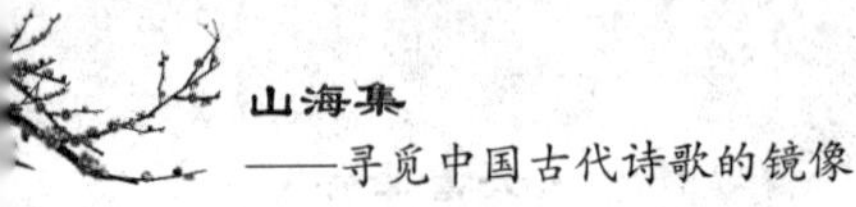

A pontoon may not presume to demand perfection.
As her song solicits the warbles in the green willow,
The dance urges its yellow geese to be drunk.
All degrees of intimacy or position have to go,
Which should not be forsaken but be rueful.

凡　是

虎兕[1]西风染霜，平推万里秋阳。
青蝇吮血成癖，吊客食人放狂。
草木雷喧浩荡，蚊虻雨躁荧煌[3]。
国中破晓蓝梦，再看浮生短长。

【注释】

①虎兕（sì）：虎与犀牛。比喻凶恶残暴的人。②吊客：丛辰名，主疾病、哀泣之事。古代星命家所谓丛辰之一。以为一岁十二辰都随着善神和凶煞。四柱神煞之一。②蚊虻：亦作“蟁虻”。一种危害牲畜的虫类。以口尖利器刺入牛马等皮肤，使之流血，并产卵其中。亦指蚊子。荧煌：辉煌耀眼。

Whatever

In the west wind, tigers and rhinoceros are frosted,
And are nudging the autumn sun to the earth's end.
When the blue flies are addicted to blood sucking,
As the crazy cannibals to the condolence call,
The vast and mighty wood burst like a thunder-growl,
Sparkling the mosquitoes and gadflies like tempestuous rains.

While the blue dream begins to dawn in the country,
We shall see more of the floating life, long or short.

樊 笼

人心守道迁变，雨脚风生隐面。
旧业天高莫知，余生水阔不见。
寒枝露下暝阴[①]，鹤唳无人乃眷[②]。
拢月年深闭门，衔泥又现飞燕。

【注释】

①暝阴：阴暗。②乃眷：喻关怀。

Confinement

The man's heart preserves the Way of changes,
That hide his face in the raindrops and windflows.
In the unending shades of his old, trackless trade,
Even the sky shall not spy what's down the wide water.
Through the gloom of the thick dews on the cold branches,
The whoops of the crane will be unworthy of attention.
Now, tuck away the moon into the deep door of the year,
Before a swallow that pecks the clods of clay flies again.

坟　墓

浪水狂夫曳①电，凌虚②仲夏霜霰。
情肠反侧千人，铁血经纶③百面。
客路风烟雨收，乡山草木芜变。
人生莫作尘沙，古冢平吞④贵贱。

【注释】

①曳（yè）：拉，牵引。②凌虚：升向高空或高高地在空中。③经纶：整理过的蚕丝，引申为人的才学、本领。形容人极有才干和智谋。④平吞：全吞；一口吞没。

Tomb

The man in the billows bellows after the lightning,
And rises high into the sneaping frost in the midsummer.
His passions toss and turn like a thousand men,
His iron blood is profoundly learned with a hundred faces.
On the way of passengers, the rain ceases in mist and clouds,
And the mountainous wood are overgrown with weeds.
To live means not to be the dust and sand,
Where the ancient tombs devoured the noble and the mean.

风信子
Hyacinth

其一：白珍珠

光含翡翠香侣，露色明珠寄语。
照影蒙茸[1]海妃，流光窈窕赢女。
回风远岫琼枝，散雪清晖几许。
户外多羞弄娇，开眉远梦幽处。

【注释】

①蒙茸：蓬松；杂乱的样子。

One: White Pearl

Sweet fellow, like the beamy green emerald,
With the message of a dewy, bright pearl,
Shines on the filmy princess of the sea,
Or the flickering, fairy lady of glad grace.
In the back draft, the jasper boughs in the distant hills
Have been scattering the snows in the sweet sunshine.
Half-shy mostly of her own charms in the open air,
She opens her brows to the far, secret dream.

其二：紫珍珠

紫气葱茏泛翅，罗裳半掩心醉。
愁眉绣带容华，笑靥菱花掩泪。
碧玉饥魂过涯，青丝怨魄求备。
烟霞澹荡寒烧，转影欺春妩媚。

Two：Violet Pearl

Spread the wing of the lush，ruddy light，
In her half-hidden，heart-broken and silken skirt；
Embroider her brow-knitted，powered face，
In the tearful smiles of the mirror；
As the starved soul of the jasper crosses the cliff，
Her black，murmuring hair asks for perfection.
In flaming chills，the cloudy wisps are softly mellow，
Her shifted shadow cheats the charming spring.

其三：粉珍珠

低容粉境回簪，漠漠[①]青筐晚蚕。
窈窕笙簧[②]隐涧，娇饶笑语薄岚。
仙姿落日风涌，月貌晴天露涵。
冷韵参差素艳[③]，凌寒抱苦如甘。

【注释】

①漠漠：寂静无声的样子。②笙簧：泛指音乐。③素艳：素净而美

丽。

Three: Pink Pearl

Glancing back, her rouged hairpin hangs her head,
With the late silkworm in the green, lonely basket.
Sweet and fair, the pipe and reed hide in the creeks,
Her cheerful, charming smiles are filmy and hazy.
With her wind-driven, immortal posture in the setting sun,
Her moon-like feature looks fine and dewy.
Of a cool rhyme, her pure but irregular colour
Hugs a bitter-sweet air in the frosty bite.

其四：巨蓝大花

应物含章[①]自贞，凌霜野霭初晴。
标格远渚牢醴[②]，品秩[③]幽行雪明。
避世清虚隐映，消忧散逸[④]轻盈。
芳蓝梦绕迁客[⑤]，次第疏阴雨声。

【注释】

①应物：顺应事物。含章：包含美质。②标格：风范；品格。牢醴(lǐ)：古代祭祀用的牲品和美酒。③品秩：以俸禄作为官员品级的标准。④消忧：消解愁闷。散逸：流散，四下流散。⑤迁客：遭贬迁的官员。

Four: Blue Giant

Her essence of beauty in response to the faithful chastity
Has just cleared up amid the frosty, unruly vapor
Far from the isle with her dedicatory personality
And her fine, serene quality like bright snow.
To avoid the world in her clear, dim and empty lights,
Her slender build goes free and relieves her melancholy.
In the arms of morpheus, her blue sweet roams about,
In the pitter-patter of the rain successively.

富贵菊

霜鳞剪翅高天，野阔晴光紫烟。
粉絮繁丝玉静，红斑嫩叶明鲜。
时节物土①多难，岁月关河未迁。
葬雪群花莫妒，痴情铁骨冬眠。

【注释】

①物土：土地所产的物品。

Pericallis Hybrida

The frost scales snip the wing that soars,
Up the wide wild that shines in purple smokes.
Pure and still, her pink fuzzes amid the lush threads
Are spotted red on the tender leaves, fresh and bright.

By the time, such a produce should be hard to get,
Though the time of the hills and rills never changes.
All the flowers under the snow! Don't you be jealous
Of such a winter sleep spoony in her steel bones.

感 觉

踏影裁诗九派，孤高玉女香界。
低迷走兔家多，散漫花鹰市隘。
富贵空明[1]浅深，冲融暗度疏快[2]。
才危莫怪贪泉，百代谁识好坏？

【注释】

①空明：空旷澄澈。②冲融：冲和，恬适。疏快：明快爽朗。

Perception

Tread the shadows of all the tailored poems,
In the sweet world of the haughty, fairy maids,
Where the sluggish rabbits have more burrows
To avoid the loose and narrow eagles.
Vast and bright, the rich and rank goes deep or shallow,
With its airy joy that slips through the sprightly freedom.
As the insatiable wit comes to be hazardous,
Who from among all the ages tells the good from the bad?

岗 位

屠龙倚剑标格[1]，蹈海回天[2]卷席。
倒扣惊魂碧水，横空动魄盘石。
云疏野鹿阡陌，雨密樵鱼广泽。
望眼红情聚散，参差几处飞白。

【注释】

①标格：风范、品格。②回天：比喻力量大，能移转极难挽回的时势。

Post

Sword! Into the dragon of a special style!
Turn the tide and then roll up the mat!
Cover the horror-stricken soul into the green water,
And stir the spirit of the flat, unstoppable stone!
Below the sparse clouds wild like the deer,
The broad marsh of fish and firewood' s teeming with rain.
To gaze out upon the red love that comes and goes,
The hand leaves a few touches of the hollow strokes.

格 局

江湖乱雨寒蓑，去日谁言苦多。
素业[1]十年斗酒，青春一曲长歌。
朦胧月道排岸，淡荡天光落波。

立马青云几度，功名最忌蹉跎[②]。

【注释】

①素业：清白的操守。②蹉跎：虚度光阴。

Framework

Whose cold cape rough in the rain
Has been swiftly gone off its dumb days?
Having measured the liquor for a decade，my gain
In youth is but a fine，crooned verse，anyways.
When the hazy moon lines up on the shore，
The idyllic daylight must be at low tide.
Astride my horse in the blue sky more and more，
The worldly fame taboos the wasted time alongside.

狗舌藤

铁脚行泥野客，狐踪隐迹阡陌。
浮生贵贱幽音，幻世贤愚物役[①]。
酷暑拉长狗舌，严寒缩短猫迹。
攀猿倒挂枯藤，古月横空朽锁。

【注释】

①物役：为外界事物所役使。

Hoya Carnosa（L. f.）R. Br

Wild through the mire, the iron feet
Trail the fox hidden in the crossroad.
High or low, this fleeting life in the serene note
Has worked as the sage or the fool in such unreal world.
Prolong the tongue of the scorching dog,
And cut short the cat's paws in the pinching cold,
While the climbing ape hangs upside-down the dead vines,
The old moon sets loose in the rotten lock.

管　理

云梯万丈灵境，半魄银钩①未定。
短褐斜风柳营②，飞蓬细雨葱岭③。
闲情莫恨花飘，丽藻④休嫌酒醒。
北鸟神清九霄，衔云挂眼诗兴。

【注释】

①半魄：半圆的月亮。银钩：比喻弯月。②短褐：用兽毛或粗麻布做成的短上衣。指平民的衣着。柳营：纪律严明的军营。③飞蓬：枯后根断，常随风飞旋，常比喻漂泊无定的孤客。葱岭：天山、喀喇昆仑、兴都库什三道山脉交汇的帕米尔高原古称“葱岭”，是丝绸之路中、南两路在喀什会合后唯一通往西亚的道路。被今人称为“葱岭古道”。④丽藻：华丽的诗文。

Management

Higher! Higher! The scaling ladder of the wonderland
Hooks its half, silver soul in the balance
Skew by the wind against the rustic garbs of the camp,
That sprinkles the fleabane all over the Pamirs.
Idle pleasure! Hate not the scudding flowers!
Colourful poems! Loathe not the hangover.
Northern bird! Up the sky in the clear air!
Poetic passions! Down the cloud in my eye.

光　明

敛屦[①]空阶暗尘，劳君俛仰[②]逡巡。
薰风旧赐芳艳，湛露新垂绿苹。
漏鼓[③]空闻月夜，芒鞋[④]望断阳晨。
飘摇醉墨双眼，野径提灯一人。

【注释】

①敛屦（liǎn jù）：摄足。踮起足走路。②俛（fǔ）仰：俯视和仰望。③漏鼓：报更漏的鼓。④芒鞋：草鞋。

Light

The dark dust along the stark steps on tiptoe
Hangs back up or down in the tenses of toil and moil.
After the old song of the southerly granted its sweet colour,

The new dewdrops are drooping their green grass.
As the drum beat announces the moon-lit night in vain,
The grass sandals are looking away unto the sunny morning.
As the eyes are floating on the tipsy ink tablet,
One single handle lantern is threading the wild trail.

归 宿

隐迹空余野风，浮云浪迹西东。
仙游忘却身后，日落还归掌中。
涧水言归地信，柴门谢客天聪[①]。
宏基竞起贤正，社稷衰于贯虹[②]。

【注释】

①天聪：上天赋予人的听力；对天子听闻的美称。②贯虹：《南齐书·褚渊传》载，渊本刘宋重臣，及萧道成篡宋称帝，渊附道成，封南康郡公，加尚书令。“轻薄子颇以名节讥之，以渊眼多白精，谓之‘白虹贯日’。言为宋氏亡征也”。白虹贯日谓其白眼珠特别大，后用以表示奸佞不忠之特征。

The End Result

Hide into the wild wind free,
Like the cloud drifts gone anywhere;
Wash away from behind, the fairy wander
Palms still the return of the sun.
The valley creek swears to the earth,
The wicker gate declines the heaven.
A grand bases mushrooms in the worthy integrity,

And the sacred shrine wanes by the yes-men.

规　律

阴晴井底明灭，树影空衔冷热。
客意烹鱼半浊，幽期载酒莹澈[①]。
穷阴[②]万里守节，正气千行烁[③]铁。
宇宙清扬里仁[④]，春秋自有一页。

【注释】

①莹澈：莹洁透明。②穷阴：古代以春夏为阳，秋冬为阴，冬季又是一年中最后一个季节，故称。③烁（shuò）：融化。④清扬：清越悠扬；弘扬。里仁：达到仁的境界。

Rule

Cloudy or sunny, the toe of hole flickers,
Cold or hot, the tree harbours its hollow shadow.
To visit the cooked fish, half-turbid,
The secret schedule stows its crystal liquor.
The last season keeps its integrity at the earth's end,
With the sense of right melting the iron in thousands of lines.
When the clear universe enchances its virtuous manners,
The spring and autumn should register its own page.

鬼　雄

项羽拔山斩龙，澄清鼎镬[1]元凶。
横枪暴怒十变，立马长驱一冲。
楚水流离片月，乌江廓落孤峰。
八千子弟豪气，怎比江东守农？

【注释】

①鼎镬（huò）：古代的酷刑。用鼎镬烹人。

The Dead Hero

Of unusual strength, Xiang Yu beheaded the dragons,
And mopped out the chief culprits of giant cauldrons.
His spear couched and roared from the heat of rage,
His steed was rapidly poised for a wide range.
One moon floated away on the southern waters,
And the isolated peak was lost in the Wujiang River.
How could the heroic souls of the eight thousand warriors
Be comparable to the farming promise to the east of the river?

过　客

万象疏狂乱絮，晴波送客来去。
闲门举酒穷通，半月吟诗毁誉。
物性明垂小康[1]，灵山暗钓仁恕[2]。
生来快意梨园[3]，死后留名几处？

【注释】

①小康：生活比较安定。②仁恕：仁爱宽容。③梨园：古代对戏曲班子的别称。

The Passer-by

Unfettered and freewheeled, the affairs of nature
Come and go on the fine waves.
Spare your door and wine for all fortunes,
Where a half-moon can praise or blame the poems.
As the physical nature droops its bright comfort,
The hill of soul angles for its dark humane pardon.
By nature, your pear orchard feels gratified,
After death, who and where would you be remembered?

含羞草

相思羽叶初醒，静理白绒粉顶。
素魄清风远游，孤魂落日闲等。
寻芳窃慕飞觥，吐艳常忧酩酊。
嫩粉秋毫触风，合羞掩敛天迥。

Mimosa

Her love-lorn leaves just wake up and comb her
Quiet, pink crown of fine and white hair.
Her pure soul travels afar in the fresh wind,
Her wandering spirit lives alone in the setting sun.
To seek the fragrance, the liquor feels envious furtively,
To bud the colours, the ebriety often feels melancholy.
While her minute, soft rouge touches the breeze,
She should shut her sheepish sky from afar.

旱金莲

香苞五角灵味，宿露搜春百卉。
镜里和风澹烟，天边细雨淑气。
黄金倒卵追游，紫萼横巢守贵。
茎蔓凌空抱星，群蝶梦醉经纬。

Tropaeolum

Her clever, pentangular sapor in the sweet bud
Seeks the night dews for the spring flowers.
In the mirror, her soft breeze heaves hazily,
On the horizon, the drizzle breathes gently.
Her yellow petals trace the oval wander,
And her purple calyces observe the noble nest.
Her stalk and tendrils nestle the stars higher,

Crooked by the drunken dream of the butterflies.

黑龙江

烟囱顾影乡陌，四望东行翠液。
塞外撕开柳边，关东涌进征客。
明花渡水维舟，暗雪蹄风振策[①]。
自古刀耕[②]女真，包容万里饥魄。

【注释】

①振策：扬鞭走马。②刀耕：指满族刀耕火种或火耨刀耕的原始农业。

Heilongjiang

Off the rural road silhouetted by the chimneys,
The green sap flowed east on the vast territories,
Whose wicker fences had been unripped,
By the famine refugees like a storm that whipped.
To wade and moor, the flowers swayed colourful,
To flip at the hooves, the obscure wind was nival.
From of old the Jurchens with the slash cultivation
Were prepared to accept all the men from food disruption.

红鹅掌

半蹋红罗玉箫，云风漫卷天骄。
沈冥[①]厚理初醉，汗漫[②]薄俗欲烧。
梦里朱门团扇，愁中满座秋飚。
通幽邂逅毒掌，钓客红尘路遥。

【注释】

①沈冥：低沉冥寂。②汗漫：漫无边际；渺茫不可知。

Anthurium Andraeanum

Half her web like scarlet gauze plays a melody,
To the proud wind and cloud, blowing and billowing.
The quiescence of her thick texture grows tipsy,
And roams through the flimsy custom to be dawning.
Her vermilion gate dreams about the round fan, and
All the seats share the autumn worries of an anabatic wind.
Were her secret to encounter a murderous hand,
The human society would be angling for the far end.

花瓣泪

高情落照斜汉，化剑垂红绣幔。
野阔江天望巢，云疏碧影离岸。
双眸弄粉枝头，一曲调红寸断。
触物层层寄情，飘忽片片伤叹。

Petals in Tears

The afterglow of her ideal soul across the Milky Way
Droops a red sword down the veil of the embroidery.
To look out on the eyrie by the wild, wide river below the sky,
The free, green clouds are clawing off the shore over there.
While her eyes at the branches are rouging,
One ruddy hue of her melody may be breaking.
Tier upon tier of the sights grow more lyrical,
And flake upon flake of her wails haunt and scroll.

话　语

岁久危辞落尽，春情最懂捷敏[①]。
西山宿燕难绝，北海残书未泯。
树下闲言正欢，楼头碎语何忍。
河鲛梦里东游，晓日长天海蜃。

【注释】

①捷敏：敏捷。此处为平仄所需。

The Discourse

The dangerous diction was long denuded
Of the most agile stirrings of love
Lodged by the swallows in the west hills
And the imperfect books on the north sea.

As the idle tongues below the tree are joyful,
Could the dribs and drabs of the towers be tolerable?
As the mermaid swims her dream east in the river,
The castle in the long sky starts to dawn.

还　乡

九陌[①]青纱玉树，荣枯不舍黑土。
虫鸣皓色轻云，鸟宿高秋绛缕[②]。
止躁孤村澹薄，粗疏[③]野店清苦。
世事冷眼沧桑[④]，到处青蝇饿虎。

【注释】

①九陌：田间的道路。②绛缕：红色丝线。③粗疏：疏略；不精细。④沧桑：沧海变桑田的简缩。泛指世事的变化。

The Return of the Native

The footpaths in the green crops and trees
Won't let the black soil go, be it there or not,
Whence the light and bright clouds are chirping,
And the cool autumn threading its red birds.
This is my village indifferent of fickleness,
Scattered where it should be stoic and stark.
In the cold eyes of the weather-beaten world,
Blue flies and hungry tigers are everywhere.

活　着

古句疏芜[①]百年，闲思散诞[②]陈篇。
花前醉倚新月，鬓上空怀古天。
怅望翻身野客，风流化作谪仙[③]。
横诗枕破秋水，带走销魂杜鹃。

【注释】

①疏芜：萧索荒芜。②散诞：放诞不羁；逍遥自在。③谪（zhé）仙：被贬谪的仙人，也可指李白、杜甫。

Alive

Overgrown with weeds a hundred years, the old lines
Went flirty, flaky in their free-spirited platitude,
Leaning on the crescent moon over the drunken flowers,
With the temples that harboured the ancient skies.
Sick at heart, the wild traveller turned over, and
In graceful pith was turned into a banished immortal.
When his poetic pillow cleaved the limpid eyes,
The cuckoos would be going off into ecstasies.

积　累

出云浩叹[①]风蕙，下笔宁知远势。
百代闲来去名，三年齿下身计[②]。
闲情乱雪朱云[③]，远目播风柳惠[④]。

世乱前程可攀，幽奇[5]不懂兴替。

【注释】

①浩叹：长叹，大声叹息。②身计：生计。③朱云：鲁人，徙平陵。少时通轻侠，借客报仇。长八尺馀，容貌甚壮，以勇力闻。④柳惠：春秋柳下惠的省称。⑤幽奇：玄妙的哲理。

Accumulation

Out of the cloud, my deep sigh to the soft breeze
Prefers to pen the farther force
Out of the fame leisurely for a hundred years,
But on the rack about the means of living just three years.
Idle pen! Plunge your red clouds down to the snow!
Far-sighted! Sow your wind unto the kind willow!
In troubled times, the journey ahead is still promising,
Though the rise and fall has been so inscrutable.

鸡冠花

万木清吟不止，长游醉卧云水。
无心暗雨流连，有意深烟转徙。
向月难寻蚂蟥，随风不返蝼蚁。
千山唱响灵鸡，遍地红罗蹑履？

Cockscomb

In the clear chants, the wood never stop
Their drunken stupor long in the cloudy water,
That lingers in the secret, careless rain,
And shifts wittingly into the deeper mists.
Under the moon, the leeches are elusive,
With the wind, the mole crickets and ants can't return.
As the clever cock crows to the thousand mountains,
Could the red crests be tiptoeing all around?

家　长

河东百辟[①]折戟，玉帐严风灭迹。
藉力[②]何曾病夫，扬尘未必狂客。
弯弧举目雄文，抚剑回观射策[③]。
叱浪峰头雾开，河西草木空碧[④]。

【注释】

①百辟：诸侯；百官。②藉力：借力。③射策：汉考试法之一。选士的一种以经术为内容的考试方法。主试者提出问题，书之于策，覆置案头，受试人拈取其一，叫作“射”，按所射的策上的题目作答。④空碧：澄碧。

Patriarch

To the east of the river, all officials collapsed,

In the icy wind, all the jade curtains were obliterated.
From the borrowed forces, they were never be a sick man,
To the fugitive dust, they were not necessarily crazy.
To curve the bows, they should be gifted with literary brilliancy,
To brandish the swords, they should look back to the academy.
After the fog was rifted over the top of the billows,
The west of the river would be covered with verdure.

坚　持

神仙百岁孤云，玉步风烟不群。
古道逍遥自负，天机澹荡羞闻。
来时稼穑无怠，去日劳思克勤[①]。
造化长思苦雨，阴阳聚散平分。

【注释】

①克勤：能够辛勤地劳动。

Persistence

The centenarian immortal like a lonely cloud
Far excels at all those steps in the wind.
On the old road, he's but a carefree fly on the wheel,
Ashamed to hear the free mystery of the nature.
When coming, he sows and reaps silently,
When going, he works his soul diligently.
When the good fortune ponders long its bitter rain,
The coming and going principle would share alike.

坚　实

自古天台半壁，飞泉铁冠凌历[1]。
归来忆梦搜奇，负杖同心扣寂[2]。
世已风尘抱肩，谁能落井沈溺？
忧人莫怪临岐[3]，俯仰朝夕怵惕[4]。

【注释】

①凌历：气势雄伟。②扣寂：构思而发为文辞的思维活动。后指作文赋诗。③忧人：忧虑他人；心情忧伤的人。临岐：面临歧路。④怵惕（chù tì）：恐惧警惕。

Stability

From of old, down the half Heaven Stage,
The imposing cliffside spring rushes off its iron crown,
Whose dream of return hunts for novelty,
To be conceived with undivided devotions,
Though the shoulders are nestled by the dust of journey,
Who would like to fall and drown in a well?
To be anxiety-ridden, blame not the forked road,
Because each day and night shouldn't be free from fear and care.

金银花

葛蔓飞墙乱冲，关山万蕊疏封[1]。
鸳鸯瑞色交颈，翡翠晴光贮胸。

傲骨何求大化，黄白自有灵踪。
尘埃悯默[②]孤苦，乱世幽驰忍冬。

【注释】

①疏封：分封。帝王把土地或爵位分赐给臣子。此处喻指。②悯默：因忧伤而沉默。

Honeysuckle

Vines and tendrils ramped over the wall,
Towards the hills sparsely sealed with the pistils.
Of lucky hues, the love-birds crossed their necks,
Like emerald, the bright light was bosomed.
With proud nature, why to seek the transformation?
The white and yellow state had its own quick trail.
While the dust suffered its tacit, lonely sorrow,
The wild times would gallop into the secret honeysuckles.

金鱼草

轻条浪迹萧疏，水色云开日初。
霭霭寒烟蔽景，霏霏宿雾凌虚[①]。
含情欲意行止，罢梦宁心卷舒。
此夜疏帘漏月，平波濑响[②]金鱼。

【注释】

①凌虚：升于空际。②濑（lài）响。从沙石上流过的急水的响声。

Antirrhinum

Deserted, her light withes are waving
To the fresh sun out of the cloudy water.
Hazy and vapoury, the cold spells are veiling
In the gathering murk drizzled in the heaven.
Her exude love desires to know the whereabouts,
To be ended in the peaceful heart that shrinks or grows.
This night when the window curtain leaks the moon,
The goldfish will flush and splash their waves.

进　化

水月长怀古今，清浊宝界游心。
松林寂寞风起，乳窦[1]深藏犬音。
落日茕茕客鬓[2]，淙流杳杳尘襟。
浮生过隙沧海，宇内无踪可寻。

【注释】

①乳窦：石钟乳洞。②茕茕（qióng）：忧思的样子，孤独无依的样子。客鬓：旅人的鬓发。

Evolution

The moon in the water bosoms long the history,
Whose saptaratna realm swims a heart, clear and muddy.
When the doleful pinewood are gusting,

The stalactite grotto deeply hides the barking.
When the temples roam in the setting sun lonely,
The dust on the garment gurgles desolately.
This life by the sea is fleeting and flashing,
The entire world offers no trail to be seeking.

九里香

清风送客乡关，九里平明[1]过山。
翠影交游壁上，浮辉逸戏林间。
玲珑哪管心草，缱绻尤含泪斑。
亮果流光梦里，红唇翘首君还。

【注释】

①平明：天刚亮时。

Murraya Exotica

The breeze sees her visitors out
Over the hills nine miles at dawn,
With the green traces associated on the wall,
And the floating splendour sported in the wood.
Outside the heart grass ingeniously and delicately,
Her tear stains are locked in affectionate intimacy.
While the bright fruit flow into her dream,
Her red lips are craned for the return of man.

决　定

江湖暗觅心曲，万里谁来眷属①？
傲岸藏修肃雍②，谈玄③乐道荫沃。
人生默默涓毫④，世路昏昏桎梏⑤。
紫陌荣华转蓬，淳俗⑥吏治无欲。

【注释】

①眷属：眷顾；属望。②傲岸：高傲自负，不屑随俗。藏修：专心学习。肃雍：庄严雍容，整齐和谐。③谈玄：讨论深奥的问题，如哲学、玄学等。④涓毫：亦作“涓豪”。喻微末。⑤桎梏：脚镣和手铐。⑥淳俗：淳朴的风俗。

Decision

Who would care for the distant
Heart song to be secretly sought?
In exquisite refinement, the haughty devotion
Delightful in the dark learning has germinated
Such a life of obscure origins,
On the way of the dark, shackled world.
And like the lustrous duckweeds by the thoroughfare,
The unsullied, political corruptions are desireless.

空　灵

风烟玉浪舒卷，大道微吟自展。
静月悬知古今，闲云莫问深浅。
菱花满目寻幽，柳叶披襟[①]辗转。
数声白鹅性灵，殊俗破体[②]虚变。

【注释】

①披襟：敞开衣襟。多喻舒畅心怀。②殊俗：风俗、习俗不同。破体：破乾坤纯阳之体。

Ethereal

Back and forth, the hazy and misty billow
Whispers on the great way of its own when
One quiet moon hangs in its learned history,
That never asks the roaming shade of colours.
To seek her secret in the mirror everywhere,
The willow leaves toss about delightedly.
Once the soul of a white goose cackles,
The different dialect breaks its virtual changes.

苦　熬

野客清觞翠羽，霓旌玉管[①]当户。
幽燕短调鸡鸣，塞外长谣犬聚。
怅望斜阳汉宫，重吟陌上秦树。

栖枝九色蓬莱，映日灵风妙舞。

【注释】

①霓旌：相传仙人以云霞为旗帜。玉管：玉制的古乐器，音乐的美称。

Torment

The clear cup on its wild wing
Plays the pipe of jade below the rainbow flags in the door:
Like the cock crow with its short, serene, north note,
Or the gathering barks of a long ballad beyond the Great Wall,
The sunset down the Han Palace has a sense of sorrow,
Chanted again by the roadside trees of the northwest.
In the nine hues of the perched branches on the fairy isle,
The bright sun dances its refined, facile wind.

快　乐
Pleasure

其一

明堂把酒长乐，浩荡春风海岳。
逸兴千觞[1]细辉，欢情四座新朔[2]。
无为竞渡风流，有意争持礼数。
烁古金石[3]易求，明珠莫过淳朴。

【注释】

①觞（shāng）：古代一种酒具。②新朔：农历每月初一。③金石：常用以比喻诗文音调铿锵，文辞优美。

One

Cheer! More wine in the bright hall!
Wine to the sea hill in the powerful spring wind!
More wine bright in spirits high and fine!
More joys for all present under the crescent!
Shiftless, but race for a graceful pith!
Minded, but stick to the grades of courtesy!
With adamantine ties, the shining joy is easy to seek,
But to be a bright pearl, rusticity comes first.

其二

淡走红尘柳市，天涯到处知己。
庄周寂历[①]言传，子美冥征[②]授技。
肃肃明德乐贫，雍雍黍稷[③]不仕。
平生一笔秋毫，写尽如烟茧纸[④]。

【注释】

①寂历：寂静。②子美：杜甫，字子美。冥征（míng zhēng）：神灵暗示的征兆。③黍稷（shǔ jì）：《诗·王风·黍离》："彼黍离离，彼稷之苗。"后以"黍稷"为感叹古今兴亡之典。④茧纸：用蚕茧制作的纸。泛指纸张。

Two

Light through the willows of the mundane dust,
My bosom friends are everywhere in this world.
By precept, Chuang-tzu went down into silence,
Spiritually hinted, Du Fu passed on his skill.
Deferentially, the bright virtue was contented in poverty,
Stately, to be official would be ignoble.
Lifelong, the perceptive brushstrokes
Could run out of the cocoon paper in smoke.

拉　手

承欢把手开眉，秋簟浮凉梦思。
物性俗薄夜雨，人心厚曲归期。
风霜客舍无限，岁月床头易衰。
落日心中反照，天涯自有情知。

In Hand

Mirthful in hand,
The cool, autumn mat flowed its thought
About the flimsy custom in the night rain
Where the heart of man counted the rhythmical dates of return.
Where the inn knew no bounds in the hardships,
The head of the time bed was prone to caducity.
And in the last radiance of the heart,

The skyline would take its own fancy.

老　夫

老大风骚墨徒，飘摇错辨贤愚。
离群海镜十载，避世云楼九衢[1]。
旅雁啼秋有寿[2]，长天叫月无虞[3]。
空庭万里眠客，陋巷残灯不孤。

【注释】

①九衢：纵横交叉的大道；繁华的街市。②有寿：年满六十岁的雅称，亦称本命年。③无虞：没有忧患，太平无事。

The Old Man

The hot-button disciple though old
Was blinded by the sage and fool in the wind.
Solitary by the sea specula for a decade,
His high-rise downtown hided from the society.
As the flying autumn honked for four score years,
The vast heaven greeted its peaceful moon, where
The empty chamber slumbered the passenger from afar,
In its last flicker of the expiring slum lamp.

连　翘

利爪疾风玉串，黄金扯地如幻。
容颜好异[①]天高，翠影寻幽日晏[②]。
对叶濯来露蝉，穿空洗去云雁。
疏狂万里生情，此境流辉顾盼。

【注释】

①好异：喜好标新立异。②日晏：天色已晚，日暮。

Forsythia

Clawed and blown, the pure strings
Have bestrewn their dreamy gold,
Whose visage ostentates higher than the sky,
Silhouetted green for its serene nightfall.
As the cicadas come to the dewy leaves,
The wild geese are washed out of the cloud.
As the unbridled chord is touched afar,
Here sheds her bright rays to the dancing eyes.

良　辰

两片兰芽盛衰，蒙笼转影缘枝。
浓云碧鸟珠缀，淡墨青花玉垂。
木冷红梨鹤见，江清碧翠鱼识。
幽情触物一醉，野性陶然此时。

The Sweet Hour

The birth and death of the two petals
Shifts its shades up the sprays dimly
Below the thick clouds sewn by the green birds,
Or the light ink that drops the blue-and-white flowers.
In the cold wood the crane sees its red pears,
And in the clear river the fish see its emerald green.
As the subtle sense touches its ebriety,
The ferity should be happy and free here.

累

怀君空余一人，楼台晓雾轻身。
新书不邀恩宠，旧史谁识苦辛。
醉后空名尚古，山中浪语失真。
孤烛世外行役，莫道乔装采苹。

Tired

Miss you, but to what avail?
I was struck with ease by the dawning fog outside the floor.
For all the new books won no favour,
My old history has failed to read the hard work.
Being so sloshed, my bare name pursues an ancient image,
In the mountains, my word of billows has been distorted.
With a solitary candle, I serve beyond the world,

Where I might not be mocked to pick the ferns in disguise.

离　职

放诞谁家醉酒，冰浆琥珀刁斗[1]。
幽怀万里横行，素志千寻在否？
雪满刚融劲风，斜拂又见丝柳。
飞云半世迷途，野渡衰容钓叟。

【注释】

①刁斗：古代军中用具，形状大小似斗，有柄。白天用来烧饭，晚上敲击巡逻。此处喻指大酒具。

Dimission

Where to fuddle my nose untrammeled?
In the amber beaker of ice wine.
To run amuck afar in leisurely hours,
But where lies the usual, lofty ambition?
In the high wind that just thaws the snow,
The swaying eyes are willowy again.
Half a century, my scud has lost its way,
For which my faded face angles in the wild ferry.

零沟通

钓玉直钩夜程，幽思望断长更。
隔帘慨叹残酒，对镜空嗟晓莺。

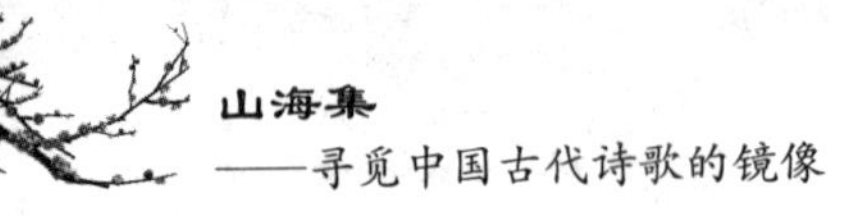

粉壁应识素面，雕梁细认娇声。
清潭大泻蟾影，夜色难停雁行。

Zero Communication

To hook the jade in the hookless night,
Long to my little, distant thoughts,
My curtain sighs its taste of liquor, and
My mirror wails the dawning warblers.
Should the white wall know her perfume-free face,
The carved beam identifies her thrilling voice.
When the Toad shade pours unto the clear pond,
The wild geese would never halt their shades.

凌霄花

苕华①月久弥贵，梦里承欢紫蔚②。
樱草殊非③圣花，冬青未是神卉。
支颐爱子三灵④，解带高堂万汇。
百尺凌霄系情，关山点泪虚费⑤。

【注释】

①苕（tiáo）华：美玉名。苕：植物名，又名陵苕、凌霄，《诗经》里就有记载，“苕之华，芸其贵矣”说的就是凌霄。②紫蔚：《唐本草》，该书在“紫蔚”项下曰：“此即凌霄花也，及茎、叶具用。”③殊非：实在不是。④支颐：以手托下巴。道教称三魂为三灵。⑤虚费：犹糜费。白白地消耗。

Trumpet Creeper

Her sweet splendour will be more precious over time,
In the violet dream of a lively mirth.
Unlike the primrose really not a sacred flower,
Or the holly unnecessarily divine,
Her three souls are adorable, with cheeks in palms,
And detached out of all others under the free roof.
A hundred feet of her amorous joys could
Answer the mountains in tears, but of no avail.

60后

听蝉梦绕幽浦，敛鬓横钗对舞。
淅淅宿雨好音，飒飒晴光池羽。
空余倦客琼英[①]，已改欢游锦缕。
岁月残滴雪霜，秋来落木吟苦。

【注释】

①琼英：美丽的花或诗文。

Born in the 1960s

Our dream by cicadas chirps the quiet riverside, and
Dances to the checked temples across the hairpins.
In the night rain rustling like a melody,
The bright light soughes and feathers in the pool.

To be tired, all the fair flowers are bare, and
Should have altered their joyous wander of silk threads.
In the last drops of the time down the snow and frost,
The falling wood of the autumn are whirring bitter.

落雪泥

飞鸿掠地凄迷，溅素初晴雪泥。
重瓣温香锦缎①，孤云冷绣春闺。
岩桐②唤醒幽梦，巨早③思归故蹊。
五色风枝落絮，闲眠醉忆山梨。

【注释】

①重瓣锦缎（Double Brocade）：深红、红色具紫色花心和白边、玫瑰红具白边、深红具深紫色花心等，矮生。②岩桐：大岩桐（Sinningia speciosa）的省称，也就是"落雪泥"的书面称谓。③巨早（Early Giant）："落雪泥"的别名。

Sinningia Speciosa

My swan sacks the forlorn ground,
That sloshes the sunny, snow slush.
As the double brocade perfumes the mild air,
The lonely cloud embroiders the cold spring boudoir.
As the sinningia speciosa rouses the secret dream,
The early giant hopes to go back to his footpaths.
As the wind branches of five hues drop the catkins,
My free nap looks back on the stoned sorbs.

旅　途

策马归心旧栈，霜潭错落青眼。
疏钟落叶折风，片月吹灯断简。
壮志啼鸡舞文，功名倒枕飞盏。
劳生倦色归途，有泪遑遑玉版。

Journey

Lashing my horse back to the old shed,
The frost pond was strewn in the dark eyes.
When the sparse bell snapped the defoliated wind,
The crescent put out the lights on the broken letters.
When the bold ambition cawed the words to dance again,
The worldly fame was pillowed by the flying cups.
On my way home, the life toiled and moiled wearily,
In its tearful hurry on the jade plate.

马蹄莲

踏破西风马蹄，垂衣唤醒晨鸡。
清辉顾步星转，素影裴回[①]月低。
荡子饱识苦泣，征人惯看酸嘶。
萧郎欲卸红粉，揽辔惊飞燕犀[②]。

【注释】

①裴回：彷徨。徘徊不进貌。②燕犀：化自李商隐“冀马燕犀动地

来，自埋红粉自成灰”。

Calla

Crush the west wind under the hooves，and
Rouse the morning fowl slouching their garbs.
Step to the starry shift with the radiant light，and
Linger its pure shade in the hanging moon.
Where the roué is fully aware of the bitter sobs，
The wayfarer has been used to the grieved neighs.
When the merry man tries to remove her red powder，
The seized reins will rouse the swallows to flight.

骂　人

幽人落日空思，紫陌荆俗[①]可欺。
次第鸡舌莫问，辛勤恶骂谁知。
剖心寸刃割面，沥胆邪风骨吹。
雾里痴情翠影，沉浮委顺[②]由之。

【注释】

①紫陌：大路，世路。荆俗：荆地的风气。此处泛指。②委顺：顺从。

Bawl

The sun went down the solitary thought，
Deceivable by the local thoroughfare.

Ask the cluck-cluck clip clop no more,
And in a hail of abuse against the toils, but who knows?
With the scalpel, cut the face and heart,
With the evil wind, split the gall and bones;
In the fogs, the green shade is spoony,
Ups and down, gone with the stream.

美女樱

香泥漫引山樱，绣伞华阳二京①。
野色蒙蒙露静，云根②袅袅风鸣。
何处宝钿红粉，此地金钗雪青。
自身蓝心不辱，孤鸾未必求荣。

【注释】

①二京：指汉代的东京和西京，即洛阳和长安。②云根：深山云起之处。

Verbena Hybrida

Oriental cherries creep with the fragrant soil,
Brightly sunned like an umbrella over the two capitals.
While the misty dews are whist and whild,
The cloud roots are catching a whiff of sough.
Where are the rose-cheeked jade pins?
Here are the gold pins hued to the violet tulip.
Blue-hearted, they will not live in dishonour,
Isolated though, the phoenix won't be necessarily in search of profit.

目　标

逸志黄肠[①]莫笑，寻仙百啭出窍。
清心紫陌风鸣，应手红楼日照。
朗抱[②]空悲险滩，高情聚首奔峭[③]。
溪鱼梦挂幽燕，肯恋烟波野钓。

【注释】

①逸志：超逸脱俗之志。黄肠：胃。②朗抱：高洁的胸怀。③高情：超逸的情怀。奔峭：崩坍的崖岸。

Target

Mock not the free will in my bowel,
Free from the twittering soul to be an immortal.
Pure in heart, the highway rustles,
Handy with facility, the red mansion gets sunbathed.
Nestled brightly, the rapids are empty but melancholy,
High-minded, let's see the avalanche of the cliffs.
Where the creek fish dreams his hanging the quiet north,
The rolling water would like to be angling in the wild.

目　的

铁马灵仙驭风，英谋作气折冲[①]。
中流翠浪和应[②]，曲岸银沙感通[③]。
展翅弯弧暗箭，高飞满引虚弓。

乾坤邂逅嘹唳[4]，安见寒云塞鸿。

【注释】

①英谋：英明的谋略。作气：振作勇气。折冲：克敌制胜。②和应：声音相应；和气感应。③感通：有所感而通于彼。④嘹唳（liáo lì）：形容声音响亮凄清。

Purpose

The sweeping horse on the immortal wind
Wisely plots the heartening conquer.
In the midstream, the green wave echoes,
On the winding shore, the silver sands are sensed.
While winging the flight, shoot your secret arrow,
While soaring high, bend your full but empty bow.
Clear and bleak, the universe may encounter
A swan in the frontier cloud, but of no avail.

能　量

清浊隐迹幽水，举目波澜咫尺。
弃世沈冥[1]一人，行心曲径双履。
惊风烈焰腾空，斗雪无声易轨。
落铁光年弃捐[2]，敲石万里沦毁[3]。

【注释】

①沈冥：幽居匿迹。②弃捐：抛弃。③沦毁：毁坏。

Energy

Pure or turbid, the hidden track in the quiet water
Raised its gaze to the billows close at hand.
One single figure hidden out of the society
Was shoed into the music of the heart
With its flying, blazing flames in the stormy power,
Against the orbit maneuver of the silent snows.
After the light year cast away the falling iron,
The knocking stones would sink to the point of ruin.

念　头

静念双轮散蹄，孤蟾旷望[①]迷离。
长歌落尽河汉，逸驾飘残素霓[②]。
寂寞嵯峨地半，清和[③]翠色天齐。
浮云对面金锁，落日垂帘玉梯。

【注释】

①旷望：极目眺望，远望。②素霓：白虹。③清和：天气清明和暖。

Idea

On its double wheels, my static mind hooves
The lonely, blurred moon out beyond the depths of yonder.
After the long song sheds all its petals of the Milky Way,
A fogbow will be faded and fallen at ease.

Half down, such loneliness has been crown ruggedly,
High as the sky, the green days are clothed mildly.
Right in front of the cloud racks, one gold lock
Will go down the jade stairs to the dossal.

炮仗花

红橙半户舒卷，莫问扬眉几转。
御苑离离地闲，仙舟眇眇石浅。
山藏晓日云浓，树绕晴波浪软。
乱序排空焰明，攀援更有黄鳝。

Pyrostegia Venusta（Ker-Gawl.） Miers

Half the red and orange hall curls and uncurls,
That denies itself to the arched eyebrows.
Though the royal garden flourishes freely,
The celestial boat runs aground uncertainly.
As the hills hide the dawn in the thick clouds,
The supple waves are looped by the fine wood.
Messy or straggly, let the fireworks fly bright,
Like the yellow eels climbing up and up.

陪　伴

世事悲欢古今，相思剪破同心。
行幽静影披雨，过耳灵犀半阴。
万象浮云指印，平川落日年侵。

烟春杳杳深隐，斜阳冥冥远寻。

Companion

In the quirks of joy and grief, the world history
Has scissored the undivided pangs of love
To be drizzled by the serene shade of the steps
Or to be partially shaded in the heartbeat in unison.
All-inclusive cloud racks like fingerprints
Are corroded annually in the open, sunset country.
Out and away, the hazy spring conceals deep
In the slanting rays of the sun farther in secret.

平 衡

翠羽交驰[①]路遥，浮云颈下多娇。
无声远陌斜日，有影疏篱短箫。
委树闲情鸟去，萦空好梦蓬飘。
鸿鹄不惹黄雀，燕雀别拼大雕。

【注释】

①交驰：交相奔走，往来不断。

Balance

The green, distant feathers passed by each other,
Below whose necks the cloud drifts its superb grandeur.
Following the toneless, slanting rays of the sun afar,

Their shadows like a short melody passed over the fence.
Out of the wood, the free birds were gone,
Hovering up, the good dream floated like a duckweed all along.
To be a swan, he won't provoke the siskin,
To be a chaffinch, he won't challenge the eagle.

70后

度鸟三秋日落，隔烟老树飞跃。
轻尘幻梦阡眠[①]，瘦骨遗幽绮错[②]。
纵目青云冷光，开襟素志寒魄[③]。
隔年鹤去空明，短棹[④]离情暗度。

【注释】

①阡眠：草木茂密貌。②绮错：绮纹之交错。③寒魄：指月亮。亦指月光。④短棹（zhào）：划船用的小桨。

Born in the 1970s

The bird of passage in the sundown of the late autumn
Soars out of the old, misty wood
Whose light, fantasy dusts thru the dense foliage
Are skinny and serectly confused splendidly.
To gaze into the cold light of the azure sky,
His white will under the open garment is coldly moon-lit.
Next year when the crane will be gone and illusory,
His short oars might slip through the parting grief.

气　概

铁马嘶风踏月，长蹄叩响筋骨。
压河暮柳笳薄，越岭朝阳鸟没。
舞羽凝心陆离，商弦[①]聚念清越。
宵行万里疏狂，裹雪扬风破讷[②]。

【注释】

①商弦：弹奏商调的丝弦。即七弦琴的第二弦。此处指马铃清脆的声响。②破讷：破讷沙，也就是沙漠的译名。泛指沙漠。

Mettle

The iron steed whinnies the moon-lit wind,
Whose long hooves are knocking on the bones.
The willowy dusk on the river flutes thin,
When the rising sun over the mountains drowns the birds.
Of varied hues the feather dances its fixed heart,
That gathers its idea into the fresh and inspired chord.
Nutty and leisurely, the night gallops ten thousand miles,
That winnow the windy snows across the great desert.

气　节

贤愚莫恋风情，素志幽藏晦明[①]。
朔雪孤魂守器[②]，胡沙散马征行[③]。
浮生不找良史，草木何求大名。

壮士从来铁血，文人自古身轻。

【注释】

①素志：向来怀有的志愿。晦明：黑夜和白昼。②守器：守护国家的重器；指所守护的重器。③征行：远行。

Moral Integrity

Wise fool, don't cling to the amorous feelings,
Dark or bright, hide your long-cherished will in secret.
Single soul, observe your integrity in the north snow,
Free horse, go out into the distant Tartar sands;
In this fleeting life, don't beg a good historian,
Like the wood, but why to woo the great name?
A stout warrior should be blood-curdling for good,
And the scholars tend to disparage each other from of old.

契　约

素志[①]人间百年，沧溟[②]几度桑田。
孤琴客子[③]犹暗，汉月江楼未圆。
细雨圆灵[④]忘返，浮光太液[⑤]流连。
清风落照鸿雁，旷世逍遥梦牵。

【注释】

①素志：同前首“气节”中的“素志幽藏晦明”。②沧溟：苍天、大海。③客子：长期远居他乡的游子。④圆灵：天。⑤太液：太液池。此处泛指池水。

Contract

The world has its will for a century,
In the evanescence of worldly affairs.
While the lonely lyre wanders darkly,
The moon goes not round near the riverside tower;
While the drizzles come and go thru the vault of heaven,
The floating light is hanging around the pond.
That breezes under the swans in the glow of the setting sun,
To be lost in the reverie carefree without peer.

矮牵牛

对客插头漏斗，留心月露情久。
寒积半片清池，霁累千条弱柳。
紫府从来断情，白衣几度执手。
轻霜扯地袭来，解梦临风对酒。

Petunia

The funnels in the hair before the strangers
Are heeding the dewy moon in the long sentiment
Half down the clear pond by the cold spells
Clear on the willows, weakly but wearily.
If the purple hall has always been heartless,
The white dress would join hands for ages.
Once shriveled up by the light, bestrewn frost,

The oneiromancy will be wined in the breeze.

强　者

黑风卷走毒龙，暴雨摧折远峰。
罩海参差雾重，横空淼漫[①]霜浓。
胡星西风缄恨[②]，汉月朔雪敛容。
壮士独刀易水，中国莫怕穷冬[③]。

【注释】

①淼漫：水流广远貌。此处喻指霜的广阔程度。②缄（jiān）恨：无奈又无处倾诉的怨恨。③穷冬：也指深冬和隆冬。

The Strong

The dark wind whirled away the viper,
And the rainstorm broke the far peaks.
The great smogs shrouded the staggering sea,
And the air brimmed with heavy frost.
The barbarian stars sealed the hatred in the west wind,
And the Chinese moon assumed its northern snow.
Like the stout warrior with a single sword,
China should never fear the deepest winter.

桥

鸟道冰河铁关，摇风堕羽空山。
灵华杳渺[①]通路，草芥连绵不攀。

百代青云世界，千年素带人间。
难得作嫁荒野，步履红尘等闲。

【注释】

①灵华：灵芝的美称。杳渺：悠远、渺茫貌。

Bridge

Thc narrow path above the ice river to the iron pass
Rocked and blew the feathers into the empty mountain
Where the ganoderma was dimly accessible
To the stretched scarp that shut out the weeds.
In the world of the blue sky for ages,
The plain ribbon arched across the human life.
It was seldom out in being married to the moor,
And any walking gait in the society was free and easy.

人　生
Life

其一

大乐流欢聿[①]变，靡谣浪雨拂面。
玄通旧曲中和[②]，至理新音上善[③]。
海静南蝉似银，潮生北梦如练。
万事赋命[④]尘埃，自古人生闪电。

【注释】

①聿（yù）：文言助词，无义，用于句首或句中。②玄通：与天相通。中和：中正平和。③上善：极致的完美。④赋命：命运。

One

Great joy flows into the vicissitudes,
Whose billowy rumours are caressing the faces.
If the old tone can test the mean, profound harmony,
The new tone will be the highest good in the wise dictum.
Once the sea calms like the south, silver cicadas,
The tide rises in the north dream smooth as silk.
All affairs of the world have to obey the dust,
Where life goes like lightning from of old.

其二

镜里人生百年，飘零几寸清烟。
朱颜不懂疾苦，皓发何谈尽欢。
梦里杯中落地，闲时酒里飞天。
黄河化作甘酿，试问谁识洞仙？

Two

About a century, life can mirror
A few inches of the clear, forsaken smoke.
If the rosy face had no ear for the sufferings,

How could the hoary joy be savoured at the full?
In dream, the cup touches down,
When free, the wine flies in the sky.
In the sweet brew of the Yellow River,
Who would know the fairy in the cave?

人 世

雾霭参差九天，徒生御气灵仙。
灵台缱绻人在，岁序苍黄数迁。
切切征帆碧海，冥冥瀑水虞渊[①]。
清晨款段[②]出世，日暮空垂老年。

【注释】

①虞渊：又称隅谷，古代神话传说中日落的地方。②款段：指马行迟缓的样子，借指马。喻指普通的生活。

The World

A heavy pall of mist slithers down the sky,
Merely bearing the spirit that drives the air.
Deeply attached to the mind of man,
The seasons have evolved with hasty changes.
Earnestly, square away into the blue sea,
Vaguely, the sunset would be cascading.
In the morn, everyman comes into the world,
At nightfall, he's very old on his deathbed.

人　性

九陌膏粱[①]燕雀，沧波棹影[②]鸣跃。
幽思降调飞流，隐迹升弦大壑。
铁柱齐天壮观，铜床钻地寥廓。
猢狲寄语苍生，利益萌生苦乐。

【注释】

①九陌：都城大道和繁华闹市；指京城。膏粱：肥肉和细粮，泛指美味的饭菜。亦指精美的饮食，代指富贵生活。②棹影：桨影。亦借指船影。

Human Nature

A chaffinch well-fed in the fields
Chirps down to the rowed shadow in the boundless waves,
Whose falling tone muses along the flying flow,
And hides its trail into the rising chord of the big gully.
Before the iron pole, the sky is spectacular, and
Down the brass bed, the drilled land is spacious, whence
The apes send word to the common people,
That benefit will create joys and sorrows.

认　识

洞里司晨[①]断梦，孤鸣指望来凤。
清尘落地涵德，润物凌空御众。

上苑[②]相欢敛眉，东风带笑闲弄。
生人看戏墙头，莫不声眠铁瓮。

【注释】

①司晨：雄鸡报晓。②上苑：皇家园林。

Cognition

The cave heralds the daybreak that breaks my dream,
With its lonely crowing to a coming phoenix.
As the clear dust grounds its moral,
Its moistening flight controls well.
In the merry garden that frowns,
The east wind teases at a leisurely pace.
To see the play on the wall,
Life will slumber its tones in the iron-clad town.

弱　点

杨花处处丝缕，镜动尘萦妙舞。
伴醉轻明绿蓑，多情磊落白羽。
池阁妙手新声，草木春深旧谱。
几许东风有违，斜吹瘦影无数。

Weakness

The willow catkins in and out of the willows
Are dancing merrily on the throbbing，dusty mirror.

In the light ebriety, the bright green cape
Opens its white, drippy feathers.
Highly skilled, the hall with its new sound
Has tuned its old growth in the fullness of spring.
A few breached touches of the east wind
Have slanted numerous thin shadows.

三角梅

满目激昂冷香，风花不改灵光。
流苏①两度银曲，彩凤别来艳妆。
伴客滩头紫径，连天岸上白荒②。
平生浩态③行乐，任尔衔杯放狂。

【注释】

①流苏：一种下垂的以五彩羽毛或丝线等制成的穗状饰物，常系在服装或器物上。②白荒：白色荒野。③浩态：仪态大方。

Bougainvillea

Her cold sweet seethes everywhere,
In the delights of nature with its divine light
That plays her silvery, melodious tassels,
Dressed most alluringly by the colourful phoenix.
Along the purple trail of the beach-head,
She stretches to the skyline of the white-wasted shore.
Life should enjoy pleasure in good time,
Now, raise our cups to take our drops!

三色堇

冰心点亮思慕，玉骨迎风问路。
紫陌晴来又新，黄尘日落如故。
红轮透满琼枝，碧浪侵薄火树。
送去无辜嫁妆，罗裙穗帐休妒。

Pansy

Your heart of ice lightens the longing,
Your bones of jade ask the way upwind.
The thoroughfare has updated fine,
And the sun still sets in your yellow dust.
One red wheel fills the jasper boughs,
And the green waves are pinching the flaming trees.
Now take away your innocent dowry,
And don't be jealous of other silk skirts and curtains.

上　帝

仙郎碾下云汉，自古沉浮聚散。
雨短漂泊暮年，云长泛梗华旦①。
方舟地角连波，抚辔天涯断岸。
几度风流使君，人神唱错一半。

【注释】

①泛梗：漂浮的草木梗。与“飘蓬”近义。华旦：吉日良辰；光明

盛世。

God

After the celestial man rolled down the Milky Way,
The vicissitudes are coming or going from of old.
In the short rains squander the declining years,
In the long clouds wander the fortunate hours.
When the ark ripples around the cape of the earth,
The bridle soothes the broken shore on the skyline.
As the true wits that touch the elegant ages,
Man and God have sung half at the wrong pitch.

少　年

龙沙紫塞残照，夜静山空虎啸。
飒飒长风露白，霏霏海月光耀。
杨洲澹荡连翩，柳岸峥嵘料峭。
逸气闲云纵横，多情莫怪年少。

Youngster

As the sun declines upon the desert of the Great Wall,
The tiger grows in the empty mountain of the still night.
As the long wind rustles in the white dews,
The brilliant moon rises thick and fast on the sea.
As the poplar isle throngs its mild ripples,
The willow shores are rugged and chilly in the air.

Like the idle cloud with a free soul,
The soulful mood blames not the juvenile.

声　名

风尘闭户催行，岁月沈沦远情。
老去归心誓志[①]，别来旧里存诚。
闲云笑我闲事，阵雨怜君阵名。
鹤静垂竿两尺，鸣群百仞流声。

【注释】

①誓志：发誓立志。

Reputation

The dust of journey shuts the pressing door,
Far from the love that sinks into the years.
When old, the oath grows impatient to return,
After gone, the old heart stows the sincerity.
The roaming cloud jests me to be nosey,
And the cloud burst pities your reiterated name.
Better angle two feet still like the crane,
That whoops its flowing tones for a hundred fathoms.

第七批中国外语教育基金项目：ZGWYJYJJ2014z30

Sponsored by the 7th Chinese Foreign Language Education Fund：ZGWYJYJJ2014z30

山海集

——寻觅中国古代诗歌的镜像

（下册）

吴松林　著/译

A Collection of Seas and Mountains

—The Mirror to Seek the Ancient Chinese Poems

Authored & Translated By Wu Songlin

东北大学出版社

·沈　阳·

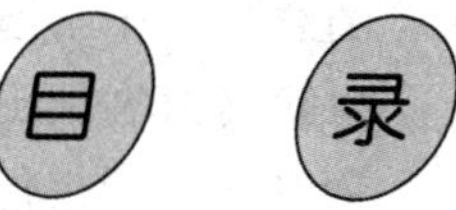

下 册

失　败

海客维舟渐远，寒瓜莫问空蔓。
桥头桂露长哀，水上菱风宿怨。
秀色侯门五千，浮云客路十万。
花深一鸟残阳，阔水沉星地远。

Failure

The mariner was moored off further,
Further off the cold melons devoid of the tendrils.
The bridgehead in dews bewailed,
And the wind of water caltrops nursed rancor,
Before the 5000 pretty faces of the lordly houses,
And the 100000 passengers like cloud drifts.
Amid the deep flowers one bird in the setting sun
Was sinking like a star down to the far, wide water.

诗　觞

山行羽翼沈冥①，散帙回飙峻屏②。
鸟雀晴虚③旧隐，烟霞净地通灵。
神游玉酒常阻，梦旅金壶不宁。
李杜瑶琴粪土，心弦素业④谁听？

【注释】

①沈冥：作“沉冥”，低沉。②散帙（sàn zhì）：打开书帙。亦借指读书。回飙：旋转的狂风。峻屏：高峻的山峦。③晴虚：晴空。④素业：先世所遗之业。旧时多指儒业，此处指本业或诗歌古俗。

The Elegy of Poems

Over the mountains in obscurity, my wings
Perused the magnificent curtains in the whirlwind,
Like a sparrow hidden in my old, clear sky,
Or the telephony of the pure land in the hazy wisps.
Roaming wild, my liquor often had its snags,
In night walking, my golden pitcher fluttered.
The jasper lute of the greatest poets was dead,
Who would listen to the plain heartstrings?

石　竹

江头落日浮柳，碧影幽姿静守。
子夜含冰去时，君竹带露归否？
萧疏①贵遇新朋，隐映闲逢旧友。
戏浪白云化蝶，红茵②淡荡秋后。

【注释】

①萧疏：冷落，稀稀落落。②红茵：红色的垫褥。

The Chinese Pink

Upstream, the setting sun was willowy
And whist in her subtle, green carriage.
As the icy midnight has gone,
Whether the dewy bamboos can come back?

Stagnated, it's lucky to have new-found friends,
Nestled dimly, an old fellow may peep out at liberty.
To sport the waves, the white cloud grows into butterflies,
That lightly swing through the autumn in the red blooms.

时　间

世累独听水流，清谈逸兴无由。
幽微岂料归轸①，律韵翻悲宿谋②。
袅袅高机弱羽，萧萧矮阪穷愁③。
殷勤晓渡沧浪，日暮平沙钓舟。

【注释】

①归轸（zhěn）：归舟；暮年。②宿谋：预先设好的计策。③矮阪（bǎn）：矮坡，下坡。穷愁：穷困愁苦。

Time

In the world that ties down, hear the water flows all along,
And an empty talk in high soul won't be reasonable hitherto.
In spiritual seclusion, who's foreseen the boat's return
To the deliberate rhyme of the merciful compassion?
It's the ubiquitous whiff that pivots the weak, high feathers,
Over the destitute rustles towards the downhills.
Before the surging wave that dawns the debonair ferry,
The strands shall be fishing until the nightfall.

识心

冰心远水如练，丽日平开扇面。
露草明行紫云，霜林暗渡白燕。
黄花两道山楼，紫叶三层海甸。
世外桃源不存，穷居陋室独善。

See Your Heart

The heart of the ice flows as silk afar
And flips the fan open to the bright sun.
Over the dewy grass, the purple cloud flows bright,
Through the frost wood, a white swallow flows secretly.
Two rows of towers in the day-lily buds on the hill
Are embellished with three layers of purple leaves by the lake.
There will never be a land of idyllic beauty, and
So, to dwell in the humble room may be immune.

世界

玄虚避世无常，客子乌啼稻粱[①]。
送月多情理短，随风寡语情长。
同游紫陌深覆，解梦红尘暗藏。
草木飘摇万里，人心盛夏流霜。

【注释】

①客子：旅居异乡的人。稻粱：稻和粱，谷物的总称。

The World

A sequestered mystery must be fickle,
And a wanderer may caw for the grains.
To send the moon, the amorous reason could be short,
With the wind, the reticent passion might be long.
Together, the highway covers deep,
To read the dream, the human society lurks here.
As the lush growth drifts to the earth's end,
The heart of man would flow its frost in midsummer.

示弱

戴水金风①弱云，连峰荡漾波纹。
贤愚北去人梦，贵贱南飞雁群。
绿蔓空愁宋玉，清声宿怨灵芸②。
连天燕雀嘶柳，铁锁铜台不分。

【注释】

①金风：秋风。②宿怨：久已积下的怨恨。灵芸：三国魏文帝所爱美人薛灵芸。

A Sign of Weakness

Weakly clouded, the Daihe River in cool breeze
Ripples around the mounds like the seedpods of the lotus.
Wise or fool, the dreams are gone north

High or low, the wild geese are flying north.
As the green tendrils are stewed for Song Yu,
The clear voice harbours the deep-seeded grudges of Xue Lingyun.
To the sky, the chaffinches are chirping in the willows,
Regardless of the Bronze Sparrow Terrace in iron lock.

睡莲

水彩和鸣翠凤，仙郎玉漏沾梦。
临窗半月涂樯，破晓连星洗瓮。
弱柳孤舟散垂，凝酥落照斜控。
出泥自守贞洁，本性无需受贡。

Water Nymph

A green phoenix full of merriment on the watercolour
Touches the dream of the merry man by the water-clock.
One crescent through the window whitewashes the wall,
And embathes the urns under the stars before dawn.
Upon the lonely boat, it's willowy loosely, and in the pure,
Soft brilliance, the slanting rays of the sun are reined.
Out of the mud, she lives chastely,
For the nature that dispenses with an esteem.

顺　性

幽姿把臂疏顽[①]，旷朗[②]薄书自闲。
益友舟惊放性，良朋露尽承颜[③]。

灵山汗漫[④]归意，骇浪颓沱[⑤]泻潺。
自古桃源劝客，贤愚莫遣[⑥]忠奸。

【注释】

①把臂：握持手臂，表示亲密。疏顽：懒散顽钝。②旷朗：开朗。③承颜：顺承尊长的颜色。谓侍奉尊长。④汗漫：广大，漫无边际；渺茫不可知。⑤颓沱：水流向下宣泄。亦指向下宣泄的水流。⑥莫遣：不要抒发；不要理论。

Compliance

In subtle, slothful arms,
The slip, sanguine sheets are idyllic.
To the salutary ship that shocks its free nature,
The compassionate dews are gone submissively.
In the intrinsic will, the hill of soul strolls back
To the fountain babbling into a terrifying billow.
To give the cheer in a Shangri-La from of old,
Voice not your wise or fool view on the loyal duplicity.

思 想
Thought

其一

楚客幽思往事，威灵澹荡精意[①]。

千回远路连天，万道行尘动地。
举世空吟苦心，谁人寂寞得志。
沧桑一缕穷达，对酒人生百戏。

【注释】

①威灵：神灵。澹荡：荡漾，飘动。精意：专心一意；诚意。

One

To roam, to ponder, to the bygone,
The powerful soul undulates into its good faith,
Whose long road stretches to the skyline a thousand times,
Whose ten thousand travel-worn steps shake the soil.
While all the world sings its bitter heart in vain,
I wonder who has got what he wants in solitude.
A plume of fortune must be weather-beaten,
By the hundreds of games in the life of wine.

其二

逆旅栖乌远思，青眸[①]唱和行迟。
吴琴著晓先到，楚客归船未离。
历历文章岁远，迢迢物象[②]时移。
君心几度留去，引棹平湖漫随。

【注释】

①青眸：瞳仁。②物象：具体事物的形象或景象。

Two

One crow perched in the free spirit of the worldly intrigues
Caws amid the late antiphony by the dark eyes.
At dawn, the zither has turned up earlier,
In the boat, the wanderer has not paddled away.
Clearly, the writings have gone far,
Remotely, the object images have shifted with time.
Come or go many a time, your heart
Popples with the oars in the smooth lake.

思与在

游思碾碎荒原，蔓草汀洲正繁。
暮雨临风抚泪，秋霜览镜难言。
休夸宦路知己，且看三朝掖垣①。
烈火烹油②过后，碣石老树鸦喧。

【注释】

①掖垣（yè yuán）：皇宫的旁垣；喻指中央部门。②烈火烹油：比喻声势气焰很盛。

Thought and Existence

The roaming idea scrunches the waste land,
While the weed vines look lush on the sand islets.
Tearful to the wind in the dusk rain,

The autumn frosts are unspeakable to the mirror.
Boast not your confidant on the official road,
Let's see the side walls of the three dynasties.
After the flames poured by the oil,
The ravens still caw in the old trees of the Jieshi Hill.

死　士

易水难酬燕丹①，消沉奋烈孤寒。
幽云悯默②犹在，壮气英威③尚残。
瘴疠④无需顾后，干戈赴死何难。
轻生谑浪插羽⑤，亮剑孰图苟安。

【注释】

①燕丹：姬姓，名丹，燕王喜之子，战国末期燕国太子。当时秦已攻灭韩、赵等国，次将及燕。秦灭韩前夕，被送至秦国当人质，受辱后于燕王喜二十三年（前232年）回到燕国。他以暗杀秦王政来阻挡秦国的兼并之势，曾策划过荆轲刺秦王事件，事情败露后，燕王喜担心秦国出兵攻打燕国，便杀太子丹，将其头颅献秦军以求和。②悯默：因忧伤而沉默。③英威：英勇威武。④瘴疠：亦作“瘴厉”。感受瘴气而生的疾病。亦泛指恶性疟疾等病。此处喻指险恶的政治和生存环境。⑤谑浪：戏谑放荡。插羽：古代军书插羽毛以示迅急。

The Man of Sacrifice

The Yishui River never requited Prince Dan,
Drooped into the isolated but vigorous cold.
Of tacit pity, the quiet cloud still roams there,

Where hangs over his heroic might of pride.
Look back not at the poisonous damps,
With the weapons of war, ready to die!
To take the life teases like a sealed feather,
Bright sword! Who'd seek momentary ease!

四君子
The Four Noble Characters

其一：梅

寒风几渡三秋，百草枯黄锁愁。
万岭虬枝劲骨，千山树干轻柔。
金霜眼底垂艳，玉露眉间凝眸。
傲雪横斜淡月，冰封誓不低头。

One: Plum Flowers

Cold snaps in late autumn days
Have locked up the brown herbs.
All ranges are framed with curled, strong sprays
All hills with the trunks in light and soft plays.
In golden frosts are hung their vivid colours
Of pure, strained brows which are dewed.
Hardened in the stress pale moon that wavers,
They won't hang their heads in the ice-bound covers.

其二：兰

玉指凝香蕙兰[1]，欣欣[2]露彩霜寒。
迎风恪守孤寂，对月何求翩跹[3]。
不与群芳斗艳，宁和野草流连。
依依[4]自抱清瘦，有泪不流人前。

【注释】

①玉指：美人的手指，此处指一茎九花的花茎。清·郑燮《题双美人图》诗："玉指尖纤指何许，似笑姮娥无伴侣。"②欣欣：草木茂盛貌。宋·司马光《小诗招僚友晚游后园》之二："麦田小雨陇微青，草树欣欣照晓晴。"③翩跹（piān xiān）：飘逸飞舞貌。唐·杜甫《西阁曝日》诗："流离木杪猿，翩跹山巅鹤。"④猗猗（yī）：柔美貌；美好貌。

Two：Orchids

On sweet，pure fingers，
A frostbiten pleasure in dewy colours
Has faced the wind in solitude
That，to the moon，has no tripping aptitude.
She never contends in fragrance，
But lingers on with the wild grass in abundance.
Tunefully stirred on the wane，
She holds no trace of tears before other men.

其三：竹

竹枝一抹金玉，惯看人间迷雾。
百代笙箫苦霜，千年鼓瑟甘露。
摇风掠地疏狂①，鼓浪排空如固。
自古谁名汗青②，寒门大写天路。

【注释】

①疏狂：豪放，不受拘束。②名：通假“铭”，铭刻。汗青：古时在竹简上记事，先以火烤青竹，使水分如汗渗出，便于书写，并免虫蛀，故称汗青。

Three：Bamboos

Precious bamboo branches of mine
Have seen enough of man's foggy line.
Frosts for the generations are fluted bitterly,
And dews for the ages are drummed sweetly.
Unbridled by nature, the wind sacks the ground,
Where they stand still in the billowing blowdown.
From of old, who's crowned with eternal glory?
A humble abode that writes the pilgrim's way.

其四：菊

本性轻肌卷面，西风更奈何堪?
冰霜四处淫威，雨雪八方阻难。
百草惊心断魂，千花动魄离乱。
孤标[①]唤醒冬梅，傲世[②]无非冷艳。

【注释】

①孤标：独特的标格。《旧唐书·杜审权传》：“尘外孤标，云间独步。”②傲世：藐视当世。

Four: Chrysanthemums

Of nature, her light flesh coldly blown
By the west wind helplessly shown
Has been rimed in despotic powers
Or sleeted at each thwarted corners.
On tenterhooks, soul of all herbs has broken,
Ghostly sighted, soul of all flowers in confusion.
Proud recluse, to arouse the winter plum-flowers,
And with contempt, her vogue cool shines invariably.

随　心

轻烟细柳别愁，隐映桃心凤楼。
翡翠飘零守道，流莺浩荡无由。
空池冷月不问，老树消息莫求。

逸兴常闻落日，长歌羽客孤舟。

At Will

The parting sorrows in the wisps of the willowy smoke
Were nestled in the peach tower of phoenixes.
Faded and fallen, like an emerald observing its truth,
The twittering oriole never wandered far and wide.
Now, ignore that cold moon on the empty pond,
And stop your message throughout the old trees.
In refined pursuits, you've often heard the setting sun,
Although the solitary boat goes with its long croon.

随意草

中禁逸客[①]玫红，放浪崩腾雪青。
静守红尘大易，恭承紫陌仙经。
披针朗玉抨火，射月晴恨溅星。
木秀连峰鸟道，淋离莫问其形。

【注释】

①中禁：内心约束。逸客：超逸高雅的人。

Physostegia Virginiana

Her unconventional, restrained heart of rose
Was transported into the burst soar of the violet tulip.
To calmly observe the *Book of Changes* in the world,

She performed the great behest of the Taoist treatise.
As the clear, needled jade stroke its sparks,
The bow at the moon sploshed the stars in fine grudges.
As the narrow path twisted thru the lush wood of the hills,
Its fantastic form should not be examined any more.

岁　觞

海客天山牧羊，江妃委地①云翔。
凌风满座狂月，荡野空骑怒阳。
艳色闲邀玉漏②，繁香倦赏东墙③。
黄莺莫信娇艳，百啭霜毛④夜凉。

【注释】

①委地：蜷伏于地。②玉漏：古代计时漏壶的美称。③东墙：喻指貌美多情的女子。④霜毛：白发。

The Wine of Time

The mariner shepherded in Tianshan Mountain,
The river Goddess crouched before soared like a cloud.
With woven wings, the wild moon filled the seats,
Roaming in the wild, it barely rode the sun in its rage.
When the fancy colour called for the vacant water-clock,
He admired the drowsy scent of aroma on the east wall.
Trust the yellow, delicate warblers, but never more,
Whose plume twitters cooled down at a frost night.

贪 腐

昨天宦侣飘摇，百尺雄心暗凋。
少壮官家虎爪，中年乐府笙箫。
东窗败露形影，北壁钳奴氛妖[1]。
治者一朝被治，风标降丧孤标[2]。

【注释】

①钳奴：髡（kūn）钳为奴者。古代刑罚，谓剃去头发，用铁圈束颈。氛妖：亦作“氛祆”，妖气。多喻指灾祸或叛贼。②风标：风度，品格。降丧：降祸。孤标：独特的标格。

Corruption

Yesterday, the official fellows were precarious,
And quietly withered their ambitious drives.
In youthful sap, they were official claws of tiger,
Middle-aged, the flutes and pipes filled their music halls.
After their criminal conspiracies had taken air,
The demons and devils must be exorcised.
One day when the rule was to be ruled,
The weather cock drooped its lonely shock.

逃 官

浮沈世道维艰，旷岁[1]劳心闭关。
虎困联翩大海，龙疲沓障[2]深山。

郎官自释匡济[3]，候吏殊伦[4]巧奸。
鹤影西游越海，逍遥汗漫[5]难还。

【注释】

①旷岁：经年；长年。②沓障：重重叠叠的山峰。③郎官：古代盖为议郎、中郎、侍郎、郎中等官员的统称。匡济（kuāng jì）："匡时济世"的略语。即挽救艰难时势，救助当今人世。④候吏：候人。古代掌管整治道路稽查奸盗，或迎送宾客的官员。殊伦：不同类；出类拔萃。⑤汗漫：无边无际。

The Officials at Large

Up or down, the world spells hard times,
Long-drawn-out, close the door to your mental perplexity.
A tiger may be trapped in the open sea,
And a tired dragon be caught in the remote mountains.
An official claims to rectify social evils and malpractices
And an inspector caps all others in his treacherous cunning.
After they cross the sea on their cranes west,
Their roaming service will not come back.

体　液

芳田静闭灵液[1]，断续朱弦细脉。
进退流年展思，离合气沮[2]魂魄。
华堂不晓霓裳[3]，洞户参同羽客[4]。
物外烟萝[5]纵横，青冥[6]扫去陈迹。

【注释】

①灵液：仙液。②气沮：气馁。③霓裳（ní chang）：道士的衣服。④洞户：洞口；幽深的内室。羽客：道士。此处指修道、修炼。⑤烟萝：草树茂密，烟聚萝缠。⑥青冥：形容青苍幽远。此处指青天。

Body Fluids

The ichor calmly shut in the sweet elixir field
Makes and breaks the veinlets of the red strings
That come or go thru the free, swift time,
And unite or separate the vital energy for or against the soul.
If the splendid hall were ignorant of the rainbow skirt,
The deep and serene cave would identify the Taoist priest.
Beyond the material desires overruns a labyrinth of the hazy ivies,
Whose vestiges would be swept off under blue sky.

天女木兰

玉魄山君雪融，仙姝醉客天工。
霜刀肃谷鸿怨，柳剪颀飙[1]树空。
慧眼千堆富贵，禅心万片穷通。
冰肌嫩舞丹芯，雪瓣流辉岁丰。

【注释】

①颀飙：狂风。

Magnolia Sieboklii

The soul of jade at the mountain top thaws the snow,
Where the drunken fairy was created and ordered by Heaven,
Where swans squawked to the solemn vale in bright frost,
Where the wild whirlwind sheared the willows stark.
Quick-sighted, thousands of stacks of riches and ranks
Are meditating ten thousands of fortunes;
Her flesh of snow dances the delicate, red pistls,
Within the brilliant snow petals through her rich passage.

天竺葵

半醉晴空紫凤，英雄一捧虚梦。
沈吟万里天竺，放浪千般信众。
鹤影清江未回，蝉声紫塞相送。
雕红弄蕊移花，点粉禅衣自控。

Geranium

Half drunk like a purple phoenix in the clear sky,
The heroine scoops a handful of empty dream,
That muses long from the ancient India,
Prodigal before a thousand sects of believers.
On the clear river, the crane shadow has not returned,
But the cicadas below the Great Wall bid farewell.
Move her red sculptured pistils now,

And touch some rouges on her robe of conscious meditation.

忘　记
To Forget

其一

攀欢欲醉闲池，柳色斜晖忘机[1]。
去恨风中此地，离情枕上相期。
萧萧落日洲浦，漠漠孤城客思。
斗酒踌躕岁月，人生几度临岐。

【注释】

①忘机：消除机巧之心。常用以指甘于淡泊，忘掉世俗，与世无争。

One

To be merry, to be drunk, by the idle pond,
The slanting sunlight goes aloof thru the green willow.
To be gone in the grudges of the wind from here,
The parting grief trickles its date on the pillow.
Desolate, as the sun sets on the isles,
My thought roams lonely in the foggy town.
To measure the liquor, I pace up and down the years,
For a couple of times, my life meets its crossroads.

其二

尘喧[1]峥嵘羁旅，陌上殷勤浪语。
倦客从未负身，欢游最易相许。
寻常造化岐山，放旷[2]沧桑水浒。
壮士谁求苟安，达人[3]莫问出处。

【注释】

①尘喧：尘世的烦扰。亦指尘世。②放旷：豪放旷达，不拘礼俗。③达人：在某一领域非常专业、出类拔萃的人物。指在某方面很精通的人，即某方面的高手。

Two

My blatant strife on the journey
Has inflamed the officious pathway.
Though tired, I never gave myself away,
To be joyous, I was quick to promise.
As usual, a forked mountain was born,
Of free spirit, a marsh could be turbulent.
To be heroic man, who'd seek momentary ease?
To be wise man, ask not where lies my origin.

望　乡

高阁式燕[1]清觞，旷岁[2]重寻绿阳。
彩笔香泥地阔，雕盘舞袂天长。

清歌欲醉江燕，玉管先调野棠[3]。
梦断疏狂冷酒，他乡也作家乡。

【注释】

①式燕：宴饮。②旷岁：经年；长年。③玉管：玉制的古乐器。用以定律。野棠：果木名。即棠梨。

Home-gazing

To feast the tower with clear liquor,
I seek the green sun agelong again.
Under the colour pen, the sweet mud measures wide,
In the carved dish, the day of sleeves dances long.
While the clear song almost drowns the river swallow,
The pipe of jade first flirts with the birchleaf pears.
Awake from the dream unbridled in the cold liquor,
The alien land could serve as my homeland.

文　化

宇内文飞碧潭，扶桑[1]水际轻岚。
明堂柳色斜映，宝鼎[2]梨花半涵。
灭影惊霜落木，消香泣雨抽蚕。
婆娑醉舞闲棹[3]，半世烟云苦甘。

【注释】

①扶桑：神话中的树名。②宝鼎：鼎的一种称呼，为了衬托其珍贵而称为宝鼎。现在，社会上的宝鼎主要是指佛教的一种焚器。③棹（zhào）：划船的一种工具，形状和桨差不多。

Culture

Fair and fine, the green pool flies in the world,
Whose tree of dawn ripples over the light hazes.
While the green willows are tilted outside the bright halls,
Pear flowers are half veiled in the incense tripod.
While the falling wood are shocking the frost shadows,
The faded sweet weeps in the rain unwinding the cocoons.
To paddle free in the drunken whirls, the wind
For half a century has tasted prosperity and adversity.

伪　僧

岭上鸡林①塔影，传灯半座斜景②。
高名待月修行，下位涵虚③不省。
客舍④多情薜萝，归心解语萍梗。
闲眠六欲七情，看惯沙弥造境⑤。

【注释】

①鸡林：佛寺。②传灯：指获得菩提智慧的人如一盏明灯，在照亮了自己的同时，有责任去点燃尚处在混沌状态中的其他灯盏，以期“灯灯相传”“亘古光明灿烂”。半座：指先往生净土者，将其莲华座留半座给后往生者。以示信心相同，果报亦相同。斜景：侧斜的影子；西斜的太阳；西斜的阳光。此处双关。③涵虚：水映天空。④客舍：供旅客投宿的处所。⑤沙弥：原语可能出自龟兹语的 samane 或 sammir，或于阗语的 samana。意译为求寂、息慈、勤策，即止恶行慈、觅求圆寂的意思。造境：在具象的基础上，进一步将语言文字还原成特定的情境、意境、心境。

False Monk

The pagoda shadows of the temple on the mound
Pass on the light half to the seat on the cross.
As the honoured name strives for virtue below the moon,
The lower-seat nature of illusion hasn't been self-examined.
In the cell drippy by the climbing figs,
The heart of return might understand the duckweed.
To take naps in the seven emotions and the six desires,
The accustomed eyes live in the fantasyland of the novices.

乌鸦嘴

老树乌衣举翅，啼杀远近名利。
三征火上时名①，九转煎熬物议②。
旷野愁闻真性，荒郊醉见儿戏。
前尘匿迹沈烟，散影连宵放肆。

【注释】

①三征：三国魏征南将军王昶、征东将军胡遵、镇南将军毌丘俭的合称。此处泛指多次讨伐或口诛。时名：当时的声名或声望。②九转：反复翻转。物议：众人的议论，多指非议。

The Chattering Daw

A daw flares its wing in the old tree,
Cawing for its fame and gain far and near,

For the fame after three flaming conquests,
From the public censure of nine-cycled tortures.
Even the open field hears its real self in gloom.
And the wild country gets its kid stuff in ebriety.
Although its history has dissolved into the air,
Its loose shadow still runs wild each night.

无　知

煮玉高风论文，书空谏草[①]孤云。
黄鹄逸志[②]何在，振羽风标不群。
岁月怀贤怅望，烟霞触类[③]殷勤。
人情好歹难定，冷暖贤愚不分。

【注释】

①谏草：谏书的草稿。②逸志：超逸脱俗之志。③触类：接触相类事物。

Ignorance

To comment on literature cooks the noble jade,
In great disillusion that exhorts the lonely cloud.
Where is the free will of the yellow swan?
Above the common, he flutters as the weather cock.
Though the years hope to be virtuous in vain,
The rosy hues would single out the urbanity.
For good or ill, the human feelings are unpredictable,
Sage and fool, the changes in temperature are indivisible.

先　衰

粉黛蛾眉解鬟①，云屏口脂思闲。
珠帘暮雨罗袂②，绣户春风玉仙。
柳叶稍觉晓箭③，菱花④渐露衰颜。
秋波化作冰雪，断梦桃夭不还。

【注释】

①鬟（huán）：妇女梳的环形发髻。②罗袂：丝罗的衣袖。亦指华丽的衣着。③晓箭：拂晓时漏壶中指示时刻的箭。常借指凌晨这段时间。④菱花：菱花镜的简称。

Premature Ageing

Down the coiled bun, her powdered eyebrows
Relax the lipstick near the cloud-like screen.
In the dusk rain, her silk sleeves behind the pearl curtain
Are like a celestial spring breeze in the boudoir.
A bit awake from the dawning willow leaves,
The mirror gradually shows her wrinkled face.
After the autumn ripples turn into snow and ice,
Her newly-wed countenance won't return in the dream broken.

现　实

芒鞋[1]踏破明月，梦里荒榛入骨。
肃穆行吟断绝，深沈立语[2]出没。
黄尘暗度银河，紫气斜穿破讷[3]。
莫作红尘路痴，人生哪有宫阙。

【注释】

①芒鞋：草鞋。②立语：立论；站着对话。③破讷：破讷沙，系沙漠译名。泛指沙漠。

Reality

The grass sandals crush the bright moon under foot,
And the wasted hazels in dream go into the marrow.
To be a solemn troubadour in severance,
He would air his deeper views that come and go.
While the yellow dust slips thru the milky way,
The ruddy light slants off the desert.
Learn not the human society that loses its way,
Where life has no palace of its own.

相对性

海内满眼明月，忆梦飘摇朽骨。
断雾穹崇[1]锁床，连云澹静突兀[2]。
冥蒙[3]翠蔓禽迷，寂历[4]红芳草没。
古墓空悲伟人，千年过后谁谒[5]？

【注释】

①穹崇：高貌。②澹静：淡泊宁静。突兀：高耸貌；突然。③冥蒙：幽暗不明。④寂历：凋零疏落。⑤谒（yè）：拜见。

Relativity

An eyeful of bright moon within the seas
Recalls its klunky bones tottering in dream.
As the lifted fog locks the bed below,
The clouds heave a detached, rolling soul.
Obscure in green vines, the fowl are lost
In the ruddy and weedy flowers sparsely.
To rue the great man for aye, to be sure,
Who would visit his tomb a thousand years later?

小　人

狂花醉惹孤竹，莫问悲欢倚伏①。
楚客别来寂寞，栖迟②语罢幽独。
渔家枕上禽类，野店窗间羽族。
巧佞无穷谄惑③，奴颜软骨匍匐。

【注释】

①倚伏：依存隐伏。②栖迟：游玩休憩。③巧佞：机巧奸诈的人；阿谀奉承的人。谄惑：谄谀并惑乱。

Little Man

The besotted, mad flowers offend the lonely bamboo,
Apathetic to the quirks of joy and sorrow.
Since the departure, the passenger roams dolefully
And lately in the breathed, quiet solitude.
As the fowl on the pillow of the fisherman,
The feathers are flaunting his window of the wild inn.
To be a sycophant, the endless enchanted flattery
Will be vulnerable to the servile, soft bones.

蟹爪兰

何方半树仙指，傲雪天工莫比。
聚散红尘苦辛，浮沈大道忧喜。
寒风浸透清虚，野径横吹妙理。

赋雪敲冰冷香，禅心幻境风起。

Crab Cactus

Where are those immortal fingers in half the wood which
Won't be compared by the nature's work proud in the snow?
In the toilsome society that separates or reunites,
The great truth sinks or swims in a mixed blessing.
When the cold snap soddens the clean hollow,
The wild trail will cross its blast of sweet philosophy.
When the ode to the snow knocks the icy sweet,
The meditative mind blows in the land of illusion.

心 态

吏隐虚阁苑墙，君行柳色春阳。
烟花世界千里，日月天人两行。
客路空山雨短，江桥满镜云长。
青山吊影芳气，万物幽姿晓光。

The State of Mind

The official hides in the empty pavilion of the walled garden,
Unlike those who walk below the green willows in the spring sun.
In the world of brothels for thousands of miles,
The nature and the man follow their own courses.
On the roaming road, the rain shortens in the empty mountains,
Full in the mirror, the river bridge has been clouded long.

Single and alone, the green hills are breathing sweetly,
And the subtle stances of the world are dawning.

行路难

疏星大旆[1]天山，铁血横行大关。
硬骨停鞭月里，尸骸覆没沙间。
钢刀万仞横路，铁戟千寻可攀。
宦场犹如战场，前行自古维艰。

【注释】

①旆（pèi）：古代旌旗末端状如燕尾的垂旒。泛指旌旗。

The Hard Way

Great banners thru the Tianshan Mountains under the sparse stars
Ran rampant with the blood of iron to the impregnable pass.
After the dauntless bones halted the scourges in the moon,
The corpses were capsized and drowned in the desert.
Massively high, the steel swords crossed the road,
Before the forest of steel spears, be daunted never more!
An official circle has been like the battle field,
The journey ahead hobbles or plods from of old.

幸 福
Happiness

其一

曲榭灵芝紫泉，回廊玉露慈缘。
南山野老汲井，北岭柴门种田。
蕙草疏窗远趣，凉风日影高眠。
人情本色恬澹，细雨荷池正鲜。

One

A tinder agaric in the curving pavilion near the purple fountain
Bears the dews of jade in its loving lot to the rural greybeard
Who lifts a barrel of water in the southern hill, and also to
The wicker gate that follows the plough in the northern mountain.
Temperamentally afar, the sweet herb before the sparse window
Breezes cool all over the high sleep of the sun's shadow.
Indifferent to worldly desires, the natural colour of the human feelings
Should taste fresh in such thin drizzles down the lotus pool.

其二

世路谋身岁久，乾坤五福[①]维厚。
安居宿愿知足，乐业浮名自守。
舞鹤悠溶[②]牧童，游鱼好事樵叟。
修得四世同堂，胜过金章紫绶[③]。

【注释】

①五福：根据《尚书》上所记载，五福：一曰寿，二曰富，三曰康宁，四曰攸好德，五曰考终命。②悠溶：平静貌；安闲貌。③紫绶：紫色丝带。古代高级官员用作印组，或作服饰。

Two

The way of the world has worked long,
For the the five happinesses richly blessed.
To secure a long-cherished life contents with the lot,
To work in peace observes the bubble glory of his own.
Like a cowboy that dances for a life of leisure,
Or the woodcutter that figures out the fish in the water,
His earnest effort for four generations under one roof
Will fetch over the purple cord and the gold medal.

训　导

身闲病眼梅心，寸步生尘几寻。
水月流萤爽气，风花玉露暝[1]林。
知音捣破嘶马，瘦影吹残晓禽。
好梦翻空岁月，朱轮[2]妙响人心。

【注释】

①暝（míng）：日落；天黑。②朱轮：王侯显贵所乘的车子。

Discipline

Idle-bodied, affected-eyed, plum-hearted,
The single step was blanketed dustily.
In the fresh air, the fireflies over the moon-lit water
Tasted the pure dews on the breezy petals of the dark wood.
Soon after their soul-mates were smashed by the whinnies,
Their skinny shadows would whiffle the dawning fowls.
Until the sweet dream turned over the time and tide,
The red wheel might be echoed in the subtle heart.

雁头红

热浪重游镜象[1]，山莓水月豪荡[2]。
红龙日去千条，紫凤春深百丈。
梦魅虚明露中，星尘启闭川上。
心随北斗初晴，振翅幽遐旷朗[3]。

【注释】

①镜象：镜中的物象；亦指水中物象。②豪荡：意气洋溢，器量阔大。③旷朗：开阔明亮。

Catharanthus Roseus

The warm wave haunted the mirror again,
Whose moon-lit water was vigorously free for the red raspberry.
After thousands of red dragons were gone in their days,
Purple phoenixes soared up to the fullness of spring.
While the goblins in dream were virtually bright in the dews,
The star dust started or stopped over the streams.
While the heart freshly cleared with the Big Dipper,
Its wings would flap up into the bright, serene space afar.

洋桔梗

敛迹[1]孤峰碧涧，临潭远近鸣雁。
阳林妙境流年，雾谷闲姿梦幻。
古翠芳蓝宝石，寒烟水色琼瓣。
仙衣饯客多愁，散作琼华欲绽。

【注释】

①敛迹：有所顾忌而不敢放肆。

Eustoma Grandiflorum

Traceless, the isolated peak amid the green gully
Faces the pool in the honks of the wild geese far and near.
Subtly located, the sunny wood alternates its swift time,
Idly posed, the foggy bottom experiences its dream of fantasy.
Like an oriental sapphire of the old green sweet,
The jade petals shine bright near the cold, misty waters.
To feast our eyes, her sentimental fairy gown
Would come loose to be the rare, budded flowers.

业　绩

远贾难知售奸，时风辣货扬帆。
贪泉①万里无事，瘴海②三年闭关。
晚稻高贤③雁水，湖田小子鱼山。
失乡莫谓迁客，数载轻肥④未还。

【注释】

①贪泉：古代一眼著名的泉水名。其泉水明亮如镜，清洌爽口。早在晋代已有盛名，于正史二十四史之《晋书》的吴隐之传中便有记载。相传人饮其水起贪心，即廉士亦贪。②瘴海：南方海域。③高贤：高尚；贤良。④轻肥：穿着轻暖的皮袍，坐着由肥马驾的车。形容生活的豪华。

Achievements

Now a far trader hardly knows to profiteer,
From the hoisted sail for the delicacies of the wind.
Without an insatiable desire, all would be kept out of trouble,
And to the sea of miasmas, close the door for three years.
Highly virtuous, the late paddy field appeals to the wild geese,
For my unworthy self, the shoaly land rises to be a fish hill.
Losing my home, though, judge me not to be exiled,
To live in luxury, why not go back for years?

一 人

雾雨长波饭涩，囊空远树蓑笠。
连茹梦里反袂[①]，吊影天边涕泣。
钓水萧萧故台，寻芳步步新邑。
空蒙暗柳垂堤，闪断潜鱼百褶。

【注释】

①连茹：形容接连不断。反袂：形容哭泣。

One Person

In fog drips, the food doubted about the billows,
Before the cape and hat with an empty bag off the wood.
In dream, he tried to choke back the spasmodic sobs,
Solitarily, the sky line dissolved in tears.

Seated by the waterside, the old fishing terrace rustled,
To seek his sweet, every step followed the new towns,
Near the willowy dyke darkly shrouded in mist,
That flashed to the hidden fish with hundreds of wrinkles.

一　天

四月披风曙鸦，帘间密语裁花。
双流远客千里，一雨临城万家。
柳色青苹曲水，莺声紫蒂长沙。
平生日落何处，回眸锦帕半遮。

One Day

April was mantled with the ravens at dawn,
That breezed and flowered the curtain by a secret code.
While the double streams devolved a thousand miles,
One torrent revived all houses of the town.
Along the duckweeds below the green willows, the streams
Meander their purple pedicles in the long shoals by the warbles.
Where the sun of life would descend?
Better glance back at the silken, half-veiled handkerchief.

一丈红

大麦晴烟陇[①]黄，闲凝远近昭阳[②]。
幽明自信高下，胜负谁怜短长。
粉紫从来淡定，红白未必清狂。

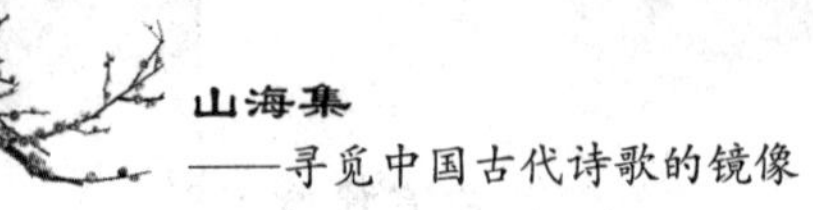

浮生自古幽梦，万里红尘践霜。

【注释】

①陇：通“垄”，田埂。泛指麦地。②昭（zhāo）阳：明亮的太阳。

Althaea Rosea

The fine, hazy barley on the yellow ridge
Curdled the bright, idle sun far and near.
Dark or light, the self-trust would be higher or lower,
Make or break, who would pity the long or short play?
Although the purple rouge exuded the sense of calm for ever,
The red white unnecessarily rode through the ruts.
The worldly life is but a secret dream from of old,
That has trampled the frost of the mundane dust afar.

遗　憾
Regret

其一

逍遥大道茫昧，铁臂横空玉碎。
放旷枯荣市嚣，留连落寞芜秽。
沈浮不懂行藏，宠辱何谈进退。
未晓田园潜心，平生错认兴废。

One

On the incomprehensible highway so carefree,
One iron arm roars to crash
The free clamours of the vicissitudes
That linger around the lonely weeds and brambles.
Sink or swim, without the trace of your whereabouts,
Gain or pain, you could be far from the ebb and flow.
Unaware of the devotion to the garden,
Your life would be misdeemed in the ups and downs.

其二

短翅劳禽应腔，飞穿漠漠寒江。
微言慨叹游士，秉志独悲异邦。
故里风霜有伴，残春隐逸[1]无双。
芳踪向晚飞渡，冷面谁人可扛？

【注释】

①隐逸：隐居；隐遁。

Two

The short wing of the wrought fowl replies to
Fly over the vast, cold and lonely river.
Its subtle sighs with regret are wandering,
Its aspiration anguishes exotically in solitude;

Homewards, the wind and frost can come along,
Late spring, it lives in seclusion past compare.
As its virtuous trail flies over the dusk,
Who can carry such a cold countenance?

意　识

风声夜坐幽台，一朵晴花乍开。
漫染华堂柳鬓，轻舒绣被桃腮。
龙韬咏调灵异，虎略吟缘可猜。
世路尘沙莫虑，薄俗有道丰财。

The Sense

The sound of wind squats at the quiet night stand,
And blooms one flower suddenly,
And freely dyes the willows outside the luxurious hall,
And lightly stretches her rosy cheeks under the embroidered quilt.
Skilfully, his aria sounds magical,
Strategically, her moan lot takes the guesswork out.
Thoughtless aware of the dust and sand in the world,
There is a way to the fortunes in the weak custom.

优　秀

灵山泻影优游，几度萍实[1]远浮。
片水遐荒九曲，祥烟旧梦常流。
千般眷爱何欲，万种风情不求。

远客轻明[2]落日，西风醉下兰舟。

【注释】

①萍实：称“浮萍”，亦称“青萍”。②轻明：薄而透明。

Excellence

Down the hill of soul wanders the shadow,
Which has floated like the duckweed many a time,
On the water zigzag into the far moorland,
Where the benevolent smoke normally flows in the old dream.
Before the thousand loves, why to be orectic?
To the ten thousand flirtatious feelings, he attempts nothing.
Light and bright, he roams far with the setting sun,
In the west wind, his tipsy boat would sail down.

诱　惑

浮名坐钓浮利，世路常思客位。
吏脸谀噱[1]倚天，氓心巧谄成器。
青云任气[2]天姿，紫禁衔恩[3]力致。
老虎乘风宦途，浮天脊背生翅。

【注释】

①谀噱（yú xué）：谄笑。②任气：处事纵任意气，不加约束。③衔恩：受恩；感恩。

Temptation

In vain, the fame fishes for the wealth,
Frequently on the way of the guest world,
Where the official faces smile ingratiatingly to the sky,
And the heart of man adulates artfully but usefully.
As the azure sky gives full rein to the rare beauty,
The forbidden city cherishes the gratitude for the devotion.
To ride the wind, the tiger in its official way
Grows wings on the back to be floated up.

宇　宙

神鞭赶走光年，玉宇①周游列仙。
碎影参差上界②，圆光历乱中天③。
乾坤百亿何往，世界三分正欢。
素色高低暗洞，新星转瞬飞烟。

【注释】

①玉宇：指太空。②上界：天上神仙或宇宙人居住的地方。③中天：星际之间的真空或天空。

The Universe

The divine whip drives away the light year,
Where all the immortals trip around the universe,
Whose milled shades in the upper realms touch on all the notes,

Whose round blips of light are tangled in the meridian passage.
Where tens of billions of stars are going now?
The great chiliocosm in its three-times-life works feverishly.
High and low, the black holes with their solid shades
Have swallowed up the novas twinkling like a wisp of smoke.

语　言

善语相逢梦里，欢言驿路天喜①。
生涯侧枕风清，四体闲檐睡美。
入室何曾小人，知音未必君子。
红尘善恶难明，美玉如同弃市②。

【注释】

①天喜：星相术士的四柱神煞之一，指日支和月建相合，如正月逢亥日，二月逢戌日，是为吉日。②弃市：在闹市执行死刑。

The Language

Good words can come into the dream, and
Merry words go in their merry way.
When the career pillows on the gentle breeze,
The four limbs sleep merrily below the idle eaves.
To burglary may not necessarily be base-minded,
And to meet the right person not the virtuous man.
Good or evil, who knows in the worldly life?
Even a man like a gem can be executed publicly.

知　止

红鳞不转双瞳，妙理深藏野虫。
饵术平垂冷雨，穷经半挂凉风。
韶光不懂人意，柳色偏求物功。
数尺竿歌野渡，春烟闭锁樊笼。

To Stop in Time

A red fish with all his eyes
Gazes at the wild bug subtly and deeply.
Where the art of bait hangs in the cold rain,
Its attention hangs half in the cold wind.
When the time has no ear for the sense of man,
The green willow prefers its course of matters.
With the fishing rod that sings a few feet wild,
The spring smoke has closed the bird cage down.

秩　序

朝衣散秩①闲居，解缆②江湖有初。
苦志奸穷③惨淡，欢情善雅安舒④。
谁家静女⑤珠履，巷里飞仙素车⑥。
返壑投林倦鸟，凌寒野渡樵渔⑦。

【注释】

①散秩（sàn zhì）：闲散而无一定职守的官位。②解缆：解去系船的

缆绳。指开船。③奸穷：奸恶处境。④安舒：安适舒坦。⑤静女：文雅的姑娘。⑥素车：古代凶、丧事所用之车，以白土涂刷。⑦樵渔：樵夫和渔夫。泛指村舍中人。

Order

Disengaged from the royal apparel,
Let the first step go for your adventure;
Though your bitter will has exhausted in the wicked gloom,
Now turn what's properly refined at ease to delight.
Who is that fair maiden in pearl shoes?
She's the nymph in her white car flying thru the lane,
Like a weary bird back to the wood of her ravine,
Where the air bites the wild fishers and gatherers.

栀　子

西窗翠带同心，素壁相思漫吟。
莫怪银衣少见，都缘翠幕闲寻。
牵肠莫探天高，望眼谁识柳林。
栀子深藏绿蒂，香凝片片白金。

Gardenia

One heart on the green ribbon by the west window
Freely chants her love knot before the white wall.
Blame not the unique silvery skin,
'Tis the spare search into the fate of the green curtain.

Probe not the higher sky in care,
Your eyes out might fail to read the willow groves.
Behold! The green pedicles hidden deep in the gardenia
Are about to shine their sweet flakes of white gold.

种　子

古道苍苍籽叶，折腰陌上一霎。
空寻羽客长风，满目流离病厌。
异壤萌蛰闭心，途中不忍开靥。
纤淋芥子横生，大树成蹊较猎[①]。

【注释】

①成蹊：蹊，田中脚步踏出的小路。喻身怀美质，勿需宣扬自然为人所知。较猎：争夺猎物。

Seed

The grey cotyledon by the old road
Broke off in a split second.
With the long wind to seek his feather in vain,
He had to fly away wearily here and there.
In a strange soil he shut his heart for the sprout
Before he could smile what was right on the way.
While the tiny seed was growing wild,
The great tree would haunt his own world.

朱顶红

临风不可求备，一爪凉霄野魅。
问路闲从对红，开山忘却独翠。
凝光鸟去烟轻，散彩云飞露坠。
小扇偷尝玉肌，多情蜜雪常醉。

Barbadoslily

In the wind, seek not to be perfect,
With your cold claw at the wild force of evil.
On the way, follow the free red in pair, and
To excavate it, the lone green would be washed away.
In the fixed light, the bird flies like a wisp of smoke,
In the loose colours, the flying cloud drops its dews.
When the little fan nibbles her pure, snow-white flesh,
The amorous, honied snow would be frequently on the go.

准　则

富贵青云阔步，人生万里平路。
丹心瘴海[①]思明，素手贪泉[②]固步。
骤雨飘摇自持，熏风乱絮相误。
金乌两寸初飞，堕落无声冷露。

【注释】

①瘴海：南方有瘴气之地。②贪泉：古代一眼著名的泉水名。其泉

水明亮如镜，清洌爽口。早在晋代已有盛名，于正史《二十四史》之《晋书》的吴隐之传中便有记载。相传人饮其水起贪心，即廉士亦贪。

Guideline

The riches and ranks like a meteoric rise
Can level its promising way of life.
Before the sea of miasmas, the loyal heart should ponder bright,
Before the insatiable fountain, the clean hand should be halted.
In the torrents of rain, try to control yourself,
In the warm breeze, the catkins are whirling a wrong story.
When the Golden Crow about two inches starts his maiden trial,
The cold dews are falling down in silence.

自　戕

长城四望芜漫①，万里桑乾历乱②。
风转关山静源，龙翻草木清瀚。
穷阴③苦雾潮平，朔雪悲风雁断。
紫禁潜结祸机，苍龙灭迹一旦。

【注释】

①芜漫：荒芜；荒凉。②桑乾：边塞。历乱：纷乱，杂乱。③穷阴：极其阴沉的天气。

The Self-destruction

Overgrown with weeds, the Great Wall
Ignited the truceless turmoils where
The phoenix sourced her still mountains and
The dragon sought his peaceful ocean down the wood.
Overcast, the sad mists rolled on the flat tide,
Doleful, the north snow blowed off the wild geese.
When the forbidden city knotted its bane secretly,
The black dragon perished on the spur of the moment.

自　然

东君欲散黄莺，杏树参差放情。
次第隔林雾渺，微茫对壑霞明。
薄光戏柳鱼过，厚影牵风燕行。
莫怪尘心不古，飞花不载虚声①。

【注释】

①虚声：空谷间传出的回声。

Nature

As the Lord of East tries to disperse the golden orioles,
The irregular apricots are clearing up
The vague fogs beyond the wood sequentially
With the bright, rosy clouds blurred over the valley.

While the fish swim past the glimmering game of the willows,
The wind pulls its thick shadows where the swallow floats.
Blame not the heart of the world which is not natural,
The flying petals will not hold any echo of the hollow.

自　由
Liberty

其一

贾客常闻近利，飘摇四海禽戏。
迷途抱玉空虚，险路开金取醉。
外物空谈自由，中流满座身累。
出笼远雨长歌，赤电扬风举翅。

One

The trader often knows his quick benefits
From the brute game that drifts about the seas.
To hug the jade, the lost way is vulnerable,
To dish out the gold, the vicious way goes drunk and incapable.
To prate any external liberty,
The whole seat of the mainstay would be sweatful.
Out of the cage, the distant rain croons,
In the red flash, the wind heaves up the wings.

其二

野马浮云逆风，闲行万里骄骢[1]。
冰棱寡义狂卷，玉峭薄情远冲。
走月嘶寒射电，流星断雪翻弓。
天涯到处阳羽[2]，四海何愁不通。

【注释】

①骢（cōng）：青白杂毛的马。②阳羽：喻指太阳。

Two

In the teeth of the wind, the cloud like a wild horse
Roams vigorously about ten thousand miles
Through the wild, ruthless sweep of the ice slushes,
And the fickle shocks from the fair, further chills.
Drive the moon that neighs and shoots its cold lightning,
Drift the stars that stop the snow with the bows,
The sunny plumes are shining upon the poles of the earth,
That will never be distressed for a passage to the four seas.

七言绝句

Seven-character Quatrain

七言绝句格律

一、两大类，四种句式

平起式两种：①平起平收，首句押韵；②平起仄收，首句不押韵。

仄起式两种：①仄起平收，首句押韵；②仄起仄收，首句不押韵。

二、四种基本句式

一般而言，第一、二、四句平声同韵；第三句仄声不同韵。第二四句倒数第三字通常为仄音；整首诗的意境高，文辞雅，寓意深。

1. 首句平起入韵式

（平）平（仄）仄仄平平◎，
（仄）仄　平　平仄仄平◎。
（仄）仄（平）平平仄仄，
（平）平（仄）仄仄平平◎。

2. 首句平起不入韵式

（平）平（仄）仄平平仄，
（仄）仄平　平仄仄平◎。
（仄）仄（平）平平仄仄，
（平）平（仄）仄仄平平◎。

3. 首句仄起入韵式

（仄）仄平平仄仄平◎，
（平）平（仄）仄仄平平◎，
（平）平（仄）仄平平仄，
（仄）仄平平仄仄平◎。

4. 首句仄起不入韵式

（仄）仄（平）平平仄仄，
（平）平（仄）仄仄平平◎。
（平）平（仄）仄平平仄，

（仄）仄　平　平仄仄平◎。

暗　香

纵横莲影闭闲房，野趣多情紫陌凉。
澹荡朱门藏脂粉，蔫红[1]落地有遗香。

【注释】

①蔫红：深红色。亦指鲜艳的红花。

Secret fragrance

The free lotus shades shut their spare seedpods with a fascinating
Charm of nature along the cool，amorous thoroughfares，where
The warm and pleasant rouge hidden in the vermilion gates
Falls to the ground that lingers her crimson flavour.

报　春

墙外衔梅柳泛青，山云匝地[1]扯金星。
平芜[2]开露吟肥瘦，纤嫩黄花在妙龄。

【注释】

①匝地：遍地，满地。②平芜：草木丛生的平旷原野。

The Message of Spring

Plums and willows are lively greenish outside the wall,
Like the golden stars down the clouds all over the hills.
As the far-flung plain chants the dewy width of figures,
Their tiny and yellow petals are coming into a tender age.

卑　宦

权奇名世问穷通①，聪辩含生马鹿惊②。
巧佞③奸声藏陷阱，负情④寡义醉功名。

【注释】

①权奇：奇谲非凡。多形容良马善行。名世：名显于世。穷通：困厄与显达。②聪辩：聪慧明辩。含生：一切有生命者，多指人类。马鹿：化自“指鹿为马”。③巧佞：机巧奸诈，阿谀奉承。④负情：违背情实。

The Humble Official

The peculiar power measures the famous fortunes in the world,
That wisely discerns and frightens the deliberate deception.
In the fraudulent pitfall which is hidden cleverly but wickedly,
The fickle, ungrateful mind gets attuned to fame and fortune.

病　变

【注释】

人小时候经常生病，每年都感冒，病历卡很厚。但是，一到发育的时候，什么病都没有了，而到七八十岁，病又回来了，也就临近死亡了。

四体别来扶病客①，穷阴②明镜闭闲眠。
波风枕上形神乱，清露忽惊雪霰天。

【注释】

①扶病，指带病，抱病。扶病客：病人。②穷阴：古代以春夏为阳，秋冬为阴，冬季又是一年中最后一个季节，故称。

Pathological Process

The run-down limbs since the last separation
Shut the bright mirror into the spare slumber in the deep winter.
When the wave whiffles the body and soul off my pillow in disorder,
The clear dews are startled by the ice rains again.

博　弈

半缘物外半缘俗，半论霓裳半论足。
斗智未曾识对手，输赢小隐对棋局。

Gaming

Half predestined in and out of the world,
Or half sized up with the skirts and the features,
The battle of wits has failed to read its rival,
Who wins or loses his secret game of chess.

才　成

才子清阳大朴[①]难，骚文振笔拜疏[②]残。
小成简傲狂桃[③]处，心镜伏波[④]久不安。

【注释】

①清阳：阳气。阳气清轻上升，故称清阳。大朴：原始质朴的大道。②振笔：奋笔；挥笔。拜疏：化自杜牧《郡斋独酌》"阙下谏官业，拜疏无文章"。③简傲：高傲，也就是傲慢失礼，是在处理人际关系上表现出来的性格特点。狂桃：化自王昌龄《香积寺礼拜万回平等二圣僧塔》"今我一礼心，亿劫同不移"。④伏波：平息变乱。

Talented

The man of parts hard to be unaffected positively wielded
His brush on the memorial, energetically but powerlessly,
Where his haughty partiality like the agrestal peach trees
Could not calm the underflow of his heart mirror durably.

差 异

云物[①]乘槎驾御席，鸟头飞过晓黑白。
摇舌欲使庭风静，心路平分咫步[②]隔。

【注释】

①云物：云的色彩；云气、云彩。乘槎：亦作“乘楂”，典出晋·张华《博物志》卷十。指乘坐竹、木筏。后用以比喻奉使。也指登天，或比喻如朝做官。②咫步：短距离。

Discrepancy

On the cloud, to sail the barque is like a royal mat,
As the bird head flies by, it can tell black and white.
While wagging the tongue to calm the wind of the court,
The way of heart takes the close realm as its right.

长城废

燕山排雪镇西风，万仞长城剑气冲。
烽火横行白刃窄，满人过后验雌雄。

The Useless Great Wall

The Yanshan Mountains were snowing upon the west wind,
Where the massive, majestic wall shot its sword light.

War flames had been rising on all sides for a close combat,
And after 1644, the Manchu measured its strength in the end.

潮流

理辩心根勿妄言，贪淫深处本清源。
黄河雪粒滴青海，九曲冲腾秽鸟喧。

The Tidal Current

No root of the reasoning heart should express itself rashly,
And in the depth of greed and debauchery, it must be sourced clearly;
After the snow grains of Qinghai are trickled into the Yellow River,
The zigzag waters are rushing down like dirty bird flocks boisterously.

成　功
Success

其一

商贾尘心钟鼓闹，铸钱刮地索铜山。
珠玑玉露方盈箧[①]，五斗折腰也不闲[②]。

【注释】

①珠玑（jī）：珠宝，珠玉。盈箧（qiè）：满箱。②五斗折腰：化自

《晋书·陶潜传》："潜叹曰：'吾不能为五斗米折腰，拳拳事乡里小人邪！'"五斗米：晋代县令的俸禄，后指微薄的俸禄。折腰：弯腰行礼，指屈身于人。比喻为人清高，有骨气，不为利禄所动。这里取其反义。

One

Fast and furious, the dust heart of the trader
Mints the money extorted from the coppermine.
Even after the pearls and jades have filled his baskets,
He would also make curtsies for the five *dou* of rice.

其二

书囊[1]薄宦任浮沈，守默缄情[2]不远寻。
阴晦[3]弥积凉飙扇，炎荒[4]裹体莫惊心。

【注释】

①书囊（nánɡ）：盛书籍的袋子。②守默：保持玄寂。缄情：含情。③阴晦：阴冷滞涩之气。④炎荒：南方炎热荒远之地。

Two

Minor officials swim or sink intellectually,
And stay silent about their search into the passions.
Having stored up their cool breath of fans gloomily,
Their souls swathed in scorches shouldn't be startled finally.

其三

好酒明月闲杯醉，顺手挥毫百首诗。
多少凄清寒暑夜，李白辛苦有谁知？

Three

The good wine in the moon-lit cup was tipsy,
And swiped at a hundred poems freely.
Cold or hot, the countless and desolate nights
Witnessed the toils and moils of Li Po secretly.

纯　情

花影澹姿闲野色，嫩茸丝雨解香苞。
幽期轻惹纤腰软，贵贱难移世外交。

Innocence

Spare in the wild, the flower shades undulate
Their soft and fine sweet in the budding drizzle.
Secretly scheduled, their slender waists are weakly desirable,
And wouldn't be transplanted wherever is high or low.

魑 魅

坐海观山雾雨长，扒开一缕漏斜阳。
北冥不见花溪钓，衣冠颠狂乱帝乡。

Ghosts and Devils

The fog showers are long on the sea down the mountain,
And claw an oblique ray of the setting sun.
By the north sea devoid of the fishing in the flower stream,
The crackbrained attires plunge the capital town into chaos.

淡 泊

乳燕连云啼小杏，青丝独钓泛舟航[1]。
草衣不问轻裘事，竹舍栖迟胜画堂[2]。

【注释】

①舟航：船只。②栖迟：游玩休憩。画堂：古代宫中有彩绘的殿堂。

The Paucity of Desires

In the cloud, a fledgling swallow chirped to the small apricots,
Black-haired, the lone fisher sailed with the stream.
A straw cape asked nothing about the light furs,
And its bamboo hut got the best of the paneled hall.

淡　荡

青枝疏雨筛夕柳，卸去兰云化水纹。
绣羽冲风[①]寻古镜，纤鳞[②]半醉月初分。

【注释】

①绣羽：鸟类美丽的羽毛。冲风：顶着风；冒着风。②纤鳞：鱼。

Leisure

The dusk sieved the green, rain-spattered willows,
Stripping the orchid cloud that turned into water streaks.
As the silk wings soared up for the old mirror,
The small fish were half drunk below the crescent.

钓鱼台

白叟无情坐钓台，清凫苹藻为君裁。
游鱼不解悬钓事，衔饵牵腮又放开。

The Fishing Platform

A ruthless grey beard was fishing where
The mallards were trimming their duckweeds.
And a swimming fish was puzzled by the angling
Bait into the gill that was let go again.

东逝水

流水无心惹是非，片石鼓浪助霜威。
青山设险谈何易，横溃[1]千年尚未归。

【注释】

①横溃：河水决堤横流。

The River Eastwards

The flowing water cares little to stir up trouble,
But slabstone billows are boosting the frost moral.
How can the green mountains arrange their strength?
A thousand years haven't regained its natural debacle.

飞　燕

日落蒹葭斜紫燕，苍苍罗带系青裳。
回瞻频点芹泥[1]觜，不厌清斋是草堂。

【注释】

①芹泥：燕子筑巢所用的草泥。

The Flying Swallow

A purple hirundo across the reeds as the sun sets
Ties up his black coat amid the green hill where
He hastens back his beak with the wetted clods of clay
And will never be wearied with his humble cottage.

妇人心

莫言裙带系青罗[①]，风化[②]同心异梦多。
晴雨[③]游丝鸡犬客，枕席暗澹[④]两蹉跎。

【注释】

①青罗：青色丝织物。②风化：隐晦的社会公德和旧习俗，往往涉及性话题。③晴雨：谐音“情欲”。④暗澹：亦作“暗淡”。不鲜艳；不明亮。

Fickle-hearted

Trust not her girdle round her skirt,
Whose moral sleep of the same heart dreams more.
Entangled by the gossamers of the erotic cocks,
The bed in dream has blackened their time's waste.

孤独

圣贤书里枕孤独，不入今朝翡翠屋。
红袖春娇啼爱语，群冰淅沥玉头秃。

Solitude

My solitude in the writings of the sages
Won't enter the house of green jade now
Where the red sleeves thrill her spring love
To the bald drizzles of the pure iceberg.

孤酒

清阴清酒坐青天，清曲清溪对小鲜。
我有清词弹海晏①，邀得明月泪珠圆。

【注释】

①海晏：大海无浪。比喻太平。

Solitary Liquor

The clear shade and liquor in the broad daylight
Faced the small fish like a clear, melodious stream.
Had I a clear libretto presented to the calm sea,
I would invite the bright moon round like my teardrops.

故乡

故园空向北风鸣，白草霜花乱雪晴。
不见儿时车马迹，但闻遍野冻鞭声。

Native Land

The north wind roars to my home town, in vain,
Where the frost work on the white grass shines fine.
All carts and horses are lost in the memory of my childhood,
That tries to snuff at the cracks of the frozen whips.

官路难

巧笑无情翠羽空，逢迎有泪锦鳞丰。
宦游荒骨荒唐事，惊梦无常四面风。

The Impossible Life for Officials

To be full-fledged, to be hollow, the dimpled but ruthless cheeks
Have been ingratiating their tears to the hearty fish.
As the officials in their wasted bones so absurd and ridiculous
Which are besieged on all sides with the fickle nightmares.

观沧海

A View of the Great Sea

其一

负日[①]晴空一鸟飞，遥遥万里碧波回。
衔来东海压沧浪，不起平洲死不归。

【注释】

①负日：喻指太阳。

One

One bird flies fine with the sun on her back,
Who flies back long from the green waves.
To the east sea her beak holds the pebbles
And fills it up with dogged determination.

其二

十里平沙对月明，从容剪雪丝绸声。
横波排满燕山树，任由情郎挎我行。

Two

Ten mile's strands under the moon
Snip the snow with a silken sound
Shearing the trees of the mountain
Where I'd go as I like by my beaux.

其三

帘卷东风看海帆，白鸥飞过玉龙湾。
万片雪花迎朝旭，飘向蓬莱有洞天。

Three

Sea sails through the waving screen
From the east the white gulls over the bay
Like ten thousand snowflakes to the rising sun
That are fluttering to a world of their own.

其四

百川灌海庄周心，承载河伯十万人。
向若[①]汪洋徒不现，障目黑夜看飞金[②]。

【注释】

①向若：假如。唐·皇甫曾《遇风雨作》诗："向若家居时，安枕春

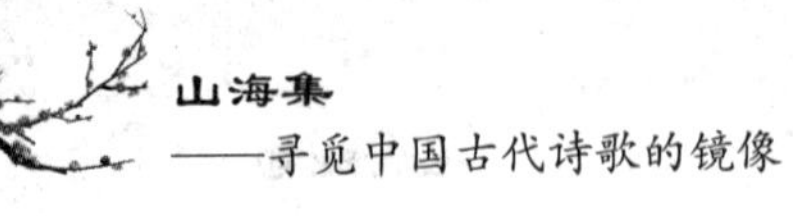

梦熟。”②飞金：喻指太阳。

Four

Hundreds of rivers pour into the sea at liberty
Carrying a hundred thousand water spirits,
Who, before a waste of waters, has seen nothing,
But a flying golden disc out of the obscure night.

其五

海上青霞四万龙，飞腾举起太阳红。
荡涤下界千层垢，金镜开云天下明。

Five

Blue glows of 40000 dragons on the sea
Scan the heaven wide in the red star of day,
Wash away 1000 layers of filths on the earth,
And open their golden mirror unto a bright world.

其六

碧天弯弯升海蟾[①]，晶莹玉暖洗清寒。
临风诗酒凭天问，李白游仙哪日还。

【注释】

①海蟾：喻指月亮。

Six

A Sea Toad rises in the curved blue sky,
And washes the clear cold brilliantly.
God! To the breeze and the wine, tell me
When Li Po turns back from his excursion finally.

其七

今夜梦中李太白，诗魂附体太阴[1]开。
平生万首惊天句，海涛缘何没我才。

【注释】

①太阴：喻指月亮。

Seven

Tonight, Li Po came into my dream,
Whose moon went down in a poetic soul.
Why 10000 world-shaking poems of mine
Was drowned by the ocean billows?

其八

清月银樽华露霜，枝头千点醉幽香。
杯酒花落笔无味，写海何如写大江。

Eight

Dews in the frost are moon-lit and wined,
By the faint sweet on a thousand tipsy branches.
While insipid flowers in the cup are fallen,
Letters on the big river are far better than the sea.

其九

汉代桃源难识秦，求仙帆影拜河神。
破浪鼓海别桑梓[1]，谁料投怀日本人。

【注释】

①桑梓（zǐ）：《诗经·小雅·小弁》中说“维桑与梓，必恭敬止”，是说桑与梓，容易引起对父母的怀念。后来，“桑梓”就用来做故乡的代称。

Nine

A Han fairyland couldn't read the Qin,
That sailed to seek its worship to the river god,

By hacking the sea from his native place,
But, who would have thought it, to japs.

其十

狂雨流星北戴河，浊泥扑海下城郭。
惊涛北斗银河落，击风原来百步多。

Ten

Cats and dogs, down to Beidaihe,
Muds and mires, down thru the town.
Big Dippers, down the surging galaxy,
In the eye of the wind, it was 100 steps or more.

闺 房

剪翠无端刀尺寒，裁红骚语梦惊残。
长宵何事摇桃脸，为妾闲眠一苇宽。

Boudoir

Untimely tailored, the green was cold by the knife and ruler,
Under the coquettish breath, the red debris of dreams was shattered.
What was paddling the pink face in the long night?
It proved to be my naps as wide as a reed.

闺　梦

平生粉字羞鸾镜，新点唇膏懒下床。
多情绣衣出锦帐，梦中飘过紫微郎[①]。

【注释】

①紫微郎：中书舍人，官名。舍人始于先秦，本为国君、太子亲近属官。

Boudoir in Dream

Her daily rouge looks shy in the mirror,
Her fresh rouged lips won't scramble off the bed.
Before her amorous nightgown goes out of the silk curtain,
Her man below the stars sails across her dream.

过　客

逸才不惮作狂愚[①]，闲钓公堂效野夫。
偃卧[②]红白皆过客，黄泉遗魄[③]尽虚无。

【注释】

①逸才：出众的人才。狂愚：狂妄愚昧。②偃卧：仰卧，睡卧。③遗魄：亡魂，亡灵。

The Passer-by

The exceptional gift fears not to be mad in folly,
Angling free like a boorish man in the office.
To lie supine in red or white is but a passenger,
Whose spectre in the hades will be empty.

桂　林

桂花十里醉银杯，酥手插头五六枚。
拔地青山千万座，月轮带雪客徘徊。

Guilin

Osmanthus blossoms ten miles drunk in the silver cup
Are pinned five or six by her fine hand
Below thousands of green peaks springing up
Under the moon's disc lingering over the snows.

海　日

戴河不愧幽燕雨，击破传说向大洋。
山客[①]不觉骑海日，从星万里任颠狂。

【注释】

①山客：隐士。

The Sea Sun

The Daihe River worthy of the serene seaside rain
Has routed the legend towards the ocean.
The mountainer bestrides the sea sun unwittingly
To chase the stars thousands of miles wildly.

酣　睡

不惜陈酿醉天仙，薄晚[①]滩头枕臂眠。
一觉十年晴雨后，管它鸡犬是非颠。

【注释】

①薄晚：傍晚。

A Sound Sleep

Aged wine! Inebriate like a winebibber!
In the evening twilight! Pillow your arm on the beach for sleep!
After a decade in such a goodly sleep, all sorts of weather
Is left to the mercy of the topsy-turvy fowls and dogs.

和金福娜

With the Rhythm of Jin Funa

其一

潇湘遍洒梅花红，携手难约百岁同。
且看霜天今又是，冰天难坐信天翁。

One

Red plum-blossoms all over the Xiaoxiang River
Join their hands hard for a hundred years together.
Behold, a new freezing weather comes again,
And to ride a quakerbird in the ice, it's not sure.

其二

蝴蝶春季一时新，惹起天边两片云。
雪月邀春春逝去，小楼且驻对酒樽。

Two

Springtime is updated by butterflies
Stirring two cloudlets at the sky line.
Spring slips by, solicited in a moon-lit
Floor that applies the brake for a wine.

其三

蝴蝶泉水映春风，不老华年弄玉声。
信手玲珑歌一曲，化成天籁给君听。

Three

Breezed by the butterfly spring,
Your never-aging time like a ring
Doodles a ducky song that turns
Into the sounds of nature for listening.

其四

清歌曼舞布依山，散落金声玉带湾。
娇艳几曾邀醉客，劝君还到彩蝶边。

Four

A clear song waves thru the hills
And falls out to the bay like a jade belt.
Delicate and charming, your tipsy treat
Advises a tour to the colourful butterfly.

红 尘

中年名利接秋水，老去樊笼[1]扣海冰。
世外野人无系累[2]，人间牵挂两难承。

【注释】

①樊笼：关鸟兽的笼子。比喻受束缚、不自由的境地。②系累：拘囿；牵缠。

Mundane Dust

The middle-aged for fame and gain near the autumn water
Beats out the sea ice caged like an aged bird.
Beyond the world, to be the savage can't be chained up,
In the lower world, to be with hopes would be unbearable.

呼兰河

呼兰河水轻舟远，柳叶拾得百鸟闲。

明镜不觉飞暑气，凉云又过一平湾。

The Hulan River

One skiff rows afar,
Below the willow leaves of the free larks.
On the bright mirror unaware of the swift summer,
The cool clouds are crossing the cove once again.

花　海

甜甜晓雾满枝鲜，莫让摇红醉眼帘。
酒内花心千古月，清辉国里几芳颜？

Flower Sea

Fresh branches in a sweet, misty morning
Are swaying their rubies to the sober eyes.
In the moon-lit wine, flower heart's shining
On a few sweet faces in aged, radiant lights.

花　觞

李艳桃明自做媒，流光四月万千回。
倾花垂泪惊天雪，玉色倏忽[①]化作灰。

【注释】

①倏（shū）忽：很快地，忽然。

The Flower Wine

Plums and peaches are matched bright
Through the April days thousands of times,
Hanging their tearful petals like the lurid snow,
Whose beauty turns into the ash in a flash.

槐　花

情忘槐花啼旧径，怪君咏性步青云。
薄蝉夹路嘶萝月[①]，万粒婆娑此夜分。

【注释】

①萝月：藤萝间的明月。

The Sophora Flowers

Unruffled by the twitters to the old trail,
The flowers are caviled to carol the blue sky.
As the filmy cicadas chirp the moon in the vines,
Thousands of petals flanking the paths will whirl tonight.

【注释】

①萝月：藤萝间的明月。

环　境

风日遐心啼柳陌[①]，晴川古道忆王孙[②]。
灵台[③]不晓人间事，万古桃源已断魂。

【注释】

①风日：风光。遐心：避世隐居之心。柳陌：植柳之路。②王孙：隐居的人。③灵台：佛教用语，指心灵。

Environment

The heart afar cries in the roadside willows,
Recalling the fine grass along the old road by the river.
If the mind were ignorant of this human life,
The eternal fairyland would break its soul.

宦　灭

少年饱饭坐学楼，壮齿雄心去宦游。
昨夜片名[①]谁可寄，风波走眼向幽囚[②]。

【注释】

①片名：化自司空图《客中重九》“楚老相逢泪满衣，片名薄宦已知非”。②幽囚：囚禁；幽禁。

The Official Ruin

The replete youth in the school
Spent the manly marrow for the officialdom.
Who arraigned his card here last night?
It was the dark dungeon that slip up in the storm.

婚　嫁

昨天论嫁青梅短，今夜白头细雨长。
锦袖不识娘窃喜，出阁晓镜扮春妆。

Marriage

Yesterday, the potential bride was so young,
Tonight, her hoary hair drizzles so long.
The silk sleeves fail to spot mom's secret delight,
Who dresses up in the mirror of the dawning light.

鸡　觞

爪翅梳风带雪寒，裘皮过客两情难。
何时飞燕啼八角[①]，再谢当途五斗盘[②]。

【注释】

①八角：八角鼓。②五斗盘：五斗米，是指晋代朝廷中信奉“五斗

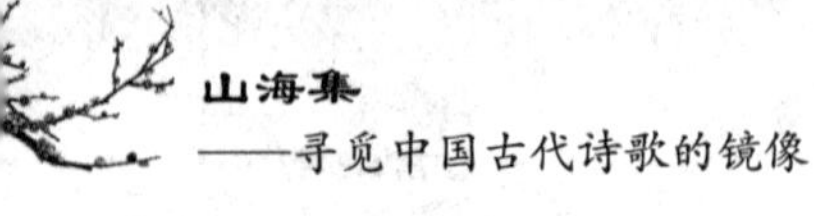

米道”的权贵。

The Cocktail Cup

As the claws and wings combed the wind cold in snow,
The passing passions in furs are stuck in the middle.
When the flying swallow chirps for an octagonal drum,
One would thank the five pecks of rice from you all.

激　情

朱顶冰泉倒影飞，翅斜迸落滚珠玑。
红闲莫教晴云转，裁下千匹做锦衣。

Passions

In the flooding ice, the red crest flies its inverted image,
And spurts out the pearls down the wings.
Don't turn the red, fine and idle cloud, but tailor it
To be a thousand bolts of damask clothes.

静　心

轻燕佩云斜曙色，幽人[①]浅卧伴林莺。
三声静躁花台后，陋室春江百日明。

【注释】

①幽人：幽隐之人；隐士。

A Quiet Mind

One light swallow wore the cloud in the slanting rays of early dawn,
When the solitary man pronated below the wood orioles,
Twittered restlessly for three times down to the flower bed,
Bright before the hut near the spring river a hundred days.

静夜思

道场心空一炷香，无边歧路印苍茫。
塞鸿替我留明月，掸去乡思雪满床。

The Night Still

The empty heart lit a stick of incense in the bodhi-site,
On the boundless, forked road that impressed the boundless sight.
Were the north swan to detain the bright moon for me,
It might whisk my full love-lorn snow off my bed probably.

镜泊湖瀑布

玉筐盛怒卸飞雷，虎爪劈山胆欲摧。
倒扣天台三盏露，黑龙入海去无回。

The Waterfall of Jingbo Lake

The wrathy basket dumps its thunder-storm,
The tiger claw blasts and spooks the cliff.
Upside down the heaven, three calices of dews
Sweep the black dragons to the sea for ever.

酒之梦

泛云[1]滴酒冰浆厚，疏放[2]横床静夜薄。
幕下摇风追玉女，醒来莫对北风说。

【注释】

①泛云：犹腾云。谓乘云飞行。②疏放：放纵；不受拘束。

The Dream of Wine

The cloud drips its wine down the thick ice slurry,
Into the thin, calm night upon my liberated bed.
After the curtain blows and traces the fairy maid,
Tell it to the awakened Boreas, never more.

绝　境

大才仙隐欲孤飞，长策飘摇罩铁衣。
世人劳心多看客，家猫变虎稻粱肥。

Impasse

A retired genius attemps to fly lonely,
Whose long-range plan totters under the iron clothes.
The world in its mental work is suffused with spectators,
Where the tamed cats turn into pampered tigers.

君　竹

竹径春深听鸟啭，苍苔委曲寂无人。
山根迸笋穿肥露，林下白石散绿苹。

The Virtuous Bamboos

The spring in the warbles of the bamboo path
Rambles deep and still along the green moss.
The foot of the upland spurts the dewy bamboo shoots
And the white wood gravels are interspersed with green herbs.

君　子

万古天刑①浮日月，乾坤大道任交驰②。
阴阳上下擎天地，四气③相磨两不欺。

【注释】

①天刑：上天的法则。②交驰：交相奔走，往来不断。③四气：春

夏秋冬四季；喜怒哀乐。

The Men of Virtue

The sun and moon float by the eterna law of nature,
And the great truth of the universe runs at liberty.
Upper and lower, Yin and Yang hold up the scope of activity,
Where the four seasons are interchanged in honesty.

空　静
Empty and Calm

其一

九土①炎凉情远近，五湖冷暖意高低。
千年五岳白石烂②，可有天鸡向海啼？

【注释】

①九土：九州的土地。指国土。②白石烂：古诗《饭牛歌》之一歌辞中语。谓山石洁白耀眼。《史记·鲁仲连邹阳列传》有言“宁戚饭牛车下，而桓公任之以国”，裴骃集解引汉应劭曰：“齐桓公夜出迎客，而宁戚疾击其牛角而商歌曰：‘……白石烂，生不遭尧与舜禅。短布单衣适至骭，从昏饭牛薄夜半，长夜漫漫何时旦？’公召与语，说之，以为大夫。”后亦用以代称《饭牛歌》。此处引申借喻并双关，指洁白的石头腐烂了，如同世道人心腐烂到根部一样。

One

The lands in temperature are affected far or near,
And the lakes, hot or cold, feel the humanity higher or lower.
If the white stones of the great mountains crumble the glorious eternity,
Would there be that Heavenly Rooster that crows to the sea?

其二

白云结梦钓龙溪，黄鸟衔枝探紫梨。
物外高情何处去？且随葱岭[①]散羊蹄。

【注释】

①葱岭：指古代称呼的帕米尔高原（Pamirs，亦作 Pamir）。

Two

The white cloud in dream fishes in the dragon stream,
The yellow bird with the branch scouts his purple pear.
Where to go with the ideal soul beyond the material desires?
Now follow the Pamirs for the goat hooves you care.

老龙头

鸾镜晴明出瀚海，惊飞黑浪百楼高。
龙头不满喧春梦，吞进幽燕万里涛。

The Old Dragon Head

Clear and bright, the mirror comes out of the sea,
That flushes the black billow high as a hundred stories.
Critical of the blatant spring dream, the dragon head
Swallows the vast tidal bores against the serene land.

老　师

浮云带走青春日，桑柘春锄[1]逗野芳。
莫叹山夫人已老，还瞧桃李正出妆。

【注释】

①桑柘：指桑木与柘木，也指农桑之事。春锄：农耕。此处泛指劳动。

Teacher

The cloud drifts with the days of youth,
When the farming hoes tease the wild sweet,
That never sighs the締 gerontic recluse,
Before the peaches and plums blooming.

梨 花
Pear Flowers

其一

五月疏狂柳岸香，柔丝醉惹两三行。
青枝几点梢头颤，剪去清白送我郎。

One

May, that' s flanked by a sweet, unbridled line,
Has been willowy and tipsy by twos and threes.
As some green branches are thrilling the heads,
I' d like to clip my innocence for my merry man.

其二

香唇回雪伤春逝，别作丝丝嫩柳轻。
千缕万丝随影去，高低上下赴清风。

Two

Savory lips are snowing in dreamy thrills

And are flying off the gentle, soft willows.
Their shadows are gone in countless ties,
And gone to the breezes, low and high.

其三

银葩一点燕山月，拢上明纱闭雪痕。
玉质冰心休去问，梨花飞雪试清纯。

Three

Silver flowers in the moon-lit Yanshan Mountain
Shut the bright gauzes of their snow marks.
Their pure, bright heart like ice touches no question,
'Cause their blowing snows can test a pure reason.

黎明湖
The Liming Lake

其一

作别家乡已六年，回眸又见雪冰天。
不知戏水冰篷下，冰上可曾同样寒？

One

Off my town, six years are gone,
Glanced back, another slush ice comes along.
Whether a game under the ice cover
Measures the same cold above, of its own?

其二

雪落平湖散玉天，飞鸿翅下舞晴川。
梨花一尺藏不住，锦鲤随心戏水寒。

Two

Snow falls on the smooth lake like jade powders
Dancing fine on the river under the wings of swans.
As it is snowing one foot of pear flowers,
Cold carps swim merrily at simple pleasures.

其三

雪柳轻装银满树，晴空点亮满湖冰。
冰心有意封寒色，冷钓无从破水声。

Three

Light snow willows like silver flames
Light up the full ice in the clear air.
Let the heart of ice seal the cold games,
And no cold angling breaks the water there.

其四

白日平开野渡风，翻花过柳车轮[1]红。
春来湖水冰消后，小桥撑开绿伞明。

【注释】

①车轮：比喻太阳。也作双关。

Four

Wild wind switches on the day,
Willowy thru their red wheels.
After a smell of spring thaws,
The bridge opens his bright green umbrella.

其五

冰锁兰洲雪正浓，飞花不见女儿红。
待到柳枝摇春絮，萍水收来脉脉风。

Five

Ice-locked isle snows heavily,
Like flying flowers out of red sight.
Await the willows to sway a new spring,
The drifting catkins will get soft breezes.

其六

晓霜百里吞油城，寒璧[1]溶溶松嫩行。
曲水流觞春何在，铁马惊散漫天风。

【注释】

①寒璧：喻指月亮。

Six

A dawning frost has swallowed the oil town,
Snapped coldly thru the vast plain all along.
To find a merry spring on the meandering stream,
The heaven' s breath comes loose like a sweeping dream.

其七

雪肥柳瘦寒风痴，遥向苍天横玉枝。
颤颤银光冰心碎，月镜秋水向西移。

Seven

Cold-snapped, the thin willows in fat snows
Are veered sideways far into the heaven.
Heart of the ice breaks in a bright silver
That quivers the limpid mirror flowing west.

其八

银柳漱冰玉蕊生，虬枝寸寸刻花明。
勾勾画画披鳞甲，逆风消融四海清。

Eight

White willows by the ice have bred the pistils
That carve each inch of clear, curled sprays,
Whose each outline has been thread-bounded
In armour against the wind for a clear realm.

其九

落花颠狂欺月明，灵台①碎影唤西风。
刀切平野寒冰阔，展开天镜照黎明。

【注释】

①灵台：指心。《庄子·庚桑楚》：“不可内于灵台。”晋人郭象注：

"灵台者，心也。"

Nine

Crack-brained, the moon-lit blossom drops have tricked
The soul of the milled shades called out into the west wind.
In the open country that's been cut by the cold, wide spells,
One mirror of heavens may be opened to beam her twilight.

其十

寒柳瘦削更放寒，邀来狂月醉华年。
风熏斗酒孤轮[①]醉，卷帘遮面向西天。

【注释】

①孤轮：喻指月亮。

Ten

Cold, bony willows can spell colder,
That rope in a mad moon pickled in lusty days.
As the orphaned wheel is pickled and smoked,
Shut the rolling blind against the western sky.

流　禅

太液晴虫照露滴，石坚闲放暗清激[①]。
浮沟开卷流香月，银镜长烟不可觅。

【注释】

①清激：水流清澈湍急。

Flowing Meditation

A fine bug on the dewdrop of the royal garden
Set loose its clear, secret tide down the solid stone
Near the gutter open to the sweet, floating moon
Whose long mists were lost in the silver mirror.

龙　腾

苍龙羊角[①]越天舟，青翰[②]银河泛水流。
兰棹[③]惊心排晓雁，金星挥手翠光浮。

【注释】

①羊角：旋风。②青翰：信天翁的别称。③兰棹：兰舟。

The Soaring Dragon

The black dragon soars up like a tornado,
And turns into an albatross thru the milky way
That paddles and shocks the dawning geese
Down the golden stars twinkling their green waves.

路

长路飞蓬寻野店，桑山连雪带荒城。
月斜系马石桥岸，枭首当头怨一声。

The Road

The fleabane on the way in search of his wild inn
Was mated by the barren town below the snow mountain.
As the slanted moon tethered the horse on the stone-bridge bank,
There came one hoot from some owl of unsatisfaction.

路 径

荡日弛云跨太行，悠悠大运数存亡。
征输断续千年事，寒雪消融水更凉。

The Route

To dart on the sunny cloud across the Taihang Mountains,
Whose remote and general destiny existed and periled,
The history in its glorious eternity made or broke the taxations
That thawed out the chilling snows which would be more cold.

猫

贪心利嘴向金银，谪宦①生民两不真。
汉网疏篱黑白处，群猫假虎惑人伦。

【注释】

①谪宦：贬官另任新职。

Cat

The sharp-tongued avarice of gold and silver
Confounds the digraced officials with the people.
Where the coarse net catches what's black and white,
The cats in the tiger's skin delude the human order.

猫之梦

牛栏端坐一匹猫，鼠辈丝罗粉黛娇。
妙体随心应世累①，如仙羽盖②任逍遥。

【注释】

①世累：世俗的牵累。②羽盖：古时以鸟羽为饰的车盖。指车辆。

The Dream of Cat

One cat sits solemnly in the cow stall,
Where some skulking rats in silk are affectedly sweet
And satisfied their subtle figures with the entangled world
Like happy-go-lucky immortals in the feathery chariot.

梦　蝶

花尘漫诱蝴蝶梦，窥见婆娑枕上明。
花露不承烟雨重，暗滴梅酒戏春莺。

Butterflies in Dream

The flower dust freely entices the dream of butterflies,
That espies the bright, whirling pillow
That can't hold the weight of the flower dews in misty drizzles
And secretly drops the plum sake to tease the spring oriole.

梦中人

汉妓轻裙不乱怀，金银台下铁石心。
双肩挑起八荒任，书剑独行不可侵。

The Man in Dream

Enchanted not by the light harlot skirt in the lap,
And hard-hearted down the tower of gold and silver,
The shoulders should bear the burdens of all directions,
Where the scholarly sword walks alone in sanctity.

米兰花

香兰结粟淡如霜，散漫虬枝作谷乡。
泛瑟[①]无声难和赋，知音四海点浮阳。

【注释】

①泛瑟：抚瑟。

Aglaia Adorata

Her sweet millets are like light frost,
Free in the curled sprays of crop land,
Where a silent zither goes in rhythmic fragments,
Before the sunny grains to her soul-mates here and there.

民　主

板荡轮回破眼[①]清，舟楫[②]逆浪不心惊。
巅峰暗落虞渊[③]处，更有垂竿在钓名。

【注释】

①板荡：政局混乱或社会动荡。破眼：围棋术语，即点眼。破坏对方眼的着法。在攻杀整块棋子时经常采用。②舟楫：行船。③虞渊：又称隅谷（yú gǔ），古代汉族神话传说中日没处。

Democracy

The choppy cycle of the clear chess game goes,
But the paddled cross-waves won't be startled.
Where the dark colours of the peaks die down,
There are some anglers for fame as one knows.

名如水

养拙经世[1]吹尘梦，心到清溪浣盛名。
浮世离思烟柳动，转蓬危浪瘦魂惊。

【注释】

①养拙：才能低下而闲居度日。常作为退隐不仕的自谦之辞。经世：治理国事；阅历世事。

The Fame Is Like Water

To live in simplicity thru the chronicle history in dream,
The heart washes down the sterling reputation in the limpid stream.
While the fickle world sways its homesick thought so willowy,
The billows shock the soul of the floating duckweeds so meagerly.

明　月

杯行片月饮长川，桃浪轻薄色正鲜。
银角孤岚如会意，窥鱼咫尺漫天圆。

The Bright Moon

The moon on the long river floats in my cup,
Whose frivolous waves are precisely delicious.
If the silver horn over the lonely cloud takes the hint,
The peeping fish near will swim into the full moon.

明　智

谁人出世赋天聪[①]？冰雪幽遐[②]玉镜中。
云水先知三五[③]夜，一轮满月正丰隆。

【注释】

①天聪：上天赋予人的听力。②冰雪：比喻心志的忠贞、品格的高尚。幽遐：僻远；深幽。③三五：每月农历十五日。

In Reason

Who's endowed with the inborn intelligence?
It's the ice and snow deep and serene in the jade mirror.
If the cloud and water foretell the third five day,

One full moon will be growing plump.

命

烟霜心苦知薄命，纵横天街有大灵。
飞动一潭夕柳月，北窗侧耳复闲听。

Fate

A bitter, frosty heart must be born unlucky,
A free, celestial street has its great spirit.
One pool of moon stirs the dusk willows swiftly,
When the north window resumes its ear attentively.

命 运

天头素月行天步[1]，大运无常祸百年。
紫露明移花月夜，秋来瘦骨谢风烟。

【注释】

①天步：天运，命运。

Destiny

One white moon on the skyline steps her fairy step
Towards the fickle, general misfortune about a century.
After the purple dews on petals glisten in the moon-lit night,

The bones in the autumn are withered in the landscape.

农家

清风清雨对青山，两亩青葱一片天。
老舍炊烟蒸米饭，谁说此处不桃源。

Farmhouse

Green mountains in a fresh breeze
Are drizzling two *mu* of scallions
Before the old hut for steamed rice
Which should be a real Shangri-la.

爬山虎

薜萝牵恨幽人[①]短，浮世青阴四壁长。
飞絮纵横别远梦，风流空染戴河阳。

【注释】

①薜萝：薜荔和女萝。两者皆野生植物，常攀缘于山野林木或屋壁之上。也借指隐者或高士的住所。幽人：幽隐之人；隐士。

Boston Ivy

The creepers grudge in short solitude
On the long, green walls of the fickle world.

As the free, flying willow fuzzes leave their far dreams,
Their loose escapades have dyed the sun in the Daihe River.

飘　蓬

薄暮疏慵[1]游子路，断云几度枕空山。
独行林下风蝉乱，野步春深梦未还。

【注释】

①疏慵：疏懒；懒散。

The Floating Duckweeds

Long-absent on the vesperal, indolent road,
The broken cloud has pillowed the empty hills many a time.
Having walked alone in the cicade chirps of the wood,
The wild step into the deeper spring has not dreamed back.

平　衡

天淆[1]一羽挂千钧，物破空峦两不真。
幽梦城头结朔雁[2]，孤飞寒水杳难循。

【注释】

①天淆：化用陈忠平《春日再雪》“天淆气象时无序，物破平衡岁有灾”。②朔雁：北地南飞之雁。

Balance

One feather in the confused sky hangs by a hundred weights,
Down the empty, untrue and broken mountain.
Such a north goose down the city wall in secret dream
Flies lonely into the far, cold water hard to be reclaimed.

气　象

山眉[①]雨后飞虹碎，大气人生易水低。
笑傲梅枝欺落雪，应知凋谢化淤泥。

【注释】

①山眉：如眉的山形。

The Prospect

The eyebrowed rainbow after the rain is fragile
Like the free life that may be heroic but tragic.
And the arrogant snow on the plum twigs in smiles
Should be readily known to fade into the mires.

牵　挂

南窗回梦到家乡，冷雨斜风几寸霜。
捆住童心知冷热，双亲为我去牵肠。

Care

My south window has dreamed back
In cold elements frosted a few inches
That'd strap an understanding heart
Of my parents kept in suspense.

将进酒

观德观酒观声色，泛酒[1]合欢醉美人。
飞燕流霞[2]得酒意，莫言传酒废青春。

【注释】

①泛酒：古代风俗。每逢三月三日，宴饮于环曲的水渠旁，浮酒杯于水上，任其飘流，停则取饮，相与为乐，谓之“泛酒”。泛指聚会饮酒。②流霞：流动的霞光颜色。

Cheers

Watch the moral of the wine and women,
Then make good cheer, and to get tight, my dear,
Let the tipsy cloud fly like the swallow,
Where the youth if dried out would be a rumour.

亲不待

地灵黄鹤当回返，人远青眸断塞云。
莫等双亲来梦里，相邀故里上孤坟。

Parents No More

To where's blessed the yellow crane should return,
To the broken cloud afar the eyes are strained.
Don't wait until the parents come into the dream,
To invite their lonely grave in the native place.

琴　女

红粉春衫袖玉鞭，绛唇一点动明鲜。
醉人不用金银盏，素指抚琴向月圆。

The Zither Lady

Her rosy spring sleeves are swirling
And her red lips are vividly pursing.
Gold and silver cups won't get more tight
Than her pure fingers to the round moon tonight.

青藏高原

史前雪野蚕丝尽，唯剩磐石任宰割。
南北东西如饮水，运来四海纵情喝。

Qinghai-Tibet Plateau

Prehistoric snow fields are spinned out
And leave over the rocks to be killed.
All the world, if hope to have a drink,
Fetch the four seas and drink your fill.

秋　菊

黄菊断柳欺白露，疏放开屏对紫梨。
泛过野晴逢九日，南山下面乱云低。

Autumn Chrysanthemum

Yellow chrysanthemums in broken willows hoax the white dew,
And bloom their free courage to the purple pears.
On the ninth lunar day of the fine open country,
The riotous clouds are hanging down the southern hill.

权　变

高柳淡薄[①]蝉雨后，江头满月泛金杯。
紫微清漏[②]飞白虎，化作飞蝇一两枚。

【注释】

①淡薄：因淡忘而模糊。②紫微：汉族传统命理学中的一种。认为人出生时的星相决定人的一生，即人的命运。认为各种星曜对人的命运具有特定的关联，又因为星曜按一定次序出现，相应的人就按照这个次序接受星曜带来的影响，源于古代汉族人民对星辰的自然崇拜。清漏：清晰的滴漏声。古代以漏壶滴漏计时。

The Ways of Society

After the rain, the light cicadas in the high willows
Chirped to the full moon like a golden cup in the river.
Down the circumpolar stars, the water clock dropped a tiger,
That turned into one or two flies, to be sure.

权　力

云梦闲思世路新，张弛洗耳莫天真。
俗流当路忠良尽，猛虎青蝇掸客尘[①]。

【注释】

①客尘：尘世的种种烦恼。

Power

The cloud in dream closed its thought on the new way,
And relaxed its attention to the air of innocence,
Because the vulgarians on the way ended the worthy men,
That brushed the dust from the fierce tigers and blue flies.

人　心
The Man' s Heart

其一

挟起燕山越大洋，送交对手又何妨。
哪年精卫穷通日，世界不须靠远航。

One

Pick up the Yanshan Mountain to cross the ocean
And deliver it to the opponent— 'tis quite a reason!
When the ocean is filled by the bird with pebbles,
The world would require no voyage on the ocean.

其二

闭心莫道开心事，闭脑提防洗脑人。
幽谷隐形难隐脑，人心各半两难真。

Two

Shut your heart against your delight,
Shut your brain against the brainwashers;
A dell steals the body but not the brain,
In that either half of the heart is hard to be true.

忍
Forbearance

其一

百年忍断望乡台[①]，不见长城北面开。
关外空吟昨夜雪，今朝戴水杏花来。

【注释】

①忍断：化自杜甫《戏题寄上汉中王三首》中“忍断杯中物，祇看座右铭”。望乡台：原指古代久戍不归或流落外地的人为眺望故乡而登临的高台。后来，随着道教鬼神观念的成熟和佛教地狱体系的引

入，道教逐步把望乡台从现实建筑演变为虚幻存在，成为神话传说中进入地狱的鬼魂们可以眺望阳世家中情况的地方。

One

Breaking my heart to the watch-tower of hell for a century,
I' ve lost the sight of the Great Wall open to the north,
Where it started snowing stark last night, but now
The apricot blossoms turn up along the Daihe River.

其二

琉璃瓦下山中客，半面蝉声半面风。
锦带无缘拴远梦，故乡夜夜小屋中。

Two

The passenger below the glazed tiles
'Mid the songs of cicadas and the wind
Failed to fasten the far dream unto his brocade belt
About his birthplace night after night in the hut.

其三

四壁行霜宿暗刀，客吟星月枕风高。
十年筋力[①]轻烟火，方寸清羸[②]划铁牢。

【注释】

①筋力：筋骨之力。②清羸：清瘦羸弱。

Three

The walls in frost are lodged by a secret sword,
That pillows the harsh wind in the moon and the stars.
The muscles for a decade have belittled the life,
Drawing a weak and feeble circle as his iron prison.

任　性

拖紫[①]骑龙戴水滑，凭胸驾海可精察。
弘窟斗玉迷阡陌，冷热清心眼不瞎。

【注释】

①拖紫：诸侯为紫色，公卿为青色。指担任高官。

Self-willed

Dignitary on the dragon, the Daihe River slides
Its breast to drive the sharp-minded sea.
For the hoard's worth, the treasure can capture all the hearts,
Which, hot or cold, should not be blind with a clear heart.

日

千亿光年千亿星，聚来驰火散如风。
豪情若为知己故，纵使焚身亦认同。

The Sun

Hundred billions of stars and light years
Come like fires and go like winds.
Lofty sentiments for a second self are
Willingly accepted though licked by flames.

柔　劲

冰泻铁声杀走马，甲胄熊虎夜衔枚。
不劳玉帐横军气，敛黛回眸骏骨[1]摧。

【注释】

①敛黛：敛蛾，皱眉。骏骨：骏马。

The Soft Vigour

The clanking icicles down would kill the amblers,
Swiftly and silently run the night corslet bears and tigers.
Why it cannot do otherwise than keep the bellicose tent?
A glance back from her frowns could break the coursers.

山　外

龙头[1]大漠苍山尽，回首獠牙万里宽。
御气摇风行虎旆[2]，细腰高枕九州寒。

【注释】

①龙头：山海关老龙头。②旆（pèi）：古代旌旗末端状如燕尾的垂旒。泛指旌旗。

Beyond the Mountains

Dragon Head at the end of the mountains
Toothed back at the vast terrain of desert.
On the shocking wind of the great banners,
Its wasp waist pillowed the nine cold continents.

上　钩

芳饵飞天垂钓线，浮沈清浅待纤鳞。
牵轮触口开俗眼，不测祸机在动唇。

Hooked

The fine bait arcs its fishing line
Up or down for the fish clearly,
That hit its laical mouth and eyes to the reel

And nibbles the fortuitous debacle.

上 妆

珠帘腻粉偷娇色，玉腕慵梳晓镜蓝。
半日斜光匀翠黛①，青桑扼臂验冰蚕②。

【注释】

①翠黛：古时女子用螺黛画眉，故称美人之眉为“翠黛”。②青桑：嫩桑叶。扼臂：抓住胳膊，形容心灵相互感应。冰蚕：传说中的一种蚕。

Make-up

Her delicate, greasy rouge peeks behind the pearl curtain
And combs her fine fingers thru the dozy, blue mirror at dawn.
Her brows evenly in the oblique light half a day
Are spiritually sensitive like the cocoons on mulberry leaves.

诗 客

普天之下存知己，曲尽瑶台①雁翅飞。
清汉②风头明锦臂，百年诗骨暗轻肥③。

【注释】

①瑶台：汉族神话传说中神仙所居之地。②清汉：天河。③轻肥：取自《论语·雍也》中的“乘肥马，衣轻裘”，用以概括豪奢生活。此处借指作诗的收获。

Poet

All over the world I have confidants,
Who would fly off the jade tower at the finale
With the silk sleeves bright on the wind of the galaxy
Where the poetic bones are secretly enervated by the luxury.

诗　画

穷诗富画古如此，富画留来换斗米。
百代诗仙都故去，灵犀片片众心里。

Verse and Painting

Poor poems but rich paintings, so it ever be,
Though the paintings are bartered for grains.
All poetic genii may have gone, but see
Their tacit sparks treasured up in man's memory!

诗　酒

冰酒冰天冰地饮，百湖初酿作清茶。
举杯常问寒风夜，莫负诗词到我家。

Poem and Wine

Ice wine, ice air, ice land! Drink
The hundred lakes that freshly brew the pure tea.
Raise the cups to the night of the wintry blasts,
Living up to the poems that come to my home.

诗　觞

富画折合万两金，穷诗不抵一根针。
凝毫销铄[1]分贫富，笔墨垂悬贵贱心。

【注释】

①销铄：熔化。

The Poetic Wine

The rich painting can be converted into thousand taels of gold
But the poor poem can not be matched for a needle in that
The same frail brush can mark off the wealth and poverty
Whose heart may be dangling with the writings.

诗之源

诗韵诗情诗路远，不如对酒释悲欢。
风言流语书桌上，愧对衔杯万句宽。

The Source of Poems

On the distant way of poetical and metrical fancies,
The alcoholic power can remove the quirks of joy and grief.
All the unfounded rumours on the table
Are unworthy of the cup widened by ten thousand lines.

石　榴

半岭石榴涂妾意，风裙剪碎露沙蝉。
霞衣醉后青丝半[①]，桃色妖姬[②]齿正鲜。

【注释】

①青丝半：“情丝绊”的谐音。②妖姬：多指妖艳的侍女、婢妾。

Pomegranate

Half the way up the hill, the pomegranates should know my hope,
Where my skirt snips the dewy cicadas in the wind and
My black hair half down the rosy coat drunk as a sow
Would taste the pink, fresh colour of a delilah.

实验治理

世路张雷鹤梦遥，天涯落木饮灵潮。
澹烟一曲门前路，醉倚青霄盼黛娇[①]。

【注释】

①青霄：清朗的夜晚。又喻指帝都；朝廷。黛娇：眉含娇态。

Experimental Control

The crane dreamed afar on the way of thunders,
And the fallen wood afar swigged the quick tide;
The melody heaved in front of the hazy gate
Was girly but tipsy below the blue sky.

书 觞

书生莫信富人言，客路吟灯枉自烦。
百卷诗书皆粪土，千层银座胜黎元[①]。

【注释】

①黎元：黎民百姓。

Book and Wine

A schoolman trusts no man of fortune,
In his rhythmic light of overcare.
All poem anthologies are but worthless muck
In the thousand-storey Ginza over the plebeians.

衰微

秦汉楼台下六朝，江花不老逗春娇。
盛唐鹉语红楼破，悲骨横陈紫梦消。

Descadence

The huge towers from the Qin and Han to the Six Dynasties
Teased the never-aging river flowers of the lovely spring.
The glorious parrots of the Tang broke the red mansions,
Where the purple dreams were strewn with the sad bones

水仙
Daffodils

其一

淡妆冷袖坐银台，玉坠金杯向雪开。
青女冰魂才触梦，风流一点是香腮。

One

On the silver stand，her cold sleeves thinly powdered

Bloom the golden cups with jade pendants to the snow.
Once the ice soul of the green nymph touches the dream,
The one amorous escapade lies in her fair cheek.

其二

檀心[1]寒梦侵风露，自信江梅玉色轻。
月魄[2]山中迎朔雪，汨罗江畔有贞名。

【注释】

①檀心：丹心。②月魄：月光。

Two

Dewy and windy，her sandalwood heart in cold dream
Affirms that the wintersweets are overshadowed
By her soul for the north snow below the moon over the hills
With the most chaste renown on the Miluo River.

其三

独立金寒抱野风，银潢[1]泣露玉颜中。
凌波澹月[2]摇珠串，逆旅[3]约来素燕鸿。

【注释】

①银潢（huáng）：天河；银河。②凌波：形容女子脚步轻盈，飘移如履水波。此处喻指犹如波涛一样的水仙。澹月：清淡的月光。亦指月亮。③逆旅：旅居。常用以比喻人生匆遽短促。

Three

Alone in the golden chills hugged by the wild wind,
The charming faces weep their dews down the Milky Way.
When the wave in the light moon sways the bright beads,
The journey invites here some white swallows and swans.

其四

乘鲤[1]清风留玉佩，长驱腊月伴宁波。
冰肌藏尽娇羞色，绝韵娥眉任婆娑。

【注释】

①乘鲤：比喻成仙。

Four

The immortal gone with the breeze left the jade pendants,
That pushes deep into the winter to be with the peaceful waves.
In the ice muscles must be hidden her virgin modesty,
Whose wonderful charm dances on her delicate eyebrows.

司法化

世间法界真难辨，鹿马[1]堂深造化穷。
万籁情长生六变[2]，千秋踪迹化八风[3]。

【注释】

①鹿马："指鹿为马"的略语。②六变：指急、缓、大、小、滑、涩六种脉象的病理变化。③八风：指利、衰、毁、誉、称、讥、苦、乐。四顺四逆一共八件事，这四顺四逆也是四对相反的事。这八种境界是人生名利、得失、盛衰、成败的总和。众生时时刻刻都被这八风所吹动，因这八风而生无穷烦恼。

Judicature

The dhamma world is less clear, but
The deep, distorted hall has used up its good fortune.
All the sounds deep in love have created the six changes,
And turned the eternal traces into the eight winds.

随缘

天地行藏任倚伏[①]，浮云舒卷自相逐。
幽怀不计烟霞[②]散，日月浮沈进小屋。

【注释】

①行藏：行迹。倚伏：互相依存。②幽怀：隐藏在内心的情感。烟霞：烟雾；云霞。

Let It Be

The whereabouts of the world follow their joy and sorrow,
Where the cloud rolls and runs so liberally.
Once the inner mind leaves the lost rosy cloud,
The sun and the moon will swim or sink into my hut.

贪腐

天下长竿垂腐宦，鸬鹚[①]笑问远来风。
守拙[②]闲步心骑虎，钓誉刚肠[③]一枕空。

【注释】

①鸬鹚（lú cí）：也叫水老鸦、墨鸦、鱼鹰。②守拙：封建士大夫自诩清高，不做官，清贫自守。③刚肠：刚直的气质。

Corruption

On the long rod hangs the corrupt official under the sun,
Where the cormorant asks the wind from afar merrily.
Honestly poor, his leisurely gait is riding on the tiger at heart,
And in righteous wrath, his angling for fame sleeps on the pillow, but empty.

逃避

逃名逃利畏天刑，世事浮沈两杳冥①。
早岁轻舟逐水去，飞琼②冷月满山青。

【注释】

①杳冥：幽暗；深广。②飞琼：仙女名许飞琼，传说中的仙女，是西王母身边的侍女。后泛指仙女。

Evasion

To flee from the fame and gain fears the natural penalty,
Upon the swimming or sinking world which is so dusky.
Had the shallop gone with the water earlier,
The fairy moon would have shone the green mountain brightly.

桃花
Peach Blossoms

其一

桃花扇底娥眉月，雪粉含晴露吐香。
闭月羞花花暗影，花飞月走两茫茫。

One

Like a crescent, her peach flowers
Are fine and savory in the snow powders.
Her flowers that shut out the moon
Will be shut out like the moon very soon.

其二

五月黄金轮[①]作马，三寻[②]灭影可追鸿。
飞扬天镜如惊燕，满目红鳞顺柳风。

【注释】

①黄金轮：比喻太阳。②三寻：指马的前后蹄一跃而过三寻的距离，形容马奔跑得快。

Two

Galloping wheel of gold in May
May trace the shade of the swan.
In the mirror flying a startling swallow,
Red scales are floating with the wind of willows.

其三

祖山莫道长城险，城下花香城上飘。
万里飞红金阳[1]去，大漠闻到海蟾[2]高。

【注释】

①金阳：太阳。②海蟾：月亮。

Three

On Mount Zushan, other Great Wall is steep, no more,
The perfume of flowers down waves up all along.
Thousands of miles, red petals are flying with the sun,
To the great desert that smells the Sea Toad higher.

桃夭

娇姿清骨放夭桃[1]，惊燕消魂粉浪高。
醉咏微风捎柳叶，休将流水作萧骚[2]。

【注释】

①夭桃：艳丽的桃花。②萧骚：形容风吹树叶等的声音。

Peaches Aglow

Pure and delicate, the peaches are running riot,
Startling the swallows in the pink, raptured waves higher.
When the tipsy ode to the breeze messages to willow leaves,
Don't mistake the flowing water as the bleak rustles.

天池

飞天凿玉卧龙池，化作群峰饰彩帷。
万仞白山悬宝镜，掩留清女翠滑肌。

The Celestial Lake

The Creator digged the jade into the pool of sleeping dragons,
Turned into the mountains inwreathed by colourful curtains.
Thousands of feet high, the white peak hangs its rare mirror,
That detains the pure nymph with her skin so tender.

天亮

风月尝闻星造浪，钓船一叶荡银声。
高情衔璧胭花[1]谢，华盖[2]涂红照大明。

【注释】

①衔璧：《左传·僖公六年》：“许男面缚衔璧，大夫衰绖，士舆

榇。”杜预注：“缚手于后，唯见其面，以璧为贽，手缚故衔之。”后称国君投降为“衔璧”。胭花：亦作“臙花”。谓浓妆艳抹的女子。旧时特指妓女。②华盖：帝王或贵族车上的伞盖。

Day Break

The moonlit night heard the starry waves,
Where one angling boat swayed its silver words,
With its ideal yet humble soul that faded the rouge,
Under the canopy that reddened the bright panorama.

特权

游燕劳生[①]竞自由，泊烟如梦任沈浮。
清浊冷暖袭人处，最是风尘一网收。

【注释】

①游燕：同“游宴”；游乐。劳生：指辛苦劳累的生活。

Privilege

The laborious swallow vies for liberty,
Berthed in the dreamy hazes, up or down.
Where the temperature assails, clean and dirty,
All the officials are roped in completely.

晚舟

清风玉露月如钩，浅草绵绵偎小舟。
两尾流云横水过，吹开一缕暗娇羞。

Evening Boat

In dewy breezes, the crescent
Snuggles up to the grassy shallop
Glided by two clouds in front
Blowing open a plume of shy secret.

望奎雪野

黑土平铺三尺雪，齐腰脆韵罩风声。
忽如冷刃飞天起，万管胡箫破胆鸣。

The Snow Field of Wangkui

The black soil outspread under the three foot snow
Was whistling crisply but rhythmically and then
Soaring up like the cold swords in the formidable
Howls from ten thousand barbarian pipes.

望眼

梁燕闲庭醉柳鞭，衔来尺素入长天。
云门举首邀心事，草木无情已九迁[①]。

【注释】

①九迁：多次变迁。

The Longing Eyes

Off the quiet beam, the swallows thru the tipsy willows
Held the letters up into the long sky soliciting what's
On the mind from the cloud door below which the ruthless
Wood should have undergone their major changes.

围城

雪月观山雾霭长，风花听鸟汽笛忙。
登楼谁见千里目，处处城郭处处墙。

Besieged

A hazy snow moon down the mountains so long
Has heard the busy hooters that shine over a drifting bird.
To ascend higher, who's seen the sight of a thousand *li*?
Here and there, it's blocked by the city walls everywhere.

文采

剑壁连云散角山，长城扬戟铁石关。
秦皇赫怒[1]碣石隐，魏武东临现海湾。

【注释】

①赫怒：盛怒。

The Literary Grace

The Great Wall into the clouds along Jiaoshan Mountain
Wielded its swords and halberds for the iron-stone passes.
The Jieshi Hill hid under the wrath of the first emperor of Qin,
But heaved out of the bay when the Emperor Wu of Wei went east.

问责

权色人情蒙厚禄，触天暗雨醉深笼。
银灯百里长裾[1]夜，度影香凝落野风。

【注释】

①长裾：长衣。

Accountability

The relationship in power and sex enjoys a fat salary,

Drunk in the deep cage that touches the high, dark rain.
In the silver lamp, her robe for hundreds of miles
Drops the sweet shades into the wild wind.

我要飞

灵禽俯仰静飞名，效仿今人适寡营[①]。
芜蔓[②]不图金玉爪，飘然一扇碧云轻。

【注释】

①寡营：欲望少，不为个人营谋打算。②芜蔓：荒芜；荒凉。

I Want to Fly

The spiritual fowl hushes his flying name, lower or higher,
As the people now who've fitted with the fewest desire.
Overgrown with weeds, he seeks no claws of gold and jade,
But flaps his fan like a light cloud to float further.

无忧

乐性寒来雨后天，飞鸿颈下欲独眠。
角山漠漠幽燕雨，一树石榴挂野田。

Free of Care

After the cold rain, the blissful nature hopes
To sleep lonely below the neck of the swan goose.
In such a foggy and serene rain down Jiaoshan Mountain,
One tree full of pomegranates hangs in the open country.

五月

扑鼻一树流红晕，满目金黄挂露音。
翡翠琼枝浮嫩柳，悠然水岸梨花魂。

May

Pinkish trees are saluting
Their dewy, golden ticking.
Green willows have tendered
The shore pears blankered.

习相远
Wide Apart by Practice

其一

碧水离愁草木新，横笛弄雨落花深。
疏风幽梦三秋后，谁按风笛在树林？

One

A green parting grief flows anew,
Thru the deep，fallen petals like a rain.
A secret dream sparsely blows the late autumn,
Which is bagpiping in the wood，somehow.

其二

春入童谣紫燕娇，烟波望断长虹桥。
云烟多少君别问，太阳出来雨自消。

Two

Purple hirundos are rhymed into the spring,
And rainbowed across the misty waters rolling.
Don't you count those fleecy clouds, whose rain
Disperses itself when the sun comes out again.

其三

春日溪山澹澹风，野生林木月溶溶。
要想洗清红尘土，摘下心来泡水中。

Three

Streams and hills in the spring are undulating,
And wild woods in the mild moon are melted.
To wash around the dust of the worldly life,
Better pick off your heart to be soaked.

其四

去年百媚石榴裙，娇艳今秋偷晚寒。
醉眼婆娑何须验，等你多少月儿弯。

Four

Her charming crimson skirt last year
Steals a late, delicate cool in this fall.
Why to test her vibrant, bleary eyes?
Quite a few crescents are lost for you.

其五

反腐东风战鼓擂，无情落叶满天飞。
苍蝇老虎乾坤外，还有袈裟财色肥。

Five

Beat and pound for the anti-corruption,
And fallen leaves are going the rounds.
Beyond the scope of the flies and tigers,
Kasayas are loose in wealth and women.

其六

寒小枝头春意薄，孤红不是百花国。
绝色出自众芳里，历尽冰霜苦难多。

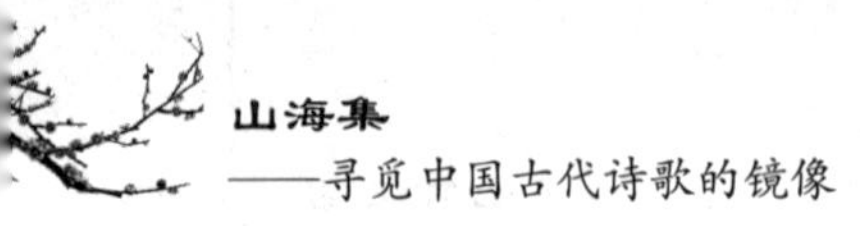

Six

Spring awakens the branches in a slight cold,
Whence an isolated red forms no state of flowers.
To be a stunner from among all kinds of flowers,
She's gone through the bitter mill in icy waters.

其七

今古兴衰万事空，几行青史月中明。
英雄有泪说成败，悔恨由来口意松。

Seven

Ups and downs, all has vanished,
A few lines in the annals may be moon-lit.
To be or not to be, a hero tells in tears,
Mouth and mind, 'tis so loose, alas!

贤能治理

贤愚旷望青云客[①]，熊虎飘摇紫禁楼。
九陌寒枝明月夜，贪廉聚散两穷幽[②]。

【注释】

①旷望：目眺望。云客：仕途显达的人。②穷幽：探寻幽深、僻静

之处。

Virtuous and Talented Control

Wise or fool, the high dignitaries are gazed out,
Bear or tiger, the forbidden mansion drifts about;
In the cold, moon-lit branches of the down-town night,
The corrupt honesty comes and goes in or out of sight.

相 煎

清气藏名飘一羽，飞红小径作蝉衣。
摩天凤驾追飞燕，幽客[①]何曾惹是非？

【注释】

①幽客：隐士。

Inhumanity

One feather flutters incognito in the fresh air,
Thru the red pathway like a cicada shell
After the flying swallow trying to be a skyscraping pheonix
For which the recluse has stirred up trouble?

心 锁

花情无法探诚心，倦鸟遥林断翠阴。

幽径不觉天欲暮，野风绿梦两相寻。

The Lock of Heart

The flower emotions can't scout the depth of the heart,
The weary bird far in the wood stops by the green shades.
While the serene path hasn't perceived the twilight,
The wild wind is seeking its green dream, or vice versa.

心　外

萧骚[1]紫陌月光斜，山鸟绵蛮[2]欲踏花。
数片紫书栖野水，幽遐[3]迷径有渔家。

【注释】

①萧骚：形容景色冷落。②绵蛮：羽毛亮密的小鸟。③幽遐：僻远；深幽。

Beyond the Heart

The moonbeam tilted in the desolate avenue
Shone the fledgling chirps over some petals
Whose purple words stayed near the wild water
Secretly lost into the maze of a fishing house.

心与事

白鸟青天玉片飞，流年一去几时归?
明泉朔雁流寒瘦，野马秋来百丈肥。

Heart and Affairs

Like the jade flakes, the white birds in the broad daylight
Have flied away into the fleeting time. Tell me when your return
To the bright fountain, your cold and lean geese would flow
From the north into the indomitable strength in the wandering air.

杏 花

杏花疏雨摇风醉，野水牵衣脸半开。
嫩色逢人羞玉露，东邻无意透春腮。

Apricot-blossoms

The spattering petals drunk in the wind
Is blooming half her face by the wild water
Whose delicate dews are sheepish with strangers for
The merry maiden isn't inclined to tell her spring cheeks.

修　炼

修心明月悬天镜，修道清风散海楼。
鸟静花湿银露脆，空江无棹[①]一浮舟。

【注释】

①棹（zhào）：划船的一种工具，形状和桨差不多。

Practice

Cultivate your heart under the mirror of the bright moon,
Cultivate the truth in the breeze over all the sea storeys;
In the crisp, silver dews, the wet petals have hushed the birds
Before the boat without a paddle on the empty river.

徐　福

横扫六国天下破，秦皇生死在徐福。
花颜五百横沧海，生下东洋野兽族。

Xu Fu

The six states were swept out and unified,
But the life and death of the emperor lied in Xu Fu,
Who crossed the sea with 500 virgin boys and girls
Giving birth to the bestial clans of Japan.

选　择

宦途破灭消荣利，人性重生断是非。
袍笏平明[1]思己过，谁能无故累囚衣。

【注释】

①袍笏：朝服和手板。上古自天子以至大夫，朝会时皆穿朝服执笏。后世唯品官朝见君王时才服用。此处泛指官服或借指有品级的文官。平明：天刚亮时；公平严明。

The Choice

Official way perished, fame and fortune vanished,
To be reborn, the human nature sized up right from wrong.
If the robes and sceptres often pondered over their mistakes,
Who could be adjudged with the prison garbs for nothing?

学　会
To Learn

其一：成长

今宵金帐金石路，晚色独眠二月天。
酒醒空留山野客，红尘岁月已千年。

One: Growth

Tonight, the golden curtain on the way of the philosopher's stone
Has slept through the twilight of February, on my own.
Awake from the stupor, the empty mountain asks me to stay
But one thousand years have passed in the world all along.

其二：承担

晴看苍山雨看河，劳生浩荡世情多。
花间不忍常年醉，家有糟糠[①]尚未磨。

【注释】

①糟糠：指酒糟、米糠等粗劣食物，旧时穷人用来充饥的食物。借指共过患难的妻子。

Two: Undertaking

Unlike the fine hill or the rainy rill,
The laborious life has known the ways of the world.
The breath of flowers can hardly bear to be perennially blind to the world,
In that the bran at home must await to be removed first of all.

其三：放下

抚掌无边修大劫[①]，禅居六度远凫鸭[②]。
灵均[③]作赋长沙地，哪料前途路短狭。

【注释】

①抚掌：拍手。多表示高兴、得意。又，犹言笑谈。大劫：总括成、住、坏、空等四劫，称为一大劫；乃一期世界之始末。②六度："度"的梵语是 Pāramitā（波罗蜜多），字义是"到彼岸"，就是从烦恼的此岸到觉悟的彼岸。六度就是六个到彼岸的方法。凫（fú）鸭：水鸭子，或指北魏所定官号，即诸曹走使。此处指走吏或官场。③灵均：词章之士。此处以屈原作比。

Three: Let Go

Rub your palms to the boundless, fearful calamity,
And dwell in meditation on the six pāramitās from the authority:
You know Qu Yuan composed his rhapsody in the penal colony,
Who must have foreseen his road ahead to go shortly and narrowly.

其四：分辨

一寸琼音惊掠影，操弦[①]入梦笼知音。
谁知野马浮云去，物外[②]翻蝶不可寻。

【注释】

①操弦：操琴，弹奏。②物外：超越世间事物，而达于绝对之境界。

Four: Recognition

One inch of the precious voice startles the skipping shadows,
With the chord to enter the dream of the soul-mate.
Believe it or not, the wild hooves have gone on the cloud,
Like a butterfly beyond the world which can't be recycled.

其五：给予

黄金有意出石濑[①]，怎奈长沙锁雾凉。
仙药帝京收玉座，谁能解取治心伤？

【注释】

①石濑（lài）：水为石激形成的急流。

Five: To Give

The witting gold comes out of the rocky stream,
Which is locked by the cold fog over the long strands.
Even the panacea to the throne of the royal capital
Would find no way out to cure the wound of the heart.

其六：理解

粉面仙郎[①]红玉软，千金理镜窥天青。
南宫明燕啼春雨，老大无由作小伶。

【注释】

①粉面仙郎：俊美的青年男子。

Six：Understanding

Creamy-faced，the man has softened the ruby
In the mirror like a blue sky by the lady of esteem.
Hark the swallow chirps of the south court in the spring rains，
He should have grown up to be a small potato，for nothing.

其七：珍惜

薄命罗裙粉泪羞，多才未免作浮囚。
汉家玉女三千万，天降胡尘万古愁。

Seven：To Cherish

Such a rush of silk skirt shy in rouge tears
Should be a come down as the versatile prisoner!
Out of the fair thirty million maids of the empire，
The barbarian dust down her was gloomy for ever.

其八：自强

行乐江头醉友欢，穷檐[1]苦月自生寒。
人生达命[2]难求贵，看取丹心五岳宽。

【注释】

①穷檐：茅舍，破屋。②达命：知命。

Eight：Self-discipline

Let the river go on the spree,
Though under the bitter moon our hovels feel cold.
If the destiny fails its glorious life,
The heart of pure loyalty should be wider than the Holy Mountains.

其九：自重

恩荣有命无修短[①]，宠辱[②]无名有暗怀。
名士古来多自重，莫执孤履到崩崖。

【注释】

①恩荣：受皇帝恩宠的荣耀。修短：长短。②宠辱：荣宠与耻辱。

Nine：Self-dignified

Gloried in honours, the life span is decided by nature,
Gain or pain, the nameless life has its secret harbour.
From of old the celebrities take themselves more seriously,
Never going their own way to the beetling cliff so pushily.

雅　贵

大雅宽情[1]嫌地窄，轻裾[2]一角释云天。
厚薄不碍春山梦，冰境消融化碧鲜[3]。

【注释】

①大雅：德高而有大才的人。宽情：犹宽心。②轻裾（jū）：衣服的大襟。指短衣。③碧鲜：青翠鲜润的颜色。原用以形容竹的色泽。后以“碧鲜”为竹的别名。

Refined and Noble

The generosity of a good taste is sour on the narrow earth,
Whose coat tail couldrelease the clouds in the sky
That, thick or thin, will not stop the dream of the spring,
But thaw the iceberg out into more fresh green.

雁南飞

北雁霜天月色愁，燕山有意也难留。
芙蓉国里黄菊瘦，自有红梅对汀洲。

Wild Geese Gone South

Frosy geese in moon-lit melancholy
Are hard to stay against the witting mountains.
After yellow mums are lean in the state of lotus,
Red plum-blossoms come onto the sand islets.

赝　僧

下界山门空野殿，良辰野客万枝香。
垂帘野僧宴嫔妓①，罗幌②诸佛坐野堂。

【注释】

①嫔（pín）妓：姬妾与歌舞女艺人。②罗幌：丝罗帷幔。

Fake Monk

To the open temple in the mortal world,
The auspicious pilgrims offered myriad incenses.
Behind the wild dossal, the monk feted his concubines,
With all the Buddhas sitting cross-legged in the wild hall.

银　滩

银沙六月叠清浪，小蟹临潮各自忙。
十里滩头吹豆粒，履声蹑影落闲房。

The Silver Beach

The silver sand waved clear in June,
When the crablets bustled about the tide,
Like the whiffled beans on the beach ten miles,
That bolted into their own burrows at the shuffling footsteps.

咏 荷
The Ode to Lotus

其一

香魂半缕吐金蕊，素影轻轻碾翠微。
淡醉桃红羞扇面，娇娇玉粉为君飞。

One

Half of the sweet soul with golden stamina
Grinds her pure shades softly into a green shadow.
As sheepish is her light, wet and peach-red sector,
Her soft, tender powders will be sliding for you.

其二

嫩风嫩玉嫩寒烟，香冷香情向月弯。
秋水相逢生媚眼，多亏此处是黑天。

Two

Breezes in the chilly mist are tender
And passions in the sweet cool are crescent.
Soft glances cross their path like autumn water,
And thanks to this place which is darkly acquiescent.

咏　梅
The Ode to the Plum Blossoms

其一

临河几树干枝雪，忍尽寒流阵阵冰。
瘦骨千磨还坚韧，香魂半缕为君明。

One

Snow trunks by the river
Have standed cold，icy waves.
Scraggy and scrawny，they're firmer,
And sweeter with half the soul clearer.

其二

看似争春片片鲜，淫风国里百花残。
柔情铁骨怀天下，大地谁来伴我寒。

Two

Each petal for spring seems to be fresh
In the lost state of all flowers.
For a world by the tender muscles of steel,
Who'd on the earth be cold another of mine?

忧　患

忧患人生复几何？金银床上也蹉跎。
青囊[①]在握须回首，客鬓[②]难明雪又多。

【注释】

①青囊：风水术的俗称。本来青囊是黑袋子，因为风水师常以之装

书，故民间以青囊代称风水术。②客鬓：旅人的鬓发。

Tribulation

How long can the life of grief be measured?
The bed of gold and silver will slip away.
The black satchel in hand should also look back,
Because the temples hardy illumine more snows.

宇　航

客心隔雨驾星回，川谷[①]激石若震雷。
银汉[②]瞬间八万里，金星送你一枝梅。

【注释】

①川谷：河流。②银汉：银河。

Space Navigation

Thru the starfall, the heart of sojourn drives back
With one wintersweet gifted by Venus, back
To the rumbling streams and torrents upon the stones
And in a split second the galaxy has gone 80000 miles,

欲　望

秦皇岛外打渔船，浪语飞花半透寒。

瘦水难填虎狼欲，捞空四海也坦然。

【自解】

每天，窗外望去，大大小小的船只在海上捕捞，使用的绝户网连厘米大小的虾子都不放过。由此，联想到了兴凯湖，总面积为4556 km^2，其中大湖为4380 km^2（我国境内为1220 km^2）。北部的中国水域水质浑浊，南部的俄罗斯水域水质清澈。中国水域的大白鱼因常年捕捞，大多跑到俄罗斯水域生息去了。由此，我开始理解起鱼心来了，便直接引用毛主席《浪淘沙·北戴河》原词平起。

Desires

The fishing boats off Qinhuangdao are yon
Snapped and half cold by the flying billows
Whose thin water can't feed the wolfish desires,
Still calm even though the seas are emptied.

元　旦
New Year's Day

其一

楼头红日戴河明，满眼寒风大野行。
几岁幽栖[①]无定处，流澌[②]地远卧钟声。

【注释】

①幽栖：隐居。②流澌（sī）：流水。

One

The red sun brightens my tower on the Daihe River,
Full of the wintry blast that lashes the open country
Upon the secluded years in my nomadic life
That flows into the hissing peals in sleep afar.

其二

门闲鹤语凉飙醉，清啸[1]留连散晓霜。
壮气纵横分海气，水仙好客数春光。

【注释】

①清啸：清越悠长的啸鸣或鸣叫。

Two

The crane whoops drunk in the cold, free door
Linger around the morning frosts that clearly howl
With its free, stout pride splitting up the breath of the sea
That opens the narcissus door to the spring.

其三

野饭前年步栈桥，荒堤不老柳丝摇。
悠扬沧海澄浅岸，更待春来妒暗娇。

Three

The picnic on the shore bridge the year before last
Was willowy beyond the barren, never-aging dyke.
When the melodious sea broke on the shore,
The coming of spring awaited the secret, tender envy.

其四

度岁风惊霜霰[①]苦，穷冬作赋玉壶冰。
忽如灵运召青帝[②]，万境流光贺水星[③]。

【注释】

①度岁：过年。此处指元旦。霜霰（xiàn）：霜和霰。又比喻恶势力。②灵运：天命；时运。青帝：春之神及百花之神。③水星：喻指太阳。

Four

The wind shocks in the sneaping frost on the bitter day
Of the deeper winter that composes an icy jar of jade.

When the fortune begins to summon Green Dragon,
Mercury shall stream down its scene of the star-studded lights.

月

月镜闲来偷古梦，幽幽摄取半分魂。
平生铁骨擎天地，只有孤蟾[①]解我心。

【注释】

①孤蟾：孤独的月亮。

The Moon

An idle moon mirror mooches the old dream
That takes in half a soul faintly agleam.
Lifelong, the steel tendons prop up the world,
That doesn't know my heart but the lonely toad.

在一起

静谷白额[①]莫令狐，衙门内外尽奚奴[②]。
清堂上下无排戟，举世风流枉作愚。

【注释】

①白额：以老虎额头喻指老虎。②奚奴：奴仆。

Together

Needlessly, the white tiger orders its fox in the quiet vale,
In and out of the offices are pervaded the lackeys.
Without rows of halberts in the clear halls, upper or lower,
All the graceful affairs will play dumb, of no avail.

再分配

经年名利牵南北，浮世荣华觅稻粱①。
羽客官鸡②啼弱柳，劳生③逆命为盈仓。

【注释】

①稻粱：稻和粱，谷物的总称。②羽客：指道士。官鸡：官家所养的斗鸡。③劳生：辛苦劳累的生活。

Redistribution

Perennially, the fame and gain hauls the north and south,
Whose fickle honour and riches are sought in the grains.
At the cock crows to the feeble willows,
The laborious life contravenes the mandate for a full granary.

征　服

长思未敢横银盏，愚智独征冷眼低。
旅梦柔服[①]穿晓月，胡沙斗酒射鸣蹄。

【注释】

①柔服：温柔顺服。

Conquest

The long thought dares not to cross the silver cup,
And the stupid wit conquers with cold eyes, lone and lower.
As the obedient dream on the trip threads the moon at dawn,
The strong-headed barbarian sand will shoot the neighing hooves.

正能量

天刀在手闯重关，国步何须论险艰[①]。
紫梦青阳行大道，中国不去拜东山。

【注释】

①国步：国家的命运，亦指国土。险艰：险阻艰难。

The Positive Energy

In hand, the sacred sword clears the hurdles,
Against the national steps irrespective of the perils.
The purple dream on the great way full of broad daylight
Should not make a Chinese pilgrimage to the eastern hill.

治　理

散吏①垂帘半梦愁，不及黠吏醉沉忧②。
俦伦反照灵均赋③，治乱悲吟月下秋。

【注释】

①散吏：闲散的官吏。指有官阶而无职事的官员。②黠（xiá）吏：奸猾之吏。沉忧：深忧。③俦伦：或同列的人；可与相比并者。灵均：楚国屈原的字。泛指词章之士。

Governance

The sinecure behind the dossal was half doleful in dream,
Falling far short of the crafty officials drunken in sorrow.
When the peers flashed back the verses of Qu Yuan,
The anarchy chanted its stirring strains below the autumn moon.

智　善

智心大小论荣枯，善道方圆对有无。
智善空薄[①]积宿愿，脱身利禄是归途。

【注释】

①空薄：空疏浅薄。

The Perfect Wisdom

Big or small, the wise heart discusses the extremes of fortune,
Round or square, the good path faces those of being or non-being.
Empty or shallow, the perfect wisdom cherishes long,
And to get out of the fame and gain should be the way back.

自　明

夜静烛红翡翠钩，梁尘[①]未染本无愁。
玉堂难懂卿家事，旷野无人枉自囚。

【注释】

①梁尘：嘹亮动听的歌声。此处双关。

Self-knowledge

The red candle hooks its emerald curtain in the still nights,
Down the dustless roof beam free of sorrowful sighs.
If the hall of jade hardly knows your weighty matter,
The unmanned, open field would be a prison, for sure.

自　强

古来弱者何其弱，弱在长期少自强。
逐鹿百年身未死，青天为尔露斜阳。

Self-reliance

From of old, the weakling has been weakened
By the chronical, deficient improvement of his own.
To vie for power but still alive for a century,
The blue sky shall smile its setting sun for you.

自　戕

一池天镜[①]两重天，雨雪阴晴各一边。
壮士不曾折沙场，敌人知道也生怜。

【注释】

①天镜：喻指长白山天池。

Self-destruction

One lake, two skies,
Cloudy or sunny, each on one side.
Heroic, but dead not on battlefield,
A conscious enemy would melt with pity.

最高处
The Tiptop

其一

昔年横目淬[①]钢刀，斩断长鲸化怒涛。
倒灌钱塘吞闽越，酿来春梦续离骚。

【注释】

①淬（cuì）：把烧红了的铸件往水、油或其他液体里一浸立刻取出来，用以提高合金的硬度和强度。

One

Out-frown, the steel sword was ever quenched
To cut the long whale into the angry waves
That flowed up to Qiantang and engulfed Minyue,

Brewing the spring dream to continue *The Lament*.

其二

圣人淳化[1]无成败，轻策[2]绝崖路也通。
朔野迷花遮柳眼[3]，难欺浩渺一飞鸿。

【注释】

①淳（chún）化：朴实。②轻策：喻指策马。③朔野：北方荒野之地。柳眼：早春初生的柳叶如人睡眼初展，因以为称。此处也做双关。

Two

Pure and simple, the sage has no success or failure,
That still runs his road on the spured, broken cliff.
Obscured by the north, promiscuous country, the drowsy eyes
Could hardly conceal that swan goose in the vast sky.

其三

君子临江坦腹[1]眠，路穷绝不上贼船。
俗流[2]得志骑金马，豺虎谋皮[3]剩几天？

【注释】

①坦腹：舒身仰卧；坦露胸腹。②俗流：流行的习俗。③豺虎谋皮：化典“与虎谋皮”，也就是同豺狼和老虎商量，要剥下它的皮。比喻跟所谋求的对象有利害冲突，决不能成功。

Three

Belly-bared, the man of virtue sleeps by the river,
To the end of the line, he will never board the prate boat.
The worldling can be greasily radiant on his gold horse, but
How long to go to have asked the jackal or the tiger for its hides?

做　人
How to Behave

其一

掠地边风百丈高，星弛颠浪裹秋毫。
微言[1]无力追天步，万里能识雪风毛。

【注释】

①微言：精深微妙的言辞。

One

A thousand feet higher, the passing wind dives and sacks the ground,
Though reeled in the billows, the star runs to swathe the fine down of birds.
When a sublime word is so delicate to chase the heavenly step,

It could still pick out the hair of the snow phoenix ten thousand miles away.

其二

进退胡为随众生？忠奸不要辨清浊。
圣贤大句应沉默，饮者之言付朽壳。

Two

Come and go, why to follow other flesh?
Loyal and evil, never discern the bass and treble notes.
Not to be a swanker, the wise man saves his breath,
Unlike the drinker's words out of the decayed body.

七言律诗

Seven-character Qctave

七言律诗平仄格式

注：⊙表示可平可仄

1. 仄起首句押韵

⊙仄平平⊙仄平（韵），⊙平⊙仄仄平平（韵）。
⊙平⊙仄⊙平仄，⊙仄平平⊙仄平（韵）。
⊙仄⊙平⊙仄仄，⊙平⊙仄仄平平（韵）。
⊙平⊙仄⊙平仄，⊙仄平平⊙仄平（韵）。

2. 仄起首句不押韵

⊙仄⊙平⊙仄仄，⊙平⊙仄仄平平（韵）。
⊙平⊙仄⊙平仄，⊙仄平平⊙仄平（韵）。
⊙仄⊙平⊙仄仄，⊙平⊙仄仄平平（韵）。
⊙平⊙仄⊙平仄，⊙仄平平⊙仄平（韵）。

3. 平起首句押韵

⊙平⊙仄仄平平（韵），⊙仄平平⊙仄平（韵）。
⊙仄⊙平⊙仄仄，⊙平⊙仄仄平平（韵）。
⊙平⊙仄⊙平仄，⊙仄平平⊙仄平（韵）。
⊙仄⊙平⊙仄仄，⊙平⊙仄仄平平（韵）。

4. 平起首句不押韵

⊙平⊙仄⊙平仄，⊙仄平平⊙仄平（韵）。
⊙仄⊙平⊙仄仄，⊙平⊙仄仄平平（韵）。
⊙平⊙仄⊙平仄，⊙仄平平⊙仄平（韵）。
⊙仄⊙平⊙仄仄，⊙平⊙仄仄平平（韵）。

安静做个美男子①

欲都粱肉②挑肥瘦，劈腿③嚼来不露牙。
艳遇好生无检束，偷情忍死快搔爬④。
奸情易为奇缘破，谗语难得慧眼查。
休道侬家掩睡脸，直男癌⑤市众人斜。

【注释】

①安静做个美男子：《万万没想到》第2季第1集中，“叫兽易小星”扮演的唐僧挂在嘴边的口头禅——“我想我还是安静地当一个美男子算了，不需要折腾和自讨苦吃”。除这个网络恶搞以外，也作为直男癌中高度患者及自恋人格的识别标签。②粱肉：粮肉。泛指美食。③劈腿：形容一个人感情出轨、脚踏两条船甚至多条船的代名词。④“艳遇”两句：化自白居易“春日闲居三首”之“饱竟快搔爬，筋骸无检束”。⑤直男癌：2014年6月出现的词汇，表示时时流露出对同性恋的苛责、打压以及种种的不顺眼，略带大男子主义的特征。

Be a Goodly Person at Peace

The orectic capital chooses its delicacies,
And chews without showing its teeth as a two-timer.
The casual sexual encounter tends to be debauched,
And the coquet exerts himself to be quickly clandestine.
The adultery may be prone to the strange, broken story,
And the calumny could escape the sharp eyes.
Let me block my sleeping face quickly as possible
From all those straight cancers tilted bakc in reverie.

傲　娇[①]

蛮横清虚斜嗲[②]眸，一颗星睨[③]闪娇羞。
娇蛮纵性垂云暮，妩媚忧烦钓月钩。
外冷恶娇翻逸致，内温善腻乱神幽。
红颜无忌蹭得累，铁汉销蚀君莫愁。

【注释】

①傲娇："平常说话带刺、态度强硬高傲，但在一定的条件下害臊地黏腻在身边"的人物与性格，主要是用来形容恋爱形态的词汇。②嗲（diǎ）：形容撒娇的声音或态度。③睨（nì）：斜着眼睛看。

Tsundere

To leer rudely, clearly and cutesily,
The star steals furtive glances in her virgin modesty.
Like a cloud hanging late, lovely but wilfully,
Her vexed charms are fishing for the crescent.
Viciously spoiled, the gruff leisure rootles her fancy,
Warmly inside, her secluded spirit stirs, clingy and needy.
To the babbles out of her rosy lips that linger wearily,
Even the man of iron will will be eroded, careless but quiescent.

白　奴[①]

小奴大扇扫燕山，翦碎蛮奴[②]紫塞间。
奴迹奇节深谷月，空名奴虏浅水湾。

奴声巧佞[③]对沧浪，婢态奴颜遗汗斑。
五岳垂藤还可越，白奴一世杳难攀。

【注释】

①白奴："白领奴隶"的简称。"奴隶主"可能是房子、汽车、奢侈品，也可能是人情世故、理想抱负。他们拥有自己的办公桌、电脑，靠为雇主服务赚取报酬。②蛮奴：奴婢。③巧佞（nìng）：机巧奸诈，阿谀奉承。

White-collar Slaves

The big fan of the small slave sweeps the Yanshan Mountain,
Cutting up the bondmaids in the Great Wall.
To entrust the queer honour to the moon in the clough,
The null name has been captured into the clear water
Whose surging waves are facing the craven toadies,
Which bow low and sweep the ground with the sweat stains.
The drooping vines on the Holy Mountains can be scaled,
Insurmountable to the white-collar slave all his life.

包公鱼

六线黑鲈行大水，塔西提[①]岛是家乡。
恣狂[②]奔北开新场，衔勇[③]司南守旧疆。
薄口钢牙方猝死，厚毒铁腺又频伤。
肉食国里不食肉，老虎皈依变作羊。

【注释】

①塔西提：印度洋塔西提岛。②恣狂：恣肆轻狂。③衔勇：怀着勇

气。

Golden Stripe Soapfish

The six-lined sea basses in the high water
Are swimming around the native Tahiti,
Reinless north to open up the new field,
And courageous south to observe the old border.
Thin-mouthed, a sudden death by the steel teeth,
Of the potent poison, the frequent harms by the iron gland
In the predacious state, they are not flesheating,
Like the tigers converted into the sheep.

北戴河

瑶池玉臂淡梳妆，明镜丝滑落北疆。
化作燕山凝翠黛，变成戴水聚清香。
天涯采药披十色，海内求仙带五光。
万古蓬莱今尚在，追随秦帝拜朝阳。

Beidaihe

Her charming arms lightly made up in Jade Pool
Fell down to the north velvety as a bright mirror
Transformed into the Yanshan Mountains like the brows of a beauty,
And then into the Daihe River tinged with gusts of fragrance
That, gay with ten colours, drifted out to gather the herbs afar,
Or, dazzled by five colours, prayed to Gods for blessing on the coun-

try.
The Fairy Land of Penglai has been still alive there,
Strung along with the first emperor of China to visit the rising sun.

不 造①

灵怪容华②柳色新，啼乌咫尺问行人。
千般豆蔻化清影，百曲丁香泻半轮。
两岸风花调睡眼，一滩雨叶戏香唇。
聚光灯下演春梦，不造枯鳞③又妊娠。

【注释】

①不造：连读或快速输入的合成音，意思是“不知道”。②灵怪：灵巧奇怪。容华：美丽的容颜。③枯鳞：枯鱼，也喻处于困境者。

I Don't Know

The bizarre beauty in the new, green willow
Caws to the foot passenger close at hand.
Thousands of round cardamons are melted into clear shadows,
And hundreds of metrical clovens are poured down half the Wheel.
While the flowers on the banks flirt with the sleepy eyes,
The rainy leaves on the strand trifle with the sweet lips.
In the spotlight, the spring dream has just started,
God knows that the withered fish should have been conceived.

财　富

铜雀窥金出紫塞，朱轮宝镜欲乘流。
金鸡玉漏女儿怨，丹凤银河公子游。
催夜金壶多契阔[1]，拂寒罗袖叹绸缪。
金波视野有宽窄，还看心胸放与收。

【注释】

①契阔：辛苦。

Wealth

The bronze crane peeps over the gold out of the Great Wall
On the red wheel like a rare mirror that hopes to flow
The water-clock of the golden pheasant thru the daughter’s grumbles
And the red phoenix on the Milky Way for the wandering son.
To hasten the night, the gold pitcher travails hard,
To whisk the cold, the silken sleeve sighs sentimentally.
In the visual field, the golden waves are broad or narrow,
Which is based on the heart that casts and reels.

沉住气

锐气藏胸不作声，面浮和气转阴晴。
心机壮气失欢洽，胆气狂言丧太平。
杀气哀声何处止，妖星怨气几时宁。
人怀才气莫失志，义气修身不可轻。

Keep Calm

The spirit in bosom saves its breath,
With the soft air that's cloudy or sunny.
As the schemed vigour loses its joyous harmony,
The courageous ravings will be denied of the peace.
Where to halt the mourning aura of death,
And when the grouching magic star will be composed?
A literary talent will not miss his morale, whose sense
Of honor in the cultivation should not be understimated.

承包鱼塘体[①]

霸气横行天不灵，河伯求退躲清宁[②]。
尽由网事多穷饿[③]，谁管芳尘不蔽形[④]。
凶暴拔根吃利刃，发飙枭首掴雷霆。
大爷天下敢开口，割掉舌头穿铁钉。

【注释】

①承包鱼塘体：流行于网络的一种霸道宣示主权式的恶搞话语，基本句式为“我要让全世界知道，这……被你承包了”。②河伯：神话中的黄河水神。清宁：清明宁静。③穷饿：贫穷饥饿。④蔽形：遮蔽身体。

The Genre of Fish Pond Contract

The sky shuts to the swashbuckling rampage,

And the river god retires into the state of repose.
The fishing nets are mostly hungry and broke,
But who cares the sweet dust in unhuman rags?
When the uprooted thug eats the sharp blade,
The owl head that freaks out slaps its thunderclap.
If anybody under my heaven dares to open his mouth,
Cut his tongue out and spike it.

出　色
Prostitution

其一

岭南玉骨洗金风①，夜夜雄鸡叫玉郎②。
屐履③寻蝶折嫩柳，浓妆宿梦醉娇娘。
莫愁流水声声短，喜看芳云阵阵长。
秋水摇枝为使君，芙蓉国里四时香。

【注释】

①金风：秋风。《文选·张协》："金风扇素节，丹霞启阴期。"此处借指卖淫。②玉郎：本意是女子对丈夫或情人的爱称，泛指男子。③屐履（jī lǚ）：着履作游屐（登临）。宋代曾巩《游金山寺作》诗："屐履上层阁，披襟当九秋。"

One

The delicate skins of the Five Ridges bathed in cool breezes
Vocalize their cocks night after night,
On their toe for tender willows like butterflies,
Soft as the maidens dressed seductively in dreams
Whose light-hearted ripples are so short though
Yet whose virtuous clouds are so long still
For her men with the limpid eyes
That rock her roses of sharon in all the seasons.

其二

冰雪娇娆[①]羞半蕊，璇闺偎傍意绸缪[②]。
萧郎月意登秦馆[③]，乱鬓风情坐楚楼[④]。
花萼引蝶花萼颤，野云招雨野云游。
赤橙黄绿青蓝紫，花好根烂几日留？

【注释】

①娇娆：柔美妩媚。②璇闺：闺房的美称。偎傍：紧靠着门，指妓女临街拉客。绸缪（chóu móu）：缠绵；情意殷勤貌。③萧郎：女子所爱恋的男子，此处指嫖客。秦馆：秦地馆舍，泛指旅舍。此处指性服务场所。④楚楼：青楼，妓院。

Two

Half pistils are coquettish before an avalanche
Are cuddled at the boudoir that's sentimentally attached
To the beaux who are mooned to the brothel
Where her flirtatious lock of hairs are bubbly
And messy like a calyx quivered by the butterfly
Or a wild cloud that wanders for the rain.
With all the colours of the rainbow,
Can a rotten root sustain its fine flowers?

穿　越

天马狂流嘶汉月，蹄风眨眼两千年。
不闻韩信忠良地，但见萧何佞幸[①]田。
过往人生鹦鹉梦，轮回天地鹧鸪眠。
白猿坐断子卿[②]路，回放持节北海干。

【注释】

①佞（nìng）幸：以谄媚而得到宠幸或以谄媚得到君主宠幸。②子卿：苏武的字。

Pass Through

In mad flows, the pegasus neighed to the moon,
And hooved on the wind that had winkled past bimillennia.
He heard not of the good and faithful land of Han Xin,

But saw the sycophant field of Xiao He.
The passing and coming life was like the dream of parrots,
And the world of reincarnation like the slumber of partridges.
Since the white ape was steeled in your way,
Now replay Su Wu's allegiance on the dry Baikal.

纯 洁

纯阳流火万条露，纯月流光花满枝。
纯水天浊能至鉴①，纯山环素②且无私。
纯心媚灶③应从矩，纯意薄俗不犯规。
世界本来一片水，都因污淖④落清池。

【注释】

①天浊：混沌初开的时候，上清下浊，沉降成为大地的为天浊。至鉴：极高的观察、鉴别能力。②环素：喻冰雪。③媚灶：比喻阿附权贵。④污淖（nào）：泥淖。

Chastity

The pure sun flows myriad dews below the bolide,
The pure moon flows her light onto the full petals;
The pure water can be perceptive of the turbidity,
The pure hill is so clean as the selfless snow;
The pure heart that fawns should follow the rules,
The pure mind in the treacherous custom shouldn't get out of line.
The world began with a clear body of water,
Which was roiled by the foul mire.

大与小

戴水横行天地广，泛舟渤海几只虾。
珊瑚探尾去狼鳗[1]，玳瑁崩涛来虎鲨。
屋里黄粱煮紫梦，院外黑土纳白鸦。
问君世界有多大，且看心藏百万家。

【注释】

①狼鳗：一种深海肉食性怪鱼。

Big and Small

On a rampage, the Daihe River under the wide sky
Drifts out into the Bohai Sea with some shrimps, where
The tails may spy thru its corals that a wolf eel is leaving,
And the turtle shells are billowed below a coming tiger shark.
Within, the day might be cooking its purple dream,
Without, the black soil taking the white ravens.
Tell me how big the world is,
The world is but your heart of a million houses.

道　路

驿路穿云过蒲阪[1]，横生绝路在崖边。
暮栖细路鸟巢挂，朝走残僧狭路牵。
甲第绝群陌路瘦，朱门迷路月秋鲜。
人生岐路万千客，天路盘空驶客船。

【注释】

①蒲阪：舜帝时代，中条山北洪水过后，河滩之处生长着大量蒲草、芦草等众多水生植物，所以古虞之地又被称为蒲阪。

Road

The post road winds through the cattail shoal,
The end road grows wild to the cliff;
The pathway hangs a bird's nest at dusk,
The catwalk leads the deformed monk in the morn;
The strange road becomes tight to the fantastic mansion,
The lost road to the red door smells fresh in the autumn moon:
On the crossroads of life there are thousands of passengers
That get on board towards the road to heaven.

倒　逼[①]

狂沙滚雪晚风逼，饥冻惊逼四野黑。
游念逼人谁谩语[②]，逼心迫物莫能识。
四隅[③]逼命出劫难，逼仄[④]侵庭去做贼。
自古都说性本善，倒逼泥淖[⑤]丧其德。

【注释】

①倒逼：一种被动行为，是“迫使”“反推”等词的升级版，该词强化了反常规、逆向促动之义。②谩语：说谎话。③四隅（yú）：四角；四周。④逼仄：狭窄。⑤泥淖（nào）：泥泞的洼地；不能自拔的窘困境地。

Retroaction

In the gusting sand that rolls the snow, the evening air forces
The cold hunger that startles its pressure on the total darkness.
As the roaming idea threatens a bald lie,
The poor-spirited heart could be unidentified.
As the four unreasonable corners come out of the adversities,
The cramped court could compel assent to being guilty.
All have declared that man is good in nature, from of old,
But its moral integrities are lost in the forced quag-mire.

点　赞

咏心论道远鸡豚，汉月胡风断旅魂。
官觅斜桥驰万乘，客寻野鸟越千门。
吟来皓魄新宾散，裁走清光旧府存。
来去焉知轻辇路，走出都市隐江村。

Thumbs-up

The rhapsodic heart on the Way standed off the fowls and pigs,
Whose souls of travel expired in the north wind below the moon,
When the officials sought ten thousand chariots thru the oblique bridge,
And the travellers looked for their wild birds over a thousand doors.
Under the coming moon that chanted, the new guests dispersed,
And in the gentle, tailored light, the old houses standed there.
To be or not, how do we know the way of the light carriage?

Better get out of your town and hide into the riverside village.

屌　丝

山穷水瘦鞭疲马，悲雪联翩嘶晓风。
旧燕迷离随叶落，矮墙慷慨对枝空。
神呆揽涕心无主，目滞凝情路不通。
翘首来生拍粉翅，肥蹄无奈羡征鸿。

Self-hater Loser

Flog the horse along, to the end of the rope,
And neigh to the doleful snow, free in the fancies of the dawn-breeze.
While the old swallow whirls and falls like a leaf,
The dwarf wall will be bounteous to the empty branches;
While the numb, tearful soul has vanquished all its powers,
The dead eye within the stiff emotion won't be free for an advance.
By birth, the raised head has been fluttering its wings,
But unfortunately, the wild geese should be the prize of its fat hooves.

东风破

少小蹉跎多少泪，寸心零落寄东风。
杨惊分袂[①]绿溪上，柳误披风粉镜中。
华馆相思长路在，荒楼润气满堂空。
辽天唱作霓裳[②]调，细雨幽燕一客鸿。

【注释】

①分袂：指离别；分手。②霓裳：《霓裳羽衣曲》的略称。

Gone In the East Wind

Countless tears wasted when young
Withered and died in the heart of the east wind.
Farewell! The poplars startled along the green stream, and
By the angry gale, the willows were lost in the mirror of the rouge.
To the luxurious hall, the long pangs of love were still there,
To the barren storeys, its moistened vigour was thronged, no more.
When the broad sky grooved on the tune of the Rainbow Skirt,
One swan soared up the soft, serene drizzle in the north seashore.

逗　比[1]

憨痴灵窍空积翠，娇态明阳人莫知。
童面须眉多醉怨，老容罗带少闲嗤。
滞呆黄狗吠霜月，流宕[2]白鹅卧水皮。
一粒灰尘不乱眼，何如逗比自先亏。

【注释】

①逗比：比较逗、略显傻缺的样子。②流宕（dàng）：不受拘束。

Dobe

In the dull wit that stacks the green in vain,

Who knows the coquetry under the bright sun?
The rosy cheeks of the beard are boozy mostly in bitter words,
The wrinkled faces of the silken girdle chuckle less sneeringly.
While the fishy, yellow dog barks at the frosted moon,
The free, white goose is sitting on the water.
If one grain of dust were not to blind the eye,
It would be far better to be a dobe to tease oneself.

断

清净思茶野水甜，色花行酒若衔钳。
是非之嘴可曾闭，方便之门何必严。
有道之人明抱瓮[①]，无情之辈暗磨镰。
人间百态是沙场，寡断终究落爪尖。

【注释】

①抱瓮（wèng）：安于拙陋淳朴的生活。

Break

Sweet like the wild water, the pure thought in the tea
Was clinched by the temptations of vice and luxury.
Whether the right-and-wrong mouth has hold its tongue?
And why the need for the door so tight all along?
A sensible person leads his simple life,
While a ruthless man secretly sharpens his knife.
The world under hundreds of shapes is but a battleground,
Where the weak knees will be seized by a claw to be found.

躲猫猫[1]

同监狱友躲猫猫，天井天光戏楚腰[2]。
飞袂犬蹄才脸破，驰颜鹰爪已肠焦。
瘦拳断铁怨无尽，肥腿折钢气未消。
墙壁早识颅脑意，行尸不会赴冥潮。

【注释】

①躲猫猫：2009年2月，云南省晋宁县警方称，一名因盗伐森林被拘押的男子，和同监室的狱友在天井里玩“躲猫猫”游戏时，遭到狱友踢打并不小心撞到墙壁，导致“重度颅脑损伤”，送医四天后不治身亡。②楚腰：女子的细腰，喻指玩细腰女童游戏。

Hide-and-seek

Playing a diabolical game at bo-peep, the prison mates'
Slender waists dallied about in the sunny courtyard where
The sleeve of the dog feet slapped and scratched the face,
Like the swift eagle-claw that would scathe the bowels.
Beneath an infinite regret, the tight fist broke the iron,
Not to be mollified, the fat leg snapped the steel.
Had the wall been awake to the fact of the brains,
The walking corpse would not have gone to the underworld.

峨眉山

竹径开合行绿烟，青霄凝黛暗明鲜。

江花斜照潇湘地，河影微醺巴蜀天。
楼曲空湾暮雨送，酒旗断岸晓云牵。
峨眉新月浣沧海，大壑佛光照我眠。

Mount Omei

The bamboo path opens or shuts its azure mists,
That fix the dark or bright brows below the fresh, blue sky.
While the riverside flowers obliquely beam down upon Xiaoxiang,
Its shadow seems to be squiffed under the sky of Sichuan.
In the late rain delivering the music floor by the empty bay,
The wineshop flag on the broken shore holds the morn clouds.
As the new moon over Mount Omei has been bathed in the sea,
The glory of Buddha shines my slumber in the bowels of the earth.

二十四情
Twenty-four Feelings

其一

一死一生孤客行，一悲一喜任流声。
伯钟依韵音符重①，管鲍分金②利禄轻。
暗道旋空还素守，明德常在两无争。
交情最在难割舍，千古人生一月明。

【注释】

①“伯钟”句：相传伯牙善弹琴，钟子期善听琴。伯牙弹到志在高山的曲调时，钟子期就说“峨峨兮若泰山”；弹到志在流水的曲调时，钟子期又说“洋洋兮若江河”。钟子期死后，伯牙不再弹琴，因为没有人能像钟子期那样懂得自己的音志。后遂以“知音”比喻对自己非常了解的人；知己朋友。②管鲍分金：管，管仲；鲍，鲍叔牙，战国时齐国的名相；金，钱财。比喻情谊深厚，相知相悉。

One

To be or not，we walk alone，
Sad or happy，let it flow in its tone.
To a soul mate，the metrical impulse falls on the beat，
Overpowered by love，fame and fortune are but a footy seat.
Though the dark way whirls there，we still hold our ground，
For the bright virtue stands there，why to scramble beyond?
Where the fellowship is most deeply ingrained，
One moon in life will be bright through all age.

其二

何事低眉斜敛手，青丝梦雪是凡流[1]。
相逢雀跃安能问，知遇联翩且不求。
思虑云藏仍未整，魂神雨到两无由。
感情微妙难开口，话到唇边心欲羞。

【注释】

①凡流：平凡之人；庸俗之辈。

Two

Why lower her eyebrows and bound up your hands,
And dream in dark-haired snow like other creatures?
Why ask her to caper while faced with each other
But not in quest of the patrons in close succession?
As the deliberate clouds hidden there are unsorted,
The rain lost in reverie would be unjustified.
Since the subtle sentiments are lost for words,
Such words on the tip of the tongue feel shy at heart.

其三

离风一叶若枯蓬，曲线牵愁落水中。
宿浪狂游谁肯问，残潮万朵又闲冲。
梦魂送我天涯断，明月迎侬何处通？
半世孤独寄明月，少年明月化飞鸿。

Three

One leaf was gone like a withered thistle,
Gone as a curve to the woeful water,
Rolling in night billows, but who would care?
Cared and buffeted by the free sprays of the last tides.
Let the dreaming soul see me to the broken horizon,
But where the bright moon is going for me?
Half a lifetime, my solitude goes to the bright moon,

Whose youth has turned into the swan goose.

其四

白鸦翻影踏霜暮，旷野萧萧无雅音。
把臂花间寻宝地，牵衣风外转空林。
素怀①独自看鸾镜，幽兴②谁来听玉琴。
满目高楼皆闭锁，真情世上最难寻。

【注释】

①素怀：平素的希望。②幽兴：幽雅的兴味。

Four

The white raven flapped into the late frost
Of the moor that rustled without a refined tone
Through the flowers in search of the treasure land,
That tugged his coat out of the wind into the empty wood.
Of a plain heart, the loner looked into the mirror,
Of a serene zest, who would come to his lyre?
Here and there, all the towers are closed down, for
The true feelings in the world are mostly inaccessible.

其五

今日游春正少年，明天白首雪弥天。
新人乘月如桃艳，老妪折风难碧鲜①。
薄宦成名欢渌水②，微臣失意累青烟。

五车宣纸犹能尽，万种心情不可传。

【注释】

①老妪（yù）：老年妇女。碧鲜：青翠鲜润的颜色。②渌（lù）水：清澈的水。

Five

Today's spring stroll reaches the age of boyhood,
But the snow will fill the whitehaired tomorrow.
The newly-wed in the moon beamed like a peach flower,
But the old woman torn in the wind is hard to be young again.
The minor official who rose to fame was lively like clear water,
But plays to hard luck overwrought to be a sudden puff of smoke.
Even five carts of rice paper could be overwritten,
But ten thousands of moods can't be conveyed.

其六

日有落时月看补，扶轮[①]明暗各开关。
世途迎客播迁[②]满，仙驾隔烟次第弯。
何事相违[③]垂枕上，所求展转落人间。
金银债务尚能破，委曲[④]人情不好还。

【注释】

①扶轮：扶翼车轮，引申为怀恩报效。②播迁：迁徙；流离。③相违：彼此违背。④委曲：殷勤周至。

Six

After the sun goes down, the moon will warm the bench
On the wheel that shuts or closes to the light and the shade.
The way of the world receives the fugitives to the full,
And the fairy chariots beyond the smoke have to wind one by one.
What has gone athwart and hangs unto the pillow?
What's sought wearily and watchfully has fallen into the world.
Even the debt of gold and silver can be repaid,
But the complaisant human feelings can't be repaid.

其七

蛾眉凝笑脸啼春，世网随形且隐身。
独抱冰霜心里恨，每弹蜜饯嘴边亲。
徘徊幽水慢开镜，索寞①青山别写真。
脑内风云顷刻变，表情无法去因循②。

【注释】

①索寞：荒凉萧索貌。②因循：顺应自然；沿袭。

Seven

Her arched brows in smiles are beaming the spring,
Whose webs of the world are freely cloaked.
To hug the rime alone, with the bad blood in the heart,
How prodigal the soul should lend the sweet tongue!

To prowl along the serene stream, with the mirror opened slowly,
But don't mirror the green hills so bleak and chilly.
When the wind within the brain changes in a moment,
The expressions on the face are unable to be followed.

其八

韬藏①十栽磨神韵，一夜出山百兽惊。
律吕②风骚犹并响，黄钟③烟月更同声。
日边天马本无事，海上飞龙故不争。
龙马云车翻五岳，金乌驰电浴激情。

【注释】

①韬藏：隐藏；包藏。②律吕：古代汉族乐律的统称，可分为阳律和阴律。是有一定音高标准和相应名称的中国音律体系。③黄钟：我国古代音韵十二律中六种阳律的第一律。本意是中国古代打击乐器和容器，黄帝发明。

Eight

Having concealed for a decade and whetted the verve,
He came out of retirement one night that startled all the animals.
In the temperament of music still ringing glamorously,
The classical bells steeped in moonlight played symphonically.
When the heavenly horse was free at the side of the sun,
The winged dragon on the sea would not be vying.
When the dragon horse on the wings of cloud crossed the Five Mountains,
The sun swift like the lightning must be bathed in passions.

其九

信笔飞鸦翻墨汁，深眉难懂羽翔集。
沉浮杯底且为念，喜怒花间还自持。
有梦逢时人渐省，凝神应物镜迷执①。
动情双眼休察色，埋在深渊不可习。

【注释】

①应物：顺应事物。迷执：迷惑执着；执迷不悟。

Nine

To scribble and doodle with the ink,
The deep brows are indecipherable to the volume on feather.
To hanker after the cup bottom, up or down,
The moody nature keeps it's desires under the petals.
To meet the dream that comes to realize the truth gradually,
The response to what's in the mirror should be attentively bigoted.
To watch the emotional eye, but never more,
What's buried in the yawning abyss can't be studied.

其十

小妇明折半卷纸，纵横志业坐屠苏①。
同僚粉署②谈高矮，异事云衢③论细粗。
朝暮阳台霞易照，往来风柳镜难梳。
参差雨雪行年齿④，日久生情结暗珠⑤。

【注释】

①志业：专心其职业。志，通“识”。屠苏：房屋；草庵。②粉署：办理公务的机关。③云衢：云中的道路，借指高位。④年齿：年纪；年龄。⑤暗珠：化自“暗结珠胎”，原为男女姻缘或两家通婚，多指使女性受孕。现指男女苟合之事或男女（多为未婚男女）因偷情而怀孕。

Ten

The little lady folded half a roll of paper clearly,
And worked in her own thatched hut freely.
In the branch office, her colleagues talked about the height,
In the cloud thoroughfare, the quirky news told the quality of work.
Day and night, the rosy cloud shone easily on the balcony,
Back and forth, the willows in the mirror were hard to comb.
To touch on all the notes, the age moved ahead thru the sleets,
In course of time, her emotion was pregnant out of wedlock.

其十一

千丝春雨杏花垂，幽户添娇可忘机①。
之子出轩本有路，咸秦②横锁却无期。
金屋攲枕③遥相望，巷陌鸣钟不可知。
自负万人难配命④，钟情一见即相思。

【注释】

①忘机：消除机巧之心。②咸秦：指秦都城咸阳。唐人多借指长安。③攲枕：斜靠着枕头。“攲”古通“倚”字。④配命：配合天命。

Eleven

The apricot petals drooped in the spring drizzles,
And the new lover in the secret door could be carefree.
Out of the door, she should have her own way,
But to the capital, the cross lock was left to the indefinite future.
In the golden bower, her pillow set its sights afar,
And down the streets and lanes, the tolls were unknowable.
In her self love, ten thousands of men couldn't deserve her,
But after captivated at first sight, she suffered the pangs of love.

其十二

一轮风月一江水，风月行潮泛小舟。
宛转蝴蝶翻梦苦，浮游雪瓣暗娇羞。
溪山轻语风弥切，洞壑闲眠月更幽。
尘世之情千百种，爱情最是到白头。

Twelve

One full moon on the river
Paddles the tides in the dream of splendour
Like a butterfly well-tuned bitterly
And a snow petal that floats her secret virgin modesty.
In the whispers of the rills and hills, the wind grows rougher,
In the free sleep, the moon down the valley looks quieter.
From among the passions of this life innumerably,

Our love should live in harmony till old and grey.

其十三

半世黑白风雨天，圆缺一任[1]两悲欢。
谋身有命眼何待，立政[2]无声心已干。
巨语挟豪惊世界，薄言恣意[3]落峰巅。
临终万事回头望，还是亲情在枕边。

【注释】

①一任：听凭。②立政：确立为政之道。③薄言：急急忙忙；浅薄的话。恣意：放纵；不加限制。

Thirteen

Black and white, in the stormy days for half a century,
The quirks of joy and grief have waxed and waned.
What the eyes were expecting in the predestined scheme?
The silent heart had run dry by the political control.
While the brave words shocked the world,
The shallow words fell off the peak arbitrarily.
On my deathbed, when I turned my head to all the past affairs,
I saw none but my family members beside my pillow.

其十四

鸿雁南飞乌雀[1]噪，铜壶[2]枕破有鸡鸣。
衔恩易水金刀在，任气[3]秋霜侠客行。

栈道齐云残月暗，乡关④摇雨落花明。
死灰方寸可腾焰，融雪消冰靠热情。

【注释】

①乌雀：乌鸦。②铜壶：古代计时器。③任气：处事纵任意气，不加约束。④乡关：故乡。

Fourteen

The swan flied south in the clamorous dins of sparrows,
And the copper clepsydra was crowed by the broken pillows.
With the great, grateful backsword by the Yishui River,
The chivalrous courage went in the coldness of demeanor.
Following the plank road in the cloud down the dim, wasted moon,
My native land might be shaking its bright petals like a rain.
If the dying embers could glow into the raging blaze,
The ice and snow would be thawed ablaze.

其十五

江帆转岸海鸥来，急雨惊竿落钓台。
春浪衔魂明月映，绿梅夺魄野天开。
故乡驾梦刚归去，前路行云正可哀。
生死别离无贵贱，同情枕泪已凝腮。

Fifteen

One sea gull came behind the sail following the river

In the torrential rain startling the rod down to the fishing table.
As the bright moon shone the soul in the spring wave,
The green plum seized the spirit that bloomed to the wild sky.
Soon after I drove my dream back from the native land,
The rolling clouds ahead proved even more lamentable.
To part for ever mustn't make clear what was noble and what base,
The cheeks of tears were freezing on the pitiful pillow.

其十六

玉钩[①]肥瘦江潭水，明灭轮回还债忙。
紫燕成行槐叶短，青莺度曲柳条长。
柴关[②]东侧两层雨，野径西边一片阳。
自古人生多醉眼，痴情睹物不堪伤。

【注释】

①玉钩：比喻新月。②柴关：柴门。

Sixteen

The width of the crescent on the deep pool promptly
Payed up its debt during the flickering transmigration.
In the short locust leaves, the purple swallows sat in line,
In the long willows, the green orioles were melodious.
To the east of the wicker gate, the two-tiered rain poured,
To the west of the wild trail, one sun shone bright.
Life peered most with bleary eyes from of old,
At the souvenir, the passions of love should be so sorely oppressed.

其十七

对酒高楼沽俸钱[1]，含春玉色复缠绵。
使君邀影行千里，薄暮闻香续百年。
音信晴窗偏旦暮[2]，相思好梦又团圆。
谁知方客[3]频偷宿，逐露绝情暗纵欢。

【注释】

①沽（gū）：买。俸钱：官吏所得的薪金。也写作“奉钱”。②旦暮：旦夕。早晨和傍晚，比喻短暂的时间。③方客：四方宾客。

Seventeen

Out your salary, to wine in the tower,
With the charming beauty of lingering passions;
For a thousand miles, drive your shadow to be invited
In the last faint glimmering of twilight sweet for a hundred years.
Dawn and dusk, the fine window should look for her news,
And in the love-lorn dream, you have met your sweet again.
God knows she should have shacked up with her clients,
Where the heartless dews give way to her carnal desires.

其十八

冷漠梨花飞似雪，香痕带雨去无归。
轻狂天翼纵烟霭，撩乱游鳞横翠微[1]。
反覆阳关迷本性，存亡歧路隐尘机[2]。

忘情[3]莫怨东风破，销尽心神空有违。

【注释】

①翠微：青翠的山色，形容山光水色青翠缥缈。也泛指青翠的山。②尘机：尘俗的心计与意念。③忘情：感情上放得下；无动于衷。

Eighteen

The offish pear petals flow like snow
Whose sweet shadows are gone in the drizzle
On the flighty wing of the heaven thru the shimmering clouds
Over the emerald hills that tease the swimming fish in confusion.
On the open，volatile road，the nature becomes lost，
Alive or dead，the worldly intrigues are hidden on the forked road.
Unruffled by emotion，blame not the east wind that breaks
And vanishes the mind against the initial intent，but in vain.

其十九

玉郎折柳送新知，敲定明珠未嫁时。
风露凄清[1]云影瘦，星辰旷朗[2]月狂痴。
灵踪[3]问遍人依旧，胜景漂泊心不移。
一夜红肌更子婿[4]，无情洒满落花诗。

【注释】

①凄清：凄凉冷清。②旷朗：开阔明亮。③灵踪：神灵。④子婿：原指子女，此处特指女婿。

Nineteen

The merry man broke the willow for the new face,
And settled the bright pearl before marriage
Below the coldish, skinny clouds so dewy and windy
With the vast, bright stars obsessively outshone by the moon.
Everywhere, her clever trail must be there as before,
To the scenic, anchorless view, his heart was convicted unshakably.
Over night, her red muscle should have changed the man,
Like the ruthless blossom drops that besprinkled the lines.

其二十

嗷嗷反哺①旧德在，天下乌鸦为楷模。
咩咩羔羊跪乳②下，觅食昏虎隐山隅③。
黑鱼④到死也知孝，黄鹤同年各上途。
虚负⑤恩情落嘴上，结交此辈有何愚！

【注释】

①反哺：化自“乌鸦反哺”。乌鸦是一种通体漆黑、面貌丑陋的鸟，因为人们觉得它不吉利而遭到人类普遍厌恶，但它们却拥有一种真正值得我们人类普遍称道的美德——养老、爱老，乌鸦在养老、敬老方面堪称动物中的楷模。据说，这种鸟在母亲的哺育下长大后，当母亲年老体衰，不能觅食或者双目失明飞不动的时候，它的子女就四处去寻找可口的食物，衔回来嘴对嘴地喂到母亲的口中，回报母亲的养育之恩，并且从不感到厌烦，一直到老乌鸦临终，再也吃不下东西为止。②咩咩（miē）：拟声词，形容羊叫的声音。跪乳：化自“羊羔跪乳”。很早以前，一只母羊生了一只小羊羔。羊妈妈非

常疼爱小羊，晚上睡觉让它依偎在身边，用身体暖着小羊，让小羊睡得又熟又香。白天吃草，又把小羊带在身边，形影不离。遇到别的动物欺负小羊，羊妈妈用头抵抗保护小羊。一次，羊妈妈正在喂小羊吃奶。一只母鸡走过来说："羊妈妈，近来你瘦了很多。吃到的东西都让小羊吸收了。你看我，从来不管小鸡们的吃喝，全由它们自己去扑闹哩。"羊妈妈讨厌母鸡的话，就不客气地说："你多嘴多舌搬弄是非，到头来犯下拧脖子的死罪，还得挨一刀，对你有啥好处?"气走母鸡后，小羊说："妈妈，您对我这样疼爱，我怎样才能报答您的养育之恩呢?"羊妈妈说："我什么也不要你报答，只要你有这一片孝心就心满意足了。"小羊听后，不觉落泪，"扑通"跪倒在地，表示难以报答慈母的一片深情。从此，小羊每次吃奶都是跪着。它知道是妈妈用奶水喂大它的，跪着吃奶是感激妈妈的哺乳之恩。③山隅：山角；山曲。④黑鱼：也叫孝鱼，这是因为鱼妈妈每次生鱼宝宝的时候，都会失明一段时间。这段时间，鱼妈妈不能觅食，不知道是不是出于母子天性，也许鱼宝宝们一生下来就知道鱼妈妈是为了它们才看不见，如果没有东西吃会饿死的，所以，鱼宝宝自己争相游进鱼妈妈的嘴里，直到鱼妈妈复明的时候，她的孩子已经所剩无几了。传说，鱼妈妈会绕着它们住的地方一圈一圈地游，似乎是在祭奠。所以，后来人们叫黑鱼为孝鱼。⑤虚负：空有。

Twenty

Clamouring for food, the old moral stayed there,
Under the sun, the carrion crow was a paragon.
In the bleat, the lamb knelt to be at suck,
To hunt for food, the tiger hid in the coign .
Till the last gasp, the snakehead was filial,
Unlike the yellow cranes that went their own ways.
It would be the height of folly to consort those
With the debt of gratitude falsely silver-tongued.

其二十一

仙果三枚遍野红，不求华盖[1]驾银风。
妄说[2]贵子和俗子，莫论天公与地公。
化作天池都柿[3]殿，浮为野水杏花宫。
长白千里开仙镜，万尺深情向海通。

【注释】

①华盖：指帝王或贵族车上的伞盖。金风：秋风。②妄说：没有根据地乱说；虚妄荒谬之言。③都柿：蓝色浆果，属越橘科，越橘属植物。

Twenty-One

Three ambrosias were red all over the wild,
Not in quest of the flowery umbrella on the silvery wind,
Not in quest of the noble men or the vulgar men,
Not in quest of the heaven ruler or the land ruler.
Transformed into the blueberry hall by the celestial lake,
It floated on the wild water around the apricot palace.
For 1000 miles, the snow-capped mountain opened its immortal mirror,
For 10000 feet, the heart strings found its way to the sea.

其二十二

刀口下边活性命，殍[1]人碗里救哀声。
地罗[2]一面放山虎，天网三层归海鲸。

效死殷勤实可重，受恩寥落也言轻。
人间凝怨知何在，为有狼心不领情。

【注释】

①殍（piǎo）：饿死。②地罗：地网。

Twenty-Two

Hold the execution, and spare the lives,
Out of the starved bowls come the faint cries for help,
Out of the snares below, liberate the tiger,
Out of the far-flung nets above, replace the whale.
Ready to die, such dedication should be commendable,
Recipient of grace, such misfortune carries little weight.
Tell me where is the fixed grudge in this world?
It lies where the ungrateful heart of wolves shows.

其二十三

凤凰台上续鸡窝，尘马江头点冷波。
笑脸婉眉行短舞，罗衣娇步作长歌。
愚公何处啄鳞角①，智叟谁人戏谷阿②。
来客多情神女庙，夜郎无处不婆娑。

【注释】

①鳞角：犹言鳞次栉比。此处双关。②谷阿（ē）：山谷凹曲处。

Twenty-Three

In the pheonix tower, nest her chicken coop,
On the river, the dust horse flips the cold wave;
Where her soft brows in smiles are dancing short,
Where her silk gown in spoiled steps is singing long.
Where can the foolish old man pick at the unicorn horn?
Where can the wise old man dally with the dale and vale?
Having visited the amorous temple of the goddess,
The night man rustles and bubbles here and there.

其二十四

人生直道修闲去，未必从俗暗里忙。
两晋寒烟凭造化，六朝暮雨任兴亡。
烂根云水寻江海，枯叶蒹葭觅稻粱。
金玉查收出虎穴，常情印证有天殃[①]。

【注释】

①天殃：天降的祸殃。

Twenty-Four

Life in an upright way elevates the free soul,
That follows the vulgar and busy taste in secret.
The Jin dynasties were best endowed in cold mists,
The Six Dynasties rose and fell in the late rains.

With the rotten root, the cloudy water seeks its estuary,
Among the dead leaves, the soul of reeds seeks its grains;
Out of the tiger's den, the gold and jade must be confiscated,
And corroborated by the common sense of natural disaster.

烦　恼

浮世常持烦恼意，网尘酸涩对闲愁。
明眸灵运入河里，盲眼虚空出渡头。
俗虑前生缘已定，心期后世业无由。
三千心火皆真理，八万法门枉自羞。

Vexation

This brief world holds a constant state of vexation,
Where the acid sorb of the net faces the needless misery.
As the bright eyes of the soul step down into the river,
The blind eyes have come out of the empty ferry.
Now that the vulgar worries in an earlier life were predestined,
An expectation for the later ages could be unaccessible to the karma.
If the three thousand heart fires were all the truth,
The eighty thousand gateways to the Law would be ashamed in vain.

反韵红莲

芙蓉团扇羞遮面，卧雪澄波招紫燕。
浅笑施红偏软语，低眉点翠乍轻颤。
满轮碧水铺冰镜，半魄长天行玉片。

闲步荣枯香满袖，高堂内外可栖禅[1]。

【注释】

①栖禅：坐禅。

Red Lotus with Wrong Level and Oblique Tones

Shy behind the round, rosy fan, the glistening waves
Like snow are catching the purple swallows.
When the rouge smiles slightly in the affectionate words,
The low brows dribbed to the green lightly quivers.
After the full wheel on the blue water paves like an ice mirror,
Half of her soul in the vast sky goes like a jade piece.
Through the loss or gain though sweet full on the sleeves,
The saunterer can sit in meditation in and out of the lofty hall.

泛桃花

桃色春来片片香，探墙窥见女儿妆。
翠纱惹动清风短，红晕迷来冷月长。
夹岸半开梳水镜，沿河放浪洗山梁。
游鱼也盼吃胭脂，弄雨娇羞片片香。

The Blooming Peaches

Each peach petal smells sweet as the spring comes,
And peeps down the wall at the hope chest.
As the short breeze stirs her green gauze,

Her pinkish, calf love extends cold into the moon.
To flank the shore bloomed half like a combed mirror,
She stays her leisure through the flat-topped ridges.
As the wandering fish hope to taste her rouge,
Her gentle and shy petals are savory in the drizzles.

福

手把长福倒玉壶，天衢①飞步是遥途。
福生巷陌拔新笋，祸起帘栊惊野凫②。
顺水祈福去苦楚，逆舟同力抗忧虞③。
大福隐市不贪贱④，物外⑤江山有且无。

【注释】

①天衢（qú）：天空广阔，任意通行，如世之广衢，故称天衢。②帘栊（lóng）：窗帘和窗牖。也泛指门窗的帘子。野凫（fú）：野鸭子。③忧虞：忧虑。④“大福”句：“隐市”化自“大隐隐于市”，说的是大隐就是隐于市之中。贪贱：贪婪。⑤物外：谓超越世间事物，而达于绝对之境界。

Good Fortune

The long fortune in hand pours its jar of jade,
Before the steps bolt into the distant thoroughfare of the sky.
The fortune born in the lane grows like the bamboo shoots,
The misfortune behind the lattice startles the wild mallards.
For the fortune, go downstream to get out of the hard lot,
United, sail upstream against the sorrow and anxiety: —
A good fortune hidden in the city has no vulgar, cheap love,

Where there must be and not be the transcendental territory.

腐　女[1]

昔日金莲未远嫁，木屋紧锁御宅族[2]。
心中恶趣已耗尽，脑内禅机还未熟。
寒露节操安步履，心潮腐道束和服。
偷眸富士百合控[3]，休道奴家不可黩[4]。

【注释】

①腐女："腐女子"（fujoshi）的简称，"腐"在日文中有无可救药的意思。但不是像"御宅族"那样具有贬低人的意思，而是一种有自嘲意味的自称。腐女或腐女子主要是指喜欢 BL，也就是幻想中男男爱情（gay）的女性。②御宅族：20 世纪 80 年代后期用于指代男性动漫迷，女性则冠名为"宅女"。③百合控：对百合感兴趣的人士。百合是 LES、GL（女同性恋）的隐性名词。④可黩（dú）：可以玷污；可以滥用。

A Slasher

The old, golden lotus has not married afar,
But locked up inside the log cabin of the otaku.
The evil paths in heart has been used up,
But the esoteric truths in the brain are still green.
The moral integrity in cold dews should go leisurely,
And the surging, klunky thoughts are girded with the kimono.
To snoop on the lesbians of Fuji,
Say not that I can not be desecrated.

腹　黑[1]

婉娈[2]对影桃花笑，妖媚[3]无言时态难。
楚楚可怜星月面，翩翩唯有虎狼肝。
亲和相问人心窄，奸恶何为客脸宽。
莫测温袍藏诡异，毒刀黑水嘴留欢。

【注释】

①腹黑：来源于日本 ACG 界，指表面和善温和，内心却想着奸恶事情或有心计的人。②婉娈：柔顺；缱绻；委婉含蓄。③妖媚：艳丽妩媚。

The Black Belly

Gentle and subtle, the shadow smiles like a peach petal,
But in wordless charms to the hard times.
Lovingly pathetic, his face shines like the moonlit stars,
With the air of thorough-bred, he has a voracious but wolfish heart.
Amiable and regardful, his narrow heart's intolerant of the undesirable,
Traitorous and villainous, but why to be square-faced?
Under his warm, unfathomable robe full of scorpions,
The honey mouth has dipped a poisoned knife in black water.

干物女[1]

高额云髻衬秃骨，明镜嚣尘却懒磨。
何处孤蓬不寂寞，家中节令[2]可蹉跎。

清心透肉乏胸罩，素面杂餐匮绮罗[3]。
暗数他人啼宿鸟，欢情难醒爱偏多。

【注释】

①干物女：泛指像香菇、干贝一样"干巴巴"的女人。干物女依然年轻，但已经放弃恋爱，凡事都说"这样最轻松"。②节令：节气时令，指某个节气的气候和物候。③绮罗：华贵的丝织品或丝绸衣服。

Himono Onna

High-browed in cloudy tresses, her bare bones
Are lazy to polish the bright mirror in the great clamour.
Where the bitter fleabane will not feel lonely?
The prime of her seasons can be staid at home.
Short of a nipple-shield, her flash flesh seems pure-hearted,
Not lapped in silks, her face without makeup grabs whatever to eat.
While counting other night chirps furtively,
Her sweet delight hardly wakes up from the loathed love.

高人处事
High-minded Relationship

其一

辩士空林欲讷言[1]，辩锋折刃有积冤。
回翔明辩才微动，巧辩凄迷又早暄。

高辩经分如坐虎，低言理辩胜骑猿。
人生误解何其少，沉默闲居祛百烦。

【注释】

①讷（nè）言：说话谨慎。

One

The debater slow of speech in the empty wood
Snaps his eloquent sword for the accumulated rancour.
Soon after the bright gift of the gab jiggles back,
The early giff-gaff will be gone，dreary and fuzzy.
The high speculation is parsed on the back of a tiger,
And the soft reasoning power runs faster than an ape.
As little as we should misconstrue the life,
The dumb leisure at home would cure hundreds of troubles.

其二

路静无尘风月夜，遥知静语叩春深。
谷虚鸟静察杨色，林静烟消看柳阴。
池静浪平应有意，木凉波静也无心。
人生低谷须平静，硬骨横尸不可寻。

Two

On the still，dustless way of the moonlit night,
The far，still words knock at the fullness of spring,

Whence the still bird takes the poplar’s cue of the hollow valley,
And the still wood watches the shades of the smoke-free willows.
Although the calm waves of the still pond are intentional,
The still waves of the cold wood later could be careless.
Even in the deep valley, our life should calm down,
And the dauntless corpse should not be found again.

其三

春心无力怨纤腰，衣带相思雪未消。
垂耳有方蕉叶颤，折腰无计柳花飘。
腰间云雨性情变，胯下江山颜色凋。
篱下分歧门下客，该弯腰处且弯腰。

Three

Powerless to grudge her slender waist, the spring heart
Suffers the pangs of love under the snow yet to melt away.
Dropping the ear proper, the banana leaf quivers,
Bending the waist, the lost willow catkins are swimming.
Upon the thigh, the temper keeps shifting like the clouds,
Below the crotch, the picturesque view washes out.
Under the another’s roof, the protégé
Has to stoop when necessary to stoop.

其四

路迷信马逢绝域，独羡深渊散野鹅。
路险云端行侧径，烟轻山肋[1]走飞萝。
路尘破镜登芒履[2]，梁燕婵娟织玉梭。
世上绝无后悔药，人间长路梦魂多。

【注释】

①山肋：山腰。②芒履：芒鞋。

Four

To ride with lax reins but lost where it's inaccessible,
The free wild geese are admired alone in the yawning abyss.
To follow the side path through the vicious way in the clouds,
The vines glide up the ribs of the mountains in the puffs of smoke.
On the dust road of the broken mirror, the grass sandals
Shuttle back and forth like the swallows under the moon.
The world has no regret drugs available for sale,
That could cure the dreaming souls on the long road.

其五

千载轩辕[1]绕紫腾，枯石过耳百王薨[2]。
汉宫征妇[3]千行泪，秦月疲氓[4]万骨崩。
铁骑虏尘[5]犹待破，天骄十万已初征。
辉煌难免临劫难，摄取全真即永恒。

【注释】

①轩辕：轩辕柏，桥山脚下轩辕庙内的柏树，树龄5000余年，相传轩辕黄帝亲手种植。此处泛指长寿古木。②薨（hōng）：古代称诸侯或有爵位的官员去世。③征妇：出征军人的妻子。④疲氓：充当隶役的平民。⑤虏尘：敌寇或叛乱者的侵扰。

Five

The cypress in wistarias by the Yellow Emperor five centuries ago
Has seen hundreds of kings dead passing by the ear like rotten pebbles.
The Han Palace called forth streams of tears of the warriors' wives,
And the Qin moon had worn ten thousand bones to a frazzle.
The barbarian dusts were yet to be swept by the strong hoofbeats,
And hundred thousands of men started the expedition by the Son of Heaven.
Even such brilliant performances can't escape the last calamity,
And so to take in the innate essence may be eternal.

其六

北阜[①]倾城冲暗雪，东邻墙外又流春。
昨天芍药檀妆[②]旧，明日芙蓉睡脸新。
仕宦[③]贤愚才作辅，权奸[④]名利且无亲。
人生行梦失颜色，活好今天才是真。

【注释】

①北阜（fù）：北面的山岗。②檀妆：浅红色的女子妆饰。③仕宦：给皇帝当仆人，做官的意思。④权奸：弄权作恶的奸臣。

Six

The north hillock was darkly snowed by the knockout,
And outside the wall, my neighbour troated again.
Yesterday, her attired peonies in the santal were old,
Tomorrow, her sleeping face will be anew like the rose of sharon.
Sage or fool, the officials joined other sustainers of the power,
Fame or gain, the political roguers turn their back on their own flesh and blood.
The life in dream has lost its colour,
And so it is true to be better off now.

其七

三闾三谏自怀羞[①]，一枕凉心一叶舟。
渔父真达情眇眇，棹歌[②]独醒意悠悠。
五湖几处刻华表，四海人人成古丘。
大道扬尘不掸袖，顺俗谙世泛浊流。

【注释】

①三闾（lǘ）：“三闾大夫”的简称，战国时楚国特设的官职，是主持宗庙祭祀，兼管王族屈、景、昭三大姓子弟教育的闲差事。屈原贬后任此职。此处指屈原三谏：多次劝谏。怀羞：感到耻辱。②棹（zhào）歌：渔民在撑船、划船时候唱的渔歌。

Seven

The cabinet minister Qu Yuan remonstrated again, but in vain,
And pillowed his cold heart that flowed with the boat.
Like an immortal, the fisherman's emotion was uncertain,
Unlike the boat song sober alone, but far away in his reveries.
No cloud pillar has been chiselled around the five lakes,
But all men have been buried like their peers within the four seas.
Don't whisk your sleeves on the broad road of dust,
But taste to the full all the flavours of the turbid flows.

弓　虽①

开弓虽未翻明月，射下青竹一叶弯。
竹叶写诗泛翠羽，柴门盛酒邀红颜。
风尘出去经年苦，诗酒归来半日闲。
飞箭无心还有意，随风一去不回还。

【注释】

①弓虽："强"字折写，还表示强的意思。多占点地盘，有利于视觉效果。强的意思就是厉害，但很多时候只是反讽，特别是拆开来写时都有点不怀好意。

Though a Bow, but Powerful

Draw your bow, though not cross the bright moon,
And shoot down one curved, green bamboo leaf,

On which to write your poems like green feathers,
For your rosy lips with the wine in your wooden door.
Into the dust of journey, it suffers all the year round,
After coming back, the poetic liquor is carefree half a day.
Let the mindless arrow fly wittingly
That, once gone in the wind, will never return.

Hold 住

暗潮击鼓半江虎，叠浪颠狂扫大荒。
骇雨鸣钟方裹电，惊云穿牖[①]正浮霜。
鬼歌满眼飞钢箭，神曲倾筐射铁枪。
丧乱[②]倏忽明月落，持节仗气[③]验存亡。

【注释】

①牖（yǒu）：窗户。②丧乱：死亡祸乱。后多以形容时势或政局动乱。③持节：保持操节。仗气：凭仗正气。

Hold It

The undercurrent beats the drums like half a river tigers,
Stacking the wild and dissolute waves that sweep the great waste.
The appalled rain rings the bell that sucks the lightning,
And the shocking cloud roves into the window that floats the frost.
In the spooky songs, the steel arrows are flying in the eyes,
And in the ghostly strains, the iron spears shoot out of the baskets.
After the bright moon falls swiftly in the wild disorder,
The moral integrity can test how to survive or perish.

蝴蝶梦

庄周年少梨花梦，不想蝴蝶采蜜来。
千点轻灵桂月殿，一川幻影柏梁台[①]。
紫烟画角莫闲剪，青嶂霓裳且漫裁。
百代轻肥[②]垂冷露，粉翅一去不可猜。

【注释】

①柏梁台：古代汉族建筑。属于汉代台名。故址在今陕西省长安县西北长安故城内。也泛指宫殿。②轻肥：取自《论语·雍也》中的“乘肥马，衣轻裘”，用以概括豪奢生活。

Butterflies in Dream

As a boy, Chuang-Tzu saw the pear flowers in dream,
Where some butterflies came to gather honey, alas!
Thousands of slender spirits flitted down the laurel hall of the moon,
All over the cypress beam terrace like the phantoms by the river;
In the purple smokes, stop that spare snip into the horns,
In the green ridges, tailor those free rainbow skirts
After a hundred generations, the luxurious life droops its cold dews,
Like their wings that once gone will be inconceivable.

蝴蝶爷鱼

冷温硬骨信岩礁，黄海依风涌暗潮。
大眼晴天唯逸兴，小头落日任飘摇。

臀鳍侧线隐八转，云路横斑映九条。
黄褐橘红秀五色，一具拖网断消息。

Azuma Emmnion

The low, bony temperature believes the rocky reef,
Springing up the undercurrents by the wind of the Yellow Sea.
Big-eyed, the fair weather has its special leisure,
Small-headed, the setting sun falls in the withering wind.
On the anal fin, the eight lateral lines hide its turn,
With the nine barred body that shines like a cloud.
Yellow, brown, orange, all their news
Of the five colours are stopped by the trawl net.

虎　穴

池塘难起翻天浪，空穴随时鼓恶风。
成虎三人人胜虎，化狼五犬犬如狼。
黑心石铁黑心硬，白眼无情愧煞钢。
有幸人生临虎穴，无缘打虎虎口亡。

The Tiger's Den

A tank has no billows,
But an empty hole invites the foul wind.
Three men's testimony creates a tiger in the market,
And five dogs from the wolves are even more bloody.
The black heart is hard as marble,

And the steel glows with shame before the white, ruthless eyes.
By accident of luck, the life is close to the tiger's den,
If the fighting luck passes, the life will perish in its mouth.

灰飞烟灭

双眼幽思身后事，谁能解语在身前。
片帆无意犹愁望，高枕多情却醉眠。
莫道升沈人各散，须知毁誉命相连。
红颜末路皆白骨，榜上封神已断烟。

Come to Dust

The eyes are pondering what will happen behind,
But who can understand what's still alive?
Unconsciously, the sail gazes out in sorrow,
Susceptibly, the high pillow sleeps tipsily.
Say not that men will break up in vicissitudes,
We know that praise and blame have been ordained.
The dead end of a rosy cheeks will be the skeleton,
Like the snapped smoke after the creation of the Gods.

回乡难

细草纤毫五月天，水国明练①片云飞。
海楼梳雨涂暝色，栈道横烟漏曙晖。
岐路笙歌还隐去，他乡鞍马且思归。
归来不见儿时路，反认他乡久莫违。

【注释】

①明练：化自许景先的《奉和御制春台望》“千门望成锦，八水明如练”。

The Hard Native Return

The fine grasses to a nicety in May
Around the bright water below the scudded cloud
Comb their dim rain before the sea floor
Near the plank road to be dawned in the mists.
On the forked road, retire from the revelry,
From the alien land, gallop to go back.
But where is the road of my childhood after return?
Better go back to the alien land, not to be long-overdue.

坚持力

长堤蝼蚁不迁穴，十载经营眨眼平。
半世蹉跎寒雨洗，浮生辗转暖云晴。
贫危落魄应劳役，贱辱持节须苦行。
烛芯摇风到泪尽，昏黑过去是黎明。

Perseverance

The causeway under the ant's cares
Could be burst after ten years in a jiffy.
In the cold rain washed and wasted half a century,

This fleeting life has floundered into the fine cloud warmly.
In the dangerous poverty, the service plays the underdog,
Chastely free of dishonour, I have to practise the self-torture.
Blown by the wind, my candlewick drops its last tear,
After the dark night, the crack of dawn comes for sure.

囧①

委郁②孤飞去灌木，凄霜旷志③任邪衷。
悲生燕婉④似垂日，恨起穷欢如落风。
无奈玉炉深院暖，岂如金梦满床空。
柴门千里无金锁，莲步三分是断虹。

【注释】

①囧（jiǒng）：光明。2008年开始在中文地区的网络社群间变成一种流行的表情符号，成为网络聊天、论坛、博客中使用最频繁的字之一，被赋予“郁闷、悲伤、无奈”之意。“囧”被形容为“21世纪最风行的单个汉字”之一。②委郁：抑郁；愁闷。③旷志：旷达的志趣。④燕婉：优美；柔和。

Sunken

Lonely and gloomy, fly into the shrubs,
Chilly and frosty, the free will has been steered wickely.
Doleful and mellow, the sun may be drooping,
And the bad blood for the vigour falls like the wind.
But unfortunately the censer warms up in the deep yard,
Not better than the golden dreams full of the empty bed.
For a thousand miles, a wicker gate has no gold lock,

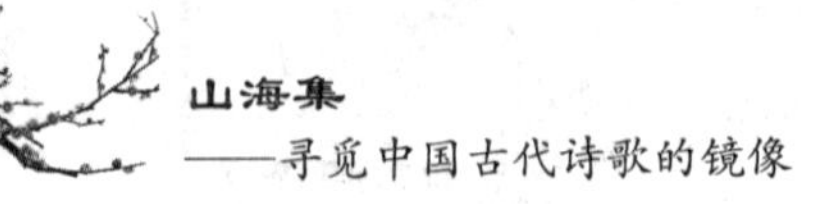

Of the little lotus feet, one step further will be the broken rainbow.

酒店试睡员

床垫横腰知软硬，空调冷暖夜翻屋。
风流下水可飞练，沐浴前池能倚伏。
内殿等闲无大小，兰房承宠有生熟。
莎鸡开眼轮轻榻，睡遍高楼走地轴。

The Hotel Sleeper

Soft or hard, the waist feels the mattress,
Warm or cold, the air conditioner controls the night house.
The smooth sewer should slide down freely, and
To be bathed in the head pond should be credible.
In the inner hall, all the leisures are created equal,
And the bed chamber lends embracements unto every stranger.
Wide-eyed, the katydid on the light couch
Can sleep in all the towers worked on the spindle.

巨斧燕子鱼

淡水飞碟腾柳阴，斜风驶浪气萧森①。
腹滑春水观潮信，背卷秋江照镜心。
银燕掠食已断古，铁鳍夺命更绝今。
灵钧大肉何足贵，天齿行空百语暗。

【注释】

①萧森：阴森。

Giant Hatchetfish

Like a flying saucer over the fresh water through the willows,
The slanting wind sails the dreary and desolate waves.
With the spring water under its belly, it watches the tidal bore,
With the autumn river on its back, it looks into the heart of the mirror.
After the silver swallow has hunted for the food unprecedented,
The iron fin claims the lives and remains unchallenged.
Before the large muscles unfit to be thought noble in the world,
Its teeth through the sky will tranquilize all other tongues.

看

清浊几度试沧浪，喜怒随风观豹斑。
断续有谁识进退，沉浮唯我辨忠奸。
推移节气难贴壁，顺逆阴阳不叩关[①]。
成败休言去问卜，舍得验取路直弯。

【注释】

①叩关：敲击城关而有所求；敲门求见。

Look

Clear and muddy, the surging waves have gone for ages,

Happy and angry, the spots on the leopard are followed with the wind.
On or off, who would get a fix on the ebb and flow?
Up or down, it's I who can distinguish the loyal and the crafty.
The solar seasons downward are hardly glued on the wall,
Because the light and dark movement can't knock at the pass.
To be or not, speak not to consult a soothsayer,
But we'd splurge on the test of the road, crooked or straight.

腊八粥

闭门晓气雪明伏，冰箭荧飞铁镜秃。
狡兔放蹄夜乱走，度云生翅日嘶逐。
黄粱几载人没老，枕上倏忽饭已熟。
醉饱浮沈仍聚散，持钱难买腊八粥。

Laba Porridge

Shut the door to the dawn with bright snow all along,
That glides the glimmering arrows of ice on the bald iron mirror;
The wily hares must have wandered freely at night,
And the cloud wings might have hooted for the day.
For years, the fond dream hasn't gone old with the man,
On his pillow, the golden millet has been swiftly done.
Dined and wined to the satiety, all comers have to go, up or down,
To whom any money can't afford the poridge not on the day proper.

狼 鱼

灰狼犬齿惊雷电，洋底花鳅噬海星。
孤胆窥天多野客，闲情守地一家丁。
丘墟低弄成前院，台榭高流作后厅。
食旅披寻耕子夜，甘从破相护精灵。

Sea Wolf

Like a thunderbolt, the fangs are shocking,
On the ocean bottom, the "spined loach" bites the sea stars.
Courageously alone, he pokes his nose into the wild sky,
In leisurely mood, he secures where it should be.
The lower mound has been tinkered into his fore court,
And the higher lodges into his back hall.
On the journey of food, he pores over the midnight plough,
Willing to be disfigured for his fair mate.

漓江茶坊

岭南云水惠香茶，醉客青阳凝紫霞。
代酒山杯尝翠叶，通神土甑[①]品灵芽。
清风蕉扇对天宝，明月竹阁封物华。
小市焙炉[②]煎腊月，闲诗烘枕作仙家。

【注释】

①土甑（zèng）：古代蒸饭的一种瓦器。②焙（bèi）炉：微火烘烤

的炉子。

Tea House by the Lijiang River

The scented tea from the cloud and water of the Five Ridges
Has intoxicated the blue sun that fixes the purple clouds.
Its green leaves could be tasted in the coarse cups like wine,
From the coarse cooking pot for these tender shoots.
As the palm-leaf fan breezes the heavenly charm,
One bright moon over the bamboo floor gives a plump wonder of nature
Where the deepest winter braised in the boiler of the little town
Could bake my immortal pillow in the free poems.

漓江游

云雨漓江腊月天，象鼻泊钓放竹船。
世间青鸟落沙渚①，海底苍山散野田。
水墨千层情倒挂，丹青万尺意垂悬。
汀州暗醉撑红伞，燕赵佳人在水边。

【注释】

①沙渚（zhǔ）：小沙洲。

My Tour on the Lijiang River

The deepest winter on the rainy river berthed or
Sailed the bamboo rafts around the elephant trunk.
The green peaks of the seabed had risen loosely into the wild field,

Where thousands of ink and wash paintings hang upside down in love,
And ten thousand square feet of such pictures were dangling there,
Whence one red umbrella was open in tipsy secret on the isle,
And a fair lady from Qinhuangdao was there on the shore.

荔 枝

荔枝青悬新雨后，春桥五月献芙蓉。
圆明红紫乡蜂厚，光润玲珑野蜜浓。
十万大山深浅出，千条小路古今从。
水晶甘露滴银碗，不负华清翠翘[①]松。

【注释】

①华清：华清宫。翠翘：古代妇人首饰的一种。状似翠鸟尾上的长羽，故名。

Lychee

Hung fresh in the rain,
The spring is bridged over the roses of sharon in May,
Swarmed with the native bees on the round and bright purple,
Strongly and naturally honeyed, smoothly but delicately.
Out of the ten thousand mountains, thick or thin,
One thousand side roads go after them from time immemorial.
With the sweet, crystal dews dropped into the silver bowls,
It was ever worthy of Her jade pins in Huaqing Pool.

龙头鱼

浅海衔泥游大口，尾鳍笼剑化三叉。
洄游触目戏红蟹，逆水惊心吞紫虾。
灰褐闲行听岸草，青黄独契看浮槎[1]。
无鳞软体还强韧，颌骨流谦[2]伏密牙。

【注释】

①独契：也作独憩。浮槎（chá）：浮行水上的竹木筏。②流谦：极其谦抑。

Bombay Duck

The big mud mouths swim in the shallow sea,
Whose tail fins like swords turn into the tridents.
Their migrated eyes may tease the red crabs,
And swallow the purple shrimps against the heart-pounding current.
Grey or brown, their free swim meets the ear of the shore grass,
Black or yellow, their lonely repose gazes upon the floating rafts.
Their soft, scaleless bodies are so tenacious,
But their humble jawbones are hidden with the thorny teeth.

绿茶婊[1]

青丝盈尺召春露，素面原来是裸妆。
心碎无痕如炼乳，泪凝有信似煎香。
多情风月倚苍霭，独宿罗裳含嫩光。

夹肉可夫衔日月，汉唐枯骨也仓皇。

【注释】

①绿茶婊：装纯的妓女，也就是出卖肉体的嫩模。

Green Tea Bitch

Her black hair induces the spring dews one-foot long
That turns out to be without makeup but nakely dressed.
Her traceless, broken heart is like the condensed milk,
Her hopeful, frozen tears are fried fragrantly.
Her drippy dream of loves lolls in the dark hazes,
And lonely lodges the silk skirt that shines softly.
Her slim slut cunt free to be fucked can clamp the sun and moon,
And scramble the Han-Tang skeletons that skedaddle shamefully.

曼哈顿悬日①

广厦琼林览宝镜，一把火伞满城金。
须臾澹荡②惊归梦，四度逍遥听客心。
纵棹西游从景命③，乘潮东望奏徽音④。
纵横南北东西路，半块棋盘明玉琴。

【注释】

①曼哈顿悬日：指在美国纽约曼哈顿出现的自然现象。由于曼哈顿街道大多呈棋盘式布局，在每年的 5 月 28 日和 7 月 12 日（或 13 日），日落时阳光将洒满曼哈顿的所有的东西向街道，呈现一幅壮观的景象，时间长达 15 分钟。而在每年的 12 月 5 日和 1 月 8 日，这样的景观将伴随着日出而出现。②澹荡：荡漾，飘动。③景命：大命；

天命。④徽音：德音。指令闻美誉。

Manhattanhenge

Among the high-rise buildings like jeweled mirrors,
One summer sun shines full in the golden city,
Shortly startling the dream in return, warmly and pleasantly,
And sauntering for four times through the heart of men.
Paddled to the west under the heaven's accession,
It takes the tide to gaze out to the good reputation.
All the roads in different directions, vertically and horizontally,
Are bright below half the chessboard that plays the lyre.

萌萌哒①

卷舌娇爱笑蛮奴②，莫向风流借昵谀③。
钓艇无人调绿岛，昏鸦隔岭戏青凫④。
树衔桃脸观吃货，蝉噪银屏逗小雏。
生眼不知梅雨⑤事，侬家⑥本相有何辜。

【注释】

①萌萌哒：同“摸摸哒”，是“mu a”的谐音，表示亲昵或亲昵的问候，多用于卖萌的语气。也可用来形容长得可爱的人或物。②蛮奴：舞姬；婢仆。此处为戏称。③昵谀（nì yú）：狎昵阿谀。④青凫（fú）：野鸭。⑤梅雨：6月至7月持续阴天有雨的气候，此时正是江南梅子的成熟期，故称为“梅雨”。此处双关“眉宇”。⑥侬家：自称。犹言我。

Adorkable

Her trill coquettes like a clinging vine,
Should not borrow a doting but voluptuous history.
The unmanned angling boat could molest the green island,
And the murky crow beyond the ridge teases the black mallard.
In the peach tree would show up the face of her epicure,
And in the cicada chirps tantalizes the chick behind the silver curtain.
If the plum rains are lost in the public eyes,
O what crime have her true features!

魔　都

塔影成林泊子夜，流光深处过重门。
蜃楼绿蚁含朱泪，仙岛青娥销客魂。
素手卷帘堆玉浪，罗衣开镜照金盆。
才高身显王侯相，岂料心中植劣根。

Magic City

The midnight berthed in the forest of stupas
Streams its light deeper into the doors.
The fantasied nectar looks on with the red tears,
And the lithe maiden on the magic isle is writhed around in ecstasy.
The lifted curtains by the pure fingers pile up the pure waves,
And the silk gowns in the mirror beams before the golden basin.
Gifted in the highest tone and the makings of lords and dukes,

Her heart should have been planted with the evil propensities!

莫　言
Hold Your Tongue

其一

无香无色无浓雪，难惹游蜂满树狂。
无浪无风无骤雨，有帆有棹有高樯。
泥章[①]几句能消惑，冥币成山不补亡。
少欲焉知是坏事，多言[②]末路有心伤。

【注释】

①泥章：又叫作“泥封”，它不是印章，而是古代用印的遗迹——盖有古代印章的干燥坚硬的泥团——保留下来的珍贵实物。由于原印是阴文，钤在泥上便成了阳文，其边为泥面，所以形成四周不等的宽边。封泥的使用自战国直至汉魏，直到晋以后纸张、绢帛逐渐代替了竹木简书信的来往，才有可能不使用封泥。②多言：说话不要太多，言多必失。

One

Short of colour, sweet or strong snow,
The gadabout bees hardly buzz loud in the trees;
Short of wave, wind or tempest,
The paddled sail should be masted high.

A few lines on the scove can clear up the confusion,
But the piled up hell notes snatch nobody from the jaws of death.
How do we know that few desires must be bad?
The dead end of many words will be heart-impaired.

其二

过隙人生行路难，泥途客雪尚衣单。
风尘归去求身逸，音信别来问体安。
灵境独眠凄肺腑，梦魂相见怆①心肝。
轻言②半句真心话，覆水成冰受苦寒。

【注释】

①怆（chuàng）：悲伤。②轻言：不要轻率地讲话，轻言的人会招来责怪和羞辱。

Two

The way of life is hard but swift,
Through the dirty slushes in the unlined garment.
To seek a free return from the times of turmoil,
I hope to make my personal enquiries since the lost touch.
In the wonderland, my heart sleeps lonely, coldly,
And sorrowfully after cut to the dreaming soul of reunion.
To get out half a sentence from what the mind is,
I can but tread in the water to be frozen bitterly.

其三

神斧飞来劈五岳，西风一曲破黄河。
酒神弱翼不堪病，花圣衰肠几欲魔。
青汉流年图自在，白云失意倦蹉跎。
倚空轻重无凭据，都是狂言①烹土锅。

【注释】

①狂言：不要不知轻重，胡侃乱说。胡侃乱说，往往后悔。

Three

The Holy Mountains were cleft by the flying ghost ax,
The Yellow River was torn in the song of the west wind.
The bacchus with the weak wings was overloaded by his breakdown,
The flower fairy with the waned bowels almost held spellbound.
In the swift time the blue sky charted its content comfort,
In hard luck the white cloud was fed up with the loss of time.
To count on an empty weight was groundless, in that
All was but the fish story to be boiled in the earth pot.

其四

狂心疏蕊撩黄莺，红粉娇羞片片惊。
六月折芳啼寸茎，三春乘兴戏垂英。
薄俗向利一身重，厚气求名四体轻。
早懂出局沦苦道，杂言①不会扯天鸣。

【注释】

①杂言：说话不可杂乱无章。杂乱无章，就会言不及义，伤害自己的美德。

Four

The sparse, mad-hearted pistils teased the golden oriole,
With their pink, bashful confusion on each amazed petal.
When June snapped her sweet that wept on the short stalks,
The late spring was kidding her drooped flowers cheerfully.
In such a frivolous world which had been benfit-oriented,
The restless search after fame was light-headed as a feather.
Had the knock-out known the resultant path of suffering,
The irresponsible tongue would never loosened up.

其五

开云洗雾调风月，野寺冰弦闻乱鸡。
马策横行常去往，龙泉[①]独步亦高低。
听声触钓青蝉落，看影翻夹[②]白兔栖。
走遍中国寻睡侣[③]，戏言[④]不可对人啼。

【注释】

①龙泉：宝剑名。《晋书·张华传》云：吴之未灭也，斗牛之间，常有紫气。及吴平之后，紫气愈明。焕到县掘狱屋基得一石函，中有双剑，并刻题，一曰龙泉，一曰太阿。焕遣使送一剑与华，留一自佩。②翻夹：化自李商隐《赠田叟》中的“鸥鸟忘机翻夹洽”。③暗指某诗。④戏言：不要不顾分寸地开玩笑，否则会引起冲突，招

来祸害。

Five

Open the cloud, wash the fog, move the moonlit night,
The wild temple below the ice chord hears the fowls in chaos,
Like the galloping horses that could come and go freely,
Or the dragon fountain that lonely measures up and down.
At the sound of the fishhook, the black cicada falls,
To the shaded, stretched snare, the white hare perches there.
And to seek another soul to sleep with all over China,
Such a humorous remark should not be cried out.

其六

刺耳冰凌惊倦魂，形骸累辱①脸犹存。
林间未必三条路，山外何曾两扇门。
职场污泥侍草野，帝乡眠粪候鸡豚。
人心不是梳妆镜，无讳直言②伤自尊。

【注释】

①累辱：劳累辛苦。②直言：不要不顾后果地直言不讳，否则也会引起麻烦。

Six

The harsh icicles startle the drowsy soul,
That toils and moils though the face can't be foiled.

The wood may be far from three roads,
And beyond my hills should there be two doors?
Where the career sludge serves the weeds,
The capital town craps and sleeps like pigs and fowl.
The heart of men is not a toilet glass,
To claim in grave tones wrecks the pride.

其七

老酒提壶一口尽，横床沈醉解春愁。
天星野水沉船尾，井月荒山没海头。
苦口是非相对峙，焦唇冷暖付东流。
尽言[①]不剩半厘地，城府干涸情未休。

【注释】

①尽言：说话要含蓄，不要不留余地。

Seven

Old flagon! Bottom up!
Stone-blind! Kiss the sorrows off your bed!
As the stars sink down to the stern on the wild water,
The well moon drowns into the desolate mountains by the sea.
Right and wrong, the bitter mouths are facing out,
Hot and cold, the parched lips are thrown into the wind.
To tell all the fractions of your thoughts,
The frank nature dries up in your ceaseless emotions, though.

其八

玄机无缝眼中迷，明月悬空百鸟低。
宫阙下方无走脉，昆仑上面有飞梯。
鱼肠咫尺贪独兕，鹅掌毫厘赛角犀[①]。
凡是密成皆顺水，漏言[②]如蚁溃长堤。

【注释】

①“鱼肠”二句：化自杜甫《故秘书少监武功苏公源明》句“青荧芙蓉剑，犀兕岂独刽”。独兕（sì）：独角兕，传说中的犀牛。角犀：远角犀，中新世至上新世早期的犀牛。②漏言：不要泄露机密。“事以密成，语以漏败”。

Eight

The hidden workings are seamless in the uncertain eyes,
And all birds are hanging low below the bright moon.
There should not be a vessel sailing down the palace,
But there must be a flying ladder on the Kunlun Mountains.
The rhinocero may gloat on the fish intertines near,
And the teleoceras can be distanced by the goose feet within an inch.
All the prudent schemes will be roses all the way,
And a divulged tongue like the ant colony bursts the long dyke.

其九

刁蛮青眼开寒浪，激濑[1]白云可浸潮。
一夜横流摇地碗，三秋乍起落天瓢。
闲居扣齿挑新恨，无事搬舌弄旧僚。
猛兽疮痍[2]犹可治，恶言[3]半世也难消。

【注释】

①激濑（lài）：急流。②疮痍（chuāng yí）：创伤。③恶言：不说无礼中伤的话，不要恶语伤人。

Nine

Open your black, proud eyes before the cold billows
And riptides tumbling frantically below the white clouds.
Over night, the cross flow rocks the earth bowls,
In the late autumn, the sky ladle falls suddenly.
In quiet life, the clicking teeth single out a new hatred,
Out of nothing, one chews the fat with the old fellows.
Even the trauma by the beast of prey can be curable,
The vicious words will be indelible half a lifetime.

其十

万态含香留客天，驰情叠破[1]为邀欢。
殷勤漫作精魂[2]绕，淅沥流光远梦牵。
销尽心冰无损益，化成脂水有芳鲜。

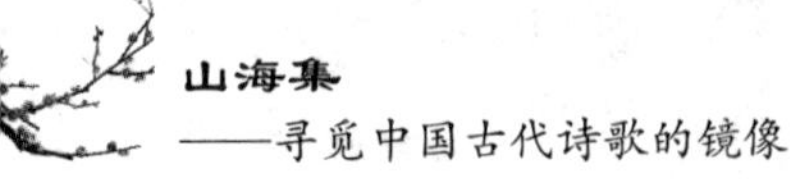

巧言[3]粉饰欺人眼，花语藏针裹木棉。

【注释】

①叠破：连续中的。②精魂：精神魂魄。③巧言：花言巧语。不要花言巧语，花言巧语的人，必然虚伪。

Ten

During the days when all the sweets ask us to stay,
The galloped passion pursues its pleasure successively.
In the kindred spirits to be dreamed around solicitously,
The rhythms of the flowing time are lost in a reverie afar.
After the heart of ice thaws without gains and losses,
It will be resolved into the fresh perfume.
The clever phrases could cheat the human eyes,
And the sweet words conceal its needles in the silk cotton.

其十一

鹦鹉无言关木所，逢人偷眼转舌关。
赪红雅调才怜欲，羽翠知音又嗜奸。
寒暑朝天谋点检，纵横向日划勾弯。
自鸣不过两三句，无病矜言[1]故弄闲。

【注释】

①矜言：不要骄傲自满，自以为是。自矜自夸，是涵养不够的表现。

Eleven

A caged, dumb parrot
Parrots its furtive glance,
With the red, refined beak in pathetic pitch,
And with the green kindred feather, shifty and wily.
Hot or cold, it checks up on the sky,
Vertically and horizontally, it ticks off the sun.
What it puffs up is but a few words,
That pine and whine in a imaginary illness.

其十二

燕赵青蝇三尺宽，啖食名利暗衔欢[①]。
安居不免赤舌断，得意岂知黑手酸。
俗子薄情易水尽，女人妒嫉戴河干。
有人就有憎心在，躲避谗言[②]此世难。

【注释】

①啖（dàn）食：吃；吞食。衔欢：心怀欢乐。②谗言：不要背后说别人的坏话。背后说人坏话，会弄得天下都不太平。

Twelve

In the states of Yan and Zhao, the blue flies were three feet wide,
Devouring the fame and gain in merry secret.
In placid contentment, their red tongue was prone to break,

On the high ropes, little did they know the harsh black hand.
Heartless, everyman might run dry like the Yishui River,
Green-eyed, a woman would dry up like the Daihe River.
The heart of hatred exists wherever the man lives,
And to seek refuge from the calumnies is hard in the world.

其十三

猫爪挠痕留旧迹，舌尖乱响愧山莺。
胡牙入叩眼先跃，霜齿相磨心不惊。
辣手明抽还有力，毒唇潜动且无声。
讦言[①]自古形器小，暗里揭疤招恨生。

【注释】

①讦（jié）言：毁谤的话。不要攻人短处，揭人疮疤。揭人疮疤的人，招人痛恨，害人害己。

Thirteen

The cat's paw has marked its scratches,
The rattling tongue tip has abashed the orioles;
The northern teeth are clenched before the leaping eyes,
The frosted teeth are ground but not spooked;
The ruthless punch whips out strong,
The vicious lips squirm silently.
From of old, the slanders have been small-minded,
And peeled away the secret but spiteful scabs.

其十四

阴阳顺逆不难寻，节序推移有定音。
度尺罗裙先整线，刀裁绣榻再穿针。
宁听壮士会行义，莫看奸豪能舍身。
信口一言①君子气，落空转脸小人心。

【注释】

①信口一言：轻诺之言。不要轻易向人许愿，轻易许愿，会丧失信用。

Fourteen

Positive or negative, it could be accessible to
The seasonal order well attuned.
To rule the silk skirt, first prepare your thread,
After cutting out the embroidered couch, then thread your needle.
We' d rather hear a chivalric man
Than a double-dealing tycoon ready to die.
Having shot off his mouth like the man of virtue,
His heart as a mean man fails and faces away.

其十五

静河迢递①无声色，怒海鳌头欲水翻。
布鼓②滞留犹纳爽，旱雷来去却空喧。
迷经怎么就三点，悟道原来只一圈。

强聒[3]鸣蝉吹噪柳，顽聋达性也心烦。

【注释】

①迢递（tiáo dì）：遥远貌。②布鼓：用布蒙的鼓。典故名，典出《汉书》卷七十六《王尊传》："毋持布鼓过雷门"。颜师古注："雷门，会稽城门也，有大鼓。越击此鼓，声闻洛阳……布鼓，谓以布为鼓，故无声"。后以"布鼓"为浅陋之典。③强聒（qiǎng guō）：唠叨不休。不要唠唠叨叨，别人不愿听也说个不停，使人厌烦。

Fifteen

The distant river stays calm,
The furious sea tumbles and billows upon the turtle.
Stopped by the cloth drum, it's still open-hearted,
In the thunder without rain, it barely bustles back and forth.
How could the sutra contains only three points like a mystery?
Cultivating the Truth proves to be one circle.
While the tireless cicadas scream in the willows,
Even a perfect deaf would be perturbed in nature.

其十六

人际升沉嘴一张，肩头上面滚炎凉。
穷途失语说高矮，末路提音论短长。
背后乱心还肆虐，人前平眼正清狂。
软嘲硬讽[1]穿空穴，无故突然扑雪霜。

【注释】

①软嘲硬讽：指讥评之言。不要说讥讽别人的话。喜欢讥讽、议论

别人的人，对自己的要求往往马虎。

Sixteen

Up or down, one interpersonal mouth
Rolls its vicissitudes over the shoulders.
The damb, dead end touches upon the height,
But not upon the length aloud.
Behind the back, the mind wanders yet rages on,
In the eyes of men, he's extremely frivolous in behavior.
With the soft sarcasm and strong satire through the hollow hole,
The frost and snow are piling up abruptly for nothing.

其十七

番薯佯愚①充土豆，角瓜吹气扮南瓜。
怀胎本是乌拉草，落地强为豆蔻花。
世代愁中行苦役，浮生梦里是官家。
各人术业难均等，出位之言②啼乱鸦。

【注释】

①佯愚：化自白居易《放言五首》之“但爱臧生能诈圣，可知宁子解佯愚”。②出位之言：不要说不符合自己身份、地位的话。

Seventeen

The sweet potato simulates the potato,
The huffed courgette plays the part of a pumpkin.

In litter, he should have been a sedge,
Newly-born, he's forced to be a cardamun blossom.
For generations, he has to do corvée labour in sorrow,
In the dream of the worldly life, he would be an official.
Professionally, each one can hardly be created equal,
But the words outside his position are cawing wildly.

其十八

胜情[①]化作酒中情，杯酒无晴天又明。
乘兴提壶才纵跃，降欢顾影又横行。
高低嘴上少生事，表里心中全摆平。
狎下之言[②]虽可近，不恭不逊坏名声。

【注释】

①胜情：高雅的情趣。②狎（xiá）下之言：亲近而态度不庄重的话语。戒狎下之言，也就是不要对下属讲过分亲密的话，以免下属迎合你而落入圈套。

Eighteen

The won wine dissolves into the passion,
Dark in the cup but up to the another bright day.
In high spirits, fill high the cups in cheers,
Before the self-affected mind runs wild again.
High and low, let the mouth of the sleeping dog lie,
Outside and inside the heart, flatten that tongue.
The intimate words may be approachable, though,
The irreverent impertinence would blacken the name.

其十九

立身坦荡浮沉路，险境愁绝①不纳针。
阅己只能付苦笑，读人无计向知音。
功名醉后无明眼，利禄尊前有暗心。
堂印烧香长跪履②，谄谀③肝胆不如禽。

【注释】

①愁绝：极端忧愁。②堂印：宰相居政事堂所用的官印，泛指权柄。跪履：《史记·留侯世家》载：汉张良游下邳圯上，遇褐衣老父堕履圯下，命良取履，并长跪履之。老父曰："孺子可教矣"。授以《太公兵法》。后以"跪履"表示向长者虚心求教。③谄谀（chǎn yú）：说吹捧奉承别人的话。吹捧奉承别人，是人品卑微的表现。

Nineteen

On the broad road up or down, the life
Won't be needled under the woeful jaws of death.
To read himself can but give a wry smile,
To read others can do nothing about the kindred spirit.
After drunken, the fame and fortune has no bright eyes,
That harbours a dark heart before the cups.
To kneel on the stomach, he burns incense for the power,
Worse than a beast with his sycophant heart.

其二十

乞丐横膝闹市中，钵盂[①]冷暖四时风。
黄粮戾气[②]一人足，烩菜膻腥[③]两手空。
浪迹衙门难肺腑，衰容宾幕[④]不由衷。
做人奴眼频摇尾，仆腿卑屈[⑤]心虎熊。

【注释】

①钵盂（bō yú）：僧人的食器。此处指要饭罐子。②黄粮：黄粱。戾气：暴戾之气。③膻腥：荤腥。亦指鱼肉类食物。④宾幕：幕府；幕僚。⑤卑屈：低俯弯曲。戒卑屈之言，不要低三下四，说奴颜婢膝的话，因为德厚者无卑词。

Twenty

Along the downtown the pauper goes on the knee,
With a begging bowl, hot or cold in the wind of the seasons.
The ruthless dream might be well fed,
Of stinking smell the hotchpotch will go empty-handed.
In the vagrant office, there's no heartfelt words,
Senescently, the aides and staffs speak with forked tongues.
Slave-eyed, they wag their tails once and again,
Lackey-legged, they kiss the ground but with the heart of tigers and bears.

其二十一

南北摇霜行易水，东西千载一荆轲。
子夫[①]巫蛊良臣少，有壬[②]招降黠吏多。
开口任从来雾雨，话心无意起风波。
正邪难辨乌鸦嘴，取怨[③]奸人落狗窝。

【注释】

①子夫：卫子夫（？—前91年），名不详，字子夫，河东平阳（今山西临汾）人。汉武帝刘彻第二任皇后，在皇后位38年，谥号思。是中国历史上第一位拥有独立谥号的皇后。于建元二年（前139年）入宫，建元三年（前138年）封为夫人，元朔元年（前128年）册立为皇后，征和二年（前91年）在巫蛊（wū gǔ）之祸中自杀身亡。②有壬：许有壬（1286—1364），元代文学家。字可用，彰德汤阴（今属河南）。延祐二年（1315）进士及第，授同知辽州事。后来官中书左司员外郎时，京城外发生饥荒，他从“民，本也”的思想出发，主张放赈救济。河南农民军起，他建议备御之策十五件。又任集贤大学士，不久改枢密副使，又拜中书左丞。他看到元朝将士贪掠人口玉帛而无斗志，就主张对起义农民实行招降政策。他在政治上曾提出过不少改革意见，采纳者少，招怨者多，甚至丢官。③取怨：招致怨恨。戒取怨之言，是说不要说招人怨恨的话，播下使人怨恨的种子。

Twenty-One

North and south，the frost rocked along the Yishui River，
East and west，Jing Ke went down to posterity.
In the witchcraft by Empress Zifu，there were few loyal subjects，

To recruit deserters by Xu Youren, there were more crafty officials.
To speak up, they counted the light drizzles,
To speak freely, they had no thoughts of an uproar.
Good or evil, it was hard to distinguish the crow's mouth,
To fall in for grudge by the wicked man, they fell into the doghole.

其二十二

是非不辨隐灾殃，腋下结胎恶语长。
钩嘴滴寒植佞惑[①]，弹舌溜雪种萧墙。
隐微易设云偏暖，明盛难防水更凉。
招祸[②]无需去卜命，人谋耕土浅深秧。

【注释】

①佞惑：谄佞，媚惑。②招祸：招来祸患。许多祸害，往往是说话不当的结果。

Twenty-Two

The arbiter of right and wrong has not a hidden disaster,
But the conceived armpit extends the rough edge of the tongue.
Down the beak drops and grows the cold, wicked demagogy,
On the facile, snowy tongue sows the internal strife.
The esoteric matter works out under the warmer clouds,
And the bright vigour seems worse than the colder water.
To provoke a disaster dispenses with the oracle,
The wise scheme can plow deep or shallow soil.

哪家强[1]

铁牢深锁闭秃阳，十载潜躯不佩光。
俯仰只愁多怨憎，屈伸空叹更夭伤[2]。
萧森一去添新岁，寥廓今来裹旧疮。
漠漠苍天行日月，盈盈人海要图强。

【注释】

①哪家强：源自蓝翔技校招生广告语——“挖掘机技术哪家强”。②夭伤：夭折损伤。

Who's Stronger?

The bald sun was firmly locked in the iron prison,
That wore the light to be hidden for a decade.
Up or down, what worried was mostly rancorous,
Flexible or tractable, what sighed fell dead in vain.
As another new year was coming drearily,
The old scars were swathed here into the open space.
Like the sun and the moon travelling across the vast heaven,
One should rise in great vigour among the seas of humanity.

嫩　模[1]

靓妆靓面靓风情，辉赫章台[2]猫步行。
嫩笋穿阶清月破，香梅滴露素圆明。
转眸翦水动三处，回首横波铺一城。

江畔软沙抚细浪，含娇野色采香苹。

【注释】

①嫩模：又叫靓模（粤语，即“嫩模”），是香港的新兴名词，指年轻靓丽的少女模特，是非传统意义上的模特。她们没受过正统训练，年纪很小，甚至不到20岁，大眼美女，卖点是可爱和漂亮，不见得很高挑。②辉赫：显赫；煊赫。章台：古台名，即章华台，喻指柳。“章台走马”指冶游之事。此处指T形台。

Tender Model

Pretty look, pretty love, pretty make-up,
Down the catwalk she struts or strides,
Like a tender bamboo shoot through the clear moon along the steps,
Or the wintersweet that drops the pure dews, bright and round.
The smart glim of her eyes has scissored three ripples,
Which are strewn all over the city when looking back on
The soft sand soothed with the ripples at the river bank
Delicately pretty and unruly before the sweet grass.

你懂的

追魂明镜半垂眼，走马莺啼心不宣。
萝蔓浮光细雨冷，柳丝远岫长云牵。
人言无处不回首，鸟散凭空难比肩。
伤感如何寻旧迹，疮疤下面怨愁眠。

You Know

The bright, soul-traced mirror drops its eyes,
Like a wordless ambler or warbler.
As the vines are shimmering their cold drizzles,
The far, willowy hills are bridled by the long clouds.
It is stated that one has to look back here and there,
And that birds gone are hard to jostle out of thin air.
But how to seek the old, sentimental traces?
Now, below the scars, the gloomy sleep grumbles there.

逆　袭[①]

暴骨荒泉风裂地，边沙云暖又新生。
剑寒负气才平虏，翅广豪歌又远征。
百战夫家知义重，三千子弟看身轻。
人生大角[②]冲绝漠，虽是疲兵还论兵。

【注释】

①逆袭，网络游戏常用语，指在逆境中反击成功。逆袭表达了一种自强不息、充满正能量的精神。多用在形容本应该是失败的行为，却最终获得了成功的结果。②大角：大角星，北斗七星指示方向的标志，亮度至少是太阳的110倍，为二十八宿之首。

Counterattack

In the wind cracks, the bare bones down the barren fountain

Were revitalized again on the sandbar below the warmer clouds.
In severe snaps, the headstrong swords conceived the conquest of the captives,
Before commencing their long compaign in the manly timbre on the wing.
A true man valued the titles of good fellowship through hundreds of battles,
And the three thousand people's soldiers stared death fearlessly in the face.
To be Arcturus in life that defied the desolate patches of desert,
The soldiers dead on their feet would still fight on paper.

女汉子①

罗裙才解换罗裤，铁臂摇风知不知。
澹荡折腰仍自负，飘摇抵掌②不喧卑。
红颜诟怒③愁飞虎，绿鉴磨牙怯吼狮。
颠倒乾坤凭胆气，女人无奈变须眉。

【注释】

①女汉子：是指一般行为和性格向男性靠拢的一类女性。形容女性可能言行粗鲁、个性豪爽、独立、有男子气概等大众认为女性不应拥有的特质，是一个有褒有贬的网络语言。②抵（zhǐ）掌：击掌。③诟（gòu）怒：怒骂；嗔怒。

The Tough Girl

To slip out of her skirt and into the pants,
Her muscled arms rock in the prevaricated wind.

Her hips are swinging mellowly but priggishly,
Her swinging high-five bustles naturally and properly.
Flying into a rage, her rosy cheeks stagger a flying tiger,
In the green mirror, her grinded teeth daunt a lion's roar.
Courageously, in the heaven and earth upside down,
A lady has been forced to be the very man.

偶稀饭[1]

酱紫高关常掩关，提鞋鸡犬上云间。
飞萝不懂水中水，瀑布难明山外山。
迢递游娱[2]无仕宦，飘摇玩物有权奸。
天朝官场偶稀饭，走马阴阳百变颜。

【注释】

①偶稀饭（我喜欢）：是网络语言的变音，走调了，还能听懂。比如“酱紫”是“这样子”，念念就能找到原形。变音都是为了趣味性。
②游娱：游戏娱乐。

I Like It

Though shut out of the high pass this way,
The fowls and dogs ascended to the clouds that way.
Though the swift dream knew not the water in the waters,
The waterfall was not clear about the mountain beyond the mountains.
Though there were not officials for a sightseeing tour,
There are political conspirators in sensuous luxury.
How I fancied the officialdom of the celestial court!
In that the light and dark pacers changed their rapid colours.

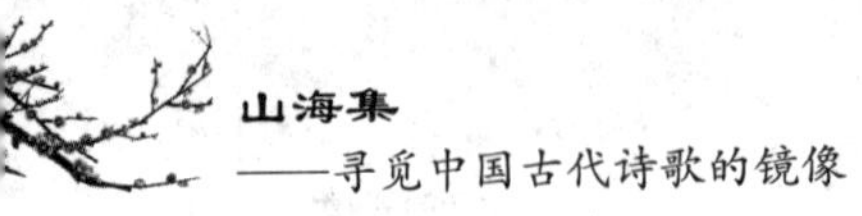

咆哮体

犬儒[1]喷箭猛于虎，杀气割寒嘶雪刀。
飒飒林禽扑叶落，萧萧野客掠风高。
纵眉连指敲孤月，横目粘屏击怒涛。
有木有人伤不起，飞云咆哮散鹅毛。

【注释】

①犬儒：玩世不恭，看透一切，政治冷感。

The Roaring Genre

The cynic shoots up arrows more dangerous than a tiger,
In the aura of death that scythes its screaming snows.
As the fowl are swooping with the rustling leaves,
The whistling loner has swept past the hard winds.
As the frowned fingers knock at the solitary moon,
The scowled computer screen clicks its angry billow.
Is there anybody entirely vulnerable to the hurt?
The scudding roars have come loose like goose feathers.

跑　酷[1]

追箭别来收野弦，满城晓镜有风穿。
两行步履千寻地，一尺开襟四季天。
月陌常闻绿蚁醉，云缰偶见跳蛙欢。
茶烟鹤迹荒萝嫩，屋顶白猫惊暖眠。

【注释】

①跑酷：来自法文的 parcourir，直译就是到处跑。此外，它还含有超越障碍训练场的意思。

Parkour

After the arrow, he controlled his string
That soughed all over the town in the mirror of dawn.
His two steps measured up thousand strands of land, with
One foot of collar unbuttoned in the circle of seasons.
Though the moon-lit road often heard the sots,
The cloud rein came upon the vigorous leapfrog.
His crane clue thru the bright, barren vines in the tea smoke
Would startle the snug sleep of the white cat on the roof.

炮弹鱼

巨卵哂食原大头，追风黄嘴在乘流。
菱形炮弹方明射，甲状枪丸又暗投。
利齿摧折龙骨架，钢牙咬断马骷髅。
曲言直语风雷恶，变色趋时皆自由。

Bullet Mackerel

Originally big-headed, the huge egg smirks its food,
After the wind, the yellow mouth flows with the waves.
The prismatic shell has just been fired openly,

The bullet out of its armour will be shot secretly.
Its sharp teeth can rip the skeleton of a dragon,
Its fangs of evil can gnaw the skull of a horse.
Direct or crooked, its tongue is like a vicious tempest,
That changes its colour adapted to the free times.

朋　友

云行雁过有朋党，撩乱朋徒纵猎声。
老酒朋情谁共醉，良朋野兴我飞觥。
交朋书剑冰壶[①]重，幕客亲朋碧玉轻。
隔岸有朋常入梦，超遥[②]此岸不虚行。

【注释】

①书剑：书籍和宝剑，指读书做官，仗剑从军。本谓做官或从军，离乡背井，漂流在外，后谓因求取功名而出门在外，久游未归为“书剑飘零”。冰壶：盛水的玉壶，比喻洁白。②超遥：高远；遥远。

Friend

Through the clouds, the wild goose flies with his partners,
Teased in confusion, the followers are free to the baying.
With who to be friendly drunken by the wet goods?
Now buddies, follow my cup gaily and recklessly.
To make friends, a chivalrous scholar should be noble and crystal,
To be a man after my own heart, jaspers are worthless as dust.
Opposite the shore, the fellows often come into my dreams,
And on this shore afar, the fame is indeed deserved.

铅笔鱼

绫梭化作一支笔，横亘清河写净云。
软水粗豪闲百对，硬风肥瘦闹千群。
长鳍张力应难见，短焰驰情更不闻[①]。
头短平牵三线过，嘴突啄朽胜八分。

【注释】

①“短焰”句：火焰铅笔鱼（Red Arc Pencilfish）是一种稀有珍贵的鱼种，因其鲜红的体色和高贵的身价而被众多鱼友垂涎。公鱼发情的时候体色会达到“血红”的境界。

Pencil Fish

The silk shuttle turns into a pencil,
Across the clear river that sketches the spotless cloud.
In the soft water, a hundred pairs are leisurely raucous,
Like the stiff wind, a thousand shoals fumble at various width of figures.
It's hard to see a long fin with its tensile force,
Still less the red arc that lives with abandon.
As the short, three-line head swims flat,
The protruded nibble at what's rotten makes a go of it.

妾　思

罗带张弛野柳宽，相思门外盼合欢。

牵衣华露尚能饮，把臂青云未可餐。
细雨遮羞愁绪在，空庭掩梦泪痕干。
不求锦翼衔春酒，夏晚当心云气寒。

A Yearning Wife

Loose or tight, her silk belt wide as a wild willow leaf
Suffers the pangs of love for a reunion outside the door.
The tangled dews on the petals may be drinkable,
But the gripped cloud can be inedible.
In the shame-veiled drizzles, her skein of sorrow entangles,
And her tear stains are covered up by the dry dream in the empty hall.
She has no desire for his spring wine on the wing,
But watches for her man by a cold air in the summer night.

青蛙鱼

椭圆一迹在台湾，鼓荡阴清沧海间。
体表红蓝镶亮点，肌肤黄绿嵌花斑。
流谦明灭转花雨，常顺盈虚①藏暗山。
凸眼平穿台海事，钓鱼岛外匿权奸②。

【注释】

①盈虚：盈满或虚空。谓发展变化。②权奸：弄权作恶的奸臣。

Mandarinfish

One oval trail in Taiwan
Wells up in the clear, hidden sea.
With a bright mosaic of red and blue spots,
Its skin may be inlaid with yellow and green dapples.
With the humble flickers shifted into the showers of petals,
It fits in well with what hides in the hills that wax and wane.
With its goggle-eyed flat through the cross-strait affairs,
There are latent traitors in power beyond the Diaoyu Islands.

人啊人

功名衰迈是穷途，不见和珅成蟹奴[①]。
邪路倾夺[②]收四海，贪泉窥霸有三吴[③]。
智人莫作衙中吏，贤者别当俎[④]上鲈。
豺虎纵横未竟日，谁人尝胆敢狂愚[⑤]？

【注释】

①蟹奴：俗称蟹子，又称蟹寄生。幼体自生生活，成体寄生。形如小袋，突露在蟹的头胸部与腹部交界处的腹面，其根状分枝突起穿入蟹体全身各部分内，吸取养料。随寄主分布于浅海。②倾夺：竞争。③三吴：指代长江下游江南的一个地域名称。④俎（zǔ）：切肉或切菜时垫在下面的砧板。⑤尝胆：化典“卧薪尝胆”，出自《史记》卷四十一《越王勾践世家》。狂愚：狂妄愚昧。

Man! Man!

Fame and fortune will wane to the last,
See that He Shen ever grew out of the crab parasite
Who rapped and rended viciously within the four seas,
And peeped over and preempt the southeast insatiably.
A wise man should not be a mandarin,
And a sage not the weever on the chopping block.
Before the ravenous beasts finished running rampant,
Who dare resolve firmly to be mad in folly?

人生礼赞

幽涧敲风一脉清，绿萝摇浪奏金筝。
凌波漱齿掠光碎，夹岸游鳞冲玉声。
万仞悬崖危梦断，千寻瀑布壮心惊。
飞流激作人生颂，半世浮沈任我行。

A Psalm of Life

A clear breath knocked by the serene gully
Waves its green vines like the golden zither
That rinse the teeth in the broken lights
Of the tinkling fish between the banks.
Off the immeasurable cliff breaks the crumbling dream,
And below a thousand strands of waterfall the stout heart startles.
If the torrent dashes down into the psalm of life,

Let me sink or swim free half a century.

人生有多远
How Far the Life Is?

其一

嗁婴转瞬成白叟，人去庭空已闭关。
今日觅升为岳顶，明朝沉陷变河湾。
蜉蝣虚翅想和运，蝌蚪实足举步艰。
且问寿夭[1]多少丈，从生到死喘息间。

【注释】

①寿夭：寿限。

One

The crying baby grows suddenly up into a white-haired man,
Whose courtyard will have emptied out entirely.
Today, the peak rises out of the underwater world,
Tomorrow, it will have sunken into a river bend.
A dayfly with its weak wings hopes a streak of good luck,
And a tadpole is now so hard to move its feet.
Tell me how long the span of life could be measured,
From the cradle to the grave, it is between wheezes.

其二

前岭谁能知后山，杨花暗度几梁弯。
东风启户铺心海，栖旅[1]凭轩点鬓斑。
玉树飘摇情乍变，朱门荡漾景长关。
从迷到悟有多远，节量[2]原来一念间。

【注释】

①栖旅：旅居之处；寄身他乡。②节量：限量。

Two

How could the front ridge understand the back hill?
The willow catkins slip through some bent girders.
As the door to my heart sea opens in the east wind,
The perched journey by the window has slightly grey-haired.
Below the tottering trees, what's promised has evaporated,
Behind the red, rippling gate, the scene shuts long.
What's the distance between the wrong ideas and the truth?
The limitation of quantity proves within the speed of thought.

其三

琪树[1]百舌鸣晓幕，骄痴过影落白鹇[2]。
丝光放眼摇花尾，素彩寻芳弄赤颜。
待雪辞恩才焕烂[3]，衔花谢宠又纷纶[4]。
青春行乐频更主，爱恨无常眨眼间。

【注释】

①琪树：常指仙境中的玉树。②骄痴：天真可爱而不懂事。鹇(xián)：尾长，雄的背为白色，有黑纹，腹部黑蓝色，雌的全身棕绿色，是世界有名的观赏鸟。③焕烂：光明灿烂。④纷纶：杂乱；众多。

Three

After all the jasper trees tweedle and warble at dawn,
The shadow of a silver pheasant falls sweetly and affectedly.
His dappled tail wags in the open, silken light,
And his white colour seeks the red-faced sweet.
The moment the graceful snow bids farewell brilliantly,
All proud flowers wither away, but again n a riot of colour.
Youth gone on the spree changes hands once and again,
Love and hate are so capricious in the blink of an eye.

其四

春芽年末长成山，崇峻[①]风流不可攀。
昨夜王侯埋帝冢，今朝公子过秦关。
惟中[②]致远结蝇翅，善保[③]高居联虎斑。
从古到今有几载，襟情[④]一抹笑谈间。

【注释】

①崇峻：高大。②惟中：明代严嵩（1480—1567），字惟中，号勉庵、介溪、分宜等，江西分宜人，弘治十八年（1505）二甲进士。他是明朝著名的权臣，擅专国政达20年之久，与其子严世蕃狼狈为

奸，贪财纳贿，卖官鬻爵，结党营私，祸国殃民。后被弹劾罢官，抄其家所得金银、珍宝、字画，数以百万计。③善保：清代贪官和坤（1750—1799），原名善保，字致斋，后由塾师重起官名“和坤”，其父为满洲正红旗人，姓钮祜禄氏。任军机大臣20多年，专擅弄权，控制官员升迁，大肆贪污。嘉庆四年（1799）定其20大罪状，赐死。查没金银、珍宝极多，时有“和珅跌倒，嘉庆吃饱”之谚。④襟情：情怀。

Four

The spring bud grows up into a hill at the end of year,
Which is nearly impassable for its towering height.
Last night, the liege lord was buried in the royal mausoleums,
Today, the patriarchal son is passing the secluded valley.
Yan Song formed his cabal out to what was remote,
And He Shen ganged up in his haughty position.
How many years have gone from the ancient times?
It only lasts from chat to laughter, to be sure.

其五

澄江披雾秦楼月，冷暖开合白玉环。
莫怪红梨无去信，多情紫豆有离颜。
朝光不问低岩瘦，阴气相杂高鸟闲。
你我距离知远近，无非善解一挥间。

Five

One moon over the gay quarters by the clear, foggy river
Opens and shuts her white jade ring, warm or cold.
Blame not the red pear that's gone without trace,
The amorous, purple bean has parted in sorrow.
The dawn light would let off the lower and lean crags,
And one bird higher stays easy before the mixed evil spirits.
How far is it between you and me?
It's but a stroke of understanding.

入　浴

七月火龙焚四野，满城脱屣[①]扑河湾。
绪风[②]摇曳裁南岭，端日飘萧酿[③]北山。
黄杏夭矫[④]留物外，红桃姝魅窥人间。
通犀[⑤]千百露光影，跳荡横波在解鬟。

【注释】

①屣（xǐ）：鞋。②绪风：馀风。③端日：农历正月初一日。飘萧：飞扬貌。④夭矫（jiǎo）：形容姿态的伸展屈曲而有气势。⑤通犀：《汉书·西域传赞》："明珠、文甲、通犀、翠羽之珍盈於后宫。"化自段成式的戏高侍御"不独邯郸新嫁女，四枝鬟上插通犀"。

To Be Bathed

In July, the open country burns by the fire dragons,
All the shoes of the city are removed into the river.
The breeze lingers and tailors the Nanling Mountains,
But brews the North Mountains drearily all day long.
As the yellow apricot stretches outside the world gracefully,
The red peach may peep over the earth seductively.
The trees of tacit understanding are checkered with shaded lights,
That may be beaming out of the eyes with the free hair.

扫　黄

玉箫载妓飞天去，绣户含娇紫月春。
客馆琼浆调润雨，灵州玉液绣芳茵。
天回①塞曲漏声旧，地隐潮声曙色新。
粉汗樱桃落玉腕，阳台天眼窥朱唇。

【注释】

①天回：天旋，天转。形容气象雄伟壮观。

Porn-purging Campaign

The whore soars up in the flute,
To the purple spring moon from her delicate door,
Where her nectar sups take liberties with gentle rains,
And embroider the fragrant carpet of the psychic isle.

As the northern heaven revolves its worn, melodious tick-tocks,
The earth hides its tides in the new light of early dawn.
After the sweet, sweat cherry falls down her pure arms,
The sky eyes on the balcony peep through her red lips.

晒　客①

一团篝火照银砂，暖卧黄鸡啼老家。
隔岭分明翠幕卷，临门又见日光斜。
曝衣子夜自然隐，承露行云不用遮。
天网平铺晒海岸，青天下面数鱼虾。

【注释】

①晒客：把自己的淘宝收获、心爱之物，所有生活中的零件拿出来晒晒太阳，统统放在网络上，与人分享，任由评说。这种分享，不为炫耀，不比金钱，只为展示生活、分享快乐。

Share

One bonfire beamed down upon the silver sand, where
One yellow cock in warm sleep crowed towards his old home.
Beyond the mountains, the green curtains rolled clearly,
Before the door, the west sunbeam was seen again.
Unlike the open-air clothes hidden naturally at midnight,
The dewy, rolling clouds would get out of the cover.
While the skynet were sprawled on the coast to be dried out,
The fish and shrimps could be counted in the broad daylight.

伤 逝

孤芳片月望汀洲，肥瘦衔环两不休。
楚客神云腾性野，湘君雾雨困情幽。
芳华一夜成枯木，翠黛三天化土丘。
岁箭仰天追绿发[①]，青肤嘶雪作孤囚。

【注释】

①绿发：乌黑而有光泽的头发。

The Regret for the Past

One flower gazed into the moon over the sand islets,
That, thick or thin, drove her constant ring.
The roamer rode on the divine, wild cloud,
Trapped in the secret emotion by the fog showers.
Over night, the sweet petals withered away,
And the pretty lady was lowered into the grave after three days.
Though the time arrow ran after the black hair in the sky,
The black skin neighed to the imprisoned snow in solitude.

射水鱼

河海神伏高架炮，连发点射一寻高。
厚薄唇里一枪管，咸淡舌尖两面刀。
白玉宽斑腾浅水，黄金窄线跃深涛。
七星吊影寻天路，灵眼青锋锁兔毫。

Archer Fish

In the river or the sea are ambushed the ack-acks,
Firing in semi or full-auto, only about 8 feet high.
Thick or thin, the lips have a rifle bore,
Brinish or limnetic, the tongue tips are two-edged.
Like white jade, the broad spots splash out of the shoal water,
Like gilded threads, the narrow lines dive into the deep waves.
As the seven stars are seeking their sky road,
The inner, blue-tipped eyes will lock a hare's hair.

失　败

军败穷荒①翻落叶，哪如官败谢秋风。
饱学常败因名满，瘦业多怀败袖空。
不见败弓引皓月，但明败箭射天宫。
古今成败写青史，一败愚蒙②再败中。

【注释】

①穷荒：绝塞；边荒之地。②愚蒙：愚昧不明。

Failure

The troop debacle wheeled like the wild leaves,
Much less of the official effect down the autumn wind.
An erudite may be crushed by his celebrity,
And an empty sleeve will mostly dissipate the job.

Don't you see the lost bow at the bright moon?
We clearly see it lost before the Heavenly Mansion.
To be or not to be, all ages are vindicated in history,
One ignorant defeat will follow on another heels.

十动然拒[①]

醉墨云书[②]十万字，扒心滴血为佳人。
满园红蜡藏幽梦，孤枕青娥生暗颦。
萧瑟春烟浮利脸，动情夜色颤香唇。
谁知蝶翅飘飞叶，相恋相怜两不真。

【注释】

①十动然拒：网络新词，“十分感动，然后拒绝了”的缩略形式。用来形容屌丝被女神或男神拒绝后的自嘲心情。②云书：典籍。

Fully Moved Then Rejected

Freely drunken, a hundred thousand words
Opened the bleeding heart for the fair lady,
Whose secret dream stored a gardenful of red candles,
Whose lithe pillow knitted her secret brows.
While the bleak spring smoke floated the faces of gain,
The emotional night quivered her sweet lips.
Who knew that the butterfly wings fluttered like a leaf,
That loved and sympathized with each other, but untrue.

史　记

谪宦穷游天有眼，幽独避世也徒然。
膏腴不可全刮尽，贫贱无因尽榨干。
得志轻狂超北海，失群落寞坠深渊。
九州何止生蝇虎，青史得逢正气天。

In the Historical Records

The officials in exile roamed below the heaven's eyes,
And withdrew from the world lonely, but in vain.
The hard-won possessions should not be scraped up,
And the paupers should not be squeezed out.
The light smug jumped over the North Sea,
But sequestered down into the yawning abyss alone.
There are far more tigers and flies, China
Has met the fair and square period of history.

熟　女①

溪桥老翠现荷开，苔雨回竿曲岸来。
烟屿静闻临幸处，风山误触过春台。
谁家艳质方初种，何处妍姿可近裁。
莫看青瓜摇碧玉，奴家生子也生才。

【注释】

①熟女：从日本传播界流传过来的词汇，泛指 30～50 岁的成熟女

人。

Cougar

The lotus bloomed near the old, green creek bridge,
Where the moss rain came punting along the winding bank.
The misty isle listened to where she was well pleased,
The windy hill touched the last spring table so wrong.
Whose graceful charm had been sown fresh?
Where her beautiful posture could be tailored closely?
Despite the green cucumber swayed there like jasper,
The fair lady can be self-fertile, of both child and gift.

戍卒叫

朱门何处少饥人，铁胆石心跋扈[①]臣。
浩荡阴违上报政[②]，迢遥[③]阳奉下疲民。
惊心渭水走娼盗，浪迹长安行贱贫[④]。
刍狗[⑤]终究有一死，渔阳星火敢当仁[⑥]。

【注释】

①跋扈（bá hù）：专横暴戾。②报政：陈报政绩。谐音“暴政”。③迢（tiáo）遥：遥远貌。④贱贫：卑贱贫困。⑤刍（chú）狗：祭祀前用草扎成的狗，祭祀后即被丢弃。用以比喻微贱无用者。⑥渔阳：征戍之地，公元前209年陈胜、吴广等900余人兵变起义的地方。当仁：勇为不辞。

The Yells of Garrison Soldiers

Which red gate had no hungry men?
The iron-hearted subjects lorded it over.
Generously, he lied and played the double game politically,
But wore out the people all the way.
Dramatically, the Weihe River delivered the robbers and whores,
Vagrantly, the paupers were hobbling in Chang'an.
Even those like straw dogs must die so that the parks
Of fire in Yuyang would consider virtue as what was devolved.

水　仙

浅草幽幽醉锦弦，仙姝点点妙孤寒。
一泓清水香盈袖，百媚冰封尽去颜。
银盏漫舒知墨韵，金台素卷懂书坛。
婷婷劲骨红梅瘦，还看冰心散玉天。

【自解】

一个寒假，45 天，这期间，梅花自然是早已开过了，人工的百合和郁金香也凋谢了，唯有分期培植的水仙花，历经了春节，不为人艳，守着一个人的办公室独自地开放着。也正如闹市里孤独的人一样，纯粹、孤独的未来也许是更深的孤独。孤独惯了，再想不孤独，反倒不习惯了。

Daffodils

Amidst a crooned chord of shallow grass,
The fairies are peerless in cold spells.
By the glittering water their sweet sleeves
Have outshone other ice-bounded charms.
Rhymed in their leisurely and silvery cups,
Their pure volume knows the golden table.
After the red plum-blossoms have thinned,
Her bright ice hearts will be pure and still.

思　维
Thinking

其一：平台思维

溪渠悬钓百人竹，难比江洋细网伏。
遮莫[①]边城居广厦，不如紫禁住厢屋。
休说乌雀行山树，且看鲲鹏化水国。
抱月飞天小四海，手边红日滚天轴。

【注释】

①遮莫：假如；或许。

One: Platform Thinking

A hundred anglers by the stream
Are no match for the mesh grids in the river and the sea.
To live in the large house of a border-town
Is not as good as the wing-room in the forbidden city.
Forget that sparrow over the wild wood,
But behold the gigantic fish transformed in the sea.
To hug the moon, the four seas down look so small,
And the red sun at hand rolls its shaft of heaven.

其二：金融思维

平田耕饭千滴汗，秋后长车粮贩忙。
织鸟擎梭没懒慢[①]，飞鹰披锦忒张狂。
日中拂地才结网，夜半相萦又启航。
自古折腰出苦力，货财[②]嗜利有劫商。

【注释】

①懒慢：懒惰散漫。②货财：货物，财物。

Two: Financial Thinking

Thousands of sweats are ploughing the farm,
And the fleet of grain mongers is busy in late autumn.
The weaver bids are shuttling, but not slothful,
While the hawks in silk are flying arrogantly.

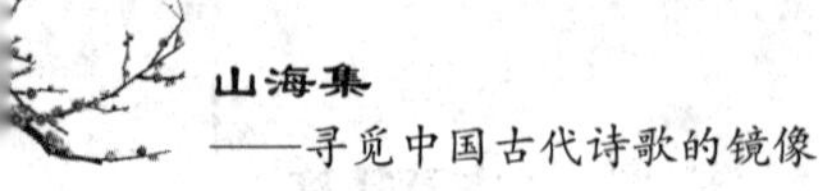

At midday, the stroked shoal is spinned,
At midnight, the enwrapped crew shall set sail again.
The coolies can break their backs from of old,
Bent solely on the main chance by the profiteers.

其三：跨界思维

右界沧茫四野宽，遐搜左界宦游盘[①]。
前朝上界驰戎马，下界人间拂翠澜。
莲界天花招鹤驾，梅天眼界会仙坛。
浮流心界浑无味，尘界扬尘水未干。

【注释】

①游盘：游逸娱乐。

Three: Cross-border Thinking

The right border is lost into the open country,
And the left border sought afar by the official pleasure,
That, a predecessor that galloped in the upper world,
Will be lower bounded to stroke the green waves.
Unlike the lotus world attracting the cranes
And the wintersweet in sight finding its celestial altar,
The heart of the swallet stream tastes so insipid,
And the world throws its dust before the water dries up.

其四：产融思维

远贾不知红粉贵，囊中摆浪杖头钱[①]。
珠钱何事连佳境，品位裘中任自然。
逐日堆钱容易见，一朝破散古难全。
休说暮齿逢衰世，空手灵犀有洞天。

【注释】

①摆浪：像浪涛一样颠簸。杖头钱：酒钱。

Four：Supplier-Financing Thinking

From afar，the trader blind to the costly rouge
Fiddled with the beer-money in the pocket.
What mated the cash strings with the fine state?
It was the quality of the fur coat free as air.
The money piled day after day can be noticeable
But imperfect once broken loose since the olden days.
Say not that the old teeth have met the shrinking time，
The tactic，free hands must have the world of their own.

其五：薪酬思维

酬功对酒入帷秋，客计[①]流年脚未休。
酬士壮心去猛虎，答君回眷[②]是幽洲。
酬身吻草时光减，敛翼含沙梦影收。
酬己价微自解语，闭门老死不相求。

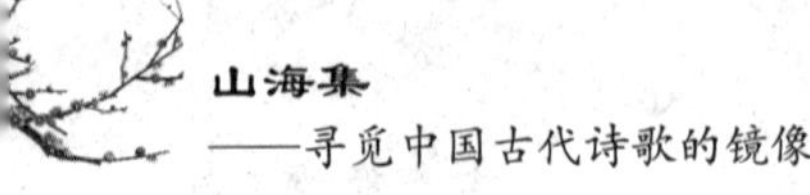

【注释】

①客计：在外地生活赖以倚靠的支柱；客中的生计。②回眷：回头看；眷顾。

Five：Payment Thinking

Curtained in the autumn，the celebratory beverages
Have roamed through the swift time without a foothold.
With the flaming heart in gratitude，drive out the fierce tigers，
To feed back what you came my way，go somewhere quiet.
In kissing the grass，the rewarded body takes away the hours，
And with the wings folded tight，the sand draws the shades in dream.
To compensate me cheap，I have to understand myself，
But will never ask for help till dead within my gate.

其六：互联网思维

三边[①]征役未牵马，大漠胡尘各自飞。
网络精粗商铺瘦，天涯疏密键盘肥。
锦囊薄暮摇轻扇，妙计平明[②]出绣帏。
自古赢家常澹定，杀伐未必做戎衣。

【注释】

①三边：边疆。②平明：天大亮时。

Six: Internet Thinking

Still on the horses in the frontier service,
All the barbarian dusts were flying in the great desert.
Crude or fine, the online shops are so tight,
Loose or solid, the keyboards afar so fat.
At twilight, the fine verse waves a light fan,
At dawn, the cunning scheme coms out of the silk curtain.
All winners must have an inner detachment since olden days,
To kill will not necessarily resort to the martial attire.

吐　槽①

微步心曲落青枝，枝上衔花凝怨思。
飞燕沈吟无解语，啭莺寂寞有谁知。
吐愁落日噪虫苦，入耳寒巢鸣客悲。
苦水一滴披冷露，衰红深处对风垂。

【注释】

①吐槽：来源于日语，“突っ込み”（黜臭）的音译。

Tsukkomi

My mind in microsteps falls down to the green twigs,
Which hold the flowers that meditate on resentment.
A flying swallow muses confusedly,
And a twittering oriole feels lonely, but who knows?

To spit the worries, the bugs are buzzing to the setting sun,
Into the ears, the cold nests are tweeting dolefully.
One drop of cold dew drops into the bitter water,
And the sapless red hangs in the deep wind.

网络暴民

指点江山吃大户，长歌愿作领头羊。
虐国蠡测[①]人心恶，弑政难名天意凉。
秽语斩伐方跳踯[②]，恶言訾毁[③]又颠狂。
键盘暴力披仁义，硕鼠横牙挖铁墙。

【注释】

①蠡（lí）测：用蠡（贝壳做的瓢）来量海，比喻见识短浅，以浅见量度人。②跳踯：上蹿下跳。③訾（zǐ）毁：也作“毁疵”。非议诋毁。

The Internet Mob

To measure out the world by force,
They crooned to be bellwethers.
Short-sighted, the tyrannized state created their nasty hearts,
Under the heaven's will, the untold control was coldly murdered.
The obscene outbursts of abuse jumped up and down,
And the backchats defamed with utmost causticity.
The violent keyboard clad in virtuous phrases
Was gnawing at the iron wall like a large rat.

网络大 V①

燕赵游侠心似铁，崩腾衢路②满城惊。
威棱③闭目千夫乱，锋刃低头四野宁。
独步西风堪负羽④，同群寒日可横行。
移山劲挺霸王气，混世无非一命轻。

【注释】

①网络大 V：网络大侠或重要人物。能称为网络大侠的都是那些“粉丝”众多的网络贵宾账户，现在，通常把“粉丝”在 50 万以上的称为网络大 V。②崩腾：奔走；奔波。衢路：歧路；岔道。③威棱：威势；威力。④负羽：背负羽箭。谓出征。

The Big V's on the Network

In the States of Yan and Zhao, the paladin was hardhearted,
Rushing and bustling through the shocked crossroads of the town.
Eye-closed, his formidable force brought chaos to thousands of men,
Nose-down, his sword blade calmed down the surrounding country.
With a bunch of arrows, he strode lonely in the west wind,
In cold winter, he could run rampant among his population.
With dogged perseverance, he conquered like a king loftily,
To wreaks havoc, his life was but a feather invariably.

望奎诗酒

高贤美酒青天色，梦里裴回[①]饮两壶。
狂客停杯辞牖户[②]，野人命酒下泥途。
他乡劝酒有高论，故里题名无大儒。
四海一瓶天下醉，横诗万卷古今无。

【注释】

①裴回（péi huí）：彷徨。徘徊不进貌。②牖（yǒu）户：窗与门。

The Poems and Wine of Wangkui

Gaoxian liquor tastes racy like the blue sky,
Lingering in the dream for a couple of pots.
While the bibbers halt their cup and shamble out,
The wild man takes to the bottle from the mud road.
In a strange land, his lofty mind inflicts the favourite drinks,
Where he was born, his scholar name should be inappreciable.
Drink the seas in one bottle now, the world would be on the go,
Before the ten thousand volumes of poems through all ages.

我的祖国

压顶三山四野空，上苍使力唱黎明。
银花闪电满天雪，火树流星遍地红。
鼠啮狼牙寻伴侣，猫出虎爪验雌雄。
三山一夜又压顶，千古家园四面风。

My Motherland

The three mountains on the head hollowed out the country,
Whose sky threw its hard drive to crow for a dawn.
As the dazzling snow streaked like silver flowers,
The flaming trees shot the red stars all over the land.
Now the rats in wolf's fangs sought their partners,
And the cats with tiger's claws measured their strength.
The three mountains bore down on the head over night,
And the homeland through the ages was dilapidated again.

惜　命

天步从容皓月高，悬梁钓日莫徒劳。
谁人竟岁捧金碗，何处终身裹绣袍。
万叶偷安烟雨啸，数枝窃静北风号。
双亲遗命应珍重，牢落[1]江湖有暗涛。

【注释】

①牢落：寥落。

The Dear Life

The bright moon steps leisurely in the high sky,
And it holds a candle to grind away at the sun.
Who can hold his gold bowl all the year round?
Where all his life wears the embroidered gown?

All the slack leaves whistle in the misty drizzles,
The twigs steal their still in the roaring north wind.
The life given by the parents should be cherished
In the wide world that billows secretly and darkly.

县　官

花雨琼浆明月升，萧郎[①]梦里递红灯。
珍馐酒影达晨壮，风乐衫光连夜征。
锦褥桃红滴玉露，银杯李白点悬冰。
风柔柳顺厌粱肉[②]，之子[③]何如侍县丞？

【注释】

①萧郎：原指姓萧的俊异男子，后泛指女子所爱恋的男子。②粱肉：精美的饭食。③之子：这个人。

County Magistrate

In the shower of petals, the bright moon rose in nectar,
Whence the merry man in dream handed over the red light.
The delicacies in the cup lasted strong till the morn,
And the gleamy dress took wreak on the metrical night.
On the silk mattress the red peach dripped its pure dews,
In the silver cup the white plum kindled its hanging ice.
Even the soft willow pursed its lips with the choice food,
How could your breeze wait upon such a county magistrate?

小鲜肉①

娇面恣游风物澹②，清歌惊笑管弦长。
三年折柳飞江燕，五载结欢吮野棠③。
香蕊冰开出谢女④，琼浆风暖卧萧郎⑤。
寻蝶轻梦别花眼，留醉啼莺有度娘⑥。

【注释】

①小鲜肉：女子眼中12岁至25岁单纯、俊俏男生。②风物：风景和物品。喻指大气候。澹：恬静、安然的样子。③野棠：棠梨。④谢女：晋代女诗人谢道韫，泛指女郎。⑤萧郎：情郎或佳偶。⑥度娘：百度的戏称。

Fresh Meat

Given the rein free, his tender face looks cosy
In the long, clear lutes and pipes that startle his smiles.
Three years, the river swallow flies with the broken willows,
Five years, the frisk lips suck the wild crabapples fabulously.
Out of the sweet pistils are thawed the fair ladies,
And in the mild nectar pronates the merry man.
Better read it right while seeking a butterfly in light dream,
And to the drunken face there's a lady to spend with in warbles.

心

虚心实腹抱文章，潜匿其德抵咎殃[①]。
迷眼平心调淡彩，定心隐面卸浓妆。
花心障日行流水，香炷抽心[②]照艳阳。
心大可容天下事，无心好运也难长。

【注释】

①咎殃：灾祸。②香炷（zhù）：点燃的香。抽心：情发于中。

Heart

The open mind hugs its full writings,
That mask the proper virtue against the disasters;
The blind heart mixes its light hues,
And the fixed heart hides its seductive face;
The heart of flowers flows like water against the sun,
And the heart of the incenses is sucked into the sunny rays:
A big heart should accommodate all the world,
And a heartless fortune would not last long.

心　态

心窗虑澹过三更，心镜凌霜也不惊。
俗眼系心方意想，尘心举目且无争。
论心有意行言重，使气乏心化理轻。
莫问离心失柳色，君心四季要分明。

The State of Mind

The heart window heaves weakly through the third watch,
And the heart mirror trembles no more by frosts;
The heart tied with the vulgar eyes imagines wishfully,
And the dust heart raises its gaze, aloof from the world;
The willful heart may change its courtesies,
And the tired heart surges under an undeserved measure: —
A heart at variance should lose its green, but no more!
In that it must be clear through the circle of seasons.

性乃迁
The Nature in Alteration

其一

红尘就在我身边，看破红尘也枉然。
自己心灵不去扫，他人世界乃云烟。
沧桑满眼别人错，反看身家几处寒。
我对人家没贡献，因何觍脸[①]让人担？

【注释】

①觍（tiǎn）脸：不知道害臊、不要脸。

One

The world stands beside me, and
To see through it would be in vain.
If the soul of mine is not swept,
The world of others will be misty.
In my eye, all others are wrong,
But brushing aside my defects.
With nothing special to be offered,
But why brazen to force another?

其二

江湖岁月横舟过，逆渡春秋看盛衰。
弱柳狂风冬雪落，强杨细雨夏云来。
苍天有信传承诺，大地无情守旧怀。
大隐人生知苦乐，为何小隐去五台。

Two

Time of the vagrant boating
Goes up through the rise and fall
Of feeble willows by winter snows
And vigorous poplars drizzled by summer clouds.
Even the worthy heaven must be committed,
The ruthless earth will act like an old fogy.
A prior life knows what' s sweet and sour,

But why follow the tonsured bonzes in yellow robes?

其三

雁过长城又一年，芙蓉国里是家园。
八千子弟[1]随风去，百万国军问老天[2]。
煮豆燃萁[3]不自省，萧墙祸起有心寒。
执著大雁还拍翅，效仿人形撇捺连。

【注释】

①八千子弟：陈胜、吴广起义后，项氏叔侄，即项羽和项梁，见天下大乱，便响应起义。于是，在秦二世元年，项羽杀死地方县令殷通，与项梁正式起义，在江东招兵，共征集八千人，即江东八千子弟兵，是项家军的主力。项梁、项羽对这支部队的感情之深厚，也非文字可语。后来，项羽垓下被围，突破至乌江时，对乌江亭长发出了如下感慨："我项籍（项羽名籍，古人自称用名，跟别人打招呼用字）带领江东子弟八千人渡江而西，今无一人还，纵江东父兄怜我而王，我何面见之？纵然他们不说，我项籍难道不有愧于心吗？"于是，自尽在乌江边。②问老天：化用"天若有情天亦老，人间正道是沧桑"。③煮豆燃萁（qí）：化用曹植《七步诗》，比喻骨肉相残。萁：豆茎。

Three

The wild geese were gone with the year,
From the Great Wall to their southern land.
Like the 8000 warriors gone with the wind,
Millions of national armymen asked the heaven.
If a fratricidal strife could not meditate on itself,

The disorder in the house would freeze the hearts.
Even the clinging geese still flapped their wings,
Trying to be stylisers that form the character "人."

亚婚姻①

万缕山情啼鸟怨，野情无畏可横行。
旅情乡梦犹悬耳，偷宿心空还挂情。
出户停眸接苦口，回身定面受丁宁。
陈仓古道应心动，暗度千年鬼不惊。

【注释】

①亚婚姻：已婚或者已有相恋对象，但感情或肉体都相当自由的群体。

Sub-marriage

All wild emotions are twittered in grudges,
And run amuck stout-heartedly.
With the toured passion, the native dream hangs in the ear,
To stay the night out, the hollow heart plays on the love strings.
Out of the door, the halted eyes receive the bitter mouth,
And turning away, the fixed face may be advised earnestly.
The old road must be heartfelt,
And the secret liaison won't disturb a ghost for ever.

颜　值[1]

人海蒙尘谁解颜，破颜不见绿云鬟。
凋颜地脉主人远，拥素天颜归客闲。
颜冷多愁幽趣躁，眼开好梦醉颜孱[2]。
颜值爆表为何事，且看红颜浓淡间。

【注释】

①颜值：网络词汇。源自日语“脸”的汉字，颜值表示人物颜容英俊或靓丽的数值，用来评价人物容貌。②孱：软弱；卑微；窘迫。

The Face Score

Who knows the face in the dust sea of humanity?
The green hair-locks are lost on the broken face.
The lord has left the wizen face of the land veins afar,
And the roamer returns without makeup at a leisurely pace.
On the cold, sad face, the delightful serenity feels fickle,
To behold, the sweet dream seems strait on the tipsy face.
I wonder why the face score has hit the limit,
Now let's see the shades of the rosy lips and cheeks.

也是蛮拼的[1]

霜爪搏风冲雪毛，万窍飞羽北风号。
翩翩旧怨不宜落，赫赫新愁无处逃。
直性秋蓬移步暗，安情春梦转天牢。

绝非鹏鸟不开翅，只怪横空峭壁高。

【注释】

①也是蛮拼的：《爸爸去哪儿2》中，曹格多次提到这句简单的口头语。意思是“挺努力，但是，即使很努力了，却没有成功”，具有反讽意味。

Much a Workholic

The frost claws against the snow wings of the wind
Are roaring from the north out of ten thousand holes.
Dancing lightly, the old hate shouldn't be falling,
Once so grand, the new sorrows could race to nowhere.
As the forthright fleabane moves darkly in the autumn,
The absurd love in spring dream enters other deep hollows.
It would be anything but expanding its wings, the roc
Might blame no one but the steep cliff in the air.

也是醉了①

一风一雨一新月，槐柳无声萤火急。
金粉学言犹可采，绣囊传信更当拾。
凌辰②虫响谁明解，薄暮孤灯我暗袭。
镜里半酣吃野酒，水星滴碗酿蓝汁。

【注释】

①也是醉了：一种对无奈、郁闷、无语情绪的轻微表达方式。通常表示无法理喻，无法交流，无力吐槽。可以和“无语”“无法理解”“无力吐槽”换用。②凌辰：凌晨。

Kidding Me?

One wind, one rain, one new moon,
Are fast and silent by the fireflies around the willows.
The gold powder that babbles can be recoverable,
And the silk sack to be mailed should be more effective.
Who could decode the buzzing bugs before dawn?
In the lonely light, the last faint glimmer sneaks me.
My mirror has been well warmed with the wild wine,
For Mercury brews the blueberry trickled into the bowl.

因与果
Cause and Effect

其一

死去金银两手空，青烟几缕化长风。
回眸娇妇嫁车里，遣梦玄夫[①]娶轿中。
簪笏[②]一朝离广殿，爵勋永世锁深宫。
严冬舍去一团火，落难收来福报功。

【注释】

①玄夫：乌龟。此处指续弦。②簪笏（zān hù）：冠簪和手板。古代仕宦所用。比喻官员或官职。

One

Gold and silver have vanished when dead,
Drifting as smokes in the long wind.
Glanced back, the charming wife came in the wedding car,
As if in a dream, the second wife came in the wedding chair.
Once the sceptres left the great hall,
The nobilties were locked into the leafy nook forever.
A fire handed out in the severe winter
Would be rewarded in distress.

其二

流落街头天已冷，烟花除岁更消魂。
宦情远道常芜没①，生事②同心早不存。
说是天堂还有路，人言地狱也无门。
忽如霄汉开青眼，化羽飞升去感恩。

【注释】

①芜（wú）没：淹没在荒草间。②生事：自专行事。

Two

Out on the cold streets,
The new year's firecrackers were more soul-consuming.
The official requirements afar were often stormed and captured, and
The undivided devotions as rabble-rousers had been socked away earlier.

With word that the paradise has more ways,
They say that the hell has no way back.
Unexpectedly, the blue sky opens its eyes,
And so better take wing for thanksgiving.

其三

恩情薄厚化浮波，穿过人生几道河。
左相苦言拦赤马①，右军香墨换白鹅②。
丹青柳艳寄清瑟③，宝镜桃明敛翠蛾。
花粉浪扑蝶翅绕，助人换取贵人多。

【注释】

①左相：唐初名相房玄龄，临终抗表进谏，请求太宗以天下苍生为重，停止征讨高丽。②右军：东晋王羲之曾任右军将军，世号王右军。③清瑟：指瑟。瑟音清逸，故称。

Three

Thick or thin, the true love has floated away,
Away through the rivers of life.
Premier Fang Xuanling remonstrated before His red horse,
And Wang Xizhi exchanged the white goose with his calligraphy.
With the smooth painting entrusted to the zither,
The bright mirror collects her eyebrows.
In the pollen billows, the butterflies are winging there,
And to help others will get more important persons in return.

其四

孤舟怨旷[①]不得意，一点禅心悬半空。
幽草荒庭堆落叶，残波废井锈回风[②]。
遗踪迁客绳床[③]下，惆怅清都[④]晚镜中。
幽咽[⑤]寒笛吹大野，无情烦恼剪双瞳。

【注释】

①怨旷：长期别离；女子无夫。②回风：回旋的风。③遗踪：旧址，陈迹。迁客：遭贬迁的官员。绳床：交椅，一种可以折叠的轻便坐具。④清都：神话传说中天帝居住的宫阙。⑤幽咽：微弱的哭泣。

Four

The lonely boat in a bad skin
Hangs its tiny, meditative mind in the midair.
The leaves down the meadow of my wasted court
Have rusted the air back to the wasted waves in the spent well.
While the lost trail roams below the hempen cot,
The pure, desolate capital looms in the night mirror.
While the wild toots on its cold, whimpering flutes,
The ruthless troubles have snipped off the eyes.

其五

禄薄居家不外求，戴河闲卧信悠悠[1]。
苔滑坐夏叠轻浪，萝密行禅熨浅流。
翠羽归航阳缕细，红鳞回沫月丝柔。
知足鸥燕自安逸，虎口贪残[2]无尽头。

【注释】

①信：果真。悠悠：从容自然的样子。②贪残：贪婪凶残（的人）。

Five

To live a deprived life, and asking for no help,
I' ve lounged by the Daihe River idyllically.
The mossy summer ripples there,
And the meditative vines are ironing the stream.
The green feathers are homing in the rays of the sun,
And the red fish are nibbling back in the soft rays of the moon.
Even a gull or swallow in contentment would be cozy itself,
The greedy and brutal mouth of a tiger never goes away.

其六

铁辔银蟾勒野树，风摇古塞断山横。
孤云荒壁隐身命，好鸟晴崖鸣不平。
过耳青刍[1]衔静恐，飞疃枯叶负遑宁[2]。
穷途有泪唯逃避，破败[3]余生瘦马行。

【注释】

①青刍（chú）：青草。②遑（huáng）宁：安定。③破败：破灭败亡。

Six

The iron bridle tight on the wild，moon-lit tree
Rocked the wind before the old，broken mountains.
The lonely cloud hided its life behind the wasted cliffs，
Where a fine bird was chirping against the injustice.
Still in fear，the ears have passed the green grass，
On tenderhooks，the dead leaves are flying into the eyes.
To the dead end，the tears could only be shirked out，
And dilapidated，the bony horse moves towards its last days.

其七

晴明江岸旷梨花，古塞南边是老家。
蝶醉浓荫偷蓓蕾，蜂痴幽径窥霜葩[①]。
连山十里人从俭，远水三秋果好奢。
典尽园辉[②]约上客，琼汁满桶作清茶。

【注释】

①霜葩：百花。②典尽园辉：倾尽菜园子里的时蔬。

Seven

Clear and bright, the pear flowers along the river
Are blooming to my old hut south down the Great Wall.
In soft shadows, the tipsy butterflies are stealing the buds,
Along the serene path, the spoony swarms spying the frost flowers.
About ten miles, the mountains have delved into frugal fashion,
And in late autumn days, the fruit-laden river stretches afar.
Let the vegetable garden treat my bright guests heartily,
And a bucketful of wine could serve as the pure tea.

其八

长川朔气攒冰雪，爽气高林枝叶新。
岚翠阴精①升地气，霞光紫气过天津。
蛮花闲气真还假，瘴气浮荣假作真。
灵气采得诗万首，水藏和气洗沙尘。

【注释】

①阴精：霜雪。也喻指月亮。

Eight

The northern chills collect the frozen snow constantly,
And the high wood take a greedy breath of fresh air.
The essence of earth goes up with the hazy, green moon,
And the rosy, ruddy glows flow through the heaven's ford.

The wild, idle flowers are true or otherwise,
And the pompous airs are false or not.
If the heart gets and livens up its ten thousand poems,
The gentle water could wash the griffy dust.

其九

举债前缘承果因，百忧十界起红尘。
贪权紫府作奴婢，好色青楼沦贱人。
暴虐黑心张利嘴，邪淫绿眼弄焦唇。
壮夫不辱中国梦，百丈悬冰看柳春。

Nine

In the predestined debt,
All sorrows have floated out of the ten realms.
The greedy power falls into the bondmaid of a purple hall,
And the carnal madam degenerates into a willing slut;
The brutal, black heart opens its sharp tongue,
And the wanton, green eyes clamp their parching lips. —
A vigorous man will not disgrace the Chinese dream,
That gazes out to the spring willows before the ice-falls.

其十

秋水结冰还作水，行云施雨更成云。
御人契阔求游宦[①]，御墨绸缪[②]偏好文。
鸡犬从来爱惑众，圣贤自古不结群。

锄文比作锄青稻，一纸行文汗两分。

【注释】

①契阔：辛苦。游宦：远离家乡在官府任职。②绸缪（chóu móu）：缠绵。

Ten

The frozen autumn will thaw into the water,
And the clouds after rain will be clouded again.
To control others, one toils to be official,
To control the pen, one fiddles at his sentimental skill.
All times, fowls and dogs have baffled the people,
From of old, sages and men of virtue never gang up personally.
To hoe the articles is like to hoe the paddy,
On whose sheet of paper the pen must pay more sweat.

其十一

福田地窄莫休耕，浅水夺鱼乏海鲸。
楼洞避风风更紧，盲人上路路难平。
梦中射箭箭无力，心里张灯灯不明。
举世如泥同醉去，醒来道远且独行。

Eleven

No fertile, narrow field would lie fallow,
No whale shall seize the fish in the shoal.

The wind blows harder through the doorway of a high-rise,
And the way for the blind could always be rugged.
The arrow fired in dream flies weakly,
And the lantern in heart can hardly be illuminated.
After drunk as a mouse together with the world,
One should wake up and walk alone down the road.

其十二

蜉蝣短寿流光彩，春夏婚飞亮羽衣。
鲲荡千层翻水厚，鹏抟①万里透云稀。
闲寻一叶能齐物②，静想三秋可忘机③。
有梦征夫怀四海，秦皇之剑照龙归。

【注释】

①抟（tuán）：向高空盘旋飞翔。②齐物：使事物齐而同之。③忘机：消除机巧之心。

Twelve

The short-lived mayfly gleams,
Swarming bright in spring and summer;
Out of the raging seas by the leviathan,
The roc whirls up through the clouds.
To seek free, one leaf can be created equal,
To think still, the late autumn can be carefree.
The man in dream embraces the four seas where
The First Emperor's sword shines the dragon's return.

鹰

秋毫风劲捕鹰眼，饥爪遐飞逞势来。
地脉千层磨利剪，天衣万尺任独裁。
白云掠影挥罗袖，明镜流光裹玉台。
坐断昆仑召日月，划开天水五行开。

Hawk

The hawk eye catches the tiny hair in high wind,
With the talons swooped down from afar.
On the earth veins, whet your scissors sharp,
And then tailor the heavenly robe as you like.
The white cloud skims over your silken sleeves,
And the bright mirror flickers about your jade table.
Steeled in the Kunlun Mountains, you summon the sun and moon,
And to rip the water from heaven, you' ve liberated the five elements.

忧宦

荣宦何知谪宦[①]难，方疑霜雪又凌寒。
两回紫燕亭边旧，一曲黄莺楼上残。
何事悲风巧佞[②]隐，苦将蔓草婢膝[③]盘。
良宵明月安可道，乱性原来一夜欢。

【注释】

①谪宦：被贬降的官吏。②巧佞：奸诈机巧，阿谀奉承。③婢膝：

侍女的膝；指下跪。

Official in Sorrow

How the honourable official knows those in trouble?
Their puzzling snow might have a new, frosty bite.
With the purple swallows gone off his pavilion twice,
One golden oriole chirps to the lost, lofty floors.
Why the doleful wind has hidden its artful flattery?
The creeping weed bows and scrapes like servile flatterers.
How to depict the bright moon in such an enjoyable night?
The nature of chaos proves to be one-night stand.

有钱，任性①

风月痴狂悬子叶②，随人臧否③去吞腥。
燕归野渡应须问，花落秋风何忍听。
富客布鞋行翠辇，穷人珠履走白丁。
人活一世谈何易，任性独来不委形④。

【注释】

①有钱，任性：起源是老头被骗事件，明知是骗子，却要看看他究竟能骗自己多少钱，直到被骗了50多万元后骗子被警察抓住为止。这件事被报道以后，被网友评论：有钱人就是任性！②子叶：暂时性的叶性器官。③臧否（zāng pǐ）：褒贬；评论。④委形：置身。

Rich and Willful

A seed leaf hangs her paradise of love into frenzies,
Free to the foul comments on its merits and demerits.
A swallow back to the open ferry should check it out,
Whether the blossom fall in the autumn wind bears to hear.
A man of wealth in cotton shoes follows the royal carriage,
And a pauper in pearl shoes walks, but a commoner.
To live through this world can not be easy,
Alone in freedom of action, but not run adrift.

宅男宅女[①]

潮信冰合连海山，青螺号角动妖娴[②]。
有宅一代封人事，无忌千人俱闯关。
冲浪偷营河汉浅，击风战地月儿弯。
蜗居一键行天下，坐看贤达与佞奸。

【注释】

①宅男/女：大都是20世纪80年代以后的独生子，在疼爱的目光下成长，步入社会难以一下子展示自我，于是，在网络虚拟世界寻找舞台。②妖娴：闲雅。

Homebodies

The sea mount has been ice-closed to the tide,
Whose conch deports itself gracefully.

The house generation keeps out of touch,
And cares not for all others' bolting their passes,
But starts web surfing, and raids the shallow galaxy,
Or braves the crescent winds on the theatre of war.
In the humble abode, one keyboard wanders thru the world,
Faced with the prominent personages and the wicked toadeaters.

涨姿势①

一双秋水剪妖歌，举袖酸风落大河。
水溅荒篱召玉雁，风摇古道采金鹅。
灵踪鞭草醒桐树，仙路诛榛睡女萝。
岐路同游穿铁网，白裘送站令狐多。

【注释】

①涨姿势：长见识。网络语言，意思不那么严肃，是让自己和别人轻松些。

Informative

Her limpid eyes have scissored the coquettish song,
Whose sleeves fall into the big river with the jealous wind.
As her sloshed, desolate fence summons the wild geese,
The old, wind-rocked road has gathered a golden goose.
As her quick trace wakes the phoenix tree on the swinged weeds,
The creepers sleep thru the cursed thorns to the immortal way.
Together, let's go thru the barbed wires on the forked roads,
Where more powerful foxes are to bid farewell in white furs.

正能量

自信燃灯醒睡客，星火一炬满城明。
千峰云梦虽凌暗，万籁天台仍动晴。
攀策[①]参差曾返顾，持权[②]迤逦更前行。
风流翰墨不轻写，萱纸银钩为正声。

【注释】

①攀策：吃力地拄着拐杖。②持权：掌权。

The Positive Energy

I believe that Dipamkara can wake up the sleepers,
And one spark can brighten the whole town.
All peaks in dreamy clouds are soaring darkly, though,
All sounds of Mount Tiantai will shine there still.
On crutches, the staggering road ever went into reverse,
In power, the tortuous route should go straight on.
Truely and heroically, a pen will not write easily,
The paper below the vigorous flourishes corrects the sounds.

中国大妈

博弈金铃形影高，抱团抄底亮钱刀[①]。
盛名谁更压枚皋[②]，雄略犹应使豹韬[③]。
不似宫音同辟命[④]，空留街舞共风骚。
做空大鳄谈何易，张嘴吞潮会套牢。

【注释】

①钱刀：金钱。刀，古代一种刀形钱币。②枚皋（约前156—?）：西汉文学家、汉赋作家。此人命卑贱，其母是枚乘的小妾。但思维"马迟枚速"，练就了一腔急才，速度快得惊人。③豹韬：韬略。④辟（pì）命：征召。

The Chinese Dama

The gold bells in game are silhouetted higher,
And are huddled with the "bottom-feeders" money.
Who else would endeavour after more fame?
The Damas are given the rare gifts and bold strategy.
Unlike the melodies that heed the rallying call,
They are left to the glamorous hip-hops in vain.
To pull of the tycoons seems not so easy,
Because to gulp the tide would be hung up.

自　题

宁词走笔越十年，窃弄[①]唐诗墨未干。
野步疏狂持五卷，闲吟苦乐握三千。
闭关危坐[②]稻粱地，回首独行鸿雁天。
冷眼古今潮起落，史书上面几人贤？

【注释】

①窃弄：盗用；玩弄。此处为贬义中用。②危坐：端坐，亦指坐时敬谨端直。

Self-composed

The quiet words have gone over a decade,
That imitate the Tang poems still in a wet ink.
Unbridled, the five tomes are deported along the wild way,
In the quirks of joy and grief, 3000 verses are chanted idly.
Closed within, I sit bolt upright for food,
And looking back, I walk alone below the swan sky.
Cold-eyed, the tides come and go at all times, and tell
Me how many men of virtue are historically recorded?

作　死

玉纤滴柳拜观音，垂目莲台不可寻。
天地无因空伫立，此身何处不长吟。
佛灯澄道醒贪兽，僧磬[①]激德警腐禽。
百度悬河迷醉眼，行棋无悔在持心[②]。

【注释】

①僧磬（qìng）：佛寺中敲击以集僧众的鸣器或钵形铜乐器。②持心：处事所抱的态度。

To Seek Death

Her fair willow makes obeisance to the Goddess of Mercy,
But unaccessible to the lotus throne with Her eyes closed.
Without reason, the world stands here in vain,

For this body, where can't it chant in slow tone?
To clear the way, the Buddha-lamp arouses the insatiable beasts,
And the sacred bell spurs the morals against the corrupt fowl.
Squiffy-eyed, the hanging river has been crossed hundreds of times,
And in chess, the preserved mind should not retract its false move.

做人七不
Seven "No" in Life

其一：梦

蓬海灵光浮玉京，春岚众籁[1]裹杂英。
兹夕独坐尘埃重，旷岁[2]安眠微雨轻。
燕雀乌纱添喜气，金银风月渡欢声。
浮生劳梦关山远，长夜幽寻难自明。

【注释】

①众籁：籁是古代的一种箫。孔穴里发出的声音，泛指各种声响。
②旷岁：经年；长年。

One: Dream

The jade palace floated in divine light on the fairy sea,
Where the haze spring swathed the flowers in profusion.
At dusk, I sat alone in the thick dust,
Over days, my slumber sprinkled.

As the chaffinch in black gauze cap was on cloud nine,
The golden and silvery nature went jubilant all over.
The rills and hills had toiled far in the dream of this life,
And canopied in darkness, my secret search couldn't be self-evident.

其二：话

新月开弧成满月，桑弓①猿臂易折弦。
兵戈御陌如难用，名秩②空门可自全。
银汉稀稠③无梦断，鹊桥聚散有情悬。
大君高论知廉退④，小子奴唇莫太圆。

【注释】

①桑弓：桑木作的弓。亦泛指强弓、硬弓。②名秩：名次。③稀稠：疏密。④廉退：廉让。谦让。

Two: Speech

The crescent grows up into a full moon,
Where the brawny arms break the bow with a twang.
If the weapons to guard the fields are invalid,
To enter the door to nirvana can be shut tight.
Thick or thin, the Milky Way breaks no dreams,
Here or there, the love hangs on the magpie bridge.
The man of virtue knows how to retreat loftily and honestly,
And the little man shouldn't round his slave lips too much.

其三：调

竹啼翠羽掩清浑[1]，深巷殷勤唤草根。
爽气杯巡谈易论[2]，薰风乐奏道朝昏[3]。
白猿垂木荡平野，飞雪惊天罩远村。
调瑟凌风下北斗，征云慷慨叩千门。

【注释】

①清浑：清澈和浑浊。②易论：《易论》共十三篇，先后为论“为君之道”、论“任官之急”、论“为臣之道”、论“治身”与“治家”之道、论“遇于人”之道、论“动而无悔”之道、论“因人”与“应变”之道、论“常”与“变”之道、论“慎祸福”之道、论“招患与免患”之道、论“心一与迹殊”之道、论“卦时”之道、论“以人事明卦象”之道。③朝昏：日子，生活。

Three：Move

Pure or turbid，the green feathers chirp in the bamboos
To the grassroots sincerely in the deeper lanes.
Gone round，the cups in fresh air comment on *The Changes*，
And play with great panache like mild breezes.
When the white ape in the wood swings as in a flat ground，
The blowing snow veils the far village that shocks the sky.
With woven wings metrically down the Big Dipper，
The forced cloud knocks on thousands of door bountifully.

其四：事

孤猿绝壁召云雨，灭迹灵芝地角边。
谗巧[①]花光偷换骨，蛇矛露气暗寻仙。
一壶轻策霸长岛，两叶扁舟横大川。
自负独刀破百万，杀伐[②]进退不相牵。

【注释】

①谗巧：谗邪巧佞。②杀伐：杀戮。

Four：Affairs

The lonely ape called up the wind and cloud,
And the lost tinder agaric was found at the farthest corner.
The backbiting flattery changed its bones lustrously and secretly,
And the serpent-headed spear sought the dewy immortals.
One pot of wine seized the long isle on the horse,
And two single sails stood in the way of the big river.
One sword was boasted to have burst through a million soldiers,
As regards its uncorrelated carnage in dilemma.

其五：情

明月风结三寸花，秦淮沽酒坐渔家。
素约[①]沾露且扶袖，微步临波还笼纱。
玉笋纤纤开玳瑁[②]，珠帘袅袅抹琵琶。
桃夭相顾方一笑，梦里三生是紫霞。

【注释】

①素约：旧约；早先约定。②玉笋：洁白的笋芽，喻指女人的纤手。玳瑁（dài mào）："玳瑁筵"（简称"玳筵"）的别称，用来描述筵席的精美与豪华。

Five：Feeling

To the three inches of flowers under the moon-lit breeze,
We sat in the fisherman's tavern on the Qinhuai River,
Where the wet, pre-agreed dews on her sleeves
Minced down the waves hung with the embroidered gauze;
Her taper fingers then held the feast in great solemnity,
And the pearl curtain plucked the graceful pipa strings.
As her rosy eyes met us in smiles knowingly,
The wonder of fate in dream must be from the purple clouds.

其六：利

造利清浊徒负累，争驰天下利前程。
锱铢求利名没起，寒暑遗名利已行。
得利入名才已暗，失心向利志难明。
无名无利不出海，载利扁舟一叶轻。

Six：Gain

Clear and muddy, the gain is but a burden,
Vying for a promising place all under heaven;

To haggle over penny before being famous,
The thermometre of wealth and fame has been advantageous.
When the gain into the fame becomes obscure already,
The lost heart in gain also loses its will clearly.
Without fame or gain, none would run out to sea,
In that one canoe for the gain sways light we see.

其七：人

假人证伪不失真，寄世堪哀无假人。
假语砺舌才入梦，假言磨耳已通神。
假田一贯是荒土，假地从来出恶民。
假眼娇娆[1]醉铁汉，假唇偷巧[2]一言亲。

【注释】

①娇娆：娇艳美好，妩媚多姿。②偷巧：取巧；浇薄巧诈。

Seven: Man

A dummy perjury will not be fuzzy,
Yet regrettably, the world has no such a dummy.
Whetted into a dream has been the artificial tongue,
And the intimate lies communicate with the divine all along.
As the false field proves to be the barren soil,
The fake farm always produces the wicked moil.
As the man of iron will is besotted by her coquettish eye,
Her feigned lips resort to the trickery of sweet words so high.